He had been framed, but how could he prove it?

Sergeant Cole, given guard duty over the prisoner, saw Danny crush out his last cigarette and pat his pockets for another. He threw Danny his own package.

"Did you do it?" Cole asked. "Fall asleep on guard? If you did, it sucks, Top getting shot and all. What I'm sayin' is, don't let it get to you. We all done it at one time or another. You just did it at a real bad time, is all. Coulda happened to anybody."

"No." Danny shook his head as he blew smoke through his nose. "No, I didn't. Smitty never woke me up. I've been sitting here thinking about it. At first, I wasn't sure—what with the confusion and all. It was a rough night."

Cole snorted. "You ain't said shit."

"No, but I'm sure now. Smitty never woke me up. He must've fallen asleep, and the miserable rat fuck is blaming me," Danny said to the floor.

"If that's true," Cole said, "and I was you, I'd kill that mother-fucker."

Danny nodded. "Roger that."

Lieutenant Chicarelli stepped through the hatchway. "They're ready for you."

Crushing out his cigarette, Danny watched the officer's face for some hint of what was awaiting him. Chicarelli would not meet his gaze. He led him up one level to the captain's cabin. Cole brought up the rear.

Danny faced the captain and all of the platoon leaders of Charlie Company. Beecher and Smitty were there as well. Danny was amazed that Smitty could look him in the eye, but he did, and the trace of a smile at the corners of his former friend's mouth looked triumphant. Danny reported to the captain and stood at attention. He saw a dog-eared copy of the Uniform Code of Military Justice on the captain's bed.

"Private Mulvaney," Captain Arnold began, "regarding the matter of your sleeping on guard during the operation from which we have just returned, specifically, last night. Do you have anything to say for yourself?"

Twenty years after he survived Vietnam, Daniel Mulvaney's memoir about it is a best seller. But success brings unforeseen attention. An invitation from a mysterious Vietnamese, to return to the land that nearly took his life, takes Danny back to when an idealistic kid was unjustly expelled from college and drafted into the US Army. The old nightmares resume. He can't work. His marriage is in trouble.

As a young man in Brooklyn in 1968, Danny was unsure if his mom's credo—everything happens for good reason—was wisdom or corny idiom, but he was determined to be a man worthy of Amanda, the girl he loved. Gino Sebastionelli, his closest friend, wanted to bolt for Canada together, but Danny wouldn't be swayed. His idealism blinded him to the horrors ahead. He'd be wounded, decorated, betrayed, face court martial, and then be saved by Tom Tyler, an officer from Danny's college town, where all his troubles began. When Danny's platoon was nearly wiped out, Tyler was captured, and Danny would have to lead a green platoon, against orders, into the U-Minh—The Forest of Darkness—in order to have any chance of saving his lieutenant...

Critical Praise for *For Good Reason*

"Wars are waged by nations, but fought by individuals. Robertson's *For Good Reason* is a fascinating study in the price soldiers continue to pay long after coming home and how, for some, the war is never over." ~ Reed Farrel Coleman, *New York Times* Bestselling Author of *What You Break*

"James D. Robertson's For Good Reason is a page-turner full of emotion and tension that will grab the reader by the throat and entertain from the first page to the end. You will care about his characters, their feelings, and their relationships. This guy can write." ~ Joseph Badal, Amazon #1 Best-Selling Author of *Obsessed*

"Some of the best war novels are written long after the war has passed into history, and James Robertson's *For Good Reason* takes its place among those classics. Robertson, a Vietnam veteran, writes with the authenticity of a man who was there, and the maturity of a man who has come to grips with his combat experiences. The battle scenes are among the best I've ever read: tense, heart-pounding, too realistic, and emotionally draining. This book will bring back memories of a time that changed all of us who lived through it." ~ Nelson DeMille, *USA Today* Best-Selling Author of *The Cuban Affair*

"From the very first page, James Robertson's *For Good Reason* brings you into an authentic, gripping portrayal of war and the devastation it wrecks." ~ Annamaria Alfierie, acclaimed historical mystery novelist

ACKNOWLEDGMENTS

This book would not have been possible without my friends and colleagues in the writing community. Thanks to my critique group: Joan, Greg, Dennis, Bev, Diane, Duke and Steve for their unwavering encouragement and to all the wonderful, talented people at the New York Chapter of Mystery Writers of America, too numerous to name, but without whose selfless support this book might never have been published. And thanks to all the dedicated professionals at Black Opal Books for their assistance and kindness in making it happen.

FOR GOOD REASON

JAMES D. ROBERTSON

A Black Opal Books Publication

GENRE: WAR & MILITARY/SUSPENSE/HISTORICAL FICTION

This is a work of fiction. Names, places, characters, and incidents are either the product of the author's imagination or are used fictitiously, and any resemblance to any actual persons, living or dead, businesses, organizations, events or locales is entirely coincidental. All trademarks, service marks, registered trademarks, and registered service marks are the property of their respective owners and are used herein for identification purposes only. The publisher does not have any control over or assume any responsibility for author or third-party websites or their contents.

DEDICATION

For Liz, my wife and steadfast cheerleader, and for my children: Tom, Suzanne, and Kate: my good reasons.

For all of my forever-young buddies who didn't make it home and for those who survived and live with it every day. Welcome home, brothers.

CHAPTER 1

1988, Cold Spring Harbor, New York:

The dream was back. It surprised Danny when it began. The experience was different now after all the years—no twisting in his guts, no ache in his heart. It felt like coming home. He was back in Nam, sitting in a bunker, alone, waiting. The sandbags were torn and drooping. Red dust dribbled from gaping rips in the fabric like dried blood. The beams were rotten and termite-infested. The whole structure was well on its way to oblivion. He found comfort in that.

Light began to brighten the timber-framed doorway. Wisps of ground mist crept in, swirling across the floor. He loved the dawn. Dawn meant he had survived another terror-filled night. Dawn promised a chance to survive another day.

In the dream he examined himself, knowing what he would find, but pleased to find it. Jungle fatigues and combat gear, everything as it had been, everything but the pain. He had missed this dream. As real as it seemed, he knew it was a dream, but that was okay. The dream was all that was left.

He waited, comfortable with the dream, expectant yet calm, content, savoring the anticipation.

One by one, his buddies shuffled in. With sparkling eyes on the brink of laughter, each one acknowledged him with a grin and a nod.

"Hey, Mulvaney," someone said, "you back for another tour?"

Unable to speak, he nodded. His brothers were with him again. Even the dead were healthy, young, and happy in this dream—the way he would always remember them. He stood. They pounded one another on the back, shook hands, embraced, and called each other vulgar names.

God, it felt good to be together again.

"What's the op?" someone said.

They all looked to him. He said what he always said in the dream. "Saddle up. We're moving out."

He woke up just as he always did at that point. Try as he might he could never alter that. Still clinging to the memory of his friends, wishing he could be with them even if it meant risking his life, he gave in to reality and opened his eyes.

His wife lay beside him, her breathing rhythmic and deep. He stifled a sob and eased himself from beneath the comforter. With his toes, he felt for his slippers. The bristly nap of deep pile carpet against his bare feet felt strange. The newness of his surroundings was getting on his nerves. He rose, holding his breath, but the mattress was so new the springs failed to squeak. He wagged his head in the darkness, stooped to snatch a terry-cloth robe from a chair in front of the window, and stole a peek at his front yard. Three dandelion stalks, seed puffs aglow in the spill from a streetlamp, mocked him from their beds where they swayed, smack in the middle of his freshly laid sod.

He chuckled softly, whispered, "Shit. 'Best lawn money can buy,' my ass," shrugged, and tiptoed into the hall.

He checked at his kids' rooms as he passed. Nary a whimper from behind those doors. He alone was haunted.

Thrusting his arms into the robe's sleeves and tying its sash as he went, Danny headed for the stairs.

Downstairs, he congratulated himself when he had, for once, successfully negotiated the living room in the dark without bashing his toe. He felt his way into the kitchen, eased open the refrigerator, and blinked in the glare as he slipped a Sam Adams from a six-pack stashed in the back. He popped the top with a bottle opener from a counter drawer and climbed onto a stool beside the center island. Sipping the tangy brew, he fished in his pocket for his cigarettes, shook loose a Marlboro and clamped his lips on the filter.

Dropping the pack on the counter, he scooped his old, worn Zippo from his pocket and spun the wheel. The lighter caught on the first attempt. He drew smoke deep into his lungs. Holding the Zippo in front of his eyes, he whispered the engraved inscription lit by the flickering flame. "When I die I'll go to Heaven 'cause I've spent my time in Hell." Nodding, he said, "Amen, brother." The clink of the cover snapping shut sounded like a shot.

With the aroma of last night's roast chicken tickling his nostrils—one homey touch in his strange new house—he drank, smoked, and thought. The letter was on his desk in his library. He could almost see it through the walls.

His wife wanted him to tear it up. As if the thought of her were a summons, he heard her on the stairs. *Now I'm in for it. Here comes the Wicked Witch of the West.*

"Dan?" she called. "What are you doing up? Are you smoking?"

The woman could smell cigarette smoke in a hurricane. Here she comes—Judgment Day in pink flannel and fuzzy slippers—Beauty *and* the Beast all in one package. *I don't need this shit now. Why can't she leave me alone?*

The overhead lights snapped on. The sudden brilliance hit his pupils like a fist.

"Yeah, I'm drinking, too." He squinted, temporarily blind. "So?"

"Don't get snotty, Daniel. It's three o'clock in the morning. The kids have school tomorrow."

"If the kids wake up," he said, "it'll be because of you. I was as quiet as a mouse."

"And as sneaky."

"Don't start with me."

"Okay." She threw her hands up, her sign of truce. "Let's start over. What's wrong?"

"Nothing."

"*Nothing?* You're slinking around the house in the middle of the night, sneaking cigarettes, and drinking beer, and you expect me to believe nothing's wrong?" With her arms folded, she leaned a hip against the counter. "It's the letter, isn't it?"

"No, I—" He clenched his fist, tapped it three times on the counter, and said, "Yes, it's the letter. I'm upset, okay? I admit it. Let's not get into it now, though. Just go back to bed. I'll be fine. Just needed a few minutes to think, okay? I'm fine."

"Honey," she said, "talk to me. I want to help. Please, talk to me."

"We'll talk tomorrow, babe. Right now I need a little solitude.

There are some things I have to sort out in my head—things you wouldn't understand."

"I want to understand, Dan. Don't shut me out."

He clenched his fist again, tapped twice, and said, "I'm not shutting you out. I just have to get some stuff straight in my own head before I can share it with you. Go back to bed. We'll talk tomorrow."

"Promise?"

"Scout's honor. Now scoot." When she hesitated, he added, "I love you."

She put her arms around him, and he felt the warmth of her body against his back, the press of her breasts through the fabric. He smelled the sleepy, woman smell of her and he was almost aroused, but it had been too long. He hadn't laid intimate hands on her in months.

He kissed her hair—a brush of the lips—and slowly turned to break contact.

"Dan, are you sure you want me to go?"

"Maybe not. Why don't you get a beer from the fridge for yourself and another one for me? Dim the lights. Let's just sit and talk like we did when we were engaged. Make believe we're in one of those cozy little pubs we used to go to late at night, dreaming of what our life together will be like. Remember?"

She pulled back. Anger flushed her cheeks. "That's all you want to do lately—relive the *good old days*." She started to pace, the way she did when she was cross. "Wake up!" she said. "I've got a news flash for you. We're not kids anymore."

He gritted his teeth and examined the floor, but she ducked into his gaze. With furrowed brow, she said, "Hello-o. Earth to Dan. Do you read me?" Snapping erect, she resumed her quick-march pacing and added finger-wagging. Pent-up energy propelled her back and forth like a ping-pong ball, firing accusations with every turn of her heel. "The past is the past. You can't go back. Since you started that damned book, you've been living in the 'sixties. 'Dreaming of our life together?' We no longer have a life together. I'm here. Now. You're in a time warp. Snap out of it!" She spun on him and stood flat-footed, fists balled, battle ready.

"That '*damned book*,'" he fired back, "is what bought you this house you always wanted. *And* everything in it. *And* the cars in the garage. *And* all the other shit you just had to have."

"Bought?" she said. "Hardly! It made the down payments. We're up to our asses in debt. You haven't made a dime in months. The advance is almost gone, and the royalties won't last forever. You've got to wake up, Dan. Come back to the world of the living." She ticked off his eccentricities on her fingers. "First, it was staying up half the night, every night, writing the first draft. Then we had to put up with the rewriting. And the *research!*" She gave up on counting and threw it all in the air. "My God! The phone bill alone. But, you know what, Dan? I'd be happy to go through it all again if you'd just get back to work. Writers do have to write, don't they? It's not like farming, is it? The government won't pay you for *not* writing, will it?"

"Keep your voice down. You'll wake the kids."

"So? Are you afraid they'll see that their father is losing his mind?"

"What the hell does that mean?"

"It means that since we moved in here, you've been acting stranger by the minute. First, there were the parties with all those weirdos from that veterans' club you joined."

"Those are my brother vets. How dare you insult them?"

"You never laid eyes on any of them until your book was published. They used you for free beer and a place to drink it. You said yourself: some of their stories don't ring true."

"My old buddies are scattered all over the country. I can't help that." It sounded lame, even to him. He looked for an ashtray, but he knew there would not be one, so he dropped his cigarette butt into the empty beer bottle. Some ashes scattered on the counter.

She grabbed the washcloth from the sink and swiped at his mess. "So, what are these people? Substitutes?" She didn't wait for an answer. "Oh, and let's not forget *paintball*." Her eyes grew wide. She threw her head back and berated the ceiling. He hated when she did that. "All of a sudden, my husband decides to be a middle-aged commando, running around in the woods, shooting perfect strangers with paint pellets." The ceiling must have had enough because she aimed those piercing brown orbs at him again. "Now you get a letter from some unknown Vietnamese, and you want to go traipsing off to the other side of the world to meet him." She clapped her hands together and locked her fingers so the knuckles went white. "Does any of this sound rational to you?"

"Come on, babe. I know how it must look, but—"

"But what, Danny? You're a writer, for God's sake. Why can't you find the words?"

He didn't know he was going to cry. He was as shocked by his tears as she. He couldn't help but cry, and he couldn't stop.

Her arms were around him again, and her sobs blended with his. "You need help, Dan. It's post-traumatic stress or something. Maybe the VA can help. They know more about this kind of thing now. Will you go see someone? Please? For me? For the kids?"

She rocked him until he nodded his submission. She stroked his hair and kissed the tears streaming down his cheek.

"Come to bed," she said. "We'll talk about it in the morning."

He couldn't meet her eyes. "Give me a minute to collect myself," he said and turned his back on her. "I'll be right up."

"Okay." She pulled back, letting her fingers trail along his arms. "But not too long. You need your rest."

"Okay," he said and wiped his eyes with his sleeve. "Go on. I'll be right up."

He waited until he heard the bedroom door close, counted to three, and went to the refrigerator. He snatched another beer from the carton, thought better of it, and took them all. Moving quickly, he slipped out the side door to the attached garage, closed it behind him with care, and caught himself just before he switched on the lights. He was safer in the dark. She wouldn't think to look for him here if he stayed quiet. Her Audi was right in front of him. He felt the cool, slick steel with the back of his hand, slid his backside onto the fender, set the beer down on the hood, lit another cigarette, and eased the lighter shut.

Alone in the dark, he puffed, sipped, and thought.

She's right. I do need to see someone—someone in Vietnam.

CHAPTER 2

1968, Brooklyn, New York:

*D*o or die time.

Danny Mulvaney sighted over the bowling ball. His target lay on its horizon. Sixty feet downrange the head pin led a wedge of wooden Spartans in a frontal assault. He started his approach. The black sphere dropped from view. The weight tugged at his fingertips. For one moment the ball hung in the air behind him at the limit of his reach. As gravity overcame inertia, he helped it along. Leaning forward, half-steps quickened to full strides as he charged the lane. His biceps bulged as he put all he had into the launch. Six feet from the foul line the black orb reappeared and shot from his fingers.

The ball rumbled over oiled hickory, spinning like a tiny planet.

He watched it hook and whispered, "If I make this strike, it means God wants me to go to Vietnam."

The whirling globe spun into the gap between the lead pin and the three as though sucked in by vacuum. Ten pins exploded off their marks.

Danny made a fist and pulled it down as his knee rose to meet his elbow.

"Yes!"

He strolled back to the ball return feeling childish, playing kid games with the most important decision of his life. How could he make a mature assessment if he acted this way? He wiped his hands on a dingy towel and looked up to see a morose Gino Sebastionelli enter the bowling alley.

Chuckling, Danny muttered, "Probably never seen the joint in daylight," and he then said, loudly, "Good morning, Gino."

"Your opinion," Gino grumbled as he slid into the scratched blue fiberglass settee.

"You look like you could use some coffee."

"Rather have a beer."

"At ten in the morning?"

"Ten here maybe but it's gotta be the middle of the night someplace." Gino's brown eyes widened. "Hey, let's drink to that. Yeah. Let's drink to time zones. I'll bet nobody ever drank to time zones."

"Probably not, but have coffee anyway. You've got the rest of the day to get loaded. I want to talk to you, and I want you sober. This is important."

Gino made a face but nodded acquiescence. When Danny hit the call button, Gino sneered, "You got a case. You think Willy's gonna pay a waitress to wait on two bums this early in the morning? On a weekday? Get a grip."

A glance at the main desk confirmed Gino's appraisal. The proprietor sat behind it, absorbed in the day's pari-mutuel statistics. Salaries were not among Willy's favorite things, winning horses were.

"Make that one bum." Danny vaulted the ball return and squeezed Gino's shoulder as he passed, heading for the snack bar. "I," he threw over his shoulder, "have a job." Turning to the man at the desk, he said, "Willy, m'man, put on your chef's hat."

Willy shot him a look of contempt but led Danny to the snack bar.

When he returned with two steaming cardboard cups, one in either hand, Gino still sat where Danny had left him, dejected, hands jammed into the pockets of his black, faux-fur ski jacket, feet crossed at the ankles beneath his flared blue-jean clad, and fully extended legs. He glowered at the scuffed, squared tips of his Dingo boots, making no secret of his displeasure at being summoned from his bed at this ungodly hour. "Speaking of your job, Dan, why aren't you there?" He blew a breath of air across the lip of the cup Danny handed him.

Except for the clunk of pins in the automatic pinsetter, the house was silent. Danny plopped down beside his pal and cast a fond eye at the empty lanes.

They had spent many hours in this building, met a few good friends and a lot of pretty girls, enjoyed some good times, and suffered through some bad ones. It was their home away from home.

"You hear pretty well for a man not yet awake." Danny nudged Gino with his elbow.

"Can't say the same for you. Answer the question. Why aren't you at work?"

"What are you? My mother?"

Gino unzipped his jacket, reached inside, rummaged around with a look of concern knitting his brow, and said, "Ah, there it is. Thought I'd left it home." His hand came out closed into a fist with the middle finger raised. "This is for you."

"Well, aren't you Joe-Funny-Man in the *ayem*? Stick that in your ear. I called in sick, okay?" Danny lit a cigarette and tossed the pack onto the score table.

"Okay," Gino breathed, "I'll play your silly game. Why did you call in sick, Daniel? You look healthy to me." He grabbed Danny's cigarettes from the Formica surface and helped himself. "I thought you loved that job." He struck a paper match and cupped it in his hands, squinting as if the smoke stung his eyes.

Danny smiled and wagged his head. Gino had lit his cigarettes just that way ever since he had seen James Dean do it in Rebel Without A Cause.

"Or," Gino went on, "is it that broad you work with that you love? I forget." He shook the match out, looking smug, and then frowned as if trying to recall. "Let's see, was it the job or the broad?" He shook his head. "Too early for me. Help me out."

"Don't call Amanda a broad," Danny said through clenched teeth.

"Why not? She got tits, she's a broad. I seen her picture, man. She most definitely got some tits."

Danny compressed his lips and blew smoke through his nose, determined not to let Gino disrupt his concentration with petty arguments. Gino was just being Gino.

Danny leaned back, and said, "I took today off to think about what I'm going to do. I wanted to discuss it with you." He flicked ashes on the floor and scattered them with his toe.

"Do? About what?"

"About this." Danny pulled a white envelope from his leather jacket on the seat beside him and handed it to Gino.

Gino glanced at the return address, and said, "Aw, shit." He slipped the folded paper from the envelope and snapped it open with a flick of his wrist. A glance confirmed what the exterior had told him. "Drafted. Fuck!"

"Yep." Danny tapped more ashes onto the floor. His blue eyes stared down the length of the lane, but in his mind's eye, he saw Coach Lembeck. The man had vowed to inform the draft board of his status the moment he was off campus. Danny had no doubts that the fat little wart had been in earnest.

"Hang on a minute." Gino looked at Danny as if he had grown a second head. "You're not thinking about going?"

Danny shrugged.

"Have you flipped? We talked about this. You're last of the line. One letter to your congressman and you're out of it. We had this all figured out. If you didn't win the scholarship, you skate on a technicality, and Gino heads for the border. That *was* the plan, was it not?"

"Well, I did win the scholarship, but that's history now, and Uncle Sam sends 'Greetings.'" Danny slapped both hands on his knees. "The plan has changed."

"Don't tell me you're back to that same old song about your old man? Daniel, we've been over this ground. War is hell? Make love, not war? This is not our fight, my friend. It ain't worth it."

"Yeah, I know. But—"

"'*But*,' my ass. What the hell are you thinking, man?"

"I'm thinking I've got to know. I can't spend the rest of my life wondering."

"Wondering what? If you can hack it? Who gives a shit?"

"I do."

Gino sighed. "Here we go again. You're determined to get your ass shot off."

"It's my ass."

"Your mom must be thrilled."

"Leave my mother out of this."

"Sure. Tell *her* that."

Danny pictured his mother the way she had been the night he came home from college in disgrace. He had never seen her so frantic, nearly hysterical, accusing him of trying to break her heart, just as his father had.

She had calmed down after a few days, and that irrepressible optimism had resurfaced. "Everything happens for a good reason," she said.

Danny thought she should have done that one up in needle-point, framed it, and hung it on the front door. If he had a nickel for every time he'd heard it...

"Look," Danny said, "that last of the line stuff doesn't hold water. I checked. My father would have to have been killed in a war. Dying of a cerebral hemorrhage twenty-some-odd years after the fact doesn't count."

"Your old man's wounds caused that bubble to pop in his brain. The doctor said that."

Hearing his father's death so coldly described made Danny flinch, but again he made allowances. Gino never meant to be cruel. It just happened.

"He said, 'It could have,'" Danny argued. "'*Could* have.' The drinking probably played a part. He said that, too."

"Horseshit. Your old man drank *because* of the war. You know that as well as I do. Cause and effect. You explained that particular bit of science to me yourself."

"We were talking about something else entirely."

"Doesn't matter. It applies. Don't you remember the dreams? He used to wake up screaming. I was there, for godsakes. I lived with you and your family for almost a year the first time my old man threw me out. Or are you forgetting that, too?"

"I'm not forgetting anything."

"No? We made a pact, Danny. You and me. We were getting out of it. What happened to the dangerous duo? Sal and Troy?"

Gino liked to brag how he and Danny looked a lot like Sal Mineo and Troy Donahue. Danny could see the resemblance to the swarthy teen heartthrob in Gino, but he'd never thought he really looked much like Troy.

Gino wasn't giving up. "We were gonna thumb our noses at the whole system. Rack up all the pussy the unlucky bastards left behind. What happened to that?"

"I can't." Danny's voice sounded small.

"Why the hell not?"

"My father wouldn't want me to."

"Yeah, right. Your old man would be real happy to know there's another Mulvaney, his only son, no less, getting ready to join him in Pinelawn. This is not World War Three, dammit. Nobody's bombing Hawaii. This is a rinky-dink civil war in a country that hasn't even heard of the Industrial Revolution yet. It is none of our goddamn business. Jesus! I don't believe you."

"Why are you getting so worked up?"

Gino smacked his forehead and talked to the room at large. "My best friend, the closest thing I got to a brother, totally loses his mind, and he wants to know why I'm getting worked up."

"Gino, you're talking to a bowling alley."

"I'll get more sense from the damned bowling alley than I'll get from you."

Danny sipped his coffee, drew on his cigarette, and stared, resolute, at his life-long friend.

Gino sighed. "I can see your mind is made up, and I know once that happens..."

Danny nodded.

"So, what did you want to discuss? So far, there has been no discussion that I am aware of. Once again you have made up your mind, and you expect *me* to go along. You're a pisser, Daniel. You had the world by the balls. You could have made the Olympics with that spear of yours."

"It's a javelin."

"Same difference. Jesus Christ, man. First, you fuck up and get booted out of college. Now, you want to get shot to prove you've got balls. What are you, some kinda *mastashist*?"

"The word is masochist, and no, I am not. And I did *not* fuck up in school. Why does everyone keep saying that? It wasn't my fault."

"You whipped a teacher and two local yokel classmates with an aerial from a Buick. I'm not Joe College, Dan, but I doubt if Street Fighting One-oh-One is a required course below the Mason-Dixon Line."

"They had me cornered. It was self-defense. *It wasn't my fault.*"

Gino cocked his head and looked up to meet Danny's eyes, making Danny aware he had jumped to his feet.

"Let's split," Gino said. "This place is a bring-down."

Gino was up and walking away before Danny's brain registered his last remark.

"Don't you want to bowl a couple of games?" Danny heard

the absurdity in his plea. He knew Gino would not ignore it.

Gino stopped, turned, and said, "Bowl? Knock down sticks of wood with a big round ball? Seems a little tame for a daredevil such as yourself. How about Russian roulette? We could use an automatic to make it interesting. You go first." He spun on his heel and headed for the door.

"Gino, wait up. I wasn't finished," Danny called to his friend's receding form. He grabbed his jacket and hurried to catch him.

Willie never looked up from the racing form, but said, "Wear my shoes in the street, and you owe me fifty bucks *plus* the lines you bowled, Mulvaney."

Looking down at the garish red and green rented bowling shoes, Danny groaned. He watched Gino disappear through the double glass doors as he yanked at the laces.

This day was not going the way he had hoped, and it would probably deteriorate from here. He still had to tell his mom.

CHAPTER 3

Republic of South Vietnam:

North Vietnamese Army Lieutenant Ngo Dinh Tran walked through busy streets in the city of Hue. Having grown his hair to sufficient length to overcome the tell-tale effect of his NVA bowl-cut and garbed in Western dress—black slacks and a white, short-sleeved shirt—he passed as a civilian. His papers—lifted from the corpse of an ARVN soldier—identified him as Captain Nguyen Dan. Forged leave orders accompanied his credentials to explain being out of uniform.

The military ID had seemed necessary to his covert mission since an able-bodied South Vietnamese of his age should be a member of the Army of the Republic of Vietnam. So far, the ruse had proven unnecessary. He had wandered unchallenged all morning.

As he moved through the ancient city, he was appalled by the lack of oppression being suffered. Hue seemed scarcely touched by the war. The city teemed with life and prosperity. He counted six people laughing in public on Hung Vuong Street.

We will see if you can laugh, he thought, *when the Americans pulverize your homes with their artillery. How rich and fat will you feel when their M-Sixteen bullets crack the air and tear your flesh to shreds?*

The poor were in evidence, of course, wherever he cared to look, but even they seemed to be bearing up under the yoke of the corrupt regime. He completed his reconnaissance, walking all the way to the Perfume River before he turned toward his meeting with the Viet Cong cell commander.

An hour later, in a squalid, empty garage a quarter mile from the Citadel, VC Captain Nguyen Duc's fiery rhetoric raised gnawing doubts in Tran's heart as to the eventual outcome of this venture. Tran had grown wary of orators. Speeches, he knew, did not win battles.

∾ↄᴇↄ

Two days later, Captain Duc's battalion of guerrillas assaulted the bridge over the Perfume River. A company of North Vietnamese Regulars followed close behind with Lieutenant Tran at their front. The surprise attack exceeded expectations. The Army of the North, side by side with their tenacious Viet Cong comrades, succeeded in taking the city. Within hours of the battle's onset, the defenders were scattered and demoralized.

Captain Duc, regaling his men with monotonous revolutionary diatribe every step of the way, died a vainglorious death. The antique French pistol he so proudly displayed as his symbol of rank, exploded with its first shot, severing his right hand at the wrist. Shock and massive blood loss finished Duc within minutes, an incredulous look on his face for all eternity.

With the city at their mercy, the conquerors wasted no time in exacting revenge on the collaborators cowering in the ruins. Political officers produced lists of names complete with the addresses of the guilty. House-to-house searches produced hundreds of the condemned. Soldiers dragged entire families into the street and shot them. Some were herded together and machine-gunned en masse. For others, a single bullet to the head was the reward for loyalty to the South. No indictment, save inclusion on a list of names, was handed down. No defense was permitted.

Scores of citizens died for the traitorous crime of simply being at home when the soldiers kicked in their door.

In the thick of it, Tran encountered a ragged old man with a wispy white beard—an ancient *papasan* dragging a rusty Japanese bolt-action rifle from another era, another war. Tran did not employ the logic to see that this confused old grandfather was merely foraging for salvageable materiel for future bartering. Instead, Tran saw only the point of the long bayonet affixed to the muzzle of the weapon and the grotesquely contorted body of a young girl lying in a doorway in the background. The juxtaposition of the two images caused something in his mind to snap. With a primal scream of hate, he shot the old man in the face at point blank range.

Tran was a mile from the scene of the atrocity before he realized that he was carrying the obsolete rifle. Astonished, he threw it to the ground. Revulsion twisted his face into a grimace. He stood transfixed, glazed eyes locked on the weapon until, with a will seemingly of their own, his shaking hands reached for the bayonet. He released the spring clip that fastened it to the rifle, slipped the blade into his belt, and walked, trance-like, to rejoin his men.

Bloodlust turned to desperation when the high command failed to exploit the early victory with the promised reinforcements. The Americans regrouped and consolidated. For nearly all of the month of February the conquerors fought desperately to hold what they had taken. The glorious people's uprising, predicted by the communist high command as preordained, failed to materialize.

The attackers became defenders, an impossible task when one considered the odds. Outnumbered, outgunned, and isolated from all aid, the NVA and Viet Cong fought valiantly.

American firepower, initially delayed for logistic and political reasons, was finally brought to bear with unrelenting potency. After twenty-five horrific days, the invaders broke contact and melted back into the countryside. Thousands had been lost.

Tran had no way of knowing the extent of the defeat, but he knew it had been decisive. The bitter rout at Con Thien, barely three months before, was being relived. Once again, he found himself at the head of a small, beleaguered band of patriots in a headlong rush to escape. Tran's company was scattered by the massed firepower of the combined forces of the imperialist South. The rain of steel the enemy poured on them thwarted every attempt at consolidation. Air strikes, artillery, mortars, and what seemed like hundreds of helicopters, harassed and frustrated his every move until the merciful order came to fall back and escape to the camps in Laos. He and the last of his harried comrades struggled to elude the American killing machines that obliterated city and countryside alike.

After three days of hide-and-seek in the jungle, Tran signaled his men to halt as he collapsed against the base of a massive teak tree. Waving his troops to do likewise, he leaned back to catch his breath. Heart pounding, lungs burning, the twenty-four-year-old veteran massaged his aching thigh muscles to alleviate the cramping his dehydrated system was inflicting upon him.

Soon, he and his decimated platoon should reach sanctuary across the Laotian border. *How many more of these accursed hills must we climb? When would the American aircraft give up their relentless pursuit? How many more of his brothers in arms would be slaughtered before they reached safety?*

He looked now at his charred left arm, oozing puss, seared by a phosphorous rocket launched from the vulture-like spotter planes.

Squeezing the smooth wooden grip of what he now thought of as his *liberated* bayonet, he swore an oath to his dead compatriots.

This foreign steel would taste much foreign blood.

An all too familiar sound penetrated his murderous mood. He froze. A glance downhill assured him that his men had heard it, too. All eyes looked heavenward as the throb of rotor blades grew in intensity until it was a clattering, angry roar above the treetops.

Short, three to five round bursts of machine-gun fire punctuated the deeper beat of the whirling blades as the helicopters zigzagged above the forest canopy, probing for return fire. Ricochets whined through the woods. Bits of bark, twigs, and leaves fluttered through the branches as bullets hacked at the foliage.

The North Vietnamese soldiers' quaking bodies pressed the earth in an attempt to blend with the rotting vegetation on the forest floor. Each man tasted the musty earth with every intake of frightened breath. None dared move lest the gunners above discern a target for their rockets and mini-guns. Tran tasted blood and realized he had bitten his lip to keep from screaming.

And then, it was over.

The artificial wind stopped whipping the treetops. The thunk and thud of high velocity rounds ceased their tattoo on wood and earth. The thrumming of the blades diminished to a receding beat until silence hammered his ears, only to be replaced by the throb of pulsating blood, telling him he had survived.

Lieutenant Tran tried to speak but found his mouth so dry he could barely croak. He tore a button from a breast pocket and shoved it into his mouth, sucking it like candy.

"Is anyone wounded?" he finally managed to say, his voice

lacking the command he so desperately sought to convey.

No one answered.

Terror knotted his belly. *Had he alone survived?*

One by one his men stood, testing their legs, mistrustful of their power to support.

Tran was tempted to thank whoever was watching over his battered men but such thoughts were for fools and women. Rising cautiously, as the others had, he said, "Quickly now, we must leave this place." The conviction in his tone amazed him. As the soldiers struggled to regain forward momentum, he encouraged them. "Take heart, my brothers. By tomorrow we will be away from the elephant's thrashing rage."

He thought of Mai then, as he often did when Death had swung his ancient sword and missed. He felt for her last letter in his pocket. It was there. Six months old, damp with sweat and turning to pulp, but still with him. Lifting his foot to resume the climb of this, another hill in a ceaseless procession of endless hills, he prayed that his prediction would become fact.

CHAPTER 4

Fort Hood, Texas:

Tom Tyler, one of the US Army's newer second lieutenants, sat on the edge of his seat outside Major Brandt's office. The summons to see the XO, the Executive Officer, had come at a bad time, in the middle of a live fire exercise on one of Fort Hood's weapons ranges. Tyler was apprehensive about leaving his platoon in the hands of his platoon sergeant, especially on a machine-gun range with live ammunition. He remembered last month's mortar practice and all those cattle blown to smithereens. The men had laughed about it for days.

No charges had been brought. The ranchers, whose herds grazed the acres of rolling grassland comprising the fort's ranges, were quietly paid for the beef. No one wanted to raise a stink. Most of the soldiers involved were *short-timers*, in army parlance, and would soon be the problem of civilian society. The army seemed as anxious to be rid of the young killers as the young killers were anxious to be gone.

So far, Tyler's duties as a platoon leader had been remarkable only in their disappointments. His men were, for the most part, Vietnam returnees finishing their enlistments with stateside duty. Few planned to stay in the army. He could understand the draftees' reluctance to play the game, but the regular army volunteers seemed equally disposed to wrap up their time with minimum effort and get out.

Tyler had gotten a glimpse of the lack of respect combat veterans had for neophyte officers. The sneering remarks prompted by any order the troops deemed frivolous, or, in the vernacular of the enlisted men, *harassment*, bordered on insubordination. A few had come close to physically challenging him. The look in their eyes left him doubtless that they were capable of killing him without a qualm. His fellow officers seemed equally at a loss to establish their authority. His commiseration with a fellow newby lieutenant had convinced him that lack of control was rampant.

"Ever seen that cartoon with the two vultures sitting in a tree?" the frustrated officer had quipped. "One says to the other, 'Patience, hell. Let's kill something.' I tell you, Tom, I've seen that in their eyes when they look at me. And this is America. What's Nam going to be like?"

Like Tyler, most of the other new lieutenants still wanted to find out.

The young officer shifted uncomfortably on the hard mahogany bench and glanced around the outer office. Apple-green paint coated walls and woodwork. That same sickening green had been the color of choice in every building he had entered since arriving on this post. When they said the US Army was uniform, they must have meant uniformly dull.

If he had known how his career was going to progress, or to be more accurate, stagnate, he might have had second thoughts about his chosen path. It had been a long, hard road getting where he was: four years of college laced with ROTC until, finally, upon graduation, he held a Liberal Arts BA and a commission as an officer in the United States Army.

He had been so proud of the crossed flintlock rifles struck in gleaming brass on his dress greens lapels and the pale blue Infantry rope encircling his right shoulder. He hadn't known when he had begun his military obligation that he would be so caught up in it. It had started as just something he had to do to repay his country for his education. He had not imagined he would enjoy it, much less revel in the sense of accomplishment he had known in recent months. He had become part of something momentous and important, something preordained. Tom Tyler had attained an essence of destiny—until they had sent him here.

Vietnam was where he wanted to be. Possessed by a wanderlust that baffled his family, the geographic location of the place fascinated him. The country was just about halfway around the world from his Mississippi birthplace. He couldn't get any farther from home without heading back, and that intrigued him. The lure of adventure in that war-torn land only heightened its appeal.

But, despite having volunteered for combat, he'd been assigned duty here—in Texas—barely out of sight of the Big Muddy—training experienced jungle fighters in the fine points of conventional warfare. The US Army was uniform all right, uniformly stupid.

He checked his watch again, grumbled, "Hurry up and wait," under his breath, and thought he saw the major's clerk grinning for a split second before the Spec/5's eyes snapped back to the form in his manual typewriter. The Specialist resumed his two-fingered pecking.

Glaring at the freckle-faced kid, Tyler shuffled through his mail and congratulated himself on his foresight in grabbing it from his mailbox on the way here. A good officer makes efficient use of time.

There were the usual letters from his parents. He looked forward to his dad's, but his mother's would be full of thinly disguised attempts to change his mind about pushing for a combat posting. He unrolled a copy of his hometown newspaper, electing to save the letters for a more private moment. He turned first to the sports page and was surprised to see the name of the third-rate college outside of his hometown in a small headline near the bottom of the page.

OKESON OUSTS TRACK STAR, the banner announced. The text went on to tell the story of Okeson College's imported best hope for the track and field championship—one Daniel *Meteor* Mulvaney—being expelled due to conduct inconsistent with Okeson's traditions and standards. The actions of which the student had been accused were not specified. The regrets of the college president and the coaching staff were expressed. The vague references to Mulvaney's shocking behavior left little doubt that *Meteor* Mulvaney had royally pissed someone off. Tyler was curious as to what, exactly, the student had done, but the story did not go beyond a strong sense that the young man had brought a great deal of shame upon all concerned. Mulvaney had been unavailable for comment.

The article brought to mind his father's humorous comments one sultry summer evening while sipping cold beer on the back porch. Alvin Tyler had been greatly amused by Okeson's attempt to increase enrollment by seeking to enhance the school's image through its athletic program. The idea had been to offer full scholarships to outstanding athletes nationwide in hopes of grabbing new glory on the playing field, thereby putting Okeson on the map as a comer in the world of collegiate sports. The problem, as the senior Tyler saw it, was that the faculty and staff of Okeson were so far out of step in the academic community that attendance by the starting lineup of the Dallas Cowboys would not help Okeson's reputation, even if they brought the cheerleaders.

Tom Tyler had traveled north to Pennsylvania for his education. The good schools in the south were out of his financial reach, and Alvin insisted some time among the Yankees would broaden his horizons. His father, Tyler had decided long ago, was a wise and prescient soul.

He grew bored with reading and folded the paper, checked his watch again, and then his uniform. The Pathfinder patch on his left pocket made him think of Grayson. He owed that award to the Airborne Ranger Captain. If he had not met him one night in the Officer's Club, he might never have gone to Panama. The ribbons on Grayson's chest and the coveted CIB—the Combat Infantry Badge—had made Tyler forget his father's standing advice. For the first time in his life, he had asked a stranger's opinion.

"Believe you me—" Grayson had been blunt. "—you don't want to go over there without some idea of how you'll fare in that godawful terrain and hellish climate."

Tyler had silently scoffed at the older man's admonition as an attempt to pee on an untried young officer's parade.

"I shit you not," Grayson had insisted, making Tyler wonder if he was that transparent. "You young fire-eaters think the schooling they give you in weapons and tactics and leadership has prepared you for what's ahead of you. Bullshit," the captain said to his unspoken reply. "They *can't* prepare you for the horror you're looking to get into. The heat and stink and insects and critters in a Southeast Asian rain forest are enough to drive civilized men bugfuck. Factor in a few million murderous gooks and a platoon of GIs, all of whom will have more savvy than you in the business of staying alive in that miserable place and you, brand spanking new second lieutenant, are in a world of shit."

Grayson paused to take a healthy slug of his Jim Beam and looked deep into Tyler's eyes. "If you're serious about doing the job right," he paused to ensure Tyler's undivided attention. Tyler's slow nod and solid eye contact convinced the captain he had it. "Then you'll get yourself some serious training before you head on over there."

"Such as?" Tyler remembered being wary. He had had enough of school.

"Panama Jungle School for starters," Grayson recited. "Then there's Airborne and Ranger School." The captain thumped an index finger on the bar top for emphasis with each one.

"Captain," Tyler interrupted. "If I take all those courses, the damned war will be over by the time I get there."

"You should be so lucky, my impetuous young friend."

Tyler remembered Grayson's sardonic smile. He saw something in Grayson's eyes then, as if the man were somewhere else for a moment. Tyler had felt surrounded by ghosts.

The captain, Tyler learned from their subsequent conversation, was not much older than he, but seemed generations wiser. Grayson avoided the subject of Vietnam for the rest of the evening, deftly sidestepping Tyler's queries. Tyler got the impression that Grayson did not believe he had the capacity to understand. He would probably never see Grayson again, but he knew he would never forget him.

Then, having somehow managed to complete thirty days of training, more grueling than anything he had imagined possible, in Panama's steaming jungles, Tyler received orders to report to the Second Armored Division in Fort Hood, Texas.

The knowledge that a month in the jungle had taken more out of him than he would like to admit was daunting. What would a year be like? Despite misgivings about his physical shortcomings, he yearned to test his mettle. The newspapers were full of the siege of Khe San, and the nation was reeling from the onslaught of the Tet Offensive. Anchormen and columnists regaled the public with comparisons to Dien Bien Phu. Student protests across the country gave no relief from the scenes of battle aired each evening on the nightly news. Hell had broken loose on the other side of the planet, and the shockwaves echoed in the streets of the United States. But here *he* was, stuck in this repository for used fighting men and abused leaders.

Tom Tyler would not be denied his right to put his training to the test. He wanted in, and he wanted it now.

"Mornin', sir," Sergeant Major Eagle murmured as he strode past Tyler on his way into Major Brandt's office.

Tyler, jolted back to the present, started. He checked himself, feeling his body tense, reminding himself that he didn't have to spring to attention for a non-commissioned officer. Eagle had that effect on him. Tyler supposed the wiry old Senior NCO had that effect on a lot of men.

A gaunt old soldier, dressed in starched fatigues with knife-edge creases, Eagle looked, at first glance, emaciated. A beak-like nose dominated the center of a weathered face. The sergeant's leathery skin reminded Tyler of portraits of old cowboys he had seen on the covers of paperback westerns. The man's white-sidewall haircut accentuated large, protruding, raptor-wing ears. The effect was momentarily comical, so bird-like did the sergeant major appear, until one noticed the eyes. They were black, flinty eyes. Tyler had never known anyone more aptly named. Sergeant Major Eagle was a strange bird, but definitely a bird of prey.

In retrospect, Tyler's first meeting with the sergeant major might have gone somewhat better. Afire with righteous indignation, he had stormed into Eagle's office the day he reported for duty and lit into the man, without overture, about the idiocy of sending him, Second Lieutenant Thomas Matthew Tyler, a highly trained jungle expert, to this wasteland known as Texas. He had slapped his orders down on the desk hard enough to make the little crossed flags in the pen stand flutter.

Glancing at the paperwork for only a second, the sergeant major said, so softly that Tyler had to strain to hear, "Close the door, would you, sir? And have a seat."

Eagle waited patiently while Tyler closed his office door and settled himself in the black vinyl chair in front of his desk.

"Sir—" Eagle spat the word with unmistakable contempt the moment Tyler was settled. "—if you ever come into my office again with the attitude I have just seen demonstrated, I will take you out behind this here building, and I will kick your fuzzy young ass upside your ears. Is that crystal clear, Lieutenant?"

Tyler still mentally cringed whenever Eagle was in the room. He would never forget the lesson he had learned that day.

Eagle came out of Brandt's office, and said, "The major will see you now, sir." The way he said, 'sir' sounded, to Tyler, more like, "sonny."

With a curt nod of thanks, Tyler marched into the major's office, reported in the prescribed manner, snapped a textbook salute, and stood at attention.

"At ease, Lieutenant," Brandt replied, returning Tyler's salute with the relaxed wave field grade officers dispense to lowly second lieutenants. "Siddown."

Muttering his thanks, Tyler sat at attention in a straight-backed wooden chair in front of the major's desk.

"Relax," Brandt said. "Jeez, you *Rotsee* pups are stiffer than three-day-old cornbread."

Tyler squirmed in his seat but said nothing.

"I've got good news for you, Lieutenant. Your orders have come down." He lifted several pages from his desk. "You can stop driving everybody around here crazy with transfer requests. You're going to Vietnam."

Tyler's face splitting grin was ample response.

"You needn't have made such a pain in the ass of yourself, you know," Brandt continued. "You were always RVN-bound. It was just a matter of Military Assistance Command figuring out which war zone you were most needed in. You can begin out-processing immediately. You'll need to get your shots up to date, of course, and all the other bureaucratic mumbo-jumbo the government requires before we ship your ass overseas." He rose to signify that the meeting was at an end. Tyler did likewise, accepted the papers handed him, and the handshake that came with them.

"Good luck, Lieutenant. Enjoy your leave."

"Leave? Is that mandatory, sir?"

"SOP, Lieutenant—Standard Operating Procedure. Personnel assigned to a combat zone get thirty days leave prior to deployment," Brandt recited.

"Can I waive it, sir?"

Frowning, Major Brandt answered, "Certainly, Lieutenant, but have you thought about it? It's going to be a long year."

Tyler had not thought about it. His only thought had been to get over there. As he considered it now, he was certain that he did not want to go home. There was nothing there for him but more wrangling with his mother and his father's steadfast refusal to intervene. Even Debbie, his former fiancée, was no longer a factor since the *Dear John* letter last month.

"I'm sure, sir. I'd like to forego the leave."

With a sigh, Major Brandt dropped into his chair. "You've got no conscience when it comes to generating paperwork, Lieutenant. I'll see what I can do. Dismissed." He shooed Tyler from his office, ignoring his departing salute.

When the door closed behind Tyler, a bewildered Major Brandt wondered aloud, "What makes a young man so all fired anxious to get hisself killed?"

CHAPTER 5

Brooklyn, New York:

Danny sipped his morning coffee, smoked a cigarette, and toyed with a spoon. He found that he could catch sunlight streaming through the window blinds and deflect it to spotlight odd defects in the tenement kitchen's floral wallpaper. His mother sat across from him, staring at the surface of her timeworn kitchen table in companionable silence. There was little left to say. Induction day had arrived much too quickly. Danny pushed aside a half-eaten bowl of Wheaties.

"Are you sure I can't fix you a hot breakfast?" Joan Mulvaney said.

He pursed his lips and shook his head. She didn't dote on him under normal circumstances. Besides, ham and eggs with home fries and toast would be too much like the last meal of the condemned. Why he was feeling so down, he didn't know. He wasn't going off to war yet, just to Basic Training. So why the second thoughts? Second? Hell, he must be past tenth by now. This was what he wanted, wasn't it?

The past few weeks had flown by. Danny and Amanda had spent as much time together as possible since his draft notice, but he couldn't shake the feeling that their relationship had taken a turn for the worse. She'd been—what? Distant? Detached? He couldn't pin it down, but things *were* different.

Danny had refused Amanda's offer to accompany him to the Induction Center, afraid of voicing his misgivings and ruining whatever chance they might have to rekindle their romance.

"Let's not make a big deal out of this," was his repetitious comment. Now, faced with the actuality of leaving, he was regretting his cavalier response.

Checking his watch for the twentieth time in the last half-hour, he said, "Time to go."

Joan Mulvaney cast an accusing eye at the clock above the stove and nodded begrudging agreement. She kissed him goodbye and gave him an extra strong hug when he rose to go. He looked at her face as he pulled back from her embrace and was shocked to see fear in her eyes.

"I'm going to be just fine. Don't worry." He gave her that lopsided grin, the one she couldn't resist. "This is *The Kid* talking. No sweat, right?"

"I'm your mother. Worrying is a large part of my job." Joan Mulvaney forced a smile and wiped a single, traitorous tear from the corner of one eye. "Fall in, soldier, or you'll be late."

"Strange expression, isn't it, Mom? Fall in? Could be disastrous in the navy."

His mother laughed. Danny felt that he could leave her now with a smile on her face. As he rushed out the door, he heard her motherly reminders as echoes in his mind, like the notes of a favorite tune.

In the hallway, he memorized every inch of peeling paint and warped wood in the two-story walk-up. The checkered linoleum—its finish rubbed to the backing in spots—had charm never noticed before. Mrs. Fioretti's tomato sauce had never smelled as sweet. Dust motes, floating in the morning rays through the roof skylight, winked goodbye. The rundown four-family building he grew up in had never felt more like home.

As he stepped out onto the high, granite front stoop, he found Gino lounging against the wrought iron railing.

"Hey, soldier-boy, want a lift?"

Danny's face lit up. "What the hell are you doing here?"

"I borrowed a car, man. Thought I'd run you down to Jamaica."

"Sounds good to me." Danny slapped his buddy on the back.

Gino led him to a late model Cadillac, a gleaming white Eldorado convertible, parked at the curb. Danny raised an eyebrow as he eased down into the roll-pleated, black leather interior.

"Wow! What idiot would loan this chariot to *you*?"

"Nicky Marino," Gino said proudly, peeling rubber as he left the curb.

"Nicky Marino, *the car thief?* You're driving me to the draft board in a hot car?"

"Not hot. A little warm, shall we say? Don't sweat it. The reggie would fool any dumb-ass cop. It pains me to know some rich dude on Long Island has to rough it and take the Chevy to work today."

"You're un-fucking-believable."

"Ain't it the truth?" Gino took it as the highest praise. They laughed all the way to Metropolitan Avenue.

He felt chilly with the top down, but Danny was enjoying his last minutes of freedom too much to complain. They soon ran out of small talk and Nicky Marino anecdotes. Danny fiddled with the radio to find some music. He caught Barry and the Tamerlanes singing "I Wonder What She's Doing Tonight" and sang along.

"Missing little Mandy already?" Gino said, with a knowing glance.

"Her name's Amanda, not Mandy. She'd whip your ass if she heard you call her Mandy."

"Ooh, stop. I'll get a hard-on."

"Watch it, asshole."

"Lighten up. It was a joke. What's wrong with calling her Mandy?"

"She says Mandy sounds like an air-head in go-go boots." Danny laughed at the mental image. "And don't call her Amy, either. She says Amy's for little girls with pig-tails and Mary Janes."

"Who's Mary Jane?"

"Haven't the foggiest."

"Okay, so what about—*Amanda?*"

"What about her?"

"Well, I haven't seen a hell of a lot of you since you dropped the bomb that morning in the bowling alley. It was pretty obvious you were spending a lot of time somewhere else. I figured the doe-eyed brunette from the office was a safe bet."

Gino maneuvered the big car through the rush hour traffic with ease.

"Yeah, we did see a lot of each other these past couple of weeks," Danny admitted.

"So, we talking true love here, or is she just the best piece of ass in the five boroughs?"

"Gino," Danny said, looking straight ahead, "I'm not going to tell you again..."

"Okay, okay! Geez, you get touchy when this chick comes up in conversation. What's with you, man? A broad is a broad. No big deal." He glanced over and met Danny's most malevolent stare, leveled like a loaded gun aimed between his eyes. "Cool it, Danny. You look like you're ready to belt me."

"The thought crossed my mind."

"Whoa. Easy, big fella." Gino adopted his Tonto persona. "Kemosabe have heap large problem with squaw. Faithful Indian companion—" He slapped his chest. "—try only to shovel buffalo shit from masked man's eyes." Seeing that Tonto was not having the usual ice-breaking effect, Gino tried indignation. "Is this any way to act? I'm doing you a solid, and you're getting pissed off? Settle down, will you? I'm sorry. I won't make any more cracks about your girl, okay?"

Danny's reply was a curt nod.

They rode in uncomfortable silence for several minutes until Danny glanced at his watch. "I was figuring on taking the bus. We're going to be way too early. Let's get some coffee or something."

"There's a Dunkin Donuts on Hillside, just past the roller rink."

"Perfect."

They talked about the army and what they thought Danny should expect—both young men citing anecdotal scraps they had gleaned from acquaintances and rumors—until they sat in a parking lot munching donuts from a pink and tan box. Danny watched the cars whiz by and imagined the drivers rushing off to work, to school, and a hundred carefree errands. He tried not to envy them.

"So, tell me about Amanda," Gino said quietly around the lip of his cardboard coffee cup.

Danny sighed. "Tell you what?"

"Will she wait?"

"How the hell do I know?"

"Do you want her to?"

Danny brushed crumbs from his blue polo shirt, and said, "I guess so."

"What's bothering you, man?"

"She's been acting funny ever since I got drafted."

"Funny ha-ha or funny peculiar?"

"You know—weird. One minute she's all over me and the next she's out of reach. I don't know. Like I said, weird."

Gino nodded, and said, "Think about this, man. She sees the handwriting on the wall. Lover boy is about to be gone for two long years. Now, I've never met this broad, but I seen her picture, and you have told me *mucho* much about her. It don't take a PhD in female psychology for old Gino to see a thoroughbred like you say she is—and from the pic, I tend to agree—is not going to wait around whilst the boyfriend trots off to play soldier-boy.

"Danny, wake up and smell the coffee. This chick is long gone. The only one that don't know it yet is sitting here threatening his lifelong friend with assault and battery every time he makes some innocent remark." He punctuated the end of his speech with a raised eyebrow and a backhand gesture, defying Danny to refute the obvious.

"Could I be that dumb?"

"You ain't dumb, m'man," Gino consoled. "That bi—" Catching the sparks in Danny's eyes rekindling, he rephrased, "—bit of fluff is a New York City girl, my friend, a Manhattan Mama, the Major League of female slickness. Them NYC chicks are the most calculating creatures on the planet. They are, uh...whatchacall?...social pathetic."

"You mean sociopathic, don't you?" Danny smiled at Gino's mayhem of the King's English.

"Precisely." Gino was pleased with his analysis. "No fucking conscience."

"Thank you, Doctor Sebastionelli." Danny rolled his eyes.

"No problem, my good man. I'll mail you my bill."

"I just don't get it. It doesn't add up." Danny ignored the exasperated gesture Gino made with his hands. He couldn't shake the feeling that Gino was jealous. They'd been inseparable until Amanda had entered his life. "She's going to NYU at night," he said. "She's going to make something of herself. Did I tell you that?"

"Only about a million times." Gino sighed.

"That's what I don't understand."

"Me neither." Gino wagged his head.

"What?" Danny said.

"Come again?"

"What don't you understand?" Danny said.

"I thought you said that."

"I did. You said, 'Me neither.'"

"Oh, yeah. College, that's what I don't understand." Gino frowned.

"It's a fairly old concept known as higher education, Gino. People go there so they won't be dumb sons of bitches like certain people I know."

"I'll ignore that, Daniel. You are obviously not thinking clearly, and I'll take that into account. Need I remind you which of us 'dumb sons of bitches' is being driven to the draft board?" Danny opened his mouth to verbalize a snappy rejoinder, but Gino cut him off. "Why would a good looking broad like that need college?"

"You wouldn't understand."

"That's what I said."

Danny shook his head. "Forget it."

"Now you're talking."

"Will you please listen to me?"

"I thought I was." Gino threw his coffee cup a sour look. "We shoulda got beer."

Danny wondered how he could expect Gino to fathom something he, himself, failed to comprehend. "Get this," he said. "Last night—our last night together, mind you—and she has to go home early to write a friggin' letter to her married sister in Buffalo. Sometimes she makes me think I'm going nuts."

"Thank God." Gino finished his coffee. "I thought it was me." He started the engine and slapped the gearshift.

They were still early. Gino parked in a tow-away zone in sight of the line of young men queuing up outside the draft board offices and waved away Danny's apprehension about attracting police attention in a stolen car.

"What are you planning to do now?" Danny asked, looking at the line of nervous young men.

"Go ahead with the plan, what else?" Gino turned in the seat with his left hand hooked on the steering wheel, his right arm stretched across the seat back, and waited for Danny to make eye contact. "Just because you're out of your tree doesn't mean I am."

"Then you're really going through with it. Canada?"

"Absolutely. By the time you finish the oath, ol' Gino will be cruising north. I ain't stopping until all I hear is French."

"How are you going to get there?"

"Behold." Gino made a sweeping gesture encompassing the car. "Bags are packed and stashed in the trunk."

"You're going to rob Nicky's car?"

"Who's he going to tell? The cops?" He mimicked Nicky's nasal whine. "Officer, my friend stole my stolen car." He laughed a short, derisive laugh. "Yeah, right? Fuck Nicky Marino. He didn't actually loan me this boat, you know. He rented it to me. Fifty cents a mile. Can you believe that prick? How many favors have I done for him? Fuck Nicky where he breathes."

Danny sighed. "Will you let me know where you are?"

"Figure I'm in Montreal. I'll have to be careful about letters and such. The Feds will be after me."

Danny threw his coffee cup onto the sidewalk and glowered at the street. "This isn't the way I thought it would be."

"Hey, man, no news is good news. I'll catch up with you when all this shit is over."

"I hope so." Danny had an overwhelming moment of help-lessness.

"Don't worry about Gino. Nobody's going to be shooting at me. You watch out for your own ass." Gino crumpled his empty cup. "You sure I can't convince you to go with me? It ain't too late. Them French broads invented the blow-job, you know."

Danny laughed. "They're Canadians, Gino. Some of them *speak* French."

"A minor technicality. You wanna check 'em out anyway?"

"Thanks, no. My mind's made up."

Gino grinned. "What mind?"

They shook hands, exchanged good-natured insults, and said goodbye. Danny stood alone on the curb and felt the isolation of the human spirit weigh heavily upon him as he watched the Caddy turn left at the corner and disappear. He whispered, "Good luck, Tonto," bit a trembling bottom lip and turned toward the line of anxious young men.

CHAPTER 6

Republic of South Vietnam:

Tom Tyler held tightly to the Jeep's seat frame as it bounced and rattled over ruts and furrows in a dusty road skirting Bearcat Base Camp.

Just days before, when his Pan Am 707 had touched down at Bien Hoa Air Base, he and his fellow replacements had been whisked to Long Binh in olive-green buses with caged windows—the apparent purpose of which was sobering. He was processed through the Ninetieth Replacement Battalion and, much to his delight, assigned to the Ninth Infantry Division. The following day, he was ordered to Bearcat—the Ninth's main base camp—for Jungle School, which was a seven-day crash course in the operational methods of the Ninth in the Mekong Delta. The basic message the school imparted was: Forget everything you think you know. We don't do it that way.

Immediately following the training—which left much to be desired when compared to Panama—Tyler was given assignment orders to Charlie Company, Second Battalion of the Sixth Regiment. He was then ushered hastily into the Jeep and sent rocketing across the sprawling camp with a pimple-faced PFC driver who kept mumbling, "Don't worry, sir. We'll make it."

The vehicle skidded to a halt in a cloud of dust. Tyler surveyed a deserted field with scattered sandbags, tent pegs and odd bits of discarded gear being the only evidence of recent occupation.

"Shit! Missed 'em," the driver snarled.

"Missed who, Private?"

"Charlie Company, sir." The kid banged the steering wheel with the heel of his hand. "Shit!"

"What do you mean, we missed them?"

"They're gone, sir." The driver's head swiveled around to punctuate his statement.

Slowly and succinctly, Tyler said, "I can see there's no one here, soldier. Am I to assume from your comments that C-Company used to be here?"

The frustrated chauffeur nodded.

"So, where did they go?"

"Delta Tango, sir. Must've left real early."

"How do you know this?"

"They're not here, Lieutenant."

"Yes, I can see that." Tyler removed his helmet and wiped sweat from his brow with the rolled-up sleeve of his new jungle fatigue jacket. He was hot and grimy from the dusty Jeep ride and the day had barely begun. "What I'm trying to determine, Private, is what or where is Delta Tango, and why you think C-Company has gone there?"

"Dong Tam, sir," the driver said. "Delta Tango is Dong Tam." Seeing this meant nothing to the lieutenant, the man made an O of his mouth, as if suddenly remembering to whom he was speaking. "Dong Tam is our new base camp. The whole Division's movin' down there. Charlie Company's due to go on the boats. They'll meet the ships down there."

Tyler had learned enough about the multi-role capabilities of the Ninth to piece together that his new company had been as-signed to Mobile Riverine duties: a joint army-navy task force charged with combat operations on the rivers, streams, and canals of the Mekong Delta. Combining ground and waterborne forces was an ambitious tactic that had not been tried since the Ameri-can Civil War.

The fact that the entire division to which he was assigned was in the process of pulling up stakes, and no one had seen fit to in-form him, was galling and somewhat humbling. "Can we catch them?" he said.

"No, sir." The man shook his head. "I'm not authorized to leave Bearcat."

While Tyler weighed this, a dust-covered deuce-and-a-half—a ten-wheeled truck rated to carry two and a half tons of cargo—

slid to a stop in front of them. None of the eight passengers, seated on fold-down wooden benches bracketing the bed, moved for several beats. As if on cue, the cab doors flew open, the tailgate banged down, and the soldiers laboriously climbed down, dragging weapons and equipment.

Of the eight men on board, the chronological senior was twenty-two years of age, but their stooped shoulders and stiff movements suggested the arthritic gait of old men. Each slung his heavy rucksack on one shoulder and, clutching his weapon in his opposite fist, stooped to inspect the tires.

The driver stalked around the vehicle, mumbling curses. Completing his inspection, he flung his steel helmet to the ground.

"Shit—*damnit!* Three fuckin' tires shot out. Son-of-a-*bitch!*" The thin young man kicked his discarded helmet, flipping it end over end to land under the vehicle.

The former passengers exchanged barely concealed grins before dropping their eyes or looking anywhere but at the enraged soldier.

"Okay. Calm the fuck down," Desmond Pomeroy, a black buck-sergeant drawled. Surveying the scattered detritus of what had once been Charlie Company's area, he said, for all to hear, "Company's split. We gotta fix this hunkajunk and sky on up." Doffing his helmet, he added, "Now, where the fuck is Top?" He spied Tyler and the Jeep driver standing beside their vehicle and loped across twenty yards of red dust to speak to them. He spotted the shiny brass bar affixed to Tyler's helmet cover at once, and said, "'Scuse me, sir."

Tyler, who was feeling disoriented in this strange new environment, was about to demand basic military courtesy in the form of a salute. But his run-in with Sergeant Major Eagle had taught him much about being sure of his ground, and he would have been the first to admit that he was not. He sat on the Jeep's fender, and said, "Sarge, I'm new here, and I don't know shit yet. Would you mind explaining to me why a non-com doesn't salute a commissioned officer?"

Sergeant Pomeroy stopped. He looked Tyler dead in the eye, raised one eyebrow, sighed, and said, "Not at all, sir." He grinned, showing big yellow teeth, but his eyes betrayed him. His disappointment was evident when he said, "We a little too close to the wire to be snappin' high balls here." He turned to indicate the perimeter with his chin. "Charley's out there, sir, and he's watchin'. Charley's always watchin'. He knows what a salute means as well as we do. We don't help him none by pointin' out our officers." He paused to resettle his grin on the lieutenant. "Snipers. Know what I mean, Lieutenant?"

Tyler felt the hair on his neck prickle. "Sure do, Sergeant."

The sergeant nodded to Tyler's helmet. "Best lose that bar, aysap."

Remembering the brass insignia pinned to his camouflage cover, Tyler uttered a sheepish, "Right," and hastily removed his helmet to pluck the gleaming symbol from its place.

"You must be our new platoon leader," Pomeroy surmised, looking Tyler up and down as if amused at the quality of officer the army was turning out these days.

"If y'all are from Charlie Company, I guess I am." Tyler stood erect to offer Pomeroy his hand. "Tom Tyler, Sergeant, pleased to meet you. And I'll be depending on you and the rest of the men to help me get the hang of all this long enough for me to get to be your *old* platoon leader."

Pomeroy shook the officer's hand, still grinning. Tyler wasn't sure if the man was friendly or just insubordinate.

"Desmond Pomeroy," the sergeant said, "acting Second Platoon Sergeant. This—" He jerked a thumb at the group around the truck. "—is the First Squad, sir."

"I'd like to meet them, but first, if you don't mind, Sergeant Pomeroy, would you fill me in on the situation? I understand from this man here—" He gestured toward the Jeep driver. "—that C-Company has moved."

"Yes, sir, to Dong Tam. We were sent out as security for a medcap at first light. We were told to hook up with our first sergeant if we didn't get back in time for the move, but he ain't here. You ain't seen him, have you, sir?"

"No, can't say as I have."

"Well, we'll just wait," Pomeroy decided. "Can't go nowheres anyway. Truck's fucked. Would you like to meet the fellas now, sir?"

Tyler nodded, and Pomeroy shouted, "*Lai dai mau,* muthafuckas. Git your ugly asses over here to meet your new boss."

When the introductions were concluded, Tyler asked, "What happened to the truck?"

A swarthy, strikingly handsome PFC, with the thickest black mustache Tyler had ever seen, outlined the event.

"Ol' Chuck let loose with a couple bursts on us on our way back. Didn't hit nobody but did a job on them tires." He scrunched his face in disbelief. "Antsiest bunch of medics I ever did see. Man, those dudes was shittin' a brick."

Tyler's look of confusion prompted Pomeroy to clarify.

"We dropped off the medics at the hospital, sir. They weren't our medics. Word came down last night that a little village north of The Rubber had a lot of sick people. Division sent out a team of medics from the camp aid station. Usually, when we pull a medcap—that's a kind of sick call for the gooks—our own docs go, and whoever's company supplies the medics supplies security.

"Well, with all our guys heading for Delta Tango, they musta decided to send some Division-type *bacsies*. Keep our medics where they belong case they're needed, I s'pose. Now, these Division dudes don't go outside the wire much. Gettin' shot at is a new experience for most of 'em. For whatever reason, we got the call to go along."

Tyler knew from his orientation that The Rubber was the Michelin plantation south of Bearcat. Division was headquarters. He had no idea what *bacsies* were but did not want to appear any greener than his new fatigues already showed him to be. He elected to wait for the definition of that one.

"So, you were ambushed on the way back?" he asked, expecting more detail of the attack.

"Oh, no, sir," Black Mustache corrected him. "It was more like a friendly warning. If they was out to ambush us, they woulda had their shit together. Naw, we was just a target of opportunity."

"Yeah, man." A red-headed kid, who didn't look old enough to be out of high school, chuckled. "Charley was just clearing his weapon before going home to pick rice, you *bic*?"

Understanding nothing other than this was going to be a very strange war, Tyler nodded. "So, let's get those flats fixed and catch up with the company, eh?"

"Not all that easy, Lieutenant," Pomeroy said. His tone was apologetic, but Tyler read mild impatience, too. "You don't just call Triple-A out here, ya' know."

Tyler had the unsettling feeling of being lectured to. Captain Grayson came to mind.

"That's most affirmative, sir," the driver interrupted. "Them tires need to be replaced and we ain't got but one spare."

"'Sides, we got to locate our first sergeant," Pomeroy added.

"Maybe he's gone ahead with the company, Sarge," Tyler supposed, trying to redeem himself, and wondering why.

"Negatory, sir." The sergeant shook his head. "Plan-B was to meet Top here iff'n the company skied up 'fore we got back. Top's here somewhere, and he'll be highly pissed off if we leave him behind."

As Tyler considered what was turning out to be his first command decision, which it seemed he was going to be obliged to make with only the sketchiest of information, the sound of an approaching vehicle drew their attention. A Jeep braked to a stop, closely followed by the inevitable cloud of dust. The men shielded their eyes and clenched their teeth in an effort to avoid billowing dirt.

A bull of a man with three chevrons and three rockers above and below the diamond on his sleeves hopped lightly from the vehicle, and rasped, "Where the hell have you been, Platoon Sergeant?"

"'Lo, Top," Pomeroy said, "I was about to ask you same-same."

"Been out trying to hunt up our new lieutenant. Seems they sent him our way, but it would appear he has gone missing."

"Negative, First Sergeant," Tyler corrected him, stepping to the front of the group. "Tom Tyler, reporting as ordered," he said, thrusting his hand forward.

"Sorry, sir. Didn't see you." Shaking Tyler's hand heartily, he introduced himself. "Andy Syzmanski, First Sergeant, Charlie Company. Glad to know you."

The Combat Infantry Badge above the First Sergeant's breast pocket had a star between the points of the encircling silver wreath, signifying a second award. Andy Syzmanski was an old soldier experiencing his second war.

"Likewise, Top," Tyler said. "We seem to have a little problem here."

Tyler and the men of the First Squad quickly related the situation with the truck and the event that had caused the dilemma.

"Anybody hurt?" Syzmanski asked.

Once assured that all of the men were intact, the first sergeant said, "Sir, might I have a word with you?" He took Tyler aside and in muffled tones suggested, "In a situation like this, with the company moving south as we speak, and it being our duty to catch up to them with all possible haste—"

Tyler's nod confirmed his agreement.

"—well, sir, we might be forced to bend a few regs, if you know what I mean."

Tyler did not, but he nodded again.

"You see, sir, you being an officer and all, it might not look too good for the men to see their new platoon leader giving his approval to acts that might be construed as..."

"Illegal, First Sergeant?" Tyler grinned, not certain what the senior non-com had in mind but getting the drift.

"That's a bit strong a word, sir, but for want of a better one..."

"Suppose I was to sit down on the edge of that ditch over there, First Sergeant—" Tyler indicated a nearby trench. "—and just thought about what we might do to extricate ourselves from this predicament, concentrating all the while on the wood-line out there." He pointed toward the perimeter.

"You might just miss any activity to your rear, sir."

"I would put my trust in you and these men to protect my ass, First Sergeant," Tyler said with mock solemnity.

"Rest assured, Lieutenant, CYA is our motto," Syzmanski vowed, his hand on his heart.

"Outstanding, First Sergeant."

As Tyler studied the exotic tropical landscape, he ignored the flurry of activity behind him as six men raced away in the two Jeeps and returned with three wheels snatched from unwary motor pools. Tools clinked, and men grunted and cursed until, ninety minutes later, they were loading up for the trip to Dong Tam.

"Sergeant Pomeroy," Top called. The lanky sergeant loped to his side as Syzmanski climbed into the driver's seat of the Jeep. "Lieutenant Tyler will ride shotgun with me. Lend us one of your people to ride in back."

"Roger that, Top. Sizemore," he yelled to the squad in the back of the truck. "Jump up here on the jukebox." He slapped the radio bolted to the fender seat. "And keep your eyes open."

A Californian, a model of the Golden State's sun-worshipping youth, leaped from the truck and sprinted toward them, his heavy rucksack and load of forty-millimeter M-79 grenades not encumbering him in any way. His bulging biceps attested to his strength, his friendly smile to his good nature.

"I like a little punch in the lead vehicle," Pomeroy informed Tyler. Turning to the first sergeant, he said, "We'll put the Sixty on the roof of the deuce-and-a-half, Top."

Tyler turned to see another man resting the bipod of an M-60 machine-gun on the gun ring above the truck cab.

"Good enough," Top approved. He fished in the cargo pockets of his fatigues and added, "Pin these on, Staff Sergeant," handing Pomeroy two black metal collar insignia.

Pomeroy looked with pride at the symbols of his promotion. "Thanks, Top."

Tyler was touched by the emotion in the black sergeant's eyes.

"Well deserved, Desmond. You're a hell of a soldier. Now, let's un-ass this dump."

As they roared out of the gate and sped south to overtake their unit, Tyler drank in the oriental beauty of the countryside, thrilled to finally be in Vietnam.

"Keep that weapon handy, sir," Top warned, interrupting his reverie. "It can turn real ugly, real quick."

Once they had cleared Bearcat, the two vehicles raced south with First Sergeant Syzmanski driving like the big truck behind them was chasing them rather than doing its best to keep up. Tyler watched the road deteriorate from four-lane blacktop outside of Long Binh to a single lane that finally became a rural dirt road.

The countryside was a lush tropical paradise with graceful palms and broad expanses of shimmering green rice paddy everywhere he looked. What was not farmland was wild jungle, and the buildings he saw were so primitive they were hard to place within his concept of recent history. The route was sometimes wide open and sometimes choked with traffic. When they barreled through Saigon in the early afternoon, Tyler was enthralled. The sights and scents of what the French called the Paris of the Orient made for a heady experience. They stopped briefly to buy cold drinks at a roadside stand just south of the city, and Tyler was pleasantly surprised to be served bottled Coca-Cola. Syzmanski had the Jeep in motion again before Tyler was settled in his seat and the lieutenant protested for the first time.

"Slow down, will you First Sergeant? What's the rush?"

"First, sir," Syzmanski replied, "it's getting late. You don't want to be on this road at night. And second, you don't want to run down Ambush Alley with just two vehicles. We've still got a ways to go and now is not the time to relax. This may all look peaceful, but never forget you're in Indian Country out here. Half of them smiling natives will slit your throat from ear to ear if you give them the chance."

"They can't all be VC, First Sergeant." Tyler watched a young boy riding sprawled across the back of a lumbering water buffalo.

"No, they can't, but you don't want to be too badly outnumbered when you find out which ones are. The captain knows we're following. He'll wait a bit for us to catch up once he gets close to Delta Tango. I figure he'll pull up on Highway Four, somewheres near the entrance to the Alley. But, he won't wait long. He's not going to risk the whole company for a squad."

"Ambush Alley?" Tyler asked, and took the first sip of his Coke. He immediately pulled the bottle from his lips to check the label and then threw a questioning look at the first sergeant.

"Aptly named." Syzmanski laughed. "The road, sir, not the Coke."

"It's different, I'll give it that," Tyler said, with a twist of his head.

"Every time, sir. Every time." Syzmanski laughed again and hit the gas.

Second Platoon's First Squad caught up with Charlie Company on Highway Four at the entrance to Ambush Alley, as Syzmanski had predicted. The ride had been uneventful, unless one counted the repeated vehicular close calls with the natives. Captain Arnold's RTO (Radio Telephone Operator), a capable sergeant named Beecher, repeatedly called on the radio until he raised Syzmanski's Jeep when it came within range of the PRC-25 field radio. They coordinated their approach so that the convoy was getting under way as the two vehicles neared.

The ride down the Alley was fast and dusty. Tyler saw the dangers evident along the road when the foliage nearly touched the speeding vehicles in some sections.

"Division would like to clear all this back a couple hundred meters," Syzmanski yelled over the wind, "but the local Province Chief won't have none of it. Says it's necessary to preserve the balance of nature. Goddamn VC sympathizer."

Tyler's hurried introduction to C-Company began when they rolled into their new company area at the far end of Dong Tam. The size of the place surprised him. The camp was already several square miles and growing.

The troops were assigned to billets. He was ushered into the captain's hootch, a squarish, one story, two room affair attached to one end of the Bachelor Officer's Quarters. The BOQ was a two-story barracks building that was a replica of the enlisted men's quarters with the exception of room dividers to afford some semblance of privacy. All of the buildings were of the same basic design. Wood planking, mounted clapboard style, but on forty-five-degree wedges to allow air circulation between the boards, comprised the walls. Aluminum screening was tacked to the frame beneath the planks. A two-foot span of open screening served as windows along the length of each floor, near the ceiling. Corrugated steel capped the gabled rooftops, and a three-foot-high wall of sandbags girdled the base of each building. Dust was the sole landscaping material available, except in the rainy season, when it would become mud.

Captain Lester T. Arnold, Charlie Company's commanding officer, was a light-skinned black man of medium height. Tyler estimated him to be about five-foot, ten inches tall. His face bore the signs of exposure to the horrors and worries of the past six months, the time he had spent in command of Charlie Company. The Ninth Infantry Division had a policy of rotating its officers to staff positions after six months on the line. Captain Arnold was fighting to stay with his company, Top had told Tyler. So far, he was winning.

"Sit, Lieutenant," the captain invited as Tyler entered the hootch. Tyler had been about to report in the formal fashion. Observing his confusion, Arnold said, "We'll imagine we just went through the motions of a new officer reporting for duty." He motioned Tyler to sit.

The captain plopped into his chair behind a battered, dust-covered camp desk in the front room of the building. The area served as his office when he was not in the field.

Syzmanski rapped twice on the door jam. Both men looked up. "'Scuse me, sirs. You wanted to see me, Captain?"

"What happened with the medcap security?" Arnold asked.

"Took a few rounds coming in. Nobody hurt."

"Did they return fire?" Arnold seemed intent on the answer.

"No, sir," Top replied, eyes downcast.

"Why the hell not?"

"It was a quick burst, sir. They were out of it before they could get a fix on him."

"Bullshit, Top, and you know it." Arnold slammed his hand on the desktop. Dust puffed out from beneath it like a tiny explosion. "They were caught napping. If they'd been alert, they would have pinpointed the son of a bitch and maybe got me a body count. You tell Pomeroy I can pull those stripes as quick as he pinned them on."

"Yes, sir."

"That's all, First Sergeant." As Syzmanski turned to go, the captain called after him. "Nice piece of field expedient maintenance on that deuce-and-a-half, Top."

"Thank you, sir," Top yelled back.

Tyler made a mental note—*the old man's tough, but fair*. Arnold seemed to forget his sudden anger and perused Tyler's 201 folder—the army's standard personnel file.

"Panama. Good. ROTC, hmm." Tyler didn't know if that meant good or bad. "Okeson, Mississippi."

He must be reading backward, Tyler guessed.

"No sense beating around the bush, Lieutenant." Arnold put the folder aside. "You're from the deep South, and I'm black. You got any problem with that?"

"Sorry, sir, but you look OD Green to me, same as everybody else on our side," Tyler said flatly, locking eyes with the captain.

Arnold fished in a drawer, produced a bottle of Johnnie Walker Red Label Scotch, smiled, and asked, "Do you imbibe, Tom?"

"Does a bear shit in the woods, sir?"

For the next hour, Captain Arnold filled Tyler in on the company's recent history and current status. Second Platoon had been without an officer for over a month. Their last platoon leader had been wounded and sent back to the States. Staff Sergeant Pomeroy was an excellent platoon sergeant, but he was also one of the men.

In Arnold's opinion, he tended to be a bit too willing to relax discipline.

The company was moving to the boats the next day after one

night's rest in Dong Tam. They would live on a troop ship anchored in the Mekong River, launching operations by way of river assault craft known as Tango and Mike Boats. The food was good on the boats. The men slept on clean sheets, and the threat of mortars was remote, since the ships changed position often. Sappers would occasionally float explosive charges downstream or swim to the ships to plant mines on their hulls but the Navy did a pretty good job of security. All in all, a trip to the boats was duty the men looked forward to. The down side was the AO—the Area of Operations. Deep mud and sodden paddies were the predominant terrain features. Enemy activity had been light since Tet, but Arnold strongly advised against becoming overconfident, saying, "Charley has a gift for nasty surprises, Tom. Just when you think he's down for the count and you're walking away, he'll bite you in the ass."

CHAPTER 7

Specialist/4 Jesse Pacheco abruptly raised his right fist. The six-man LRRP team on the jungle trail behind him froze. He listened for a moment and then hand-signaled the team to scatter into positions of concealment beside the trail. Silently, the small unit melted into the foliage. Pacheco, the team's point man, had heard someone approaching from the west. This close to Laos and this deep in the jungle it was logical to assume that anyone they met was unfriendly.

The team's mission was to locate enemy troop movements along this branch of the Ho Chi Minh Trail and to pinpoint them for air strikes if they were too numerous to tangle with. If an enemy unit were small, the team would ambush it and vacate the area immediately thereafter. Reconnaissance was the job of the Long Range Recon Patrols—*Lurps* in GI slang—but the highly trained and motivated soldiers who proudly wore the black beret often found themselves in situations where they were forced to fight.

The team watched and waited, adrenaline pulsing through every man. A uniformed North Vietnamese Army soldier stepped cautiously around the bend in the trail that had concealed him from view. Head swiveling from side to side, he moved steadily toward the hidden team members, searching each square foot of the surrounding jungle as he came. Alert, but relaxed, he seemed sure that he and his comrades were still safe in these mountains, so closely bordering Laos.

The enemy point man moved more quickly than Pacheco considered prudent, but, apparently, he felt more at home in these mountains than did the Americans. A decidedly bad habit,

Pacheco was convinced, squeezing the pistol grip of his M-16, gently easing the selector switch from safe to semi-automatic. The team let the lead enemy soldier pass unmolested as they watched to determine the size of the force behind him. Ten minutes later they had counted more than thirty heavily armed troops equipped with AK-47 assault rifles, RPG-7 rocket propelled grenade launchers, RPD machine guns, .61-mm mortar tubes, and plenty of ammunition. Several lugged backpacks bulging with supplies, obviously heavy and, judging by the rest of their lethal loads, probably explosive charges. Still more men marched behind.

These boys are loaded for bear, thought Pacheco. *They are going to bring smoke on somebody's ass.*

The team remained hidden and motionless as the vastly superior force moved through their midst. Engagement would be suicidal. No one had to be told to hold his fire. They would observe and report after the unit had passed. Headquarters would determine whether they were to follow or call in fire support. The task at the moment was to remain undetected. The North Vietnamese Regulars were passing within arm's reach of some of the team. A light rain began to fall.

This would be snow if I was home, Pacheco daydreamed for a second, his mind in the Sierra Nevada.

The last man had passed. The team breathed a collective, silent sigh of relief. They had counted over fifty enemy troops.

Richie Thompson's eyes moved with the last man in the file, but the rest of his body was as still as the ground itself. He couldn't wait for this mission to end. The plan was for this to be a quick, three-day patrol—in and out. Last night had been hellish. Chills and sweats had kept him awake. He thought he must be coming down with something. He had been afraid to sleep, lest he cry out or make some careless noise in a fevered dream. One more night out here, and then he could get back in, load up on antibiotics, and knock this bug for a loop.

Cold rain was soaking through his shirt. The NVA rear guard was almost out of sight. Something salty and moist was running over his upper lip. He needed to wipe his nose. As he started to reach for the leaky nostril, it happened.

He sneezed. The trooper fought to suppress it, but the muffled sound was audible.

Startled, the enemy rear guard whirled to fire his AK on full automatic. The Lurp team reacted instantly, returning fire on full-auto, as well. The heavy air crackled and popped. The enemy soldier nearly disintegrated as a storm of bullets ripped him to pieces. Excellent marksmen to a man, the Recondos could not miss at this range, barely forty feet.

Sergeant Jan Ogilvy yelled, "Run!" jumped to his feet and sprayed the trail to the east with lead to cover his team. Four Americans burst from the brush and crashed through the undergrowth, fleeing for their lives. Pacheco, now the farthest from the action, hesitated a second to look back. He saw three of his teammates hurtling toward him, wide-eyed with fear. Ogilvy, his team leader, was switching magazines. Walking backward and firing again, Jan frantically searched for the last man, Thompson, who had been walking tail-end-Charlie before they had gone to ground. Thompson lay where he had hidden, a bloody hole where his left eye had been. His left hand was still clapped to his nose and mouth, where it had been when he died trying to stifle the sudden eruption that betrayed them all.

The North Viets rallied quickly and came at them through the woods, on line, pouring out a large volume of suppressive fire. Ogilvy was lifted off his feet and flipped backward by the slugs that smashed his torso. Pacheco and the others followed their leader's last order and ran.

"Spread out!" Pacheco bawled. An RPG whooshed past them to explode on the bole of a huge tree to their front. Heinz, the M-79 man, screamed as shrapnel slashed his carotid artery. He fell in a shower of blood. His fingers clenched in pain. His weapon discharged, sending a 40-millimeter grenade into the open mouth of Schachter, the radioman beside him.

The round failed to explode, its short flight not allowing it to arm, but the impact ripped the top half of the man's head off.

Pacheco ducked at the sound of the RPG's passage but slipped on wet leaves on the forest floor and tumbled over a fallen log to slide downhill. A large rock stopped his headlong skid ten yards down the slope when his shoulder slammed against it with a numbing jolt. Dazed, he felt the rain soaking his head and thought for a fleeting second to look for his boonie hat.

Firing from above cleared his mind. He rolled onto his back in time to see Farley, his last surviving comrade, drop to his knees above him. Arms hanging useless at his sides, Farley bore a look of utter amazement when he fell forward, as if in slow motion, to land with a thud, face first in the mud between Pacheco's feet.

Jesse's right arm was paralyzed. He had no feeling beyond a sensation of dead weight on that side. Scrunching his chin down to his chest, he could examine the shoulder out of the corner of his eye. It looked odd. Dislocated at least, maybe broken. His rifle was nowhere to be seen. He bent his left arm double to extract his Kaybar combat knife from its inverted sheath on his pack strap but saw an enemy soldier standing over him, weapon poised. The 7.62 mm muzzle was pointed between Jesse's eyes. It looked like a tunnel. His hand rested on the butt of the knife. He relaxed and began the Hail Mary in his mind, a prayer he suddenly realized he hadn't said in years. Rain was dripping in his eyes, and he hoped the enemy soldier wouldn't notice the tears running into his ears. *Now, and at the hour of our death, amen,* he finished his prayer to his Blessed Mother and closed his eyes. Seconds passed. He grew impatient.

Why don't they finish me?

Jesse Pacheco expected no quarter. There was little given on either side in this brutal contest in the jungle. He opened his eyes to see several more NVA troops surrounding him, some smiling knowingly, most grim, eyes filled with hate. They parted to let another draw near.

Pacheco couldn't help admiring how quietly they moved. These boys were good. Professionals.

The newcomer was an officer. He wore no emblem of rank, but his authority was unmistakable by the deference of the others. Squinting through the rain, which had grown heavier as he lay there, Pacheco noticed this man's badly mangled left hand. A burn that had healed badly, he decided. The officer said nothing but stooped to slap Jesse's hand from the knife hilt. He withdrew the blade and examined it, squatting beside Pacheco's head.

Feeling the point with his thumb, the enemy officer said something to his men that caused them to laugh. The bloodthirsty gleam in their eyes told Pacheco that something unpleasant was about to happen. *Momma is going to have a visit from an army officer with terrible news. Will he speak Spanish? They have to have Spanish-speaking officers, didn't they?*

Captain Tran slammed his mutilated paw over Pacheco's

mouth and leaned his full weight onto the man's face, muffling his scream. He cocked the knife-wielding arm back in a wide arc and plunged it into the top of Pacheco's skull. The rigid blade punched through the squirming soldier's cranium with a snap. Pacheco's eyes bulged. His body went rigid, nearly lifting him from the earth as his back arched. His boots beat a tattoo in the mud, and then he was gone.

The grotesque mask of unspeakable torment on his victim's face pleased Tran. The image of the dead boy's face, the knife handle protruding from his brain, blood mixing with mud flowing freely down the steep grade, was a picture he wished to savor. He stared at his handiwork for several moments, imprinting it on his memory. Then, using his Japanese bayonet, he sliced off both of Pacheco's ears.

Finally, he rose and issued orders to strip the American bodies of anything useful. He admonished his men to be quick but thorough. They must be on their way. He cocked an ear for the dreaded sound of the American war machines, scanning the treetops with his eyes. The Americans probably had not had time to get a message off to their support elements, but it was unwise to be too certain.

Tran had two weeks to reach the rendezvous. He did not know what his superiors had in store for him when he got there. After the defeat at Hue, he would not have been surprised to be disciplined, perhaps even reduced to enlisted rank. Instead, he had been promoted and given command of the finest soldiers he had ever been honored to lead. He remembered his oath and reaffirmed his promise to kill many times this small band of foreign pirates before this war was over.

CHAPTER 8

Fort Jackson, South Carolina:

The sky was a dust-streaked blackboard. Thunder rumbled somewhere over the horizon. Rain smell permeated the air. Leaves on the trees trembled and showed their petticoats as a chill wind spread news of the coming storm. Up and down Drag-Ass Hill, ranks of World War II vintage barracks stood empty, as if at parade rest, evidence that another Basic Training cycle was over. The trainees, now soldiers, were gone. There was a brooding stillness in the company areas that would last until 0400 when, with the influx of another batch of raw recruits, the clamor would start all over again. The approaching storm turned afternoon into twilight, but in one cream-colored clapboard building, lights burned.

Private E-2 Daniel Mulvaney sat on an olive-green plywood footlocker, at the end of his steel-framed bunk, sipping cold Budweiser from a can. He found it hard to believe that he was drinking in the barracks with some friends from his Basic Training Platoon and, of all people, their Drill Instructor, Sergeant Pauley. Danny couldn't help but stare at the man who had, until today, been the worst enemy he had ever imagined. *Could this be the same guy who was bent on making my life a living hell for the past two months?*

Outwardly, nothing had changed. Pauley still looked like the same deranged animal whose mission in life had been to demoralize and torment Danny and thirty-nine young men like him for the past ten weeks. The barracks looked like the same drab wood frame building it had been since its erection more than a quarter

century before. From the wavy glass in the quarter-pane sash
windows, to the exposed beams encased in decades-old layers of
high gloss paint, to the mirror-like surface of the asphalt tile floor,
nothing had changed.

But today, the place, even the people, didn't have the usual
tinge of misery. Basic Training was finally over. They had graduated. They were soldiers now, and nothing could undo what had
been done.

"Sergeant," Danny was compelled to ask, "was all that bullshit these last ten weeks an act? I mean, really, Sarge, up until
today, hell, even this morning, every one of us thought you were
certifiably insane."

The rest of the men exchanged I-don't-believe-Mulvaney-
said-that glances. No one dared breathe.

Pauley pinned Danny with his penetrating, ice-blue gaze, daring the young troop to look away. When Danny failed to squirm,
Pauley smiled.

"Mulvaney—" He paused, sipped some beer, and said, "—you
know what I've always liked about you?"

"Sergeant, I wasn't aware there was anything you liked about
me."

It broke the tension. His platoon mates snickered.

"You weren't supposed to be," Pauley said. "Anyway, what
I've always admired in you is your guts."

Danny frowned in disbelief.

"I've seen you so mad," Pauley said, "I thought you would try
to kill me."

Danny remembered the day Pauley made a fool of him during
bayonet drill.

"I've seen you so whipped, I thought you'd collapse."

Double-timing through the sand pits.

"I've seen you so outraged, I thought you might cry."

The day the cadre kicked Bartholomew until he puked.

Pauley took another taste of his beer. "I rode you hard, kid.
You got a cockiness about you that I've seen in city boys before.
The cocky ones usually got no depth. They knuckle under soon
enough. But you never quit. It ain't in you. That's guts, soldier."
He toasted Danny with his beer can.

Danny was too embarrassed to speak. His face flushed, deep-
ening his distress.

"Every swingin' dick here," the sergeant said to the group, "was wondering the same thing." He looked each man in the eye, one at a time. "How come old Sarge is all of a sudden a regular Joe? Suckin' suds with us and shootin' the shit. But Mulvaney's the only one with the sand to say it."

Pauley rocked back on the hind legs of his chair, and said, "Since graduation this afternoon, you boys are soldiers. You're not dumbass trainees anymore. You're members of the fraternity, my fraternity, the US Army. I don't have to treat you like shit-birds anymore 'cause you made it. I don't have to get your attention anymore 'cause you got the message." The pride on the faces of the new soldiers prompted him to temper his praise. "Don't get the idea that it's all downhill from here, though. You've cleared the first hurdle, but there's still AIT ahead of you and most likely Nam after that."

Verbalizing the dreaded name cast a pall over the group.

"Don't sweat it, gentlemen. You'll do okay. You're good men. Hell, I trained you!"

Setting his empty can on the footlocker, Pauley rocked forward and stood. "I'll say goodbye and good luck now, men."

They each, in turn, took the callused hand he offered and murmured some words of thanks for pulling them through, for making them soldiers. He took a little more time with Danny.

"I've a feeling I'll be hearing more from you, Mulvaney. Keep your shit together. You're okay, kid."

"Thanks, Sergeant." Danny felt he should say more but was unable to find the words. He could not explain the feeling—more than gratitude, more than pride. He was sorry to say goodbye as the sergeant strode out the door.

"Clean up them cans and shut off my lights when you go," was Pauley's parting shot.

The young men stood staring at the exit for several moments.

Lance Corporal broke the mood. "Do you believe that shit?"

Lance, whose unlikely name had earned him much more than his share of grief from the cadre, had been at a loss to understand the concerted effort to bombard him with abuse until Danny had explained that his name was also a rank in the Marine Corps. The marines—better known as jarheads among the training cadre—were not exactly held in esteem by their army brothers-in-arms.

Danny had met Lance on the bus from the draft board in Ja-

maica on the fateful day that now seemed a lifetime ago—
induction day. They had bitched about everything as the Grey-
hound rocked on its springs like a ship on a rolling sea. Their
draft board was in Queens because they lived on the north side of
Brooklyn, so they had to leave Brooklyn to report, only to be
transported to Fort Hamilton—in Brooklyn—for the physical ex-
am. They saw this as proof positive that the government had no
idea what it was doing.

They passed the tests that declared each of them 1-A, along
with a guy in tiger-striped panties and a pink tank top. He had
polished finger and toenails, a touch of rouge on his cheeks, clear
lip-gloss and eyebrow pencil, and he smiled invitingly at the
NCOs as he minced through the halls. No one wanted to be in
front of him in the long lines in which the inductees were obliged
to wait, clad only in underwear.

At the end of the medical checkup, when the recruits were
told to dress in their civilian clothes, Tiger Panties, still in his
feminine underwear, was ushered into a room with three burly
sergeants. He emerged pale, in spite of his makeup, and stood
between Lance and Danny for the oath as they were sworn in.
There was much speculation as to the individual test that had
been administered in that room, but no one dared ask.

"Nice try, Ace," Lance whispered as they raised their right
hands.

Tiger Panties shrugged and declared, "It was worth a shot."

Leon Weislogel brought Danny out of his reverie.

"Fuckin' guy," said Leon, amazement all over his angular face
as Sergeant Pauley disappeared.

Weislogel was from a small town in Ohio. His two-word epi-
thets, the first of which was invariably the F-word, had become
the adopted slang of the entire platoon. The *Weislogel Preamble*
had grown to be the humorous response to any situation, individual, or inanimate object that presented itself. Leon was truly a
man of few words, but what he lacked in vocabulary was more
than offset by his generous heart. He was always the first to bolster a lagging comrade, lest he fall out of a forced march. His wry
wit was a mainstay of the unit as the young trainees struggled to
comprehend the intricacies of their masters' demands. Leon's
most endearing quality was his ability to relate, in the most comical terms, the twisted reasoning behind the cadre's commands.

Early in their training, Danny wondered aloud at the gleeful brutality of the drill instructors. Leon had replied, quite seriously, "It's these fuckin' GI boxer shorts. They get all knotted up under your balls. Jesus Christ himself would turn mean if he had to wear these goddamn things every day."

The platoon had laughed so hard it took forty push-ups to wipe the smiles from their faces. Leon was everyone's friend, impossible to dislike.

Smitty said, "Bet you never thought you'd be getting compliments from old Low Crawl Louie, eh, Danny?"

"Not in this lifetime," Danny had to admit.

Smitty was the spark plug of the platoon. His exuberant, get-it-done-and-be-on-to-the-next-thing attitude was exhausting but nonetheless irresistible. A recruiter's dream, he appeared every inch a soldier. He had drive and zeal. He used phrases like *zero-defects* and talked about why they should strive to be the best. Smitty's persona out-classed, if it did not overshadow, Leon's every-man appeal. In truth, his square-jawed, rugged good looks were—through genetic happenstance—the only manly thing about him. He was a charlatan by nature, playing roles that brought him attention and admiration. His current character was a dashing soldier of fortune, a man's man. With the ease of a gifted thespian, he donned the mantle of the All-American Hero and worked his audience for all he was worth. With a memory close to photographic, he absorbed the details of every classroom instruction, every field exercise, every weapons manual, anything that would further his role-playing. Lance alone had pegged Robert J. Smith for the fraud that he was.

Danny laughingly dismissed Lance's instinctive perception of Smitty as jealousy. Lance kept his own council regarding Smitty after Danny's good-natured rebuke, but he watched him carefully.

They had all been sent to Fort Jackson, South Carolina, for Basic Training. Lance and Danny gravitated toward one another early on as fellow New Yorkers. They helped each other through the toughest times, laughing at the preposterous contrivances of the training cadre, whom, they were convinced, must stay up nights collaborating with psychopaths to dream up the humiliating insults and degrading tasks they inflicted upon their charges.

They had shared the disgrace of being refused entry to a nightclub in Columbia on their first weekend pass because Lance

was black. Lance insisted, thereafter, that they go to town sepa-
rately, with their own kind.

"Don't be ruinin' your weekends because of me, Dan," Lance
had said. "I know you're my friend, and I know how bad you feel
about this shit, but it ain't your fault, and you shouldn't suffer for
it. There's a black section for us brothers to go to, and you ain't
gonna be welcome there. We can party together back on the block.
This here's the South, and they still pissed about the Civil War
and shit. When in Rome, you go with the flow. End of story."

Danny had been outwardly reluctant to give in to the bigotry
but was inwardly ashamed at his lack of conviction to his princi-
ples. He desperately needed to get off post on weekends, to have
some time away from the army. He suspected Lance knew and
understood.

He didn't realize that Lance's mixed metaphor was his way of
hiding his own shame. Rationalizing what they felt powerless to
change didn't make either of them feel any better about their ina-
bility to stand up for their rights. It infuriated them to know that
their countrymen would let them die together but shun them if
they lived as equals. Vietnam, they suspected, might be an improvement on South Carolina.

Now, Danny looked fondly at his friends. He had known them
for only a little more than two months but he had no doubt as to
their friendship and the strength of their bond.

"Looks like you impressed the sergeant, Daniel," Smitty was
saying. "Did you notice, however, that he never did answer your
question?"

"I think he did, Smitty." Danny chucked his empty beer can at
the garbage pail at the end of the bay. It clattered loudly against
the galvanized steel.

"On target as usual, Private." Lance grinned. "You got a gold-
en arm, m'man."

Danny acknowledged Lance's praise with a nod of thanks and
said to no one in particular, "I think I'm gonna miss ol' Sergeant
Pauley."

"Yeah! Like I'd miss poison ivy," Lance hooted.

"Fuckin' right," Leon agreed. "What time does the truck pick
us up?"

"Sixteen hundred," Smitty volunteered.

"What the fuck time is that in civilian, Super Troop?" Lance crushed his beer can. Exasperation with Smitty was something he could no longer hide.

"Four o'clock," Danny translated. "Just enough time to get squared away and knock out a letter to my girl."

The four men were the only graduates in the platoon who were not leaving Fort Jackson for Advanced Individual Training. They had all been earmarked for Infantry School and were being shipped across the post to begin the next cycle on Monday. They were to report to their new training company today, Saturday, but have Sunday off. Failure to get leave or be blessed with a change of scenery in the form of another post had been a bitter pill. Their training had instilled in them grudging resolve to the whims of the Green Machine, however, so they accepted their fate with a minimum of complaint once the initial disappointment had worn off.

Finished with packing his belongings, Danny perched on the exposed bedsprings of his bunk to lean his back against his rolled-up mattress to begin a letter to Amanda. As he tried to focus his mind, Pauley's remarks kept intruding on his thoughts. He found himself reliving the last two months. The physical demands of the training had taken their toll on his out-of-shape body, at first, but before long the athlete had re-emerged, and he had excelled in PT. His keen eyesight and depth perception, coupled with razor sharp reflexes, made him a natural with weapons. He qualified expert with the M-14 rifle and threw hand grenades farther and more accurately than any of the DIs had seen before.

What Danny had been surprised to learn was how easily Sergeant Pauley could push his buttons, to scrape away the veneer of the civilized man, exposing the latent killer he felt emerging. He resisted the efforts to release his baser instincts, despite the cadre's warnings that not to learn was to die in combat. He learned out of self-preservation but insisted it was merely a precaution. They would never make a killer out of him.

He folded the barely started letter, his mind too full of cascading thoughts to get past *Dear Amanda*, and tucked it into his duffel bag. He told himself he would write later when he was settled in his new billet, when he could concentrate on her.

At the moment, he kept hearing the litany of bayonet drill in his mind.

"What is the spirit of the bayonet?" the DIs would begin the mantra, their eyes shining as the trainees roared back, red faced, "To kill! To kill without mercy!"

CHAPTER 9

Republic of South Vietnam:

Tom Tyler slung his rifle on his shoulder and lifted his helmet to wipe his forehead with the olive green towel he wore around his neck. Half of the Second Platoon was behind him, spread out across a rice paddy. The rest were lined up on the dirt road that had been the morning's objective. Vietnamese peasants scurried past him on foot or in various forms of wheeled transport. He was getting used to the mix of conveyances—bicycles, Lambrettas, oxcarts, buses and trucks. The smells of fossil fuel exhaust, sweat, wood smoke, excrement, and rotting vegetation combined to create a unique scent that he thought would stay with him for the rest of his life.

The midday heat of South Vietnam reminded him of summer in Mississippi, with one distinct difference. Back home you could always get out of the heat: just step into the nearest air-conditioned building or get in your car and let the breeze cool you down. Not here. Here you had to take your punishment and keep going. Panama had been hot, but most of the training had been in the jungle where you could at least get out of the sun. The land here in the Mekong Delta was as flat as a pool table and nearly all of it wet, the ideal climate for rice farming, and for thousands of years that was what the people of this land had done here. *Which was fine for them*, thought Tyler, *but we occidentals like our shade.*

"Sergeant Pomeroy," he shouted.

"Sir?" Pomeroy turned from his conversation with one of the men.

"Get 'em off the road. Spread out on both sides and take five. When you get them squared away, I want to see you."

"Yes, sir." Pomeroy turned back to the men already on the road and issued the orders. He then turned to the men still slogging through the mud in the paddy. "Let's not take all day, people. You're on your own time now."

The platoon shuffled off the road and, in groups of two or three, found shade under the trees lining the road. Some lit cigarettes, some opened C-ration cans for a quick snack. Most drank water from their plastic canteens, and some just sat and stared at nothing.

They had been shaping up, Tyler thought, until today. He had led them on a few short and uneventful operations since his arrival, but he still didn't feel comfortable as their leader. The sidelong looks to see if Pomeroy agreed with his orders were less obvious now but far from over. They still didn't trust him with their lives. Why should they? He wasn't sure of his own worth as a commander.

On this operation, just when he had been starting to think they were coming around, he was appalled by the utter lack of discipline he observed. They played transistor radios on patrol and danced on rice paddy dikes, oblivious to any form of alert security. They smoked cigarettes in the bush and made enough noise to break the deepest slumber of any enemy within a thousand meters, better known as a click. They joked and grab-assed as if they were on holiday in a park.

Tyler and his RTO dumped their gear and flopped beneath a tall palm. The lieutenant stuffed a fresh piece of chewing gum in his mouth and waited for Pomeroy. As soon as the sergeant arrived, Tyler pointed to the ground. Pomeroy dropped to one knee.

"What the fuck is going on, Desmond?" Tyler snapped. "I've never seen anything like the shit I've seen today. Has the whole platoon gone Asiatic?"

"I know, Lieutenant," Pomeroy replied. "They's acting like a bunch of assholes. Most of it's testing you to see how much you gonna let 'em get away with. They know that this here AO's a cake-walk. Charley don't fuck with nobody 'round Nha Be. It's kind of like an open town. They kick back here, and so do we. Battalion sends us out here for a rest. They can't let these boys hang out in base camp too long 'cause they get in trouble. So, when they need a breather, they send us out to sweep around Nha Be. They know it," he indicated the platoon with his chin, "and it pisses 'em off. They deserve a stand down, and they're letting *you* know it—"

They were interrupted by Tyler's radioman.

Extending the handset to Tyler, Pomeroy said, "Sir, Cap'n's on the horn."

Tyler took the black plastic phone. "Charlie-Six, Two-Six, over."

The phone crackled. "Anything, Two-Six?"

"That's a negative, Six. Quiet as a church, over."

"Roger, Two-Six. No surprise. Wait one."

Tyler listened to the static of squelch as Captain Arnold put him on hold. "Two-Six, Six," came from the phone moments later. "Higher recommends you reccy the ville, over."

"Roger, Six. Understand you want this element to recon November Bravo."

"You copy, Two-Six. Proceed. Out."

"Battalion wants us to check out the village, Sarge."

"You're shittin' me?" Pomeroy's mouth fell open.

"Am I to believe that my platoon sergeant is as daffy as the rest of this bunch of clowns? Why are you gaping like an idiot, Sergeant Pomeroy? It's a simple order."

"Yes, sir. Sorry, sir. I'll get the men moving." He got up and walked along the road, saying, "Saddle up. Let's go. We're movin' out."

As they trudged in the direction of the village, Tyler noticed the men becoming excited as they passed whispered comments, pointed ahead, and slapped high-fives.

He sidled up to Pomeroy and asked, "Why are the men so enthusiastic about sweeping a village?"

"It's not any village, sir. It's Nha Be."

"So?"

"Like I said before, sir, Nha Be's kind of wide open. You'll see."

And he did. They advanced into town in textbook fashion, staggered in standard road-march formation. The platoon became military precision itself. Tyler, in the center of the column, watched as the point element entered town, trotted up to the nearest hootch—standard GI lingo for a native dwelling—and with the following men providing cover, entered, presumably to search.

The lieutenant was pleased at the transformation as his men did their jobs with practiced skill. The platoon was proceeding rapidly with the sweep. Half of the men who had thus far entered the town were in the buildings, supposedly seeking enemy contraband. The rest provided cover.

As he entered the village, Tyler saw that Nha Be was a strange blend of East and West. The buildings lining the main road all seemed to be shops. His map, and his observations as he walked along the road, showed that most of Nha Be's buildings were indeed, on the road. Nha Be was a linear village, not spread out like most. The combination of thatched huts and corrugated steel was becoming the norm, even after such a short time in country, but unlike other villages Tyler had seen, there seemed to be a great deal of activity in the huts. He heard many voices, both male and female, and much laughter and music. The blazing sun made the interiors inky so that it was difficult to see into the buildings from the road.

He heard the drone of generators and noticed electric wires strung between some of the buildings. He was surprised to see a pink neon sign in the pane-less window of one establishment that blinked *COLD BEER*, but it was not until he overheard one of his men complaining to a buddy that he began to assimilate what Pomeroy had been trying to tell him.

"Come on, Dawson. What are you, on your honeymoon in there? Pay the bitch and give somebody else a chance."

Tyler was shocked. He stood in the center of the street and looked from building to building as the realization dawned: nearly every hootch was a business. There were tattoo parlors, makeshift bars, tailor shops, barbers, and a butcher stall with dried bats hanging by spread wings tacked to the eaves. Fresh fruits and vegetables, as well as every type of black market goods imaginable, were displayed openly, proudly, for sale. Prostitution seemed to be a sideline practiced in each hut.

"Sergeant Pomeroy!"

"Sir." Pomeroy sang out, rounding the corner of a nearby building, hurrying to his side.

"What the—" Tyler spun slowly in an all-encompassing circle, wide eyed.

"Nha Be, sir. Party Town, RVN." Pomeroy grinned. "This is

why I was so surprised when you said our orders were to sweep the ville. This sinful spot has been off-limits for a year."

"But—"

"Colonel knows all about this place, sir. If'n he wants us in here, he knows what will happen. I'd guess this is a little unscheduled R and R."

Tyler sighed. "This is not turning out to be what I thought it would, Sergeant."

"Nha Be, sir?"

"Vietnam, Sarge." Tyler shook his head. "Viet-fucking-nam."

Tyler advised Pomeroy to be sure to see that the men used condoms. He envisioned his entire platoon queued up at the medic's door, awaiting penicillin in massive doses. He found a shady porch to sit on and accepted a frosty 33-Brand beer from a giggling crone of a *mamasan* with a wicked gap-toothed leer. Signaling his RTO to get the captain on the phone, Tyler sat, wondering what had happened to his idealistic dream of saving these people from the communist scourge. When Sp/4 Wilson handed him the handset, he identified himself and stated his compliance with the captain's last order.

"Any contact?" Tyler could hear the mocking grin in the captain's tone.

"Beaucoup contact. Negative Victor Charley."

"Understood." Arnold chuckled. "When your men have thoroughly inspected the dwellings, and you are certain of the absence of the enemy, move to map reference..." Tyler pulled his Pictomap, known as the funny papers, from his thigh pocket and, jotting down the coded map reference, transcribed the coordinates. They were to set up an ambush about a thousand meters from the village, around some sort of structure out in the paddies. "That will be your November delta papa, Two-Six. Do you copy? Over."

"Roger. Wilco. Out.

"Night Defensive Position is here." Tyler showed Pomeroy the position on the map.

"What's this here, sir?" Pomeroy poked a digit at an indistinct blob that seemed to be man-made.

"I was hoping you could tell me, Sergeant."

"No, sir, never been over that way. Damn piss-poor photography on some of these funny papers. Wish we had some old-fashioned, hand drawn maps. Be a lot easier to read."

"I agree, but it's not likely Charley will hold up the war while the Army Corps of Engineers surveys the whole of South Vietnam for us, is it, Sergeant Pomeroy?"

They moved out at dusk, easily covering the flat, sparsely wooded terrain. The Second Platoon of Charlie Company was noticeably relaxed with the exception of their leader. The gray blob on the map—its distinctive architecture masked by overgrowing vegetation—turned out to be an ancient temple with carved stone oriental lions and dragons guarding its portals. Its moss shrouded, pillared entrances were foreboding in the rapidly gathering gloom.

"What the fuck? Over," Wilson said.

"Sergeant, send Second Squad to check it out," Tyler ordered, huddled behind a rice paddy dike fifty meters from the structure.

He was pleased with the smooth deployment as the squad moved up in stages, half of the men covering the rest as they rushed the temple. They moved warily inside and emerged moments later with three uniformed, but unarmed, South Vietnamese soldiers in front of them.

Sergeant Cole, the squad leader, waved the Americans in. "Arvin deserters, sir," he advised when they were together. "They live here from what I can gather."

"Weapons?" Tyler asked.

"No, sir, unless you count the potent shit they're brewing up in there." He motioned with his head at the temple. "Rice whiskey. Beaucoup. Stuff will melt your teeth."

"What do we do with them?" Tyler asked Pomeroy.

"If we turn 'em in, they'll be shot, or worse."

Tyler couldn't imagine what could be worse than being shot but decided he'd rather not know.

"Okay. Keep an eye on them. Post a guard to watch them until we leave." He looked quickly around the temple and issued orders as to where to set up automatic weapons to cover possible avenues of approach. "Twenty-five percent alert, Sergeant?"

"That'll do fine, sir." Pomeroy was obviously pleased that the lieutenant was smart enough to seek his advice. He relayed the orders to the squad leaders, and the men settled into their assigned positions.

Tyler took the first watch for the command position. As an officer, he wasn't supposed to pull guard, but he was so unsettled he knew he would be unable to sleep.

The day had been one more curious episode in a string of odd happenings that had begun with Captain Arnold's ad hoc orientation on his first day.

The CO had said nothing about probing whorehouses for VC with your pants down around your ankles or rooming with allied deserters. Indeed, Tyler felt there was a great deal Captain Arnold had left out of his little briefing.

When his hour was up, Tyler shook Wilson awake for his turn on guard, but instead of sleeping himself, he sat with his RTO. He needed to talk.

"Nha Be's a trip, huh, sir?" Wilson whispered, intuitively knowing what was on his platoon leader's mind.

"That is an understatement, Wilson. Is it true, what Pomeroy says? That there's some kind of undeclared truce here."

"It's more like a deal, sir," Wilson frowned in the darkness, trying to explain. "You saw the tank farm we passed on the boat this morning, didn't you?"

"Sure. I was surprised to see it, too. You'd think all that oil and gasoline would be a very attractive target for Charley's mortars."

"Roger that, sir," Wilson nodded. "Damn near impossible to protect. Which, I guess, is why things are the way they are."

"And how are things, Wilson?"

"Nha Be is considered pacified, sir. Leastways, that's the political jargon for the arrangement. The VC leave the tank farm alone as long as the oil companies, who lease the land at the river's edge, pay their rent on time."

"You're telling me that US oil companies pay off the enemy to leave them alone?"

"Not just American oil companies, sir. There are lots of foreign outfits in there, too."

"But, they *are* paying off the VC."

"I doubt if the check goes to Ho Chi Minh personally. They lease the land from the South Vietnamese government in Saigon. What doesn't stick to our ally's greedy little fingers, finds its way to Charley."

"It's incredible!"

"No, sir, it's business. This whole damn war is a business.

You saw some of them tanks all crumpled and burned this morning, didn't you?"

"Yeah."

"That's what happens when the check is late."

Tyler pondered the level of corruption he had just heard so casually described. Did the lives of his men hang on late payments or arguments over increased fees? According to Wilson, so long as the multi-national cash cows forked over the green, Nha Be was safe.

With sleep now completely out of the question, he told Wilson he was going to check the perimeter.

"Just be careful, sir. The guys ain't so relaxed they won't shoot if you surprise 'em."

Tyler tucked that piece of advice in the front of his mind and set out to tour the positions. When he came to Second Squad's assigned sector, he got the biggest shock of the day.

One man sat smoking a cigarette huddled under his poncho to hide the glow of the butt. The rest of the squad was nowhere in sight. Tyler crouched beside the green plastic hump and whispered, "What the fuck do you think you're doing?"

The cigarette dropped between the man's feet, and he scrambled to crush it with his heels. "Jesus, sir, you scared the shit out of me," PFC Jackson whispered as he whipped the poncho from over his head. "Just having a smoke, sir. I didn't show no light."

"Where the hell is the rest of your squad, soldier?"

"Uh, gee, sir, I don't know."

"Last chance, Jackson. Lie to me again, and you're going to finish your tour in LBJ." Long Binh Jail was the military's in-country Leavenworth, somewhere no one in his right mind wanted to go.

"They, uh, went to town, sir."

"To town? What the hell for?"

"I guess they wanted a little more nooky, sir. I got the short straw."

Tyler was dumbfounded. He held his head in his hands in the gloom. "Jesus Christ! Is there no end to this bullshit? Find Sergeant Cole. Bring him to me."

"Yes, sir," Jackson hissed and hustled off.

Tyler covered the position until Jackson returned with Cole, who had already been filled in on the situation.

"You stay here, sir," Cole whispered. "Me and shit-for-brains—" He jerked a thumb at Jackson. "—will go get those assholes and bring 'em back."

"Where were you, Cole? Why weren't you with your men?"

"I went to talk to Pomeroy, sir. Only been gone a few minutes."

"Unbelievable." Tyler sighed. "Take two more men, Sergeant."

"No sweat, sir. This is fuckin' Nha Be. They'll be okay. And I volunteer to head up the firing squad when we find them jerks."

"Don't tempt me. Just take two more men and bring them back."

Tyler covered for them with false situation reports to the captain until the errant squad was found and bullied into returning.

The perpetrators tried to appear contrite, but Tyler saw the conspiratorial winks and grins.

"I'll deal with you idiots when we get back in," was all he said.

The truth of the matter was he didn't know exactly what he was going to do. The day's events had left him feeling stupid and naive. He was angry—angry with his men, his country, the people of Vietnam, and mostly with himself.

With the prodigal squad manning its position, Tyler found his way back to his CP, but one last shock awaited him. Just as he was bedding down for what little sleep he might steal before the new day began, he smelled something he had not smelled since college. The pungent scent of burning marijuana crinkled his nose. He started to get up but hesitated. The smokers would be watching for him, and he didn't want to go sneaking around in an attempt to catch them. He'd look foolish at the very least, and he might even get himself shot. With a sigh, he lay back down, closed his eyes, and wished he could talk to his dad.

CHAPTER 10

Captain Tran waited until his unit was well clear of the site of the LRRP massacre before pausing to radio a report of the contact. Radio silence was the rule, but Tran's orders stipulated that he report anything that might compromise his mission. Because of the distance between the NVA troops and their command structure, his message was relayed several times before it reached its destination. Consequently, he and his men traveled three kilometers deeper into South Vietnam before a reply was received. When his radio operator decoded the transmission, Tran was uneasy. He gathered his element leaders together.

"Comrades," he said, "we have new orders. The mission is canceled."

The reaction was unanimous: silent, blank stares. His noncommissioned officers were well trained. Their expressions revealed none of the consternation Tran saw in their eyes.

"We are to move quickly east, back across the Laotian border." Squatting, he spread a map on the jungle floor, pointed to a place several kilometers inside Laos, and said, "We are to rendezvous in forty-eight hours—here—with a team that will lead us to our next checkpoint."

The men waited for elaboration, but Tran stood. "We must begin at once. Such a march will not be easily accomplished in so short a time. Get the men moving."

Forty-six hours later, Tran and his exhausted men rendezvoused with a pathfinder squad inside Laos. After a brief rest, they force-marched through the forest for an additional seven hours. Their guides then handed them off to a transportation unit waiting in two battered, camouflaged trucks parked beside a winding mountain road. For the next twenty-four hours, Tran's men, riding in the back of the trucks, bounced over a bone-jarring road. Outside of a nameless Laotian village, they became part of a supply convoy headed south over the ever-changing track that was the Ho Chi Minh Trail.

For twelve harrowing days, they were passengers on a suicide express. The convoy traveled by day through the twilight of triple canopy jungle that hid them from the air. When the foliage became sparse, movement was restricted to the hours of darkness. The American CIA's Air America and Raven spotters hunted them day and night. Discovery meant bombing or ambush further on by American SOG teams or indigenous guerrillas led by local warlords. Twice in the dozen days they ground southward, the jungle erupted around them, and the air became filled with the roar of automatic weapons and the screams of the dying. Three times their route was diverted to detour around sections of the track pulverized by bombs and once they raced through a burning village as American fighter-bombers blasted the Pathet Lao unit encamped there. On the twelfth day of the trip, Tran's fighters became laborers as all available hands pitched in to repair a washed-out bridge across a swollen stream. For eight tense hours, they toiled in the heat, ever mindful of their vulnerability as they watched the underbrush and the sky for a surprise attack. With the bridge completed, Tran's troops piled back into the trucks for the crossing, only to be told to disembark on the other side.

A bewildered Captain Tran was ordered by the convoy commander to wait to be contacted with further instructions.

"Comrade Dai-ui," Tran said, "surely you can tell me more."

"You will be met, Comrade Dai-ui. That is all that I know," the captain said. With that, he and his men drove off.

"Sir," Sergeant Vinh said, after the convoy had passed, "we have no food and little water. How long must we wait?"

"Until we are met, Sergeant. See to the men."

The men scrounged berries, coconuts, edible roots, lizards, and even a monkey to ward off starvation. The temptation to use the radio to summon assistance was strong, but Tran forbade it. Three anxious days passed before the NVA soldiers saw another human being. When truck motors were heard in the distance, grinding their way over the steep track, discipline nearly collapsed as half-starved men pushed and shoved one another in an effort to be first in line to meet the approaching vehicles. Captain Tran and his NCOs barked orders, and by the time the convoy was in view, the men stood in formation, at attention beside the road.

"How are you enjoying Cambodia, Captain?" a grinning major greeted Tran as he dismounted from the lead vehicle.

Tran hid his shock well. He had no idea they were in Cambodia. He saluted and said, "It's rather boring, actually, sir. My men like to fight."

"How do they feel about river excursions, Captain?"

e/ɔe/ɔ

Three days march through the Cambodian hinterland, led by two sullen guides, brought Tran and his people to a tributary of the Mekong River where they were met yet again, this time by a Cambodian river pirate and his crew aboard a decrepit junk. Tran made no attempt to hide his distaste as he looked over the filthy scow's rotted, waterlogged wood and peeling paint. One gold tooth gleamed in the center of a row of crooked brown teeth as the captain of the vessel handed Tran written orders. The documents said no more than that he and his men were to accompany this man to their final destination.

Reluctantly, the NVA troops climbed aboard. The grinning pirate gave orders to his men and Tran and his soldiers were escorted below to a fetid compartment, rank with rotten fish. The first mate explained in halting Vietnamese that they were to remain out of sight in daylight hours. The thrum of twin high-powered inboards surprised Tran when the captain hoisted anchor and set out. Ten monotonous days later, Tran and his men found themselves once more on solid earth with new guides—sharp-eyed NVA brothers—who led them, at a quick pace, up steep, well-defined trails.

e/ɔe/ɔ

Cambodia

From a rocky outcrop high above a valley, Tran sat alone and watched the sun climb the Annamite Mountains, thinking that all places are beautiful at sunrise. Within the hour, the heat of the day would begin, and the strange beauty of this wild and ancient land bordering his beloved homeland would be forgotten as men fought to survive another day beneath the merciless ball of white.

Looking east across the peaks, where Vietnam was awakening, he felt a hollowness in his breast, a void where his heart had once been. Twice, in less than half a year, he had been driven like an animal from his country: driven by the power of a corrupt, insurgent nation whose meddling would not cease until he and all his people lay broken and bloated, putrefying in the tropical sun. He was ashamed and in despair. The cost of the Lunar New Year attacks was incomprehensible. The hope he had clung to with his new assignment had withered with the cancellation of their original mission and the blind trip south. Tran had mistaken the swift pace since the rendezvous for efficiency until he learned, on the march, that the guides' speed was inspired by fear rather than enthusiasm. He had tried to put an end to their depressing diatribe of defeat, but like whining old women, they bemoaned their demoralizing losses whenever he relaxed vigilance.

The Viet Cong guerrillas had been smashed in nearly every engagement from the highlands to the far south and could no longer be counted as an effective fighting force. The soldiers of the North had suffered to a lesser degree, owing only to their smaller part in the attacks. Hanoi's strategy to preserve their main force regulars by throwing the Cong headlong into the battle had deepened the enmity between the guerrillas and the NVA. He did his best to maintain the facade of resolve, but he knew his spirit was withering. On this, the second day of inactivity since they had arrived at this place, Tran's despondency grew.

"Dai-ui." A voice roused him from his misery. He turned to see a corporal at attention, saluting him on the narrow path to his limestone perch.

"Yes?" He was irritated by the interruption. "What is it?"

"Sir, the commandant will see you now," the corporal said, eyes locked to the front, never meeting Tran's angry stare.

"Very well, Corporal." Tran slapped dust from his trousers as he rose. "Tell him I'm on my way."

"Yes, sir!" The corporal dropped his salute and turned on his heel to trot back down the trail.

With a sigh of resignation, Tran followed at a leisurely pace.

General Nguyen Van Quoc's hootch, which served as living quarters and command post for this small garrison, was quite comfortable in a modest way. He stood, waiting on the verandah of a sizable thatched-roof hut fashioned of bamboo and reed mats. Set on short stilts, the building allowed air circulation from below as well as all sides. In the shade of the lean-to style awning, the general smiled, watching the young officer's approach like a benevolent parent pleased to see the long-awaited return of a wandering son.

"Welcome to Cambodia, Captain." The general beamed, descending the plank steps.

Tran snapped to rigid attention, bringing his right hand up sharply to the brim of his cap in salute. He could not help but be impressed by the confident air of the legendary general officer.

The general returned Tran's salute and then surprised him by coming abreast and linking arms with him to guide him along a path that led to the rear of his quarters.

"Please, Captain Tran," General Quoc said, patting his arm, "there will be time enough for military matters. I hope your frequent encounters with the Americans have not caused you to adopt their caustic disposition."

Brought up short by the senior officer's gracious rebuke, Tran apologized. "Forgive me, sir. I have had a long and arduous journey."

"As I know well, my dear Captain." With a casual backhand gesture, the general motioned to a shelter comprised of four stout bamboo poles supporting a thatched, pyramid-shaped roof. In its center was a weathered French Colonial pedestal dining table with four matching chairs. The round top was covered with a fine linen tablecloth as white as snow. The setting was bizarre in the remote jungle camp.

"Sit please, Captain, rest," the general ordered.

Tran could not hide his astonishment.

"I find it helpful to incorporate some of the finery of gentler days, even here in this wilderness." General Quoc ran his tiny hand over the crisp textile. "This table once belonged to a French General who commanded a garrison of Legionnaires near Danang. I took it when my men annihilated the French invaders' camp. I was a young lieutenant then, serving with the Viet Minh. It has traveled many kilometers with me. It serves as a reminder that the spirit of the people of Vietnam is indomitable." He stared into Tran's eyes as he took his seat opposite the young captain.

Tran felt shame for his doubt in his cause and in his countrymen.

"How are your men?" the general said. "Fit? Comfortable?"

"Yes, thank you, sir. Your staff has been most hospitable."

At a barely noticed signal from the general, an aide set out a porcelain tea service and poured, filling both men's cups. Tran took the welcome intrusion as an opportunity to break eye contact with the general. He looked, as casually as he could, at his surroundings.

Other than this island of gentility in the middle of the camp, it was no different than many others he had seen—another secret sanctuary Hanoi denied, on a daily basis, to the world at large.

"My congratulations on your promotion, Captain," the general said.

A slightly built man, even for a Vietnamese, General Quoc had a reputation for cunning and ferocity that belied the refined gentleman by whom Tran found himself being entertained. He was anxious to know what interest the general might have in him and was disturbed by being withdrawn from the field so soon after his force had successfully infiltrated South Vietnam.

He was wise enough to know, however, that he would be told only what the general chose to tell him, and at the great man's leisure.

He resigned himself to patient conversation. "Thank you, sir," Tran replied, but the general continued as if he had not heard.

"Richly deserved from what I understand."

"Sir, I—"

"Ah! No false modesty, eh, Captain? Your exploits at Con Thien have been recounted to me in detail."

"But, sir, I—"

"You led brave soldiers out of the jaws of the tiger to fight another day." Quoc froze Tran with his tone. "Such tenacity in the face of overwhelming odds is the mark of a true leader, Captain. And again, in the glorious battle of Hue, you, Captain Tran, rose to the challenge and led your brave fighters to distinction."

Tran was speechless. His mind reeled at the slaughter he had witnessed.

"I see by your face, Captain, you doubt the veracity of my

words," the general said, a hard edge on his voice.

Tran made no reply, but stiffened in his chair, his fingers tightening on the delicate teacup.

Inexplicably, the general's tone softened, reverting to the avuncular mien of moments before. "You are young and a fine soldier, Captain, a brave fighter full of zeal and impatience. But wars are not won by warriors alone in the modern age, Captain Tran. Politics and world opinion hold sway as well."

The general paused to sip his tea, never letting his gaze fall from Tran's. "The American press has accomplished what we soldiers, with our blood, could not." He smiled wolfishly at some irony still unknown to Tran. "They have taken our military defeat and forged it into a knife point aimed at the heart of the American people."

Tran was so unabashedly confused that the general mistook his befuddled expression for fatigue.

"But you are weary from your journey, Captain. Compose your thoughts. Enjoy the peace of this place. My aide will bring you a meal and show you to your quarters afterward. Forgive me for not joining you in your repast, but I have a staff meeting to attend."

General Quoc rose to leave. Tran jumped to attention. Quoc extended his hands to brace Tran's shoulders as he said, "After you have rested, we will talk. Take heart, valiant warrior. Things are not as black as you imagine." He left Tran to wonder about his meaning.

The general's aides arrived with the promised food a few minutes later and, after the best meal he had eaten in months, Captain Tran retired to his hut and slept soundly despite the heat of the day. Before he drifted off, he was again mystified by the general's comments.

The North had suffered one humiliating defeat after another. If the rumors were true, even partially, and personal experience suggested they were, the situation was bleak. The army was still ill-equipped and unprepared to march in force on the South. His perilous journey along the infiltration routes through Laos had been fraught with danger. The tenacity and endurance of the column were impressive, their determination heroic, but the eventual outcome when one considered the might of their opponent, was death. What could battered trucks and bicycles accomplish against such overwhelming power? Surely, the leadership must soon be forced to sue for peace. Maintaining the status quo seemed the most the North could hope for.

When he awoke, the general's aide brought him cool water to drink, a clean uniform, and personal hygiene gear. He then led Tran to a nearby stream and stood guard as Tran bathed in a clear pool.

Refreshed and invigorated, he returned to the meeting place to await the general. The sun had lost its punishing heat as it was now early evening. The general took Tran by surprise, approaching silently from behind, his hand lightly on Tran's shoulder the first indication Tran had of his arrival.

"Be at ease, Captain," he said gently. "Let us enjoy a peaceful supper together and discuss the future of our land."

When the food was brought, and the soldiers serving it stood back awaiting their commander's wishes, Quoc said, "So, Captain, you are not convinced of the inevitable victory of the Vietnamese people over their current invaders."

Tran said nothing, aware that the statement was merely a preamble, and waited.

"That bayonet you arrived with lashed to your pack—Japanese, is it not?"

"Yes, sir."

"An artifact of still another race that came to our beloved country to enslave us." The general paused, smiling. "But where is the Japanese Army who brought these weapons to conquer us?

"They are gone, as are the French, and the Chinese, and a host of others with visions of empire. So too will the Americans, one day soon, be gone from Vietnam. We are not easily conquered. Our mission is to free the people from the adventurous whims of foreigners. No more, no less. We do not seek world domination, as have the nations who have sought to usurp us. We accept, albeit temporarily, the aid of those who do. Hence the Communist Bloc weapons that we now arm ourselves with to continue our fight. But, when the battle is won, even these mighty powers will learn that it is a formidable task indeed to control the Vietnamese people. In the end, we will be the sovereign nation that we wish to be—incorruptible, purely Vietnamese."

Tran chewed his rice slowly, eyes glued to the general's every move.

Refilling Tran's cup, Quoc went on, "Young warriors, such as yourself, are able to see only their present situation, the narrow focus of the immediate battle without the benefit of its ramifications." He nodded, as if agreeing with himself. "My aim is to broaden your scope, to enlighten you to the 'big picture,' as the Americans are so fond of saying." Quoc smiled at his own humor.

"The recent battles fought so heroically in the South are, if taken at face value, a cataclysmic defeat." The general paused as if expecting agreement from Tran, who nodded, feeling obliged to do so.

"However, if one analyzes the American media reaction and the uproar it has aroused, a different perspective is possible." He paused again, searching for understanding in the younger man's eyes.

"They are crying out for the heads of their leaders. Asking how this could happen. Large scale attacks on major population centers? From an enemy the American Army has said they are defeating? They take no notice of the victories of their soldiers. Incredibly, they discount them as preordained. They wring their hands and bemoan the insignificant losses they have suffered. To our vain enemy, one American is not worth one hundred of us, the backward savages of an impoverished third world country. And that, my dear captain, is why we will win. Not because of great victories on the battlefield, but because of the price we will exact from our tormentors. A price the Americans have demonstrated in their free press they are unwilling to pay. We will win because our mighty adversary simply has no stomach for war."

Tran sat silently weighing the general's words.

"There is much that we can do to help ourselves in this, Captain Tran. We must pay heed to the lessons we learn from our foe. We know that the American forces can summon death, en masse, at lightning speed, with their advanced technology. We have learned to hug his belt in any engagement to forestall the effects of his immense aerial firepower and bombardment capabilities."

Tran nodded again, recalling the doctrine of close contact. The Americans had a phobia for killing their own.

"We must watch his tactics closely and never underestimate him. Take lessons from history, Captain Tran. Look to those who have fought this beast before. A Japanese officer in the South Pacific proclaimed that the Americans are truly the greatest jungle fighters in the world. 'They do not fight in the jungle,' he said, 'they remove the jungle.' Is this not what they are attempting to do yet again, with their chemicals that turn lush forests into wasteland?"

Tran was reminded of the decimated tracts of land he had seen in the north.

"Thankfully, they have the conscience, possibly superimposed by their press, not to eradicate every living thing in our land with their defoliants." Quoc gestured toward the food before them. "The rice bowl is safe, as of now, and that is where the fight must be taken at this juncture—to the South, deep into the agricultural heart of Vietnam, the Mekong Delta. He sipped his tea and examined a tiny rice cake before popping it into his mouth. "You have a sister serving in the Delta Region, do you not?"

The off-hand aside, Tran thought, was calculated to startle. It worked. He was impressed with this man's knowledge of his life, but Quoc was not the famous hero of the war for his lack of thoroughness. He would undoubtedly have much more information than he let on.

"Yes, sir. Mai. She is a nurse, working with our brave brothers in the Viet Cong Seventh Division." He added sadly, "I haven't seen her in more than two years."

He remembered his sister leaving for Hanoi to complete her nurse's training. She had been the prettiest girl in their village, near Long San in the far north. Their family had been traders in the region for generations. His father's wealth, accumulated over a lifetime of dealing with the Chinese caravans traveling south through the mountain passes, had paid for the university education Mai had been privileged to receive. Her fervent desire to return something of her good fortune had led to her medical pursuits. Once in Hanoi, she had rallied to the communists and their lofty promises of equality for all of the peoples of Vietnam.

In hindsight, it had been inevitable that she would take up the cause and back her convictions with action. Mai had always been as brave as she was beautiful. Tran prayed that she was safe and well.

"Hopefully, you will have the chance to be reunited with her in your mission, Captain," Quoc said.

The unexpected statement brought Tran out of his reverie. "Sir?"

"You are going to upset the rice bowl, Captain Tran." The general's smile was gleeful. "You, along with the best of those fine men—" He nodded toward the enlisted barracks. "—are going to disembowel the Americans. The Mekong Delta is your ultimate destination."

CHAPTER 11

Fort Jackson, South Carolina:

The quiet in the barracks on Sundays was something Danny enjoyed. Noise had come to be an expected by-product of military life. The drumming of many boots on pavement, the sing-song cadence of marching commands, the clatter of equipment, and the never-ending drone of male voices had become so much a part of his every waking moment that the absence of background noise was pleasant.

He stretched his arms over his head, sitting cross-legged in his bunk, and let the peace wash over him. Being broke and stuck on post while others escaped to town had its advantages. The four-man rooms of AIT, Advanced Infantry Training, were a marked improvement in privacy over the platoon bays of Basic Training, but Columbia, the nearest town and the state capitol, wasn't exactly the most swinging spot he had ever seen.

What was Leon's joke? *See Columbia and die. Better yet, die first*.

The air-conditioner started that thrumming sound again. He groaned as he unfolded his legs, walked across the glistening floor, and kicked it. It settled down to its previous insignificant hum.

Danny mumbled, "That's what you get when you go with the lowest bidder," and went back to his bed.

Being grounded had its disadvantages, too. There was too much time to think, to be lonely, homesick, and horny.

Heartache was something Danny thought he fully understood after so many long weeks of enforced celibacy. Well, not entirely.

There had been that night with the hooker on E Street. It had probably done more harm than good, he mused. Twenty dollars' worth of sexual release, with a woman he wouldn't normally be seen in the same neighborhood with, followed by several anxious days waiting for his dick to fall off, wasn't exactly Danny's idea of passionate love. It had only made him miss Amanda more.

The ache in his middle was becoming monotonously predictable. Spend some time alone and there it would be—heartache.

The doubt was the worst of it. *Does she really love me? Do I really love her? How the hell am I supposed to know? Where do love and lust differ? Shouldn't I be able to think of her without picturing her naked?*

He unfolded and reread Amanda's letter.

Hi, Lover,

News from the home front. I bought a car. It's a red Volkswagen Beetle. Not exactly a luxury vehicle, but solid transportation. My promotion gives me enough extra cash to be able to afford it. I bought it so we can have a real vacation when you get home.

Which brings me to my other news. Jeannie and I rented a house in the Hamptons for the summer. You have to let me know soonest exactly when you'll be home on leave so I can take my vacation then. We'll spend two glorious weeks soaking up the sun on Tiana Beach by day and soaking up the suds by night. You'll love it. They have the most fabulous clubs out there.

Don't forget. I need the exact dates. Jeannie sends her love. She says bring a friend if you can find one like you.

Mom and Dad send their love. Me too. I miss you so. Write back NOW!

Love and stuff,
Amanda

Advanced Infantry Training was almost over. Soon he'd be winging his way back home and then, after thirty days of glorious leave—Vietnam.

What would Amanda say? He had to tell her eventually. Why was he putting it off? Could it be that he didn't trust her? Could Gino be right? Was she just a Manhattan Mama?

Lance suddenly appeared in the doorway to Danny's room.

"Put down the letter and follow me," he said.

"What's up?"

"We are faced with one of them irresistible opportunities that is just too damned tempting to pass up." Lance paused, building suspense, savoring his friend's anticipation. "That dumb shit Smitty locked himself out of his room. He knocks on my door and has the gall to ask me if I would pick the lock for him." Lance did a parody of Smitty's serious tone, "'You know how to pick a lock, don't ya?' he says. This dumbass Nebraska farm boy assumes that any black dude from New York must know how to pick a lock."

"You're shitting me?"

"If I'm lyin', I'm dyin."

"This I gotta see."

Danny leaped from the bunk and trotted after Lance. They skidded to a stop in front of Smitty's door. Smitty stood beside the locked portal, thoroughly chagrined.

"What gives?" Danny asked.

Before Smitty could reply, Lance cut in, "Smith, m'man, I've brought Fingers Mulvaney. Best damn lock picker this side of Brooklyn."

Danny's mouth fell open, but he saw the quick frown from Lance and elected to play along. "Got a bobby pin?" he asked Smitty, as serious as death.

Tears were forming in Lance's eyes when Smitty patted his pockets as if he might have one. Danny kept a straight face and told him a paper clip might do. It came as no surprise when the notoriously by-the-book martinet had one in his pants pocket.

Danny jiggled it around in the keyhole for a minute, and then told Smitty that this must be one of the new government locks that were, "Almost unpickable." It took all of Danny's self-control to keep from laughing when he saw the dismay on Smitty's face. Warming to the game, Danny said, "Why don't you go out my window, walk the ledge to your room, and climb in the window."

"Two stories up? I don't think so."

"You'll be perfectly safe. That concrete ledge is at least two feet wide."

Lance said, "If you're afraid, man. We can go down to the orderly room for a master key. I'm sure they got one."

"Who said I was afraid? I'm not afraid."

As soon as Smitty was midway between the rooms—edging along the two-story high span like he was walking a tight rope— Danny and Lance ran to a pay phone to call the CQ.

"There's a jumper on the ledge of Building One-oh-Five," they told the soldier on Charge of Quarters duty.

Then, they ran back to the barracks to await developments.

e⁄ɔe⁄ɔ

After the fire trucks left, Smitty spent a mortified hour trying to explain it to the MPs.

He spent three more hours with a psychiatrist at the base hospital before they released him.

Danny and Lance laughed until tears came to their eyes upon their victim's return. Smitty played the hapless, good-natured, yet sorely taxed recipient of a beautifully executed practical joke, but Danny was sure he saw anger in Smitty's eyes.

He wondered, for the first time, if Lance might be right about Smitty, but decided he was reading too much into it. Smitty was a buddy. A joke's a joke. No big deal. Just a little side trip on the boredom express. Smitty would forgive and forget. Private Smith adopted a new role that day, one that required finesse. In addition to being the perfect soldier, Smitty now took on the covert persona of a double agent. He now had a secret mission known only to him.

CHAPTER 12

Republic of South Vietnam:

Tyler kept his temper in check until the platoon was safely on the troop ship the morning after the Nha Be operation. In the privacy of the platoon compartment, he lit into them.

"You men of the Second Platoon have the highest number of decorations for valor in the company," he began.

With smug grins and sly winks, his soldiers showed their pride until Tyler added, "You also lead the company in Purple Hearts. Your performance on this little jaunt around Nha Be has shown me why." The stunned looks were almost comical, but he was not finished assaulting their affronted egos. "That sophomoric stunt you people pulled last night could be considered desertion in the face of the enemy, and that, gentlemen, can get you court martialed and shot."

"Sir?" Sergeant Cole raised a hesitant hand.

"What, Cole?"

"My squad fucked up, sir. Not the whole platoon. Is it fair to blame the whole bunch?"

"Your squad put every man in this unit in jeopardy, Sergeant. *They* dragged the whole platoon into this, not me. You and I are ultimately responsible. So, you and I are going to square their asses away." He directed his next remarks to the entire platoon. "Inspection in two hours. That means everything, gentlemen— weapons, field gear, lockers, bunks, uniforms, haircuts—the whole nine yards. We will stay cooped up in this compartment until you *all* get it right." He raised his voice to be heard over the chorus of groans and complaints. "You are confined to quarters

until I say otherwise. No smoking and no food or drink. No one
goes to the can without an NCO as an escort. Get it done, people.
Staff Sergeant Pomeroy, I want to see you in my stateroom. Right
now."

⌀⌀⌀

Pomeroy closed the door behind him as he entered Tyler's
quarters. He was grinning when he said, "They're none too happy
with the dressing down you gave 'em, and they definitely pissed
about the inspection, but they respect you for not rattin' to the old
man, Lieutenant. You handled it just right. I guess most of 'em
figure you're gonna be okay."

"Sergeant," Tyler said, so sternly that Pomeroy was visibly
taken aback, "I don't give a rat's ass what the men think of me.
My job is to see that as many of them go home in one piece as is
humanly possible, while seeing to it that Charley Cong's men
don't. I would advise you, Sergeant Pomeroy, to regard this as
your prime objective as well. And stop being one of the guys,
goddammit. Unless you won't mind writing the letters to their
mommas and wives explaining that, although you got them killed,
they were having fun when they bought it."

"Will that be all, sir?"

"No, that will *not* be all. Top said you were a helluva soldier,
Staff Sergeant. Start acting like it. I need you. The men need you.
If you resent me taking over your platoon, I understand, but I'm
not going away, so maybe you should."

"No, sir, I'm not goin' neither. It's just..." Pomeroy stood like
a man wary of the next step.

"Let's clear the air, Dez. Forget the rank. Talk to me."

"I guess it's just that I thought I could take a little breather
now. You know? Coast a little, I guess. It's been all on me for
awful long."

The sergeant's unexpected human frailty touched Tyler. Before confronting the platoon, he had had a long talk with First
Sergeant Syzmanski. According to Top, Desmond Pomeroy was a
walking success story. Born in a shack in rural Alabama, the son
of migrant farm workers, Pomeroy had lied about his age to join
the army at sixteen. On ability alone, without having attended
NCO School, he had overcome the barriers of race, education,

and social standing to attain the rank of buck sergeant while still in the States. He had proven his courage, stamina, and resourcefulness on numerous occasions in Vietnam. When the Second Platoon's lieutenant had been killed on the Y Bridge during the Tet Offensive, Pomeroy had taken over instantly to lead his people out of a very bad situation with minimal casualties. Syzmanski said Pomeroy was a natural leader. His only fault—and Top didn't see it as such—was his almost parental love for his men.

"Sorry, Desmond." Tyler wanted to add words of consolation, but he knew it would be wrong. "No rest for the wicked. We going to do this together?"

"Right on, sir."

Pomeroy was as good as his word, and the platoon, seeing that their hero was soldiering, did so as well in the operation that followed. Operation Toan Tang, an effort by the ARVNs—the Army of the Republic of Vietnam—and the Ninth Division, to rid the area surrounding Saigon—an area the men called the *Rocket Belt*—of VC, resulted in increased contact with the enemy. It seemed to the grunts in the field that the net outcome was to have "pissed Charley off."

℘∽℘∽

Cambodia:

Soldiers cleared the crockery from the table as the general and Captain Tran strolled the path to Quoc's quarters. As they neared the headquarters hut, aides lit lanterns, rolled down reed mats to cover the windows, and retreated to the shadows outside the front room.

A small table set with crystal goblets and flanked by two chairs filled the center of the space. A wicker umbrella stand contained rolled maps, and a weathered side-boy against the far wall held bottles of Napoleon Brandy, rice wine, and water.

"Would you care for a drink, Captain?" General Quoc offered.

"Thank you, no, sir."

"Fresh fruit?" The general raised a finger and an aide appeared as if by magic.

"No, sir. Thank you."

The finger dropped, and the aide disappeared.

"Militarily," Quoc said, motioning Tran to sit, "the National Liberation Front and the North Vietnamese Army are no match for the power of the United States."

Tran's jaw dropped, but the general went on as if he had taken no notice. "Man for man we are equal, if not superior, to the Americans, but we cannot hope to win against the immense firepower that the imperialists can bring to bear. Cunning and political maneuvering will win in the end. Cigarette, Captain?"

Tran took an American Salem from the gold case the general proffered. Quoc lit Tran's cigarette with a Dunhill lighter and started one of his own.

"One must look with an objective eye at the American's successes and analyze them," he said, as smoke curled from his lips. "See what they do well," the diminutive general counseled, "and emulate it. Note how they learn to out-guerrilla the guerrilla. Note well how their Special Forces—their Green Berets, Seals, Rangers, and Recondos in their Long Range Recon Patrols—master the terrain and, with small unit strikes, wreak havoc in our rear and along our infiltration routes. Note the results of their Phoenix Program, militarily and psychologically."

The general paused to let Tran absorb this. With fire in his eyes, he added, "Now, look also to the American people. They know little of this struggle beyond the reports given nightly on their television screens, and they care even less for the world beyond their immediate borders. They see nothing worth the lives of their precious youth here, so far from their fat, indolent land. As one examines the pulse of America through her reactions to the media's outcry, one begins to see that a certain aspect of the conflict results in outrage disproportionate to its importance. The Americans are far more vulnerable to what they consider atrocities than to ordinary battlefield deaths. Prisoners of war are a high-priority issue to the American public. Mistreatment of prisoners is regarded as despicable. They wail about their precious Geneva Convention.

"Can you imagine, Captain, a treaty that promises kind treatment of one's mortal enemies in war?"

General Quoc looked with amazement at Tran, obviously expecting the younger man to agree. Tran nodded his head, but his eyes never left the general's.

"Can you further imagine a highly motivated and well-trained unit—acting alone—with minimal support, deep in the South, striking at American weak points—for the sole purpose of taking prisoners?"

Tran was flabbergasted to learn that he had been selected to lead the unit the general was describing, a unit whose mission was to shatter the morale and undermine the enemy soldiers operating in the Mekong Delta.

"Is it logistically possible to mount such an operation, Comrade General? Are there facilities in the South for holding more than a few men at a time? Transporting them to the North would be difficult, I would think."

"An understatement, Captain, but it will not be necessary to transport these prisoners to the North, or even to the sanctuaries in Laos and Cambodia. The purpose would be to create an atmosphere of terror. It would not be essential to keep these men alive, only to leave the impression that they had been spirited away. The propaganda wizards will handle the rest."

Tran mulled this over in his mind. The general was, in effect, telling him to take prisoners and then to kill them. He said, "To be effective, the operation would have to be massive, would it not?"

"Massive? No. Sustained? Yes. If a few soldiers disappear each week from a given area, that area will soon acquire a reputation among the Americans as a very bad place to go."

"Intriguing."

"Exactly." General Quoc rose to walk across the room to the side-boy. As he poured two snifters of brandy, he said, "My plan is simple."

❧❧❧

Later that night, Captain Tran sat alone in his hut. An oil lamp cast a pool of light over maps of southern Cambodia and Vietnam's Mekong Delta spread out on the floor around him. Stacks of after-action reports of engagements with American Special Forces troops lay beside him. Dozens of photographs of enemy troops, their equipment, and installations were piled alongside.

General Quoc's plan was daring. They would strike terror in the hearts of their enemies and use the American press to compound their successes.

Once his unit's training was complete, they would have a journey of over two-hundred-twenty-five kilometers to reach their objective. More than half of that would be in South Vietnam. It would be no simple task to remain undetected for such a long march through hostile territory. Much of the terrain was flat, open ground. Rice fields and scrub jungle were the predominant features and, of course, the innumerable streams and rivers that meandered like capillaries across the landscape.

He and his men would seldom be dry. The monsoons were about to begin. Not the gentle rains of the Northeast but the punishing torrents of the Southwest. Rain would swell the rivers and flood the region, causing discomfort, but aiding them in their covert insertion. Once he and his men left the relative safety of the Elephant Mountains, it would be a harrowing trip indeed.

Tran set down the magnifying glass he had been using to discern every detail of his intended line of march. He walked to the window of his modest dwelling. Bamboo, cane, and reeds: these were the construction materials of the poor and the hasty. How tired he was of living in such rudimentary conditions. He was homesick. Odd, he thought, that such feelings came so overwhelmingly at times. He smiled at the prospect of being reunited with his loving sister, Mai. A remote possibility, he knew, but far less remote than in the highlands. The Delta—the Mouth of the Dragon—that was where she was. He would do all that he could to locate her. The Viet Cong network of agents in the South was effective. He hoped the units ordered to assist him would be of help in that regard.

His most fervent hope was that she was well and unchanged. He looked at his mangled hand and saw the disfigurement in his heart. Bitterness and hatred had left permanent scars on his spirit. Sweet, gentle Mai must not be forever marked.

He saw her twinkling eyes in his mind and remembered the joy of her smile. The picture of goodness and love that was Mai was indelibly imprinted in his memory. He did not need to carry a photograph of his sister to remember every contour of her glowing countenance. He remembered the day she had taken his picture when he was a young lieutenant. It seemed such a long time ago. He wondered if she still carried it with her as she had vowed.

A sentry on patrol caught his eye, returning him to the present. Reluctantly, he resumed his work. He lit a cigarette as he studied the charts and paused to watch the smoke rise, curling in the lamplight. He thought once again of the general's briefing and how enthralled he had become as he listened to the senior officer's plans. No pipe dream was this. Not the opium-induced rhetoric of the late Captain Duc. The people would not rise up and free themselves. Tet had proven that. General Quoc's schemes were far more realistic. Best of all, he, *Captain* Tran, would have complete control over the operation.

Quoc had not mentioned that the perpetrators of these acts might be subject to criminal proceedings if the North lost the war. Although it had been on his mind, Tran had not broached the subject either. It did not matter. Winners in war do what they will. Losers are left with the ashes.

The U-Minh Forest, the largest mangrove swamp in the world outside of the Amazon, a thousand square kilometers of the thickest, most impenetrable terrain in the South, had been selected as the base of operations for this mission. Any incursion will instantly educate the ignorant as to the reason for its forbidding pseudonym—The Forest of Darkness.

With his hand-picked team of thirty seasoned sappers, Tran felt confident in the success of this bold thrust into the breadbasket of Vietnam. He would truly upset the rice bowl.

This thought sparked another. While absorbed in his studies of the American Special Forces methods and modes of operation, Tran had taken notice of the American penchant for symbolism. He riffled through the photos again. Each American unit sported a distinctive patch. Many depicted death's heads or weapons and had ominous slogans accompanying their insignia. He decided his men should have some sort of distinctive emblem as well.

Sweeping his maps aside, he snatched up a pencil and began to sketch on a scrap of notepad. Finished, he called out to his sergeant, standing guard outside his hut.

"Bring Corporal Dinh to me at once," he snapped.

Tran waited, impatient, tapping his pencil to the beat of a Vietnamese marching song playing loudly in his mind.

Corporal Dinh arrived within minutes, rubbing sleep from his eyes. Tran seemed not to notice the man's salute.

"Look," he commanded, pointing to his drawing.

Dinh stared at what appeared to be a knife or a sword piercing a half circle.

"Sir?"

"It is our unit emblem, Corporal," Tran announced proudly, pointing. "A bayonet. This bayonet," he drew his Japanese souvenir from the scabbard at his hip, "plunged through the inverted rice bowl of the South. The bowl has no rim, signifying its emptiness. You were a tailor before the war, were you not?"

"Yes, I was," mumbled Dinh.

"Can you embroider this design onto some cloth?"

"Certainly, sir. It is quite simple."

"Good!" Tran smiled. "Make it a circle to signify the unbroken fidelity of the people of Vietnam. Make the cloth green, to remind all who come to know it of the forest from which we will strike. The bayonet and bowl should be black, for the despair which we will bring to the enemies of our cause." Grinning, he added, "It will also not make a good aiming point in such subdued colors." Slapping the man on the back, he ordered, "Make one for each man's headgear. Start now."

ೞಲೞ

Republic of South Vietnam:

For the first time in weeks, Charlie Company was getting a breather. Tom Tyler looked out at the muddy expanse of the Mekong River from the deck of the Benewah, the troop ship that was home to the battalion while working with the Mobile Riverine Force. He flipped the butt of his cigarette out over the guardrail and watched its lazy arc as it plunged thirty feet into the muddy water. Tyler rested both elbows on the ship's rail to look down at his men as they laughed and clowned on the flat-decked barge known as the pontoon. The members of C-Company were the guests of honor at a beer party thrown by the ship's officers and crew. Cases of the golden brew were on ice in metal garbage cans lined up on the deck of the barge, which served as a floating pier when lashed beside the ship. From there the infantry boarded the assault craft that took them up- or down-river to do battle with the VC. The arrangement was a marked improvement in safety over the days of cargo net disembarkation.

An ancient, but still enforced, regulation forbidding alcoholic beverages on United States Navy ships caused the party to be confined entirely to the pontoon, which was technically army property. The fact that most revelers returned aboard with cylindrical bulges in shirts and cargo pockets, and walked with a distinct clank, was studiously ignored.

They needed this break. Things had gone from bad to worse since the operation in Nha Be. Tyler chuckled in spite of his remembered fury. As he watched his platoon below, he marveled. They really were kids at times. They were men when they needed to be, as well. The past few weeks had shown him that more often than he would have liked.

Booby traps had taken a heavy toll as the troops slogged through the sodden paddies or searched likely wood lines for enemy presence. Snipers and small ambushes were commonplace, whittling away at the strength of each unit involved in the sweeps. Charley seemed to evaporate moments after he struck, leaving the survivors to rage at phantoms as they nursed their fallen comrades. Frustration ate at the men as they faced the daily grind, wondering when it would be their turn to fill a body bag.

At night, rockets and mortars rained down on base camps and cities as the communists launched their May Offensive. Tyler's pride in his platoon had grown as he watched their staunch determination to survive, helping each other as they waited for their chance to hit back at the elusive Victor Charles. His only doubts still lay in his confidence in the platoon's faith in him. They still hadn't fully accepted him as their head. He hadn't made any serious errors so far, but he could feel the tension as the men waited for him to screw up.

Tomorrow's operation was to be different. They would travel upstream by Tango Boat to where they would sweep another village and then, in what was hoped to be a surprise move, Eagle Flight—as helicopter assaults were known—to a new area some distance from the AO they had been searching. They hoped to catch Charley with his pants down and annihilate him. Optimism for success was not widely held. Veteran troops quipped, "If you want to know what's going down, ask mamasan." The Cong spy network was infamous.

Tyler went down the gangplank, mingled for a few minutes to keep up appearances, and slipped two beers into his shirt. The men were noticeably inhibited while he lingered so he made a show of checking the time, made his excuses, and slipped back onto the ship. He went straight to his room where he downed one can of beer and fell asleep halfway through the second.

The next day, the morning of the assault, the men of Charlie Company were remarkably well rested and fit to go after the night's festivities. There was something to be said for youth in fighting troops.

The operation proceeded as planned with no contact on the river or in the village. The helicopter assault yielded some sporadic sniper fire upon insertion but nothing that could be called a hot L-Z. It had become apparent, however, that the enemy was in the area. The remainder of the day proved fruitless as the platoons cleared areas assigned to each. Fresh bunkers were found as well as old ones. Punji pits, spider holes, and assorted explosive booby traps were uncovered, most without mishap. The two casualties of the day were in the other platoons and minor. The Second counted its lucky stars. Even without anyone being wounded, immersion foot, dysentery, and a wide variety of skin disorders added to the strain. By nightfall, they were relieved to set up their separate platoon ambushes. Each man hoped that Charley would not be so foolish as to venture into his unit's field of fire. Sleep was more valued than revenge.

ひなひ

Shortly after two in the morning, Second Platoon's guards heard the sound of paddles being pulled through the waters of the narrow river they had set up adjacent to. Wilson quietly roused Tyler and passed the word.

"Movement," was the single whispered scrap of information. One word was all that was necessary. They had done this many times.

Tyler strained his pupils to expand to the limit of their capacity to gather what light was available in the moonless night. Although tempted to use his Starlight Scope—a night vision device—he decided against it. The scopes gave out an audible, low-pitched whistle as the circuitry fired up. The sampans were close enough that the sound might be detected. He opened his mouth and rotated his head slowly to increase his hearing range.

Rowers in two sampans tried to muffle the sound as they glided down-river but the drip of water from an oar was unmistakable.

Hand signals, given inches from the faces of the recipients, advised the platoon that two craft were approaching with seven or eight bodies in each. The men lay motionless in the undergrowth along the banks with weapons cocked.

As the tiny flotilla reached the center of the kill zone, Tyler opened up with his M-16 on automatic. The platoon responded instantly with a deafening crescendo of fire. The sampans and their inhabitants were ripped apart in seconds. Rapidly changing magazines, each man emptied a second clip into the hapless targets, caught in the stuttering light of muzzle flashes, floundering in the black water amid geysers of spray kicked eight feet high by the impact of high velocity rounds. The *bloop* of M-79 grenade launchers was nearly lost in the crackle of automatic rifles and machineguns. The flat *Ca-rump* of the exploding rounds sent splinters and body parts cartwheeling in the air.

"Cease fire!" Tyler repeated, three times, at the top of his lungs, until the slaughter was halted. The silence amid the smoke was total.

Partially blinded by the flash of their own weapons, the keyed-up soldiers began to shoot short bursts at shadows. Cries of, "He's moving!" and, "What's that?" sent fusillades of supersonic steel into the darkness.

"Cease fire, goddamnit," Tyler yelled to end the pot shots. "Listen!"

When three tense minutes had passed, someone said, "Not so much as a moan."

"Quiet!" Tyler hissed, loudly enough for all to hear. "Wait! Rear guards, watch our backs."

They lay silent until dawn revealed the carnage they had wrought. Bodies bobbed in the sluggish stream, entangled in wreckage or snagged by protruding branches along the water's edge. When they were certain they were alone and unobserved, several men were dispatched to enter the water to haul the bodies, weapons, and equipment ashore.

The men soon determined that they had bagged two sampans loaded to the gunwales with troops and equipment. Nine bodies were recovered. The excited after-action report pieced together by the officer and his NCOs concluded that fourteen enemies had been observed in the strobe-light flash of the weapons. None had survived. Each one could be accounted for as having been hit by someone's fire. Scouting parties were sent a short way along the banks to search for the remainder, but no more bodies were found. The others had sunk or drifted downstream. The men examined the corpses.

"Lieutenant Tyler," Cargill, Fourth Squad's M-79-man, called, "this one's a woman."

Tyler, Cole, and several others gathered around the body.

"Look at this, sir," Cargill said, kneeling over the corpse. "One Sixteen round went in below her eye." The entry wound was a small hole in the woman's cheek. "Blew the back of her head out." He fingered a flap of scalp that seemed to be hinged. "Left this piece of skull like a trap door. Not too bad lookin' for a gook," he added, turning her face for all to see.

"Not anymore," Cole interjected.

Tyler was still amazed at the young men's blasé attitude toward violent death.

"Looks like a nurse," Cargill continued, as he searched the person and then the effects of the young woman. "Got this fifty-caliber ammo can still held tight in her fist. It's full of gook medical shit." He picked through the contents, displaying each item as he did so. "Bunch of silk scarves. They use 'em for bandages. Morphine—ours. Scissors, aspirin, rubber tubing…" He rattled on, cataloging the contents of the aid kit. "Dig this." He handed Tyler a faded black and white photograph. "Must be her boyfriend. Lookit the scarf around his neck. That's an NVA officer, sure as shit. We oughta mail it to the son of a bitch with a note." He laughed. "'Sighted pussy, sank same.'"

The surrounding group joined in the black humor.

"Not bad tits for a gook," Cole observed, peeling back the bloody shirt. Someone suggested they tie the body to a tree and take turns in necrophilia.

"That's *enough*," Tyler said. "Pack that shit up for S-Two. See if the Intel dudes can get anything useful from it." With that, he left to check on the rest of the men.

Cole slipped the photo into his helmet liner webbing.

Cargill said, "You heard the lieutenant, Sarge."

"Shut up, Specialist." Cole looked left and right. The others had wandered off. "This might be worth something to the rear-echelon guys. They buy all kinds of shit so they can tell war stories when they go home. Why should the remfs in S-Two make money on our hard work? You be cool, and I'll split it with you. Anybody asks, it got lost. Right?"

"How much you think it's worth?"

"Hard to say. Just keep your mouth shut, and we'll see when we get in."

"Sir," Wilson said, sidling up to Tyler, "Charlie-Six is on the horn. Says, 'Nice work,' but we gotta sit tight here. Some general's coming out to congratulate us."

"Great," Tyler said to the sky, "just what we need. A dog and pony show."

"Give Chuck plenty of time to prepare a little thank-you party for us," Pomeroy said.

"No shit. Goddamn rear-echelon motherfuckers."

"There it is," Pomeroy sighed.

Tyler knew they were safe enough for the moment. Their ambush position was in a small patch of woods on the riverbank. The surrounding area was open rice paddy for a thousand meters in every direction. They were out of small arms effective range, and Charley was not in the habit of letting mortar crews roam about in daylight, especially where such sparse cover was available. The gathering cumulonimbus clouds were the most pressing concern. A storm front moving in could cost them their air assets, forcing them to walk out. It would be child's play for Charley to set a trap.

Tyler scanned the horizon for the approaching helicopter bringing the PR boys.

"Laffin!" he called to the platoon medic. "Foot check. Make sure they're taking their malaria tablets, too."

"Roger dodger, fearless leader," Sp/5 Hadley Laffin, the platoon medic, replied in his sing-song cadence. "Let's have a peek at them piggies, gents. And everybody gets a taste of Doctor Laffin's travelin' medicine show elixir, which Uncle Sadist has seen fit to disguise in these pretty orange wafers," Laffin joked as he shook malaria tablets from a plastic bottle in his aid bag.

Laffin's disrespectful humor had taken some getting used to, but Tyler ignored it now. He was the best medic in the battalion, possibly the brigade, and his irrepressible good nature was invaluable to morale. Pomeroy had cautioned Tyler to be patient with the medic's irreverence. Second Platoon drew strength from their resident stand-up comic. Hadley Laffin's legend had begun on the day he enlisted in the United States Army as a conscientious objector. The look on the face of the Chicago recruiter when the long-haired Laffin had strolled in grinning must have been priceless. Dressed in faded bell-bottom jeans, sandals, sleeveless teeshirt, and a truly remarkable assortment of peace symbols, Hadley said, "I hear you assholes are giving a war. I'm coming along. Somebody's bound to get hurt."

The men had re-christened Hadley. They called him "*Always* Laffin." It fit.

The heat was becoming oppressive by the time Tyler heard the far-off beat of rotor blades. Wilson switched to air-to-ground frequency and confirmed that the inbound *slick* was the awaited general officer and his inevitable entourage. Two Huey *Hog* gunships circled the area as the slick flared to land on the yellow smoke grenade Pomeroy tossed.

The general, a one-star that Tyler had never heard of, dismounted and strode with a hand extended in greeting beneath teeth bared in a plastic smile.

"A pleasure to meet you, Lieutenant Taylor. Excellent night's work, I understand."

"'Morning, sir. Thank you, sir." Tyler shook the general's hand, his smile in close competition with the one-star's for lack of sincerity. He failed to correct the general's mispronunciation of his name, neither annoyed nor awestruck. He simply didn't care what the general called him as long as he made this quick and let them get out of there.

They went through the drill of the general shaking many hands while his photographer snapped away, showing the folks back home and the army worldwide the good time they were all having out here in the middle of nowhere, killing and posing for snapshots. The general helped himself to the best of the captured weapons and did everything but stand with one foot on a dead body for the great-white-hunter shot that Tyler fully expected. They gathered all of the documents and personal effects of the slain Cong for analysis.

Suddenly, the general was gone in a swirl of rotor wash and, along with him, the protection of the gunships. He had been kind enough to apologize for the loss of their chopper ride back in. The weather was turning nasty, as they could see.

"Hell, boys," he said, "if I don't leave now, I'll be stranded right along with you." Nobody wanted that to happen, especially the general.

They left the bodies laid out in a row on a dike for the VC to find for burial and started walking, in column, in the direction of the Mekong's nearest tributary. Every man was hoping that Charley wasn't waiting along the way and that the boats would be there when they arrived. In an hour, they came to a wide, built up dike, the surface of which was five feet above the paddy. It could have passed for a road if it had not been so overgrown with trees and brush. It led in the general direction they needed to go. After conferring with Pomeroy, Tyler decided to "take the high road" to speed their march. The rain had begun and was making the narrow paddy dikes slick and the deep mud was a sure bet to cause them to spend another night out here, so slowly would they advance.

Tyler knew the dikes were dangerous. They were often booby-trapped, but it was a risk he deemed necessary.

They did make better time on the "road." Tyler had Morgan on point. The man had an uncanny eye for spotting trip wires and all of the assorted tricks Charley left for the unwary. Tyler was learning the signs. The VC never set a trap without marking it, lest they blow one of their own to Kingdom Come. There might be nippa palm tied in a knot, a straight stick pointing down a trail, or even an actual sign.

Tu Dia was Vietnamese for Kill Zone. Charley would carve it on a grave marker or a tree, or place a sign on a road, or even nail a piece of cardboard to a tree with this inscription. He knew most GIs weren't here long enough to get any firm grasp of his language. They would assume they were reading the name of the nearest village or the resting place of the departed. Charley had a diabolical sense of humor.

Tyler called a halt after another hour and some particularly tough going past a break in the dike. A thirty-foot section was gone, blown away, it appeared, by some tremendous blast. The muddy breach, half a dozen feet below the road, was like walking through hip-deep glue. The men emerged red-faced, covered in slime, and winded.

"Take five. Pass the word," Tyler ordered.

The men collapsed in place, strung out over nearly a hundred yards. Tyler was just forward of the center of the column. The rain was steady but light. He was just about to tell the platoon to saddle up when he heard the *bloop* of a grenade launcher. Looking to the rear, the direction of the sound, he began to ask who was firing and at what when he heard it again and the explosion immediately thereafter as the round hit nearby. Seconds later, the next explosive shell landed in their midst. Tyler realized, with shock, that the fire was incoming and increasing.

Men crawled into any depression, no matter how slight, or rolled up against trees, even bushes, seeking any sort of cover from the forty-millimeter projectiles exploding among them. They could not return fire. Half the platoon was behind them in the direction the rounds were coming from. There was no room to spread out on the confining dike.

Pomeroy shouted, "Let's blow this taco stand."

"Right," yelled Tyler. "Come on. On your feet. We gotta get out of here."

Several soldiers slid down the six-foot embankment into the paddy. They were knee-deep in mud at the bottom.

"No good," Tyler hollered. "We'll be sitting ducks. Back up here. Keep going along the dike."

The platoon began a shuffling run in the same direction they had been walking. Tyler waved the men by as he crouched behind a sapling. He grabbed Pomeroy by the hand and pulled him down beside him.

"What do you figure, Desmond?" he asked, breathless, relying on his platoon sergeant's experience.

"One, maybe two gunners," Pomeroy said, breathing hard. "Rounds're coming too slow for more. Nobody hit yet, far's I can tell."

"You keep 'em moving." Tyler rose to his feet, stooped low. "I'm going to hurry up the rest."

"My job, sir. You should lead."

"You're the one they follow without question. I'm still the new guy." Pomeroy's look of uncertainty prompted Tyler to add, "He who hesitates…"

Pomeroy nodded and began to move forward through the mob, yelling, "Intervals people. Keep your intervals. One round'll get y'all."

The platoon sergeant was more concerned by what might lie ahead than what was behind. This type of harassing fire was typical of Charley Cong, prodding you toward someplace you didn't want to go.

Tyler retraced his steps, urging each man he passed to keep going. When no more soldiers bustled past him, he stopped.

Something was wrong. There should be another squad. He ducked behind a banana tree and watched where the men should appear. He tried to gauge how far back he had run. He was sure that they could not have been separated by much. The grenades were sighing softly overhead, still sporadic, but walking further along the dike. Charley was adjusting his fire or closing on them. Smoke hung in the still, damp air to his front. The rain had stopped for the moment. Several shells had landed here just moments before his arrival. The missing men may have hit the dirt and were awaiting orders. Or Charley had overtaken them and finished them off. He saw a vicious, hand-to-hand battle in his mind. Maybe he was alone here. Maybe the squad was dead, and Chuck was slithering up to slit his throat.

The rain began again, this time in a torrent. Tyler strained to see the road. A muddy hand rose up from behind a small mound ten feet away. The forearm was bare.

Tyler took a bead with his rifle, held his breath, and prepared to put a round through Charley's head as he raised up. He spotted the Octofoil, the Ninth Division patch on the mud caked shirt just before he fired at the wet, black hair that followed the arm.

"Rodriguez," he hissed, seeing the striking Latin face of the man with the thick moustache.

"Lieutenant! Give us a hand. Edwards is hit."

Tyler dashed to the man on the ground. As he drew near, he could see the rest of the squad, dragging the wounded man, slipping and sliding in the muck as they fought to make headway while stemming the bleeding from the man's buttocks.

"How bad?" Tyler asked, as he slid to the ground beside them.

"Not bad," Laffin advised. "He got it in the ass. Shrapnel, small piece. Hurts like hell. Looks deep. He can't run."

Tyler saw Simms, Second Squad's M-79-man. "Put some rounds back there," he told him. "Keep their heads down." He got them all to their feet as Simms cut loose. Simms was good with the grenade launcher. He could put four rounds in the air before the first one struck and each one would be on target. Tyler shucked his pack and told Rodriguez to bring it along. As soon as

Simms's first grenade exploded, Tyler threw Edwards across his shoulders in a fireman's carry, and said, "Let's *di di mau*," and took off at a run. They caught up with the platoon and fashioned a field stretcher from rifles and a poncho as Simms and Cargill laid down suppressive fire to slow Charley up.

As they resumed their forced march, they realized the grenade attack had stopped.

"Watch it now, sir," Pomeroy warned. "We may not be out of this yet."

Three AK-47s opened up to prove the advice prophetic. The platoon hit the dirt. The fire was coming from a wood line two hundred meters parallel to the dike. No one was hit in the first volley, but the rounds were coming dangerously close. Tyler heard the whine as one zipped past his ear.

"Return fire," he screamed, rising to his feet and spraying the trees.

The platoon rallied and poured out an enormous volume of fire as every man followed suit.

"Let's get the fuck outta here," Tyler bellowed, sending a long burst at the woods and running. The rain increased in intensity until they could not see more than five feet ahead. Tyler urged them on as the enemy fire slackened and quit.

They slowed to a fast walk, adrenaline fueling their muscles. They continued for fifteen minutes until Pomeroy advised, in an undertone, "Better slow up, sir. We don't want to walk into any-thing else."

Two hours later, the road ended in a village. They halted a hundred meters from it, reconnoitered, and leapfrogged in. The rain had tapered off to drizzle. The village was deserted.

"Guess where the welcome wagon came from," Pomeroy said.

Tyler nodded, "Good bet." He called the captain on the radio to advise him of their progress, as he had several times along the way.

"How's your whiskey India alpha?" Arnold wanted to know. Laffin's thumbs up told Tyler his wounded-in-action soldier was doing well. Arnold advised him they were half a click from the boats.

"Five hundred meters," Tyler told Pomeroy. "Thataway," he pointed, after checking his map. "You think Charley's waiting?"

"Naw. We know where the son of a bitch lives now. He probably won't fuck with us less'n we fuck with the village."

"Then let's not. Saddle up and stay sharp."

They made it to the river without further trouble. On the Tango, Pomeroy offered Tyler his canteen. Tyler gulped greedily.

"How'd you know I was out?" he said.

"Bein' scared makes a man thirsty." Pomeroy grinned. Looking over the soaked and exhausted men huddled in corners, he said, "You won 'em over today, sir. They's yours now."

"I don't know, Sergeant."

"I do. They'll follow you to hell now. Goin' back for them stragglers done it."

"Let's not mention that to Captain Arnold, shall we?"

"No, sir. Too bad, though. Be worth a medal, surer'n shit."

"I don't think the captain would see it that way."

"Mebbe not. What counts is—" Pomeroy pointed to the platoon with his chin. "—they would."

CHAPTER 13

Republic of South Vietnam:

D anny twisted his head around until his helmet bumped against the crazed Perspex porthole. Fascinated, he watched the scene unfolding below the twin-engine C-7 Caribou transport plane carrying him and his friends high above the reflecting mirrors of flooded rice fields. He had never seen such vibrant shades of green. Where rays of sunlight spotlighted the verdant foliage, it fairly glowed, in stark contrast to the patches shrouded in the shadows of thunderheads scattered like gray mountains as far as his eyes could see.

The agile aircraft wove in and out of passageways between the clouds as the pilot maneuvered for smoother air. The map-like tableau of the Mekong Delta spread beneath him would have been beautiful from Danny's vantage-point had it not been pockmarked with bomb and shell craters. The number of holes in the earth suggested three possibilities, hostilities had been ongoing for a long time, the enemy was resilient, or the gunners were inept. The first was a certainty, and the second and third choices gave him little reason for optimism.

Danny couldn't shake the sense of unreality that he was actually here in Vietnam. Perhaps, he mused, the life of a soldier was surrealistic by nature. His leave had been no less dream-like. The days had slipped from his grasp—ethereal strands of time that seemed to evaporate. Thirty days that may have been his last taste of the life he loved were gone.

Danny thought that funny. He had never known he loved his life until now.

New York City had rudely dampened the exhilaration of homecoming after he had completed his training. Vietnam was on every front page, every newscast, in every conversation, yet distant, removed from the business-as-usual hearts of the citizens. His country was at war but the people—his people—seemed barely affected. Only those citizens with loved ones involved bore any resemblance to what he expected the "Home Front" populace to be. For the rest, it was fodder for political debate. At times he had wanted to shout at strangers, to say: "This isn't just prime-time discussion stuff. This is war! People are dying! And I might be one of them!"

He wondered if it had been like that for his father. All he had to go on were old movies and newsreels, and he wasn't so naive that he didn't know that much of that was propaganda. He hadn't asked his mother or Uncle Mike, the only people from that era he trusted enough to bear his soul to. What good would it have done to speak of his misgivings? They were worried sick about him already.

Even Amanda had not reacted as he had imagined. She had told him to be careful, made him promise to come back to her, but not with the level of passion he had hoped for. He might as well have been going back to school, rather than to war. Was she being brave? Or didn't she really care? To be fair, she *had* been uncommonly distracted. Things couldn't have gone more wrong. The idyllic vacation in The Hamptons had turned out to be a few feverish weekends. It wasn't Amanda's fault. How could she have foreseen that her job promotion would force her to change her vacation to fit the supervisor's she replaced? And her sister, Cathy, losing the baby. That had been awful. Maybe he should have gone to Buffalo with her. And done what? Sit in the hospital waiting room making consoling noises? Try to comfort her family, people he hardly knew? No. He would have been as conspicuous as a bald Beatle.

Danny had often fantasized about having a brother or sister, and he believed that the loneliness he had known growing up as an only child qualified him to understand the closeness siblings must feel. He was being selfish. Knowing it only made it worse. Amanda didn't know how reluctant he had been to say she should go to her sister. It had been the right thing to do. But it seemed so unfair.

At least they had the last few days together, although that could have been better, too. That silly fight on the beach. Didn't she realize he had been penned up with nothing but guys for months? So what if he watched a few bikinis. Looking wasn't a crime.

And his mother—fussing like that. It gave him the creeps. He couldn't remember ever having seen her cry except when his dad died, but she had been on the brink the whole time he was home. And that scene at the airport. Good God. He had felt like he was at his own funeral.

That thought shook him.

His mom's last words had been, "Don't forget to follow through." He knew she'd said it for the old man. That was his father's catch phrase before a meet, and it had nothing to do with his form. The old man knew his mechanics with the javelin were superb. The phrase was to encourage him to go for broke. His mom wanted him to know they were both with him spiritually, but his dad's pep rally cheer didn't fit. This was no game.

The aircraft crew chief, sitting with his back to the quilted gray blanket insulating the flight deck wall, clapped his hands to his earphones to hear the copilot's words through his headset.

"Five mikes out," he yelled above the roar of the engines.

Danny, Lance, Leon, and Smitty exchanged what-the-hell-does-that-mean looks. The veterans stirred, some for the first time since takeoff. A few came grudgingly back to consciousness. How they could sleep in this pitching, rattling crate was a mystery to Danny. Most fastened their seat belts and shifted in the hard, plastic saucers that served as fold-down seats. The backs-to-the-wall style seats had been a disappointment. He found it to be reminiscent of subway car seating. Except in the tunnels beneath New York City, there was nothing to see but blackness and streaks of light whizzing by. Here, there was a world straight out of *National Geographic*, and he wanted a good view. The four replacements had not removed their belts, as instructed, and Danny was getting a crick in his neck from straining to see behind him.

He caught a glimpse of Dong Tam Base Camp as they lost altitude and began their approach. He was surprised by the extent of it. He'd expected a lonely outpost in the jungle. Not this—this place was huge.

The steep dive was expected after the Bien Hoa landing. Danny recalled the stewardesses closing all the pull-down plastic shades over the windows and the pretty brunette's nervous grin as she explained in a whisper, "We always do this for night landings. Charley doesn't like to waste ammo on an empty bird. With the windows dark, he can't tell we're full."

Now, Danny watched the palms race by, growing in size from tiny plants to full size trees as the craft zoomed low over the land. His first glimpse of the runway panicked him. He was looking down its length. He was getting a pilot's view of the rapidly approaching asphalt strip while looking out of the *side* of the aircraft.

They were crashing!

As Danny struggled to find his voice to scream a warning, the plane fishtailed and landed with a spine numbing bounce, heading, to Danny's amazement, in the right direction.

An amused soldier sat opposite, watching him and laughing softly.

"They side-slip for drag," the man yelled to be heard above the racket. "It's the only way to slow this sucker down enough to land on a short strip."

"Oh," was all Danny could manage in reply.

On the ground, Lance swore as they exited the plane. "That's the last time I fly with them filthy muthafuckas. Somebody shit in my seat."

They laughed all the way into the terminal area.

The familiar litany of boring instructions, recited by soldiers equally bored with the daily ordeal, was endured with stoicism as they stood sweating in the tropical humidity. Two hours later, a deuce-and-a-half, with *2nd of the 6th* markings stenciled in white block letters on its bumpers, arrived to collect them. Minutes later, they were on their way to their new home. Happy to be assigned to the same unit, the four young men did not question their good fortune and left unsaid their misgivings at having been shipped to the Ninth Infantry Division.

Stateside training had focused on First Division tactics and modes of operation. Much had been made of the need to know how to dig a First Division foxhole. The war had been hottest in the highlands when they had been drafted. The army had stressed the basics of survival in the mountainous terrain to the north. The fact that the Mekong Delta would be the scene of increased activity by the time of their arrival in-country could not have been foreseen. Each of them had heard reports from veterans they met at the Ninetieth Replacement Battalion that the Ninth was getting hammered.

A short trip across the base camp ended in a sudden stop followed by the driver hollering, "End of the line. All out."

First Sergeant Syzmanski greeted them upon their arrival in Charlie Company's area. Everyone called him Top. He was the top-kick, the highest-ranking non-commissioned officer in the company. He invited them to lunch in the company mess hall, but Top ate alone at a table perpendicular to and set apart from the larger portion of the dining room. They sipped lukewarm cherry Kool-Aid and munched cold, tasteless hamburgers as they listened to snatches of conversation from the other diners.

"Did you see me kill that motherfucker?" a freckle-faced, red-headed sergeant asked his friend as he wolfed his food.

A black PFC at another table laughed. "Sliced his dick like a salami, man. Bitch had razor blades in her pussy."

"Short round got 'em." A tall Spec/4 nodded to his three comrades. "Nothin' left but teeth."

Danny and his friends ate silently, convinced they were surrounded by maniacs, avoiding all eyes but each other's as they mentally planned and rejected methods of escape from this nest of insanity. Although they wore the same uniform, none of the replacements had any delusions that they were soldiers in anything but a loose definition of the term in the company of such callous killers. Smitty alone seemed to be enjoying the proximity to the veterans. He smiled and nodded to everyone he could make eye contact with. Danny wondered anew about Lance's opinion of Smith. Their relationship had been less than close since the ledge prank. Danny thought he had caught Smitty watching him several times. The look in his eyes had not been friendly, but it had always vanished at the instant Smitty realized he was being observed.

After lunch, the first sergeant collected them and preceded the group to the Orderly Room. He welcomed them once again to the company and explained that they would be staying in Dong Tam for a few days. The company was on an operation, and it would be necessary to wait for them to come back up-river where they would join them on the boats. They were billeted on the top floor of a two-story barracks hootch and shown where to store their belongings. The rest of the day was spent with issuing of field gear, weapons, and the assorted paraphernalia of the infantry soldier in Vietnam.

As they lay back in their bunks, their gear stowed in footlockers or hanging on hooks that were nails pounded into exposed two-by-four studs, a grinning Spec/5 with a large nose tramped into the building.

"You FNGs all squared away?"

They sat up, glancing to one another for some sign of an appropriate response. No one felt squared away, but it was unknown if it was proper etiquette to admit it.

"What's FNG?" Leon asked.

"Fuckin' new guys," the new arrival informed them.

Danny leaned close to Leon and whispered, "This one speaks your language."

The man shot them a hard look before continuing. "I'm Sedarius. Company clerk. Top says to march you guys over to the mess hall. You're on KP."

He left, assuming they would follow. As they raised themselves from their beds, groaning, Leon whined, "Fuuuck me."

Lance shook his head. "Too hot."

They laughed as they followed the tall, skinny clerk across the street. A sudden downpour drenched them as they neared the chow hall. They started to run but noticed no one else had increased his pace.

"These people don't know enough to get in out of the rain," Lance proclaimed, wide-eyed.

They worked nonstop in the hundred-forty-degree heat of the kitchen until the Mess Sergeant allowed them a break to eat. Wringing wet from perspiration, as well as the dousing they had received in the street, they picked at what they labeled mystery meat, swimming in a gelatinous grease they supposed was meant to pass for gravy. The mashed potatoes had to be sliced, or the pasty white clump came off the plate in one gluey mass. The string beans were recognizable but cold.

"I never thought I'd die of starvation over here." Danny threw his fork down in disgust.

They worked until after dark. The Mess Sergeant inspected

every utensil and surface in the hall before he released them. They trooped back to the barracks, dejected.

Not ten minutes after they had collapsed into their bunks, another Spec/5 poked his head into the hootch.

"Now what?" Lance groaned.

"I'm Thatcher," said the newcomer. "How you guys doing?"

They looked warily at each other, afraid to answer.

"Can I buy you guys a beer?"

The four young men were up in a flash, bombarding Thatcher with questions.

"Whoa! Whoa!" Thatcher cried. "I'm too thirsty for bullshittin' here. Let's go to the club and talk." He caught a whiff of them as they stampeded to the door. "You guys smell like three days in the bush," Thatcher complained, wrinkling his nose. "Didn't anybody tell you where the showers are?"

Their looks of confusion answered him, and he led them to the enlisted men's showers.

"Sundown's the best time to shower," he informed them. "The sun's had all day to heat up the water." He pointed to a jet fighter's wing-tank atop the building. "That's the water storage container. Never come here in the morning after they fill up unless you like to freeze your ass off. And don't dawdle or you'll wind up scraping the suds off dry. These things can hold just so much water, and they only fill them once a day."

"How come they didn't teach us any of this shit in the States?" Lance inquired while scrubbing his hair.

"They must figure the desertion rate's already high enough," Danny joked.

Once they were clean and dressed in fresh fatigues, Thatcher took them to the Artillery Club.

"It's the best club around," he told them, "and not too many people know about it yet. The main EM Club's too tempting a target for Charley."

They talked and drank for several hours. Thatcher, who worked in the S-2 shop, the intelligence section, answered all of their questions freely and good-naturedly. He dispensed welcome advice on a host of topics. Danny and he hit it off immediately. Thatcher had been *on the line*, as the men called infantry field duty, until the captain had given him his present job as a reward for excellence and as compensation for his three Purple Hearts.

"Three Hearts used to be a sure ticket to the rear but not any-more," he told them. "They're too shorthanded since Tet."

Lance mouthed, *Three?* and the new men rolled their eyes in unison.

By the time the barrage of questions Thatcher's remark had aroused subsided, he said it was getting late, and they strolled back to the hootch to fall into dreamless sleep.

Two hours later, Danny awoke to the sight of red flares light-ing the sky. Everything was bathed in a crimson glow.

"What the—" he mumbled. His training came back to him slowly. Red flares meant something. *Attack! Red flares meant they were under attack.*

He dressed with haste born of terror, fighting his way into his uniform. After donning his fatigues in seconds, he struggled to arrange all of his combat gear and lace his boots. The sound of distant explosions came to his ears. He hurried all the more.

Just as he completed his battle preparations, the blasts came closer together and increased in volume. The flash of a mortar round's impact outside lit up the room. The blast shook the build-ing. He heard the pounding of feet as Lance came into view from the far end of the bay, similarly attired in full equipment, running flat out. As the concussion rocked the hootch, Danny heard a sound like gravel being thrown on a cellar door and the whine of steel fragments buzzing through the air. With that, Lance became airborne and sailed past Danny to land with a sickening thud in the aisle.

Don't be dead, Danny thought, stooping to help if he could, terrified of what he was sure he would find.

"Lance," he called, shaking his friend's shoulder. "Lance, buddy, what should I do?"

"Get down, asshole. Them fuckers ain't kiddin'."

Danny laughed with relief and fell upon his friend.

"Get your skinny ass offa me, muthafucka," Lance wailed. "Let's get the fuck outta here."

Danny chuckled, giddy from fear and relief. "We ain't gone *yet?*"

They hit the doorway in unison and bounced back as their rucksacks caught in the tight space. Laughing, close to hysteria, they tumbled down the steps together. A shell blew the front off the first sergeant's hootch across the street as they hit the muddy ground. Lance grabbed Danny's hand and pulled him upright.

"Feet don't fail me now," he mimicked a line from an old movie as they ran to the nearest bunker.

They rolled into the sandbagged structure in a tangle of arms and legs. A flashlight blinded them when its beam fell on their frightened faces. Danny saw the muzzle of an M-16 lift as the inhabitants, dressed only in skivvies, burst into laughter.

Somebody laughed. "John Fuckin' Wayne."

"Yeah, and his faithful sidekick, Shithead," another voice chorused. Hoots and catcalls mingled with the pounding reverberations outside.

"Fuckin' new guys," a voice proclaimed.

As Danny and Lance disentangled themselves from one another, four loud reports shook the earth as Charley walked his mortars across the compound.

"Gangway," someone yelled from just outside the bunker doorway. A split-second later, two bodies tumbled down the steps, one on top of the other, to sprawl across the dirt floor.

Gary Thatcher crawled from beneath the nude body of Tony Sedarius.

"It's definitely our turn in the barrel tonight," he wheezed, trying to catch his breath. "They're plastering the whole battalion area. Blew the shit out of your hootch, Top."

Danny was surprised to see the first sergeant sitting in the back corner.

"He hit?" Top asked, beginning to get up to assist Sedarius.

Sedarius, Danny saw, was bleeding from the nose. Lance and he recoiled at the sight. Everyone else rushed forward, ready to do what they could for their fallen comrade.

"Relax." Thatcher waved them back. "He's dead drunk, is all. Found him flat on his face in front of the showers. Damn near got a hernia dragging his worthless ass over here."

"Should have left the little prick," a tough-looking, older man growled. Sergeant First Class Jellicks, clad in underwear, with his hairy belly protruding from beneath his olive drab T-shirt, exuded authority with or without his stripes.

"Don't be so hard on the boy," Top said. "I've seen you shit-faced on more than one occasion, Jake."

"Yeah, and likewise, Top, but this is getting old. He's blind every night lately."

"It's the mortars. The kid can't take mortars. I'll have a talk with him tomorrow."

"I still say he's a little prick," Jellicks persisted.

Someone rolled Sedarius's naked body on its back. Jellicks made a show of craning his neck to confirm his observation.

"I rest my case." He smiled a wicked smile.

Top, placing his hands on the shoulders of two men in front of him, rose up to make his own examination.

"Seein's believin'," he murmured as he sat back down.

The raucous laughter of the men huddled in the darkness of the musty hole in the ground seemed ludicrous to Danny and Lance as the earth shook with the impact of falling bombs.

In twenty minutes, it was over. The men shambled back to fall wearily into their beds, hoping this was the last for this night.

An hour later, it began again.

ℰ∽ℴ∽ℰ∽ℴ

"Harassment, that's what it is," Gary Thatcher advised the new men as they ate bacon and eggs in the mess hall the next morning. "Been going on for a week or so now. Chuck lobs a few rounds into somebody's area every night. Gets everybody out of bed and into the bunkers—and then he stops. He waits an hour or two for us to get back to sleep—and then he does it again. Harassment, pure and simple. Keeps everybody edgy."

"Can't they stop them?" Leon asked, his frazzled nerves evident by the tremor in his hand as he raised his coffee to his lips.

"They try," Gary said. "Counter mortar fire, arty, gunships, air strikes, the works. A whole shit pot of stuff goes out every time we get in-coming. Problem is: Charley's real good at this. Been doing it for a long time. They know just how much time they've got to set up, fire, break down the tube, and *di di* before we can react."

"*Di di?*" Danny asked.

"Vietnamese for: Get the hell out of here."

"What about ground attacks?" said Lance. "They ever follow up with an assault on the berm?"

"Rarely. A sapper team got into the lumber yard a couple of weeks ago. They raised holy hell before they got them out. Started some fires. Blew up a couple of trucks. Killed two guards.

Nothing major," Gary shrugged, shoveling eggs into his mouth.

"Unless you're one of the guards," Danny mumbled.

"Roger that," Gary nodded.

"What happened to you guys last night?" Danny asked of Leon and Smitty. "Lance and I were the only ones in the barracks when we saw the red flares."

"We booked when the siren went off," Leon answered. "Didn't you hear it?"

"There was a siren?" Danny said.

"Guess that answers that," Gary said. "Listen up. Unless you guys want to pull details all day, I suggest you make yourselves scarce after breakfast."

"First Sergeant said to report to the orderly room when we were finished," Smitty said.

"If you do, he'll have some filthy job for you to do," Gary promised. "It's up to you. I'm just telling you the way it is."

"Won't we get in trouble if we don't show up?" Danny asked.

"What's he gonna do? Send you to Vietnam?"

With that, Thatcher left to go to work. The four friends discussed their options and decided Gary had the rank and the experience to go against Top if he wanted to. They were less confident in their ability to risk his wrath. They lined up with the rag-tag formation they found outside of the orderly room.

The heat and humidity were already unbearable at this early hour. First Sergeant Syzmanski assigned most of the men to various tasks around the company area. Danny, Lance, and Smitty were put on a truck and driven to a far corner of the battalion area where they were put to work filling sandbags to repair a collapsed drainage ditch. In an hour, their heads were swimming from exertion. Their mouths were dry as cotton and their fatigues were soaked with perspiration.

At noon, they dragged themselves into the truck and lay sweating in the bed as the vehicle rolled back to the company area. The sergeant in charge of the detail told them to be back at the truck at thirteen-hundred hours.

"Super Troop?" Lance gasped.

"One o'clock," Smitty panted.

In the mess hall, they guzzled Kool-Aid until their stomachs swelled. No one had an appetite. They shuffled across the muddy street to collapse in their bunks.

Leon was already there, clad in his skivvies, his filthy uniform in a stinking ball on the floor beside his bunk.

"What have you been doing?" Danny asked.

"Burning shit." Leon groused.

"What kind of shit?" Lance asked.

"The kind that comes out of your asshole, dummy."

"You're kidding," Smitty said.

"You've all been to the latrine?"

They nodded.

"Maybe you noticed there's no fucking plumbing. Did you think there was a Shit Fairy to cart it away?"

The three of them still had their noses scrunched moments later when Thatcher rapped on the doorframe.

"Learned your lesson?" he grinned.

Their groans said that they had.

"Anybody want to go to the pool?" he asked, arms folded, leaning against the jam.

"They've got a pool?" Lance croaked.

"Over near the PX," Gary nodded. "But maybe you guys would rather go back to work." He turned to go.

In silent agreement, the four replacements were on his heels before he cleared the doorway. Leon struggled to get into clean pants and a shirt as he hopped along behind. It started to rain before they had walked very far. It felt good on their sweaty bodies, and the new men began to see why no one hurried to get out of the sudden downpours.

"This should stop soon," Gary predicted. "This early in the rainy season it's like this. Rains on and off all day. In about a month, when we really get into it, it'll rain nonstop, sometimes for days. That sucks."

They hitched a ride on a passing three-quarter ton pickup truck and rode the rest of the way to the Post Exchange. They had lunch in the snack bar, finding the cooling rain had done wonders for their appetites.

The food was by no means good, but it was still better than the fare they had sampled in the mess hall. Smitty commented on this.

"Sergeant Krales is new," Gary told them. They had met the mess sergeant, much to their disenchantment, the previous evening. "Our old mess sergeant was a wizard. The guy could cook *shit* and make it taste good."

"Krales seems to have gotten it backward," Danny suggested.

"You got that right," Gary laughed, brushing longish, thick, black hair from his forehead. His steely, blue eyes were alive with mirth, but Danny sensed a depth of wisdom there. Gary Thatcher, he decided, was good people. "Anyways, he'll get his shit together by the time the company gets back from the boats. You'll like the food on the boats. Navy's got the best chow in the AO. Captain Arnold—he's our CO—he don't put up with lousy chow. He'll square Krales's sorry ass away or bounce him out of here." He looked through the screen doors at the rain. "Guess I was wrong. This may not stop for a while. Sorry about the pool."

"No sweat, man," Lance said for all of them. "This beats the shit out of digging ditches."

"Roger that." Smitty grinned, proud of his grasp of the GI lingo he was hurrying to master. You could not play the role, he knew, if you didn't know the lines.

CHAPTER 14

Cambodia:

With General Quoc observing from his porch, Tran issued final orders to his men as they made ready to begin the long trek into the southern reaches of the Mekong Delta. The troops stood at attention, lined up in three parallel files, laden with gear, facing their leader, sweating in the sun.

"Comrades," Tran said for all to hear, "we will travel in three groups of ten. Small units can move faster and are easier to conceal. Dividing our force increases the odds that at least two-thirds of the unit will reach its objective. I remind you to avoid enemy contact and to remain hidden by day once you reach the broad expanses of flatlands. You are to move quickly where possible, but remember that secrecy is of prime importance until we are established in the U-Minh. We will rendezvous at a predetermined point outside of the coastal town of Rach Gia. Each of you has been advised of that location. In the event an element has to scatter to evade the enemy, every man can find the rendezvous point on his own. Once the rendezvous is achieved, we will make contact with agents of the Viet Cong to plan our best route and disposition of forces from that point.

"Comrades," Tran paused for emphasis and raised his voice slightly when he continued. "Under no circumstances are you to allow yourselves to be captured. Is that clear?"

The affirmative response was loud and in unison.

"Excellent," Tran said, "Sergeants, take charge." As he turned to order his contingent to fall in, he stole a glance at the general's quarters. The porch was vacant. Tran was mildly surprised that the general would not address his men. He tried to shrug it off, but he had to admit that he felt slighted. With a conscious effort, he focused his mind on the mission and his men. So many things could go wrong. Contingency plans had been made, but Tran hoped they would prove unnecessary.

Departure times were staggered over two days to allow for differences in the routes each unit was to cover. Tran's unit, with the shortest route along the coast, was last to set out. He had toyed with the idea of amphibious landings to cut the time to reach their objective to days rather than weeks. The only vessels available for water-born insertion were sampans and junks. These would be open to scrutiny from an array of unfriendly eyes.

The American, Vietnamese, and Thai Navies were attempting to search everything afloat off the shores of South Vietnam. Discovery on the sea would be disastrous. They would be overmatched in every way. The overland avenues of approach were arduous, but prudent.

As Tran and his team began their march exhilaration gave spring to his step. His disappointment with General Quoc had lessened as he excused his apparent dismissal as unavoidable. The general had an army to command, and he had already given much of his valuable time to encourage a young captain who should need no encouragement.

He felt shame for what he now considered his childish sense of injury. At last, he had a mission that dovetailed with his thirst for vengeance.

The First People's Provisional Captive Force would teach the invader the meaning of fear. The thought of the terror he had known under the guns of the enemy stiffened his resolve. Now, he would see *their* fear at close range. They would feel the power of *his* fury. And they would die.

ᘓᘏᘓ

Republic of South Vietnam:

The Second Platoon of C-Company fanned out on the steep bank of a wide, swift river close beside a bombed-out steel bridge. Lieutenant Tyler wiggled his fingers, and his RTO gave him the handset.

"Charlie-Six, Two-Six. We got a problem here." Tyler explained about the bridge. "River's too deep and too strong to ford, Six. Current will drag my best swimmers under. There's enough of the structure left above water to climb over but I'd like a little more firepower backing us up before we try it."

"Roger, Two-Six. Three-Six, do you copy?"

"That's affirmative, Charlie-Six," the Third Platoon's lieutenant responded on the company net.

"Roger. Move your people up to support the crossing. How copy, Three-Six?"

"Roger. Good copy. We are moving to the blue, over."

With the Third Platoon providing additional cover, Second climbed onto the twisted wreckage, one squad at a time, with every man spaced in fifteen-foot intervals. The men negotiating the bridge were defenseless and exposed with weapons slung and both hands needed to hang onto the mangled girders as they inched their way across. If the enemy opened fire while they were weighed down with all of their gear, and dangling above the rushing water, the choice would be to drop into the river and drown, or be shot and *then* drown. Jittery young men with sixty-pound loads, balancing on narrow beams, stretching to grasp any method of purchase, grumbled and cursed until the first squad made it safely across to set up security on the far bank, fifty yards from where they had started.

It took most of the day for the entire company to cross and move to their objective: a village, three hundred meters down the road from the destroyed bridge. Second Platoon swept the ville while the balance of the company surrounded it.

The reception the soldiers received was extraordinary. Villagers greeted them with warm smiles, bows, even handshakes—a western custom alien to most peasants. The headman ushered Tyler and his CP group into his hootch. His wife served tea and rice cakes. Chickens and pigs were slaughtered, dressed, cooked, and served to the men of the platoon. People chattered introductions for their entire families. The young girls were not hidden and, strangest of all, there were young men.

While the usual searches were conducted, the people still smiled. Most helped, gladly moving furniture, opening cupboards, offering to share anything they had.

Pomeroy said to Tyler, "This is the damnedest thing I ever seen, sir. These folks are glad to see us."

"Is this some kind of government village or something, Dez?" Tyler wondered.

"There'd be Arvins up the ass if it was. Nope." Pomeroy removed his helmet and scratched his head. "This here looks like a boneyfide pacified ville. Didn't think there really was any."

Tyler reported to Captain Arnold, describing in detail the welcome reception.

"Don't get careless, Two-Six," Arnold warned.

"Roger that, Six. But you've got to see this to believe it."

Captain Arnold elected to do just that. He and his group joined Tyler in the center of the little thatched town, took tea, and had a pleasant discussion—through an interpreter—with the village chief. The old man insisted no Viet Cong had been in the vicinity since before Tet. The presence of the young men was explained as laziness on the part of the local draft board. No fighting had taken place in the area for so long that the government ignored the village. Many young men came home on leave from the army and stayed, working the fields as they had done before their induction, and no one came looking for them. The chief thought the destruction of the bridge probably had a lot to do with that.

"Arvin soldier no like wet boots," he said, laughing.

Captain Arnold had to admit, it seemed they had found a spot bypassed by the war. Still, he advised Tyler against becoming lax before the captain and his CP group moved out of the village to set up for the night with the First Platoon.

"Wait until last light and move your people to ambush positions on the blue lines here and here," he ordered, pointing out on his map where he wanted Tyler's men. "The canals crisscross just outside the ville. It's a likely avenue for moving supplies."

"Ambush positions, sir?"

"No matter what you think you see here, Tom, this is still Indian country. This whole area is a Free Fire Zone. Chuck may not be anywhere around, or he may be right under your nose. Do not be lulled by the friendliness of these people. You don't want papasan's smile to be the last thing you see."

"Yes, sir."

Second Platoon loitered in the village longer than they should have. By the time they set out, it was full dark. Several young women walked with the soldiers, bidding fond farewells and pushing last minute gifts on the troops. The men loved it, but Tyler and his NCOs passed the word to lose the indigenous personnel before setting up. Tyler elected to set his ambush positions closer to the village than Arnold had planned and radioed the captain of his intentions.

"Say reason for change," Arnold snapped.

"Took too long to shake the friendlies," Tyler honestly replied. "Don't think it wise to stumble around in the dark."

"Okay, but watch your backs." Arnold's terse reply told Tyler he had displeased his commander.

Half an hour after the positions were set, before anyone fell asleep, Tyler heard the whispered warning, "Movement."

He heard laughter and female voices in the direction of the village, upstream, coming closer, moving along the canal he had placed his people on. The men were less than a hundred yards south of the intersection of the canals. Another platoon was set up on the north corner in such a way as to preclude friendly fire accidents but giving interlocking coverage. The other platoons were on the same canals but farther upstream.

"Hold it," Morgan whispered. "It's the villagers. Look, sir, they got lanterns lit fore and aft."

Tyler crawled through the reeds to get behind a tree, poked his head up, and saw three conical hatted women in a sampan, chatting amiably. They were exotically attractive in the flattering light cast by the flickering paper lanterns. Several more boats followed, most lighted, making no secret of their movement as they crossed the confluence of the canals. He saw what appeared to be families in most of them.

"Jesus! Are they nuts?" Morgan whispered.

The flotilla turned to travel in line along the canal covered by the Third Platoon. Tyler thought to call on the radio to advise the Third to hold their fire but decided it was unnecessary. Surely, no one would ambush women and kids, especially after the day they had had with these people. Before moving out tomorrow, he thought, someone should warn the headman about the carelessness of his people. This was no way to behave, no matter how pacified the AO.

He had just decided to do it himself and personally thank the people of the village for their graciousness when the crackle of many M-16s on full automatic froze him in mid-thought.

Someone yelled, "They're killing those poor people, Lieutenant. *Do* something!"

CHAPTER 15

Back aboard the Benewah, early the next morning, Tyler waited, seething in the companionway, as the captain finished his orders to the first sergeant. He heard them say something about replacements arriving. Arnold wanted two of the new men for his headquarters group. The rest would be allocated to the platoons, according to need.

Tyler caught himself wondering if the Second would get any of the new guys, and if so, how many. Thinking of the platoon had become reflex, he realized, a habit that would have to be broken now. He wondered if Pomeroy would continue to lead them in his absence or would Arnold take this out on him as well. He marveled at how much could change in one night. Things had been going well since the day he led the platoon out of that situation on the road dike. The men had accepted him since then, and the platoon was getting a reputation for being lucky. No one had been seriously wounded in weeks.

And now, *this*.

Whatever the captain decided to do, Tyler was determined to go to the wall with him. If Tyler ever got his hands on the jerk who had dreamed up this last little soiree, he would strangle him bare-handed.

As Top backed out of the captain's quarters, Tyler heard Arnold's staccato commands.

"Head back to Dong Tam. Get the new meat ready to rock and roll. And square away those rear echelon candyasses while you're at it. I want every able body humping the paddies with the rest of us. You get those pussyass goldbricks hiding out in the rear out here. Understood, First Sergeant?"

Acknowledging the order, Syzmanski reminded the captain of Tyler's presence in the corridor.

"Send him in," Arnold snapped.

Tyler sucked air into his lungs as he thrust himself from the bulkhead, steeling himself for what was to come.

Captain Arnold sat on his bunk, his back propped against the gray steel wall, one leg thrown across the surface of the fold-down desktop, the other dangling. The look in his eyes was ferocious.

Tight lipped, Tyler snapped to attention, only to be told, "Sit down, dammit."

Tyler dropped into a metal chair.

"If you ever disobey a direct order again, Lieutenant Tyler, I will throw your ass in Leavenworth so fast it will make your head spin," Arnold barked, stabbing a grimy finger at Tyler's face.

"I am sworn to obey all *lawful* orders, Captain," Tyler stated in flat, hard tones. "That was murder."

Arnold bit back his retort, shook his head violently, and balled his fists in his lap. He yanked open a cupboard at his side and pulled a fifth of scotch from a shelf. Lips clamped in a thin line, he splashed two fingers into a glass and knocked it back in one pull. He grimaced as the whiskey went down. "Where the fuck do you get off calling me a murderer?" His voice was like the rasp of wind-blown sand. "That was a Free Fire Zone, and you know it. Rules of engagement dictate anything that moves is fair game."

"It was a well-traveled river outside of a friendly village," Tyler snapped back. "No one's worked that AO for months. You said that yourself." His voice was rising. He knew he was going too far, but he didn't care. "In your pre-op briefing, you said that it had been ignored as pacified by Division since before the Tet Offensive. You know as well as I do that somebody, some blood thirsty, remf, brass-hat-motherfucker, sitting on his fat ass in a concrete bunker, worrying about his next fitness report, got pissed off at the lengthening casualty lists from booby traps and snipers, so he ordered up a slaughter—a sure thing. Lots of warm bodies out this way, fellas. Let's harvest a bunch."

"*They knew the rules,*" Arnold screamed.

Tyler reached, like a very old man, for the bottle without waiting to be asked, shook his canteen cup free of its case, and poured a large dose of liquid oblivion for himself. He slurped the whiskey noisily, and then said, softly, "There were women and kids in those boats. They had fucking lanterns lit. They thought we were there to protect them." He slammed the cup down on the table between them with such force, Arnold jumped. Tyler's features twisted into a snarl. "And you and your fucking butchers tore them to pieces."

"That's *enough*. You think what you like of me, but don't you ever slander the men of this company, Lieutenant. They followed orders, as your platoon would have done had you not commanded them to disobey."

"Commanded them?" Tyler laughed without humor, a flat painful sound. "When they heard the ambush was blown, they were stunned. They pleaded with me to stop it, for Christ's sake. They would have mutinied had I given the order to fire. We spent the night trying to save some of those poor bastards in the river. By the time they got to us, they were mincemeat. What did you want us to do? Make sure there were no witnesses?"

"What about the secondary explosions and the booby traps this morning? Do you think those were set by the Tooth Fairy?"

Arnold's smug, bloodshot stare further enraged Tyler. Realizing he could not win, Tyler rose, and said, "If you're asking me if there are VC in that village today, I'd have to say, yes. Every survivor in that godforsaken place will hate the US of A, and all of its sons, until the day he dies. Yeah, there are VC there today, Captain Arnold. You recruited 'em last night." Tyler grabbed his dented canteen cup, and asked, "Shall I consider myself relieved of command, sir?"

"You're relieved when I say you are, Lieutenant. Now get the fuck out of my face."

Tyler returned to a morose Second Platoon. The morning's booby traps had wounded two men seriously enough to be evacuated to the Third Surgical Battalion in Dong Tam. They were down to twenty-six men, including their officer and NCOs.

Pomeroy sighed, tugging the collar of his fatigue jacket. "I never thought I'd be ashamed to wear this suit."

"It ain't the uniform, Desmond. It's some of the cruds wearin' it."

"I hear you, sir. They's lower than whale shit," he indicated the men with his eyes. "They're disgusted by what was done to them poor people and mad as hell that they took the punishment for it."

"I know, Dez. It's done. At least they know they had no part in it. They have to live with the memory, but, thank God, not the guilt."

"They got you to thank for that."

"Do they? I like to think that they would have refused to fire if I had told them to."

"I know this: if you asked for volunteers to shoot that man upstairs right now, you'd have your pick."

"It's not his fault, Sergeant. Battalion wanted a body count. He did as he was told."

"That's what the Nazis said."

Tyler had no reply. Captain Arnold had lost his respect. He hoped that he would never be in a position to be judged so harshly. He pitied the man.

At the same time, he wondered: *Am I wrong? Could these people be so duplicitous? Could an entire village fool me and all of my men? Could the VC be so blinded by hate that they would risk their families to dupe their enemies?*

He was sick at heart of it all.

CHAPTER 16

Danny stepped into the barracks after dinner, his third night in Dong Tam. He and his friends had managed to avoid any manual labor since the first day. Top didn't seem to care as long as they were not hanging around the company area. They had learned to make themselves scarce.

Danny's plan this evening was to get off a letter to Amanda and one to his mom. He tried to write every day. He knew they would be worried. The five- to seven-day delay for the mail to reach them made it worse. Each letter would only serve to assure them that he had been all right a week before the letter arrived. The media would be a constant reminder of how much can happen in this war in a week. By writing often he hoped to alleviate their fears, but it was difficult to think of things to write about. He could not mention the nightly mortar attacks. That would worry them unnecessarily. He resolved not to tell them any bad things but to keep his letters as light as he could. Once his letters were written, he would have a few beers with the guys at the club and then try to catch some sleep before Charley's alarm clock woke him up.

None of the new men were anxious to join the company in the field. Stories from the veterans convinced them that rolling out of the sack to dive into a handy bunker every night was light duty compared to tangling with the VC in their own backyard.

A stranger was sitting on the bunk opposite his when he entered the hootch. A serious looking young soldier with longish, medium brown hair, dressed in camouflage fatigue pants and an OD T-shirt sat cleaning an M-14 rifle. Danny was surprised to see this older weapon. He thought that everyone was armed with the newer M-16, the weapon he had been issued. He stood staring at the disassembled parts, neatly laid out on the bed.

"Don't touch anything," the soldier said, without looking up.

"I wasn't. Just looking. I thought those were obsolete."

The man looked up, and Danny saw the hardest, amber-brown eyes he had ever encountered. He took an involuntary step back, as if he had found himself face to face with a hawk.

"This is a match grade M-Fourteen, an XM-Twenty-One," the man said, as if he were reading from the manual. "It is precision tooled and a delicate instrument. Do not fuck with my weapon— ever."

"Sure, sure. No problem. Danny Mulvaney," he said, smiling, and offered his hand.

The man reached back for his camouflage fatigue shirt without taking his eyes from Danny's face. He held the shirt up with the nametag displayed for Danny to see. Danny read *F-U-Q-U-E-T-T-E*.

"What's that say?" the man asked, unblinking. Danny noticed a faint accent he could not place.

"Fookay." Danny properly pronounced the French name.

"Thank you, Lord," the man prayed, looking gratefully to the heavens.

He sprang to his feet and, pumping Danny's hand, said, "It is a distinct pleasure to meet an educated man. I am David Fuquette, C-Company sniper *par excellânce*, at your service. Where you from?"

"New York," Danny grinned, amused at the sudden change he had just witnessed. The man's eyes had lost their forbidding glare. He was hail-fellow-well-met in a blink. "How about you?"

"Yes, how about me? Magnificent, am I not?" Fuquette preened like a bantam rooster. Danny couldn't help laughing. "Baton Rouge's most infamous son, a ragin' Cajun."

That was the accent Danny could not put his finger on.

Fuquette made no apology for his initial rude behavior, but Danny sensed it had been an act, some sort of defense mechanism the man used to establish his place in the pecking order. He made his excuses, retrieved his writing materials from his locker, and set to his nightly task of a letter to Amanda. Fuquette left him to it. Danny was pleased to have something new to tell her. She would enjoy the tale of his meeting with *the great* David Fuquette.

As he began the last paragraph, Sedarius popped in.

"You and your buddies will be leaving for the boats in the morning," the clerk said to Danny with a self-satisfied grin. "Get your shit together and be ready to rock and roll at o-eight-hundred." With a nod to Fuquette, he added, "You too, Fuckit," and left.

Danny sat, agape.

Fuquette, scowling, muttered. "*Merde*. Must I suffer the ignorance of uncouth assholes forever?"

Danny laughed so hard he fell on his side.

"Ah, yes. Laugh my friend. They do not call *you* Davy Fuckit, King of the Wild Frontier." Fuquette's attempted look of scorn did not hold up under the slightest scrutiny. He too began to laugh as Danny tried in vain to control his glee. This parody of his boyhood idol promised to be an unforgettable associate.

David Fuquette, he would soon learn, had racked up eighty-three confirmed kills and so many probables he had stopped counting. David Fuquette, formerly of Baton Rouge, Louisiana, was a hunter of men, a virtuoso among lethal professionals. On his next birthday, five months in the future, Fuquette would be twenty-two years of age. But he would never again be young.

CHAPTER 17

Captain Tran watched the cautious approach of the last group to arrive at the rendezvous in South Vietnam. All three elements had reached the wooded knoll within twelve hours of each other. A low-pitched whistle issued from his guard's lips. The approaching squad's point man returned the recognition signal. The unit spent the next several minutes engaged in a boisterous reunion until he reminded them that they still had more than half of their journey ahead of them.

They let the new arrivals relax and eat a meal of rice flavored with a spicy fish stew. The persistent drizzle had convinced Tran that it would be safe to light a fire. The smoke was invisible against the background of the moisture-laden air. While they ate, Tran, Lieutenant Sau—his second in command—and Sergeant Vinh, having each led a contingent to this place, compared notes on the journey.

No enemy contact had been made. All three leaders recounted close calls, but each had successfully evaded the American and ARVN patrols they encountered. Tran ordered them to establish camouflaged positions. They were two days early for their meeting with the local VC agents who were to lead them to the headquarters of the sector commander. The early arrival was intended to give Tran time to reconnoiter the area surrounding the contact point. He did not trust anyone in South Vietnam.

The First Peoples Provisional Captive Force set up shop, albeit temporarily, on a remote rise in South Vietnam several kilometers from the town of Rach Gia. They would rest there for the night. Tran and his team would scout the contact point in the morning. Tran slept more soundly than he had in many days.

CHAPTER 18

The boat ride to the USS Benewah was a pleasant diversion for the new men. The sluggish brown water, the exotic tropical scenes along the Mekong River's banks, and the smiling natives that waved to them from sampans made the trip almost languid.

The small boat, known as a *Tango*, was a modified beach landing craft, similar to what Danny had seen as a boy in war movies—the ramp falls, and the screaming Leathernecks storm the beach—but the Tangos were specialized for Riverine duty. In addition to its capabilities as an assault craft, the Tango had a steel deck welded above the troop compartment to serve as a floating chopper pad.

Landing a helicopter on one of these small boats seemed a dangerous, even desperate thing to attempt. Danny thought he might like to see it done—but from a safe distance.

There were no seats below decks in the troop compartment. Leon complained of this to one of the crew.

The sailor pointed to the forward ramp, which still served as the main method of landing men on an unfriendly shore, and said, "The quickest way for you grunts to un-ass this boat is a straight line. The seats got in the way, so we took 'em out."

The four new men climbed atop the sluggish craft to sit on the flight deck with legs outstretched, leaning against their rucksacks, soaking up the sun, which had obligingly shone since they boarded the boat.

Before embarkation, Fuquette had instructed them all on what to take to the field and what to leave behind.

"Weight will kick your ass out there," he warned. "You got to hump a bunch of shit that you need, but you don't want to carry one ounce more than you have to."

They had taken his advice on all of the gear except their bayonets.

Fuquette insisted, "If they get that close, you can't miss. Shoot the motherfuckers."

But the new men agreed a knife might come in handy.

"Davy," Danny yelled, lying prone, poking his head below the edge of the deck to look in on Fuquette. "Come on up and join us. It's beautiful up here."

"No, thank you. Charley likes to shoot stupid newbies who ride on top," Fuquette answered without taking his eyes from his Playboy magazine. The next sound he heard was the clanging of boots on the steel ladder. He chuckled, wagged his head, and mumbled, "Fucking new guys."

The four complained bitterly about the disturbance of their pleasure cruise.

"This is a war, my friends," Fuquette said, "a serious business for serious men. To die laughing is the destiny of fools."

Smitty cocked his head, and said, through clenched teeth, "Then why in the hell didn't you tell us before we got on the damned boat?"

"Understand something," Fuquette said. The icy stare that slid from man to man ended any thoughts of joining Smitty in his rebellious challenge. "You FNGs are a liability to everyone. You have no idea what you're doing, and the odds are that you'll fuck up and get someone else killed before you learn."

Danny started to apologize for them all, but Fuquette stopped him with one raised forefinger. "Do not mistake kindness for responsibility. I am not in the least responsible for keeping you alive. I cannot tell you everything you need to know to survive. Most of it you will learn on your own. Until you know your shit, watch those who do and listen when they tell you things. Your life depends on it. And so does mine."

They stayed below the screen of the Tango's steel walls for the rest of the trip.

Boarding the Benewah was an experience in itself. The river undulated with a mild swell due to the ship's proximity to the South China Sea and the fact that the tide was changing as they drew near. The Tango bobbed beside the pontoon so that it was necessary to time one's jump with the movement of the decks. A simple task in normal attire, but with the weight of their gear, the men were off balance.

It took several minutes for them to acclimate themselves to the motion and summon the nerve to jump. A slip meant drowning. The weight of their loads assured it. Or, if they were truly unlucky, they could be crushed between the two colliding vessels.

Fuquette watched with amusement as the four negotiated the breach, clumsily but unharmed. He then stepped across with the grace of a figure skater.

Several men greeted Fuquette as they made their way through the ship to Captain Arnold's cabin. Danny noticed that the French lilt in Fuquette's speech seemed to come and go. He decided that Fuquette was an exceptionally odd character. He liked him all the more for it.

Captain Arnold, who made it a habit to meet every new man personally, was cordial but abrupt.

"Welcome to Charlie Company, gentlemen," he said, after they had reported as a group. "You two guys— he pointed to Danny and Smitty. "—will be my new RTOs. You—" He indicated Lance. "—are assigned to Second Platoon, and you—" He pointed to Leon. "—to Fourth. Sergeant Beecher here will escort you." A sour faced buck sergeant with a lean, angular jaw, nodded confirmation before the captain finished his speech. "Get your gear stowed. Beecher will show you where. Get to know the men you'll be working with. Tomorrow's a stand-down day, but we'll be going out again the day after. Dismissed."

As they turned to leave, he stopped them. "Wait one. Did you men zero your weapons before you left Dong Tam?"

"No, sir," they mumbled together.

"Shit! Okay." He sighed. "We'll have to get somebody to take you ashore tomorrow and get that done."

Danny and Smitty were dismayed when they learned they were to be separated from their friends, but they were still in the same outfit, and Beecher assured them they would see a lot of each other. The sergeant, they learned, was to be their mentor. He was Charlie Company's senior RTO, an acronym for Radio/Telephone Operator.

SOP was to have two such men with the CO, one to handle the company's radio traffic, and the second to stay on the battal-

ion net. The new men were curious as to the reason for the vacancy but were afraid to ask, hoping the missing man had simply
finished his tour and gone home. The captain, Beecher told them,
wanted to try having a spare RTO on hand. At times it was necessary to talk to the platoons and battalion at once and to air crews
or artillery batteries as well. Switching frequencies in a fire-fight
was confusing and potentially dangerous but often necessary.
Arnold's idea was to have that extra radio available at all times as
insurance against overloaded communications and broken equipment. The captain, Beecher proudly explained, was renowned for
his unorthodox methods.

The stern buck sergeant said he would train both new men to
see which one took to the work best. The other would act as the
spare man.

Though apparently humorless, Beecher was good at what he
did. He wasted no time in beginning their indoctrination, showing
them to their sleeping area, demonstrating the use and shortcomings of the tiny storage compartment each man was allowed for
his personal effects, and then getting right to radio procedure.

After chow that evening—a marvelous improvement over
Dong Tam's mess hall—Danny and Smitty found themselves on
radio watch in the ship's wireless room. The windowless little
cabin soon had Smitty fidgeting like a cornered rodent. Danny
took advantage of the quiet space and light radio traffic to write
several letters home.

By the end of their shift they had learned a great deal about
military commo procedure and that they got on each other's
nerves in a short span of time. No words were expressed of their
dissatisfaction with each other's fellowship, but when the shift
ended, both were relieved to part.

Danny searched the ship until he located Lance and Leon.
They went to the galley for coffee and cigarettes and to discuss
their new status. None of them could impart any great insights
regarding their fast approaching introduction to jungle warfare. It
seemed the veterans shared a "you'll see" attitude when queried
on the lessons of combat.

Smitty was neither missed nor mentioned.

એવા

The next day, a squad from Second Platoon accompanied

them ashore to pull security while they zeroed their rifles. Fuquette went along to practice. He had just returned from R & R in Sydney, Australia, and expressed a need to "get the kinks out." He entertained the admiring group with awesome feats of marksmanship, dropping coconuts from trees at distances that made the trees themselves hard to discern with the naked eye.

The new men zeroed their weapons on less challenging targets—ammo boxes at one-hundred meters. When their sights were set to their individual eyes, target practice became a game of one-upmanship. The veterans baited the new men by picking out smaller and smaller targets at greater and greater range. Like freshmen at a frat party, the new men accepted every challenge, but Danny alone stayed in the game.

After watching Danny's considerable talent with his M-16—a weapon notorious for its inaccurate tendencies at long range—Fuquette complimented Danny on his prowess.

"Good enough for Sniper School?" Danny asked.

Fuquette squatted down beside Danny's prone form. "When you shoot at a gook with that thing, my friend," he said, looking upon the black rifle with disdain, "you are usually blasting away on automatic, firing at the sound of your opponent's weapon, or snapping off wild shots at his fleeing form." Displaying his own weapon as one would a work of art, he went on. "When I get Charley in my scope, he does not know I exist. He is at peace, secure in his belief that he has a future." Fuquette paused to look with his rock steady gaze into Danny's eyes. "When I squeeze the trigger, I see his face go from placid to shock, and sometimes agony. The crack of the round that kills him comes after the impact. If he hears it, his last emotion is fear, the powerless fear of the mortally wounded. If God is merciful, he never hears it."

Standing erect, with the sun behind him so that Danny had to squint to see the sniper's face, Fuquette asked softly, "Is this what you want to be?"

Danny was shaken by the isolation, the soul-deep loneliness in Fuquette's eyes. Fuquette turned and walked slowly to the river's edge as Danny watched him go. He hadn't answered Fuquette's question. He didn't have to.

On the boat ride back to the ship, Fuquette sat alone, apart from the rest, reading a paperback novel, his desire for solitude obvious and respected by the men. Danny resisted an urge to speak to him, knowing that he had unwittingly intruded on the man's inner self. He was ashamed without knowing why.

Once back on the ship, they were informed that the operation scheduled for tomorrow had been scrubbed in light of new information of a VC unit's movements a few clicks upstream. They were to move out late this afternoon in hopes of intercepting the enemy. The strength of the enemy force varied with the rumor-monger relating the information. They were after something between two kids with AKs and a reinforced regiment.

Danny tried to locate Fuquette to no avail. Asking repeatedly if anyone had seen him, he was told, wryly, by a soldier from Delta Company, "If Fuckit wants to be found, you'll find him. If he don't, you won't. That son-of-a-bitch could be standing right next to you, but if he don't want you to see him..." He made a gesture with his hands to show that the sniper was indeed nowhere to be seen. Danny couldn't resist the urge to look over his shoulder. The soldier laughed and moved on.

At the appointed time, Smitty and Danny strapped on their gear. Beecher supervised and helped where needed. They were awestruck by the burdens that they were expected to carry. Extra ammo, Claymore mines, rations, spare radio batteries, mortar rounds, and assorted grenades were dumped at their feet or stuffed into their packs. Danny had been chosen as the first to take a turn with the radio. Beecher assured Smitty that he would get his chance and explained that he could not possibly evaluate them both at once.

"One cherry on the horn is bad enough," he growled. "Two of you is more than even *I* can handle."

The vets seemed to enjoy their flabbergasted expressions as they increased their burdens. The two young men walked to the gangplank ladder bent under their loads, wondering how it was possible to fight a war so encumbered.

At the bottom of the gangway, the pontoon was crowded with men equally buried by the mountains of equipment that the new men found so daunting. The vets seemed to bear up under their loads with stoicism, if not ease. Danny struggled to shift the radio and his web gear to a comfortable position. The pack straps cut into his shoulders, the rolled poncho tied to his rucksack frame was coming loose, and his ammo bandoleers slapped against his groin when he walked.

"Should I put these in my pack?" he asked a passing soldier.

"Good idea," the man said. "Just remember to yell *'time out'* when the shooting starts or Charley might not wait for you to reload."

The men within earshot had a good laugh at Danny's expense. His ears reddened and his jaw clenched.

The jokester said, "Chill out, newgie. Ask a stupid question..." He pulled roughly on Danny's bandoleer straps, knotted them so that they were shortened, and then adjusted them so they rode across his chest.

"Like that," he said.

"Thanks," Danny said.

"You want to thank me, stay the hell away from me," the man said, walking away.

Danny was standing near the edge of the pontoon, awaiting orders as to what to do next, when he glanced down at the brown water and noticed, with annoyance, that his left bootlace was untied. He stooped to correct the problem and bumped rear ends with the man behind him, who was similarly bending over to adjust some article of his equipment.

The weight of his load sent him pitching forward. The muddy river water rushed to meet him. He straightened his body in a desperate attempt to right himself. His only accomplishment was to hit the water feet first instead of in the dive he had begun. The weight of his gear dragged him down like a falling elevator. Before he had time to grasp his situation and make any attempt to shuck the pack that was attempting to drown him, he stopped. It felt like a puppet master had pulled his strings. He was rising. His head broke water, and he gasped for air. Rough hands grasped his shoulder harness straps and jerked him from the water. He was sitting on the pontoon deck, his feet hanging just above the murky stream, wondering what had happened, when he heard, "Mulvaney, you all right?" He turned, dazed, to see Beecher squatting beside him.

"Yeah. Think so. What happened?"

"There will be no more unauthorized swimming," Captain Arnold quipped. "Lifeguards go off duty at sixteen-hundred."

"You fell in," Beecher told him. "If Davy hadn't grabbed your antenna, you'd be fish food."

"Thanks," Danny gasped.

"No sweat," Fuquette nodded. "You owe me a beer."

"I'll buy you a case," Danny promised.

"If you plan to make a habit of this, forget it." Fuquette walked off, feigning insult. The men surrounding Danny helped him to his feet as the Tango Boats came into view down river. He did his best to wring the water from his sodden uniform while they waited.

Beecher double-checked his charges' gear on the ride to the insertion point. He was pleased to find that the dunking had not damaged the radio. The plastic bag in which the handset was wrapped and secured with a rubber band, had remained in place.

Ludicrous as it might be, the sergeant told Danny, the black plastic phone was highly susceptible to malfunction when wet. A result, Beecher felt certain, of Pentagon penny pinching.

Danny, still squeezing water from his clothing, asked if every company had its own sniper.

"Hardly," Beecher snorted. "Snipers work out of Division HQ. They get assignments all over the AO. They're here-today-gone-tomorrow type dudes. Travelin' men, to be sure. Why?"

"Fuquette said he was C-Company sniper. How come?"

"Ol' Davy Fuckit's a special case," Beecher answered, looking at Fuquette's back as the sniper leaned against the ramp to peek through the grillwork atop the door. "He was originally a rifleman in Second Platoon. When they started the Sniper School, they came around interviewing guys that had qualified expert with the M-Fourteen in Basic. A few they tested on the range. Fuquette was the best. He worked with every outfit in the Division like the rest of them, at first. He went out with us when the captain had a need for him. As it turned out, he bagged the greatest percentage of his kills when he was working with his old unit. Charlie-Six convinced Division that it would be a good idea to have him along permanent-like. He stays with us most of the time now, although Division does call him away now and then for special jobs, like the one he was on before his R and R."

"What was that?"

"Classified," Beecher whispered. "If I told you, I'd have to kill you." Danny was taken aback until he saw the sergeant's grin. Beecher's rare attempt at humor was gone as quickly as it had come. "Keep quiet when we hit the beach," he said, all business once again, "and for God's sake, keep up."

"I'm kinda disappointed—" Smitty began.

Captain Arnold turned from studying his map. "At what?"

"At not getting to ride in a helicopter." Looking around at the interior of the boat, he continued, "I never expected to be going into battle in one of these."

"You'll get plenty of chances to ride on choppers," Arnold assured him. "You'll learn to appreciate a nice boat ride."

"Maybe so," Smitty grinned nervously. "At least you don't hit any hot LZs in these things."

"You'll learn to appreciate those, too, if you ever hit a hot beach," Sergeant Beecher put in. "When that ramp drops," he indicated the steel door at the front of the boat, "we're like fish in a barrel. If Charley's expecting us... Well, it ain't pretty."

"Just stay low and get off fast," Charlie-Six advised.

The beach was a cold one. The boats nosed into the bank, dropped their ramps and the troops climbed carefully off of the mud slick trap doors. They struggled up the steep embankment, slipping and sliding in the ooze. Danny and Smitty soon found out that, "Get off fast," was an order more wishful than relevant.

Upon reaching level ground, the men hunkered down, spread out on line with every other man facing the rice fields to their front. The rear-facing soldiers scanned the opposite bank, protecting the unit's back. The sun was dipping rapidly on the horizon. Danny got a brief glimpse of the flat, alluvial plain that was the Mekong Delta. His impression was one of looking across a soggy green and brown tabletop. Low dikes and narrow wood lines bordered the paddies. The outline of tall, graceful palms in the distance would have been romantic had he not been so frightened.

Engines growling, the boats backed off the beach and spun in mid-stream until, once again in column, they reversed throttle and headed back the way they had come. Most of the men watched them go. Danny wondered if they all felt as uneasy about being left out here on a hostile shore as he did.

After checking his map one last time, the captain gave the order to move forward. Beecher relayed the command to the company via radio and Charlie Company crossed the line of departure. A wood line, roughly two hundred meters to their front, was their first objective.

"Keep it on line and stay off the dikes," Captain Arnold spoke into the handset as Beecher moved up with him.

The mud, Danny soon discovered, was difficult to move through. He seemed to sink deeper with each step. He was falling behind from the start.

"Step on the plants," a friendly soldier advised.

By placing his feet on the growing rice shoots, Danny found that he did not sink as deeply into the muck. With the quickly gathering dusk, it was becoming impossible to find the helpful foliage. The mud stuck to his boots like paste, and he was soon dragging pounds of the stuff on each foot. So absorbed was he in watching his footing, he failed to notice that he was being left to negotiate the paddy alone. When he glanced up, breathing hard, all he could see of the company was a few ghostly forms as the soldiers disappeared in the gloom. He was tempted to cry out but remembered Beecher's admonishment: *Keep quiet and keep up.*

His next step sent him sliding down the sixty-degree slope of a neck-deep drainage ditch. Danny lost sight of the company completely as he lodged in the bottom of the trench. His legs were spread in a split, the left sunken in the mud to the hip, the right trailing behind, with his boot nearly even with his head.

Clenching his teeth, he dragged his trailing leg down until the weight of his pack toppled him on his side. Grunting and cursing under his breath, he managed to right himself to a sitting position. With Herculean effort, he lurched erect and yanked one foot free, trying to swing it forward, only to pitch face first against the muddy slope. Try as he might, he could not make any headway up the bank. The more he struggled, the deeper he sank.

Realizing he would never get out with the crushing weight of the radio driving him deeper, he shrugged the rucksack from his shoulders and hoisted the offending burden to the precipice. The effort lodged him in the slime to his waist. It dawned on him that he had just put his only means of communication out of reach.

Danny desperately dug into the slope with the stock of his M-16, using it like an oar to gain purchase. He succeeded only in pulling more of the sickening sludge down on him. The lip of the ditch seemed farther away than before. It was fully dark now and the stars, twinkling brightly in the heavens above, gave just enough light to distinguish solid objects from space.

Fighting panic, Danny grasped the stock of his weapon and tried to snag the straps of the radio with the front sight assembly. Stretching for all he was worth, he felt something catch. He pulled. The smooth plastic stock slid from his mud slick fingers. The weapon teetered on the edge and came to rest out of his reach. The butt, protruding into space, was only tantalizing inches from his outstretched fingers. He fell back, panting, to sit in the mud. Aware that he was now all but defenseless, he resigned himself to wait for someone to come back for him, or at least until he caught his breath. Danny was, once again, unfavorably impressed with the heat.

A faint rustle of shrubbery sent his spirits soaring.

Thank God. Someone was coming.

The sound had come from behind and above him, not from the direction the company had gone. He had a flashback to a poster on a bus in Fort Jackson: a USO ad depicting a lonely soldier, sitting beneath the caption, *DOES ANYBODY KNOW I'M HERE?* It had been a standing joke among the trainees. *You better hope not, young troop*, the gag went. *If Charley knows, your ass is grass.*

The recollection got Danny's adrenal glands pumping. He twisted his torso around just in time to see a small shadowy form lunging at him. He threw himself backward as the man hurtled past. A machete sliced the air and sank into the mud beside him with a faint ringing sound.

Danny grabbed for the man. His hands seized cloth and flesh. The assassin threw his weight against Danny's breastbone. The air was forced from his lungs. He thought his ribcage would rip through his skin. His eyes bulged. His vision blurred. While his mind tried to will his body to breath, he saw the man scrabbling to right himself, trying to extract his weapon from the mud. The slippery muck would not allow his fingers to get a firm grip on the handle. Danny smelled rancid fish on the man's breath. He knew that if he didn't overpower this man he would be dead in a moment.

His left hand got tangled in his attacker's shirt. Danny stiff-armed him back, trying to dislodge himself from the man's clutches. The man's weight, as he fell away, pulled the knot of material tighter around Danny's wrist. As the machete came free and the man raised it to strike, Danny's right hand found the bayonet at his belt. In one swift movement, he drove it deep into his opponent's abdomen. The man screamed. Danny imagined a horde of machete-wielding fanatics descending on him to hack him to pieces. He tore his left hand free from his opponent's shirt and clawed for the wounded man's mouth. Hot blood and bowel content gushed from the belly wound. The stench nearly made Danny vomit, but silencing his antagonist was his most urgent need and, clutching the man's throat, Danny pulled him on top of himself.

"Shut up, you gook son of a bitch," he hissed as he pulled the blade back and thrust it home again, higher up, under the ribs.

The man coughed blood in Danny's face and went limp. Danny thrust him away, revolted, terrorized. He lay back, gasping for air in the stinking trough.

"Mulvaney." He heard an urgent whisper from the lip of the ditch. Sobs of relief were all he was capable of in reply.

Several men slid down to pull Danny from the trap he had made for himself. A red lens- filtered flashlight played over the scene as they extracted him from the mud. He caught a glimpse of a young Asian face, frozen in agony, splashed with something dark and wet. Once on firmer ground, he was helped to his feet.

"You all right, son?" Captain Arnold said. "We were looking for you when we heard the scream. Are you hurt?"

"No," Danny heard himself say, and then he was crying. He felt strong arms embrace him and heard words of comfort. He was helplessly distraught, shaking with grief at what he had done, jubilant beyond description that he had survived, mortified by his tears, and powerless to stop them. Someone picked up his gear and led him away, stumbling across the paddy.

He heard Captain Arnold say, "Let's shag it, people. That gook's buddies are around here someplace, and they are gonna be *beaucoup* pissed off."

Captain Arnold humped Danny's radio until they were safely in the trees. Fuquette handed him his rifle with, "Clean it, first chance," as his only comment. They set up briefly in place while Charlie-Six radioed the colonel of Danny's encounter. Danny eavesdropped.

"Body count is one." A pause. "Confirmed Victor Charles," Danny heard him whisper. Another pause, and then, "Negative. No rifle." Another pause and then, "Because he tried to cut him in half with a goddamned machete."

They lay in the woods for what seemed to Danny several hours. In fact, it was less than one. They watched and waited until the captain said, "No one seems to be missing our little friend. Let's boogie."

A quick march through the brush began. Danny felt the tension of the men around him as they traveled. Night moves were dangerous. Both sides waited in ambush for anyone foolhardy enough to move in the dark. Everyone seemed to breathe easier once they settled in for the night a hundred meters from where they had entered the woods.

ون

Captain Tran watched the hootch in the clearing for nearly an hour after sunset. No one entered; no one left. Sergeant Vinh reported the same inactivity from his vantage point on the other side of the hut. Vinh and two men walked warily to the entrance where Vinh called out softly for the occupants to show themselves. A curtain parted in the doorway, spilling yellow light at Vinh's feet.

"I am the one you seek," a man's voice said. The speaker was silhouetted in the doorway. "Enter, please." The man stepped aside but held the curtain open.

Vinh hesitated before he stepped inside, the muzzle of his cocked assault rifle preceding him.

The other two men stayed back, watching the jungle.

"Welcome to my home, comrade." The smiling middle-aged man, bowing slightly as he greeted his guest, seemed less than sincere to Sergeant Vinh. Vinh did not trust spies, farmers, or merchants. Vinh trusted only fellow soldiers, fellow North Vietnamese soldiers. He had no respect for the guerrillas in the South. The Viet Cong were amateurs as far as he was concerned. Careless amateurs at that. He was not going to let one of these farm boys get him killed. "You are the officer with whom I am to discuss the needs of the unit from the North?" the polite man asked.

"I am the man who will slit your throat if the 'unit from the North' is carelessly mentioned again," Vinh told him. He watched the man's eyes widen in fear.

"Comrade, you have no need to worry. All is secure here."

Vinh did a rudimentary search of the man's dwelling. It took him less than a minute to check the one-room shack. There was nowhere for another person to hide in the sparsely furnished thatched hut. Still, he opened the door of the only cupboard in the room and even peeked under the plywood bed, never letting the snout of his weapon leave the obsequious stranger.

Vinh was a proud soldier and disliked this sneaking-around business, meeting with a sniveling merchant who traded with the enemy by day and plotted against him by night, leaving the fighting and dying to better men than he could ever hope to be.

Satisfied that no one was concealed from his view, he poked his head out of the curtained door and spoke quickly to one of the men there. In a few moments, Captain Tran entered the hootch. Vinh introduced his commanding officer and stood in the corner where he had a clear view and a clear shot at everything in the room.

"I am here to discuss the logistics of re-supply with you, Comrade Nimh." Tran related, taking a seat at the man's small table. "Do you have tea?"

Nimh visibly bristled at the arrogance of the NVA officer. Vinh was enjoying the spy's discomfort. He kept his rifle pointed at the floor but always in Nimh's direction. Nimh obediently scurried to prepare the beverage. The captain's startled reaction, when Nimh boiled water by lighting a small ball of C-4 plastic explosive, brought a sly smile to his lips. His brief moment of superiority collapsed when he saw the disgusted scowl on Vinh's face. The heat produced by the burning plastique was sufficient to bring the water to boiling in seconds.

"Is that not wasteful?" the captain asked.

"Perhaps, but we have so much..." He left the sentence unfinished. Tran and Vinh exchanged a glance that told Nimh not to overplay his hand.

They sipped the tea while discussing the provisioning of Tran's troops for the next few months. Vinh watched Nimh's mental abacus calculating behind his eyes. By the amount of food required, Nimh would be able to assess the size of the force Tran led. Merchants trade goods for profit. Spies deal in information. Vinh considered both equally larcenous. The emblem on the captain's hat seemed to intrigue the spy, but he knew better than to ask.

"I understand you will require a guide into the U-Minh," Nimh said. Tran nodded. "Then, I think it best you meet directly with the area commander. His scouts know the terrain from here to the sea as if it were their own. He can assist you in establishing caches and advise you of the location of existing stockpiles. He may be of some help in accomplishing your mission in a more active role as well."

Nimh waited expectantly for Tran to reject or accept this suggestion of direct aid. He was casting his net in hopes of gathering a few scraps of information he had no need to know. His orders forbade direct inquiry into the specifics of the mission but knowledge was life in the intelligence field, and he obviously chafed at being left out of the picture.

The captain made no reply, and the lack of expression on his face gave Nimh no hint as to the scope or objective of his mission.

Promising to have word of the planned meeting with the local cadre chief in two days' time, Nimh bid Tran good night.

"Do not keep me waiting," Tran said in parting.

"Sound advice—comrade." Vinh leered, showing his teeth as he slipped through the curtain behind his captain.

Nimh sat at his table for nearly an hour after the men left. A gentle rapping on the bamboo doorframe signaled the arrival of another guest.

"Come in, Mui," Nimh said quietly. A young man slipped into the room. Eyes downcast, he stood awaiting instructions.

"How many?" Nimh asked.

"At least twenty. There may be others, but I saw twice ten."

"Any hint as to their mission from their equipment?"

"No, Comrade Nimh. They carry only light weapons, nothing unusual."

"Maybe that is extraordinary in itself," Nimh mused, speaking more to himself than to the young man.

"Shall I follow them?"

"No. Go instead to the camp of Colonel Van Dinh. Tell him of the arrival of our friends. Tell him that they need supplies for at least two-dozen men for an extended period of time and a guide into the Forest of Darkness. Tell him their commander would like to meet with him in three days' time. Go, Mui. Be quick." Nimh shooed him into the darkness.

As the young VC flitted through the forest, much like his namesake, the mosquito, so light and abrupt were his movements, Mui realized that this was the chance he had been waiting for.

He had been disenchanted with the life of the guerrilla for

some time. He had joined the Viet Cong out of boredom rather than a conviction for any cause. Dashing through the jungle with an automatic weapon had seemed far more adventuresome to a boy of thirteen than picking rice on his father's land. He would give anything to return to the simple existence he had once despised. He could not. One did not quit the Viet Cong. They would wipe out his entire family if he disappeared. He had decided, after long weeks of deliberation, that his only chance was the *Chieu Hoi* program. Literally translated it meant: *Open Arms.*

The Saigon government was offering amnesty to all rebels who would turn themselves in and denounce the communists. The Chieu Hois, or Hoi Chan, were given jobs as interpreters or scouts, living and working side by side with the rich Americans. The family of a Hoi Chan was repatriated to a secure hamlet where they would be safe from the revenge of the Cong.

The rich Americans were probably going to win anyway. Mui thought it simply good sense to be on the winning side in the end. He had a leaflet stashed in the forest. You were supposed to bring the leaflet with you when you surrendered. You were supposed to turn in your weapon, as well. He didn't have one. They had never trusted him with one of their precious AK-47s. Mui knew where the village chief at Ap Bac hid his old M-1 rifle. He would steal it before he went over. The information about the regular soldiers from the North might prove to be very valuable to the Americans. He might be a rich man in a few days' time.

Mui smiled as he ran.

CHAPTER 19

Danny sat bolt upright, less startled to see that it was daylight and he was sitting in the mud surrounded by nippa palm and banana trees than to realize he had slept at all. He shivered, surprised at the unexpected cold. He looked down at his sodden uniform, caked with mud, feces, vomit, and blood. The events of the previous night replayed in his mind. His stomach heaved.

"Mornin', Slick," Doc Laffin said, looking Danny over with a clinical gaze. "You look like shit over easy."

"'Bout right," Danny agreed. He looked around to find the men of Charlie Company stirring to life. Most were preparing breakfast. Doc offered him a green C-ration can of steaming coffee with the lid bent back to form a handle.

"Here. Get your heart started."

Danny thought, *And hopefully my brain.* He found it unsettling to admit to himself that he had been so absorbed in his private thoughts that he had not been aware of the medic kneeling close beside him. After last night he knew that any lapse in vigilance could easily cost him his life.

Doc waved the can under his nose, and said, "Last chance before the kitchen closes."

"Thanks, Doc, but I couldn't take yours."

"Damn straight." Doc grinned. "It's yours." He indicated Danny's opened pack with a jerk of his head. "I could have cleaned you out. You were dead to the world."

Danny accepted the piping brew, mumbling thanks.

"Natural reaction," Doc said, in answer to his unspoken question. "The body shuts down when faced with severe mental or physical shock. You probably thought you'd never sleep again after what happened to you last night." Laffin stirred hot cocoa in a canteen cup and continued his assessment of human survival instincts. "Lucky for us all we have inbred self-preservation mechanisms. How else could sane creatures deal with this?" He indicated their surroundings with a sweep of his hand. "End of speech." He chuckled. "Best brush them skeeters offa you before they carry your grungy ass away."

Danny saw, in the gathering light, that his uniform was covered with dozens of black mosquitoes and a few with white striped tails. Balancing his coffee with one hand, he roughly slapped and brushed at the bloodthirsty little creatures with the other. Then he noticed that his body was covered with welts.

"Them bumps won't last," Doc said. "Better learn to cover up at night out here. The little bastards like you. Wanna watch out for the striped ones, especially. Malaria, you bic? Some guys think malaria's a great way to get off the line but, while I understand the sentiment, I disagree with the logic. Malaria's tricky, like Charley Cong. Just when you think it's gone for good, it can come back and kill your ass."

Smitty and Beecher ambled over while Danny sipped his coffee. Doc asked if he was hungry, but Danny had no appetite and elected to skip breakfast. He dug in his breast pocket for his cigarettes when he saw the other men smoking. His fingers extracted a mass of soggy pulp.

"Better keep your smokes in a baggy," Smitty advised through a pompous grin, pulling a fresh pack tucked in a plastic pouch from his own pocket. He gave one to Danny and lit it for him, still grinning, smug with his early grasp of jungle survival. He was showing off, Danny realized.

"Some shit last night," Smitty allowed, seeming to enjoy the adventure of it all.

Beecher stepped into the group just then, aborting Danny's angry retort to Smitty in mid-thought, when he told them, "We're going to sweep a village near here. Get your shit together and be ready to *di di mau* in zero five."

As Danny assembled his gear, he watched those around him for tips on the do's and don't's of the morning ritual. The immediacy of the present situation suppressed all thought of Smitty's arrogance. Danny didn't have much to do. He hadn't unrolled his poncho, his liner, or his air mattress. He had fallen asleep lying on his belly in the mud, expecting Charley to come for him. No one had awakened him for guard duty. He correctly assumed that they had let him sleep in recognition of his ordeal in the ditch. He was grateful but chagrined. Danny wanted no special consideration. He knew he was expected to pull his own weight. Vowing to measure up from here on out, he swung the radio onto his back, keyed the mic and called, "Charlie-Three-Six-Oscar, this is Charlie-Six-Oscar. Commo check, over." He waited patiently, but no reply came. Danny tried again and again with no response. Something was wrong. He was proud of himself for having the presence of mind to check his equipment before starting out, but as he turned to Beecher to report the malfunction, Beecher reached over his shoulder and twisted a knob. Danny immediately heard the hiss of static as the radio came alive.

"Works better when it's on," Beecher growled. Mumbling, "Fuckin' new guys," the sergeant turned to follow the captain through the woods. Without turning to face Danny, he flipped his hand in an impatient beckoning gesture.

Danny followed, red faced. He did another commo check to salvage what he could of his self-esteem. This time, Third Platoon's RTO came back, "Six-Oscar, Three-Six-Oscar. Lima Charlie, hotel mike?" Danny was pleased to be able to understand the operator's jargon—Loud and clear, how me?

"Same-same. Thank you much. Out," he replied.

Beecher glanced back, snorted a laugh, and walked on, nodding his head. Danny felt somewhat redeemed.

The company walked through the morning, slogging through rice paddies, crossing what seemed like dozens of streams. The first was a blessing to Danny as he saw his chance to rinse some of the filth from his body but the refreshment of the dip was short lived. The muck on the far side clung to him anew as he fought to climb the shallow slope. Before long, it became evident that being dry was a rare experience out here. His uniformed chafed wherever the wet cloth made contact with his skin. His pack straps cut deep into his shoulders. His rifle seemed to weigh more with each step. He was apprehensive about its condition as well. He had followed Fuquette's instructions and cleaned it as best he could, last night, in the dark, anxious and hurrying to reassemble it before the Cong attacked. He was paranoid about being defenseless.

His terror of the night before faded as he became consumed with his present agonies. When the captain ordered a break for lunch, he collapsed to the ground, thigh muscles twitching in painful spasms. He found himself praying for the rain to resume.

"Sergeant," Captain Arnold said to Beecher, "have one of the medics take a look at Mulvaney. He looks kind of gray around the gills."

Laffin trotted up in response to the radio call. The headquarters group was heating C-rations and talking amiably among themselves when he arrived. Danny sat against a tree, panting like a whipped mongrel.

"Afternoon, gents," Doc Laffin greeted them. "Somebody request a house call?"

"Check out Mulvaney, Doc," Beecher said, punctuating the order with a twist of his head.

"Ah, yes." Laffin smiled, sizing up Danny's obvious symptoms. "Hard day at the office, Daniel?"

After a cursory sampling of Danny's vital signs and placing a palm on his forehead, Laffin announced, "Heat prostration, dehydration—the usual." He shook salt tablets from a white plastic bottle in his aid bag, told Danny to swallow them, and reached back for one of Danny's two canteens hooked to his rucksack. The first was empty and the second less than a quarter full.

"You've got to learn to make your water last," he told Danny, as he gave him a drink from his own canteen. "Two quarts won't cut it. Carry four. And don't expect anybody else to be as generous as your friendly, country doctor. Water is like gold out here."

Danny looked around at the sopping wet landscape.

"I know: 'Water, water everywhere, but not a drop to drink.' The guy who said that must have been here." Laffin grinned. He gave Danny a small, brown bottle. "Halazone tablets. They purify water. Fill up at a quick-running stream. Pop two of these in a canteen. Wait a half-hour, and you can drink it. Don't fill up in a paddy. Nothing can kill the shit in them. The water will taste like piss, even from a stream, and it'll probably give you the squirts, but it won't kill you."

Turning to the captain, he said, "He'll be all right. Try not to run him over fifty until he's broken in. The warranty doesn't apply to abused vehicles." To Danny, he added, "Eat something. Canned fruit is best, peaches or pears if you got any. Dextrose and fluid." He winked. "Doctor's orders. Afternoon, gents," he threw over his shoulder in parting.

Danny found a can of pears in his rations and did as he was told. He sat apart, spooning soft fruit into his mouth and drinking the juice, trying to gather his strength as the others spoke in hushed tones.

"Beecher?" The captain raised an eyebrow.

"Too early to tell, sir." Beecher cast a sidelong glance at Danny. "It's not uncommon for new guys to get winded on their first op. He did have a hairy beginning." Spreading his hands, he said, "We'll have to wait and see."

Smitty chimed in, "Mulvaney's a good guy, sir. His heart's in the right place—"

"Okay, Smith," the captain insisted, "out with it. All our lives depend on each other's out here."

"Well..." Smitty said, seeming reluctant. The impatient stares from the CO and his RTO urged him on. "Danny had a tough time in Basic and AIT, you know? He used to fall out on runs and such. Had a hard time keeping up. But he tries damned hard."

The knowing glance exchanged by the two vets was gratifying to Smitty. He had interjected the lie at just the right moment.

Smitty had no intention of playing second banana. He longed for the prestige he was sure must come with the close working relationship between an RTO and his officer. He needed to get Danny out of the equation.

"Watch him," Captain Arnold instructed Beecher, leaning back on his elbow to study his map.

Smitty said, "Excuse me," and got to his feet. "I better check on my buddy." He sidled up to Danny, sat beside him, and put a benevolent arm around his shoulders. Danny sat with his arms locked around his drawn-up knees with his head resting on his forearms. "You'll be okay, Dan," Smitty cooed. He glanced at Beecher, nodded assurance with what he thought was just enough concern in his frown and patted Danny's back.

The first seed was sown.

After lunch, the company moved through the woods following hard-packed trails, watching for booby traps. They sighted the village an hour after the break.

All seemed normal as the people of the hamlet went about their daily routines.

The only indication that they were aware of the approaching soldiers was an occasional furtive glance toward the trees where C-Company had stopped.

"First and Second Platoons," Arnold ordered, "move in by squads. First from the north, Second from the south." Charlie-Six handed the radio handset back to Beecher. Hand signals to the platoon leaders told Third and Fourth to spread out and cover. Leon was suddenly beside Danny as the men deployed. Danny was shocked to see the state his friend was in.

"Jesus, Leon," Danny gasped, "what the fuck happened to you?"

Leon looked like he had been dragged every inch of the way from the boats. His uniform was caked with mud and stained with white splotches of dried sweat. His skin was pallid and his eyes were sunken and bloodshot.

"Nothin'." Leon blinked, insulted. He looked down at his filthy fatigues and then at Danny's. "You don't look so hot yourself, old buddy. This hasn't exactly been a fuckin' walk in the park."

Danny laughed for the first time since the ship. "A master of understatement, as usual, Leon. What the hell is that thing?" he asked, squinting at the large black tube balanced on Leon's shoulder.

"This ugly motherfucker," Leon grunted as he hoisted the weapon and placed the muzzle on the toe of his boot, careful not to let it touch the ground, "is a ninety-millimeter recoilless rifle. The Fourth Platoon is the weapons platoon. *Heavy* fuckin' weapons."

"Definitely looks that way."

"You should see the rounds for this sumbitch," Leon wheezed.

"Weislogel!" a gruff voice yelled from their left. "Git your ugly ass over here and set up that ninety."

"My master's voice." Leon grimaced. "Coming dear," he answered, loud enough for Danny's ears only. "See you later, Dan. You got to tell me 'bout the gook."

As Leon scampered off, Danny thought again of the man he had killed. Was that just last night? He knew, from his brief time in the field, that it was going to be a long and harrowing year.

Second Platoon leapfrogged by squads into the village. The picturesque beauty of this example of ancient civilization was marred by the fear in the villagers' eyes. The people watched with studied disinterest as the soldiers moved in, avoiding eye contact, hoping to avoid the inevitable questions: *Where VC? You VC?* These questions had been asked of them more times than they could count. They were impossible questions. Whatever answers they made could mean their death.

Lance ran along a dike with his head darting in all directions, feeling naked and exposed midway between the woods and the nearest hootch. The man trotting ten meters ahead of him suddenly stopped, stood up straight, and raised his hand to halt his comrades.

"Buffalo pen," he called out, no louder than was necessary to be heard. He gave Lance a shooing motion with his hands and backed away, never taking his eyes from the wooden railed enclosure.

"What?" Lance asked when they had retreated to an intersection in the dikes.

"Water Buffalo," PFC Rodriguez said, spitting into the paddy. "Mean bastards. Hate GIs. Seen one damn near level a village once. Had to shoot the bastard with a Seventy-Nine round. Our Sixteens wouldn't stop him. Like a runaway freight train when they're pissed."

"What do we do?"

"Find another way."

Lieutenant Tyler came up behind them, and said, "What's this clusterfuck?"

"Water buff pen, sir. I was just explaining to Private Corporal," he grinned as he said it—the men got a kick out of the games they could play with Lance's name—"about how them beasts hate us. Must be the sight of our weapons or something."

"I've heard a rash of myths," Tyler said, "about the violent reactions these creatures have to American soldiers, Rodriguez. Everything from our height to drug-induced hypnosis by the VC." Tyler laughed. "The facts are much simpler, if not as colorful."

He had their interest, he could see by the expectant looks on their faces. It amused Tyler how the American soldier would stop whatever he was doing, wherever he was, to discuss some odd bit of information.

"Vietnamese diets," he resumed, "consist mostly of fish and vegetables. They eat very little red meat. Poultry and pork comprise most of the flesh they consume and not much of those."

Like patient pupils, the men waited for more. Tyler glanced around to see the platoon proceeding with the deployment. The captain would be watching. He started to walk, angling away from the buffalo pen as he went.

"We, on the other hand, consume large quantities of red meat, almost daily. We smell different than the gooks because of it. We smell like what we are to the buffalo—carnivores. To these big, dumb beasts we are simply predators."

Lance was astonished. "They think we're gonna bite 'em?"

"A-plus, Private First Class Corporal." Tyler grinned.

"Holy shit," Rodriguez said.

The village was clean, as far as they could see. The headman denied any knowledge of VC in the area. No surprise. Vietnamese peasants had learned to be like the famous brass monkeys. Captain Arnold radioed a report to the colonel. He was told to wait in the hamlet for a re-supply helicopter. The men were glad for the extended break. They set up perimeter security and found shade wherever they could. Danny leaned against the wall of a hootch and slid to the ground. Beecher and the captain went inside to take tea with the elders.

"Geez, Davy, it is always this hot?" Danny asked Fuquette.

"Nope. Sometimes it's hotter. You'll miss the monsoons when the dry season rolls around. Dry season's a motherfucker."

Grubby children scurried about the soldiers, chattering, giggling, and begging. They never seemed to tire of ogling the funny-looking foreigners.

"You give me chop-chop?" they repeated again and again until a GI or an adult villager would chase them away. Chop-chop meant food, candy, cigarettes, soap—any consumable. The sing-song voices rang through the village in an all-pervasive mantra. Danny watched, amused, and sad that he had nothing to give to them.

"Git lost, you little beggars," Fuquette snarled as he sat down beside Mulvaney.

"It's okay," Danny said, "they're kind of cute."

"You won't think they're so cute when one of 'em steals your watch or drops a grenade in your lap."

"They're just kids, Davy. Give 'em some slack."

Danny smiled through his weariness and spread his hands to show he had nothing to give. In twos and threes, the children turned away to search out more lucrative targets. The last little boy snarled, "You numbah ten cheap Chollie," to Fuquette, as he ran from them.

Doc Laffin joined them in time to overhear the boy's parting shot. "Maybe the Diplomatic Corps isn't the best career choice for you, Sergeant Fuquette."

"Fuck you, Doc," Fuquette said. With that, he was up and gone.

Bewildered, Danny said, "What just happened, Doc?"

"Not to worry. Davy's still getting back in the saddle, is all." Danny's wrinkled brow prompted Doc to elaborate. "Our intrepid sharpshooter just got back from R and R."

"I know, but—"

"He's going through withdrawal."

Danny's eyes grew wide. "Davy does drugs?"

Doc chuckled. "Hell, no. Davy's a Southern boy. They do mostly bourbon." The confusion evident by Danny's expression brought a wide grin to the medic's face. "What I meant was that Davy, like a lot of guys when they come back to this place after being in a semi-civilized state of mind for a spell, has to get back in the game. He's dealing with the fear, putting it back in that deep place it needs to be in if he plans to make it out of here."

"I thought I was the only one who's scared."

"Hah! You a funny fucker, Dan." Before Danny could respond, Doc said, "Well, lookie here," pointing to a little doe-eyed girl about nine years old, who stared, enthralled, at Danny. "I think baby-san over there is sweet on you, Daniel. That blonde hair and them blue eyes seem to be to her liking, my friend."

The little girl was fixated on Danny, they could see. Lance sat down as Laffin was noting this.

"No shit, Danny. She looks stoned in love to me," he said, nudging Danny with his elbow.

The other children in the village milled about, probably due to the sparse pickings available from the rest of company, since all of the men were equally short on rations. Baby-san kept her distance but never took her eyes from Danny. He downed the last of his water, shook the empty canteen, and gave it a forlorn look.

The little girl came forward then, taking hesitant half steps. She had a natural poise he would more readily associate with a woman. It struck him as curious in one so young.

"*Nuoc?*" she asked. Danny looked at Doc.

"She's asking if you want water," Doc said, scratching designs in the mud between his feet with a stick.

"No. No, thank you." Danny shook his head, remembering tales of ground glass and battery acid from Jungle School.

"Don't be a shithead," Doc advised. "She loves your sorry ass. Go with her. She'll get you some good water. I'll mind the radio. Just don't leave the village," Doc called, as Danny followed the young girl.

Danny felt awkward as he walked beside the little girl, so big and clumsy beside her petite, graceful form. She wore the standard peasant dress: a dirty white blouse and loose-fitting black silk pants. Her feet were bare, and he marveled at the smooth surface of the village street, beaten to a polish by farmers padding to and fro for hundreds of years as they toiled away their lives.

There was something in the little lady's bearing. She was almost regal as she walked. Head high. Confident.

She led him to a large earthen jar, removed the wooden cover, and showed Danny the contents. The jar was filled to the brim with clear water. "*Beaucoup nuoc*," she proclaimed.

Danny filled his canteen and popped in two Halazone tablets to be on the safe side. When they returned to the hootch, he described the jar to Doc.

"Rain water collector. Good water. She's waiting for you to drink," Doc said, pointing with his chin at the smiling face of the pretty little girl.

"I'll wait half an hour for the pills to work."

"Oh, man. You mean you fucked up sweet water with that iodine shit?"

"You said…"

"I was talking about finding water in the bush. There's nothing wrong with that water, and you'll break her little heart if you don't accept her gift."

"You sure?"

"Look around, man," Doc said. "You're in downtown Povertyville, RVN. These people have nothing. Anything they offer you is a big deal. Trust me. This is important to her."

The bright-eyed little angel squatted at Danny's feet, shielding her eyes from the sun with her hand as she watched him sitting in the shade. She really did look hurt. He took a swig of the water. It was cool and quenching. The only thing wrong with it was the distinctive taste of iodine. The girl's bright smile told Danny he had done the right thing. He drank again and smiled his thanks.

The radio interrupted with a call from the re-supply chopper.

"This is Charlie Six-Oscar," Danny replied. "Say status, over."

"Uh-Roger, Charlie Six-Oscar," the pilot drawled, his voice a throbbing vibrato. "We are inbound your poz with the groceries. Five mikes out. Pop smoke in zero-four, over."

Danny relayed the information to the Second Platoon, located at the edge of a clearing large enough for the helicopter to set down.

"Smoke out," someone yelled a few minutes later. Danny saw purple smoke billowing beyond the trees and repeated the message to the pilot.

"*I*-dentify Goofy Grape," the pilot responded to Danny's announcement.

"Roger that," Danny said. "Confirm purple. Come on down."

The chopper flared and touched down. The crew chief kicked out a pile of rations, water, and ammo, keyed his intercom to tell his pilot to go, and sat down behind his door gun as the tail kicked high. The bird did a nose down run across the paddy and then climbed into the sky.

"A pleasure doing business with you, Six Oscar," the pilot called. "Y'all have a nice day."

Sergeants supervised the distribution of the delivery, while the men kept the kids at bay. The tiny beggars followed each group of soldiers in screaming knots of frenzied energy as they dispersed. There were definitely spoils to be had now.

Danny watched as Lance and Doc threw unwanted articles to the kids in the street and laughed as they clawed for whatever they could grab. Danny was impressed as his personal angel stood back and watched with sadness as her friends debased themselves. *What class*, he thought.

She stayed when the others had gone to squabble over their booty. As Danny prepared his meal, she sat on his shin to watch. She was as light as a feather. He ate with gusto, the food tasting better than anything he had eaten in weeks. Her smile of delight at his enjoyment touched his heart. He found a chocolate covered mint patty at the bottom of the C-rat box, unwrapped it, and offered it to her. She shook her head.

Doc said, "You opened it, man. She can't sell it once it's open."

"You're a cynic, Doc, she's just being polite."

Danny broke the candy in half and, munching with exaggerated delight, offered her the other piece. Her expression could not have shown more pleasure had he offered her gold. She bowed deeply and took the wafer with delicate fingers. They ate, smiling at one another, thoroughly enjoying the moment.

Doc shrugged and, laughing softly, said, "Now I've seen it all."

When they saddled up to move out, the little girl took Danny's hand and walked with him to the edge of the village. He bent down, kissed her hand, and said, "*Merci beaucoup.*"

She stood where he had left her, waving goodbye with a wistful smile as they shuffled along the track. Danny looked back until he could no longer see her. His load seemed lighter. His heart uplifted, and his opinion of the world much more charitable as they marched back out into the boondocks. If they could save that one little girl, he thought, it would all be worth it.

That night, they set up in separate ambushes, dropping platoons as they went. The weapons platoon was intermingled with the others to add firepower. They humped one eighty-one-millimeter mortar, three ninety-millimeter recoilless rifles, a fifty-caliber machine gun, two sixty-millimeter mortars and four M-60 machine guns. The balance of the platoon was armed with M-16 rifles and M-79 grenade launchers. They bristled with firepower. Ammo bearers prayed for an opportunity to fire up some of the ordnance to relieve their burdens but, in truth, most prayed never to be in a situation that would warrant using the heavy stuff.

The night passed uneventfully. Danny pulled his radio watches, kept his sleeves rolled down, and slept wrapped in his poncho liner with his helmet for a pillow.

In the morning, he was dismayed to find the hungry mosquitoes had bitten through the blanket wherever it stretched over his skin.

"Keep it loose around you," Beecher advised over breakfast,

"Viet mosquito's got a stinger like a hummingbird's beak. Even go through the rubber of a poncho."

There was so much to learn.

They walked across a field of craters that morning, some big enough to drop a small house into. Each was filled with crystal clear water. The devastation was mind-boggling. The holes went on for a thousand meters.

"Arc Light," Beecher answered Smitty and Danny's quizzical looks. "B-Fifty-Two strike. Whispering death," he said, looking to the heavens. "Fuckers fly so high you can't see 'em. Charley don't know he's about to be dead until the first bombs hit. Nothin' gets out of the area in one piece."

"Why here?" Danny wanted to know. "There's nothing."

"Not any more. A few days back this might have been a village, a staging area, or a bunker complex. Only people know for sure ain't sayin'."

"Jesus," Danny whispered.

"You keep concentratin' on the whys and wherefores," Beecher said, "instead of keeping your eyes peeled for the little bastards this was dropped on, and you might get to talk to Him face to face."

The boats were waiting for them when they reached the river. Danny had never been so happy to take a boat ride. As he dumped his gear and collapsed onto the deck, Fuquette asked, "So, how did you enjoy your first operation, young troop?"

"I have never been more pleased to see something come to an end," Danny exhaled, his chin on his chest.

"Too bad." Fuquette grinned. "'Cause we get to do this again tomorrow."

CHAPTER 20

Mui dug quietly in the darkness, wanting to be long gone when the moon rose. Having relayed his messages to Colonel Van Dinh, the young man had set about stealing the old chief's rifle. He found it, wrapped in clear plastic, buried beneath the dung heap on the outskirts of the village. It started to rain just as his hands felt the vinyl beneath the stinking mound. He pulled. The weapon came free with a sucking sound. Mui darted for the safety of the woods, his prize held lovingly in his arms as he ran.

He ditched the plastic tarp in the underbrush as he entered the forest. The weapon was heavy. He wondered if it worked. It didn't matter. He needed it only to add credence to his tale of long years fighting beside the hated Viet Cong, trapped by their evil power over his family. He would say he had only fired his weapon in the air in the many skirmishes he had been forced to participate in. He would tell them he would never willingly harm an American. All this time he had been waiting for his chance to rally to the Saigon government and their beloved saviors from the United States. They would believe him and shower him with praise and maybe a few small gifts.

He waited, impatient, outside of a small, American fire support base, until sunrise.

With a white rag tied to the muzzle of the old M-1, he stepped into the road near the gate. Holding the rifle above his head with both hands, he walked smartly to the entrance, flapping his leaflet from his fingers.

"Chieu Hoi." His voice shook. He tried to smile as he watched the base for some sign of life. Nothing happened. Afraid he had not been heard, he repeated the phrase of surrender with greater amplitude and conviction.

Two astonished soldiers peered cautiously over the berm at the scrawny youth in tattered shorts and shirt standing at the base of the earthen wall.

"Plug the motherfucker," one said to the other.

"You kiddin'? That little asshole is a three-day pass to Vung Tau."

"No shit?"

"If I'm lyin', I'm dyin'."

"You got that right."

They cautiously climbed down the loose earthen slope until they were face to face with the grinning turncoat.

"Take his weapon," the first soldier said.

Mui was pleased as the fellow disarmed him. This was going well. He smiled and bowed repeatedly to show sincerity and respect. On the fourth bow, his forehead met the stock of the M-1 as the second soldier flattened him with a vertical butt stroke.

Stunned, nearly unconscious, crumpled in a heap in the muddy road, Mui didn't understand the Americans' words, but he understood their cruel laughter.

CHAPTER 21

First Sergeant Andy Syzmanski let the Orderly Room screen door bang shut behind him and stood facing the rising sun. Hands on hips, he rotated his broad shoulders back until he felt the comforting pop between his shoulder blades, then he stretched his six-foot frame to ease the morning stiffness.

"Getting too old for this shit," he growled, thinking of what lay ahead this day. The ruby dawn bathed him with warmth that barely hinted at the coming furnace climbing inexorably over the horizon. His blue-gray eyes absorbed the fleeting beauty of the tropical sunrise making silhouettes of the distant palms. Syzmanski's wide face shone with a power reminiscent of his former rugged good looks. Never known as handsome, but never shunned by pretty ladies, he had, as a young man, had few complaints regarding his appearance. His chosen path had made its indelible mark on his features, and the laugh lines of his youth had matured to amused, if cynical, creases. Running meaty fingers through his close-cropped, iron-gray hair, he noticed again the thinness becoming more apparent these days.

Mary would want me to let this grow a bit, he mused. His wife missed his thick black locks. He knew he could get away with it over here, with the army relaxing the haircut regs to appease the preponderance of young draftees, but he'd worn the buzz cut for two decades now, and it was part of him. He was not vain enough to worry about things as mundane as middle-aged baldness. The thought of his wife, half a world away, preparing dinner about now, to eat alone, choked him with unexpected loneliness.

He jammed his olive-drab baseball cap onto his head, pulled the bill low over his eyes, and brushed an emerging tear from his cheek. Syzmanski stole a furtive look around the company area to assure himself his moment of weakness had gone unobserved.

"Jesus," he whispered, "I'm falling apart."

Twenty-two years in the United States Army Infantry had not prepared him for the torment that this godforsaken place inflicted upon him daily.

Syzmanski gulped lungfuls of warm, humid air to calm himself. He glanced down at his hands, held flat, palms down in front of his middle, and whispered, "Steady. No shakes. Better."

His inspection revealed another hallmark of his years. His gut, no longer washboard tight, was hanging over his belt a tad more than it had been when last he had noticed. He knew it was as much from the beer he had consumed in recent months as from lack of enforced exercise. As first sergeant, he'd been in the rear much more than he was accustomed to. The frustration of sitting in the orderly room while his men—hell, they were babies for the most part—got chewed up by the Viet Cong, had been agony. The misery of filing mountains of useless and widely ignored reports on the day-to-day carnage suffered by his boys stretched the limits of his strength. Drinking had graduated from recreational distraction to self-prescribed antidote for an anguished heart.

That was ending now. The captain must see that he would be far more valuable in the field with the troops than pushing papers in the rear. He was going out today, orders or no.

Syzmanski rubbed his freshly shaven jaw with his hand, feeling too much flesh there as well. Grinning, eyes crinkled, sparkling with resurrected youthful lust for adventure, he thought, *I'm going back where I belong. If the captain don't like it, he can get himself another first shirt.*

As he strode across the compound to rouse the chopper pilots for his ride to the field, he had a flash of premonition, dashing his elation. The jagged scar on his knee, inscribed by a Chinese bayonet on a frozen hilltop in Korea fifteen years ago, ached fiercely for a moment. The stink of battle filled his nostrils. His mind recoiled from the memory. He smelled blood, and he felt—for the first time in his forty-two years—dread.

CHAPTER 22

Charlie Company's long, predawn boat ride had been almost enjoyable until a B-40 rocket flashed from the underbrush choking the bank. The flaming wolf tail exhaust of the rocket motor in the darkness startled the sleepiness from the eyes of all who beheld its terrifying flight as the black blur of the warhead arced harmlessly over the top of the lead boat. The thunderclap explosion on the opposite bank roused any souls so stupefied as to have missed the missile's flight.

The navy responded with a deafening roar of automatic weapons. Every gun that could be brought to bear cut loose on the source of the projectile. Stuttering gouts of yellow flame lit up the river.

They did not heave to and assault the bank as the soldiers feared, content, it seemed, to rip up the real estate as they sailed past. No further enemy fire was forthcoming. The contact, with its exact position, was radioed to task force headquarters so that any available Monitor gunboats or Zippo flame boats could be diverted to the spot.

When the company disembarked a mile upstream, the sniping began. Charley Cong was playing his version of tag. A few pot shots from the VC would be answered by a fusillade of American small arms fire, followed by artillery called in by the ton. The troops swept the offending patch of woods before the smoke cleared but ol' Chuck was long gone.

This scenario was repeated several times. After three hours of this, the company stopped, deployed in the trees surrounding a broad expanse of rice paddies. Danny called on air-to-ground to the helicopter he could hear approaching in the distance. He was keeping up so far, this, his third day in the field, and getting the opportunity to do his job.

"Eagle-Five. Eagle-Five. This is Charlie-Six-Oscar, over."

"Six-Oscar. This is Eagle-Five inbound your location, over," the vibrating voice of the pilot came back.

"Roger, Eagle-Five, I have you in sight," Danny said, as the chopper cleared the trees in the distance. "Throwing smoke, over." He held the handset to his chest and yelled, "Pop smoke!"

A man ran from the wood line, splashing across the flooded paddy. He threw a smoke grenade as far into the middle of the field as he could.

"Smoke out, Eagle-Five," Danny said into the horn. "Identify."

"*I*-dentify green smoke," the pilot drawled in the bored fashion of hotshot American pilots the world over.

"Roger, affirmative green. Lima Zulu is cold. Come on in."

As the bird flared to land in a man-made hurricane of rotor wash on water, Danny puffed with pride at his professional cool during his first combat radio transmission on his own. He was surprised at how much he had learned.

Four figures scrambled from the helicopter's cabin. Ducking beneath the whirling blades, they ran toward the waving soldiers in the woods.

"One too many, sir," Beecher called to the CO.

Captain Arnold came forward to see. "Who the hell?" He squinted to recognize the men rushing toward him. "It's Top. What's he doing out here?"

The chopper's tail kicked high, and the machine skimmed the surface of the water, gaining speed, until it lifted off just short of the trees to climb into the sky.

The offloaded men clambered out of the paddy to be met by the waiting troops. Syzmanski, all smiles, was the only one who seemed glad to be there.

The sullen expressions on the faces of the three younger men with him left no room for doubt as to their disenchantment.

"First Sergeant," Arnold said, as Syzmanski pumped his hand, "what brings you out here?"

"I thought I'd make sure they didn't get lost." Top indicated the three new arrivals with a jerk of his thumb.

"You shitbirds." Charlie-Six scowled at the men. "Report to

your platoon leaders. Beecher, show these three candyasses where their people are. If any of you have any ideas about getting sick or having an accident to get out of the field again, forget it. You'll go in with the rest of us, or you'll go in a body bag. Got it?"

The men nodded and mumbled, "Yes, sir."

Beecher got them quickly out of the captain's sight.

"Now, Top, would you please enlighten me as to what my first soldier is doing in the field when he's supposed to be in Dong Tam."

"Sir, my CIB was starting to corrode. I'm going Asiatic being in the rear with all them remfs. I needed a break. Thought I'd tag along on this one. I hear tell there's a regiment out here."

"Don't go feeding the rumor mill, First Sergeant." Arnold cast an uncomfortable glance at the anxious looks of the men within earshot, and said, loudly enough to be overheard, "We are investigating reports of activity of a unit of undetermined composition that may be operating in this area. That's all."

Syzmanski disapproved of the captain's penchant for telling his men the barest details of any action. He believed that the men should be trusted with the facts, that they should know what they were risking their lives for. Dissension in the ranks, he felt, was born of keeping the troops in the dark.

"So, we're trolling for trouble, sir? Hanging our asses out for Charley to shoot at?"

Arnold wagged his head. "Something like that."

"Sounds good to me." Top grinned. "How's it going so far?"

Captain Arnold recounted the morning's sniping.

"Sounds like they're disorganized or not strong enough for a direct challenge," Top deduced. "Or they're sucking us in."

"Right. Well, seeing as how you are here now, First Sergeant, let me fill you in. We're going to move through this area ahead." He outlined his plan as he spread his map on the ground. "It's mostly scrub jungle. Third Herd will take the main axis with First and Second on the flanks. We'll maintain radio contact and try to keep it on line. Fourth is broken down to beef up the rifle platoons. Chick is traveling with the CP group to act as FO and coordinate his people's fire if it's needed."

Syzmanski knew that the Fourth Platoon, the weapons platoon, was usually integrated with the other platoons in this type of sweep operation. Their crew served recoilless rifles, mortars and heavy machine gun were cumbersome, murderous loads to hump through the jungle, and all but useless in a mobile operation. The purpose of the heavy stuff in a sweep was to provide enough fire-power in the event of contact with VC Main Force units to keep the bad guys at bay until support arrived.

Lieutenant "Chick" Chicarelli, their platoon leader, was also a capable Forward Observer.

"We'll sweep to the blue line—" Arnold pointed to the river on the map. "—and take it from there. If there are no questions, we'll move out."

There were none.

"Mulvaney," the captain said to Danny, "give 'em the word. Saddle up. Execute plan Alpha." He folded his map and flipped open his lensatic compass to shoot an azimuth.

Danny tried to raise the platoons. He was acting as company radio operator today and being evaluated. When no one answered his calls, he looked to Beecher.

"You're still on air-to-ground, numbnuts," Beecher grumbled, standing to twist the dial on Danny's radio to the proper frequency. He looked disgusted with his pupil's performance.

Danny blushed as he made the calls.

Charlie Company moved through the woods slowly and care-fully. Trails were suspect, as the Cong were known to booby trap them, but moving through the undergrowth was slower and made it more difficult for the platoons to stay abreast. The men used the trails to ease their travel, despite warnings to the contrary.

First Platoon hit a grenade trap half an hour after they began the march. The blast sent every man to the ground. The radio crackled with calls for help from the First and queries from the others as to the nature of the explosion.

Sergeant Beecher took over to answer the calls. Danny was amazed at the man's calm as he answered them, first as a group once he had assessed the situation, then individually, as he re-layed the captain's orders. A medivac helicopter was dispatched to evacuate the wounded point man, his legs and groin ripped by the explosive set in the roots of a tree beside the trail, triggered by an artfully camouflaged trip wire.

They resumed their march when the Dustoff had removed the injured soldier from the field. Soon, they found punji pits along one trail, old but intact. The Third Platoon discovered a deserted bunker complex and blew the fortifications with grenades. Danny marveled at the ingenuity of the VC. The structures were small igloos of mud, reinforced with logs, impossible to detect until you were almost upon them. They were incredibly solid. Danny shuddered to think what would have happened if Charley had been waiting in them.

Near mid-day, Second Platoon reported a trail wide enough to be classified as a road. The trail was not on the map and was concealed from above by overgrowing trees and vines that were tied together where they did not overlap naturally.

"Watch it!" Arnold told Tyler. "This AO is hot. Keep your eyes open."

Third Platoon hit a clearing. The point man signaled a halt. Word was passed to the command element that he thought he detected movement on the far side. The captain hurried forward to see for himself, his entourage keeping up with him.

"Fuquette," Arnold said as they lay down, just short of the tall grass, "check it out."

Fuquette trained his scope on the woods on the other side. After several long moments of observation, he said, "Bingo."

Danny strained to see anything suspicious. His heart was thudding against his ribs. The wood line was deserted as far as he could tell with the naked eye.

"Got one lone gook moving east to west," Fuquette whispered, although it would be impossible for the man to hear him at this range. It must be a hundred yards, Danny thought. "He's in the trees, and I don't think he knows we're around yet."

"Is he armed?" Charlie-Six asked in an excited whisper.

"Negative." Fuquette sounded disappointed. "Wait one. He's bending down." Fuquette nodded and smiled. "The little fucker just picked something up. Hang on. I can almost see it." He twisted a knob on his scope. "It's a BAR, sir. The little shit's got a BAR."

The Browning Automatic Rifle was an old US weapon dating back to World War I, a highly accurate and deadly piece of equipment. One man could pin down a company with it if he knew what he was doing.

"Any more?" Arnold asked.

After sweeping the area again, the scope never leaving his eye, Fuquette said, "Don't see any. I think he's alone."

Captain Arnold considered this for a moment, and said, "Kill him."

Danny was shocked by the offhand way the captain said it. His mind was still weighing the casual order to take a life when the crack of Fuquette's rifle made him jump.

"Eighty-four," Fuquette breathed.

They waited until they were sure that there would be no response from any other enemy soldiers in the vicinity before moving across the clearing to examine the body. Danny relayed a situation report to the other elements as they walked.

Flies were swarming on the gory hole in the enemy soldier's head when they found him. Fuquette had put the bullet through his right ear. The exit wound on the opposite side was the size of a man's fist.

"He didn't hear it," Danny heard Fuquette mumble as they captured the dead man's weapon and searched the corpse. Fuquette looked on, detached. Danny fiddled with the radio to get his mind off of his churning stomach.

Syzmanski said, "They don't arm trail watchers with BARs."

"First line of defense." Arnold nodded. "Early warning guard post. Chuck's version of the DEW Line." He scanned the trees. "But why only one man? Something weird going on here."

"Charlie-Six. Charlie-Six," from his handset startled Danny into answering a call.

"Second's found a village on that road," he told Captain Arnold after he'd taken the report.

The map showed no populated areas in the vicinity.

"Two-Six, Six," the captain said into the phone. "Watch your ass. I think you've found the nest."

CHAPTER 23

Sam Hellinghausen had a problem. As CIA section chief in Saigon, it was part of his job to evaluate turncoats such as the one in the next room. The Chieu Hoi Program was something he viewed with mixed emotions. It had given him the occasional intelligence windfall, but it had also caused some embarrassing episodes. More than one VC soldier had seen it as the tempting entree it was into the camp of the enemy and part of Sam's job was to weed these enterprising types out before they became troublesome.

The kid in the adjacent interrogation cell was too stupid to be a double agent. Sam smiled, thinking the punk didn't have the brains to be a *single*. The really dumb ones often turned out to be the biggest pains in the ass. In his zeal to show good faith, this one had named one name Sam would rather not have heard. If he had come straight to Saigon to offer his services, it would have been as simple as a bullet in the head. But, no. He had to tell his story to every Tom, Dick, and Harry from here to the ass end of nowhere, way out in the boonies where he had started his pilgrimage to the land of the big PX.

"Major Co," Hellinghausen said to the South Vietnamese officer seated across the table from him, "you're certain our little friend has IDd Colonel Van Dinh to the CO of that little fire base he walked into."

"Absolutely, Sam, and he, in turn, reported this information to his superiors. It was all I could do to prevent a raid on the colonel's headquarters." The major looked as troubled as Sam. "This will not go away. Van Dinh has been suspect for quite some time. Confirmation of his activities, even from such an insignificant source as that idiot boy in there—" He gestured with his hand at the wall to the adjoining room. "—will create enough pressure from the local commanders to force us to act."

"And if we do, his relatives in high places will lose a great deal of face," Sam said.

"Alas, yes. With your senators due for their annual fact-finding tour, we do not need any more scandal."

"Suppose we leak word to the colonel that he is blown?" Sam offered. The major's raised eyebrows prompted him to add, "Through an untraceable back channel, of course."

"It would be hoped that the colonel would have the good sense to flee." The major smiled. "A shame to lose him. He was convenient."

"Yes. Well, that's the way it goes. We'll just have to hope his replacement is as greedy."

"Not likely, but one can hope. Suppose he doesn't run?"

Sam smiled in turn. "If he doesn't, he'll have to meet with an unfortunate accident."

"I shall see to it." Major Co rose to leave. "And the boy?"

"The mosquito? Aptly named little son of a bitch, flitting around the countryside buzzing in people's ears. A real pest." He thought for a moment. "Give him the hero's welcome," Sam said. "Let him know how proud his countrymen are of him and his brave deed. But sit on him until we see which way the wind blows. And for God's sake, don't let him talk to anyone else."

When Co left, Hellinghausen lit a cigarette, rubbed the back of his neck with both hands, and laboriously stood up. "God, I'm tired."

The QC guard outside the cell snapped to attention as Hellinghausen stepped into the hallway. Sam nodded and smiled as he let himself into the interrogation room.

The square, windowless cell reminded him of a stateside public restroom. The dun-colored ceramic tiled floor and walls may not have done much for the atmosphere in the place but it did make it easy to clean up after a messy Q & A session.

Mui looked up from the steel bench through exhausted eyes. He had not thought that he would have to stay awake for the rest of his life when he had begun his change of sides. He prayed that the American in the bright flowered shirt would have no more questions. They must let him sleep.

"Mui, my friend," the man said in accent-less Vietnamese, "tell me about these visitors from the North."

CHAPTER 24

"Chow Em. Chow Bo. Chow Ba."
Hadley Laffin beamed as he greeted each villager he passed, smiling and nodding to them as if they were not watching him and his fellow soldiers with undisguised contempt. Tyler had not seen such cold hate in the population of any village since he had arrived in Vietnam. If these people were not hardcore VC, then he was the Queen of the May. There were few men present, as usual. There were not even boys here. Toddlers and very old men made up the entire male population in evidence.

The troops were aware of the hostility. Their eyes shifted constantly as they walked, watching everything and everybody at once. No one played with the kids. The children did not want to be bothered. They clung to their mothers, fearful of the monsters invading their town. Even the sight of a pretty, young mama-san suckling an infant, her bare breasts unabashedly exposed, failed to bring the usual round of adolescent hooting and hollering from the nervous GIs.

Everyone was markedly uncomfortable, with the exception of Doc Laffin, who smiled, waved, and joked with every citizen as he gamboled down the street.

"What a beautiful neighborhood," he said repeatedly between greetings.

Always Laffin was acting like Mister Rogers wandering into Disneyland instead of downtown Charleyville, as the village had been dubbed.

Tyler had halted his platoon when he had first observed the hootches. The captain had radioed battalion headquarters for orders.

"Higher says to round up the whole population and send them in for questioning," Arnold had radioed back after ten anxious minutes.

"Say again?" Tyler shot back.

"They're sending out a hook to ferry them all back to a detainee camp for questioning."

A hook was polite radio language for a shithook, GI slang for the Ch-47 Chinook, twin-rotored helicopter used for hauling large numbers of troops or heavy cargo.

"Move through the village and set up as a blocking force on the other side," Charlie-Six ordered. "We'll circle around to come in from your present poz and drive 'em to you. There's a clearing beyond the village according to my funny paper. That's our Lima Zulu. Do you copy, over?"

Tyler rogered the call and went over the plan with Pomeroy.

"This is nuts!" Pomeroy said.

As the last man cleared the village, walking backward with his M-16 leveled to guard their backs—with Laffin still singing the praises of his *quaint little neighborhood* —half a dozen AKs opened up from the woods on full automatic. Second Platoon hit the dirt and rolled for cover.

Landing with a bone-jarring thud in a ditch, Tyler heard Simms yell, "Hey, Doc! There goes the neighborhood."

The entire platoon laughed so hard that no one returned fire. Tyler found himself giggling as well, as he tried to give orders to establish suppressive fire to break up the ambush. The release of the tension had been so abrupt, so craved, that it had triggered a response akin to laughing in church. The men were helpless with mirth as the rounds cracked overhead. The pop-pop-popping of the enemy weapons went unanswered for several moments until Tyler managed to raise his weapon, one handed, above the ditch, to squeeze off a burst in the general direction of the incoming fire.

The platoon regained control, a few men at a time, until they were all firing. The Viet Cong's shots withered and died as the crackle of M-16s and the roar of M-60 machine guns replaced their sounds.

"Cease fire!" was the cry heard up and down the line as squad leaders determined that they were unopposed.

"Anybody hit?" Tyler sang out. The lack of response amazed him. The Cong had pumped at least a hundred rounds at more than twenty exposed targets and missed them all. He thanked God and the range instructors of the VC training units.

By the time the Second had secured the LZ, Third Platoon had encircled the village and was herding the inhabitants toward the clearing. The villagers spat and cursed. Many had to be dragged bodily to the landing zone. Thankfully, the chopper was not long in coming and the now terrified people were loaded and lifted away.

"From the state of the bunkers in those hootches," Charlie-Six decided, "and the fighting holes we found, I'd say this is most definitely a VC village. Wouldn't you agree, First Sergeant?"

"No doubt in my military mind, Captain."

"Instead of risking our necks on booby traps, of which I am sure there are many, let's just call in some artillery and blow the place off the map."

With all in agreement, the captain made the call.

"Permission denied," was the reply. "That's a populated area, Charlie-Six."

"Who said so?"

"You did."

The rules of engagement forbade support fires being brought to bear on population centers.

Arnold flipped the handset to Beecher, and said, "Burn it," to the men.

"Big-Six is on the horn," Beecher cut in. He was monitoring the battalion net while Danny covered the company frequency.

With a hand signal to wait, Captain Arnold stopped the men reaching for their cigarette lighters.

"Charlie-Six-Actual," he answered the radio call. After a few minutes of listening and muffled disagreement, the captain signed off. Handing the phone to the sergeant, he said, "Higher has had word from Higher-Higher. We are not to destroy this little hamlet in the trees. Orders are to search it thoroughly and remain in and around this location for the night to see who shows up."

"Guess who *that's* gonna be," grumbled a rifleman standing nearby.

"It won't be the Easter Bunny." Top smiled ruefully, shaking his head. "Sir, every Victor Charley from here to Tan An knows we're in this ville by now. They'll mortar the shit out of us as soon as it gets dark."

"Would you care to discuss your misgivings with the colonel, First Sergeant?" Arnold asked. The coolness in his tone told Top he had already argued the point and lost.

"Stating facts for tactical evaluation, sir. No disrespect intended."

"None taken," Arnold said.

"You heard the orders," Syzmanski announced. "Let's get it done."

Second Platoon was instructed to conduct the search while the First and Third, reinforced by the Fourth, established a perimeter in the surrounding forest. The headquarters group remained in the village to establish a command post.

A painstaking inspection of every building, pen, and bunker revealed a variety of contraband. More rice than the population could have eaten in a year was discovered in straw bins above ground and in concealed caches in large holes below. Web gear and various articles of military equipment were uncovered. Ammunition was found secreted in small quantities in thatched roofs and under walls. A large pile of sharpened stakes was unearthed just outside of town. No weapons were discovered. No booby traps were found or tripped. The consensus was that even Charley was not so callous as to wire his own backyard. The village had been full of kids.

Danny, bored with sitting by the radio in the largest hootch, asked the captain if he might take a break to stretch his legs. Captain Arnold nodded assent and told Smitty to monitor the company net. Danny grabbed his rifle and went out in the street to have a look around. Fuquette turned down his invitation to come along for a stroll.

Danny walked halfway across the street and noticed a slight movement on the floor of the hootch facing him. He thought it had been his imagination, a trick of the fading light. He wondered what the captain's plan for the night would be. Surely, they must be finished with the search soon. There was about an hour and a half of daylight left. He had been tempted to ask when they had their evening meal but thought better of it when he saw the pensive mood of his commanding officer.

There it was again.

He ambled toward the open door of the hootch. Five guys must have been in and out of there. They couldn't have missed anything. He was three feet from the entrance when he saw the floor lift and drop. Something rolled toward him and came to rest at his feet.

"Grenade!" he screamed, rooted to the spot.

A wooden-handled pineapple grenade lay before him. His weapon jumped in his hands as he fired half the magazine into the earthen floor of the building. Dirt danced inside the darkened room. The floor moved again, raised up suddenly, and fell back. Danny unloaded his rifle at the spot without knowing he had pulled the trigger. A long, piercing scream accompanied the snapping of the M-16. The grenade lay where it had stopped. Danny gawked at it through a wreath of smoke.

Fuquette said from behind him, "Don't move, Danny."

Suddenly, he was lifted off his feet and flung aside. Fuquette landed on Danny's back, knocking the wind from his lungs. There was no explosion.

"It's a dud," Fuquette finally called out to the platoon.

Slowly, men inched toward the spot. Top gently lifted the trapdoor of a spider hole inside the hootch with the muzzle of his M-16. The outline of the door was visible since Danny had riddled its cover with lead. Everyone stayed clear of the grenade.

A bloody mess that had been a young man, moments before, lay in a heap at the bottom of the hole.

"Don't look, Mulvaney," Top said.

Danny should have listened.

"Two fer two," Smitty sang cheerfully. "You got another one, Danny."

Danny's face was ashen.

The Second Platoon made a hash of the floors of the rest of the hootches. No other holes were found. The enemy grenade was pushed into the pit with a bamboo pole and blown with an American fragmentation grenade.

"You're lucky them Chicom grenades got no quality control, m'man," Lance quipped.

Captain Arnold called a meeting of all platoon leaders in the CP hootch.

"Dennis," he told Lieutenant Booker, "Third Platoon's got the road in, the south side. Set your people up to watch the trail and the woods on that end.

"Marv. First takes the road out. Same deal. Watch the far side of that clearing. Good place to set up a tube. Better put your LP on the other side."

An LP, or Listening Post, was the second most feared duty in the field, outside of walking point. Two to four men would be sent forward of their lines to sit silently and listen for the enemy's approach. They would act as an early warning for the main body. The hope was that they would alert the unit to a pending attack in time to prepare and still be able to make it back without getting shot by either side—nerve-wracking work.

Marvin Fredericks, First Platoon's commander, nodded compliance.

"Tom," Charlie-Six said to Tyler, "Second stays here. Divide your men up to cover both sides of the village, east and west. You'll be thin, but you'll have the best cover."

Every hootch in Vietnam had its own bunker, and there were shallow fighting holes scattered around the outskirts of the hamlet.

"Stay out of the hootches unless you'll leave too big a gap by doing so. Charley will expect us to homestead. He'll target the hootches if he comes. I want LPs at both ends and both sides."

Arnold methodically continued with his orders. "We'll use each of the platoon radios for the LPs. Sit-reps every hour, staggered in one-minute intervals. No noise. Break squelch twice for negative. Set up a schedule with Sergeant Beecher. Tell your operators to use voice only for contact or urgent transmissions. Fifty percent alert."

Arnold saw the dismayed glances. "I know they're tired, but after the events of the day, I think you'll all agree we'll be damned lucky to spend the night unmolested. We stomped all over Charley's patch today and locked up his whole family to boot. He's gonna be pissed." Arnold saw the grim looks of agreement in the officers' faces. "Questions?"

"You sure the Coast Guard's full up?" Chick Chicarelli asked, deadpan.

"Last I heard," Arnold answered with a wry grin.

The handsome, young lieutenant smiled. "Just askin'."

Nervous laughter from the group ended the meeting. Chicarelli took the officers aside to discuss placement of the heavy weapons. They agreed that the mortar crew would set up somewhere near the middle of the village, but the tangle of branches that hid the enemy base from the air would also make it difficult to effectively use the weapon. The specialist in charge of the crew was to make his best judgment before firing. Mortar rounds that fall back or explode in the trees above your head are not favorite things to mortarmen.

Top volunteered to pull radio watch with the RTOs. It would give all of them more sleep. Beecher would take the first watch, Smitty the second, Danny the third, and Top, the last. First and last watch were the most coveted as they were the only ones that might allow an uninterrupted night's sleep. As the senior men, Beecher and Syzmanski had preference.

The captain, Lieutenant Chicarelli, and Sergeant Fuquette would not be disturbed unless they were needed. At dusk, the platoons moved into prearranged positions. The command post settled in for a long night beside the hootch.

Danny, still shaken from his close brush with death, sat with Beecher in the shadow of the building. They watched the village disappear in the rapidly growing darkness.

"You're a lucky son of a bitch, Mulvaney," Beecher whispered.

"My girl says I'm charmed or something," Danny whispered back. He had a brief picture of Amanda pop into his mind, remembering the night in her bed in the house in the Hamptons as she kissed away his worries of the days to come. Then he saw her expression change to horror as he imagined her knowing of the men he had killed. It took him a moment to recover his train of thought as he realized Beecher was continuing the conversation.

"Must be, man." Beecher shook his head in disbelief, recalling the dud grenade. "You fucked up, you know. You froze. You shot that gook out of reflex, but the grenade should have blown your balls off. Like I said, you're a lucky son of a bitch."

"What would you have done?"

"Let's hope we never get to find out," Beecher ended the discussion. "Get some sleep. Smith will be waking you up before you know it."

Danny crawled to his spot, a dip in the ground beside what had been a chicken pen before the men of C-Company had scattered the flock. He curled up in his poncho liner and stared into the surrounding shadows. He could just make out the supine forms of the soldiers near him. He was surprised to find that he did not feel the remorse and revulsion he had felt after killing the man in the ditch. He had been as close to death as he had the first time but shooting the man through the cover of his hiding place had been less personal in some way. Danny felt nothing really, and that bothered him.

Exhausted, he fell asleep two minutes later.

ℰↄℰↄ

Sergeant Beecher awakened Smitty at the appointed time. He made sure the new man was fully awake and manning the radio before he allowed himself to drift off.

Smitty heard the static break in four double signals as the LPs reported negative situation reports, the first on the hour, the others in one-minute intervals thereafter. The boredom of listening to nothing but the hiss of static from the handset, as the second hand of his watch ticked off the seconds in hypnotic jerks, made him drowsy. Instead of sitting up or kneeling to awaken himself, Smitty curled up next to the radio and lay with the receiver to his ear.

Might as well be comfortable, he thought. *I'll just relax a bit until I can wake up Danny.* He was asleep almost before he completed the thought.

ℰↄℰↄ

Syzmanski woke up. Some sixth sense, common in combat veterans, told him something was wrong. He raised his head to survey the area. All seemed quiet. That was what was wrong. Everybody was lying down. No one was on guard. He started to sit, and a knifelike pain lanced his knee. Sleeping on the damp earth had aggravated his old wound. His leg was stiff. He'd have to stand on it, maybe walk a bit to loosen it up. A light rain was beginning to fall. He looked at his watch, covering the luminous dial with his cupped hand. Mulvaney's supposed to be on watch, he thought, I'm going to have to teach that young troop a lesson. As he struggled to his feet, the sky suddenly opened, and rain fell in sheets. Lightning flashed. Top was lit up like a deer frozen in headlights on a dark road.

The crack of a rifle was almost lost in the thunderclap. A single green tracer round cut the night and disappeared into the first sergeant's belly. Syzmanski fell back, doubled up like a man punched in the stomach. With the thunderbolt, the rifle shot, and the sudden downpour, every man in the company was instantly awake. Captain Arnold accurately assessed the situation in an instant.

"We got a sniper in close. Check the LPs. See if anybody got a fix on him. Is anybody hit?" He saw Top sitting on the ground in front of him. Syzmanski's massive shoulders were slumped, his head was bowed, his hands were holding his middle.

"*Andy.*" He grabbed his weapon and crab-walked through the mud to reach Syzmanski's side. The CP group was all movement as the men raced to form a defensive circle around their first sergeant.

Smitty had recovered enough to realize he had fallen asleep on guard and that he'd have to think fast to cover his mistake. He had rolled away from the radio when he'd been startled awake, instinctively setting his body in motion to minimize the threat.

"Get a medic over here aysap," Arnold ordered, "Top's hit." He put his arm around Syzmanski's shoulders and tried to ease him onto his back. "Take it easy, Andy. Where'd you get it?"

"Gut." Top groaned. "*Nooo.* Don't lay me down. Hurts."

Arnold could see the agony on Top's face. "Help me get him inside," he ordered. "Where the fuck's that medic? Who's on the radio? Get those LPs in and nail that fuckin' gook."

"Danny," Smitty hissed. "What the fuck are you doing over here? Get back on the radio."

Bewildered, Danny went to the radio and called the listening posts. Post two, in the woods across from the CP had seen the muzzle flash and the tracer. The rain had made it impossible to fix the enemy's position without revealing their own.

"We can fire him up, but he's probably split," the sentry advised.

"Negative," Danny replied. "Come on in. All lima papas, come in. Report to your element commanders." That seemed like the right thing to do. Captain Arnold had ordered them in but had given no further instructions.

As the posts pulled back, Charley began sporadic sniping. AK-47s and SKS bolt-action rifles sent grazing fire through the village. Several perimeter guards returned fire, which served to increase the incoming rounds as the soldiers gave away their positions. Danny huddled close to the wall of the hootch, terrified.

Beecher slid to the ground beside him. "We dragged Top inside," he whispered. "He's hit bad. I'll take the radio in. You get to Lieutenant Tyler. He's on the other side of the road. 'Bout three hootches down. That way," he pointed. "Tell him we need Laffin, and quick. *Go!*"

He slapped Danny on the shoulder. Danny hesitated for only a second. Gripping his rifle, he bolted from the wall to run in a crouch across the street and in the direction Beecher had indicated. He heard bullets whine through the air as he ran. His sphincter tightened. His stomach was in a knot. Every step, he felt certain, increased the likelihood of his being shot. He ran, doubled over, as fast as his legs would carry him, all the while wishing he could get lower. He dove to the ground as he reached the spot he thought the lieutenant and his men should be.

"Lieutenant Tyler," he whispered, seeing no one. A shadow spun in the darkness. Danny closed his eyes as he waited for the bullet that would end his life.

"*Jesus Christ.*" He heard an urgent whisper. "Don't fuckin' do that. Who the hell is it?"

"Mulvaney, sir. Top's hit. Captain says to get your medic, right now."

"Doc," Tyler said, "go with him, and for Christ's sake, keep your asses down."

The two men retraced Danny's steps. The enemy fire slackened as the VC maneuvered for position. Danny and Doc dove into the CP hootch out of breath.

Top was writhing on the floor in front of the bunker as the men with him struggled to stem the bleeding from his middle.

Laffin tore open his aid bag and went to work.

"He's got a belly wound. Help me get him on his side so I can have a look," Doc ordered. "Top, I'm gonna need your help. Try to lie still for a minute so's ol' Doc can have a look-see."

"Hurts real bad, Doc," the first sergeant said through clenched teeth.

"I know, Top, and I'm gonna give you something for that in a minute, but first I gotta see what we've got here." To the captain, he said, "Sir, I could use some light. Cover the windows and the door with ponchos so I can use my flashlight."

Arnold sent Smitty and Lieutenant Chicarelli outside to retrieve their packs.

"Fuquette, cover them," he snapped.

Fuquette grabbed Danny's M-16 from his hands and knelt in the doorway.

"Mulvaney. Get us a dustoff," Arnold told Danny, pointing to the radio that was tuned to the battalion net.

Doc worked on Top while the others performed their tasks. With the openings covered, Laffin switched on his light. Fuquette kept his head poked through the hole between the doorframe and the poncho covering it to preserve his night vision. Laffin spoke soothing words to the brave first sergeant, who fought valiantly to not cry out as the medic tended his wounds. When he'd done all that he could, Doc covered Top with a poncho liner and stroked his crew cut head.

"Hang in there, Andy. We'll get you out of here," he whispered as a parent might to a badly injured child. Laffin rose to take the captain aside when the first sergeant passed out.

"It's real bad, sir," he whispered. "Bullet tore up his intestines, and I think it shattered his pelvis. Hard to tell. Peritonitis will set in without surgery and lots of antibiotics. There's an exit wound where his rectum used to be. He's in for a lot of pain. That shot of morphine won't hold for long with that much trauma." Laffin sighed. "If we don't get him to a hospital quick, he hasn't got a chance."

"*Mulvaney!* Where's that dustoff?" Arnold barked.

"Coming, sir. But they don't know if they can get here in this weather. They're gonna try."

"We'll have to get him to the clearing if the bird can get here. That's the only place they can touch down," Arnold said, more to himself than anyone else. He felt the weight of command. His friend would die if they didn't get him some serious help. How many others might die in the attempt? "Tell the LPs to get with their platoon leaders," he said to Beecher.

"Sir, I did that when I called them in," Danny interjected.

"Good," the captain said. "Tell First Platoon to secure the LZ."

Beecher made the call. A few minutes later the north end of the town crackled with automatic fire.

"Six, One-Six," came from Beecher's radio. He had turned on

the bitch-box, a speaker that allowed all to hear the transmissions. "They're all over the place down here," Lieutenant Fredericks yelled. The fire-fight erupting in First Platoon's location could be heard from outside and as it echoed over the airwaves. "We can't move. They've got us pinned."

CHAPTER 25

A *boy?*"
Tran's menacing gaze made Nimh squirm in his seat. The captain's two-word onslaught pressed him against the rickety back of the cane chair. There was no one to help him here. He began to doubt the wisdom of meeting this man alone in his brother-in-law's house. When Captain Tran stepped closer, Nimh blanched. Sergeant Vinh's finger slid to the trigger of his weapon. He watched Nimh closely. Nimh saw the look in Vinh's eyes and sat perfectly still while Tran raged.

"You tell me that we have been betrayed by a boy, and you expect me to place no blame on you? You are a fool. Or perhaps you think that I am." His hand went to the hilt of the long blade at his belt.

"Comrade Captain," Nimh replied with all of the indignation that he could display, "the boy was a trusted agent. He gave no hint of his duplicity. His family has paid for his treachery."

"Is that supposed to appease me?"

"We are not so inept as we appear to be," Nimh offered in defense. "Are we not aware of the identity of the traitor? Have we not acted swiftly in informing you of the situation?"

"Once again you miss the point, Comrade Nimh," Captain Tran breathed, sounding to Nimh like the hiss of a cobra. "I am not concerned with the vengeance meted out by the Viet Cong, nor am I impressed because you are aware that you've been undone. If the buffalo shits on your foot, do you revel in knowing what has occurred?" Tran slammed his mutilated fist on the table. "I want to know what you are going to do to fulfill your part in my mission."

Sergeant Vinh's eyes flicked to the door. It would not do for the wrong ears to be attracted to this house.

"Captain, Captain," Nimh pleaded, his thoughts running parallel to Vinh's, "let us reason this out. All is not lost. We are faced with a serious setback, to be sure, but we are not undone."

Tran was incensed. Nimh was belittling the calamity. Colonel Van Dinh had disappeared. The man who was to have been the source of their supplies was gone. True, the VC seemed to be aware of the turncoat and of the damage he had done to their organization, but where did that leave *him*? He was cut off with no assets beyond what his men carried with them, and he wasn't even in place to begin his mission. The shortcomings of this operation were all too apparent at this late date. General Quoc had thrown him out here with the barest essentials, relying on his zeal and ego to send him charging into disaster.

No. The general had not foreseen this fiasco. He had, Tran was sure, not taken the trouble to envision such an outcome. The more he dwelled on it, the more he was convinced that his little band was but one insignificant cog in a complicated mechanism.

How many more audacious schemes did Hanoi have blindly stumbling about in the field? The general had taught him to look at the conflict as a multi-faceted gem. By way of the same logic, if enough wild plans were afoot, a sufficient number of them should succeed to accomplish the desired final result. General Quoc was placing so much turmoil in the enemy's path he must throw up his hands in the end and walk away.

Tran's predatory gaze met Nimh's prey eyes. The spy cringed as if the bony fingers of death gripped his heart.

"Continue," Tran commanded.

"Your mission is of the highest priority, Comrade Captain. Were I privy to its details, I might suggest some way to rectify the situation." Nimh paused to see if the captain's tongue would be loosened by his anger.

"Keep fishing, you little fool," Tran said. "This fish's teeth may be far more than you bargain for." The captain's chilling smile was enough to convince Nimh to abandon curiosity.

"I myself am in the gravest jeopardy," Nimh whined. "If Mui has revealed the colonel to the Saigon puppet masters, then surely he has informed them of my existence as well. Still, I have taken the trouble to wait for your man at the message drop and have him bring you to this village so that I might apprise you of the situation."

Nimh waited for some token response. Receiving only an icy stare in answer, he carried on. "I am unable to return to my home, as I am certain it is being watched. As a true patriot, loyal to the cause, I risked my chance of escape to assist you." Actually, Nimh knew he might need this fellow's aid to escape the trap himself. "Through agents unknown to the traitorous youth, I have made arrangements for you to be led into the U-Minh. It is best that you go quickly. We do not know to what extent the enemy will exploit this intelligence he has been given. Certainly, you will be safer if you leave now."

"Details, Comrade Nimh, give me details," Tran demanded. "Save your pathetic pleading for someone with compassion."

Nimh swallowed the bile that rose in his throat and set about explaining the specifics. Two men, with intimate knowledge of the U-Minh Forest, would meet Tran and his men a day's march to the south. He wrote exacting instructions as to the route they should follow to arrive at the rendezvous. Naturally, he said, they should memorize and destroy the directions.

Tran nodded, impatient.

Once they met with their guides, Nimh warned, they would be wise to enter the forest and establish a base. It would be less dangerous to contact the local VC cadre once they were stabilized.

"The enemy fears the U-Minh," Nimh concluded. "You will have greater latitude once you are in place."

"And what of you, Comrade Nimh? Is my latitude improved with you running around the countryside?"

"I will accompany you, if you wish, Captain." Nimh ignored the veiled threat in Tran's words. "I am not, however, a fighter in the physical sense. Nor am I trained in the sapper's stealth. I am afraid that I would be more hindrance to you than help. I had planned to fade into the populace, to blend into the urban background as would a chameleon. In time, I shall re-establish my network elsewhere, to fight on in my own fashion."

Tran openly enjoyed the power he held over this man, silently studying him like an odd insect. Nimh, to his credit, met his gaze with detachment.

"Wait here until morning, Comrade Nimh," Tran ordered. "Let us hope we meet again as victorious brothers in arms."

Nimh had no desire to ever lay eyes on the NVA captain again. The heat of the man's gaze melted his innards. Tran's oily grin gave him no doubt of his chances for survival should they meet in some isolated spot. Nimh gladly stayed the night in the home of his brother-in-law, who had wisely found business elsewhere needing his attention. Nimh was sure his legs would have failed him, had he been required to leave now.

ℰↄℰↄ

The Charleyville nightmare was something Danny could not have imagined. The VC thwarted every attempt to secure an LZ for the dustoff ship that Top so urgently needed. Charlie Company was harassed from every angle throughout the night. The Cong countered every attempted maneuver. The woods surrounding the tiny hamlet were alive with enemy. They made no attempt to re-take their homes but seemed satisfied to snap at the Americans' heels like wild dogs.

Artillery proved ineffective. The enemy stayed in too close for the rounds to be put on them directly.

Charlie-Six would not call *Danger Close* fire support unless they were being overrun. The Cong seemed to know that. They made no rushes at the American positions but darted through the jungle in small groups to snipe and probe all night.

The Weapons Platoon's fifty-caliber machine gun got the enemies' heads down, but its blinding flash advertised its position so that the crew was forced to cease fire and seek cover from the deadly hail their bursts attracted. The recoilless rifle had the same result. A solitary shot from the mortar ended that defensive tactic. The shell caromed off a tree limb and very nearly landed on the Third Platoon.

Rain came down in torrents, blinding attackers and defenders alike. The VC used their familiarity with the terrain to better their advantage when visibility approached zero. The constant shifting of the enemy positions made confusion the order of the day. A machine gunner in the First Platoon became so disoriented at one point that he let loose a long burst into the village.

C-Company blew every Claymore mine it had and had nearly depleted its supply of hand grenades by four a.m. Small arms ammunition became so critically low that word was passed to return fire on semi-automatic and only at clear targets. Men with bayonets fixed them to their weapons in the dark.

Throughout the night Andy Syzmanski thrashed in agony on the floor of the hootch. Doc Laffin pumped as much morphine into his veins as he dared. It seemed to have no effect, so great was the big man's pain.

Valiantly, the dustoff crew made repeated attempts to get to him. With no secure landing zone and the weather, as well as enemy fire, threatening to down the ship, they were forced to turn back when their fuel ran low.

Gunships were unavailable. The pilots would not risk their machines until the storm let up.

"Thank God the damn gooks don't have mortars," Lieutenant Chicarelli whispered from the hootch floor next to the bunker where he and Fuquette lay, desperately trying to quiet the first sergeant.

Leon Weislogel was hit early in the fight. A team of VC infiltrators crawled within three feet of his position. He killed one with the .45 caliber pistol he carried as a back-up weapon. The other two retreated, but not before lobbing a grenade toward the flash of the pistol. Leon grabbed his stunned ammo bearer's M-16 and kept the VC at bay. He tried to stem the flow of blood from his neck with his free hand, where shrapnel had ripped a nasty gash, while firing with the other. The heavy recoilless rifle lay in front of him, more useful as cover than a weapon. He bled to death without telling anyone he had been hit.

Forty-five minutes before dawn, the firing stopped. The only sounds were the hiss of the rain in the trees and the moans of the wounded. As the sun rose, the rain ceased, as did the life of First Sergeant Andy Syzmanski.

Three Cobra gun-ships circled the village like angry wasps when the sun came up, sending rockets and mini-gun fire into the woods, vainly seeking revenge on an enemy who had gone.

Colonel Conte personally came out in his Command and Control ship to assess the situation. After a huddled discussion with Captain Arnold, he left with Top and Leon Weislogel's mortal remains.

Danny knew Leon well enough to surmise that his friend had not wanted to risk his buddies' lives by calling for aid. Danny wished he had gotten to know Leon better. Sure, they were friends, but he hadn't been as close to Leon as he had to Gino back home. He didn't know Leon's history, his favorite foods, his girl's name, his mom and dad, his plans for the future—the one he'd never have. He just knew the man, a helluva guy. And he knew his favorite word.

Fuckin' Leon.

The company waited a short time for a re-supply chopper to land with ammunition, food, and water. Nine men had been wounded, none serious enough for dustoff. All would walk to the boats with the company for extraction. There was room enough in the clearing to land only one helicopter at a time. The river was two hours away. It took Charlie Company five hours to reach it.

An hour after the last man walked out of Charleyville, a flight of F-4 Phantoms incinerated the place with napalm. The men of C-Company watched the jets dive in the distance. They saw the silvery, oblong shapes of the canisters tumble from the wings of the fighters to disappear into the trees.

Boiling clouds of black smoke rising from the jungle told them Charleyville was no more.

"If they'd done that yesterday," Beecher said to the captain, "Top would be alive today."

Arnold sighed and turned to continue the march.

The men quietly endured their physical and emotional pain as they concentrated on placing one foot in front of the other. They watched the jungle. They saw no one. Considering their mood, it was lucky for the local farmers that none crossed their path. Today, everybody was VC.

On the Tango Boat, Chicarelli said, "What the hell was Top doing standing up, anyway?"

"Standing up?" Captain Arnold asked.

"Yeah. One of my people looked our way as a flash of lightning lit up the area. He said he saw Top standing between the hootches like he was looking for something and a tracer came from the woods and hit him in the gut. He lost his night vision from the flash, so he couldn't see anything afterward for a few minutes." Chick paused to think. "I can't figure what the hell Andy was looking for."

"Who was on radio watch at that time?" Charlie-Six asked Beecher. "What time was that, Chick?"

"Just after midnight." The lieutenant nodded. "I remember

looking at my watch. I was estimating the time for the dustoff to arrive."

"Mulvaney," Smitty volunteered. "It was Mulvaney's watch."

Danny looked like he'd been clobbered with a two-by-four.

"You fell asleep, didn't you?" The captain was on his feet, glaring at Danny. "Top was looking around to see who was on guard. That's why he was up. You sorry sack of shit. My friend is dead, and I've got to write to his widow and tell her her husband died because a wimpy little shit couldn't keep his eyes open."

Danny's mouth worked, but no words would come. He was flabbergasted.

Arnold leaned so close to Danny's shocked face, spittle sprayed his cheek. "I oughta kill you right here."

"Take it easy, Les." Chicarelli seized the captain's arm. Arnold turned his maddened eyes on the lieutenant. "Let the kid talk, sir." He turned to Danny. "Well?"

"N—No, sirs. It wasn't me, s—sirs," Danny stammered, confused and terrified. His mind raced to sort this out. He was sure he wasn't up at the time. He was so tired. They had interrupted his solitary mourning for Leon, and of course, the first sergeant. He hadn't known Top well, but he had liked him. And now he found himself accused of causing the man's death. He wasn't on watch. *Was he?* His exhausted mind reeled. He doubted himself for an instant. They sensed it.

"Sergeant Beecher," the captain said without taking his eyes from Danny, "who was supposed to be on the radio at twenty-four hundred hours?"

"Mulvaney, sir. It was Mulvaney's watch." It sounded like a death sentence. The boat was silent except for the throb of the engines. All eyes were on Danny.

"Smith," the captain said, his madman's stare still pinning Danny, "did you wake Mulvaney for his shift?"

"Yes, sir, right on time," Smitty lied.

"Was he up and pulling his watch when you went to sleep?"

"Yes, sir. He said he was tired," Smitty ad-libbed, "but I thought he was okay, so I left him and bedded down. If I'd known he couldn't stay awake, I'd have stayed up with him."

"I'll see you rot in Leavenworth for this," Arnold hissed at Danny through clenched teeth. "Place this man under arrest, Lieutenant Chicarelli. We'll discuss court martial when we get in."

CHAPTER 26

The air conditioning on the ship, usually a blessed relief, served only to heighten Danny's discomfort, dressed as he was in the same wet uniform he had worn in the field. Shivering while lighting his fourth cigarette in a row, he weighed the case against him as he awaited the decision of the hastily assembled panel in the captain's quarters, one deck above. He knew enough about military courts to know that if the court martial was convened he would be considered guilty until proven innocent. The military version of justice was opposite the American system he had sworn to defend. With Smitty lying through his teeth to cover his own ass, he would probably be convicted. Anger burned in his belly.

Sergeant Cole, given guard duty over the prisoner, saw Danny crush out his last cigarette and pat his pockets for another. He threw Danny his own package.

"Did you do it?" Cole asked. "Fall asleep on guard? If you did, it sucks, Top getting killed and all. What I'm sayin' is, don't let it get to you. We all done it at one time or another. You just did it at a real bad time, is all. Coulda happened to anybody."

"No." Danny shook his head as he blew smoke through his nose. "No, I didn't. Smitty never woke me up. I've been sitting here thinking about it. At first, I wasn't sure—what with the confusion and all. It was a rough night."

Cole snorted. "You ain't said shit."

"No, but I'm sure now. Smitty never woke me up. He must've fallen asleep, and the miserable rat fuck is blaming me," Danny said to the floor.

"If that's true," Cole said, "and I was you, I'd kill that mother-fucker."

Danny nodded. "Roger that."

Lieutenant Chicarelli stepped through the hatchway. "They're ready for you."

Crushing out his cigarette, Danny watched the officer's face for some hint of what was awaiting him. Chicarelli would not meet his gaze. He led him up one level to the captain's cabin. Cole brought up the rear.

Danny faced the captain and all of the platoon leaders of Charlie Company. Beecher and Smitty were there as well. Danny was amazed that Smitty could look him in the eye, but he did, and the trace of a smile at the corners of his former friend's mouth looked triumphant. Danny reported to the captain and stood at attention. He saw a dog-eared copy of the Uniform Code of Military Justice on the captain's bed.

"Private Mulvaney," Captain Arnold began, "regarding the matter of your sleeping on guard during the operation from which we have just returned, specifically, last night. Do you have anything to say for yourself?"

"Sir, I was not awakened for radio watch by Private Smith," Danny said flatly. "If anybody fell asleep on guard, it was him. He's lying to protect himself."

Arnold's eyes narrowed. He looked at Lieutenant Tyler.

Tyler shrugged.

"So, it boils down to your word against his," the captain said. He stood to look directly into Danny's eyes. "That's exactly what Lieutenant Tyler said would happen. I think you fucked up, Private. I think you dozed off, and you don't have the guts to admit it. But I can't prove it. So, I'm going to have to let the matter drop. I won't bring charges without proof. I can, but I won't. You're getting off lucky—this time. But I won't have a liar and a screw-up in my headquarters group, so I'm transferring you to the Second Platoon. Lieutenant Tyler seems to think you're salvageable, so you're his problem from here on out. Pack your shit and get the hell out of my sight."

Danny felt hot tears forming in the corners of his eyes.

The captain sat. "Dismissed." His anger was unabated as he stared holes in the young man whom he was convinced had carelessly cost Syzmanski's life.

"You'll regret this, sir," Danny said, returning Arnold's scorn.

"Are you threatening me?" Arnold screamed, springing to his feet so abruptly that his chair toppled backward and crashed to the deck.

"Absolutely not, sir," Danny yelled back. "The threat is sitting behind you. Private Smith is the liar. I was warned about him back in Basic Training, but I didn't listen. If this is your idea of fair, Captain, you'll probably get along just fine with him."

"That's enough, Mulvaney." Tyler seized Danny's arm and, applying firm pressure, turned him from his confrontation with the captain. "Get your stuff and move on down to the Second Platoon's area. *Now.*"

"Yes, sir," Danny hissed. He turned and left.

"Will that be all, sir?" Tyler asked of the captain.

Arnold dismissed him with a backhand wave. "Leave me be, all of you. I've got a letter to write."

Beecher and Smitty left Danny alone in their compartment to gather his belongings. After stuffing everything in sight into his laundry and duffel bags, Danny grabbed his rucksack. He stopped to unbuckle the PRC-25 from the frame and tossed the radio on Beecher's bunk as he left. Fuquette was waiting in the corridor. Danny stopped and stared at the sniper.

"You tell me this is bullshit," Fuquette said, "I'm gonna believe you. I don't think you're the kind to lie."

"It is bullshit."

"Good enough for me." Fuquette nodded. "Let me help you with that."

Danny handed him one of the bags. "Thanks, Davy."

"No sweat. Let's get you settled in your new home."

Sergeant Pomeroy told Danny to park his stuff on a vacant bunk in the platoon area. "We'll wait and see where the lieutenant wants to put you before we put your shit away. Better put on some dry fatigues before you see Two-Six."

Danny nodded and looked questioningly from Pomeroy to his gear. Theft of equipment was commonplace. They had all been taught: *A good soldier does not do without.*

"I'll keep an eye on it for you," Pomeroy promised.

Danny had to climb back up to officers' country after he had changed. He found Tyler sitting on his bunk, clad in clean fatigue pants and a t-shirt. His feet were bare. Danny noticed the lieutenant was showing signs of immersion foot. Tyler stopped him when he snapped to attention.

"Skip it," Tyler said. "Have a seat."

A steel chair next to a fold-down writing desk bolted to the bulkhead and one other bunk were the only places to sit in the tiny compartment. Tyler apparently shared his billet with another officer. Danny selected the chair.

Tyler perused some mail as Danny made himself comfortable. "Smoke if you got 'em," Tyler drawled. "This is an informal kind of talk, Mulvaney."

Danny absentmindedly fished in his pocket for his cigarettes until he remembered he had none. Tyler motioned to a pack on the desk. "Help yourself."

Thanking him, Danny lit up and waited for the man to begin. The lieutenant seemed to be in no hurry as he sorted his mail. Danny wondered if his own mail would ever catch up to him.

Tyler picked out one letter and smiled, and then his eyes strayed to a rolled-up newspaper, and finally came to rest on Danny. "I've been bothered by your name since first I heard it," he said. "What I mean is, it struck me as familiar, but I couldn't get a handle on it. Until just now, that is."

Danny said nothing. He smoked and waited for the officer to get to the point.

"That newspaper triggered me. Anybody ever call you 'Meteor,' Mulvaney?"

Danny warily answered. "Back in college. I was on the track team. Meteor was a nickname the coach hung on me."

"Okeson College, wasn't it?"

Danny nodded, raising one eyebrow.

"I was raised on a farm near there." Tyler smiled. "Small world."

"Too small," Danny blurted.

"You got kicked out of Okeson, as I recall," Tyler stated. His furrowed brow showed he was becoming uneasy at the turn the young soldier's attitude was taking. "I read it in the paper, but I don't recall why."

"It's not important," Danny mumbled.

"When I said this conversation would be informal," Tyler's tone became brittle, "I didn't mean that we would completely dispense with military courtesy."

Danny took a moment to get the officer's meaning. "It's not important—sir."

"Better," Tyler placed both hands on the edge of the bunk and leaned forward. "Let's get something straight, soldier. I just saved your ass. Don't ask me why. Call it a hunch. Or maybe I just believe in giving a man a chance. Whatever." He dismissed further conjecture with an offhand gesture. "I would not like to think that I was mistaken in my judgment. When I ask a question, it's because I wish to know the answer. It's not for you to decide what is and what is not important to me."

Danny stiffened.

"Now," Tyler said, "why, exactly, did they boot you out of school?"

Danny began his story quietly, calmly reciting the facts. "I won an athletic scholarship to Okeson. A full-blown free ride. I threw the javelin in high school, and I was pretty good. Won a bunch of trophies and medals. Okeson was trying to bolster their enrollment by beefing up their athletics department."

Tyler nodded.

"It seemed like a good idea at the time," Danny went on. "A free education. New horizons. That's what I thought, anyway." The image of his downfall played like scenes from the coming attractions of a B-movie in his mind. He wondered how the lieutenant would react to his tale if he told it all. He didn't care. "So, there I was, Daniel Francis Mulvaney: track star, javelin master, scholarship winner. Yes, sir. World by the balls. Had it made in the shade. Except it was bullshit. Okeson turned out to be a backwater college in the armpit of the South. No offense—sir."

Tyler folded his arms and leaned back against the bulkhead to stare down his nose at Danny.

Danny misread the body language. He gave out a short laugh of derision. "There was a big meet one day," he continued. "We were going up against one of Okeson's biggest rivals. I can't even remember the other school's name now." He looked to the overhead, trying to recall. "Cracker U or some shit."

Tyler started to say something, but Danny went on as if he hadn't noticed.

"Anyway, just before start time a bus pulls up, a school bus loaded with black kids. No name on it or anything, just a run-of-the-mill school bus. It stops in full view of the stands, right at the end of the track, and a guy climbs up on top with a bullhorn and starts spouting off about freedom and equality."

Danny could see that proud, ballsy, young black kid now. Standing there with his chin held high, eyes burning defiance, sweat shining on bronze, ropey muscles, Afro glistening in the sun, leading the others in a chorus of *We Shall Overcome*—a tune definitely not on the hit parade at Okeson College.

"He had to know what would happen. The whole school was in the stands. They couldn't let them get away with it. This stupid bastard had to stand up and challenge the whole school to wax his ass. And the son of a bitch dragged me into it."

"How so?"

"All I wanted was to get along, win a few medals, maybe, and graduate in four years. No fuss. No problems. Danny Mulvaney, Bachelor of Arts, thank you very much."

"So, what happened?"

Danny was startled by the lieutenant's intrusion into his story. Coupled with his present troubles, his recollection of humiliation at Okeson had served to bring his anger to the boiling point. He flicked the long ash from his cigarette into an artillery-casing ashtray and stubbed out the butt.

His questioning glance at the pack on the table prompted Tyler to nod and say, "Go ahead."

Danny lit up again. Smoke curled from his lips as he resumed the telling of the end of his college career. "I knew this was not the best place to be at the time. The sheer hate on the faces of everyone around me told me to make myself scarce. I started to back away when Coach Lembeck grabbed me by the arm." Danny could smell the booze on Lembeck's breath, even now. "He slapped a javelin into my hand like Doctor Zorba passing the scalpel to Ben Casey. 'Skewer that nigger for me, Danny,' he said, like, '*Pass the mustard, would you?*' The little bastard reminded me of a fireplug with a mean streak. You couldn't tell if his muscle was turning to fat or the other way around. He was an ugly little shit, clear to the bone.

"I almost laughed, then I saw his eyes. He was fucking *serious*. It all happened so fast after that. I remember standing there, dumbstruck, my mouth flapping like a fish on the beach. I dropped the javelin. They turned on me then. The whole damned team chased me from the field. There wasn't one of them could have caught me." A small, proud smirk lifted the corners of his mouth. "They didn't call me Meteor Mulvaney for nothing." The humor vanished as he recounted the rest. "But I couldn't run forever. They cornered me in the parking lot with my back to a Buick—Lembeck and three shot-put goons—glaring at me.

"I snapped the antenna from the fender and slashed the closest guy across the face." He winked. "Old Brooklyn street fighter's trick. A car's aerial makes a good whip if you know how to use it. It kept them at bay. They would have killed me, or I would have killed a couple of them if Professor Shields hadn't shown up. They were closing in, gathering their nerve for the charge, when Shields ran into the lot and asked what the hell was going on.

"Lembeck never missed a beat. He said, 'We caught Mister Mulvaney inciting them niggras to riot. Ain't that right, boys?' Naturally, the rest went along." Danny blew smoke at the overhead. "And that's it—*sir*."

"So, they kicked you out on some trumped-up charge of being a radical."

"You know the drill."

Tyler visibly bridled at the implied accusation but let it pass. "You're not impressed with Southern hospitality, I take it?"

"Never heard of it," Danny said.

"Can't say as I blame you." Tyler grinned. "I'm from there, Mulvaney, but if you choose to paint everyone from down South with the same brush, you're the stupid one." The smile vanished as quickly as it had appeared.

Danny was off balance.

"What you said to Captain Arnold," Tyler said, "was it true? About Private Smith, I mean."

"Yes, sir," Danny maintained eye contact. "That rat-bastard framed me."

Tyler stared into Danny's steady blue eyes for a moment. He slapped his thighs with both hands, and said, "That's that then. Captain Arnold's got a snake in his pocket, and I've got myself a new RTO."

Danny was shocked.

"I believe you, Mulvaney. Wilson, my RTO, is scheduled to DEROS in a few weeks. He's got a wife and kid. I'm going to pull him off the line as of now. You take over his duties immediately. Sergeant Pomeroy will help you get set up. Any questions?"

"Just the obvious one, sir."

"Why?" Tyler laughed. "Damned if I know. I ask one thing of my men, Danny. Be straight with me. I'll always be straight with you. Fair enough?"

Tyler extended his hand. Danny took it. A contract was formed. Both men knew it. Neither could have explained it. Although wary, Danny begrudgingly decided to give the redneck lieutenant a chance. Something made him think of his mother and what she'd have had to say about this. He wasn't sure what it would be, but it would be corny. Of that he was certain. But it would also be incredibly accurate. He missed his mom more than he thought possible just then.

CHAPTER 27

Sergeant Pomeroy found room for Danny with the second squad after introducing him to Wilson, the man most pleased to meet him. Lance came over to sit with Danny as he stowed his belongings.

"I thought it would be a little strained," Danny said. "You know, with what I was accused of and all. These guys seem pretty friendly, though."

Lance said, "Two-Six says you're okay, and that's good enough for these dudes. They talk about Tyler like he was God's kid brother. I think you lucked out. Second Platoon is the place to be, old buddy."

"Maybe so, Lance, maybe so. At least we're together. I can't believe Leon's gone."

"Well, he is. He's dead, and we ain't."

Danny started to object to so cold a dismissal of their friend, but he heard the quiver in Lance's voice and saw his lips tremble. "Fuckin' Leon," he whispered.

"Fuckin'-A." Lance sniffed, wiped his nose on his sleeve, and dug a stack of letters from beneath his pillow. "'Bout time the mail got here, ain't it? Where's yours?"

"I guess I didn't get any."

"No way, man. With all them letters you wrote, must be some for you. Lemme check with Pomeroy."

Thirty minutes later, the platoon sergeant dropped a bundle of mail on Danny's bunk. "Got misplaced up in HQ," he said.

Danny raised an eyebrow. "Misplaced?"

Pomeroy shrugged and walked away.

Danny tore open each envelope and devoured the contents like a starving man at a banquet. Before long he realized that they made more sense when he read them in chronological sequence. He arranged them by postmark date and began again.

He set Amanda's aside to save for last so that he could savor them and let her fill his mind. Mom's letters were just like her, full of confident hopes and stiff upper lip stuff. Uncle Mike's rambled. Danny pictured the big bear of a man, straining to find words to scrawl across the pages, the love in his heart struggling to leak through the ballpoint. His father's brother had never played much of a part in his life. He had lived in New Jersey ever since Danny could remember so they had never had as much contact as Danny would have liked. Since his father died, Uncle Mike seemed to be more accessible. He still didn't come around much, but always seemed to pop up when Danny needed a father figure. Danny decided to make a point of spending more time with his uncle when he went home.

Amanda's missives were sunshine and flowers. They were light and cheery, and I-miss-you-my-darling was between every line. At least he read them that way. The summer was winding down in the last of them. She said The Hamptons had lost most of its beauty when he left. Cathy was doing well, considering. Her mom and dad were hurting but picking up the pieces. They sent their love.

Jeannie and Amanda were talking about getting an apartment. They had grown fond of their newfound freedom in The Hamptons and were not anxious to give it up. Her job was going well. She had gotten another raise.

Everyone said to keep his letters coming. Danny realized he had not written a line since before that night in the ditch with the VC.

"You dropped one," Lance said from the bunk below him, scooping an envelope from the floor.

"Thanks," Danny mumbled as he checked the return address. The letter was from Gino, and it had a Brooklyn postmark. "What the hell—" He tore it open and began to read.

Dan,

Got your address from your mom. I figured you'd be some-what curious as to what happened to your old buddy, so this is to inform you of Yours Truly's untimely induction into this man's army. You will undoubtedly notice the RA prefix on my service number when next we correspond. No, I didn't go Gung-Ho in your absence. I joined under duress, you might say. I got busted with the Caddy on the Triboro Bridge. Don't go blaming yourself. The chauffeur bit was my idea and I had always planned to swipe one of Nicky's stolen cars to make my way to the border. Driving you to the draft board just gave me a reason Nicky would swallow.

Anyway, the reggy held up as advertised at first, but there was a minor problem with my license. No big deal, a trivial detail, like I don't actually have one. I told the pig I left it home. He asked for any kind of ID, but I didn't have anything that wasn't forged on me so I said I lost my wallet. That was stupid because it was in my back pocket and a quick pat was all it took to prove the lie. Next, he tossed the car. Unbeknownst to me, that asshole Nicky left two joints in the glove compartment. I took the big fall when they impounded the car and ran the VIN numbers.

Okay. At that point, I was looking at one misdemeanor traffic violation, two counts of felony forgery, possession, and the biggie: Grand Theft Auto. Not so good. Spent some time in the clink waiting for a trial. The DA seemed to think I might not show up for court if they let me out on bail. First impressions never were my most shining moments. On my fateful day in court, the judge gave me a choice between enlistment and the Tombs. The old rock-and-a-hard-place pitch. So, here I am back home, finished Basic, which sucked the big one. Got a delay en route before heading for Commo School. Uncle Sam's gonna make me a Communications Specialist, whatever that is. Came home to see if I could catch up with you on leave, but you were already gone.

What the hell. Probably would have been too cold in Canada for my hot blood anyway. I figure, even if I go to Nam, I'll be in some air-conditioned bunker with a teletype machine because that's what they're going to train me on. I'll let you know where I am. Maybe we'll meet up someplace and see if the Frogs taught the Viet chicks any good sex tricks whilst they were in residence.
Gino

Danny sighed. "Gino, you poor bastard."

The letter was dated six weeks ago. Gino would have been on his way home at about the time Danny was leaving. He wondered what took him so long in mailing it and if he would write again to update his address. With Gino, anything was possible.

He rummaged through the storage bin beneath his bunk until he found his writing paraphernalia. Propping himself against the bulkhead, he stared at the blank page on his knee. What could he say? Should he tell them about the VC in the ditch? Or the one in the hole? Or Leon and Top? Charleyville? His near court martial? Maybe just a light note about his jailbird pal who was now caught up in this mess.

He started with Amanda, wondering if he could get away with just commenting on her news and neglecting to say anything about what was happening to him. Amanda had her job and a life. She was making plans and looking forward to the next adventure in her bright future. He didn't know if he would survive tomorrow. He stared at the crowded compartment, filled with soldiers celebrating surviving another day. His eyes glazed over and he saw only horror and death. Fear gripped him.

"You a popular sumbitch back home, ay, Daniel."

Danny came back to reality to see Fuquette standing beside him, looking at the letters strewn around the bunk.

"Hi, Davy." Danny tried, unsuccessfully, to sound glad to see him.

"What'sa trouble, bro?"

"I don't know what to say." He spread his hands over the blank page.

"Say everything is hunky dory. Lie like a motherfucker."

"Is that what you do?"

"It's what most of us do, man." Fuquette sat on the edge of the bed. "Would you want them to know what this place is really like?"

"I see what you mean."

"Don't make it sound too good. Tell them you're on the line but that it's not so bad. You don't want to lull them so completely that it comes as an even bigger shock if the officer comes to the door one day. Friend of mine told his old lady he was a clerk typist in a big concrete bunker under a mountain. He was really a tunnel rat up around Cu Chi. She had a complete breakdown when he got killed and came home in a sealed coffin marked: Remains Unviewable."

Danny grimaced. "You know what I wish? I wish we could go

the Artillery Club and have a couple of beers. I'd like to get mildly plastered tonight. These navy guys may eat well and sleep on
clean sheets, but this bucket is like a prison."

Fuquette looked at his fingernails, and said, "Can you keep a
secret?"

Danny nodded. Fuquette crooked a beckoning finger, then
placed it to his lips and turned. Danny swung down from his bunk
and followed. Fuquette led him up on deck and to the stern.
Without a word, he climbed into the twin-forty gun tub and produced a silver flask from a cargo pocket in his fatigues.

"French brandy," he whispered.

"Where'd you get it?" Danny said.

"From a general. Being a living legend has its advantages."
He took a taste and handed the flask to Danny.

Danny sipped some of the liquid and passed the container
back. It burned all the way down his throat. They passed the flask
back and forth several times and then sat with their backs against
the splinter shield. Fuquette lit two cigarettes, cupping the match
expertly to hide the light. He passed one to Danny and they
smoked in companionable silence for a few minutes.

"Have you ever read *For Whom the Bell Tolls?*" Fuquette
asked.

"No." Danny shook his head in the darkness. Stars shone
brightly in patches between the clouds. "But I saw the movie."

"Read the book if you get a chance." Fuquette smiled. "You
thought you understood the end, didn't you."

"'It tolls for thee,'" Danny said.

"Do you think you might understand it a little better now?"

Danny thought for a moment, and then nodded, "I guess I do."

"You know more about yourself already than most men learn
in a lifetime. Combat does that. Its lessons, once learned, are with
us always."

"When I picked up that pen," Danny whispered, "it struck me
that I wasn't the same guy they wrote their letters to. I felt like I'd
be lying to them if I pretended to be. I felt...I don't know...lost?"

"You're a good man, Daniel. It's hardest on the good ones."
Fuquette seemed to be talking to himself, as if Danny wasn't
there. He chuckled in the darkness but didn't say why. Danny saw
his profile in silhouette against the lighter gray of the steel well
that contained them. "Do you have a girl back home, Daniel?"

"Yeah, Amanda. She's beautiful."

"Do you love her?"

"I think so." Danny paused, rethinking the question he had asked himself a hundred times. "She's a year older than me. More mature than most of the girls I've known. A little richer, too. She lives on the East Side in Manhattan. Sometimes I wonder if I'm good enough for her."

Telling this to Fuquette seemed natural, but Danny didn't know why.

"Remember this, my friend," Fuquette said, "we have to live with ourselves. The opinions of others are less important. Forgive yourself for the things you do here. Those who love us will understand that we are changed men when we return home. They may pity us, at first, but they will understand because of their love and still love us in the end. Never doubt your worth. Amanda is a lucky woman."

"I'll tell her you said so."

"No, you won't. But maybe you should."

"How about you, Davy? Got a girlfriend waiting for you?"

"Heavens, no. My wife would kill me."

"You're *married?*"

"Does this seem so impossible?"

"No, of course not, I just didn't—"

"Her name is Patrice, the most beautiful, raven-haired temptress a man would care to meet."

"Do you write to her often?"

Fuquette sighed. "Rarely."

"Why?"

"I enlisted against her wishes. Her father is a big man in New Orleans. Big fishing magnate. They say, 'If it swims in the Gulf, Papa Jacques owns a piece of it.' Patrice and I met when I was a freshman in college. We fell in love and eloped. Her daddy was not pleased with his daughter's new husband—a swamp Cajun, sometime fisherman, sometime alligator poacher, all time loser. We soon found out that two *cannot* live as cheaply as one. I was barely scraping by before the wedding, doing odd jobs—not all of them legal—to pay my tuition. Her father offered me a job as a manager in one of his canneries. Suit and tie. Not my cup of tea.

"We needed the money, so I quit school and went to work for him. I hated it. The men under me made no bones about their anger working for a man who latched onto his rich wife's petticoats. To be frank, I agreed with them. Patrice and I began to fight. I began to drink. One day I walked into the recruiter's office. The rest, to coin a cliché, is history."

"Do you think she'll be there when you get back?"

"I am sure of it. We love each other very much, and we have both learned from this." Fuquette took a drag on his cigarette and exhaled slowly. "One thing is certain. There will be no more cannery for this man. I'm going to buy a fishing boat and get rich on tourist charters. Maybe. If not, we will sail off into the sunset, my lovely *cher* and me, and be happy with who we are and our love for one another."

Fuquette stood in the darkness. "Get some sleep," he said. "Charley is a farmer. He gets up early."

Fuquette went to bed. Danny walked the deck and watched as the sailors lobbed concussion grenades into the water to keep saboteur swimmers away from the ship. They laughed after every muffled explosion, and said, "Sorry, Charley."

Back in his bunk, Danny found he could fill his letters with news and comment on the Vietnamese people and their country without telling war stories. He started to explain his transfer to the Second Platoon as a way to fill a vacant slot before replacements arrived, but decided that would prompt questions about the reason for the vacancy and cause worry about a shortage of replacements. He had to avoid anything that would give the impression they were losing people. After some thought, he made up a story about how the RTO from the Second Platoon had traded places with him because the other guy had seniority and demanded the better slot. This scenario his blue-collar family and his white-collar girl could relate to. They would only know what he chose to tell them. Fiction was more fun to write, anyway.

When the lights went out, replaced instantaneously by the soft glow of the Navy's darkened-ship red lamps, someone on the far side of the compartment did a good imitation of the ship's 1MC intercom, which the navy used to pipe orders to the enlisted swabees.

"Now hear this. Now hear this. All hands on dicks."

Danny found that he could smile, if not laugh along with the rest, and fell effortlessly into dreamless sleep.

CHAPTER 28

I understand the way you feel, Les," Colonel Conte sympa-
thized with C-Company's commander seated opposite him
across a wooden desk in his Dong Tam headquarters. "Andy
was the finest senior NCO in the brigade and a good friend. It's a
shame, but that's all it is." He saw Arnold stiffen. "You know as
well as I do that when your number is up, it's up. Blaming this
kid won't bring Andy back. From what I understand, you can't be
certain which one of them screwed up, either. After the shit storm
you raised over it, we can hope that neither of them will ever do it
again. Let's move on. We can point fingers when the war's over
if we still want to. Now, let's get down to business. I'm pulling
you off the boats."

Captain Arnold's face showed his surprise.

"I know you're not due for rotation for a while yet, but something's come up."

The colonel rose from his desk and walked with Arnold to a
large wall map of the Mekong Delta. Grease pencil marks in several colors showed the boundaries of the Division's AO. Pins and
markers showed the deployment of units, friendly and enemy.
The former was known, the latter suspected.

"Division wants a stronger presence in the Camau Peninsula,"
Conte said, pointing to the area with a telescoping baton. "We're
going to set up a fire base here," he tapped the map, "just outside
the U-Minh Forest. There's been a lot of raw intelligence lately
from SEAL teams and Lurps that suggests a buildup down there.
Nothing concrete as yet, but enough to make it worth a look-see."
He faced the captain and said, "C-Company will head on down
there to secure the site. The engineers will move in and build it as

soon as you're ready for them. The rest of the battalion will stay on the river and look into this hornet's nest your boys kicked over on your last op. We'll move down there in force as soon as the base is ready.

"You'll go in two stages. First, we'll airlift you into an area midway between Long My and Sac Trang. Sweep it for a day or two, and then we'll jump the rest of the way.

"You'll be dropped right where the base will be built. You won't even have to walk." The colonel grinned as if he had just handed Arnold a prize. "We start in two days. Get rested up. I'll have an Intel packet sent over to you to brief you on the logistics."

Arnold shook the commander's hand, saluted, and returned to the Benewah.

CHAPTER 29

The rendezvous with the VC guides outside of Hang Don went smoothly, and Tran could see they knew the area as well as they claimed. The trip to the U-Minh was slow. They moved only by night. Daylight was far too dangerous. Enemy air traffic was plentiful by day. They avoided the many hamlets along their route. The eight million inhabitants of the Delta saw as little as possible of any military movement out of self-preservation, but one careless word could bring the wrath of the gods down upon them. Once into the forest, they would breathe easier.

The rain became more frequent and increasingly more violent as they moved south by southwest. They risked daytime advances when the deluge became so heavy and unceasing as to preclude air attack. The men were restless and edgy. They longed to take vengeance on the enemy who forced them to skulk and slither through the mud like serpents. When, at last, they reached their objective, Tran could see visible signs of improvement in their stride, their bearing, their determination. There was even an occasional smile.

The chosen site was adequate, but Tran made no move to set up permanent housekeeping until the guides had left them, promising to return with news of their contact with the VC infrastructure. As soon as they were gone, he told his men to prepare to move. He would not risk betrayal a second time. They would set up elsewhere and send teams to watch this place.

Half a kilometer from the original site, Tran found what he was looking for. He halted his men and looked with satisfaction at the surrounding foliage. They were deep in a swamp. Mangrove trees stood on twisted roots like stilts above fetid water. Where the jungle floor rose above water, it was mossy and sodden. The tangle of limbs and vines overhead was sufficiently thick to provide good concealment from the air.

"Here," he said. "Here is where we will build our camp."

His men looked to one another and cast their eyes down as Tran met their nervous glances.

"The solid ground of the first place was more to your liking, was it not?" Tran said to them as a group. "That is precisely what the Americans would look for. A place such as this would be overlooked as too inhospitable. We are not the usual troops. We are highly trained and strong. We will make the most of this place and be all the more secure." He pointed to the treetops. "We will build sleeping platforms and guard towers up there, where we can look down upon anyone who blunders into our domain. We will camouflage all of our emplacements. We will be invisible until it is too late for an enemy to escape us.

"Sergeant Vinh, get the men into a perimeter. We will eat and plan our camp. Lieutenant Sau, join me."

While they ate, Tran outlined the layout of the camp, as he pictured it. They would keep ten men on guard while the rest worked. The forest would supply their building materials. Sau suggested they use a nearby stream to supply their water.

"It moves swiftly, and there are many fish. Perhaps we could divert it and dig a fish trap. We would have a source of food at our threshold," Sau offered.

"See to it," Tran ordered. "We must patrol the area surrounding the camp, as well. I want to know every wrinkle in the soil for a kilometer in every direction. It is imperative that we know every trail, every hole, every conceivable hiding place, as well as every way in and out of here."

"This will take time with the small band we have, Captain."

"Yes. There is much to do but do not let the size of the task, nor the limits of our manpower hasten you," Tran cautioned. "Work swiftly, yet carefully. We are far from the aid of Hanoi, and I do not place a great deal of faith in the efficiency of the Viet Cong. We can catch or steal food. Ammunition is our greatest problem. Once we begin our mission, it can quickly become critical. Remember, our main objective is the taking of prisoners." Tran smiled. "At least, that is the impression we must give to our enemies. Soon, the Forest of Darkness will have a whole new meaning for the Americans." Tran thought for a minute, then said, "When all else is completed, construct tiger cages, just in case we wish to have guests.

"You will take charge of the construction, Comrade Lieutenant. I will accompany as many of the patrols as possible so that I can familiarize myself with our new home."

CHAPTER 30

The promised intelligence packet came with the afternoon supply boat. Charlie Company's commanding officer read the warning order that accompanied it and cursed, chastising himself for not realizing that the company would be required to stage from Dong Tam. They would have to move with all their gear at dawn tomorrow.

"'Rest up,'" he sneered. He called a meeting of his officers. There was the expected grumbling and grousing from the platoon leaders when he gave them their instructions.

"We just got here," Marv Fredericks whined.

"Then you shouldn't be too attached to this bucket," Charlie-Six said.

The officers settled down, their obligatory bitching spent. "There's a bright side," Captain Arnold resumed. "Our air assets aren't available until zero-seven-hundred, the day after tomorrow. We'll be up half of tonight getting our shit together, but once we get to Dong Tam, we'll have most of the day and all of the night to stand down. I've laid on a pallet of beer and some steaks. We'll have an old-fashioned barbecue for dinner and let the troops kick back for a few hours."

The captain hushed their cheers. "We're heading into who-knows-what on this next one though, so I don't have to tell you to warn your NCOs to keep a lid on the festivities."

Thoughtful nods assured him they understood.

"Have your men assemble on the flight deck, topside, at seventeen-hundred for a memorial ceremony for First Sergeant Syzmanski and Private First Class Weislogel. Clean fatigues, pistol belts, and helmets. Questions? No? Okay, that's all."

That afternoon, atop the Benewah, with a hot, damp wind rustling the troops' freshly laundered uniforms, the Chaplain read a brief service and appealed to their faith in the Lord to comfort them in their grief. The company stood at attention for Taps and a twenty-gun salute. Danny held back his tears as Charlie Company snapped a final salute to their fallen comrades that would put the army drill team to shame. You could almost hear the collective intake of breath as the men were dismissed.

Captain Arnold left the preparations for the move in his officers' capable hands and flew to Dong Tam in a Huey sent to the ship to collect him. He ran through a mental list of things to do to make ready for the return of his men once he got back to the company area.

As the slick carried him over the Mekong River, Lester Arnold wished for the hundredth time that he had sent Andy Syzmanski back to his desk the moment he had set foot in the field.

CHAPTER 31

Mamasan chewed beetlenut and smiled with blackened teeth at the MP sergeant as she waited in line to be searched at the main gate of Dong Tam Base Camp. He frisked her quickly but carefully when her turn came. The military policemen didn't mind searching the young women. The MPs found it fun to cop a feel, and they could get away with a lot. The girls took it stoically, the price one paid for the well-paying jobs on the American base. Pride was the quickest way to be declared persona non grata and ejected for all time from the camp.

Mamasan had seen outraged Vietnamese arrested and held for questioning for refusing to let the long-nosed foreigners run their hairy paws over their bodies. She was far too old and ugly for the guards to give her more than a quick pat. This one, however, was thorough. She could see the grimace of distaste as the young soldier slid his hands up her thighs and brushed her crotch. Her breasts hung like bean pods beneath her grimy blouse, and she smiled as the soldier ran his hands over them.

He laughed as he finished his search. "*Di di mau*, you horny old bitch."

She bowed and smiled again as he wiped his hands on his pants. Comrade Dan would be greatly pleased at the information she was bringing to him. She repeated the particulars over and over in her mind as she hurried along the muddy road.

A gracious young woman offered her seat on the bus to My Tho. The old woman was glad to see that respect for age was not entirely at an end. The girl obviously came from a good family.

She hoped that the commander would have time to prepare a suitable welcome for Charlie Company of the Second of the Sixth.

She was far too old and pragmatic to still hope to live to see the victorious end of the revolution, but she would do her part to make the prophecy fact while there was life in these old bones.

CHAPTER 32

The rain had let up long enough for the men to fill their pockets with cold beer from the ice- filled garbage cans and to down one or two while they waited in the chow line. A hastily erected GP-Medium tent housed three fifty-five gallon drums split lengthwise and welded to angle-iron frames. Filled with charcoal briquettes and covered with wire grills, they made excellent barbecue braziers.

Back in the hootches, the soldiers wolfed their food and guzzled beer until the company area took on a party atmosphere. A word of warning from each of their squad leaders—usually administered with a wink—about moderation in their imbibing, was as quickly forgotten as yesterday's lunch.

Danny and Lance sat with the second squad and enjoyed the lies and ribald stories of their hosts, who were showing off for the new men. David Fuquette slipped in quietly and sipped a beer as he listened.

"Davy Fuckit, you short-timing son of a bitch," Morgan slurred when he spotted the sniper. "How many, man?"

"Thirty-two and a wake-up," Fuquette grinned, "you sorry ass lifer."

"Lifer this," Morgan laughed, tugging his crotch. "I'm so short I haven't got time for any long conversations, man. Two weeks, baby, and I'm on that silver dustoff, skyin' up for the land of round-eyed pussy. I already told my old lady to start sliding down the banister to warm that sucker up. What's the second thing *you're* going to do when you get home, Fuckit?"

"Probably repeat the first thing," Rodriguez said, laughing.

"Roger that," Fuquette said with a grin.

"You're going home soon?" Danny asked, saddened that he would lose his new friend so soon and immediately ashamed of his selfishness.

"If Charley don't change my plans," Fuquette said soberly.

"Don't talk like that," Morgan snapped. "It's bad luck."

"It's all luck, my friend."

An uncomfortable silence followed.

And then Paco, the squad machine-gunner, sang, "Every party has a pooper, that's why we invited you."

The squad chorused, "Party pooper. Party pooper."

As the laughter fell to scattered snickers, Simms sang, "Daveeeey, Davy Fuckit, King of the Wild Frontier."

The squad, and then the entire platoon, joined in with a raucous parody of the famous song that Danny had learned as a kid. Lance and he sang along for the choruses and laughed at the comical stanzas between. Fuquette blushed behind a good-natured smile as the platoon rattled the rafters with their drunken rendition.

He really is a legend in his own time, Danny thought.

Lance put his arm around Danny's shoulder. "Better here than with those pricks in Headquarters, ain't it, Danny." His eyes were rolling in their sockets. He was getting very drunk. Danny had been feeling no pain either until Lance reminded him of his humiliation.

"Lance, old buddy, how'd you like to help me get even with that cocksucker, Smitty?"

"In the words of the late, great Leon Weislogel," Lance whispered, "Fuckin'-A."

They excused themselves for a piss stop, stopping at Danny's footlocker for a pack of cigarettes. Danny slipped something in his pocket besides the cigarettes, and he and Lance zigzagged their way to the door, stepping over and around their platoon mates, many of whom sat on the floor. Danny swiped a CS tear gas grenade from a rucksack hanging conveniently near the exit.

"You gonna frag him?" Lance asked, wide eyed, as he watched Danny loosen the pin.

"Nope." Danny leered, exposing the gray, yellow-banded cylinder for Lance to see. "Gonna make him cry like a baby."

They did have to stop at the piss tube now as their laughter weakened their bladders. The piss tube, as the open-air urinals were called, was a cardboard sleeve stuck into the ground at a forty-five-degree angle and surrounded by a square of crushed rock for drainage. Four corner posts with a band of corrugated steel nailed to three sides, and a slanted roof of the same material, were the extent of the design's privacy and protection from the elements.

Lance said, "This is gonna be good," as he buttoned his fly. "Gassin' that prick is the best idea…"

"Sshh," Danny warned. "We gotta be quiet or we're gonna wind up in the stockade."

They crept to the rear door of the Headquarters enlisted hootch, a small structure at the back of the orderly room. The building was dark and silent.

"Nobody home," Lance announced after peeking inside.

"Probably in the latrine for the nightly buggering," Danny quipped. He had to clap a hand over Lance's mouth to end the giggling fit that followed.

While Lance stood guard outside, Danny crawled into the hootch. Retrieving the sewing kit from his pocket that he had taken from his locker, he used thread to tie the grenade to a rafter above Smitty's bunk. The masking tape label on the footlocker at the foot of the cot confirmed its owner's identity. Danny fastened a length of black thread to the ring of the arming pin. He then ran it down to the springs beneath the bed, pulled it taut, and tied it to the middle of the steel web. He checked to be sure that the cotter pin was amply loosened so that the weight of a body on the mattress would release the handle.

"Fuck you, Private Smith," he whispered.

They resisted the urge to hide and watch the fun, knowing an alibi would be the best defense. They rejoined the party and tried not to giggle at any inappropriate moments.

Soon, the men reluctantly drifted off to bed. Danny and Lance were beginning to wonder if something had gone wrong when they heard, *"Gas! Gas!"*

The entire company stumbled into the street and ran in the direction of the alarm. The men scattered like ants as the cloud hit them.

Danny and Lance, with tears streaming down their cheeks, were the last to run. They waited until they saw Smitty roll out the door, crying and retching as he spun in the mud. Beecher toppled to his knees behind him and vomited his steak dinner all over himself.

"A double!" Danny exclaimed.

"That, my friend, is a fuckin' home run," Lance corrected him. They laughed until they choked.

Fuquette shook his head in the dark. He couldn't help admiring the ballsy kids from Brooklyn who lay giggling like schoolboys in their bunks. There would be hell to pay over this, but it would be worth it. Fuquette had followed the two jokesters, watched them set their trap, and admired his skill when Danny wired the bunk. The man was a natural. He hoped his nerve would not make him reckless. He would teach him all that he could in the time he had remaining.

Daniel Mulvaney was a worthy pupil. Fuquette hoped he would survive long enough to learn.

CHAPTER 33

Charlie Company waited beside the Dong Tam chopper pad
as the allotted lift-off time came and went. Hurry-up-and-
wait was alive and well in the United States Army. Last
night's gas attack on the Headquarters Element and speculation as
to who might be responsible for the deed led the list of topics of
conversation among the officers and men. Threats of dire consequences for the perpetrator had been the extent of retaliation for
the act.

With a new operation about to begin, Captain Arnold had decided to ignore regulations and forego the requisite CID investi-
gation that should have been convened. No one had been seriously injured, and Arnold had doubts about the net result of digging
too deeply into the affair.

If there was animosity among his men, interrogations and, in
all probability, severe punishment for whomever the investigators
deemed culpable, might spread the cancer. That was especially
likely since condemnation would come from outside the company.
Arnold knew that formal military inquiries rarely resulted in un-
solved mysteries. Innocent people could be trampled in the rush
to justice. Besides, the commander inevitably shared the blame. A
good officer cleaned his own soiled linen in private whenever
possible. With a blot like that on his record, he could kiss the War
College goodbye.

To a man, the officers thanked their lucky stars that they had
not been the targets of the vengeful marauder. Arnold suspected
Mulvaney but had no foundation for accusation other than the
fact that the grenade had been planted over Smith's bunk and not
his own. Mulvaney had a grudge against Smith, but Arnold had

no way of knowing if he was alone in that. He wondered if the motive for the gassing was the outrage of one wrongly accused, revenge for righteous indictment, or something of which he was not even aware.

Whatever the reason, he would have to make certain that there would be no escalation. Feuds among the troops were rare but occasional clashes were inevitable. They were, after all, robust, young American males with all of the tendencies that the high levels of testosterone present in their youthful bodies produced. At the same time, there was more brotherhood among these men than you would find anywhere back home. He had seen them bleed on one another and watched their tears fall freely for their buddy's pain, regardless of race, ethnicity, religion or social standing. They would lay down their lives, thinking only of their friends' safety, never of any differences. This was how it should be. These kids were everything good about America. They *were* America. That's why he wanted to stay with them—that and the fact that he wasn't ready to go back to proving himself better than the white officers he would have to compete with in a staff job.

Arnold also realized that, with the passion that drove the men to sacrifice for each other, came the danger of the mob. Paranoia was like hot iron on wax paper. It burned away the film of civilization, quickly exposing the animal reactions just beneath the veneer. Arnold had seen too many examples of that growing up in Philadelphia. He would never forget the white cop who had rousted him one night downtown. He had not so much as jaywalked, but the policeman grabbed him off the street, hauled him in, had him fingerprinted, photographed and held for six hours on suspicion. To this day he did not know what he had been suspected of. When they finally let him make a phone call, he dialed his uncle, an attorney.

He was released half an hour after Uncle Ed showed up. Despite his furious demands for an apology from the arresting officer, it didn't happen. Afterward, over coffee in a local eatery, he had asked his uncle why the police had singled him out.

"Lester," Uncle Ed had said, "remember this: When in doubt, the nigger did it. The gospel according to bigotry."

The army had been the only place Lester Arnold thought he could be judged on merit alone. What was it Tyler said? *We're all OD green here.* Well, not really, but it was as close as it would ever get. Despite that remembrance of wisdom, Tyler's holier-than-thou attitude still rankled. Calling these kids *murderers*. The smart-mouthed rebel would learn when it was his turn. You don't have an army if you question orders. You have anarchy.

Arnold looked at the crimson countenance and swollen eyes of Private Smith. He had taken the gas full in the face. He was lucky not to be blinded. The captain wondered if the man who had done this knew he was using riot gas and not the more potent Combat CS. Smith, although distressed, was fortunate. It could have been much worse. It could, just as easily, have been a frag.

Arnold remembered two black privates in Bearcat who had fought over toothpaste. One had sworn the other had stolen his new tube. Without so much as a "Yo, motherfucker" he had load-ed his M-16 and shot the other boy in the head as he stood naked in the shower.

Arnold shook his head and rubbed his brow with his fingers. The shame he had felt, not so much as their commander, but as a black man, still sickened him. Worse, the satisfaction he had felt last night in knowing that these two *white* boys could equally dis-honor themselves, disgusted him. He'd thought he was better than that. He marveled at how fragile men really are. He was having the kind of maudlin thoughts that he believed sapped a com-mander's strength.

Lester Arnold suddenly realized that he had acquired a buck-etful of unaccustomed doubt. Maybe it was time to take that desk job at Battalion. A man can just take so much. Losing Andy Syzmanski had cost him more than any of the men that had gone before. Maybe Top was the last straw. Maybe it was time to step down. He just couldn't bear the thought of it.

"First lift inbound," Beecher declared, kneeling beside the ra-dio.

"Get 'em ready," Charlie-Six ordered, shaking it off.

The men ran to the pad and dispersed in groups of four to op-posite sides of the landing point of each slick in a prearranged pattern.

The choppers could not ferry the entire company in one lift. There were not enough helicopters available. Three waves would be required to deploy the unit. First Platoon would go on the first lift, to be followed by Second, and then Third. The Fourth was being held back for their fire support role at the new base. The

Headquarters Element would go on the second lift, once the LZ was secured. If the landing zone was hot, it was deemed best to have the commander clear to evaluate before insertion.

Once airborne, First Platoon enjoyed the cool breeze at two-thousand feet, above the effective range of small arms. At the end of a twenty-minute ride, the *Hogs*, as the gunships were known, flying shotgun, prepped the woods nearest the LZ. The flight descended with the door gunners spraying the surrounding area. The method was used to prematurely trigger any ambush lying in wait for the *Eagle Flight*. There was no return fire as the birds flared and set down in a rough diamond in open paddy.

First Platoon trotted to the dikes and deployed to cover the next lift's approach. The second wave landed as uneventfully as the first, with the exception of Morgan, who, in an attempt to demonstrate his ingenuity, attempted to jump onto a dike as his ship skimmed over it. His plan was to get down dry, avoiding the shin-deep water in the paddy. Morgan mistimed his exit and caught his heels on the lip of the earthen barrier. He fell, face first, into the mud with a sizable splash.

"Nine-point-five," Sergeant Cole cackled from the next dike, where the chopper deposited its load, high and dry. "Good style, but you entered the pool at too sharp an angle."

The humor was lost on Danny, whose mind raced with all he had been taught in AIT. He was off the bird and racing for the nearest dike the instant the skids touched the water. He was chagrined at the laughter of his platoon mates walking slowly behind him as he crouched close beside the dike.

"Must be Jesus Christ himself," Paco marveled. "I swear the man walked on the water."

Lieutenant Tyler stood where the chopper had lifted off, beckoning Danny with his forefinger.

"Rule one," Tyler said, as Danny slogged back to meet him. "You follow me, not the other way around."

Nodding, Danny handed him the handset. Tyler checked in with Charlie-Six and got his instructions. The last flight joined the troops on the ground, and the company moved into the woods.

The paddies were wet but firm, and the going was easier than in their last area of operations. Heavy clouds kept the sun from frying them as they walked but the rain held off for the moment.

After sweeping several wood lines and finding nothing but

more paddies on the other side, the company emerged from one line of trees to see two Vietnamese in peasant dress running across the next paddy. Several men had fired on them, although they were at extreme range. Danny questioned the fact that the men shot at these people who did not seem to be armed.

"Running away is tantamount to admitting to be Victor Charles," Tyler advised.

Or being scared, Danny thought. The captain ordered pursuit, and the company sped up. There were three of them when they broke out of the next wood line, and four disappeared into the trees after the next.

"Uh oh," Rodriguez murmured.

"Affirmative," Tyler nodded. "Get Six on the horn, Mulvaney."

"Charlie-Six, Two-Six-Oscar. Two-Six has traffic for you, over."

"What'cha got, Two-Six? Over." Captain Arnold gave no indication that he knew to whom he was speaking when he rogered Danny's call. But he must know, thought Danny.

"I think we're being suckered, Six," Tyler said, taking the phone.

"You're learning, Two-Six. I concur. We'll slow up some and watch for a reception committee. Funny, paper shows a village on the other side of the next green belt. Get on line in the woods and advance to the far side of the green. Do not, repeat, do *not* move into the ville until this element advises you to do so. How copy? Over."

"Roger. Good copy. Two-Six, out."

When they reached the edge of the trees, they saw a broad plain of rice paddies with hootches spread out at wide intervals. A lone Vietnamese stood in front of the nearest. He waited until he was sure he had been spotted before ducking into the thatched hut. He carried an AK-47.

"Sighted confirmed Victor Charley, Six," Tyler drawled into the handset. "Request permission to engage." The men lay down on their bellies without being told.

"Say method of confirmation, Two-Six," the captain called.

"Subject carrying alpha kilo four seven, over."

"Roger that. Fire him up."

"Simms," Tyler ordered, "put a round in that hootch."

The hut was within range of the grenade launcher, but Danny knew it was a long shot.

Wetting his sights with a moistened thumb, like Gary Cooper in Sergeant York, Simms asked, "Door, window, or through the roof?"

"Just hit the fucking hootch, Simms," Tyler said.

Shaking his head and mumbling, "No class, LT," Simms took aim and thumped an HE—high explosive—shell downrange. It exploded with a loud crack inside the hut. Danny craned his neck for a better view. Tyler slapped a hand on top of his helmet and forced him back down.

"There's a bunker in there, remember?" Tyler said. "We probably just gave him one hell of a headache but now he's going to get mad."

A few seconds later they saw the twinkle of a muzzle flash from the shadowy interior. The rounds zipped overhead as they heard the popping of the burst.

"See?" Tyler grinned. "Now, we fuck him up. Simms, fire for effect. Paco, put a long burst into the walls when the first round lands."

The two professionals worked the hootch over. Simms let fly with four grenades in rapid sequence. Each found their mark. The M-60 machine gun ripped thirty rounds from the disintegrating belt, every fifth one a tracer. The hootch caught fire. The VC dove through a side window just before the flaming tinderbox collapsed. He disappeared in the smoke before the platoon could draw a bead on him. Danny found himself wishing Fuquette was with them. Fuquette would have greased the little son-of-a-bitch for sure.

He was startled by his own bloodthirstiness. He was appalled at how easy it was to get caught up in the thrill of the hunt.

Charlie-Six ordered, "Recon by fire and move on in. Two-Six, lead off. One and Three, cover and follow in turn."

Second Platoon peppered the huts within range before jumping off. They reached the edge of the village proper and sought cover while First Platoon advanced on their left. Third mirrored the First on the right. What followed was a running skirmish as VC popped from holes, dikes, and various places of concealment to crack off a few rounds before fading into the woodwork once again.

Danny hustled to keep up with Lieutenant Tyler, who seemed bent on being anywhere his men were involved in any contest. They were spread out due to the configuration of the village. The layout seemed, to Danny, more in keeping with his idea of a farm community than the type of villages he had seen until now.

Through the day, Charlie Company played tag with the elusive Viet Cong. By the afternoon, they had reached the far end of the village and were stopped in a rough horseshoe formation facing a large, thick knot of nippa palm across a broad expanse of dry paddy. The vegetation rose above the surrounding fields like an island. Second had crossed in front of First as they advanced, pursuing two fleet-footed snipers. The Second made up the left prong of the horseshoe when they halted to take stock.

"They could have a battalion in there, sir," Sergeant Cole warned.

"Or they could be running like hell on the other side," Tyler countered.

"And if pigs could fly, they'd get pigeon pussy," Cole spat tobacco juice into the paddy.

Danny giggled and wiped his mouth with his hand to silence himself.

"We having fun yet?" Doc Laffin strode up behind them.

"Mulvaney seems to be enjoying himself, Doc," Tyler said. "Would you mind getting down in the dirt with us mortals? I wouldn't want to get hit by a round with your name on it."

"There is no such animal, sir," Laffin said but obliged and assumed a prone position. "I'll get my pretty green suit all dirty, though, if it will make you happy."

"Doc thinks he's immortal." Cole nudged Danny. "Says they ain't made the bullet with his name on it. That right, Doc?"

"That's affirmative, Sergeant," Laffin nodded.

"You best be careful of the ones marked: To whom it may concern." Cole shook with glee at his own joke.

"Everybody's a comedian." Doc feigned insult. "No wonder us professionals can't find work. Would you believe that *I* would be doing *this* for a living?" Doc asked Danny.

"Were you a professional comedian back in the world, Doc?" Danny asked.

"A disc jockey, actually," Laffin said.

"Really? Where?"

"Fort Wayne, Indiana," Doc answered, "Station TWAT."

Danny was still assimilating the call letters when the men within earshot chorused, "It's kind of fuzzy but you can always get it in."

"Time for some new material, Doc," Tyler advised.

"Not as long as my Uncle Sammy keeps replacing the audience."

"Captain's calling," Danny said, as he heard his call sign on the radio.

Tyler took the call, listened and acknowledged, before saying, "We're going to sweep the nippa patch. Second and Third Squads lead. The rest cover and follow when we reach the trees. Third Platoon will be on our right. Link up as we go in: I don't want to wind up in a fire-fight with our own in there. Let's go!"

They hadn't gotten ten steps into the paddy when the VC opened up.

"Back!" Tyler yelled. The men splashed back to the dikes and dove over them, returning fire as they turned to face the enemy.

"Cease fire!" Tyler bellowed. "They're too far away."

It was true. The nippa palm patch was at maximum effective rifle range. The enemy had opened up prematurely. No one had been hurt. Most of the bullets had impacted in the mud, well short of their targets. Charley wasn't usually this sloppy or free with his ammo. There was still sporadic fire coming from the trees.

"What the fuck?" Tyler asked of Danny, who shrugged in reply, not understanding the source of the officer's consternation.

"Six, Two-Six," Tyler radioed Arnold. "You get the impression that Chuck wants us to hang around here for a bit?"

"Looks that way, doesn't it, Two-Six? I've requested a light fire team to ruin his day. Should be here in one-five mikes," the captain advised. "Hunker down and wait. You've got front-row seats, so I'll turn the orchestra over to you for direction when they come on station. How copy? Over."

"Roger. Good copy. We'll make pretty music when the band gets off the bus. Two-Six, standing by. Out."

Danny found himself smiling along with the rest of the men as they waited for the gunships to arrive. Was he too stupid to be scared, he wondered, or was he beginning to enjoy the action? He was not thrilled with either choice.

Three Huey *Hogs* made up the light fire team. They circled

the nippa once to eyeball the target. The VC reacted with a flurry of automatic fire.

"Brave or stupid, sir?" Rodriguez asked of Tyler.

"Hard to say." Tyler shook his head. "There's a very fine line between the two."

"You got that right," Sergeant Cole said.

Danny saw a huge peace symbol, painted in white, on the belly of the lead ship. The second chopper had *LOVE*, scrawled with the same brush, on its undercarriage. The third was marked KILL, in a similar fashion.

"Peace, love, and kill," Danny read aloud.

"Amen, brother," Rodriguez remarked devoutly.

Danny saw that all eyes were on the woods as the choppers began their runs.

Rockets and machine gun fire from the electric Gatling guns, called mini-guns, mounted to the ships on either side, showered down on the tangle of growth like steel rain. The enemy answered each pass with a burst of parting shots as the gunships pulled out of their dives.

"They've got some good bunkers in there, Charlie-Two-Six," the flight leader called when they had nearly expended their ordnance. "Suggest you call for something with a bit more bang for the buck, over."

"Roger. Thanks for trying," Tyler replied. Switching back to the company frequency, he advised Captain Arnold of the pilot's assessment.

"Roger, I monitored, Two-Six. Sounds good to me. Sit tight while I try to rustle up some fast movers. Six, out," the captain signed off. Not having initiated the call, Arnold was technically not supposed to end it, Danny knew, but he thought it best not to bring it up.

They munched C-rations while they waited for word on the jets. Danny saw two soldiers trying their skill in a dugout canoe in the paddy behind the hootch they were set up adjacent to. They seemed to be having fun. Danny said so.

Tyler threw his empty ration can down in disgust when he saw the men in the boat. "What the fuck do you think this is?" he bellowed. "Six Flags? Get the fuck out of there. *Now!*"

"They're bored, sir. We've been here for hours," Danny said in the men's defense.

"Yeah, I know, but Jesus Christ on a crutch, Charley's right over there and those two clowns are paddling around like they were at summer camp."

"Charlie-Six, this is Tiger Flight, do you read? Over," Danny heard over the bitch box.

"This is Two-Six, Tiger Flight. I will be your Foxtrot Oscar," Tyler responded.

"Roger, Two-Six. We are a flight of four foxtrot-fours. We are zero-two mikes out. Suggest you pop smoke to mark friendly positions as we ingress. Throw smoke now, Two-Six. We'll be there by the time it's out," the fighter pilot predicted.

Danny heard the roar of the big F-4 Phantom fighter-bombers and turned in time to see them swoop low over their positions.

"Wow!" he said, as they climbed into the clouds.

"Two-Six, Tiger Lead. We have two-fifty iron bombs, rockets and twenty mike-mike cannon. Where do you want it?"

Danny thought the flight leader sounded bored, as if he was delivering a pizza.

"Put it on the big nippa patch to our front, Tiger Lead. Charley's in the bush. We are in the village."

"Roger, Two-Six. We'll make our runs from the northwest, if that's all right with you."

"Affirmative. Northwest to southeast will keep us from getting pelted with your brass," Tyler said.

The storm of spent cartridge casings that would fall from the Vulcan Guns mounted in the nose pods of the Phantoms could be as lethal as any bullet.

"That's the idea, Two-Six," Tiger Lead said.

"Smart-ass jet jock," Tyler grumbled without depressing the talk switch.

The four fighters thundered over the trees, spewing death as they came, one at a time, pounding the nippa grove. When the fourth jet peeled off, a single VC ran into the rice paddy to send a burst from his AK at the retreating fighter-bomber.

"*Holy shit!* Did you see that ballsy little fuck?" Sergeant Cole asked Danny.

Danny nodded but said nothing. He was too enthralled with the air strike. The next run ended with the same lone gunman hosing the tail of the departing Phantom.

"Watch your butt, Tiger Lead. That little sucker's in the tail plucking business," Tyler warned.

"He's going *out* of business before I leave here," Tiger Lead swore.

What followed was a black comedy of monster machines versus the lone Cong and his assault rifle. He would time each run to be safe in his bunker—and it had to be a solid one—when the bombs fell, and be back in the open as the attackers climbed out. The VC had a free shot at their tails. They could not roll over and catch him in time.

Frustrated in trying to preserve their ruffled egos the jet pilots switched tactics several times to no avail. They shortened their intervals, split into pairs, rolled out at different angles. Nothing worked.

Luke the Gook, as the men of the Second Platoon dubbed the VC, anticipated their every move.

Finally, Tiger Lead called to say they had expended their ordnance and had to return to base. "I've got one two-hundred-fifty-pounder left, Two-Six. Might as well try one more time," Tiger Lead said.

Maybe he was tired. Maybe he was wounded. No one could say. But Luke's timing was off this last time, and he found himself face to face with an oncoming Phantom. He froze for a moment and did a double-take as he looked from the diving jet to the safety in the trees. The ship lifted as the last bomb tumbled from its wing.

Luke did not have time to duck back in his hole. He stood flat-footed in the paddy and fired at the bomb screaming toward him from on high.

It must have hit him between the eyes. He never flinched. His finger never left the trigger. He disappeared, vaporized in a ball of black smoke.

The fighter pilots cheered their leader. The men of Charlie Company silently said goodbye to a brave little bastard. He was the enemy but he had a pair of stones that would hinder an elephant. Company C respected that.

Tyler spoke to the captain and then said, "We're going to sweep. On your feet."

The Second Platoon looked at the smoking hole that had been the infamous Luke only a short time ago. They looked beyond, to the thick growth he had sprung from. They thought of his friends, waiting there. This might get pretty hairy. No sooner had they stood up than the Viet Cong resumed their fire.

"This is getting ridiculous," Tyler complained as he rolled back over the dike.

Because it was getting too late for another flight of jets to be diverted to assist Charlie Company, Battalion suggested that they dig in and wait for sunrise to continue the air strike.

"That's cool," Rodriguez snarled when the captain had passed the word. "We sit here and wait for ol' Chuck to *di di mau* or to come out and cut a few throats tonight."

Tyler gave him a look that said *Save it*.

Undaunted, Rodriguez added, "You know I'm right, sir. They know exactly where we are, for Pete's sake. At the very least they're gonna drop a few mortar rounds on our asses. Don't the brass ever learn?"

Snatching the handset, Tyler called the captain. "-Six, do you think it might be possible to get Puff on station for the hours of darkness?"

Puff the Magic Dragon was what the men called the C-130 transport planes the Air Force had converted to gunships. Mini-guns lined their fuselages, interspersed with automatic grenade launchers and Vulcan automatic cannon. One even mounted a .105 Howitzer. They could flatten a wood line in seconds, leaving a mulch heap in place of a thriving forest. The men loved them.

"No Puff, Two-Six, but I got us a Spooky." Spooky was a C-47 flare ship with enough fuel for hours of loiter time. "He can circle all night and drop illumes. Keep them from creeping up on us, anyways."

"Like Indian underwear," Cole sneered.

The night passed peacefully except for the moaning of the spent flare canisters that dropped from two-thousand feet.

Lance crawled to Danny in the darkness between flares. "Are these people nuts? We're lit up like daylight out here." His eyes looked like saucers in his black face.

"You'll be fine," Danny assured him. "This guy Tyler knows what he's doing." They both flinched as a flare canister plowed into the mud, thirty feet away. "As long as one of those things doesn't land on your head."

CHAPTER 34

At the proposed site of the battalion's new fire support base, the Viet Cong were preparing the main event. The delaying action in the nippa palm grove was keeping C-Company occupied as planned. Tomorrow's LZ was being painstakingly prepped to maim and kill as many GIs as possible in the initial assault.

Hand grenades were sown about the grassy field like seedlings to burst forth in flowers of death. Most of the bombs were simply primed and laid on their handles. Their own weight would prevent detonation until careless feet disturbed them. Others were trip wired to bushes or saplings. Shallow pits were hastily dug. Some were implanted with punji stakes. The sharpened sticks were fire hardened and dipped in human excrement to guarantee infection.

In others, a second smaller hole was scooped out in the middle of the first. Two short wooden boards, pierced at the outside ends with steel spikes, with a scrap of rubber inner tube tacked to each, were placed over the inner hole. A foot falling into the hole would be pierced at the ankle when the rubber gave way to bring the boards slamming together like a bear trap.

Mats of turf, complete with growing grass, were placed to hide the pits. Five-foot bamboo poles, with sharpened sticks protruding from one end and a perpendicular board nailed to the other, were laid out in tall grass. When a soldier ran across the board, the result would be akin to stepping on the head of a garden rake, with a more lethal outcome. Sun baked balls of mud, bristling with ten-penny nails, were strewn about to pierce frightened bodies as they dove to the ground, seeking cover.

The VC worked from one end of the field to the other, taking great pains to get it right the first time. No one would be able to go back across the meadow once it had been fully mined.

The commander regretted not being able to haul larger charges for his traps. A few artillery rounds or anti-tank mines would have been far more desirable. The speed with which he had been required to assemble his force had precluded more elaborate preparations. This would have to do.

The last man stood in the darkness and whistled. The guards were summoned from the perimeter and the group moved to the woods to set their sixty-one-millimeter mortar tubes. Marksman scrambled to treetops or sought suitable defiles in the earth to afford cover and concealment. Once each man was in place and knew his part, the commander retreated to his command post several hundred meters into the jungle.

This was to be a hit and run attack. They knew their chances against the American fire support were nil. The grassy meadow would yield some nasty surprises for the American infantry when the helicopters landed, and the fusillade of fire that followed would compound the damage. They would give the assault force a bloody nose and disappear.

e/ɔe/ɔ

As the sun rose behind the now semi-permanent cloud cover, the men of Charlie Company greeted the new day with the usual complaints and grumbling. A transistor radio, which someone had accidentally turned up, blared, "Goooooooood morning, Vietnam." Its owner was not swift enough to prevent it being booted into the paddy.

The troops crouched low as they prepared their C-ration breakfasts. Sergeant Cole stood erect to light a cigarette, ignoring Tyler's warning to stay down.

"Chuck is in the next province by now, sir." Cole smirked. A single rifle report put the lie to his statement. "Son of a bitch," he roared, as he sprawled in the mud. "This shit is gettin' flaky, Lieutenant. Let's call in B-Fifty-Twos and erase that patch of weeds."

CHAPTER 35

In the jungle, adjacent to the field where the Americans sought to build their new Camau Peninsula artillery base, Major Xuong was impatient. Although he had been fighting the enemies of Vietnam since he was a boy, he had never gotten over pre-combat jitters. Patience was a characteristic of a good soldier, but in the hours before a fight, his grew thin. He resisted the urge to have his radio operator query the lookouts again. It would not do to let the men see his anxiety. The lookouts were to guard against surprise from unexpected avenues of attack. They would not be needed to warn of the air assault. The American flying machines were as stealthy as stampeding pigs.

The ARVN compound could prove troublesome, but that was unlikely. His snort of derision for his misguided brothers in the South Vietnamese Army brought startled looks from the men in his command post. His baleful glare caused them to resume their duties with exaggerated concentration.

No, thought Xuong, the women in soldier's uniforms in the tiny outpost three kilometers from this spot would not poke their noses out this morning. They would know Xuong's troops were in the area, and know too, from experience, the folly of opposing the Viet Cong. They would mind their own business until the battle was over and make a great show of rushing to the rescue after the slaughter.

Why didn't the American helicopters come? Their information was accurate. Did not the brave fighters in the diversionary force report the successful action to the north? Perhaps they had not disengaged soon enough. Perhaps the Americans were still chasing them.

The sun was brightening the sky more every moment. He wished to engage the enemy before the road opened. The highway was in sight of the meadow. Major Xuong did not wish to involve innocent women and children. The road would be jammed with buses, trucks, and cyclos before long, going to and from Camau. The morning mist would burn off and expose his troops to greater peril as well. His plan had been to inflict swift and terrible punishment on the Americans and then vanish into the jungle. His troops were not equipped or deployed for a protracted fight. The Americans must come soon.

CHAPTER 36

Captain Arnold pounded his fist on the dike he lay behind at the edge of the village. They were still pinned down. He had moved his CP during the night, to the center of the horseshoe but even with binoculars, he could not get a better view of the enemy positions.

"That shit is so thick they could hide a regiment in there. What the hell is so important about this place?"

"It is weird, sir," Beecher mused. "They led us right to what would have been a hell of an ambush and then tipped us off before we got in range. Doesn't make sense."

"Maybe Charley stepped on his weenie. Wouldn't be the first time."

"I don't know, Six. This has all the earmarks of a setup." The radioman suddenly spun his head around to look to their rear. "Maybe they're holding our nose so the knockout punch can come from behind."

The entire command group followed his gaze.

"Nah." Charlie-Six scowled. "If that was their game plan they would have hit us last night. Even the dumbest gook knows what happens in daylight in open country."

"Maybe they just want to hold us up for a while," Smitty offered, "so they can set something up where we're heading."

"That presupposes they know where we're going, Smith," Captain Arnold said. "That would mean a leak in high places."

Or anywhere between those high places and us, Beecher thought. Charley's penetration of the chain of command was legendary, bordering on mystical. The sergeant had learned, however, that second-guessing the CO was not the best way to climb the promotion ladder. He kept his disloyal thought to himself.

"What's the latest on tac-air?" Arnold asked.

"No change." Beecher shook his head. "We're near the bottom of a long list of priority targets. Chuck is keeping the flyboys busy this ayem."

"Well, we can't lay here all day." Arnold turned to Lieutenant Chicarelli. Proffering the binoculars, he said, "Keep an eye on them, Chick. I wish we had your mortars."

Although the mortars and their gunners had been left in Dong Tam, Chicarelli had elected to go along with the insertion to be on hand to direct the engineers' preparation of their firing pits.

Motioning for Beecher to follow, Arnold crawled to the rear of a nearby hootch. He sat with his back to the thatched wall and lit a cigarette. "We're going to have to assault. I don't like it, but it's that or walk away and that's not an option the colonel will sit still for," he said, studying the glowing tip of his cigarette.

Beecher knew it wasn't like his commander to throw an order out for speculation. He wondered about this shift in the captain's style of command. It was obvious that he was waiting for some comment.

"How about artillery, sir? Can't we get some arty?"

"Nothing within range. There's a One-Five-Five battery waiting to go. They're supposed to move into the base we're going to set up, but they're still in Delta Tango. We're weak in this area. That's why they want to build the new base. But right here," he pointed to the ground beneath him, "there wasn't supposed to be anything. It's so wide open it wasn't considered viable for Charley to operate effectively. Further south, where we're headed, is another story. Lots of hidey holes for Chuck to run around in down there." He threw his cigarette butt down in disgust.

"So why the pit stop, sir? Why not go all the way in one jump?"

"Air assets," Arnold said. "We couldn't get enough damned birds laid on to take us all the way yesterday in the time allotted. And if we don't get our asses moving soon, we'll lose them today."

"So why didn't we wait until today?" Beecher asked the next logical question.

"If I knew the answer to that one, I'd be a general and I wouldn't have to answer to the likes of you and me." The captain grinned. "Let's get our people on the horn and give them the bad news."

"Same deal as yesterday," Tyler announced when he handed the handset back to Danny. "Move up on line and sweep. Link up with the Third Platoon as we enter the bush."

"No more bombing?" Sergeant Pomeroy asked.

"Can't get the *zoomies* to come to the party," Tyler answered. "One sniper doesn't rate wasting taxpayers' money today. We can call for gunships if we get stopped." Inserting a fresh magazine in his weapon, he said, "Stay close to me, Danny. If we need to make a call, I don't want to have to look for you. Sergeant Pomeroy, pass the word. You stay on the right flank." Tyler took a deep breath. "Let's get it done."

When both platoons were in position, they stepped off into the paddy. The ground was wet but solid beneath their feet. Scattered puddles lay like mirrors on the flat plain. Danny felt his mouth go dry as they began the long walk across the open ground. Every nerve ending screamed: *This is stupid. Run!*

The men of Charlie Company swallowed their fear and swept toward the enemy's lair. The distance seemed to grow as they walked. A glance behind them confirmed that the safety of the sheltering dikes was becoming a thing of the past. The tangle of vegetation ahead loomed larger. Danny could see that this patch of short palm trees was actually an overgrown mound in the middle of all this flatland. He speculated on its origins. Was it harder soil than the surrounding countryside that had resisted the erosion that leveled the plain? Could it be manmade? Something the industrious Cong had constructed to house a fortress? Was it the remnants of some long dead civilization? The tomb of kings passed into oblivion in antiquity? Was his imagination working overtime to distract his conscious mind from the reckless thing his body was doing? Why doesn't Charley open up and get this over with?

They passed the bomb crater where Luke had lost his tussle with the jets. A bare foot lay at the rim of the hole, the torn and bloody appendage the only evidence of the courageous stand.

"If they're not afraid of that," Danny whispered, "I must be a joke to them." He was amazed to realize they had reached the trees.

"Hold up here," Tyler ordered. "It's too thick to stay on line."

The men crouched at the edge of the brush. After conferring with the captain, both elements found trails and sparse growth to serve as entrances. They moved in by squads.

The heat became palpable as they went deeper into the woods. Humidity, trapped by the dense tangle of foliage, caused sweat to spring from every pore. By the time they had reached the center and formed a loose perimeter, every man was wringing wet.

The lush green of the growth was splattered with gray mud from the churning effects of high explosives. Shattered trees lay strewn across the jungle floor. Ruptured bunkers dotted the landscape. A single enemy soldier lay like a discarded rag doll behind one smashed earthen mound. His bloody back, evidence of the mortal wound in his chest, explained the reason for his silent rifle, still held tightly in his dead hands.

"Cole!" Wendford sang out, "Here's your attempted murderer. Looks like he was too far gone to drag along. Must've left him behind to ruin your day. Hey! That's an SKS. Finders keepers." He stooped to retrieve the souvenir.

"Freeze!" Tyler ordered. "He may be booby trapped. Check for wires, and don't roll him over."

Once they had determined the body's hands and arms were not rigged, they cautiously pried the dead man's fingers from his weapon. Then they tied a length of rope to his wrist. When everyone was clear and under cover, Tyler yanked the rope.

The dead VC was blown to bits by the home-made mine beneath him.

Wendford wet his pants.

When it was plain that they were alone in the nippa, the company backtracked and returned to the village. Captain Arnold radioed that they had a body count of one and blood trails to suggest several possibles. He was told to ready his company for extraction and the next phase of his mission. The men deployed to their pickup formation to await the arrival of the choppers. Enough ships had been scrounged to lift the company in one flight. Charlie-Six was gratified to learn of this, the more men in the first wave of the assault the better. If the LZ was hot, it could seem like a very long time waiting for reinforcements. Still, the landing zone wasn't large enough to drop the entire company at once. The second wave would orbit until the first cleared the field, then follow in close succession.

As they waited, two figures were reported emerging from the trees in the direction they had come the day before. Wary eyes watched two women slowly wend their way along the dikes. More guns were trained on the two bodies, clinging to one another, than would have been required to kill them fifty times over. A rifleman halted them while they were still a safe distance from the nearest position. Radio inquiries were made for instructions.

"Call it, Two-Six," Arnold ordered. "I can't see the subjects from here."

Tyler sent three men to evaluate. They escorted the two women to him.

"The old lady seems to be sick," Rodriquez reported. "I think they want to go home."

A young, attractive Vietnamese woman supported a very old and chronically ill mamasan. Laffin and Fuquette were summoned. Doc, to see if the old woman's suffering might be eased, and Fuquette to help translate. Both men could communicate passably in Vietnamese.

They soon learned that the women were residents of this village. The Viet Cong had driven the people off the night before last. They had returned to find the Americans and had gambled that the fight was over. Mamasan was very ill and would be much more comfortable in her own bed. Their hootch was the one closest to Tyler's group. They were allowed to enter after submitting to a search of their persons and their home.

Laffin conducted an examination and gave the old woman some medicines from his aid bag. The younger woman, her daughter, was extremely grateful. The tears in her eyes evoked tenderness and sympathy from the men. It surprised Danny. He was learning that his brothers-in-arms were not so different from himself. They could be as kind as they could be cruel.

"The old girl's dying," Doc said to Tyler when they had made the woman as comfortable as they could and left them to their privacy. "TB, I think. She won't last much longer."

"We've done all we can," Tyler said. "Let's get ready to go. Slicks are ten mikes out."

The choppers landed in a standard pattern. The men scrambled onto the birds and flew over the nippa patch. Danny sat on the floor with his feet hanging out the door. His left hand gripped the doorframe tightly as he enjoyed the cooling breeze and watched the ground beneath him. The flight did a slow right turn, coming back over the village to proceed in the direction of their next landing zone.

As they soared above the farms, the beauty of this land once again struck Danny. He found he could pick out the hootch the women lived in. Suddenly, he heard the rattle of an M-60 machine gun. The door gunner, sitting beside Lance on his right, said something into his lip mike, laughed, and fired another long burst toward the ground. Danny watched, horrified, as the tracers lanced through the women's hut.

"You son of a bitch!"

Lance had to restrain Danny as he tried to stand to reach the gunner. With one more burst for good measure, the door gunner leaned back to light a smoke, the sign of a veteran in the windy perch he occupied. He noticed Lance struggling with Danny. The look on Danny's face was unmistakable.

"What's his problem?" he yelled above the racket of the shaking machine.

"There were civilians in that hootch," Lance yelled. "Women, man. One of 'em was sick."

"Fuck 'em." the gunner snarled. "Trail says we was taking fire from the ville. *Xin loi,* motherfuckers." He turned to stare at the sky and smoke.

"Maybe they got to the bunker," Lance yelled in Danny's ear.

"Mamasan was too sick," Danny said, "and her daughter wouldn't leave her. They're dead. All they wanted to do was go home and be left alone." He sobbed. "God, I hate this place."

⌘

Major Xuong was seriously considering withdrawing his men now that it was full daylight. The road was open and traffic was heavy. The ARVN, no doubt, had reported the road clear, as they habitually did without venturing from their compound. If a vehicle hit a mine, they would insist it had been command detonated and undetectable. Their utter disregard for the safety of those they were sworn to protect appalled and disgusted the major. He had always tried to avoid civilian casualties. They were the reason for the struggle, were they not?

The beat of helicopter blades interrupted his musings and ended his disquiet. The time for reconsideration was past. They were committed.

℘℘℘

Tyler, in the lead ship, leaned over the pilot's shoulder and yelled, "Where are the gunships?"

"Supposed to meet us," the man answered, looking like some two-legged insect behind the dark green visor on his flight helmet. "That's your new home." He pointed through the windscreen at a grassy field less than a mile ahead. "Can't wait. Not enough fuel. We'll have to go in without 'em."

"What's up, sir?" Danny asked.

"Snafu!" Tyler hollered—the time-honored army slang for *Situation normal, all fucked up.* He called Captain Arnold to report the bad news. The captain had just learned of it, himself.

"No choice," Arnold came back, "we're committed."

Highway Four seemed normal, Tyler noted. No sign of anything amiss. He hoped it would be as peaceful an insertion as the scene suggested.

The Eagle Flight broke into two. Tyler's half descended in landing formation. The rest went to stagger trail right and began to orbit.

As the ships flared to land, the rotor wash flattening the tall grass disturbed several of the primed grenades. Fused with instantaneous detonators, in place of the normal four-second delay, they exploded as soon as the handles were released. The Viet Cong opened fire with machine-guns and rifles. Mortar shells were dropped into tubes as the sounds of battle began. The landing zone became the kill zone.

A grenade blew in front of Tyler's ship. The pilot instinctively yanked back on the collective to abort the landing. An AK round snapped through the windshield and split his helmet like an eggshell. He threw the ship to the right as he died. The aircraft commander, who was also the co-pilot, hauled his control yoke in the opposite direction to correct the attitude and prevent them diving into the ground.

The ship still slewed to the right as the man fought to regain control. The craft on their right was dodging the inferno as well and jigged to the left, rapidly closing the safety zone between aircraft. With whip-like reflexes, the co-pilot of Tyler's ship reacted to the hurtling buzz-saw coming fast on his right. Dropping the nose to gain airspeed, he kicked the rudder to hurry his reversal. He overcorrected. His wingman's main rotor clipped the tip of his tail rotor. The whirling blades bit off two feet of his tail. The severed tail rotor blade broke free of its tenon and spun in a flat arc toward the road like a boomerang. A Vietnamese farmer, momentarily stunned by the abrupt eruption of the attack, stood watching the violent drama unfolding in the sky. He was still watching when the errant tail rotor cut him in half. His torso toppled forward and landed at his feet, spurting blood like some grotesque fountain. His lower body remained standing for several seconds before it keeled over. The damaged chopper went into a wild spin. The co-pilot flattened it out with skillful use of the main rotor but the ship drifted toward the road, still spinning as he wrestled the vibrating controls.

Danny watched the horizon rush by at incredible speed, like a runaway carnival ride. He strained to hang on to the doorframe with his left hand and clutched Lance's shirt with his right to prevent his friend from being pitched into space by centrifugal force. The ship spun crazily, dropping like an elevator. The tail boom slammed into the windshield of a bus, crushing the driver who had time only to begin a scream of panic. The wounded bird bounced down hard on the road, directly in front of and perpendicular to the bus. The right side, Danny's side, faced the enemy gunners.

The bus driver had braked in time to stop short of the plummeting war machine, but the thrashing tail was an unforeseen complication. His passengers—those who survived the impact—bailed out of the vehicle. The whirling main rotor blades cleared the roof of the bus but not the baggage piled high on its top. Chicken cages, suitcases, and parcels of every description were sliced and scrambled by the spinning blades. The other damaged ship, with its clipped main rotor, swung low over the tops of the downed slick and the bus. For a second, Danny saw the belly of the ship descending on them through a blizzard of debris, a dying bird, poised to crush and slash—and then it was gone. The pilot had managed to regain control of his injured craft at the last moment.

The men tumbled from the ship into the road. Danny fell to

his knees on the ground beside the downed chopper. A sharp pain stabbed at the base of his spine. His helmet was gone. He saw the smoke and heard the roar of battle. The rest of the flight was evading the ambush any way it could. Bullets kicked dirt in his face.

Got to get out of here, he thought. He pulled his left foot under him and felt a stabbing pain in his thigh. He looked down, startled to see blood oozing from his leg.

"Motherfuckers!" he shrieked and fired a full magazine at the woods across the field in one burst. He reloaded without thinking and, struggling to his feet, began walking to the co-pilot's door, snapping three round bursts from the hip at the sparkle of muzzle flashes in the trees. Wrenching open the door, he hauled the man in the seat from the ship.

"I'm okay," the man said. "George," he called to his friend in the left seat.

"He's dead," Danny yelled. "Let's get out of here."

The rest of the flight aborted the landing and swung around. They dropped the company on the road, chopping holes with the rotors in the overhanging branches.

Danny heard his buddies' withering fire as they rushed up to support their stricken comrades. He and the airman rolled into the ditch on the far side of the road, behind the crashed chopper, protected from the enemy's fire for the moment. Tyler and the rest of the passengers and crew lay panting beside them.

One of his lieutenants radioed Major Xuong that the enemy was down and organizing a counter attack. Xuong ordered an immediate retreat. Firing on both sides ceased in minutes.

Danny's gaze swept the battlefield. Women and kids were staggering to their feet. Native men saw to their families. Most were crying, many were bleeding, many lay motionless in the mud. Litter was everywhere.

"Jesus, somebody help these poor people," Danny cried.

As he stood up, everything went black.

e/se/s

Soldiers were loading Danny on a medivac helicopter when he regained consciousness. He saw Doc Laffin winding a bandage around a native woman's head, tried to call out to him, and slipped away again as the chopper lifted off. The next thing he knew he was in the Third Surgical Battalion in Dong Tam. Medics met him at the chopper pad and ran with his stretcher into the cool shadows of the emergency ward. He was stripped of his uniform. They cut it off of him and threw it away with no regard for the money he had paid mamasan to sew on his name tag, rank, and insignia. With practiced speed, they checked his vital signs and examined his body. A portable x-ray machine was wheeled in. The doctors, nurses, and medics disappeared from his sight while the machine took pictures. Minutes later, a doctor studied the negative images in a lighted view box on the wall.

"Private..." the radiologist asked.

"Mulvaney, sir. Danny Mulvaney."

"Okay, Danny." The doctor smiled. "Glad to see you're with us again. You're not in bad shape. There's a small piece of steel in your thigh, just under the skin. Your spine isn't permanently damaged, thank God, but you're going to feel like you've been kicked by a mule for a couple of days."

Danny remembered the chopper crash. He'd been flung into the air as the ship dropped, and then slammed on the deck like a hammer when it met the road. His tailbone had taken a terrific wallop. He lay still and listened.

"You've got a nasty bump on your head and a mild concussion. That's why you conked out. I'm afraid you'll have a headache to match the pain in the ass." The doctor's broad, toothy grin attested to his admiration for his own humor.

His helmet had fallen off as he bounced, Danny recalled. He must have hit his head as he was thrown from the ship. He remembered the burning pain in his leg as he'd tried to get up. That must have been when he caught the shrapnel. He also remembered the insane rage with which he had reacted. He was trying to kill every gook in the wood line by himself. His temper was something Danny thought he'd learned to control. It depressed him to realize how completely he could be immersed in a killing frenzy.

They administered a local anesthetic and proceeded to cut the bit of Chicom steel from his leg. When they were finished, what had been a pinhole was a four-inch scar. It looked like a zipper.

The medic, who had performed the surgery—more like butchery in Danny's eyes—held the forceps for Danny to see the thing that had punctured his body. It looked like a ragged BB.

"Want this for a souvenir?"

"Sure. It'll make a great paperweight."

The medic was not impressed by Danny's sarcastic wit. He left the tiny scrap of metal on the bedside table.

Danny threw it at the closing door as the team left. The effort caused his head to pound. He spent the day and the night in the hospital for observation. Awake, he worried how the platoon was making out. Asleep, he dreamed of smoldering children and bloody mamasans.

The next morning Danny awoke to find two medals, a Bronze Star and a Purple Heart, pinned to his pillow. An orderly soon delivered a bland breakfast of oatmeal and Tang.

Danny pointed to the medals, and asked, "What's with these?"

"Must be yours, man."

"I don't think so."

"You're here, so unless you was in a jeep wreck or you slipped in the shower, the Heart is for the wound."

"Oh. But the Bronze Star has to be a mistake."

"Did you do anything brave while you was getting yourself wounded?"

"Not that I know of."

"Somebody musta thought you did." The orderly shrugged and left.

A pretty nurse came by to check his bandage and take his vital signs. Danny inquired again about the Bronze Star. She explained that Colonel Conte had come while Danny slept and pinned the medals to his pillow.

"I still think it's a mistake," he said.

The nurse smiled and, like the orderly, shrugged and left.

He was released shortly thereafter and was glad to leave the halls of pain.

With the medals in the pocket of his powder-blue hospital pajamas, he thumbed a ride back to Charlie Company's area. He'd get it all straightened out and get the Bronze Star to its rightful owner when he felt a bit better.

Danny slipped unnoticed into the Second Platoon hootch and sacked out. At noon, Tony Sedarius shook him awake. His headache had redoubled its intensity.

"Sergeant Jellicks wants your young ass in the orderly room, aysap," Sedarius told him. "Get into fatigues and quick march on down there if you know what's good for you."

Danny wasn't sure if Tony was his latest bad dream. He was tempted to tell Sedarius to piss off but decided to play it safe. Jellicks struck him as a mean tempered cuss. He dressed slowly and strolled to the small office. Jellicks was sitting behind the first sergeant's desk when Danny entered.

"You want to see me, Sarge?" Danny asked in a friendly tone.

"More than Bob Hope," the motor sergeant sneered. "I been waiting to get my hands on you, Sleeping Beauty." Danny was taken aback by the menace in the sergeant's tone. "Git your sorry ass over to the ammo bunker and start filling sandbags," Jellicks ordered. "I want that entire structure covered in bags, and the roof, too." He threw an entrenching tool to Danny, which the younger man caught out of reflex.

"I—I'm on light duty, Sarge. I'm supposed to rest."

"Seems that's all you think you're supposed to do," Jellicks snarled. "This *is* light duty, goldbrick. If you want to see what *hard* duty is, gimme an excuse."

Danny followed orders and spent the rest of the day filling and stacking the green woven bags. Sedarius took pity on him and brought him a bush hat and a canteen filled with water. Dizzy from the heat and the work, Danny gratefully accepted the gifts, asking, "What's he so pissed at me for?"

"You got Top killed," Tony said, as he walked away.

Danny was so hurt and angry he had to fight back tears. He labored until darkness made it impossible to continue and then staggered, exhausted, to his bunk, where he fell asleep in his filthy clothes.

In the morning, he showered and dressed in a clean uniform, planning to confront Sergeant Jellicks after breakfast. Sedarius found him in the mess hall and told him he was assigned to burn shit. Danny demanded to speak to his tormentor.

"Sarge left at first light on a convoy to bring some shit to the new fire base," Tony told him. "Jellicks is Acting First Shirt until Battalion gets us a new one. You buck him, he'll throw your ass in the stockade. Top was his best friend. He's not a forgiving man."

"I had nothing to do with Top getting killed, Tony."

"Not what we heard," Sedarius said. "Best get over to the shitter. I mean it."

☙☙☙

Greasy black smoke billowed from the pots, fouling the air with putrid plumes. Danny twisted his neck to wipe the slick sweat from his soot-smeared brow with his rolled-up sleeve. The heat of the flames crackling in the blackened tubs combined with the hammering tropical sun made his head swim.

With a steel engineering stake, he stirred the stinking mess in the cut down oil drum. The contents bubbled and hissed beneath the roaring flames licking the lip of the pot. Muscles bunched, back painfully bent, head low to dodge the smoke, Danny twisted the steel stake, pulling it with both hands to stir the putrid sludge.

Holding his breath to escape the stench he felt sure would make pigs vomit, he forced the stake another turn and, dropping the shaft, back-pedaled several steps before collapsing to the earth. The impact sent a stab of pain lancing up his spine. Sitting on the moist ground, he wiped his hands on his fatigues to rid himself of the vile corruption in his palms. Pulling his knees into the crook of his arms, he sat staring into the burgeoning smoke.

He hungered for a cigarette. The pack was buttoned in his left breast pocket. He would have to touch one with his filthy hands to put it in his mouth. The thought revolted him. Still, he craved a smoke. With the delicacy of microsurgery, he unbuttoned the flap, pulled the pack from its resting place and shook one cigarette out until he could withdraw it with his lips. Replacing the pack, he snapped his lighter open and spun the wheel to ignite the wick. Smoke filled his lungs. He exhaled with an, "Aah."

Hate radiated from his eyes as he stared at the blazing tubs before him. What had he done to deserve this miserable detail? Burning shit was a job for new guys and screw-ups. Danny was a veteran now, despite his short time in-country. His mind clouded with rage at the injustice of it all.

His head still throbbed and his back ached. He could sit, but with care. Danny thought of the letters still unopened on his bunk that had piled up while the army tried to track his movements these past few days. He had planned to read and answer them after he had cleared the air with Jellicks. He could not think of soiling them with the filth on his hands and he knew the black fury that pounded in his temples could not be suppressed. He would not write to those he loved in such a mood. He must finish this, once and for all.

He watched the bare boards of the shitter dance in the shimmering heat. The smoldering pots were going out again. He'd have to splash more diesel fuel into them and stir it in before igniting the slop. The stuff resisted ignition as if it had the will to live.

With a sigh of resignation, he hauled himself to his feet and stooped for the five-gallon can, but found it empty. He trudged across the muddy ground to the fuel tanker, parked out of harm's way. He grabbed the nozzle gun and yanked the hose until it spun from the reel at the back of the truck. As he depressed the trigger and watched the amber fluid bubble into the can, he glanced back at the outhouse. His mind focused all of his anger on that dirty wooden box of a building.

"They made poor Leon do this," he whispered, "the rotten bastards. Someone should teach them a lesson."

He looked from the building to the tank truck and smiled.

Danny dragged the hose with him as he walked back to the shitter. He dragged the still smoking pots to the rear of the building, propped the trap door at the bottom of the building with a piece of two-by-four, and manhandled the three drums into their slots beneath the holes in the plywood seat. He then ran inside with the fuel can and poured equal amounts of diesel oil into each of the tubs.

Back outside, he aimed the gun at the back of the building and sprayed gallons of oil over the back wall. He snapped open his Zippo and started to hold a rag over the flame but snapped the lighter shut when he considered the fuel stains on his uniform and his proximity to the structure.

"Don't want to end up like a Buddhist Monk," Danny cautioned himself.

With the engineering stake, he scratched out a furrow in the earth and made a trench halfway back to the truck. Into this, he pumped more diesel fuel from the hose. The soil was damp, so little fuel was absorbed. It floated on the wet ground.

Whistling, Danny cranked the hose back onto its reel. He lit a cigarette and then the rag, held at arm's length, which he tossed into the little ditch. The diesel fuel caught with a *whump*.

A stream of fire raced unerringly to its target. It ran up the back and spread to the roof. The entire structure was engulfed in flames in seconds and reduced to ashes before Danny had smoked half of his cigarette. He strolled through the small crowd of excited soldiers who came running to watch the spectacular blaze.

He was stepping out of his filthy clothing when Sedarius ran into the barracks, wide eyed and spluttering, "What did you *do*, you crazy son of a bitch?"

"Nothin'," Danny assured him. "It was an accident." He stepped to within inches of the clerk. "Just like the one you're going to have if you don't get the fuck out of my face."

Sedarius left without another word.

CHAPTER 37

Tyler swished his boots in the brown water of a huge puddle at the side of the road. There was no sense in trying to keep them dry. At best he could dislodge some of the heavy mud that clung to them like cement. He took a swig from his canteen and wiped his brow with his shirtsleeve.

Across the road, the new base was beginning to take shape. Bulldozers and road graders rumbled and squeaked as they pushed the mud into shape. The engineer unit from Cantho had come barreling down the road scant hours from the time C-Company had signaled that the field was secure. EOD— Explosive Ordinance Disposal—had cleared the area of the remaining booby traps.

The VC had melted into the forest like so many ghosts. The only sign remaining of their presence was the carnage and destruction they had inflicted. The second half of the company had been landed on the road, shielded by the trees from the small arms fire that erupted from the woods. After the fight, they had swept the edge of the forest for two hours and found nothing but spent brass. The still-unnamed base had been christened in blood. A short road in and an earthen berm around the whole thing had been completed before dark. C-Company had spent the first night inside their new camp huddling in shallow foxholes that rapidly filled with water from the incessant rain.

Charley had lobbed four mortar rounds into the camp two hours before sunup this morning. Pomeroy caught a shard in the back and was dusted off.

Laffin said the wound was more painful than serious and the sergeant should be back in a week or so.

Tyler wondered how Danny was doing. He hoped the decorations he had put him in for had been approved.

The convoy arrived as Tyler sat resting his aching body. He roused some of his men to lend a hand with the unloading. As always, they complained.

"Come on," he chided them, "that shit on those trucks is to build nice solid bunkers. The sooner we get it unloaded, the sooner our engineer friends can build us safe, dry places to sleep. Let's go, people."

Tyler grabbed Rodriguez's shoulder as the man tried to slip by him. "Stay out of the garbage dump, Rodriguez. Your dick is gonna fall off if you keep screwing them mangy whores."

The handsome young soldier leered. "No sweat, sir. Us Latino lovers can grow a new one."

"Really? Let's see if you can use your amazing appendage to lift some of that lumber." Tyler patted the man on the back. "Come on, Second, we're burnin' daylight."

The quiet field of two days before had been transformed into a hive of feverish activity. Tyler was proud of the engineers who worked tirelessly to construct their new base. With luck, they would sleep dry tonight with sandbagged roofs and beams above them to shield them from the deadlier things that fell from the sky.

CHAPTER 38

Tran heard the news of the American incursion onto his doorstep with mixed emotions. He found it disconcerting to know that the enemy was establishing a strongpoint so close to his tiny encampment. At the same time, it would bring his prey within his grasp. This infant fire support base might be a blessing in disguise. The VC major seemed to know his business. His information was up to date and relevant. The arms caches he boasted of should prove ample to meet the needs of his men. Major Xuong's plans for the enemy, however, might get in Tran's way. The type of pressure he was planning to exert could easily bring the Americans down on them in force. This was something Tran was not equipped to handle.

His plan was to strike at small units and unwary rear area troops, to spirit them away in the night, spreading terror instead of determined response. He would have to dissuade the major from doing anything reckless. It would take skillful guidance. The major was not a man to be easily duped. He must be convinced he was acting in his own best interests.

Tran's camp was nearly complete. He would have liked to show it off to the VC commander but he had convinced the man that secrecy was of the utmost importance in his mission. He would continue to meet with him at prearranged times, in this, the site of the originally planned camp.

When the major and his security team arrived, Tran asked him if he knew the whereabouts of his sister's unit.

"The Three-Oh-Second Battalion has been withdrawn to Cambodia for rest and rearming."

"My sister is with them," Tran said. "I had hoped to see her while I was in the South."

"Disappointing, I am sure, but at least you know she is well."

CHAPTER 39

In Dong Tam, Danny stacked his mail in chronological order and sipped a cold beer in the cool interior of the Artillery Club. A letter without a stamp, marked *In Country* in the upper right-hand corner, caught his eye. PFC G. Sebastionelli topped the return address. He tore it open and read.

Danny boy,
Guess you've been wondering what happened to your old buddy since my last. Mucho shit, my friend. As you can see from the return address, I am now in the land of the little people. I finished Commo School and got shipped over here right after. I didn't get the usual thirty days leave, just two weeks. It seems I lost track of time and was a little late reporting for school. I don't know what the big deal was. What's a couple of weeks here and there? But, as I'm sure you know, the army's got no sense of humor, so they deducted my bad time from my leave and were kind enough to send two MPs to escort me to the plane.
Too bad we missed each other back home. I stopped by to say hey to your mom. She writes to me regular. Guess who was visiting when I dropped in? I got to hand it to you, that Amanda is some chick. Now I know why you were so strung out. Hang on to this one, Daniel, or at the very least, let your old pal know when you're done with her. Just kidding.
Anyhoo, you'll never guess what happened to me. I get over here expecting to get some dick job as a teletype operator or something, and I get sent to a Green Beret compound way the hell up north. It seems they needed a skilled commo man so I got drafted into the green beanies. No shit. The CO here is a Gung-

*Ho son of a bitch but a cool dude. He tells me he ain't having no
"legs" in his outfit. I gotta be Airborne qualified if I'm going to
hang with his people. I had to make five parachute jumps, from a
helicopter no less. I got my jump wings and a green beanie to
boot. I'm probably the only OJT Green Beret in the war. Our
camp is up on top of a mountain in spitting distance from Laos.
Camp A-666, The Devil's Own. That's us. I was scared shitless at
first, but I'm getting the hang of it now. What's happenin' in the
Infantry? Write soon.*

Gino (Airborne)

"Holy shit!" Danny said.

He did not know whether to be pleased or dismayed for his
friend. His mother mentioned Gino in her latest letters but she
made no reference to his status beyond the fact that he had joined
the army and that she hoped he was straightening himself out.
Maybe Gino left things out of his letters too, like stolen cars and
two weeks AWOL. He wondered how long his mom's indefati-
gable optimism would hold up if she had all the facts.

Amanda's letters depressed Danny. He was at a loss to explain
why. Perhaps it was because he missed her so, or maybe it was
because he was drinking and feeling sorry for himself. He was
only aware that her letters did not lift him up as they had in the
past.

He read that the apartment hunt had gone into full swing. She
wrote of many things that would have interested him greatly a
few short months ago. They seemed trivial now.

Amanda must never know what went on here. She must never
know of the brutality and bitter hatred. She must never know of
his ability to sink into the mire of man's most evil deeds. She
must never see his dark side.

Danny drank the day away. The master at arms left him alone.
He had no reason to intrude. The kid was reading his mail, in obvious pain, and hurting no one.

Danny staggered back to the barracks well after dark and very
drunk. Sergeant Jellicks was waiting for him. Danny was too
soused to be afraid. He was beyond caring.

"Fuckin' beautiful," Danny slurred, swaying in the doorway.
"The perfect end to a perfect day."

"I had a long talk with Lieutenant Tyler today," Jellicks said.

His chest swelled as he took in a deep breath. "I guess I owe you an apology."

"No sweat, Sarge." Danny entered the barracks like a man walking on a pitching deck. "I owe you a shitter." He then collapsed, unconscious, across his bunk.

Jellicks covered Danny with a poncho liner. "I'll make it up to you, kid."

℮ᴧℰᴧ

Danny regained consciousness about mid-morning the next day. He found his head did not fall off when he raised it from the musty pillow, but he wasn't sure if this was blessing or curse. Sitting up, he decided on the latter. His mouth tasted like the pots he had stirred yesterday. That thought brought a wave of anguish. Danny didn't feel capable of dealing with the consequences of his actions in his present state. Jellicks was going to chew him up and spit him out. Vaguely, he thought he recalled having seen the grumpy old soldier last night, but Danny was still alive and not in jail so he dismissed the memory of Jellicks as a nightmare. He vowed to never drink alcohol again.

Danny didn't have the strength to venture outside until noon when his bursting bladder forced the issue. He barely made it to the piss tube. Danny was almost finished when he heard Sedarius rasp, "Jellicks wants to see you, Mulvaney."

Danny squinted through bloodshot, tear-filled eyes at the company clerk, who seemed to be evaluating Danny's equipment.

"What's the matter, Tony? Never seen one of these before?"

Sedarius left without retort. *At least*, Danny thought, *I've put the fear of God into that little shit.* His anger was returning. Buttoning his fly, he resigned himself to get this over with. He would go to jail if necessary, but first he would have his say.

Jellicks nodded to a chair in front of his desk when Danny entered the Orderly Room. Danny sat and leveled a sullen stare at the acting first sergeant.

"Coffee?" Jellicks asked.

Surprised, but unable to resist the tantalizing aroma, Danny nodded. Jellicks stirred in powdered cream and sugar after he inquired of Danny's preference.

The flavor of the strong brew lacked in actuality of Danny's expectations and caused sweat to break out on his forehead.

"Hair of the dog?" Jellicks proffered a pint of bourbon.

Danny shook his head emphatically. The sergeant dropped the bottle in a drawer and slammed it shut.

"Get yourself cleaned up, soldier," the master sergeant told him. "Clean fatigues, helmet, pistol belt, your weapon, and ammo. Shine up them boots. Pack a grip with whatever you'll need for one night. Bring your Class-As. You and me are taking a little trip."

"If I'm going to be court martialed, Sergeant Jellicks, there're some things I'd like to say first."

"You're going to Saigon with me to escort a prisoner back here. Nobody said anything about a court martial. Get started, soldier. Chopper leaves at sixteen-hundred. Meet me here at fifteen-thirty. Dismissed."

As Danny walked, dazed, across the company area, he saw a five-ton wrecker lowering a new outhouse, a replica of the one he had torched, onto the concrete pad that had supported the original.

"Prefab," Sedarius said from behind him. "Damn things burn up so often the engineers started stocking 'em."

෬෨෬෨

In the jeep, as Jellicks drove to the airstrip, he said to Danny, "Andy Syzmanski was the finest man and the best soldier I ever knew. He was also a good friend. A man's judgment can get clouded when he loses a friend like that." The sergeant's eyes never left the road as he spoke.

Danny sensed this was as close to an apology as the man knew how to give, so he said nothing, and waited for Jellicks to continue.

"This prisoner we're going to pick up. Name's Kowalski, *Andy* Kowalski. Named after his uncle." He looked at Danny to see if the young man had made the connection.

"Top? This guy's Top's nephew?"

"That's a rodge." Jellicks nodded. "And he's as screwed up as his uncle was squared away." He shook his head. "Now this ain't common knowledge around the company, mind you. You keep this to yourself, hear?"

Danny nodded his understanding.

"Andy didn't want no one saying he was playing favorites with his kin. We put young Andy in the motor pool so's I could keep an eye on him. His ma begged her brother to keep him out of combat. Went against Andy's grain to interfere even that much, but it being his sister's kid and all...well, what could he do? We made him a truck driver. Not as dangerous as the line, but not as safe as the Orderly Room, either. Sort of a compromise, you might say."

Danny could imagine the guilt a man like Top, a man who lived the code of Duty, Honor, Country, had carried around at this breach of his own code of ethics. *Blood is thicker than water*, Danny mused.

"Young Andy went on R and R," Jellicks was saying. "No special privilege, he was due. Picked Taipei. He was due back the day his uncle died. He's been AWOL ever since. We've been covering it up on the morning report. Figured he'd turn up before long. MPs bagged him coming into Ton San Nhut last night. I pulled some strings, called in a few favors. They're holding him for us. No charges will be filed if we collect him. I owe it to Top. If it was up to me, I'd shoot the son-of-a-bitch."

"How'd you know he'd come back?"

"Where's he gonna go?" Jellicks snickered. "He's got no passport and no way to get enough money to bribe anybody. If he wants to live the rest of his life in the hills of Taiwan, he can, s'long as he steers clear of the government. They frown on deserters. Ours *and* theirs. Only plane he can get on is the one that brings him right back here. Kowalski's smart enough to know he'd get his throat cut on a ship. Sooner or later he's got to come back. He probably figures his uncle will bail him out, and the worst he can do is some crumby details until Top cools down."

"He doesn't know?"

"Nope." Jellicks sighed. "I've got to tell him."

ぐっぐつ

Danny gripped his weapon tightly on the ride to Saigon. He wasn't as comfortable in helicopters as he once had been. They checked into the Caravelle Hotel upon their arrival. Jellicks refused Danny's offer to share the expenses.

"Master sergeants do a little better in the payroll department."

Jellicks smiled. "It's the least I can do. Tonight, Mulvaney, you and me are going to give ourselves a pass 'cause tomorrow I gotta do something I dread."

Danny wondered what had caused the change in Jellicks's attitude. What had Tyler said to him?

They shared a room, and Jellicks helped Danny make his khaki dress uniform presentable. The Caravelle was as close to class as the Vietnamese could get, Jellicks explained.

"If you put on the feed bag here," he said, "you dress for the occasion."

There was little that could be done with the wrinkles in the stiff cotton uniform, but he showed Danny how to shine his brass with a piece of nylon stocking and how to wear the ribbons he had been issued. Jellicks insisted Danny wear the Purple Heart and the Bronze Star ribbons above the three ribbons every soldier in Vietnam received as symbols of his service. Danny had brought both of his new medals along in the hope that Jellicks would know how to trace the Bronze Star's rightful owner.

The master sergeant convinced Danny that the medal was his. Lieutenant Tyler had put him in for it for his action at the LZ. Danny could not imagine why.

They went downstairs for dinner and drinks in the bar. The Caravelle had seen better days. It had once been a magnificent edifice, a landmark in this city, the Paris of the Orient. Now it was run down, bordering on seedy. Even this grand old dame of a hotel was tired of war.

The clientele was on a loftier plane than that to which Danny was accustomed. He saw more brass than he thought existed, and all in one room. He was also amazed at the profusion of civilians from many nations. Everyone seemed to be having such a good time, it was hard to remember that they were in a country racked by war. Most astonishing were the women. Beautiful women— Asian, European, and even American women—ate, drank, and laughed while men doted on them. The civilians all seemed well-to-do or at least comfortable among the rich and powerful. Danny felt distinctly out of place. He was glad to be here, rather than out in the mud with his platoon, but he felt a nagging guilt.

Jellicks entertained Danny with tales of daring-do and humorous anecdotes of his adventures during his career. He had been a soldier since "that Kraut paper-hanger invaded Poland" as he put it, insisting that this was the German's first mistake. He had fought in Europe in that one, Korea in the next, and was finishing his thirty years here, in Vietnam. "It's all different now." He sighed. "This used to be a great life for a man. Not anymore." He shook his head. It bobbed drunkenly. "Too many asses to kiss. Too many tickets to punch. Nah! It ain't what it used to be. I'm glad I'm gettin' out."

They drank in silence for a time, each man weighing the master sergeant's words—one contemplating his future, the other mourning the loss of his past.

Danny helped Jellicks up to bed when the crowd in the bar grew thin. He considered going back down for a nightcap when the old soldier was snoring. Instead, he cracked open the bottle of Jack Daniels Jellicks had left on the night-stand. Danny sat up in bed and alternated between sips of the whiskey and drags on a cigarette. He chuckled as he remembered his temperance pledge of the morning. "Didn't stay on that wagon for long, did I? Following in my old man's footsteps."

As his eyelids grew heavy, Amanda came to mind. *What would she think of me if she saw me now? Maybe she'd be better off without me.* He put out his cigarette and curled up on the frayed sheets. A B-40 rocket crashed into a street four blocks away.

"Fuck you, Charley. Missed me," he mumbled as he dozed off.

CHAPTER 40

Major Xuong read his after-action report, signed it, and gave it to a runner. One helicopter destroyed, another damaged, several enemy soldiers wounded, and at least one killed, with no losses among his VC troops. Not a bad tally. The few minor wounds his men had sustained would not limit his effectiveness in any way, and the civilian casualties did not diminish the success of the action. The VC propagandists would point out that no innocent Vietnamese would have come to harm had it not been for the imperialists sticking their long noses where they did not belong.

The new American base, he knew, would make operating more difficult for his forces. He must maintain pressure on them to prevent them from becoming too well established. How to do it was his immediate problem. Surprise was the best weapon the guerrilla had: surprise and overwhelming power. He could muster the manpower to attack the American camp. Three-to-one was the ratio needed to assault a fortified emplacement. But with the American aerial bombardment and reinforcement capability, that time-tested equation wasn't sound. Even if he hit them now, before they were fully manned and ready, he would lose more men than victory was worth. The Tet Offensive had bled his Main Force units badly.

Now was not the time to engage the Americans in large numbers. If he did drive them out they would be back, and in greater strength. He had to draw them out, bleed them, and withdraw before they could organize a determined response. Advance intelligence had led to the trap in the meadow. He might wait a long time for such valuable information to fall into his hands again.

The Americans were not stupid. They would know that such a carefully laid ambush was not coincidental. For a time, they would be doubly watchful of Vietnamese with access to sensitive data. It would not be wise to risk such carefully placed operatives. Patience was the key.

Still, the temptation to repeat such a bold stroke was tantalizing, and intelligence was a double-edged blade. If the seeds were carefully sown, the right words to known American sympathizers could draw the hunters to become the hunted yet again. This time he would choose a location more to his liking. If he acted quickly, before the Americans had time to tighten their security, he just might compound the damage at the meadow.

Summoning his element leaders, he spread his maps on the ground to study them while he awaited his officers' assemblage. This had to be planned carefully. The bait must not smell so strongly that it would bring the enemy in strength. He must attract a reconnaissance force, not an invasion.

CHAPTER 41

Captain Arnold toured the completed emplacements at the new fire support base with Colonel Conte, pointing out sites of proposed positions and fortifications.

"It's coming along fine, Les," the colonel complimented him. "You're doing a great job."

"Thank you, sir, but we're still too vulnerable here. We need more concertina wire, engineering stakes, PSP, and sandbags. I could use a shitload of Claymores, drums of Foogas, some beehive rounds for the one-o-sixes and nineties. A couple more fifties would be nice. We need enough ammo to blow a few mad-minutes, too. Nothing bolsters the men's confidence more than a demonstration of their own firepower." Pointing over the berm, he went on. "I want the engineers to clear the kill zone back another hundred meters, at least. Most of all, I need more men. This is supposed to be a battalion-sized base when it's completed, and we're still just a company. As it grows, we get thinner along the perimeter. We have to patrol more aggressively to keep the gooks off our backs. I've only got three platoons that are mobile. The weapons platoon is totally occupied with its support role."

"I know all that, Les." The colonel nodded emphatically. He did not like to be reminded that this venture had been begun in half-measure. "The rest of the battalion is still tied up on the river. Our relief unit was badly mauled just when they were due to move into the AO. I simply cannot disengage your sister companies to come trotting on down here just yet."

"Then get me some replacements," Arnold pleaded. "My men are tired, Colonel. They're putting in long hours helping to build this frontier town during the day, and going for midnight strolls in the woods afterward. Tired men make mistakes. Mistakes in this business get people killed, and I don't have to remind you of that."

Colonel Conte said, "I'll see what I can do."

"Please, sir. These kids deserve a chance."

Conte left Captain Arnold with a promise to get on it, first thing. The captain closed his eyes and tucked his chin into his shirt to avoid the debris whipped up as the colonel's chopper lifted off.

"Got two new men, Six," Lieutenant Chicarelli said, and fell into step with his commander as he walked back from the chopper pad. "Just got off the convoy."

Chick was acting as Executive Officer and thereby second-in-command at the base. His promotion to First Lieutenant had made him the obvious choice. Arnold would have assigned him the job in any case, but the rank made it easier to avoid the jealousy of his fellow officers.

"Who's light?"

"Who isn't?" Chicarelli quipped. Arnold's frown erased his grin. "Tom's lost his RTO and platoon sergeant," he continued. "He's got a few near-crippled with foot problems and skin diseases, but so does everybody else. Marv's got two on R and R and one on emergency leave. Everybody's under strength to begin with."

"Okay, okay. I know the situation. Give one to Tom and one to Marv. Big Six promised me a flock of them, soonest. Let's hope he delivers."

"You want to meet them?"

"No, but it's expected. Bring them to the CP."

Privates First Class Verde and Blalock were unremarkable as far as new men went. If their new fatigues did not give them away as FNGs, their puzzled expressions did. Arnold sleep-walked through his perfunctory greeting and wished them luck. He could see, by their expressions, that both of them felt that if they'd had any, they would be somewhere else.

એએએ

In his bunker, Tyler worked at his makeshift ammo box desk, composing a letter to his mother, a chore he did not enjoy, but felt honor-bound to accomplish at least once a week. His letters to his dad were easier. One page of mindless pap closely resembling the one to his mom, the rest devoted to the truth—an anthology of his experiences and observations. He knew he did not need to explain the reason for the duality in his correspondence to his dad. His father would read only the first page to his mom, keeping up the pretense that they had no secrets from her. They had started this charade when he was in college and in need of fatherly advice regarding certain women. He saw no reason to change now.

He looked up from his writing to find a brooding soldier standing before him. Sergeant Cole stepped in behind him and elbowed the man aside.

"Private First Class Verde, Ezekiel J," Cole drawled. "XO says to give him a home."

"I'll bet they call you Zeke." Tyler smiled, extending his hand. "Welcome to Second Platoon."

The man shook Tyler's hand as if he had just been introduced to the custom and was not particularly enamored of it. He did not return the smile.

"Where you from?" Tyler tried to put the man at ease.

"Utah," Verde mumbled.

"I'm a Mississippi boy, m'self."

The blank look Tyler got in return caused him to abandon any overture of welcome. Something in the new man's eyes told him to be personally watchful with this one. The cornered prey demeanor most new men seemed to share was missing. This one was either fearless or exceptionally stupid and, to Tyler, the two were synonymous.

"You'll be my RTO, Private Verde, until my regular operator gets back. Sergeant Cole will get you squared away." Tyler sat and returned to his letter.

Verde turned to go and turned back, a question on his face.

Tyler felt the man's eyes on him and looked up to see him standing half-in and half-out of the bunker. He squinted, and said, "What is it, soldier?"

"What's a…"

"An RTO?" Tyler guessed.

Verde nodded.

Tyler sighed. "Didn't you have infantry training? Basic? AIT?"

"Yessuh. Basic twice."

Cole said, "A goddamn recycle." He shook his head and waited for the lieutenant to change his order.

"At ease, Sergeant Cole," Tyler said. "Give this man a refresher course in radio telephone operation and procedures. Private Verde, you will pay *strict* attention to the sergeant's instruction. I'll expect you to be standing tall and ready to rock and roll when next we meet."

Verde glowered at Tyler. He nodded after a moment and left.

Cole said, "Sir, I—"

Tyler cut him off. "It's just until Mulvaney comes back, Sergeant. Get it done."

"Couldn't we make him a rifleman and give one of the older guys the radio, sir?"

"We could, but *we* don't run this platoon, Sergeant, *I* do."

"You're the boss." Cole sighed and followed the new man outside.

Tyler almost called him back but decided to go with his first instinct. Picking up his pen, he said, "Dear Mother, if the VC don't get me, the FNGs will." He wrote, instead, of the many similarities apparent to the Mekong and the Mississippi Rivers.

CHAPTER 42

Tran explained the exercise he had in mind to his one officer and four non-coms. Half of the force would leave the now completed camp to march through the forest. They would follow a predetermined route to the edge of the heaviest jungle, timing their arrival at the outskirts to coincide with nightfall. They would then proceed to reconnoiter an area two kilometers beyond the U Minh. Contact with the enemy was to be avoided unless they ran across a target too tempting to ignore. Tran knew the value of first blood in this alien environment, but he had doubts about his men's readiness. They had been stationary for too long. He knew he must refocus their energies in stages. Even champion martial artists train for a match. His troops were lean and fit but out of shape mentally. He must tune their reflexes before combat.

"Do not let impatience interfere with good judgment, comrades," he warned. "We have been occupied with organization and defense for too long. The skills we worked so hard to sharpen have dulled, whether we admit it or not. This is a training mission. We will lay up in this area, here," he pointed to the map, "for a day, and then circle back to the camp when we are once again cloaked in darkness. Those left behind will follow a similar plan when we return, but in a different area. Only when I am certain that we are at peak performance will we begin operations in earnest. I will lead both patrols."

CHAPTER 43

Andy Kowalski did not look at all the way Danny had pictured him. From the master sergeant's derogatory comments, he had envisioned a weasel-like spoiled brat. Kowalski was a strapping young man of six-foot-two. His pale face and puffy eyelids attested to the hard drinking he had done of late, but he was still a handsome specimen. Bloodshot though they were, there was intelligence and a mischievous twinkle in his pale green eyes. A shock of thick black hair kept falling across his brow. He swept it back absently, an innocent, almost boyish gesture.

The military police seemed genuinely fond of their prisoner. They went so far as to wish him luck and shake his hand when they released him into Jellicks's custody.

"Master Sergeant Jellicks," Kowalski beamed. "My favorite lifer. How the hell are you?"

"Can it," Jellicks snarled, "before I bust you in the mouth."

They walked through the gate in the chain link fence as they left the Provost Marshal's compound. In the street, they hailed a cab to take them back to the hotel where they had left their gear in the concierge office under lock and key.

As the tiny white and blue Citroen cab bobbed and weaved through the Saigon madness—laughingly referred to as traffic—Kowalski asked Jellicks, "Aren't you going to ask me where I've been? And aren't you going to introduce me to your bodyguard here?" He indicated Danny, sitting beside him in the cramped back seat, with a jerk of his head.

Jellicks turned in his seat beside the driver and, fixing Kowalski with a scowl, said, "Danny Mulvaney—Andy Kowalski."

"*Private* Kowalski." Kowalski grinned, shaking Danny's hand. "I *am* busted again, am I not, Master Sergeant?"

Danny noticed the Spec/4 eagles on Kowalski's rumpled khakis.

"Most affirmed," Jellicks growled.

"Ah, well." Kowalski laughed, "these little birds always seem to be flying away before we get acquainted. It wasn't my fault, you know," he said to Danny. "I was kidnapped."

Danny couldn't help but smile at the gleam in Kowalski's eyes as he waited for Jellicks to react.

"Here we go," Jellicks grumbled.

"God's truth," Kowalski swore, raising his right hand. "I met this gorgeous little Chinese girl my first night in Taipei. Barbie. That was her name. Not really, but I couldn't pronounce her Chinese name. They all have American names for us GIs, you know," he said to Danny, with an exaggerated air of confidentiality, as if imparting some brilliant observation. "Anyway," he went on, "I met Barbie my first night in town. It was love at first sight. Not me—her. She was nuts about me. Took me home with her that first night."

"What'd it cost you?" Jellicks sneered.

"Don't get the wrong idea, Sarge," Kowalski said. "This was no chippy. Good old Taiwan family and all." He paused and took a deep breath. Letting it out in a rush, he continued his story. Danny thought he might get high from the alcohol fumes that engulfed him. "I did have to lay some bread on the slope who owned the bar. You know," he winked at Danny, "sign a contract and all the formalities. They have somewhat different customs in these foreign countries."

"He means he bought a bar girl for a night," Jellicks interrupted.

"Sarge, you make it sound so crude. Wasn't like that at all. I'm telling you this chick was really head over heels about me."

Jellicks shook his head and made a point of watching the traffic outside the cab.

"We wound up spending my whole R and R together." Kowalski concentrated on Danny. "I couldn't get away from her. She was glued to me." He wagged his head slowly, grinning. "What a broad. Anyway, my last night, she begs me not to go back to Nam. 'I gotta go,' I told her. 'It's my duty. My country is at war. I'm a soldier, and I gotta go back. My friends are there right now, fightin' and dyin', stickin' it out in the mud and the blood. I gotta go back,' I told her. 'I'm sorry, but I gotta.'" He hung his head to emphasize the drama and then raised his eyes to gaze sadly into Danny's. "She drugged me," he said, "slipped me a Mickey Finn." With that, he again raised his right hand, and said, "I swear to God." He then brought his left hand up and spread them in a gesture of disbelief. "I missed my plane."

"Gimme a break," Jellicks moaned.

"No shit, Sarge." Kowalski became animated as he resumed his tale. "I was furious when I came to. I yelled at her. I told her she had done a terrible thing. She cried like a baby. 'I do for you, Andy, I do for you,' she kept saying over and over. I felt sorry for the poor kid. I forgave her, but—" Kowalski raised an index finger and an eyebrow. "—I made her promise not to do it again. I'm a sucker for a pretty face, especially when they cry. So, I figured, what the hell. I'll leave tomorrow. What's one more day? To show her I really forgive her, I take her to dinner. We have a few drinks and—*son of a bitch*—she dopes me again. I miss another flight."

"And another, and another," Jellicks said.

"Exactly." Kowalski threw up his hands and let them fall in his lap. "When a woman loves you, she'll do anything to hang onto you."

Danny had to look away to keep from laughing. Kowalski, he could see, was enjoying watching Jellicks's slow boil.

"Do you really expect me to believe that cock and bull story?" Jellicks said.

"Who told you about the cock and the bull?" Kowalski asked, amazed. To Danny, he explained, "We went to a cock fight one night and this guy brought a bull—"

"*At ease, soldier*," the master sergeant roared. The cab driver nearly swerved into oncoming traffic. "Shut your lying yap, or I'm going to shut it for you."

Kowalski made a zipping motion across his lips and winked at Danny, who nearly choked. They rode in silence until they reached the hotel where Jellicks instructed Danny to wait at the desk while he took Kowalski aside.

When they rejoined Danny, Kowalski bore no resemblance to the wisecracking, brash young man he had been in the cab. He was shattered. Kowalski spoke not a word all the way back to Dong Tam.

Danny lay awake in his bunk that night, feeling forsaken and alone. Kowalski's grief was contagious. He contemplated the pain caused by the passing of any man. Top, Leon, the chopper pilot, the enemy soldiers he'd killed—they all left someone behind to feel the pain, someone who loved them.

His back was sore from the chopper ride. His head ached. The wound in his leg itched. It was healing. He'd be back out there soon. He was afraid.

Sleep was impossible. He got up and dressed. Walking through the empty platoon bay, he almost wished for mortars to send the few men in the company area diving for the bunkers. At least he wouldn't be alone.

Outside, he wandered aimlessly until he saw the glow from a cigarette as someone left the mess hall by the side door. He ambled toward the red dot of light, drawn to it by his need for companionship. Gary Thatcher met him at the little bridge over the drainage ditch, a cardboard cup of coffee in his hand.

"Hey, Gary. What's happenin'?" Danny said, relieved to find a friend. They exchanged small talk for a while. There wasn't much he could tell Gary in the way of news that Gary didn't already know.

"I *do* work in Intelligence, you know?" Gary smiled. "And contrary to popular opinion, we do get our heads out of our asses now and then."

Gary offered to "buy" Danny a cup of coffee from the mess hall. They filled their cups at the perpetually recharged urn and left the building to escape the heat. They walked until they found themselves on the road above the Motor Pool. Gary scaled the drainage ditch and motioned for Danny to follow. They skirted the ammo bunker and climbed onto the hood of a truck. With their backs against the windshield, they sipped coffee and smoked cigarettes. Danny unloaded his heartaches and misgivings while Gary listened, responding only in terms of agreement and understanding. He had no advice to give. No one had answers to these questions. Only a fellow soldier would understand the deep, aching need to verbalize them, to expel them by giving voice to the torment.

As Danny's anger and pain ebbed, his words trailed off. The

moon peeked from behind its veil of clouds. The sleeping base camp was almost pretty in the pale blue glow, and from their vantage point on the truck's hood, he could see over the berm. Even the jungle looked peaceful. Gary leaned over to crush his cigarette out on the side of the cab. They both heard a snap. They looked in puzzlement at one another for an instant until Danny saw the spider-webbed hole in the windscreen. He pushed Gary and rolled the other way. Both men fell to the ground on opposite sides of the vehicle.

"Sniper," Danny whispered to Gary from across the undercarriage.

"No shit," Gary replied.

"What do we do?"

"Go to bed," Gary whispered back. "Charley says *Nighty-night.*"

CHAPTER 44

Tyler returned from a mid-morning briefing at the fire base CP bunker accompanied by David Fuquette. They entered the Second Platoon's area, and Tyler called his men together. "Ambush tonight," he announced. "S-Two says a VC paymaster will be coming through a village a few clicks from here tonight. We're supposed to greet him."

Several of the men rolled their eyes. Some chuckled. Fuquette sat on a wall of sandbags and wagged his head with a wry grin on his lips.

"What?" Tyler asked.

"Lieutenant, don't tell me you bought the ubiquitous VC paymaster spiel," Fuquette replied.

"There's a two-dollar word," Tyler said with a short laugh.

"I read."

"No offense intended, Sergeant Fuquette. Would you care to elaborate?"

"Sir, the VC paymaster is S-Two's way of saying, 'Something's going down, but we haven't got the foggiest.'" There were nods of agreement from the platoon. "If we bagged all the paymasters they sent us out after, we could buy this miserable country and pave it for a parking lot. Whenever they get a glimmer of any kind of unit moving through an area that they don't have solid intelligence to put a label on, they become the VC paymaster and his guides. Bottom line—we don't know what will be out there. Maybe nothin', maybe a meat grinder."

"We'll find out tonight, won't we," Tyler said. "Squad leaders, and you too, Davy, assemble outside my bunker in fifteen minutes. We'll go over the map and the op order. Sergeant Fuquette is going with us on this one," he said to the men. "Captain thinks his unique talents may come in handy."

The choppers picked them up outside the camp after a canned lunch. The men were looking forward to the completion of the mess hall. The cooks would be brought out then and hot meals would be served instead of C-rations. For the moment, the vacuum-packed tins were their sole diet.

After a short chopper ride, insertion was accomplished a kilometer from the targeted village. Second Platoon would walk to the ambush point. The plan was to circle around behind the village before moving into position at dusk. The ambush site was on the opposite side of a small river that skirted the southern end of the hamlet.

A rough road, little more than a wide footpath, ran through the village and into the jungle on the south side of the river. A rickety wooden bridge spanned the stream at that point. Tyler planned to place his men in the trees on both sides of the road and hit the VC as they crossed the bridge. If the enemy obliged and approached from the expected direction, the Americans would have a clear field of fire and the VC would have no cover.

They crossed the river upstream. Everything went well until Verde slipped and slid down the embankment to land with a splash in the swift current. He panicked. His head went under and he fought to get his feet under him before he drowned. He lost his rifle as he struggled to right himself. Rodriguez dropped his pack on the bank and dove in after him. Seizing his harness, he yanked him to the surface and hauled the spluttering new man to the far side.

Tyler said to Cole, "Put Rodriguez in for a Soldier's Medal when we get back."

"You mean another Oak Leaf Cluster, don't you, sir?"

"Another?"

"Rodriguez is Puerto Rico's answer to Johnnie Weismuller, Lieutenant. Last guy he saved was me."

They wasted twenty minutes while three men took turns diving for the missing rifle. Rodriguez found it on his third attempt.

With the platoon assembled on the far side, Cole checked the radio and attempted a commo check. The handset was soaked. They couldn't raise the company.

Cole growled, "I told you to keep the baggie on the handset when we cross streams, didn't I?"

"Keep it down, Sergeant," Tyler admonished Cole. "It's done. Dry the damned thing out as quickly as possible. Let's get moving."

Cole disassembled the black plastic ear-piece, shook the water from it, and disconnected the coiled cord from the radio. He would carry the parts and wait for them to dry enough to try again later. He glared at the back of Verde's neck as he walked.

"Dumbass recycled son-of-a-bitch," he grumbled.

They were completely on their own without the radio. The platoon had no lifeline to the company. No help could be summoned if they got into trouble.

Tyler moved his men quietly into position as the sun dipped below the horizon. Cole lay down with the lieutenant and his RTO.

"I think it's dry enough to try again, sir," he whispered. After attaching the cord to the set, he made his call. The radio was still dead. "I'm sure it's dry enough, sir. Maybe the battery's done for."

"Put a fresh battery in, Verde, and try again," Tyler ordered. Verde's worried look and failure to move told the story.

"You didn't bring a spare battery, did you?" Cole asked. Verde looked down at his hands. "Jesus Christ," Cole hissed. "I told you this guy was an asshole, sir."

"Knock it off, Sergeant," Tyler said. "We're in trouble. We'll settle Private Verde's hash when we get back. Meanwhile, pass the word we've got no commo. Stay sharp and let's hope Charley decides to stay home tonight."

They lay quietly in the brush, praying for an uneventful night. It started to rain just after nine o'clock. By eleven, they were drenched and cold. Not a soul had moved in the village.

Cole indicated the village with a nod of his head. "Awful quiet."

"Too quiet," Tyler whispered the Hollywood cliché and smiled.

At midnight, they heard the chunk, ka-chunk of mortar rounds exiting tubes.

"Oh, shit," Cole whined, pressing close to the mud.

Two of the first three shells landed in the river and sent geysers of muddy spray into the air. The third blasted the bridge into splinters. By the time the shrapnel stopped whizzing through the trees, the next volley was in the air. Charley's gunners knew their business, and the corrected rounds landed on Second Platoon's side of the river.

"They're on us!" Cole yelled.

"*Di di mau*, people," Tyler bellowed. "Fall back into the woods."

They scrambled to their feet and plunged pell mell into the brush.

"Keep your buddy in sight," Tyler yelled amid the explosions. "Don't get separated."

They ran a hundred meters until the rounds stopped falling around them. Tyler ordered a halt to regroup. Charley found them a moment later, and the bombardment resumed. They broke cover and ran deeper into the woods.

CHAPTER 45

When sleep still proved elusive, Danny arose again to prowl the battalion area, this time careful to avoid the Motor Pool. He spied a light burning and moved toward it like a moth to a flame.

"Buy you a beer, Kowalski?" Danny asked from the doorway to the Headquarters Company hootch.

Andy Kowalski turned from his footlocker, which he had been using for a desk. Danny saw crumpled balls of paper and a ballpoint pen. "Sure." Kowalski sighed. "I'm not getting anywhere with this anyway."

"I know what you mean," Danny said. "It's hard to find things to say."

"Especially when you're trying to console your mother on the death of her only brother from ten thousand miles away."

"Were you and your uncle close?"

Kowalski thought about it for a minute. "I guess. But we didn't get along too well once I enlisted." He laughed at Danny's startled expression. "Yeah, I'm an RA. I guess I did it for Uncle Andy. He loved the army. Don't ask me why. It sucks. He busted my balls from the beginning. Always talking about what a good soldier should do and what a good soldier should be. I was more interested in having fun. We fought a lot. When I got orders for Nam, he pulled some strings and got me sent here. I'll bet my mom had something to do with that. I've been in one scrape after another since I got here." He sighed again. "Now he's gone, and I've got Jellicks to ride herd on me."

"You restricted, or anything?"

"Naw. Jellicks must figure I've got enough troubles. He seems content to bust me again. I'll probably get another Article Fifteen. At the rate I'm going, by the time I get out I'll owe the army about a year's pay."

"How about that beer?"

"Lead on, Macduff."

"Mulvaney."

Kowalski laughed. "Whatever."

At the Artillery Club, a Philippine USO band was twanging out country western. The lead singer did an impersonation of Johnny Cash that was astonishing. Danny would have sworn *The Man in Black* was in the room when he closed his eyes.

"Wish I knew how Uncle Andy died," Kowalski said when the band took a break.

"Jellicks didn't tell you?"

"Only that he was shot by a sniper."

"I was there."

Kowalski looked startled. "Was it bad?"

"It happened in a village we named Charleyville," Danny hedged. The pain in the young man's eyes convinced him of his answer. "He never knew what hit him."

"Thank God for that," Kowalski breathed. "Maybe that'll make Mom feel a little better. Thanks."

Danny nodded. "Let's get drunk."

CHAPTER 46

Lieutenant Tyler lay panting on the muddy ground near the center of a peninsula of scrub jungle. His poncho was draped over his head and torso to block the light emitted by his army-issue flashlight. Sweat stung his eyes as he attempted to ascertain his platoon's location on his Picto-map. The air under the plastic rain gear was like a steam bath. By orienting the map to his compass, and shooting a back azimuth to his last known position, then trying to pick out some prominent terrain feature that looked like his surroundings, he knew he should be able to pinpoint his position. No easy feat in the Mekong Delta. Even in daylight, one rice paddy looked very much like another, ditto the wood lines.

Best guess is here, he thought, poking a grimy digit at what appeared to be the wooded finger he and his men occupied. Quickly, he scribbled the coordinates of the location on his palm. Rain and perspiration would wash the ink off in a matter of minutes. No matter. He could not read it in the dark, once he crawled out from under the poncho, but if he wrote it down it would be committed to memory—an ingrained habit from college.

Snapping off the light, Tyler emerged from the plastic tent gulping air, which seemed much cooler than it had before he entered the light trap. He sat up, looked around, and picked out the silhouettes of his platoon. They had fallen into a hasty perimeter defense after running for most of the night in a deadly game of tag with the Viet Cong.

"Jesus, what a fucking mess," he breathed, removing his helmet and running his hand through his sweat-soaked hair.

"Roger that, sir," a disembodied voice whispered at his side.

"Morgan," Tyler whispered to his point man, "do you think we lost them this time? How are the wounded?"

"Not bad, considering," the sharp-eyed veteran disseminated the information in his cool, pragmatic way. "Mostly small shrapnel wounds and splinters from tree bursts. None serious. Cole was bleedin' pretty bad from his shoulder, but I think Doc's got it stopped. As for your first question—maybe, maybe not."

This operation had been a series of catastrophes. Tyler had been opposed to the plan and its theoretical objective from its inception. Sending an already under-strength platoon on a night patrol, far from its equally under-strength company—which was further burdened with the Herculean task of manning a battalion-sized base—smacked of incompetence. Captain Arnold was proving to be a difficult leader to follow. Privately, Tyler thought the man was a blazing asshole, but concern for his platoon kept his tongue in check. Dissent among officers was bad for morale if apparent to the troops. His last confrontation with his captain, he was sure, was not forgotten. Disloyalty, as his superiors would see it, was bad for the career. So, he kept his mouth shut, tried to follow orders, and hoped that his continued presence as platoon leader could forestall disaster for his men.

Captain Arnold had reasoned that sitting around waiting for Charley to get the upper hand was ill advised. The company's purpose was to find and kill the enemy. Tyler agreed with the premise. His problem was with the odds. There were supposed to be elements of a VC Division bopping around in this AO. His own commanders couldn't say what size those elements were, never mind where they were holed up. And you didn't have to be a mathematician to figure out what would happen to an under-strength platoon if it ran into a battalion. Theoretical equations were moot at the moment. Survival was the driving force behind his thinking right now.

If his reckoning was accurate, they were being driven toward the U-Minh Forest, the Forest of Darkness, the closest thing to real jungle in the Mekong Delta, and somewhere he didn't want to go. The U-Minh was an infamous VC stronghold where entire units had disappeared. Army intelligence—a contradiction in terms in some circles—believed that the Seventh VC Division had set up shop there and was responsible for the increased enemy pressure on the surrounding countryside. Charlie Company was part of the battalion that Division had assigned to patrol the outskirts of the forest, to make contact with, and fix the suspected VC unit. Once contact was established and the identity and strength of the enemy force was confirmed, the substantial might of the Division could be brought to bear. Sound military hypothesis. To the grunts given the task, it was tantamount to insanity. C-Company was alone at the sharp end of the spear, and things were getting ragged. The great schemes of generals always had the ring of madness to the soldier on the ground.

Tyler could not comprehend the laziness of Verde, the new kid from Utah. Going to the field without a spare radio battery was nothing short of criminal negligence. *Didn't he realize the spot he had put them in?*

"Pass the word to pull in tight and hunker down," Tyler whispered to Morgan. "We'll hole up here 'til first light. One hundred percent alert. No noise and no smoking."

They strained their eyes and ears to penetrate the incessant rain. Tyler felt Morgan's elbow in his ribs and was startled to realize he had dozed. He forced his mind to concentrate and his eyes to discern what the point man was staring at in the darkened woods. His breath caught in his throat. Two men, moving warily through the trees, emerged from the gloom.

They were coming right at them.

CHAPTER 47

Danny and Kowalski staggered along the road to C-Company's area. They had closed the Artillery Club and decided that what they needed were women. The rarity of such companionship in this place created a problem.

"The Donut Dollies!" Kowalski exclaimed.

"The what?"

"The Donut Dollies, man," Kowalski repeated. "You know, the Red Cross chicks that bring donuts and coffee to the fire bases and shit."

He was referring to a group of American young ladies who voluntarily came to Vietnam to bring a touch of home to lonely soldiers in the field. Their crisp powder-blue jumpers with the Red Cross emblazoned on the bodice were a welcome sight to GIs far from home. They were treated with respect, if not reverence, at least to their faces. Even the crudest of the men watched his mouth in their presence. By and large, they were a pleasant addition to any man's day, giving young soldiers an opportunity to be what they had been before they had come to this place.

Danny had not met them yet. He didn't really believe there were American girls right here in Dong Tam and he said so.

"I know every one of them Biscuit Bitches," Kowalski winked. "Some in a biblical sense," he lied. "There's always a party in their hootch. Come on. I'll introduce you."

The hootch turned out to be a floodlit, air-conditioned, permanent bunker of concrete and steel surrounded by a razor wire-topped ten-foot tall cyclone fence, practically in the shadow of Division Headquarters and patrolled by armed MPs with large German shepherd attack dogs. The drunken pair was told to leave or spend the rest of the night in the stockade.

"Fuck 'em," Kowalski grunted. "Place is probably lousy with officers, anyway. Let's go to My Tho."

"Okay," Danny said. He would have agreed to hand grenade juggling in his alcoholic fog. For the first time in many days his body didn't hurt and, best of all, his heart didn't either. "Who's Me Toe?"

"It's not a who." Kowalski laughed. "It's a what. My Tho is the biggest city in these parts. Beaucoup pussy in My Tho."

"Where is it?" The voices of conscience and caution were re-awakening in the back of Danny's brain. He wondered if he should mention the sniper that had nearly killed Gary.

"Few miles down the road." Kowalski waved in the general direction.

"Don't they call that road Ambush Alley?" Danny heard his little voices rising.

"Only the first few miles." Kowalski burped. "It's too far to walk. We'll have to steal a jeep."

They were weaving across the company area. Danny was try-ing to come up with some sensible argument to this wild scheme without looking like a wet blanket. Uppermost in his mind was the fact that he didn't want to be unfaithful to Amanda. It came as a surprise that he should suddenly be thinking of her. His inebri-ated brain was debating with itself on whether he had sinned in thought when Thatcher stopped them.

"Hey, Gary. How the hell are you?" Danny wheezed.

"Jesus, Mulvaney, you're fried," Thatcher noted as he stead-ied his rocking friend with both hands on Danny's shoulders. "Better get your head straight. Second Platoon's missing."

Danny was trying to understand what Gary was telling him. He squinted through bleary eyes. "Say again."

"That's right," Gary confirmed. "They went out on an ambush. There's been no commo with them since they cleared the LZ. Charlie-Six sent the Third Herd out to look for them. They left the fire base on foot, couple or three hours ago. That leaves eve-rybody's shit weak. Sober up. They may need you." With that, he turned and was gone.

Danny stumbled to the showers with Kowalski following. The sight of two fully clothed men taking cold showers at three o'clock in the morning might have aroused some measure of hilarity had anyone been watching. No one was. All eyes were glued to the radios in the TOC, Tactical Operations Center, as if by staring at the sets, the men could extract from them the all-is-well messages they prayed to hear.

CHAPTER 48

Tran crouched behind a stately palm as his point team moved forward to check out the jungle ahead. He had decided, as a last exercise, to try to locate the arms cache that Major Xuong had informed him was hidden in this sector. They should be able to find these places in the dark if they were to operate efficiently. He was anxious to finish this patrol and get back to camp. They had heard sporadic firing and explosions for most of the night. It had been impossible to fix the range, although he had a good idea of the general direction. Sound carries in the rain. The firefights might have been nearby or a good distance away. He did not wish to stumble upon some VC action unaware. That was a good way to wind up on the wrong end of an ally's weapon. He would have to arrange some sort of liaison with Major Xuong to prevent unfortunate incidents. He would send a runner tomorrow to arrange a meeting.

※※※

Tyler let his chin sink lower until it touched the muddy earth. He held his breath as he watched the enemy soldiers come. They seemed to be looking for something. They were coming from the wrong direction to be the people that had chased them through the night. Could they have passed him in the darkness and doubled back? Was this a point element or two wayward souls as lost as the Second Platoon? He willed his men to lie quietly and let them pass. To tangle with anyone while they were without communications before knowing the tactical situation would be foolhardy.

The pair was veering to the left, away from the platoon, when

Verde, who had nodded off, awoke with a start. His eyes grew wide as he saw the ghostly shapes twenty feet from his nose.

"*Gooks!*" he screamed and emptied his rifle in one burst.

Second Platoon cringed but opened up. Both enemy soldiers flew back into the brush, hit by dozens of slugs. The platoon ceased fire without being told. Every man tensed for the retaliatory fire from the dead men's comrades.

Nothing happened.

కూసిక

Tran froze in mid-step when he heard the shots. His hand went up, and then slowly came down. He and his men sank to the ground, coiled to spring like pit vipers. Every nerve ending tingled. Fingers took up slack on triggers. Frightened minds willed pounding hearts to be still. The sound of one's own breathing became a nuisance.

కూసిక

Rodriguez's hand was clamped on Verde's mouth to still his whimpering.

"Only two?" Morgan whispered. The hope in the question was painful to hear.

"Not likely," Tyler whispered back. They waited for what seemed an interminable time. The jungle was still. Maybe they'd been lucky. "We can't stay here," he whispered to Morgan. There was no cover. The scrub had afforded good concealment, but that was gone thanks to Verde. Tyler pictured the map in his mind. Flooded paddy on both sides. Woods in front and behind. Not a good idea to go where these two had come from. If the dead men were scouting for a larger force, they might walk right into them. Better to go back the way they had come. They had probably lost their pursuers or the enemy had somehow gotten ahead of them. If the latter was the case, mortar tubes were being cranked to firing elevation right now. Time to go.

"Pass the word," Tyler hissed. "Move out by squads. Back the way we came. From the far left. Keep your intervals, but don't lose anybody in the dark. And for God's sake, be quiet."

The men began to file past him. Every snapping twig sounded

like a rifle shot. Weapons clinked against rucksack frames. Boots made sucking sounds in the mud.

Tyler loved every one of his men, but in his mind at that moment, they were all dumb shits who should have paid closer attention to his lectures on night movement.

As the last men trudged past, Tyler, Morgan, and Verde rose and turned to go. At that second, Tran's men opened fire and charged.

A round creased Tyler's helmet. It rang like a bell. He collapsed in a heap. Morgan dove to his side, directly into the path of a speeding slug. He was dead when he hit the ground. Half the platoon, lined up like clay pigeons, were cut down in the first few seconds. Verde stood stunned, his empty rifle hanging useless at his side. Rodriguez tackled him. They crashed into the bushes with the handsome young Chicano screaming at him to fight for his life. A grenade killed them both as they got to their knees. A bullet through the kneecap toppled Sergeant Cole. A light machine gun cut his squad to pieces around him. Panicked men fired in all directions, killing their friends. Fuquette rolled under a fallen log as the men around him pitched in agony in their death throes.

At the front of the line, the point farthest from the screaming sappers, Paco pulled Simms and Lance into a depression. He blazed away with his M-60 until the barrel glowed red. Simms pumped out shotgun rounds and high explosive from his M-79 regardless, grabbing the next round in his ammo bag and letting fly. Lance fired one magazine after another and prayed he would not run out.

The NVA ran through the demoralized platoon shooting anything that moved. Cole got a bayonet through the chest for his valiant attempt to raise his weapon. The long, four grooved blade stuck in his ribs. The sapper behind it stepped on his face to pull it out and then butt-stroked him so viciously that Cole's jaw shattered and his neck snapped.

Moments after the melee started, the only men returning fire were the three frenzied souls in the last-stand pocket at the end of the line. Tran began to issue orders to flank and reduce this small, but determined, force until he realized that he could see the man on his left more clearly than he had only moments before. He looked up at the lightening sky and was dismayed to see the trees growing more distinct. Dawn was overtaking him. He quickly amended his orders, and the NVA fell back. Tran knew they must seek the cover of the forest before they were caught in the light of day.

Like vampires gorged on blood, The People's Provisional Captive Force retired in good order. They grabbed what American weapons and equipment they could and ran for the safety of the U-Minh.

Sergeant Vinh dropped to his knees and summoned his captain to show him what he had found. Tran dropped down beside his NCO.

"Look, *Dai ui*," Vinh whispered, excited. An American lay beneath a bush, unconscious but alive. Tran yanked his bayonet from its sheath to cut the man's throat. "Wait, sir," the sergeant said, grasping the collar of the stricken soldier's fatigues. "*Trung ui*," he said, holding Tyler's embroidered black bar for Tran to see.

An American lieutenant. Tran smiled. "Good, Sergeant. Very good." He barked orders and two men hurried to raise the man to his feet. Tyler's head lolled drunkenly, but he took some of his own weight.

They forced him to move with them.

Fuquette drew a bead but could not risk the shot without hitting Tyler. He looked at the spot where his friends still poured fire into the trees. If he called out, he might wind up in a crossfire. He crawled from cover and followed the enemy.

℮⊰℮⊰

After a risky, forced march in the dark, Third Platoon reached the Second's planned ambush site at the village just after dawn. The shattered bridge and the tail fins of a Chinese mortar shell in a water-filled hole bore silent witness to the drama that had unfolded there.

"Looks like they went that way," Ted Stark, the platoon sergeant, said to Lieutenant Booker.

"Yeah, brush is all trampled," Booker observed. "Any sign of wounded?"

"Been raining all night, sir." Stark shook his head. "Blood trails would be washed away if there were any."

"Let's hope there weren't," Booker said. "Let's try to pick up the pace a little. Tell the point to move quick but careful. We won't do anybody any good if we get ourselves bushwhacked. Stiles," he said to his radioman, "get Charlie-Six on the horn. Tell him what we found and that we're following Second's trail."

ᔥᔥᔥ

Lance poked leafy twigs into the loops in his helmet cover before raising his head, an inch at a time, over the lip of ground they had huddled behind for what seemed like years.

"Nobody out there," he whispered.

"That's what we thought last time," Simms said.

"Sun's up," Paco noted. "They're gone. Our guys'll be looking for us. Charley knows that. He ain't gonna tangle with gunships to nail three dudes."

"*Hey,*" someone yelled from the trees. "Anybody there? Give me a hand. I'm stuck."

The three men ducked, their weapons up and ready.

"That sounds like Doc," Simms whispered.

They cautiously rose from their position and moved in a knot, toward the sound, weapons pointing out, muzzles shifting constantly, trying to cover every possible threat.

They found the medic in a hole about five feet deep and six feet square. He was wedged between two moldy crates. The thatched carpet of palm fronds that had concealed the cache had given way under his weight when he ran across the mat in an effort to get to a wounded man. Lance and Simms extricated him from the hole while Paco stood guard.

Laffin made a futile attempt to minister to his fallen comrades while the three last-ditch defenders sat around the hole and smoked cigarettes. Doc sat down heavily by their sides with a fist full of dog tags when he had checked every body.

"We're it," Doc sighed. "Now what?"

The four young men exchanged vacant stares, too much in shock to cry or even to think.

ᔥᔥᔥ

"Jerry," Chief Warrant Officer Harlan Appleton said to his pilot, "swing back over that last wood line. I think I saw something."

The teardrop shaped LOH, Light Observation Helicopter, lay over on its side and buzzed back the way it had come.

Warrant Officer Jerry McPartland throttled back as he skimmed the trees. They darted forward and back and side to side as they searched. Hovering too long in a helicopter, at this altitude, was unwise. A Loach, as the army called the swift little ships, was a sitting duck at treetop level.

"Oh, my God," Appleton whispered. They could see many bodies sprawled in death's contortions on the jungle floor.

"Looks like we found them." McPartland swallowed to hold down his breakfast. "Better call it in."

"Take another pass. Maybe there are survivors," Appleton said.

A purple smoke grenade gushed its familiar cloud into the air.

The pilot yanked back on the stick and groped for altitude.

"Unknown station, this is Hound Dog," Appleton called on the radio. "*I*-dentify smoke, over." It would be just like Charley to suck in any rescue attempt. Appleton repeated his call several times as the chopper danced in the air.

"Briefing said they lost commo with these fellas," McPartland reminded his aircraft commander.

"Yeah, I know," Appleton said, "but do you want a bullet up your ass to find out?"

"I'm open for suggestions, Harlan."

"Shit," Appleton snapped. He poked the muzzle of his CAR-15 through the aperture in the Perspex bubble. "Okay, let's be stupid."

CHAPTER 49

The convoy rolled as soon as the road was open. Danny rode shotgun in the third truck, his M-16 pointed out the window of the speeding deuce-and-a-half with his finger on the trigger and his thumb on the selector switch. Kowalski drove.

"How long?" Danny asked when they had cleared Ambush Alley and were barreling down Highway Four.

"Four hours, if Charley don't blow the road," Kowalski estimated, "and if the Arvins don't sidetrack us for a priority convoy, or if a truck don't break down, or if we don't get ambushed, and if the bridges aren't down, and—"

"Okay, okay, I get the picture," Danny said.

"Take it easy," Kowalski said. "I'll get you there. How's your head?"

"It's funny," Danny said, "I should still be drunk. So should you. But I'm cold sober. Don't even have a hangover."

"Amazing stuff, adrenaline," Kowalski said. "Burns alcohol like a flame."

Danny nodded, settling into the seat. He'd have to keep his cool and hope and pray for the best. There had been no word of the missing platoon since Third Herd had reported finding their trail into the woods. At least no bodies had been found. They *had* to be all right. Tyler was with them.

The convoy roared through a settlement. Shacks of tin and thatch clustered along both sides of the road. People and farm animals scrambled to get out of the way of the speeding vehicles lest they be crushed beneath the ten-wheeled monsters.

"Here's the first bridge," Kowalski announced. A steel-framed arch with a concrete bed loomed before them, rising on pilings to fifteen feet above the road at its apex. "High tide can be as much as twelve feet," Kowalski said. "The steep angle is the only way to keep the bridges from washing away."

The truck hit the up-ramp without losing any forward momentum and Danny would have sworn they flew across the top without touching the roadbed. The truck bounced on the down-ramp without so much as a tap on the brakes. Danny saw a Vietnamese man in the side view mirror as he plummeted from the bridge to splash in the brown river.

"Happy landings, you little shit," Kowalski laughed. "We're supposed to slow down to twenty miles an hour when we go through populated areas," he yelled above the sound of the engine and the whine of the tires. "Some asshole at the Puzzle Palace put out that stupid reg. Don't want us disturbing the tranquility of the locals," he sneered. "The fact that every anti-vehicle rocket launcher known to man is set to lead a truck at twenty-mikes-per makes no never mind to those bastards. They don't get out here and haul shit through hell and high water. The gooks know we ain't slowing down so they stand aside or get knocked on their flat little asses."

Danny said nothing but looked askance at his friend.

"We do slow down for certain situations, mind you," Kowalski continued. "A good-looking chick can cause a pile up, but that don't happen very often." He scanned the road ahead while Danny focused his attention on his friend's dissertation.

Suddenly, Kowalski slammed on the brakes. The truck slid on the wet pavement. Kowalski skillfully corrected for the skid and veered around a mangy brown dog cowering in the middle of the road with its tail between its legs. He downshifted and was building speed again, slamming gears without missing a beat. "Humanitarian reasons is the other contingency," he said with a broad grin.

Danny couldn't help laughing at the warped sense of values. He was beginning to understand the cynicism of the men he had come to admire in this strange and terrible land. Charley got no slack. He'd kill you without a thought. The problem was in recognizing him. He could be anyone. Many of the civilians they passed on this battered road were VC. They would smile at you in the daytime and do their level best to kill you when the sun went down. *Kill 'em all and let God sort 'em out* made more sense to him now than when first he had heard the hideous phrase. He knew now that it was the will to live, survival of the fittest, the law of the jungle in twentieth century form. Frightened young men with nothing to strive for, except to protect their friends and try to get home, had mutated into the most dangerous thing known to man—cornered animals. It disturbed him that he not only understood it, he was beginning to become one of them.

Amanda came to mind, as she did lately at the oddest moments. Her cheerful letters had become offensive at times. She was back home, living a real life, dealing with day-to-day problems that didn't begin to approach his new meaning for the word. He was stuck here, wondering if every day was his last. He realized, with alarm, that he could no longer envision a future. There was only now. Maybe that was the lesson he would bring home from Vietnam—*if* he went home. He was not one of them anymore—those everyday people leading everyday lives. He was bloodstained and unfit to be among the innocents of home. Maybe it was better that he learned it now before he ruined her life. He thought it sad for a man to discover that he wasn't who he thought he was.

"One down, six to go." Kowalski said, bringing him out of his introspective depths.

"What?"

"Bridges," Kowalski yelled. "There's seven of 'em before we get to the fire base."

"Oh."

CHAPTER 50

Thanks much, Hound Dog. Good work. Blackhawk-Six, out," Colonel Conte ended his transmission to the Loach crew. "Break, break," he called to clear the net, "Charlie-Six, Charlie-Six. This is Big Six, over."

"This is Charlie-Six, go," Captain Arnold said, from his bunker at the fire base.

"Roger, Charlie-Six. Your Three-Six is moving into the area now." Arnold heard the colonel's voice with the whine of the helicopter turbine as background. Colonel Conte had boarded his Command and Control helicopter as soon as the call had come in from the Loach. "Hound Dog is returning to base. He's low on go-juice. Meet me on alternate push. I'll turn you over to your Three-Six. He's in a better position to assess the situation on the ground."

Obviously, Arnold thought, *that's where he is.*

"Charlie-Three-Six, Big Six," Conte called on the company push. "Your Six is standing by. I will monitor and give assistance where needed."

"Roger, Big Six. Break. Charlie-Six, Three-Six, over," Booker picked up the conversation.

"Roger, Three-Six. Say sit-rep, over," Captain Arnold ordered.

"Uh, roger. We have reached the site. It's bad."

Arnold could hear the emotion in Booker's voice. The Third Platoon leader was close to tears. Arnold took a deep breath.

"Slow and simple, Dennis," he said softly. "How bad?"

"We have confirmed Hound Dog's estimate as fact," Booker sighed, "Four echo mikes, that's all."

Four enlisted men, Arnold understood, that's what was left of the Second Platoon. He brushed a tear from his cheek and snapped his fingers at Private Smith. Smitty hurried to hand the Second Platoon roster to his CO.

"How many W-I-A?" Arnold asked.

"Negative whiskey India alpha," came Booker's sad reply as he looked around at the grisly scene. Bodies lay everywhere. Flies swarmed on the wounds of the dead boys. Red ants marched steadfastly to the sound of silent drums as they industriously sought to clean up the mess the humans had left. Vultures wheeled in lazy circles overhead, waiting for the living to depart so that the carrion eaters could feast. The smell was overwhelming. The tropical heat took little time to begin decomposition of tissue. The jungle hungered never-endingly for nourishment. Four survivors of the massacre sat dazed on the ground around a rectangular hole. Their brothers from the Third Platoon ministered to them, offering water, food, cigarettes, their love and compassion.

Anguish infested the place.

"Will you give me the names of the survivors, please?" Arnold asked, as if requesting a desperately needed favor of a cherished friend.

Booker read from a list his platoon sergeant had provided. He began to spell the names phonetically.

"Don't bother Dennis," Arnold stepped on his transmission. "Send it in the clear."

"Roger," the lieutenant cleared his throat. "Spec/Four Laffin, Hadley, A."

Beecher, listening to the speaker, said, "The medic."

"PFC Corporal, Lance, N-M-I."

"One of the new guys."

"Spec/Four Simms, Bertram, P."

"Seventy-Nine man."

"Spec/Four Cortez, Alejandro, M."

"Paco, the gunner."

The horribly short list ended. Arnold started from his mental image of a formation of ghosts waiting to hear their names read. He saw the faces of men he knew he would never see again, kids whose families would never be the same. He wanted to say he was sorry but no one would hear.

"Six, do you want me to give you the kilo India alphas now?" Booker was asking.

"Negative, Three-Six," Arnold's voice was full of gravel. He cleared his throat. "There'll be time enough for that when you return." He did some mental arithmetic. Four survivors on the ground, two previously medevacked. "Anybody on R and R?" he asked Chicarelli, hoping.

The forlorn shake of the XO's head would have been bad enough, but he added with a cracking voice, "Rodriguez was due, but I held it up because we were so short of people."

Arnold closed his eyes and shared Chick's pain. He motioned with his hand to say: You didn't know, it's not your fault."

Chicarelli would never believe it. "Do you roger two-two KIA?" he asked Booker, wanting to confirm his figures.

"Negative, Charlie-Six," came Booker's confused reply. "We have two-zero KIA."

"Be certain, Three-Six," Arnold ordered.

"Roger, wait," the lieutenant replied. He sent his men to do another count and confirm the dog tag count with the platoon medic.

They came back with some exciting news.

"Charlie-Six, we have two mike-India-alpha," Booker reported in a loud voice.

"Two MIAs," Arnold said to the men gathered in the bunker.

"We are expanding search radius at once," Booker continued.

"Who? Three-Six," Arnold said. "Say names of MIAs."

Booker returned to the businesslike jargon of the professional soldier. He now had a job to do that offered hope. His training took over. "One Oscar type and one November Charlie Oscar, the sierra, over," he said.

If Charley was listening, and these men were trying to escape and evade, he must protect their identities as much as possible in case they were captured.

"An officer. Tyler," Beecher translated unnecessarily, "and an NCO. The sierra?" He snapped his fingers. "The *sniper*. Tyler and Fuquette got away!"

"Maybe," Captain Arnold said, "or maybe they haven't found the bodies yet."

"There's one other possibility, sir," Smitty piped up.

"POWs?" Arnold raised an eyebrow.

"Charley don't take GIs prisoner, Smith," Beecher snapped.

"Maybe they would an officer and a sniper," Smitty said.

Beecher's derisive snort left no doubt as to his opinion of Smitty's theory.

CHAPTER 51

For two hours the NVA team ran flat out in the shadow of towering prehistoric trees through the tangle of vines, thorns and brush that was the U-Minh Forest. Dragging their prisoner over mangrove roots and across bogs and swamps, they raced.

When their officer finally signaled a halt, all eyes went to the treetops. Motionless, they listened.

Davy Fuquette, winded and trembling from his exertions, watched through his scope from beneath a bush bristling with thorns the size of framing nails. "Damn, these fuckers are tough," he said under his breath.

The enemy troops were as still as window mannequins. It was all he could do to remain motionless as well.

Tyler said something that Fuquette could not hear. The officer shot his guard a look filled with menace. Instantly, a hand was clapped over the lieutenant's mouth, and a blade appeared with its point under his chin.

The group remained frozen for two minutes more until their leader said something. Immediately, the men sank to the earth in place. Their relaxed body language told Fuquette a rest had been ordered.

More orders were given. Half of the enemy troops formed a perimeter while the remainder gathered together in the center, surrounding their officer, talking quietly. In spite of their obvious jitters, they were jubilant with their victory. Fuquette saw smiles and gestures of congratulations. He understood.

They had launched a devastating assault on his friends. His vision clouded when he remembered the way the Second Platoon had been eviscerated. *Like a turkey shoot*, he thought. *They never had a chance.* He blinked back the tears and focused on the task at hand. He had to make a tactical assessment of the opposition and look for an opening to get Tyler out of their grasp. The loss of the two point men and the few minor wounds the enemy troops had suffered was something they could handle. These guys were pros, no doubt about it.

Fuquette made a mental list of what he knew from his observations. These dudes were in excellent shape, even for NVA regulars. *Special troops. The North Vietnamese equivalent of our Green Berets.* They had accomplished a forced march in very tough terrain after a wild fight, kept their cool, and gotten away clean.

There were no English speakers among them. He knew that by the way they communicated with Tyler. Hand signals, fists, and rifle stocks got the messages across. They vented their anger nose to nose, faces contorted in hate, but it was plain they didn't expect him to understand.

The NVA soldiers were beginning to examine the souvenirs they had snatched as they vacated the battlefield. The officer saw that his captive was secured and began to make the rounds of his men, complimenting them as he went, and studying the captured booty. One man showed him an American helmet. From his animated speech, Fuquette saw the man was making a joke. He put the helmet under his butt, squatted over it, and then made a scooping motion with one hand before he put it to his mouth. The officer laughed and waved a finger in front of his nose.

"Regular fuckin' comedian," Fuquette whispered.

The soldier laughed. He pulled the helmet liner from the steel shell. A piece of paper fluttered to the earth. He set the liner down as he stooped to retrieve the paper. It looked like a black and white photograph. He laughed again as he turned it over in his hand and made a comment that made the other men laugh. His facial expression changed to anger as he examined the photograph. He snarled something as he showed the photo to his officer.

Abruptly, the officer's face froze. A shocked look of pain replaced his smile. A cry of anguish broke from his lips. He snatched the photo from the enlisted man, wheeled, and ran to his prisoner. Tyler cringed as the NVA officer began to kick him savagely, screaming incoherent curses. Tyler curled up into a fetal ball to protect himself. Bound hand and foot, with his arms behind his back, he had little success. The crazed officer drew his bayonet. Fuquette's finger tightened on the trigger of his rifle.

The officer stood screaming over the crumpled American. Fuquette could hear the man's bellowing from his hiding place, a good seventy yards from the men he watched.

The NVA officer screamed a question in Vietnamese that Fuquette could not make out. The officer dropped the picture in his fury. The man who had shown him the helmet looked helplessly at his comrades who watched, baffled. The officer seemed to have lost his mind. The soldier retrieved the photo, looked at it, obviously puzzled, and spoke to his officer. The officer whirled on him, slapping the photo from his fist with his gnarled left hand. Out of control, the officer seized his bayonet with both hands and swung the long blade like an ax. The enlisted man parried it with his AK-47, just in time. The force of the downward blow drove him to the ground. The officer raised the bayonet again, one-handed now like a gladiator, but he froze with the knife above his head. He had his back to Fuquette, but his body language was that of a man who had suddenly awakened to find himself in strange surroundings. The man on the ground said something, and the officer's arm, holding the bayonet aloft, dropped. The officer turned, scooped the photo from the jungle floor, stalked back to Tyler, and bent low to put his face within inches of his captive. He screamed his question again.

The NVA soldier on the ground got to his feet, walked purposefully to stand behind his crazed officer, stood at attention, and rattled something off.

The officer spun on him, his entire body trembling, speechless with rage. The soldier continued with his speech, still at attention. He could have been making a report, but Fuquette saw, by the expression on his face, that he was pleading.

The officer stood rigid, the bayonet pointed at Tyler. The soldier kept speaking until the officer looked skyward. Abruptly, he squatted in front of Tyler, and the lieutenant flinched. With swift, economic movements, the NVA officer cut the bonds that secured Tyler's ankles and then did the same to his bootlaces. He yanked the jungle boots from his feet so that the socks came with them. He growled some unintelligible threat in Tyler's face that no one else could hear.

The NVA officer stood erect, barked an order, and turned to resume the march. His men followed, one of them prodding Tyler with the muzzle of his weapon and all of them exchanging apprehensive looks.

Fuquette lowered his rifle. "What in the hell was that all about?"

CHAPTER 52

Danny saw Kowalski pull his .45 caliber pistol from its holster and watched his eyes flick from the road to his left repeatedly. Kowalski shifted gears with the semiautomatic in his right hand, gripping the shift knob with his fingertips.

"What's up?" Danny indicated the weapon with his eyes.

"Arvin compound's just ahead."

"I thought they were on our side."

"Shows how little time in country you've got, Daniel," Kowalski said. "Half the South Vietnamese Army is VC. It's a great place to hide, plus you get free ammo and pick up all sorts of good info."

"So, what are you saying? This Arvin camp up ahead is VC?"

"About six months ago, we made a run to Camau. Had to deliver some shit to some Special Forces types trying to win the hearts and minds of the kids in a school down there. Our previous colonel—an even bigger asshole than Conte—played poker with the CO of this little contingent of green beanies. One night the pot was more than the colonel could cover, so the snake eater conned him into putting up a load of office supplies. You know, paper and pencils, shit like that. Stuff the kids could use in their school. The colonel lost. Way I heard it, the idiot tried to fill an inside straight.

"The colonel promised to deliver the supplies to Camau. Keep in mind, when a full bird promises to do anything, he means he'll have his slaves—meaning us—do it. So, we got to haul all this shit way down into the ass end of nowhere. Three trucks. One with the loser's stake, one full of troops to protect this shit, and a diesel tanker. Shell Stations are pretty scarce down here if you haven't noticed." He shook his head with a rueful grin, remembering. "It was the dry season. We ate dust all the way from Bearcat.

"Anyway, we got held up outside this Arvin compound. They had some scrawny-assed old man with a cart full of sugar cane stopped in the middle of the road, and they were beating the shit out of him. We never did find out why. Now, my friend Benny was driving lead. Benny was a good old boy from Georgia. He loved to drive. God, how that man loved to drive. All he ever talked about was getting out of the army and buying him an eighteen-wheeler. He said he was going to get rich hauling produce for truck farmers all over the South."

Kowalski's hand tightened on the wheel. His face turned to granite, but he continued in the same matter-of-fact tone, "So, Benny climbs down to ask these nasty little motherfuckers to kindly get their asses out of our way. We could care less what the squabble is with papasan. They can beat him 'til his eyes go round on their own time. We got some shit to deliver, and we're history, man. So, how's about dragging his ass off the road so we can get on with it? Maybe he was a little forceful in his choice of words. Benny didn't have much patience with these slant-eyed pricks. For whatever reason, this gook lieutenant shot him dead. Just raised his weapon and wasted him. Didn't so much as blink."

Danny's jaw dropped.

"Swear to God." Kowalski crossed his heart with the .45. "Happened right up here."

They rolled past the compound, and Danny saw the baleful looks from the soldiers in the lookout towers.

"We had some pussy captain from Supply as convoy commander. He stopped us from wasting the place. Far as I know, the son of a bitch got away with it. Least ways we never heard of any punishment. Benny had two weeks to go to ETS."

Danny wondered if anybody in this country was sane.

Ten minutes later, they turned right onto a new dirt road that led, a hundred yards off of the main road, to the fire base. The base looked like a sawed-off anthill from the road, a lot of dirt pushed into a pile with two sandbagged observation towers rising from opposite corners and the whole heap surrounded by row after row of concertina wire.

The convoy slowed to negotiate the muddy zig-zag entrance through the gate, built to prevent direct fire into the compound. Once inside, Danny was amazed at the progress the engineers had made in the few days that he had been away.

Sandbagged bunkers dotted the perimeter berm, interspersed by fighting holes reinforced with corrugated steel culvert. Mortar pits and gun emplacements crowded the majority of the open ground in the middle of the circular camp. A battery of .105 Howitzers was being towed into the positions as he watched. The TOC bunker dominated the very center of the camp like a mountain of sandbags, bristling with antennae. A huge, square tower of scaffolding rose up from beside the TOC to scrape the sky with its long-range Two-Niner-Two radio mast protruding like a needle from its top, complete with blinking red warning light.

Kowalski snorted. "Ain't that one hell of an aiming stake." He dropped Danny off in front of the CP bunker, promising to see him later. Inside, Danny was surprised at the welcome he received from Beecher, who seemed genuinely interested in his health.

Danny confirmed that he was healing well and that he was fit for duty.

"What's the word on the guys?" he asked, at the first chance to get a word in.

Beecher's face fell. "I thought you knew."

"When we left Dong Tam, nobody knew shit." Danny had a bad feeling in the pit of his stomach.

"They were wiped out, Mulvaney," the sergeant whispered. "All but four."

"Jesus." Danny's head felt light. He thought he might pass out. He leaned against the sandbag wall. "Four?"

"Doc, Paco, Simms, and Corporal. Tyler and Fuquette are missing."

Danny moaned and sat on the dirty wood floor to avoid keeling over. Beecher rummaged in the captain's desk and came up with his scotch.

"Six won't mind," he said, as he poured three fingers into a canteen cup. Handing it to Danny, he poured some for himself. He straddled a wooden chair and faced Danny, leaning his forearms on the backrest. "Drink," he ordered.

Danny gulped the amber fluid. He had never tasted scotch

whiskey before. It tasted like iodine. He thought of the little girl in the village, the one who had shared his cookie. It seemed like a million years ago.

"Did you say Fuquette and Tyler are missing?" he asked, when he could control his breathing.

Beecher nodded.

"Why was Davy with them?"

"His idea. Charlie-Six didn't think it could hurt, so he told Tyler to take him along."

"And there's been no word?"

"Not since Booker and his guys found the—the bodies. Colonel's ordered them to search until dusk. Choppers will pick them up then and bring them in. Captain doesn't think it safe to leave them out another night. Charley's got to know how thin we are here. Everybody's bushed. We've been on alert since late last night."

"Where's Six?"

"Colonel picked him up in the C and C. They went out to try and find them from the air. Got gunships, Loaches, and a coupla FACs out looking, too. Your friend Smith went along to help with the radios."

"He's no friend of mine."

"Tyler said we were wrong about you, Mulvaney. If we were, I'm sorry."

"You were, and you are. Sorry, I mean," Danny said, locking eyes with the sergeant, anger bubbling up from past injustices.

"I guess you're entitled to be bitter. Helluva way to treat your host when you're drinking his whiskey. I figured we were even after the CS."

Danny heard the forgiveness and the wry humor in the sergeant's tone. His frown softened, and he searched for the right words.

"Besides," Beecher continued, "I figure we got the shitty end of the stick."

"How so?"

"We're saddled with Smith." He shook his head as if mystified. "That guy is weird. He looks and talks like a West Point poster boy, but something's missing. I can't put a name to it."

"Substance?"

Beecher snapped his fingers. "Bingo!"

"I thought he was Joe Army myself when we were in Basic. Lance tumbled to him early. Said he was all smoke and mirrors. I should have listened."

"Well, he ain't fucked up lately, but I hate to have to watch him all the time. Six won't dump him 'cause he thinks it'll look like he was wrong. Leastways, that's what I think. Not that you would give two shits." He grinned openly.

Danny said, "I bet whoever rigged that CS grenade—and I have no idea who it was—didn't mean for you to get it, too."

"Forget it," Beecher said, offering his hand. Danny stood to take it. "Second's bunker is on the south side, behind the mess hall," Beecher continued. "Get settled in. I'll send someone for you if there's any news."

Orienting himself by facing the main gate, which faced the road, Danny figured out where the south side of the camp was located and soon found Second Platoon's quarters. The interior of the bunker looked like pictures he'd seen of concentration camp housing. Four by four posts served as uprights for rude, bunk bed-style sleeping platforms. The same flat springs used in the steel bunks at Dong Tam rested on two-by-four frames with thin, lumpy, striped mattresses thrown over them. What light there was came from the two doorways at the ends of the structure. Both faced the interior of the camp. There were no shooting ports. These were sleeping quarters.

Wooden ammo crates stored under the bottom bunks served as lockers for the men's personal items. American ingenuity was alive and well in the American soldier. The same artillery shell boxes that the men used for storage became furniture, sidewalk paving, even the very walls of the bunkers. Filled with dirt, stacked in interlocking fashion like bricks, nailed together and to the sixteen-inch beams that comprised the framework, the sturdy cases made solid building materials. The flat roof was built of abutting beams laid the length of the building. The exterior was covered with several layers of sandbags.

"They built this to last," Danny whispered, brushing the wall with his fingertips. He read the names of his dead friends, printed in black ink on white tape on the personal lockers. Tears burned his eyes. He found one with his name on it. All of the gear he had left behind when he was wounded was stored under the bunk. Grief twisted his gut as he realized they had been waiting for him to return. Unable to stand another moment in this dreary tomb, Danny dumped his rucksack on the bed nearest his locker and ran outside.

Leaning against the green bags, he wiped his eyes and fumbled in his pocket for a cigarette. He looked up at the cloudy sky and heard a chopper beating the air from a long way off. He scanned the horizon. A flash of sunlight on the windscreen caught his attention, and he stood watching as the tiny speck grew to become a Huey. He ran to meet it as it settled to the ground outside the camp.

Expectant men surrounded Captain Arnold when he climbed down from the cabin. With a grimace and a quick shake of his head, he told them there was no news. Shielding their eyes from the bits of grass and garbage thrown into a cyclone by the whirling blades, the captain and Smitty walked swiftly to the berm and climbed over into the compound as the colonel's ship lifted off.

"Mulvaney," the captain said when he noticed Danny. "How are you?"

Danny shrugged and mumbled, "Okay, sir."

"I'm glad you weren't—" Arnold began, but cut himself short.

"They find anything, Captain?" Danny asked as they walked together to the CP.

Smitty hung back, apparently deciding to give Mulvaney a wide berth.

"No sign of Lieutenant Tyler or Sergeant Fuquette. Third Platoon is still searching. Come inside, and I'll tell you what I know."

When Danny looked, Smitty had vanished.

Danny found the captain's kindly tone and polite conversation odd. This man hated him, at least he had not so long ago. Captain Arnold's entire personality seemed to have changed. He lacked the confidence he once exuded. He seemed humbled, almost apologetic.

In the bunker, the captain motioned Danny to sit and poured scotch for the three of them. He offered cigarettes and sat heavily behind his camp desk as he said to Danny, "I understand Private Corporal is a friend of yours from back in The World."

For once, it didn't sound funny. Danny nodded.

"He's okay. He, Specialist Simms, Specialist Laffin, and Specialist Cortez survived the battle," the captain continued. "They were dusted off along with the—casualties." He paused to take a sip of his scotch. "They'll be checked out at the Third Surge. They aren't hurt physically, but they are in shock. They'll be debriefed afterward. The army needs to know how this happened—to prevent any re-occurrence, you understand."

Danny nodded, but Beecher said, "'Scuse me, sir, but I'm sure Mulvaney does *not* understand. Somebody will have to take the blame for this, Danny. The goddamn press will be on it like white on rice. It will probably be Tyler, poor bastard. Division will be thinking damage control. Shit, sir, those motherfuckers may come after you."

"That's my problem, Sergeant, not yours. We have more important things to worry about."

Beecher started to say something else, but Arnold said, "Shut up, Sergeant. We lost a platoon last night, and the last thing I wish to discuss is the effect on anybody's career."

Beecher said, "Yes, sir," and went back to his drink.

"The colonel has advised me that he will get us some replacements aysap," Arnold went on, changing the subject entirely. "The old man swore to me that he would go to the Ninetieth Replacement personally, if he has to, and bring back enough people to rebuild the Second Platoon. Until they get here and your friends return, as the only member of that unit present, Mulvaney—"

Last of the Mohicans, Danny thought.

"—I'd like to ask a favor of you," Arnold finished.

Danny swirled the scotch in his canteen cup and waited.

"We have to send the personal effects of the dead home," Arnold said. "Normally, that's handled by S-Four." He made a face that showed the distaste he harbored for the rear echelon. "They're supposed to go through the deceased's stuff and discard any embarrassing items."

Danny looked puzzled.

"You know. Fuck books, dirty pictures, drug paraphernalia, love letters from women other than wives—that sort of shit."

Danny nodded. "Oh."

"Anything that might make the family uncomfortable," the captain resumed. "What happens all too often is those pricks in the rear steal anything of any value or use. I don't want that to happen to our people. Normally, the platoon leader is asked to do the preliminary. In his absence, the platoon sergeant gets the job. Staff Sergeant Pomeroy has not been released from the hospital as yet—"

Danny's lowered head snapped up. "Pomeroy's *alive?*"

"Yes, of course, I—"

Arnold's astonished look prompted Beecher to interrupt. "That's *right*. You wouldn't know," he said to Danny. "Pomeroy took some shrapnel just after you left. He wasn't with them."

Tears of joy streamed down Danny's cheeks. Such unexpected good news lifted the pall from the room.

"Sure, sir." Danny sniffed and wiped his nose with his sleeve. "I'll do what you want. They deserve to have one of their own do it."

The irony of his now belonging to the platoon he had felt barely a part of days before was not lost on Danny. He was saddened to feel so close to them now that they were gone. In their honor, he promised himself, he would be a man they would have been proud to call brother, a living memorial to the Second Platoon of Charlie Company.

"Take the crates in the bunker back to Dong Tam," Beecher said. "Go through them and the foot lockers in the platoon's hootch. Sound okay, sir?" he added, realizing he had chimed in without being asked.

The captain nodded. "We'll get some help loading them on a truck. You can wait in Delta Tango for the replacements and help Sergeant Pomeroy bring them down here."

"You're sure I won't be needed here?"

"I'll need you more to help rebuild my Second Platoon."

The captain seemed tired. His face had the look of a man who couldn't bear his load.

"You can count on me, sir," Danny promised.

CHAPTER 53

Y ou say this came in yesterday?" Sam Hellinghausen asked of the pudgy US Army colonel seated across the gray metal desk in his office. He was talking about a bloodstained khaki bush hat that the colonel had deposited on his desk blotter.

The colonel nodded and sipped a Coke straight from the can. "Yeah, Sam. The action took place the day before. A real mess. Twenty dead, two missing in action, the platoon leader one of them." The overweight colonel snorted. "He may be hiding. He fucked up and got his whole platoon greased. If they find him, they'll probably hang him."

Hellinghausen smiled to show he was one of the boys, the ones who looked down their noses at other people's mistakes and found comfort in watching them take their lumps. He didn't feel that way, but he knew the Agency was as rife with the type as the military. He had found it best to pretend to share the viewpoint of those who were in a position to do him good. "I wish they hadn't blown the cache," he said. "Might have been some valuable information in there."

"The officer in charge thought it best. They were running out of daylight," the fat colonel explained. "I'm sure he didn't relish spending the night out there with whoever waxed his buddy's outfit still stalking the woods. Besides, the hole was filled with boxes of dynamite, real antique stuff, unstable as hell. They say the kid who fell in the hole, the medic as I recall, was damned lucky not to have been blown to kingdom come."

"Guess it couldn't be helped." The CIA operative sighed. He held the bush hat up. "Can you leave this with me?"

"If you think it will help," the colonel said, "but I can't imagine how. The general will want it back, though. It makes a nice conversation piece in his trophy case."

"Of course." Hellinghausen stood to indicate the meeting was at an end. "Thanks for taking the trouble to come down personally, Joe."

"No sweat, Sam. Gave me a chance to get out of the office." He smiled and shook the spook's hand. The colonel had a reputation as a man who took great pains to ingratiate himself to anyone who could help his career.

As soon as the corpulent colonel had departed, Hellinghausen unlocked the four-drawer filing cabinet that was the only office furniture in his tiny cubicle besides his desk and two chairs. He riffled through some files until he found the one he sought. He laid it on the desk beside the bloodstained bush hat. Flipping through the folder, he hummed tunelessly until he extracted a folded sheet of paper. Spreading it on the desktop, he compared the drawing on it to the emblem on the head gear.

A call to Major Co confirmed that Mui was still on ice and readily available for questioning. He instructed the major to rustle him up. He dialed the black phone again.

"General." Sam smiled when the G-2 answered the phone. "Sam here." He listened and then said, "Yes, sir, Joe just dropped it off. His briefing was informative and complete, as usual. That's why I'm calling. I may have something on that unit crest. I've got some artwork on file that bears a striking resemblance to it." He paused once again while the general asked another question. "Yes, sir, I'll know more this afternoon once I've had a little talk with the artist. Will you have any time for me today?" Hellinghausen nodded. "Sixteen hundred would be fine, sir. I'm buying."

Sam hung up the phone and leaned back in his swivel chair to light a cigarette, thinking: *Sometimes it's nice to have a sledgehammer in your pocket.*

CHAPTER 54

Danny lay supine on his bunk in Dong Tam, asleep atop a poncho liner blanket. A large electric floor fan blew a stiff breeze across his face, keeping hungry mosquitoes at bay. He had worked at examining and sealing the dead men's belongings from the time they had unloaded the truck until the wee hours of the morning when, physically and emotionally exhausted, he had collapsed. A shaft of sunlight burning through the slats in the walls of the hootch struck his eyes and awakened him. He sat up, disoriented. The sad sight of the footlockers, neatly stacked on both sides of the aisle, reminded him he was nearly finished. Five remained in the unopened pile.

Having skipped dinner with no appetite, and having slept through breakfast, he was famished. After packing the box he had been working on when sleep had overtaken him, he nailed it shut and scratched an X on the lid with a piece of chalk. His wristwatch said he could still make lunch if he hurried. Rubbing the stubble on his jaw, he walked to the mess hall. He downed two cups of lukewarm Kool-Aid from the stainless-steel urn before going to the chow line. Hot dogs and sauerkraut were the entire bill of fare.

Danny took two shriveled wieners, pumped mustard on them from the yellow squeeze bottle on the nearest table, and turned to refill his cup.

"Mulvaney!" Master Sergeant Jellicks called from the rear of the dining room. "Join me. You looked about a million miles away," Jellicks said, as Danny took a seat across from him. "How goes it?"

"Almost done," Danny said around a mouthful of frankfurter. "Five more to go."

"I would have been glad to help," Jellicks told him.

"I know, Sarge, and I appreciate it." Danny took a breath. "It's just..."

"I understand." Jellicks raised his cup in salute, bowing his head slightly. "They were family. You needed to do this for them."

Danny sat motionless for a moment, staring into his tray. He could not have verbalized it as well. "I guess that's it."

"I lost a squad in France." The master sergeant sighed. "Screaming Mimis caught us in a street in this pretty little town near the Seine. Never knew what hit us. Whole thing was over in seconds. I walked away. Never knew why. It took a long time to understand that it just wasn't my time. Strange how surviving can make you feel so guilty."

"I'm okay, Sarge," Danny assured him.

"If you need to talk, or you want to tie one on or something..."

"I know where to find you."

"Good. Anything we need to dispose of?" Jellicks asked, more to change the subject than from any genuine curiosity. A soldier's private affairs were just that. He was trying to make conversation.

"A few Playboys, some French postcards, couple of torrid letters from girlfriends. Not much." He didn't mention the hash pipes, marijuana, opium, and an assortment of pills that would shame the average drug store. The contraband was found in only a few of the lockers, but it seemed that the men who had been into drugs had been serious in their pursuit of a good high. He would dispose of this stuff in secret so as not to stain the memory of his friends. Maybe he'd keep some of the grass. He hadn't decided.

"Let me know when you're through." Jellicks pushed himself from the table. "I'll have Sedarius do the paperwork and get the stuff on its way."

Danny was feeling better after his talk with the master sergeant, and as he pounded the last nail in the last locker, Pomeroy walked in. They embraced like long lost brothers, neither hesitant nor ashamed of their grief. Danny was clapping Pomeroy on the back when the staff sergeant winced.

"Easy, Daniel," Pomeroy sniffed. "It's still a bit tender there."

"Jesus, I'm sorry, Sarge. I forgot. They told me you took one in the back."

"It's all right. Just a little sore is all." Pomeroy smiled, wiped tears from his eyes, and sat on a bunk.

"Shrapnel?"

"Yup. Mortar." Pomeroy nodded. "Long sucker. Couple or three inches. Jagged sumbitch. Slow moving. Didn't go deep. Knocked me flat on my puss. Funny thing was, I heard it coming. Whoop, whoop, whoop." He made a tumbling motion with his hands. "And then, *wham*. Hit me like a baseball bat between the shoulder blades."

"You were lucky."

"Bullshit!" Pomeroy laughed. "If I was lucky, the fucker would have missed."

Danny had to laugh at the truth in that statement.

"Whatcha doin' here?" The sergeant's sweeping hand took in the piles of footlockers.

"Getting the guys' stuff ready to be sent home," Danny said. "Just finished."

"What say we get the hell out of here for a spell? This shit gives me the creeps."

They went to the NCO Club. Pomeroy waved aside Danny's fears of being caught and expelled as a private.

"You ain't wearin' no rank, and I'll vouch for ya. After you, Sergeant." He did an exaggerated bow as he held the door for Danny to enter. The master at arms took no notice of either of them.

The club was dark, cool, and quiet at this early hour. A pretty Vietnamese girl in a skintight mini-skirt served them. Danny watched her buttocks wiggle as she walked away. Pouring his beer into a tall glass, he realized that he had probably done more drinking since his arrival in Vietnam than he had in all the time since he had turned eighteen. It didn't seem worth worrying about at the moment.

"Here's to the best goddamn platoon the US Army ever had," Pomeroy said solemnly, raising his glass.

Danny clinked glasses with the staff sergeant and drank. He began to put his beer down when he saw that the sergeant was chug-a-lugging his bourbon and Coke. Danny imitated him.

"Baby-san!" Pomeroy yelled with two fingers held aloft, "*Lai de mau.*"

"Do you think Tyler and Fuquette are alive?" Danny asked the question to which he dreaded the answer.

"No, Daniel. I'm very sorry to say, I do not." The sergeant's brow wrinkled as he shook his head. "If they was, they woulda turned up by now."

"Then you don't think they were taken prisoner?"

"I hope not." Pomeroy saw Danny's shock. "They'd be better off dead, Danny. Charley don't take a helluva lot of prisoners in the Delta. He's got no place to keep 'em, first of all. Second, he's not willin' to risk his people tryin' to get POWs across the border. And third, the average GI's simply got no value. He don't know shit. Leastways, nothin' Charley don't know already."

"So, if Charley catches them, he's going to kill them?"

"Bet on it." Pomeroy guzzled his drink. "And he ain't gonna be merciful about it." He looked at Danny as if he was weighing something in his mind. "You might as well know. Best chance a man has over here is to know all there is to know." He rocked back in his chair and set his glass in his lap, holding it with both hands. "Chopper got shot down a few months back. Right after Tet, as I recall. They sent us out to burn the ship and rescue the crew, or at least get the bodies back. When we got there, the bird was in one piece. Shot up some, but they got it down without cracking up. The crew was gone. We followed their trail, and we could see from the sandal prints mixed in with the jungle boot tracks that Chuck was either hot on their tails or with them. We found them late that afternoon—tied to trees—spread-eagled. The gooks had cut their dicks off and stuffed them in their mouths. There were no other wounds, so they done it while they were alive."

Danny felt sick to his stomach.

"Like the man said," Pomeroy growled, "'War is hell.' But actual combat is a motherfucker. Now, drink up. Let's enjoy bein' just you and me for a time. When we go back down to the company, we go back to bein' staff sergeant and private first class."

"Not so loud," Danny whispered.

"Drink, Mulvaney, or forever be known as private no class."

CHAPTER 55

Tyler shivered in the tiger cage, wet and cold, hanging two feet above the ground in a bamboo prison. At least the NVA officer had finally left him alone. His bare feet were torture enough after more than twenty-four hours in wet boots. No sooner had the enemy soldier stripped him of his footgear than the maddening itch had begun. It felt like thousands of tiny insects had swarmed from heel to toe to devour his shriveled, fish-belly white flesh. The itch turned to burning. Saw grass and thorns had sliced and punctured his soles as they ran from the battlefield. Instead of relief, immersion in water amplified the sensation of walking on hot coals. Walking through the swamp was agony. Then, a tree branch had been thrust between his back and his bound arms to further hamper him. It caught on every limb and vine, spinning him around and frequently causing him to lose his balance. When he fell, he was kicked, punched, and poked with rifle muzzles until he regained his feet. His captors cursed him and spat in his face.

The blindfold had been unnecessary. His vision was so badly blurred by the blow on the head, he could not have seen enough to find his way back. He still didn't know what the enemy officer had been carrying on about. He must be an officer: he gave orders. What had he been waving in front of his face? A gray and white blur, he thought, square in shape, like a photograph. Why would an enemy officer be so upset about a photograph and why was he showing it to him? And what had happened to his men? His last memory was of a terrific volume of fire at close range. The next thing he knew he was a prisoner. He prayed that the platoon had survived the fight.

Night in the jungle was always frightening, but tonight, locked in a bamboo cage, was worse than anything in Tyler's memory. The ceaseless rain seemed to soak through to the very marrow in his bones. The enemy camp was quiet, except for slithering sounds in the brush and the occasional shriek of some animal falling victim to a predator. Tyler prayed more fervently than he had in his lifetime. He prayed for salvation. He prayed for an end to his misery. He prayed for a peaceful death.

℮∕ℨℰ∕ℨ

Fuquette slit the wrapper of a LRRP ration pouch with a stiletto he kept in his boot. He set the plastic bag on the thick bough of the tree he occupied so that rainwater would soften the dehydrated meal. The meals were tastier hot but could be eaten cold. He had three more of the lightweight meals stuffed in the cargo pockets of his jungle fatigues. When they were gone, he would have to live off the land. His biggest worry was not food and water—he was well trained in survival. His greatest concern was the risk of discovery.

Having trailed these boys back to their hideout, he now had to watch and wait for his opening. If they gave him a chance, he would snatch the lieutenant and be gone before they knew it. He'd had plenty of chances to kill a few and make his escape but not without getting Tyler killed in the bargain. He needed to know much more before he would risk his neck or Two-Six's.

These guys were good, of that there was no question. Their noise and light discipline went way beyond the average enemy soldier. They were not VC, he was sure. They were too good, even for the NVA. It would be helpful if he could ascertain their identity, if not their mission. Patience is the sniper's religion. He would bide his time, build clever hides and watch. For the present, he needed to find a likely spot for his base of operations. He needed to sleep. Better to do it away from the perimeter of the camp, then here, fifteen feet in the air. They were smart enough to supplement their guard positions with roving patrols. If caught, his weapon and camo fatigues would identify him. American Snipers were not among Charley's favorite people. If they found him napping—

He decided it would be better not to think about it.

CHAPTER 56

Captain Arnold held a meeting of his officers and NCOs. He had to raise his voice to be heard over the cacophony of the rain that drummed steadily on the tin roof of the unfinished mess hall. It would have been safer to hold the meeting in a bunker, but the men were weary of the close quarters of their protective dwellings. The stink of unwashed bodies combined with the ever-present odors of mold and mildew made the bunkers unpleasant. During mortar attacks, the comfort of several feet of wood and dirt overhead made the whine of flying hot metal less frightening. At all other times, the men preferred the open air. A round through the still un-sandbagged corrugated steel roof of the mess hall would, in all probability, decimate C-Company's command structure.

With three hours until nightfall, and the Arvins running a sweep of the nearest wood lines, it seemed an acceptable risk. Half-joking remarks about the Arvins mortaring the base were met with nervous laughter. An imaginative discussion regarding the elimination of VC infiltrator rats on the base was beginning to yield some creative solutions—foremost of which involved nuclear weapons and the annihilation of every living thing within a click—when the captain called for attention.

"Gentlemen," Arnold began, "you are here to learn of the situation in which you will be operating in the immediate future."

The captain paused as the room settled down. This was the kind of briefing that got everyone's attention. They were hopeful they would leave here with information that directly affected their lives and the continuation thereof.

"The battalion commander has informed me that we can ex-

pect to welcome several dozen replacements in short order." He
paused for the cheers to subside. "As you know, the devastating
loss of our Second Platoon sufficiently reduced the manpower of
this unit to render it combat ineffective in its present role." He
paused again to let the grumbling and bitching die down. "I know
we had our asses put into a sling from the word go, but Higher
felt it imperative to get this base under way soonest. The reception we received upon arrival and the action that took our brothers
in the Second serves to underline the need for a strong presence
in this AO. Charley has had his run of this neck of the woods for
too long. We're going to put an end to that. The rest of the battalion is still involved in mopping up around Charleyville. We hope
they'll conclude their mission and join us here shortly. Until that
time, it's all on us.

"With regards to the new men, I have decided to use most of
the replacements to form a new Second Platoon. The survivors of
the massacre will stay with their element and act as trainers for
this new unit. They await the FNGs' arrival in Dong Tam and
will take a few days to orient these people to their mission and
responsibilities before bringing them down here. Once they arrive,
they'll be primarily employed on perimeter defense and close-in
patrol duties until I feel they are ready for a wider role. This will
impact the veteran platoons in several ways. You'll bear the brunt
of most field operations."

The groans nearly outdid the pounding of the rain on the tin
roof.

"But you'll get more rest when you're in the camp. Garrison
duties for the veterans will be kept to a minimum. That should
help you sell it to the troops. As far as a platoon leader for the
Second, Colonel Conte has hand-picked a man for the job. He
will also be coming down with the replacements after the initial
indoctrination. I will keep you informed of further developments.
Dismissed."

As the officers and noncoms filed out of the building, First
Lieutenant Chicarelli scooped two cups of coffee from the Mer-
mite cans at the end of the serving counter.

"Thanks, Chick," the captain said, as he took the offered cup
and lowered himself into a chair.

Lieutenant Chicarelli took a seat at the table opposite his
commander and stirred his drink with a plastic spoon. He avoided

Arnold's eyes as he said, "You think this is a good idea, sir? Manning an entire platoon with green troops, I mean."

"As I recall, the army defends the democracy but does not operate under its ideals," Arnold said.

"I'm not questioning your orders, Captain, I—"

"Then what the hell are you doing, Lieutenant?"

Arnold could see, by the look on his face, that Chicarelli realized he had overstepped his bounds but was determined to voice his opinion. "Sir, don't get me wrong, it's just that I—" the lieutenant began, but the captain stopped him.

"Could it be that you doubt my judgment after the massacre of one of our platoons? Maybe you think it's time I took command of a desk and leave the fighting to better qualified people such as yourself?"

"That's not fair."

"Life isn't fair, Lieutenant. War isn't fair. It isn't fair to put the responsibility for the lives of all these kids on the back of one man. But that's the way it is, goddammit. If I start second- guessing myself the odds of keeping those young men alive goes way down." He sipped his coffee, grimaced, and threw the contents of the cup on the ground. "And if my officers start questioning my orders, it will only serve to undermine the foundations of this company. Do you understand what I'm saying to you, Lieutenant?" he finished, his jaw set like stone, his eyes unblinking.

"Yes, sir," Chicarelli said. "I'm sorry if the captain misread my intentions." He stared into Arnold's eyes. "The lieutenant was seeking clarification."

raised one eyebrow. "Of what?" Arnold

Chicarelli had no answer.

Arnold had accomplished what he had to. Chicarelli's squirming in his seat, as he racked his brain for an answer, was sufficient. Lester Arnold had great respect for the young man seated across from him, but he could not tolerate hesitation or misgivings with regard to his decisions. It was time to let his second-in-command off the hook now that the lesson had been taught. "If you're looking for logic in this decision," Arnold said in a gentler tone, "sound reasoning, or mathematical probability...well, there isn't any." He lit a cigarette and blew smoke at the steel ceiling. It hung in the still, humid air, flattening out below the exposed rafters. "It's more gut feeling. Spreading the replacements around like so much seasoning and pulling members of our other platoons from their accustomed teams strikes me as stirring the pot before reading the cook book." He smiled at his domestic metaphor, somehow appropriate in the present surroundings. "The men would feel unjustly penalized for the misfortune of Tyler's people." He leaned his elbows on the table, and said, "Right or wrong, that's the way I'm going to play it. Until now, I've been right more often than wrong. If you have doubts, you can always request a transfer."

"Not doubts, Charlie-Six." Chick bowed his head briefly and then looked Arnold squarely in the eye. "I guess I'm just scared. The Indians are surrounding the fort, and the cavalry is nowhere in sight. This whole deal gets flakier by the day."

"Roger that." Arnold sighed. He rose to go and motioned with his hands for Chicarelli to keep his seat. "Have a word with Sergeant Krales about the quality of his coffee, Chick. Either square it away or hang a non-potable sign on the urn." He winked and left.

CHAPTER 57

Second Lieutenant Jasper T. Johnson stepped gingerly from the Jeep, lest mud mar the glistening spit-shine on the toe caps of his new jungle boots. Once on solid ground, he took his first look at Charlie Company's portion of Dong Tam Base Camp, and said, "My God, what a hell hole."

He still wasn't sure whose sensibilities he had ruffled in order to draw this assignment. Someone had shafted him, of that, he was sure. His Infantry MOS—Mode of Service—had been an unfortunate but necessary happenstance required to get a slot in Officer's Candidate School. If he had to fulfill his military obligation, it had seemed better to do so as an officer. The Combat Arms being the only way open to him to achieve that status at the time had seemed only mildly troublesome. Infantry won out over Artillery and Armor. One had all that noisy, heavy equipment to contend with in the other two branches. Besides, he had never dreamed his National Guard unit might be activated.

Still, he had managed to avoid the unpleasantness associated with the life of a foot soldier by wheedling his way into one cushy job after another—until now.

Lieutenant Johnson shrugged off this temporary setback. He thought it not in his nature to dwell upon the vagaries of lesser beings. Through malicious mischief or blind stupidity, someone had deigned to test his mettle as a platoon leader. So be it. He would master the trade of leading ruffians in battle and move on to pursuits worthier of his talents.

Master Sergeant Jellicks met him at the steps to the Orderly Room, welcomed the new platoon leader to Charlie Company, and directed him to the Second Platoon hootch. Johnson declined his offer of accompaniment and set out on his own.

Leaning against the doorjamb, Jellicks watched the new Two-Six step nimbly around puddles as he wended his way to the Second's barracks.

"That's the colonel's hand-picked honcho, eh?" he threw over his shoulder. "Where'd he pick him out of? His ass?"

"He was supposed to be the new Battalion S-Four," Sedarius commented as he finished the replacement's paperwork. "Colonel figured Supply got along fine without him 'til now so he sidetracked him to us."

"Where's he been?"

"Saigon," the clerk replied, consulting Johnson's 201 file. "Ran a women's work camp for MACV."

"What's an infantry lieutenant doing ramrodding a bunch of mamasans in Saigon?" Jellicks asked under his breath.

"Hiding," said the sharp-eared clerk.

෴

Johnson's nose wrinkled at the smell of stale beer when he entered the platoon bay. Six men, in varying degrees of undress, lay sprawled across as many bunks. The colonel had briefed him on the ordeal that four of these men had endured. The other two had most certainly commiserated with their fellows. *Well, they had had their binge*, he thought. *Time to soldier.* "Gentleman!" he rapped in his best command timbre. "Formation in the company street. Up and at 'em. Let's go. Off and on. Move it, soldiers. You're on my time now."

Amazing, he thought, how the lessons of Basic Combat Training came back to you when confronted with leadership responsibility. He did an about face, marched smartly into the street, and stood at attention to await his men.

Lance groaned and said, "What the fuck? Over."

"I'm havin' a nightmare," Simms whined. "I'm dreaming some lifer lieutenant just called a formation."

"Must be a day-mare," Danny groaned. "And I'll thank you to leave me out of your horrible dreams."

The remnants of the Second Platoon had been drinking since shortly after their reunion the previous day.

Once the initial shame at having survived their comrades subsided, they had loosened their tongues with alcohol until grief had broken the floodgates. They had cried on each other's shoulders, cursed capricious fate and Charley Cong for wasting the young lives of their brothers. Then they had begun the slow, painful process of healing. Lieutenant Johnson had rudely disrupted the pattern.

"Better go see what he wants," Pomeroy advised, peeking through the screen. "Don't look like he's going away anytime soon."

They shuffled outside and into a ragged formation.

"Sir, Staff Sergeant Pomeroy reports," Pomeroy barked, stepping forward to snap a salute. "All present and accounted for, sir."

"Where are the snipers when we need them?" Paco whispered.

Johnson returned the salute with a crisp snap. "At ease," he ordered. The men fell into a relaxed parade rest.

"Gentlemen, I am Lieutenant Jasper T. Johnson," he stated proudly.

"I won't tell nobody if you don't," Lance mumbled.

Danny almost wet his pants fighting to keep a straight face.

"I am your new platoon leader," the short martinet continued.

"Dat's it, I quit," Lance whispered.

"Answer to your names, please, as I call the roll," the lieutenant said. He read from an index card, calling them one by one, according to rank, with Pomeroy first. Each man answered in turn. Johnson studied their faces to familiarize himself with their names. "Specialists Simms and Cortez," he announced, "are hereby promoted to the rank of sergeant. Specialist Laffin to spec/five. PFCs Corporal and Mulvaney are promoted to corporal. Congratulations, gentlemen," he said, looking up from the slip of paper, "the new Second Platoon will be proud of its leaders, I am sure. The replacements for your fallen comrades will be arriving within the next day or so. Sergeants Simms and Cortez, as well as Corporals Mulvaney and Corporal, will be my squad leaders. Please take the time remaining to get your uniforms squared away and see to your grooming. Haircuts will be mandatory as well as some polish on those boots. That will be all for now. Dismissed."

He did a perfect left face and marched to the Orderly Room.

"*Madre de Dios*," Paco breathed. The others, as if struck dumb, stared at the receding back of their new leader.

"Why do I feel like I've just been screwed?" Danny asked as the group wandered toward the piss tube to relieve themselves of the remnants of last night's three cases of beer.

"Because you have," Simms answered. "Sarge," he said to Pomeroy, "you're not going to let him do this to us, are you?"

"You boys are acting mighty ungrateful, seein's how y'all just got a raise in pay," Pomeroy said. "Y'all non-commissioned officers now. Best be cool and act the part. Specially seein' as how the lieutenant is watchin'." They followed his eyes to where Johnson was standing in the Orderly Room doorway, hands on hips, studying his new subordinates with the air of a man examining livestock on an auction block. "We'll talk in the hootch."

"I'm not givin' up my gun, man," Paco led off when they sat in a circle back in the barracks.

Doc was making C-ration coffee from water he boiled over burning C-4 explosive on the concrete floor beside his bunk and passing canteen cups of the eye-opening brew to his friends.

"Never heard of a squad leader carrying a Sixty," Pomeroy said.

"Then I don't want to be no squad leader," Paco sneered.

"He's right, man," Simms interjected. "Paco's the best gunner in the company. Be stupid to take his gun away, and I'm not giving up the blooper," he vowed.

"Don't suppose you'd have to." Pomeroy nodded. "Nothing says a squad leader can't carry a Seventy-Nine."

"What about me and Lance?" Danny asked. "We've only been in country a couple of months. What the hell do we know about being squad leaders?"

"A damn sight more than the newgies you'll be headin' up," Pomeroy stated flatly. "Now listen up, people. We don't know shit about this new Two-Six we got here. But we do know more than he does 'bout what goes on outside the berm. I didn't see no CIB on his shirt. Did you hear those commands? He's as wet behind the ears as a catfish. It's gonna be up to us to get his shit straight before he gets his ass blown away and ours with it. You may not like it much, but there it is."

Danny looked at Doc as the disgruntled group chewed on their platoon sergeant's words. Laffin quietly blew air over his steaming cup. "What do you think, Doc?" Danny asked.

Doc had been uncharacteristically reticent since his return to Dong Tam.

"Don't mean nothin'." Doc shrugged.

"Well, Doctor Always," Simms said amiably, throwing an arm around his friend's shoulder, "I have never known you to be a fence-sitter on any issue. Do you mean to tell me that the sage of the Second Platoon doesn't have an opinion on our present sitch-e-ation?"

"What difference does it make?" Doc sighed and went to his bunk to lie down.

"He'll be all right," Simms promised, his voice little more than a whisper, as the others stared in disbelief at the silent figure of their once outspoken buddy. "He's takin' it hard. He feels like he coulda done somethin' if he hadn't fallen in that hole."

"He coulda' died is what," Lance said.

"Yeah, I know, maybe he thinks that would've been better."

"He's gotta snap out of it, Bert," Danny said. "We're going to need him."

"Roger that," Simms nodded.

Lance broke the pitying silence with, "Where do you think they dug up this Johnson clown?"

"Can you believe that name, man?" Paco laughed. "Jasper T. Johnson. His momma and papa musta hated him."

Lance spread his thighs and pointed to his crotch. "Now *this here* is a Johnson. And this bad little mutha stands as tall as our new platoon leader at attention. Anybody care to salute?"

He was answered with a round of single digit salutes.

"What do you suppose the T stands for?" Danny asked.

"The," Lance suggested to howls of approval.

"Corporal Corporal." Pomeroy winked at Danny and turned to Lance as he said, "You should be the last dude to goof on people's names."

Lance waited for the jeers and laughter to die down, and said, "Mebbe so, but something tells me the new Two-Six's name is the only thing funny about the muthafucka."

Danny stole a glance at the Orderly Room. Johnson was still in the doorway and still in the same posture. When he looked back at his friends, he saw that each of them was absorbed in his own private thoughts. When Lance looked up, their eyes met, and Danny remembered his prophetic words about Smitty.

CHAPTER 58

A long, hand-painted plank hung over the fire base gate, notched on both ends with a series of triangular cuts like Hollywood's version of a western ranch sign. The lettering proclaimed the fledgling Second Platoon's new home to be Fire Base Dagger.

The Second rolled in on the morning convoy and fell out in platoon formation at Lieutenant Johnson's order. Most of the veterans stopped what they were doing and watched with amusement as the new platoon followed their officer's commands. He marched them around the ring road to the CP, calling cadence all the way, ignoring the catcalls and jeers from the vets. When he halted the platoon, he sang out the appropriate commands.

"Right—*face! Dress right—dress!* Present—*arms!* Order—arms!*"

The men performed the movements like a practiced drill team, which was what Lieutenant Peckerhead, as he was becoming widely known, apparently thought he was leading. Their time in Dong Tam had been spent in what might best be called Basic Training review. The new men simply did as they were told through it all. The veterans never seemed to get the looks of astonishment off their faces.

Once the new Second Platoon had completed the abbreviated manual of arms for the incredulous defenders of Fire Base Dagger, Second Lieutenant Jasper T. Johnson stood proudly in front of his charges, whipped a crisp salute, and bellowed, "Second Platoon, C-Company, reporting as ordered, *sir!*" to Captain Arnold as he emerged from his bunker.

The captain stepped quickly back inside. From the doorway,

he beckoned the befuddled officer inside and called Staff Sergeant Pomeroy to the door.

"Dismiss this clusterfuck and get them to their bunker," Arnold rasped. Looking down, he added, "And get the shine off those boots, all of them. You know better than this, Pomeroy," he said with an accusing stare.

"Yes, sir, I do," Pomeroy agreed. He looked past the smoldering captain at Johnson. Arnold nodded.

Pomeroy loitered outside the door long enough to hear Charlie-Six's first words to his newest platoon leader. "If you ever salute me in a combat situation again, Lieutenant, I will shoot you myself. What the fuck do you think this is? Summer camp?"

Pomeroy's self-satisfied grin shone like a beacon as he led the men to their place.

ยจยกยจ

Danny sat cross-legged with his back to the innermost sandbagged wall atop Fire Base Dagger's west-facing lookout tower. He looked up from the letter he was trying to write, squinted in the sunlight, and craned his neck to peer over the top of the wall past the new guy sharing his turn on guard.

The sun was bright for the first time in days, but the mounting clouds to the west promised an end to the welcome relief from the monsoon. The rice paddies and the tropical wood lines, shimmering in the heat, were exotic—if you ignored the barbed wire and shell holes. In the distance, an old peasant farmer stood motionless on a dike, bent over something in the paddy that had his undivided attention.

Papasan produced a stout bamboo pole, slapped furiously at something in the mud, paused to peer intently at the object of his beating and, raising the pole with both hands tightly grasping one end, brought the stick sharply down one last time. In one motion he stooped and retrieved a large water rat from the muck and began a dance of joy on the narrow dike while clutching his catch by the tail.

"What the hell is that old guy doing, Corporal?" Cliff Wyman asked.

"Bagging dinner," Danny replied, bored.

"But isn't that a...a..."

"Yep. Rat, water type, black in color, one each," Danny confirmed, mimicking the government nomenclature American soldiers had learned to expect stenciled on everything they used.

"You mean he's going to eat it?"

"That's a rodge. These people will eat almost anything. When he and his family are done with that little morsel there won't be nothin' left but bones. Waste not, want not." Danny grinned. "Haven't you noticed the scarcity of dogs and cats?"

"*No!*" The innocent Kansas farm boy looked horrified.

"*Yes!* Pets are a luxury these people cannot afford. Rover must look mighty tasty to starving eyes."

"They're animals," Wyman said.

"Aren't we all," Danny replied, frowning at the blank page.

"You go ahead and write your letters, Corporal. I'll keep a sharp eye," the new man declared. His gaze swept the fields surrounding the new base.

"Yeah, right."

Danny hadn't written a letter since he'd been hit. Too much had happened. He'd either been too busy or too depressed. The worrying phrases from his loved ones in his most recent mail had prodded him to answer. He supposed he had spoiled them with his daily epistles in the beginning. Now they feared the worst if they didn't hear from him.

He was angry with the people who wrote to him for putting more pressure on him. Didn't he have enough on his mind? That wasn't fair, he knew.

They loved him and had no way of knowing if he was alive or dead unless he wrote. He just didn't know what to say. He couldn't tell them the truth, could he? Fuquette had told him to, *Lie like a rug.*

God, how he missed Davy.

Dear Mom, he began in his mind, *everything's fine, except all but five of my friends are dead. Two more are missing in action, but we figure they're most likely dead too. It's boring here except for the mortar attacks at night. Did I tell you I was in a helicopter crash and I got shot? Not really shot, it was just a little piece of steel from a rocket or a grenade or something. No big deal. We've got a bunch of new guys who don't know their asses from their elbows, and a new lieutenant who makes them look like vet-*

erans. I got promoted. I'm a squad leader now, mainly because there's nobody else left. I get to give orders that can get six guys killed if I fuck up. Sorry about the language, Mom, but everybody talks like that here. Besides, it was Leon's favorite word. You remember my buddy Leon from Fort Jackson, don't you? Did I mention he's dead too? We're in a new camp that's bigger than we can properly defend and we have no idea when we'll get help. They don't censor our letters like they did in Dad's war or they'd cut all this out. They say it's because our mail is more secure but we know it's because the enemy knows everything before we do anyway. Otherwise, everything's peachy keen. How's the weather there? It rains a lot here.

He snickered at his own black humor. Wyman looked back a wordless question.

"Told myself a joke," Danny said.

The new guy nodded as if that was the most natural thing in the world and made a show of watching the horizon.

He must think we're all nuts, Danny thought. He remembered his first reaction to combat vets. Maybe the kid was right. *Did I look that stupid when I got here?*

His thoughts turned to the new men. They were so painfully green. He hoped they would shape up quickly. Those who didn't would die or go home minus limbs. He didn't want to get to know them, at least not as friends. It hurt too much to lose them. He would, though. Getting close was unavoidable. They shared so much. Mostly they shared fear and uncertainty. Few could bear the burden alone.

The *new* Second Platoon—*F Troop* to the rest of the company—had been on berm guard since their arrival two days prior, with work details interrupting the boredom for a few men at a time. KP, trash hauling, sand bag filling, police calls, rat patrol and shit burning soon made berm guard glamorous duty.

Danny thought of Amanda. He was having trouble remembering her face. At night in his dreams, she was so real he could smell her soft hair, feel her soft skin and be lost in those dark, smoldering eyes. He loved her more each day. He couldn't stand the nagging premonition that he would never see her again. It grew like a cancer in his heart. She was lost to him. Danny hated the swelling rage for revenge that burned within his chest. He wanted to kill and keep on killing to quench his thirst for the blood of his enemy. Amanda would run from him if she saw the beast within him. And she *would* see. He could hide nothing from her.

Had this violent nature always been a part of him? He suspected it had. He had always had a hot temper. He thought he had curbed it, outgrown it, until he came to this awful place. It seemed, in his current state of mind, that it had outgrown *him*. He had never imagined such hate. The remorse for the gooks he had killed was gone. His only regret was that there hadn't been more. There would be. He was determined.

He forced himself to begin the letter to his mother, starting with an apology for his neglect. The rest he made up. The central theme was of being busy with make-work duty and boredom.

When he finished, he read his own words. They were dull. *Perfect.*

So much for Mom, now for Amanda. He skimmed her last three notes. She didn't write every day anymore. Her letters were shorter, as well. Probably losing interest in him. Maybe that was for the best.

Amanda and Jeannie had found an apartment somewhere on the Upper East Side. They would be moving in as soon as the landlord finished painting. The place was furnished, but they would still have to buy a lot of odds and ends. Danny wondered who would be invited to the house warming party. He was certain there would be one, although there was no mention of it. Those girls loved to party.

He realized he hadn't opened her last one. The platoon had been preparing to move and he'd forgotten it on the ride down Highway Four. Johnson had kept them too busy since. He thumbed through the stack until he found it. A newspaper clipping from the New York Times fell out as he unfolded the sheets. He decided to peruse the article first.

GREEN BERET COMPOUND OVER-RUN was the headline. His eyes flicked back and forth in anxiety.

Camp A-666, a Special Forces outpost near the Demilitarized Zone in South Vietnam, was attacked and over-run by a large North Vietnamese unit, sources inside the Pentagon announced today. Initial reports are sketchy, but it is believed that a battal-

ion of ARVN Rangers sent to relieve the beleaguered camp found no survivors.

Danny dropped the scrap of newsprint and hurriedly read Amanda's letter. She didn't know how to tell him, but she thought he'd want to know. Gino was missing in action, presumed dead. Danny's mother had refused to tell her son until she was certain. Amanda was writing against her wishes, but she had been afraid Danny would read about it or hear of it from someone else. She wrote of her sorrow and how she wished she could be there to comfort him in his loss. She said she had met Gino only once, but she had liked him and understood why Danny thought of him as a friend. She hoped she had done the right thing and begged him to write soon so that she would know he was safe.

Danny stared at the paper, frozen in shock and disbelief. *Not Gino. They couldn't have gotten Gino. Nothing could touch him. Gino always came up smelling like a rose. He was invincible.*

Danny wondered why he couldn't cry.

CHAPTER 59

Fuquette's jaw was going to sleep from pressing the stock of his rifle so tightly to his cheek. The eyepiece of the scope was causing his head to throb with the rhythm of his pulse. His finger cramped from restraining the pressure on the trigger. Through the circular lens, he watched the gook commander raise the green bamboo whip again, to bring it down with a *thwack* on Tyler's stomach. The lieutenant was stretched out on the ground, his limbs tied to stakes, his naked body running with sweat in the stifling heat.

⊙≫⊙

Tran had begun the beatings the day after their arrival at the camp. He would make this murdering scum tell him where Mai was being kept. He had convinced himself she was a prisoner. He would not accept that she might be dead. One of this pig's soldiers had carried the picture Tran had given to his sister a lifetime ago. He must know her whereabouts.

As the American's stomach muscles contracted with the pain of the blow, his eyes grew wide with fear and apprehension. His tongue twitched against the filthy rag stuffed in his mouth to muffle his screams.

Tran smiled evilly, tapping the slender stalk in his palm. He had found that systematic beatings exacted the most terror from the American dog. The pain was enhanced when the subject knew where the next blow would strike.

Tran never varied the order. He'd start with the soles of the feet. Next, the biceps would get some brief attention, then the shins, the chest, the thighs, and the stomach, until the American's nostrils flared and perspiration ran in rivulets along the welts. Tran would hesitate before the final phase, savoring the agony in the eyes of his victim. Two rapid strokes to the groin completed the ritual.

Tyler's eyes bulged, and tears ran from their ducts. Every muscle in his body contracted. He shook with strain. Tran dropped the switch and barked orders. Two soldiers hurried to untie the prisoner. They yanked the rag from his swollen lips and left his crud-caked uniform in a heap between his feet.

Tyler moved like an arthritic, every effort sending waves of pain through his body. He puffed like a steam engine as he struggled into his clothes. When he was dressed, the guards brought two low stools made from split logs and bamboo lashed together with vines. Tyler dragged himself to the one nearest him and, with difficulty, hoisted himself to a sitting position. His head hung between his knees as he panted. Tran sat opposite him on the other perch, waiting for the prisoner to gather his strength.

Once Tyler sat erect, his head bobbing like a drunk, Tran began his questioning. Each session was the same. First, the picture would be displayed. Tran would nod his satisfaction when the American lieutenant focused on it.

"*Bacsi de?*" the captain would say. "*Bacsi de?*"

Tyler would feign incomprehension and confusion. He had given up the defiant stare. He no longer had the strength, and it seemed to inspire more painful punishment. Tyler had recognized the photograph when his vision cleared. It was the one they had found on the dead nurse. Gradually, he had understood that this man was asking where it came from. The photo was of the man before him when he was much younger. *Bacsi*, he had learned from Pomeroy, was a doctor. *Bacsi de* was a medic or nurse. He had pieced together that the dead VC nurse was someone close to his tormentor, possibly his wife. Tyler logically assumed that the only reason he was alive was that the man wanted to know what had happened to the woman. If he told him she was *craci dau*—killed—he would meet the same fate. At times, he was tempted, but the will to live still surpassed his despair. He shook his head and slid to the ground.

Snorting his disgust, Tran ordered his men to return the American to his cage. He summoned Sergeant Vinh and gave some

curious orders. Vinh set about accomplishing his task by rounding up two men and relaying the captain's commands.

❧❧❧

Sergeant Vinh was troubled by his captain's behavior. Nothing was being done to continue their mission since the capture of
the American officer. Captain Tran was obsessed with learning
something from the prisoner. All Vinh knew was that it had
something to do with the photograph. The captain tortured and
questioned the man incessantly but would not permit anyone to
know what about.

Lieutenant Sau was leading the few patrols that ventured from
the camp, but Tran had ordered that they not go far. He wanted
them available at a moment's notice. For what, they didn't know.
They were becoming tense. Communication with Hanoi, via their
radio relays, had been halted with no explanation. Now, this.
What in the name of Ho's beard was the captain up to?

❧❧❧

Fuquette watched, puzzled, from beneath the twisted roots of
a banyan tree as the NVA soldiers cut bamboo poles and constructed a tripod over some sort of pond that was fed from the
stream. The tiny pool looked manmade. Fish trap, he realized. He
watched, moving only his eyes. The leeches would soon force
him to abandon his inundated hide. This spot was the only place
he could watch in daylight with minimal risk of discovery, but he
couldn't risk infection, and his motionless form was a tempting
host for the slimy little vampires.

As the NVA officer stomped back to his command post Fuquette swore to kill him no matter what. But he was not ready to
die to avenge Tyler just yet. The sniper could play this waiting
game better than most. Tyler's condition was his primary concern.
The lieutenant was going downhill fast. Fuquette would try to get
him out, if possible. As for himself, capture was not an option.
Two-Six's treatment would be like room service compared to
what they would do to him. If it came to it, he'd take Tyler out
first and then himself. The only certainty was the gook officer. He
was a walking dead man.

CHAPTER 60

Johnson's pained expression, as he looked on his muddy jungle boots with revulsion, said volumes about his opinion of his present status. Captain Arnold's careless attitude regarding grooming in the field confounded him. Johnson saw no reason why a soldier should not look the part, regardless of his surroundings. The argument that glossy boots would give away a soldier's position was, in his opinion, the rationale of a slovenly individual too lazy to enforce discipline. Worse, the captain sought to mask his slipshod habits by failing to be an example to his men. Johnson thought it obvious that this man lacked the fundamental prerequisites of a good commander.

He lacked imagination as well. Johnson's carefully developed plan to dress a squad of short soldiers in black pajamas, conical hats, and sandals, and thereby close with the VC disguised as their fellows, had been met with a blank stare and a curt negative response. Surely, they had enough captured weapons and equipment to outfit such a force with authentic communist gear. And the clothing was plentiful.

Was this not a guerrilla war? *Who dares, wins*, as the Special Forces types were so fond of saying. Risk was part of the equation. Could it be that Captain Arnold was a coward? Johnson had heard from many of his fellow officers that the black soldiers were the first to panic in combat. Many refused to fight, proclaiming that this was a white man's war, or so he had been told. Rick Partridge, his dear friend in the Quartermaster Corps, had said this many times. Rick had been in Vietnam three times. Surely, he must know.

The fact that his good friend Rick had never been shot at in his three tours never occurred to Johnson. In truth, he had never associated with the *grunt* officers, even in the States. He had no reason to. His world was made safe by the risks taken by men he looked down upon, men he considered too lacking in the gray matter to find more comfortable postings.

Johnson was not afraid of combat. He didn't have the sense to accept his own mortality. Born in Peabody, Massachusetts, of upper-middle-class parents, he had breezed through the first twenty-one years of his life as a carefree intellectual. Jasper Johnson, he had concluded while in college, was a philosopher. His urbane, simplistic views on worldly concerns had been the subject of much debate among his peers, none of whom had an ounce more experience in the realities of which they spoke than did Johnson. This had deterred them not a bit from pontificating upon the causes of the problems foisted on the masses *by* the masses. It boiled down to a lack of basic intelligence, they had all agreed.

The national guard had been a lark, a chance to taste the forbidden fruit side-by-side with lesser beings, from a distance of course, and only on weekends. It had seemed a logical solution to the annoying imposition of active military service. Upon activation of his unit, Johnson had bravely pronounced his call-to-duty as kismet. He was obviously destined for great things. Perhaps he would become a general. First, he had to make first lieutenant. If handled correctly, this combat thing was a stepping-stone. A Combat Infantry Badge would look impressive on his custom-tailored dress greens. Several rows of campaign ribbons beneath it should do wonders for his career. The primary objective, as in all endeavors, was to be noticed. Every book he had read on successful soldiers—and he had read many—emphasized individual flair. Great men of arms were dashing figures. He must work on his dash.

CHAPTER 61

Rain bounced off of the hood of the truck and ran like a waterfall down the flat windshield panes. Lester Arnold cautioned Kowalski to slow down.

"Charley can't aim any better in this shit than we can. Take it easy until it lets up."

Kowalski turned the windshield wipers to high and let up on the pedal enough to drop down to fourth gear. Highway Four ran straight for more than a mile at this point, and he felt confident of his ability to keep them on the road. Pedestrians and cycles would have to watch out for him. He wouldn't see them until it was too late. *Xin loi.*

They were half of a two-vehicle convoy racing to reach Dagger before dark. Captain Arnold had flown to Dong Tam on the returning supply chopper that morning for a briefing from Colonel Conte. The storm, which was now overtaking them, had socked in the birds at Dong Tam. Arnold had elected to return to his command by road, rather than spend the night away from his company. The vehicles, a jeep and the truck they were riding in, would have to spend the night at the fire base and Arnold knew they would probably attract some mortars tonight. Charley loved to mortar trucks. No one knew why, but every time a vehicle stayed overnight, the base got mortared. Regardless, Arnold had decided to commandeer both vehicles for as long as he could. He had plans for them.

The jeep was somewhere ahead. The captain had lost its outline in the downpour. It would come in handy for road security south of the camp. They could also utilize it for ice runs to the Vietnamese ice factory in the village about a mile into the forest.

Cold American beer and soda would be a welcome change from the lukewarm, home-brewed garbage the young Vietnamese girls sold outside the wire.

The truck would have a more conventional military role. Arnold planned to employ it tonight to take a squad up the road and insert them as an ambush element near the ARVN compound. If G-2's information was accurate, they should meet with some success.

The rhythmic beating of the wipers had a hypnotic effect as his mind panned back to the colonel's words.

"Our best information indicates enemy activity to be on the rise in your sector, Les."

No shit, Arnold had thought. He managed to look absorbed in the briefing, even as he wondered what happened to their *worst* information. They always gave out the *best* information. Who decided which was which?

"Elements of the VC Seventh are running scattered ops through a wide arc in the Camau Peninsula," Conte had continued. "We have no evidence of massing of troops, only broad-based activity. G-Two doesn't feel that Dagger is in danger of imminent heavy attack."

The colonel looked at Arnold as if he expected him to be pleased with this news. Arnold thought it would be nice if G-2 was always right in its feelings. Charley, sadly, had little respect for those feelings. The warm reception the company had received upon its insertion into the empty meadow had proven that.

Arnold nodded to show his thoughtful regard for the wisdom of G-2.

"We have good information that Charley is planning a raid on our counterparts. We expect them to be hit tonight or tomorrow night." The colonel frowned to show the gravity of the situation. "Soon, anyway," he hedged.

Lester, disappointed in the lack of more *best* information, covered his sorrow with another thoughtful nod.

"I know you're under strength, but I want you to send some men up there to reinforce our allies," the colonel ordered.

Arnold had no intention of putting his people in jeopardy by placing them under South Viet command. He would come up with some creative solution to the colonel's orders.

"Now for the juicy part," the colonel grinned, rubbing his

palms together like a miser in a gold mine. "We have some interesting intelligence on the people who jumped your Second Platoon."

The colonel had Arnold's undivided attention for the first time.

"This patch was found on a bush hat at the scene of the massacre." Conte produced an artist's rendering of the insignia of the People's Provisional Captive Force. "Now you know why I named our fire base Dagger."

Arnold did not but remained silent so that the colonel would tell him.

"It's this symbol that inspired me," Conte said with a flourish. "We don't know what unit goes with this patch. A thorough search of the archives hasn't yielded a clue. We assume that it is a new outfit, a specialty force. Their purpose is a mystery, but we believe them to be operating in your backyard. The audacity with which they attacked your people, and the efficiency with which they dispatched them, suggest a highly trained and dedicated force. I've been directed to make all possible speed in getting the rest of the battalion disengaged from their present contacts and on to Dagger. Our primary mission will be to hunt down this unit and destroy it. We're to make an example of them, to show that no one can decimate an element of the United States Army and live to brag about it. I've been promised all available firepower to accomplish this mission. Once we find them," Conte pounded his fist on the table for emphasis, "I can bring goddamn B-Fifty-Twos at dress-right-dress on their asses if necessary. Any questions?"

"Is this the unit that's expected to pay a call on the Arvins, sir?"

"Negative," Conte wagged his chin. "Our info is local VC. It's a punitive raid for the Arvin's mistreatment of some village chief's daughter. It seems she was abused, fondled actually, by the slopes during a recent sweep. The chief has turned to the Cong for justice." Conte's shrug was all the explanation Arnold expected. The colonel had long ago given up trying to fathom the oriental mind.

"How do we know that these guys," Arnold pointed to the sketch, "are still in the AO?"

"Because they haven't turned up anywhere else," the colonel replied.

The captain thought: *Now you know why you're not a colonel, Les. Logic like that bit of brilliance is totally beyond you.*

Arnold suspected the colonel had not been privy to all of the wisdom of G-2. More likely they were guessing and didn't care to enlighten their subordinates to their fallibility. He nodded once more. The colonel assumed understanding. In fact, Arnold had just counseled himself: he would not resist the pressure to rescind his command when next it came. Either the army was nuts or he was. He had too much time invested to walk away, but this was turning into a circus. He nodded in agreement with his own assessment.

"Almost there, sir."

Kowalski's remark brought Captain Arnold back to the present. He reached into his shirt pocket for a cigarette. The foul taste in his mouth changed his mind. Even the Vietnamese, formaldehyde-spiked Thirty-Three beer would taste good tonight.

CHAPTER 62

*D*ear Pop, Tyler began another mental letter to his father, *I never realized how much a man can miss the sound of his own language. All I hear during the day is gook gibberish. At night, I'd welcome even that. At least, Captain Tran—he's my jailer —has taken the trouble to introduce himself.* Dai ui Ngo Din *Tran, he boasted to me on the first day. He went on for a while after that, strutting like the cock of the walk. I think he was giving me his resume but the name is all that I understood. I think he's trying to cow me with his power. Identifying himself is a way of showing me that I have no hope of rescue. What he's done, inadvertently, is give me a name to attach to the object of my hatred. Somehow, it helps.*

Tom Tyler had begun composing letters to his father on the second night in the cage. It occupied his mind with something besides fear. He hated being so afraid. Tyler pictured his father in his mind and realized he did not need to write imaginary correspondence. He could talk to his old man, just like they did on the porch on summer evenings.

"You don't look so good, son," the conjured Alvin Tyler said.

"I'm okay, Pop," Tyler reassured his parent. "The accommodations at this tropical resort are a little rustic, is all."

"I know you always had itchy feet, Thomas." Alvin always prefaced his admonitions with understanding phrases. "But there's much to be said for staying at home."

"At the moment—" The younger Tyler smiled. "—I'd be inclined to agree with you." He breathed a sigh of despair. "I'm afraid I may never see you again, Daddy. Things don't look so good for me. This feller, Tran, is going to get tired of this game sometime soon. He'll either kill me outright or bust me up bad, and I'll die of exposure. I've been feverish the last two nights. A lot of these cuts are getting infected, and the skeeters are eating me alive. I feel real bad about this whole thing. Tell Momma not to blame herself. This was something I had to do. Lord knows she tried to get me to change my mind. Funny thing is, I feel worse about not seeing more of the world than I do about not coming home. Dying young is something I hadn't planned on."

"You get some rest now, Tom. Things always look blackest before the dawn. We'll be together again, in this life or the next. Don't be afraid. I love you, son."

 e/o e/o

Fuquette slithered from between the roots of a banyan tree and lay still, listening. If he could get to the cage without being seen, they had a chance. Every exposed square inch of his skin was covered in mud. It kept the mosquitoes away from him by disguising his scent, and it made him virtually invisible. It also accelerated his body's submission to skin diseases. Ring Worm and Impetigo were spreading. He had to act before he became sick. Time was his enemy.

He watched the sleeping platforms in the trees for movement. The structures were excellent observation posts and, compared to the wallows he had been using as quarters, luxurious. The guards could hit anything that they could see from up there, so he had to remain under cover in daylight. In the dark, the dense foliage worked for and against him. He could be surprised and overpowered if he stumbled into a group of them. Movement had to be planned and enacted with care.

A squishing sound a few feet to his left alerted Fuquette. He eased backward into his hide. A shadow moved slowly through the trees until it stopped a few feet in front of him. It sank to the ground and disappeared in the undergrowth.

Roving guard, Fuquette correctly surmised. He would not get to the lieutenant this way: too many sentries and no discernible pattern to their patrols. Perhaps it was time to bring in the cavalry. Tyler could die before he got his chance if he played the waiting game too long. He was confident enough in his sense of direction to be able to get back to the fire-base and return to this spot. His granddaddy had taught him well in the ways of woods craft. The lessons learned during many days and nights prowling the Okeefenokee, with nothing to sustain him but a boy's thirst for adventure, an old rim-fire .22 rifle, and granddaddy's wisdom, had served him again and again in this place called Vietnam.

His time with the Green Machine, however, had made him distrustful of its ways. Fuquette had been on enough *Sneaky Pete* operations to know that a great deal of time would be wasted in debriefing upon his return. He also knew that he would have no control over the method of the lieutenant's rescue. They were just as likely to come crashing in here with a regiment as they were to carpet bomb the place, cross their fingers, and hope Tyler survived. They would be more intent on the destruction of the NVA than on the rescue of one half-dead trooper.

No, he thought, *no good to bring in the heavies.* This had to be done with stealth. He backed out through the rear entrance to his shelter and padded, barefoot, to his nest. The distinctive imprint of a jungle boot near the camp would raise an alarm, so he had stashed his boots and nonessential gear in a rotting log two hundred meters away. He would need his footwear now to make better time through the forest. His decision was made. He would go back for help. What kind of help he would determine on the march.

CHAPTER 63

Sergeant Beecher flipped through his codebook. There was nothing in it that was of any interest, but he needed something to divert his eyes from the outraged lieutenant who stood in front of him and the captain.

Johnson, having just returned from the ARVN compound, pleaded with Charlie-Six to take some action.

"They robbed us blind, sir," he whined. "Stole anything that wasn't in a man's hand. C-rations, poncho liners, bush hats, socks—anything. They rifled my men's rucksacks while they slept. My Rolex, for God's sake." He thrust his naked wrist at them as proof. "I dozed off for a couple of minutes, and it was gone. My mother gave me that watch, sir. What are you going to do about it?"

"The Rolex, Lieutenant?" Captain Arnold barely hid the smile that was curling the corners of his lips.

"No, sir," Johnson sputtered. "I mean, yes, sir. That and everything else. My men are very upset."

Beecher cleared his throat to stifle the laugh that was bubbling up.

"There isn't much I *can* do, Lieutenant," Arnold responded. "Those people are supposed to be our allies. This is their country. Technically, we are their guests. I did tell you to keep an eye on them, didn't I?"

"Yes, Captain, you did, but they seemed so friendly, so genuinely glad to see us—"

"Like kids seeing Santa Claus," Beecher could not resist saying.

Before Johnson had a chance to digest the sergeant's remark,

Arnold said, "I sent you along on this little sojourn so that our people would have an American officer in command. Your job, Lieutenant, was to look out for them. I suggest you take this as an object lesson on a platoon leader's myriad responsibilities. The colonel will expect another detachment to go to the Arvin compound tonight. Send the other half of the platoon this time."

Johnson's horrified expression made Beecher wish he had a camera close at hand.

"There'll be no need for you to accompany them this time, Lieutenant Johnson. We'll do things a bit differently tonight. Send your platoon sergeant over. I'll explain the situation to him. He can lead the patrol."

It took a moment for Johnson to realize he had been dismissed. He stammered. Arnold raised an eyebrow. The hapless lieutenant caught himself in time to check his reflexive salute. He stomped out of the bunker.

ↄↄↄ

Pomeroy arrived several minutes later, to find his CO and his RTO wiping tears from their eyes, trying in vain to suppress their giggling.

"'Scuse me, sir. You wanted to see me?" Pomeroy grinned, infected by the contagious mirth.

"Yes, Sergeant, have a seat," the captain said, indicating the chair in front of his desk. He filled Pomeroy in on the events of the previous evening regarding Lieutenant Johnson's unfortunate experience at the ARVN camp. "I want you to take Mulvaney's and Cortez's squads up there tonight. G-2 insists our friends are going to be hit. If nothing happens again tonight, I can beg off this detail. In the meantime—" He produced a map of the area. "—you set up here." The captain pointed to a small copse of trees north of the compound, just off the road. "It's too small to tempt Charley to use it to stage an attack. It's surrounded on all sides by open ground, and it gives you a clear view of the camp. If Chuck comes, he'll probably come from here." He pointed to a large wood line, closer to the camp. Pomeroy saw that it stretched far out into the paddies. "There's good cover, and he can get within easy range undetected."

"Isn't that the place for us to be then, sir?"

"If you weren't leading a bunch of FNGs, Sergeant, I'd agree with you. Besides, I don't think it's wise to put our people between the enemy and our allies."

"I see what you mean, sir. Could put us in a nasty crossfire."

"Exactly." Arnold leveled his gaze at the sergeant. "Your orders are to assist the friendlies with fire support, should the need arise. By that, I mean *indirect* fire support."

"We call in arty on 'em and be cool."

"Roger that." Arnold nodded. "I don't want them to even know where you are. You'll run up there at last light, pass the place, disembark around the next bend in the road and walk back through the paddies to your position. We'll have the truck go out under canvas and return with it down so it'll appear to be a different vehicle. Impress your people with the need for quiet. Any questions?"

Pomeroy nodded his head. "You want it to look like we kept right on goin'. Just might work."

෨෨෨

Jasper Johnson's rubber sandals slapped his heels as he strode along the road to the shower point outside of Dagger. He had pestered the engineers throughout the day to make haste in assembling the water purification equipment. The installation was now complete, and Charlie Company had their own means of producing potable water from the tiny stream that ran beside the road. As a bonus, the industrious engineers had erected shower stalls with the setup. The fact that it was outside the berm deterred many from using the refreshing ablution equipment. By the time they had completed the job, even the daring engineers were convinced that they would have no customers until the next day.

Having tested the equipment, they prepared to shut it down for the night when they spied the lieutenant bustling toward them. With a fluffy white terrycloth towel wrapped tightly around his middle, his soap and shampoo in one hand, and his back brush in the other, Johnson was a sight.

The soldiers warned the officer of the risk of being caught outside the wire in the fading light. He scoffed at their warning and ordered them to turn the appropriate valves.

So enthralled was he in the luxury of cleaning the filth from his body that he failed to notice the sun dipping below the trees until he could not see to rinse the soap from his skin. Belatedly heeding the operators' strident caveats, Johnson hastily wrapped his towel about his waist, trailing after the departing engineers with the flap-flap-flap of his rubber soles counting double-time cadence as he squeezed the rubber thong with his toes to keep from walking out of his shoes.

The first mortar round exploded with a white-hot flash two hundred feet behind him. The next two walked up the road, following him like impatient swats at a pesky fly. Johnson, clutching his flapping white towel, struggled to increase his speed but the loose-fitting rubber slippers were not designed for sprinting. The blasts sent men inside the camp scurrying for cover or scrambling to their defensive positions on the berm. The sight that greeted the few who ventured a peek over the earthen barrier aroused a chorus of disbelieving yelps.

Charley corrected and let fly with another salvo. The engineers left the scampering lieutenant far behind as they ran for the cover of the camp. A rooting section lined the berm to watch the show. Some cheered the terrified officer on. The majority applauded the Viet Cong gunners.

"Lead him! *Lead* him, you sorry sons of bitches," one of Johnson's own men roared above the rest. "He's getting away. Add twenty and fire for effect, goddammit."

The last round came close enough to let Johnson feel the heat of the blast. Shrapnel buzzed past his ear. The concussion shoved him on his way. He gave up on the towel and, dropping it along with the rest of his paraphernalia, sprinted the last fifty yards buck-naked. He dove headlong through the gate to land with a splat in a huge mud puddle churned to the consistency of glue by passing vehicles. The incoming fire stopped, as he rose from the slop, to be replaced by counter-battery fire from the .81 mm mortar pits inside the base.

"Enjoy your shower, sir?" Johnson heard from the darkness.

ℰↄℰↄ

Pomeroy heard the distant thud of mortar round impacts and accurately assessed the target. He signaled the men to keep going, urging them to resist the instinct to fall flat in the mud.

"Dagger's gettin' it again," he whispered to Mulvaney. "I hope our driver got back okay."

"Kowalski? That crazy polak's curled up with a beer, snug in his bunk by now. The guy drives like his pants are on fire."

They stopped behind a dike, sixty meters from the trees. Pomeroy sent Danny and Wyman to check it out.

The little island of trees was perfect. A natural depression at its center would serve as a command post while the squads lay in a circle to watch the fields and the ARVN compound. Danny waved Pomeroy in when the recon was complete. The men slipped noiselessly into position. After checking his men and establishing a guard roster, Danny went back to the CP to confer with Pomeroy.

"Looks good," he whispered, "they moved in better than I expected, but I don't think Chuck is going to head this way after stirring things up at Dagger."

"Don't be so sure. That could be just what he wants everybody to think. Could be a diversion." He indicated the direction of the ARVN camp with his chin. "You got your Sixty pointing down the road?"

"Most affirmative. We'll be ready if they come."

"Just keep in mind we got us a bunch of trainees here. Our job is to call in support as needed. We don't go mixing it up unless they come right at us."

Danny sighed but nodded. What he wanted most was revenge for his friends. He wanted to see gooks fall under his sights, to hear their screams as they died. They would suffer for what they did to the guys and to Gino. He crawled back to his position beside Wyman. The new guy was wide-eyed and jittery.

"Relax," Danny whispered. "Probably be a long night."

                                  ᙅᘓᙅᘓ

A light rain was falling at about three o'clock in the morning. The initial apprehension experienced by the troops set up outside the ARVN compound had given way to boredom and discomfort. Danny slept fitfully, instantly awake at the slightest breeze or rustling of cloth.

A B-40 rocket initiated the attack on the compound. It landed inside the walled perimeter, lighting up the area with its flash.

Mortars, small arms, and RPGs quickly joined in the onslaught. Danny was momentarily stunned. The ferocity of the attack and the thunderous response from the ARVNs split the night. Green and red tracers etched crosshatch patterns in the sky. Danny saw one of the defenders, lit by the flash of his thirty-caliber machine gun, flip backward and somersault from his guard tower.

The camp was inundated in explosions. Silhouettes of men darted and fell as the South Vietnamese soldiers ran in panic to reach the parapets or to vacate them. The Viet Cong clearly had the upper hand. Danny felt an urgent need to aid the underdogs. A solitary ARVN soldier ran into the road, threw his weapon behind him, and ran in the platoon's direction. A VC marksman put a bullet in his back. The fleeing man threw his arms out and fell on his face.

Danny recalled Kowalski's story about Benny, the truck driver. It occurred to him that these bastards had it coming. Quickly, he duck-walked along the line behind his men, telling each of them to hold his fire.

"This isn't our fight," he repeated. "Be cool."

Pomeroy slid to the ground beside him, the new RTO in tow. "Let's get some fire on those fuckers," the sergeant said, grabbing the handset.

"What's your hurry, Dez?" Danny grabbed his hand. "We've got gooks killing gooks. It's their country. Why interfere?"

Pomeroy ripped his hand free and, glaring at Danny, called, "Fire mission. Troops in the woods. Give me a marking round." Turning away from Danny, he recited the prearranged targeting information. "They're right where we expected them to be. Shot!"

"Shot out," came the casual reply from the .105 crew back at Dagger.

The smoke round exploded in the air directly above the attacking VC.

"On the money," Pomeroy whispered. "Fire for effect."

Six shells screamed in to explode in bright flashes in the trees. Pomeroy called in volley after volley, correcting the fire with, "Up fifty," or, "Left seventy-five," moving the destruction up and down the wood line until all firing had ceased from the attackers.

"Cease fire," he ordered when all was quiet from the enemy. "Nice shootin'."

"Why not add two hundred and finish the job?" Danny suggested. The correction would place the fire on the ARVN compound.

"Not tonight, Mulvaney," Pomeroy sighed. "What the fuck is eatin' you?"

Danny was disturbed by the pitying look in Pomeroy's eyes.

Charlie-Six called for a report. Pomeroy related the effect of the artillery bombardment. Captain Arnold congratulated them on their work and ordered them not to show themselves until daylight. He would lead a relief force in the morning to survey the damage. Pomeroy signed off and sat staring at Mulvaney. Danny curled up in his poncho and pretended to sleep. He shut out the screams of the wounded and the wailing of the dependents in the compound.

👁👁👁

Ground fog lay in every depression as the Americans heard the sound of vehicle engines grinding up the road at daybreak. A jeep, followed by a deuce-and-a-half, both loaded to overflowing with troops, rolled slowly into view. They stopped short of the wood line where the Viet Cong had fought the night before.

Captain Arnold threw open the door of the truck and stood on the running board, barking orders.

Men poured from the olive-green carriers to disperse beside the road. Arnold yelled again, and half the men moved cautiously into the woods. The rest took covering positions, their weapons trained on the underbrush.

The truck moved toward Danny and the two squads hiding in the observation post.

Kowalski leaned out of the driver's window when he was abreast of them. "Come out, come out, wherever you are."

The men slowly filed out onto the road.

"Keep it spread out," Pomeroy hollered. "One round'll get ya all."

The soldiers moved away from one another.

"Mornin' Andy," Danny said, the butt of his M-16 braced against his hip.

"Back at you." Kowalski grinned. Motioning behind him with his head, he added, "I hear you brung smoke on old Charles last night."

Danny nodded without looking at his friend.

"Six says move back into the bush and watch his ass," Pomeroy ordered after a brief exchange via radio with the captain. "Kowalski, you can sit up there like a big fat target or you can unass that thing and come with us."

"How could I resist such a warm invitation?"

"It's okay to eat," Pomeroy said when they had settled into their previous positions, "but keep your eyes peeled. Mulvaney, I wanna talk to you."

Danny shrugged in response to Kowalski's questioning look. He dropped his pack and walked into the trees with Pomeroy.

"I want to know what that shit you tried to pull last night was about," Pomeroy said when they were alone. Danny opened his mouth, but Pomeroy spoke again before he could answer. "I think you think you know, but I want to be sure," the sergeant said evenly.

Danny looked through narrowed eyes at his platoon sergeant and said nothing.

"You think because these people killed a bunch of your friends, you got the right to hate them all."

"Don't you?"

"No, I don't," Pomeroy snapped. "I don't hate an entire people because some of 'em are no-good rat bastards. There's a word for that. Bigot." He spat the word like something vile.

"Sarge, I—"

"You're acting like an ignorant fuck," Pomeroy snarled through his teeth. "Lieutenant Tyler thought he saw something in you. His judgment was always good enough for me, but you're making me doubt him. No one, Mulvaney, *no one* has more right to hate for what happened to our people than I do. Those guys were my family. You didn't know them like I did. You didn't know the names of their sweethearts, their kids, their wives. You didn't know their dreams for when they got back to the world. I did. And I'll carry those memories around with me for the rest of my life. This is a fuckin' war, Mulvaney. I don't know who's the good guys and who's the bad guys. I don't know if there are any bad guys, 'cept maybe the bastards that started this thing.

"What I do know is that if you become one of the ones who love the killing, you're wearing the wrong suit. You best trade it in for a white sheet and a pointy hat, 'cause that's the kind of man

who hates everybody that don't look like him." He paused, looking—Danny felt—into his soul. "Think about it."

Danny watched Pomeroy stomp back to the men. His mouth
tasted foul. He gulped water from his canteen. The face of the
little angel in the village sprang into his mind's eye. His cheeks
burned with shame.

ৎৡৎৡ

The wood line sweep yielded little. A few blood trails were
found amid a lot of shattered trees and shell craters. One smashed
AK-47 and bits and pieces of clothing and gear were all that remained of the Viet Cong.

"They had plenty of time to drag the dead and wounded out,"
Beecher observed.

"Yeah," Captain Arnold conceded. "Call in a body count of
six probables. Good a number as any." He winked at his RTO.
Higher liked body counts. If he didn't make a claim they'd do
their own figuring. The captain estimated they had already wiped
out all of Southeast Asia on paper.

"Three-Six says the Arvins got their asses handed to them,"
Beecher informed him, holding the handset, waiting for a reply.

"Tell him I'll be along in a minute," Arnold said. "We must
have caught Chuck flat-footed. He didn't even leave us any booby traps. Score one for the good guys." Arnold's eyes swept the
brush one last time. Taking a long breath, he said, "Okay, let's go
see how our brave counterparts made out."

The Third Platoon was tasked with securing the compound perimeter until reinforcements arrived. Helicopters were dispatched
to ferry the wounded to the hospital. The dead would be transported home by their families for burial. The Americans patently
ignored the anguished weeping of the women. There was little
compassion for these local troops among the men of Charlie
Company. This was *their* war. *Xin Loi.*

CHAPTER 64

Notify Captain Arnold at Firebase Dagger that he can put out the welcome mat," Colonel Conte told the radio operator on duty in the battalion TOC in Dong Tam. "Alpha Company will be joining him on the morning convoy." The RTO scribbled the message on a pad while consulting his codebook for the day's ciphers.

"Bravo and Delta will follow in a few days," the colonel said. "I'll be with them. The Second of the Sixth is going hunting."

⋐⋑⋐⋑

Smitty decoded the message and, with a whoop, ran outside the Fire Base Dagger's CP to shout the news to C-Company and the artillerymen.

The captain, riding in the jeep as the patrol returned, heard the news upon entering the camp. Smitty's booming voice would shame any town crier. Arnold watched the many peasant camp followers outside the wire who made their living selling things to the GIs. Although they were forbidden to enter the camp proper, they were privy to much of the gossip and speculation that went on among the soldiers who came to sample their wares.

Arnold sighed. "So much for secrets."

⋐⋑⋐⋑

Alpha Company rolled into Fire Base Dagger without fanfare. Unit pride forbade the men of C-Company from showing the relief they so deeply felt at the sight of assistance. A hastily scrawled addendum to the signboard over the gate read: Courtesy of Charlie Company.

The reinforcements were greeted with good-natured ribbing.

"Y'all feel safe enough to come on down heah with us men?" a Texan specialist drawled.

"Hope you dudes brought your own baby-sitters. We're too busy to be lookin' out for Alpha remfs," another soldier quipped.

There was also a good deal of back-slapping and hand shaking as friends were reunited. Cat calls and insults were exchanged as the men settled in, displacing homesteading C-Company troops. The extra firepower was welcome if the loss of coveted space was not. Eventually, the distribution of forces was sorted out, and the new arrivals began to put their own touches of home on the primitive living quarters.

The convoy was quickly unloaded so that the drivers could turn around and repeat the dangerous run back to Dong Tam. Kowalski surprised everyone, including himself, by volunteering to stay on as the base truck driver.

Lieutenant Johnson carefully picked over the piles of supplies until, with a broad smile of sheer delight, he located the parcels he had been seeking. Second squad was detailed to haul two heavy crates into the platoon bunker. Inquiries as to the contents were met with brusque, vague answers that were no answers at all.

The lieutenant, it was apparent, had no desire to advertise his windfall. The men were suspicious of anything that pleased him.

"Good old Partridge," Johnson mumbled several times. He fussed over the storage of the cases like a proud new mother. Swearing his platoon to secrecy, he promised they would be happy with the surprise, once revealed.

"The CO can't say no to what he doesn't know about," Johnson assured himself, covering the crates with a tarp.

The platoon speculated but kept their wild suppositions to themselves. If it was something good, they didn't want to share it, especially with Alpha.

"A pair of raving nymphomaniacs would be nice," Simms commented.

"Male or female?" Paco winked at Danny.

"All nymphos are female, at least in America," Simms said. "I suppose human would be variation enough for you, my Mexican friend."

"Woof." Danny groaned. "Target destroyed. Crashed and burned."

"Come on, wetback," Simms said with a brotherly arm around Paco's shoulder. "I'll buy you dinner." They strolled toward the mess hall. "Now don't embarrass me. Eat with a fork tonight."

Danny raised two fingers, shaking his head. "Quit while you're able, man," he told Paco. "This boy's on a roll."

Paco's black eyes sparkled as he laughed. White, even teeth gleamed when he smiled. He seemed about to rake Simms with his own sharp wit when Doc joined them.

"Did you guys hear what the colonel's got planned?" Laffin's agitated expression erased the humor the three had been enjoying.

"What?" Danny asked.

"The whole battalion's going after the gooks that hit us," Doc whispered, breathless, "the ones that wiped us out."

"Where'd you hear that bullshit?" Paco asked.

"Alpha," Doc persisted. "It's true. Their CO told them before they came out here. He says they're NVA and Division wants them—bad."

"Okay by me," Simms proclaimed. "It's about time for a little pay-back."

Laffin stopped. His cheeks were sunken and there were dark rings beneath his eyes.

"You don't understand," Doc said, in almost a whimper. He turned abruptly and walked away.

"You guys go ahead. I'll catch up," Simms said, as he hurried after the medic.

"Do you think we should go with him?" Danny asked Paco.

"Nah." Paco pursed his lips and shook his head. "That gringo got a mouth on him like a rusty razor sometimes." He smiled in admiration. "But he can be a silver-tongued devil, too. Let him talk to Doc alone. Come on. Let's eat. I'm starving."

"You won't eat with your hands, will you?" Danny grinned.

"*Madre De Dios.* Another one."

ᏋᏯᏋᏯ

"Hey, man. Wait up!" Simms called to Laffin.

Doc looked confused. He hesitated, and then stopped, looking at the ground.

"What's the matter with you, man? Why'd you run away from us?" Simms looked into his friend's eyes as Doc's head came up. "The doctor looks like he needs a doctor. Talk to me, man. Get it out. It'll fuck you up if you don't."

Laffin watched other men hurrying by. With a jerk of his head, he beckoned Simms to follow. They walked to a deserted howitzer emplacement where Doc sat on a sandbagged parapet. Simms sat close beside him and waited.

"I'm scared, Bert," Laffin said, with a quiver in his voice.

"Don't feel like The Lone Ranger," Simms joked.

"I mean it, man," Hadley scowled. "I never was before—not like this. I can't sleep. I can't eat." Laffin looked up and Simms could almost see the terror emanating from his friend like a physical force. "We don't stand a chance against those gooks. Look what they did to us last time. We had Tyler then and they creamed us. This peckerhead clown hasn't got a clue. He's going to get us all killed."

"We got you, me, Paco, Danny, and the infamous Corporal Corporal," Simms said slowly, deliberately. "And don't forget Pomeroy. He can run the platoon. Once we get outside the wire, Johnson will shut up and listen, or he won't come back. The new guys will do as we tell 'em. We'll be fine," he put his hand on Doc's shoulder, "as long as we stick together."

"Think so?"

Laffin's pleading look made Simms want to hold him, to tell him he'd be all right. Instead, he punched Doc's shoulder and laughed, "Course I do. Shit. Pay attention when a sergeant speaks to you. Now smile or we gonna have to start callin' you Never Laffin."

Doc laughed a small, nervous laugh.

"Come on," Simms said as he pulled the medic to his feet. "Let's go get some chow. We can teach the Mexican how to eat like Emily Post."

CHAPTER 65

Gentlemen," Captain Arnold said, prefacing his speech, "we are going to stretch our legs tomorrow."

He leaned against the wall of the TOC bunker and lit a cigarette. His officers took this as permission to smoke, and all but Lieutenant Johnson, who refrained from what he considered a disgusting habit, lit up as well. The confined space was quickly engulfed in a blue haze.

Johnson was noticeably displeased. His colleagues intentionally blew smoke in his direction.

The room fell silent except for the hiss of static from the radios and the occasional hushed conversation between RTOs and patrols. The dim lighting added to the portentous atmosphere.

"Colonel Conte has received orders from Higher-Higher to hunt down and kill the unit that took out our Second Platoon."

Johnson appeared miffed.

The captain amended his words. "Former Second Platoon, that is."

Somewhat mollified, Johnson adopted an air of attention.

"We believe this unit to be a specialized detachment of NVA. G-Two suspects some sort of mobile strike force comprised of highly trained troops, probably sappers."

The captain raised his voice to quiet the hubbub that this bit of information created.

"Sappers, as *most* of you know—" Arnold looked directly at Johnson, who pretended not to notice. "—are the North Vietnamese version of Special Forces. They are not suicide squads whose sole mission is to blow installations with satchel charges strapped to their backs. True, they have been known to do just that, but understand that this is a sign of their determination and will to win. They are the best the North has to offer. If G-Two's intel is accurate, and I'm sure none of us here doubt it—" He paused for the expected laugh and was not disappointed. "Then we have a job cut out for ourselves." He pulled a map down from its roller, like a window shade. Sergeant Beecher snapped a floodlight on.

Red grease pencil markings indicated the fire-base and friendly units within the AO.

"Here we are." Arnold pointed with his finger. "And here," he circled the green mass adjacent to Dagger, "is the U-Minh Forest." Tapping the center of the area, he went on. "G-Two believes our quarry is somewhere in here."

Raised eyebrows and frowns of concern appeared on every face in the bunker, with the exception of Jasper T. Johnson.

"Alpha Company," Arnold nodded to Alpha's commander, First Lieutenant Brad Hartman, "is the first to join us in this quest. Bravo and Delta are due within the next day or so.

"I have discussed the planned op with Big Six. I think it best to begin right away. The colonel agrees.

"That's a big hunk of real estate," Arnold indicated the forest again, "and it would take months to search it with a division. We don't have that kind of manpower so we'll have to narrow the field a bit. C-Company's First, Second and Third Platoons will head out at dawn tomorrow. First will break trail right through here." He indicated a point directly opposite the base. "Third will eagle-flight to here. This is near where the massacre took place. I use that term to remind you all who you're up against." He paused for effect.

"Dennis, you and your people will move through the battle site and try to find some sign of the enemy's movement. You'll work your way south along this axis." He traced a line on the map with his finger. Third Platoon's commander nodded.

"Second will proceed by truck along Highway Four to this point," Arnold tapped the spot with an index finger, "and set up a blocking force a little ways into the forest—about here." He pointed to a spot about five hundred meters from the road. "First and Third will sweep toward Second. Simple hammer and anvil. We'll estimate three days to complete the operation. Alpha takes over base security until we return. If we haven't found and killed these people by then, they get a crack at them. Any questions?"

There were many. Artillery support, air assets, types of ordinance most effective in this terrain, re-supply, reaction forces, communications and medivac were among the topics the officers wanted clarified. When the discussion had ended, with all but Johnson voicing questions and opinions, Johnson cleared his throat.

"Sir? May I ask why the Second has been relegated to such a passive role in this operation?"

"Certainly." Arnold paused for a moment before continuing. His tone, when he did, was patient, like a teacher explaining the obvious to a slow student. "First of all, Jasper, if these cats come your way, your assignment is going to be anything but passive. Secondly, you are leading a green platoon. Let's give these kids a chance to get their feet wet before we throw them in the deep end, shall we?"

Johnson bristled. "The Second is ready to fight."

"Let's hope they don't have to," Arnold said. "CP will travel with the First. We'll expand on this scenario when the battalion is at full force. We're not going too deep this time. This is more to get a feel for the logistics. Personally, I think we'll have to hunt long and hard to catch up with these boys. Alert your platoon sergeants and squad leaders. Good evening, gentlemen."

Johnson lagged behind as the officers hurried out to begin preparations for the operation. He waited patiently for Arnold to finish his instructions to his radio man.

"Sir, might the lieutenant have a word with the captain?" Johnson recited, his eyes fixed on a point on the wall, his chin tucked in, his chest out.

Arnold, becoming impatient, replied, "What is it, Jasper?"

"Sir, the Second Platoon would respectfully request to be more actively involved in the forthcoming exercise."

"At ease, Lieutenant," Arnold grumbled. "You'll find you get more out of me if you act like a human being and not a marionette."

Visibly ruffled, yet undaunted, Johnson relaxed his posture slightly. His voice resisted the familiarity his body sought to convey. "Yes, sir. I just think my platoon is capable of more than waiting for the enemy to come to us."

"I sincerely hope so, Jasper. I just want them to be around long enough to find out. You'd do well to stop referring to this operation as an exercise. This is no war game. What you've been assigned to do is important. If the other platoons flush these bozos and herd them your way I'll need a solid anvil to swing the hammer on. I'm counting on you to do that for me."

Johnson said, "Might I offer a suggestion, sir?"

Captain Arnold nodded. He could always say no.

"May I?" Johnson asked, reaching for the map roller.

Arnold nodded again. Johnson smiled as he unrolled the map. "Sir, as I understand it, I am to travel by road to this point." The lieutenant paused for confirmation. Arnold nodded once again. Johnson smiled, as if immensely pleased with his little victory.

Arnold thought, *Congratulations hot-shot. You can follow simple instructions.*

"At this juncture, we're to proceed into the forest and establish a line here."

Arnold nodded impatiently.

"Suppose we were to disembark from the vehicles here." Johnson pointed to a spot about a kilometer north of the intended line of departure. "We would then sweep south to the original destination through the forest."

Arnold weighed the value of such a change in plans.

The lieutenant continued. "We would gain valuable experience in patrolling, while still near enough to the road to be relatively free of concern of contact far from support."

Captain Arnold looked for the flaw in the logic. None was apparent, but he didn't like his lieutenants second-guessing a plan without some basis in fact. He opened his mouth to reject Johnson's alteration, but Johnson beat him to the punch.

"Although, on the surface, it would seem pointless," he interjected, "I feel it would mean a great deal for the men's morale to have a sense of doing something, rather than just waiting. As the captain has pointed out, they are untried troops. Men need to be trusted with responsibility, I have always felt, in order to be most effective."

Arnold nearly said, *Bullshit. Soldiers do as they're told.* He believed a good commander demanded unquestioning adherence to orders. The burr that had been irritating his conscience since the loss of Tyler and his people stopped him. Self-doubt made him teeter on the edge of giving in.

Johnson pushed him over. "If the captain feels that a note of flexibility in his operational orders is disruptive..." He let the question hang in the air, like a guillotine waiting to fall.

"Okay, Jasper," Arnold hissed. "What harm can it do? Maybe after humping through the toolies, your men will be more disposed to sit and wait. Make this your approximate line of march." The captain traced the route with his finger. "Check in when you reach this blue line and again when you reach this clearing."

"Yes, sir."

"Just be at the designated position by nightfall."

Johnson nodded abruptly and turned on his heel. He was gone before Arnold had a minute to reconsider. Arnold looked at the map for a moment before turning to Beecher.

"You sure this is a good idea, sir?"

Arnold snapped, "When I want your opinion, Sergeant, I'll give you one." He stalked out of the bunker.

Beecher yanked the map. It spun into its casing. "Bite my head off, why don'tcha?"

CHAPTER 66

Lieutenant Tyler hung upside down, trussed like a deer for gutting, from a bamboo tripod erected above the fish trap beside the stream in the center of the NVA encampment. The ropes around his ankles and his wrists sawed into his water-softened flesh. His head was out of the water only as long as he could keep his body bent forward in an L. When his burning abdominal muscles failed, the fish nipped at his hair and the back of his scalp. As his body went limp, he was immersed in the pool to his chest. He could hold his breath for mere seconds after the strain of flexing weak, tortured sinew. With his lungs on fire, Tyler again resigned himself to drowning and coughed what he hoped was his last breath into the dark water.

Captain Tran let him gulp a mouthful of the green slime that covered the fish trap and then ordered his men to push Tyler, like a pendulum, with bamboo poles jammed into his back, until his head broke the surface. Tyler vomited and choked, his head pounding with the blood thudding in his temples. The pain from the poles thrust between Tyler's shoulder blades was a minor annoyance compared to his torment of moments before.

Tran waited for the convulsion to subside. With the photograph held upside down so that it would appear upright to Tyler's bulging eyes, Tran crooned, *"Bacsi de?"* until he decided another dunking was required.

Tyler had lost track of time. It seemed he was under water more than he was not. His confusion was becoming absolute. He no longer knew what the enemy officer wanted him to say. He wished he could remember.

It would be nice to tell him what he wanted to know. Maybe

he would leave him alone if he told him. Maybe he would let him die.

ᏇᎧᏇᎧ

David Fuquette was exhausted. He had traveled day and night since leaving the enemy encampment. Movement in the thick forest was difficult. What was not jungle was swamp. Trails were dangerous. He avoided them wherever possible. He moved slowly, warily, knowing he was not alone in these woods. Twice he caught sight of VC patrols and twice more he heard them nearby. The fire-base was not far now. He could reach it by early morning if he continued on, but Fuquette realized he could not. He was beat.

The sniper had studied a map of the U-Minh before they had flown out on the last operation. There should be a small river, just out of sight, ahead. Fuquette had a rare gift. He could memorize maps and charts and see them in his mind's eye as clearly as if they were in front of him. That ability, coupled with an extraordinary sense of direction, allowed him to travel unerringly anywhere in the wild. He was like a human homing pigeon. Fuquette had never been lost in his life.

Moving as silently as a shadow, disturbing nothing, he crept to the riverbank. Skilled predator that he was, he hunkered down to watch and listen before emerging from the underbrush for a drink. The water was clear for such a slow-moving stream, which told him it had not been disturbed recently. Fuquette filled his canteen and sipped sparingly. His bowels cramped again, and he fought to control the spasm. His Halazone tablets were gone. He had been drinking unpurified water for a day and a half. His strong body resisted disease, but the effects of amoebic dysentery were inevitable. He'd just have to control it a while longer.

He also knew that water attracts living things. It would not be the best idea to stay too close to the river. Charley gets thirsty too. He would backtrack a bit and hole up for the night. Tomorrow he would follow the waterway to where it came close to the road. *It should be easy to stop a Lambro or a bus when the road opens*, he thought. No question, it would be better to ride than to walk. Fuquette still hadn't decided on the best way to approach the base. He didn't want to walk in and alert the entire division. The more he dwelled on the possibilities, the more convinced he became that the hard chargers in headquarters would screw this up if given half a chance. Getting Tyler killed was not in his plans.

Fuquette crawled under a thick patch of briars and, cradling *Old Betsy* in his arms, he closed his eyes. He smiled at the kidding he imagined he would take if the guys knew of his pet name for his rifle. The song parody they sang to him played in his mind. He wiped a tear from his cheek as he remembered the last time he had heard it. Tyler's sweating and bruised body appeared in his thoughts. The enemy officer stood over him, gloating. Fuquette whispered, "You're gonna be number eighty-five, motherfucker," and drifted off.

e∕ɔe∕ɔ

Tyler retched. His guts felt like they were trying to crawl up his throat. He lay soaked in his own vomit at the bottom of his cage. He tried to sit up, but his brain swam with the effort. Dizzy, he collapsed.

Alvin Tyler had deserted his son. That was the only possibility that Tom could imagine. His fevered mind slipped in and out of reality. How he longed to talk with his daddy.

"Please, Daddy," Tyler moaned, "just stop by and say goodnight."

A guard shook the cage with a blow from his rifle butt. The enemy soldier spat something unintelligible. Tyler waved a sluggish hand to signal he would be quiet. The guard disappeared from his field of vision. Closing his eyes, the younger Tyler strained to concentrate, to take himself away from here. The gloom parted to reveal his mother's kitchen. She was dressing a turkey. Was it Thanksgiving already?

Emily Tyler stopped in the middle of lacing the bird's belly. Tom's mouth watered at the sight of the bread stuffing oozing out of the partially closed cavity.

"Thomas Matthew Tyler," his mother gasped, "get out of those wet clothes this instant. Do you want to catch your death?"

Tyler clapped both hands over his mouth to stop his giggling from arousing the guard.

"Captain Tran will only get them wet again, Momma," he said. "I knew something like this would happen if you went over there." Mrs. Tyler sighed. "What have they done to you? My poor baby."

Tyler wished his father had been the one to answer his plea. He could tell him about the fish trap. Momma would be traumatized. "Have you got any of that cool apple cider, Momma? I'm real thirsty."

His mother smiled and magically produced a brimming pitcher of the sweet drink that Tyler had loved to help her make as a boy. She poured a large tumbler full. His mouth watered. He reached for it with trembling hands.

His mother said, "Let me help you," and threw the contents of the glass in his face.

Tyler sat bolt upright in the pen. His eyes could not pierce the darkness surrounding him. He hurt. Cold rain slapped at his skin. He ducked his head to breathe. The rain fell with such force that he feared being washed away in its floodwaters. At the same time, he thanked God it wasn't apple cider. He forced his mind to take stock. He was alive, awash in a dark green watery hell, but alive. Shivering in the blackness, he held his breath and lifted his face to the icy shower. Opening his mouth, hesitantly at first, and then greedily, he gulped the cool, fresh water. His stomach rebelled and regurgitated.

Tyler spit the bile from his mouth and resumed drinking until his belly was full. Curling into a ball, his arms wrapped around his head, his chin tucked into his chest, he breathed fresh air.

He was asleep before the rain subsided.

ℰↃℰↄ

The Viet Cong camp was orderly chaos. Men scurried everywhere as they hastened to follow Major Xuong's commands.

"You are certain they are coming out?" Xuong scowled at the messenger that had brought him the news of the enemy's movement.

"Absolutely, Comrade Major," the man insisted. "Our watchers report a great deal of activity in the American base. They were reinforced today, and the signs indicate preparations for the field. We have word from our operatives in Dong and Go Cong that our visitors from the North have attracted attention. What else could it mean? They are going to enter the U-Minh."

"I wish we had more information," the major grunted.

"If they knew the location of our brothers' base you can be certain they would mount a large-scale attack," the courier thought aloud.

"Then this is a fishing expedition," Xuong concluded. Abruptly decisive, he ordered, "Keep the men moving. Small patrols. Nothing larger than a squad. We must attempt to divine the American commander's plans. Once we have determined his objectives, we must pick at him and lead him away from where he wishes to go. Do not give him any fat targets for his air power. Strike and vanish, but always lead him away from the area our visitors occupy."

"Yes, sir."

"If only the weather will hold," Xuong prayed as he watched the rain gush from the eaves of his shelter.

CHAPTER 67

Bare, frosted light bulbs, strung between the rafters in the mess hall, bathed the young soldiers below in a warm glow. Window shutters made from ammo crate covers prevented the light from spilling over into the predawn darkness outside. The clatter of stainless steel trays and flatware was background noise for the hubbub of the morning meal as brash young men practiced their bravado while the quiet ones watched and listened. Were it not for the green uniforms and black rifles it could have been a scene from a college cafeteria. The soldiers might have been pupils intent on the rites of passage but for the look in their eyes. There were no bell curves here, no make-up tests, no next semester. Those who could not pass the course the first time would not have to worry about failing anything ever again.

Doc's eyes scurried about the room, never resting for more than an instant. A bowl of Cheerios sat uneaten in front of him. When his dancing brown orbs met Mulvaney's across the table, he looked away.

Danny froze with a paper cup of hot coffee poised midway to his lips.

"You okay, Doc?"

Laffin held up his spoon and, as he studied his inverted reflection in the shiny metal, said, "It's true, you know."

"What is?"

"Cowards do die a thousand deaths."

"Welcome to the club."

Doc laughed softly, without humor. "Bert said the same thing. You're both full of shit. Hey, you mind if I tag along with your squad this trip?"

"You mean you don't want to hang out with our fearless leader?" Danny jerked his head toward the door, where Lieutenant Johnson stood at parade rest, his eyes examining the men—a scientist studying lesser life forms.

"I thought I was," Doc said.

Danny smiled. "Keep the yucks to a minimum. These FNGs act like escapees from nursery school to begin with. A little fear might do them good. If they get the impression that horsing around in the bush is okay—"

"I copy. Don't worry about it. I'm not feeling all that funny this morning anyway."

"It's okay to cheer up your friendly neighborhood squad leader, though."

"I'll see what I can do." Doc tried a grin. It didn't come off.

Danny looked at the faces of the men he was about to lead into combat. Self-doubt threatened to strangle him. He gulped his coffee to moisten his tongue.

Cliff Wyman would be all right, he decided. The gutsy farm boy had impressed him with his quick grasp of the lessons he had attempted to impart while they gabbed on guard duty. The kid was good with a rifle—at least he had been when they zeroed their weapons from the berm. How he would hold up in a fight remained to be seen.

E.Z. was an enigma. Edward Z. Phillips was a muscular black street punk from Detroit. He said Ed and Eddie were honky names—call him E.Z. or don't call him at all. He would not tell anyone what the Z stood for. He did as he was told, with a permanent sneer on his broad face. He kept to himself and trusted no one.

Lance had warned Danny to watch E.Z. after Lance's abortive attempt to befriend the man. "That black muthufucka called me a *nigger.*"

Wyman proclaimed E.Z. to be an equal opportunity bastard. "He hates everybody."

Danny had dubbed Cooper and Soloway—two irrepressible practical jokers from Minneapolis/St. Paul—the Katzenjammer Kids. They were inseparable. You never saw one without the other. Their hometown, Danny was certain, must be celebrating the absence of their most mischievous sons. The two not only behaved like twins, they had such a strong resemblance to one another that either man could have used the other's ID and gotten away with it. Simms said their matching brown hair and eyes were because they were so full of shit.

The biggest disaster, by far, was Berger. If ever a man epitomized the term FNG it was Berger. Danny watched him make his third attempt at bringing a forkful of runny eggs to his mouth. The food slipped back into his plate again. Berger pouted, looking up and down the table as if trying to discover the secret to mastering breakfast. If aliens from space were to abduct Berger they would surely throw him back and laugh about it all the way out of the solar system. How he had gotten through training alive was a mystery. That he would not survive Vietnam was a foregone conclusion.

Danny was once again reminded, by his own thoughts, of the hardening of his heart. He was appalled that his most prominent concern regarding Berger was that he would not take anyone with him. Danny realized it was becoming a conscious battle to hang on to his humanity.

Kill! Kill without mercy! echoed in his brain.

Amanda would never understand. No one in *The World* would understand.

"Saddle up!" Pomeroy barked.

Startled, Danny blinked. He noticed the staff sergeant watching him as he rose from the table. He ignored it and went outside with his squad to gather their gear.

ᘓᘐᘓ

Steel hinges squealed in complaint as the drivers pulled the locking pins to let the tailgates bang against the trucks. Second Platoon clambered aboard their two vehicles in the predawn light.

Lieutenant Johnson noted that Charlie-Six was occupied with last minute instructions to Chicarelli, whose task was to stay behind as base commander with his weapons platoon in their fire support mode. Johnson saw his chance. He whispered hushed orders to the third squad. The two mysterious crates were loaded. Four six-foot-long engineering stakes and a length of rope were tossed beside them to facilitate carrying them in the bush.

The chaplain waved his hand in the sign of the cross to bless the men as they climbed aboard. He tugged at Danny's sleeve. Danny snapped his head around.

"Relax," the padre smiled, "it's only me. I missed you at Holy Mass last night, Mulvaney. Are you trying to give the Catholics a bad name?"

"I was busy."

"Too busy for God?"

"He seems too busy for me lately."

The astonished look on the chaplain's face made Danny flush. He regretted having said it because it was disrespectful, and he had been taught always to be respectful to priests. His mother would be ashamed of him. Turning abruptly, he shook off the sky pilot's hand and hoisted himself over the tailgate to sit with his back to the clergyman. The chaplain stepped back and, as much to recover his bruised ego as to perform his function, mumbled a prayer to bless the vehicle and its passengers.

Captain Arnold led the First Platoon out of the gate and onto the road. From atop the trucks, Second watched their brothers walk past the water point and then turn right into the field beyond the wire. When the last man had traversed the open ground to disappear into the mist-shrouded trees, Lieutenant Johnson gave the order, and Kowalski started his engine. The Second Platoon drove over the tracks of their dismounted comrades and headed south on Highway Four.

"Everybody facing out," Simms instructed the men in the first truck. "Lock and load. Safeties on. If we get hit, return fire and watch your squad leaders for orders."

The metallic clack of rifle bolts slamming home rattled from both vehicles as Pomeroy issued similar orders in the following truck. The men knelt on the wooden benches, one hand holding the side rail for balance, the other firmly gripping a weapon. The new men's eyes were like saucers as they strained to penetrate the darkened forest. The veterans, in exaggerated postures of nonchalance, hid the awe each man felt as he gazed into the primeval tangle of massive trees and impenetrable vegetation.

The fire base had disappeared from view, and the darkness was rapidly receding when the platoon braked to a halt at Johnson's order. The men dismounted with knees buckling and leg muscles bunched to reverse the inertia of their heavy packs. Squad leaders ushered them into the ditch beside the road, spreading them out, facing every other man in opposite directions. Johnson banged sharply on the side of the vehicle when he saw the platoon deployed. The drivers executed three-point turns to head for home. The sense of all pervasive evil brought on by the proximity of the woods made the urging of their shotgun guards unnecessary. The drivers hit the gas, and both trucks accelerated quickly away.

"Play nice, kiddies. Don't fight," Kowalski called as the vehicles gathered speed.

No one laughed.

In the gray dawn light, shrouded in mist and shadow, the U-Minh was forbidding.

"Spooky," Paco whispered.

"Nice place for a war," Doc suggested. There was a ripple of nervous laughter.

Danny grinned. Good old Doc: Johnny Carson in jungle fatigues. He looked for Simms and found him watching Doc as well. Their eyes met. Simms threw Danny a thumbs-up.

"Let's form up," Johnson hollered. "First Squad, take the point. Third and Fourth, follow in that order. Second Squad, bring up the rear. And don't forget my boxes. Sergeant Pomeroy, you direct the line of march. I'll be in the center. Move out."

"Why not use a bullhorn, asshole," Pomeroy mumbled under his breath.

Simms took point, not trusting any of the new guys with the dangerous job.

Danny walked beside the lieutenant long enough to whisper, "If you want to be alive tomorrow, sir, keep it down."

He fell back to his squad without waiting for a response.

Johnson huffed but took a careful look at the pale faces of the men in the gathering light against the shadowy backdrop of the U-Minh. After an unconscious glance over his shoulder, he fell silent.

With the sun came the heat. Before they had walked for an hour, the men were feeling the punishing effects of exertion in a tropical rain forest. Johnson called a halt. He sank to the ground near collapse. Pomeroy checked the line to make certain the men did not relax.

"Search your front. Don't goof off. You're in Indian country," he said repeatedly. He saw that his squad leaders were on top of it and hurried to the lieutenant. He shook his head in disgust as he knelt beside the panting officer.

"You're haulin' too much shit, sir," he said, as he examined Johnson's bulging pack. "My god, is there anything you *didn't* bring? Let's deep six about half this junk."

Johnson shoved Pomeroy's hands from his rucksack.

"This is all necessary issue, Sergeant. I just need some time to get acclimated."

"You may get dusted off, first," Pomeroy grumbled.

Pointing to his map, Johnson told him, "Advance to the blue line, Sergeant. We'll halt there for a bit before we continue."

Pomeroy went ahead to pass along the order. He glanced back to see the lieutenant struggling to his feet. It started to rain before they had walked ten minutes more. Although the heavy downpour impeded their progress, it provided welcome relief for the over-heated soldiers.

After three hours of pushing through thorns and climbing over slippery roots, Simms saw the river. He signaled a halt as he moved up with his slack man to reconnoiter.

Danny checked his squad and moved them forward again when the signal was passed. They were on a well-used trail now. The rain let up. Something caught his eye—a thin white line stretched across the trail at chest level. The man in front had disappeared around a bend. As he drew near, Danny could see a trip wire strung across his path. He knew it was impossible that the men ahead of him had missed it. Someone should have waited to show the next man the trap. Something funny was going on.

Danny carefully approached the wire and saw it was monofilament—the kind they used on trip flares. He traced it to a tree on the left. The hairy end of this thing, he knew, should be on the other end. Following it, he found the right side was also tied to a tree.

"Weird much."

He was still puzzling it out when he heard giggling. The *Katzenjammer Kids* were peeking around a tree at the bend in the trail. Danny was incensed. He started to break the line when he saw them frantically signaling him to not do so. He ducked under and jogged to confront them.

"What the fuck do you two assholes think you're doing?"

"Just a little fun, Corporal," Cooper whined. "No harm done."

Danny was about to give them hell when Soloway shushed him.

"Here comes Berger. This oughta be good."

Curiosity got the better of Danny. He ducked behind the tree with the two jokers.

Berger shuffled along like he was on a grammar school field trip. His M-79 Grenade Launcher dangled uselessly by its sling as he continually adjusted his ammo bag to find a more comfortable position. As rear guard, Berger's job was to continually check behind the platoon, but not once did he look back. When he hit the wire, the tension made him stop. He looked down with a frown of puzzlement. Annoyed, he leaned into the string until it snapped, and then continued along his carefree way.

"Boom," Cooper whispered.

Danny's displeasure was evident by his look. The Katzen-jammers hoisted the heavy crate, hung by rope from the steel stake they had rigged to carry it. They trotted off to catch up with the column. Danny lectured Berger on the stupidity of breaking trip wires until he realized the platoon was getting too far ahead.

"Get in front of me, asshole," Danny snarled at Berger. "You fuck up one more time and I'll waste you myself. Now get that fuckin' weapon off your shoulder and wake up."

Danny paused to let Berger lead him by the ten-meter interval necessary to limit casualties in case of contact or booby traps. Berger was out of sight around the bend in the trail when he set out again. Danny cast his gaze to the rear one last time and, as he turned back, nearly ran into the Vietnamese man who appeared in his path. Bringing his rifle up sharply, Danny leveled it at the man's chest. His thumb flicked the selector switch to semi-automatic without conscious thought. The man froze. Danny's eyes bored into him. He saw a flicker of fear and then it was gone. The man smiled stupidly.

"*Dung lai.*" Danny barked. The command to halt was unnec-essary: the guy was like a statue except for that idiotic grin. "Hey! Hold up," Danny yelled. "I got a prisoner."

Berger ambled back to see what the commotion was all about. His stupefied expression seemed welcome to the Vietnamese who bowed his head over and over again, grinning like a fool.

"Don't get too close, Berger. You might want to point your weapon at him," Danny snapped. "This is Charley Cong."

Berger squinted through his steamed-up horn rims, completely baffled.

"*Come on*, dammit. Where the fuck's the lieutenant?"

Johnson strolled up to them, scowling his annoyance at this intrusion on his mission.

"What have we here?" he said.

"VC, sir," Danny answered, too eagerly. Johnson gave Danny a look that adults use when confronted with miscreant children.

"He walked right into me, sir," Danny said, excited and determined to convince his openly skeptical officer. "Must be a trail watcher. He didn't see me and Berger switch places. Figured the last man had passed and he walked right out."

"How do you know he's VC, Corporal?" Johnson said in his condescending tone. Pomeroy and Doc stood behind him.

"Come on, Lieutenant," Danny pleaded. "What the hell else could he be? He's bopping around out here in a free fire zone. Look at him, for Christ's sake." He reached out with his free hand and tore the buttons from the man's dirty white shirt. The garment fell open to reveal a muscular chest marked by several small scars. Danny made a shrugging motion, his weapon's muzzle never leaving the center of the man's body. The Vietnamese, still grinning, obligingly removed his shirt.

"Frisk him, Doc."

Laffin patted the man down below the waist. The Vietnamese smiled coyly as Doc checked his crotch.

"He's got both his balls if that means anything." Doc shrugged.

"You see, Corporal? The man's unarmed." Johnson gloated.

"Where the hell's his ID card, sir?"

"Why don't you ask him?"

"*Cancuk*?" Danny asked.

The Vietnamese man's blank stare was his only response.

Johnson said, "Maybe he forgot it."

"They don't forget that, Lieutenant. It can be the difference between life and death. This bastard's Victor Charley."

"Corporal, this man's a farmer. Probably lost his way. Let him go."

"*What?*"

"You heard me. Let him go."

"Mulvaney's right, sir," Pomeroy interjected. "No *cancuk* means VC, especially out here."

"Then where's his weapon, Sergeant?" Johnson demanded.

"Probably on his way to get it."

"Damned straight," Danny said,

"I said, let him go," Johnson commanded.

Danny flipped the selector to automatic and took up the slack in the trigger.

"If you shoot that man, Corporal, I'll have you court martialed for murder," Johnson proclaimed in his most imperious tone.

The Vietnamese man's smile evaporated. He saw the determined set to Danny's jaw, the hammering pulse in his neck, the white knuckle of his trigger finger.

Danny saw the fear return. His malevolent stare bored into the man's wide black eyes. He could see the VC understood. This was no bumbling trainee. These cold blue eyes might be the last he'd ever see.

That moment of recognition was enough for Danny. He dropped the muzzle of his weapon, nodding to the shirt in the mud. The idiot smile returned to the man's face. Bowing again and again, the Vietnamese scooped up his sodden garment. As he edged past Mulvaney, Danny kicked him in the seat of his pants hard enough to lift the man off the ground. Without turning around, the VC continued on his way.

"If you don't mind, Corporal, we have a job to do." Johnson smirked. He shook his head as he walked back to his place in the column.

"Good call, Mulvaney." Pomeroy patted Danny's shoulder. "Watch your back."

Five minutes later, Charley blew the ambush.

The entire platoon dropped to the ground. Some lay flat, some crouched on one knee. Everyone looked frantically for orders. They could hear a lot of automatic weapons firing. The vets knew from the sound that they were AK-47s, but no rounds were coming their way.

Johnson was near panic. His head swung right, then left, with such force that he nearly dislodged his helmet.

"Easy, sir." Pomeroy spoke calmly. "We're okay." He nodded toward the trees to his right front. "Charley jumped the gun. They're far enough off the trail to have to fire blind. They timed us to be in the kill zone now." Motioning with his head to the rear of the column, he explained, "That gook Mulvaney found was their lookout. The kid threw their timing off when he ran into the son of a bitch. When the signal didn't come, they took a wild-assed guess. They don't know where we are."

"We should return fire," Johnson whimpered, rising to give the order.

"Negative, sir," Pomeroy restrained the lieutenant by holding his elbow. "It'd just give our position away."

"I'll call in artillery." Johnson made a grab for the handset clipped to his RTO's shoulder harness.

"On what? They won't be there when the stuff comes in." As if on cue, the firing stopped. "They know they fucked up. They'll pull back and try again later. We gotta shake 'em. Pass the word," Pomeroy ordered in a hoarse whisper, "on my command, Seventy-Nine men only, fire three rounds in a high arc, that way." He pointed to where he estimated the enemy to be. "Then *di mau* that way." Pomeroy indicated the opposite direction, into the forest. He waited a few seconds for his instructions to be relayed up and down the line. "Now," he mouthed, bringing his arm down sharply.

The foop-like sound of the grenade launchers firing was heard from the nearest gunners, followed a split second later by the others. Berger got off one round and then fumbled with his ammo bag for the next.

"Like this," Danny said, pulling the sack around from the inaccessible place that Berger had shifted it. Plucking a grenade from the bag, he wrenched the weapon from the rattled soldier's hands and cracked the breach loader open. Danny thumbed the round into the chamber and flipped the barrel up to snap shut. Bringing the muzzle up, he yanked the trigger and then repeated the process. As the shells burst in the woods, the platoon bugged out. The echoes of the flat *crump* of the explosions had barely faded when the men halted, breathing hard.

Pomeroy held a hand up for stillness. They listened.

"They're not following. Let's move."

Picking their way through heavy brush, the platoon resumed their column formation. Pomeroy checked his map and compass bearing. He corrected their heading and sent a runner to the point to tell Simms to stay on this side of the river and to follow it north for three-hundred meters. They would cross the blue line there and work their way south on the other side to bring them back to a line near their original course.

Johnson was put off by the presumptuous assumption of his command but said nothing. He could not argue with the sergeant because he did not know what to do. In order to regain some semblance of control, he said, "Let's pick up the pace, Sergeant. We haven't got all day."

Pomeroy was speechless. Johnson brushed past him. Pomeroy closed his mouth and bit his tongue. He waited beside the trail for Mulvaney.

Pomeroy watched two men in the Third Squad struggle with the cumbersome load they had been ordered to carry. What was in those cartons worried him. From what he had seen of Lieutenant Johnson so far, he did not believe that there was anything in them that would be good for the platoon.

"What's in this thing?" Soloway groaned, echoing Pomeroy's thoughts, as the second musty package was hauled past.

"Damned if I know," Pomeroy had to admit.

E.Z. answered the sergeant's look of concern with a baleful glare. He followed the two friends and their burden at just the right interval. His eyes swept the brush ceaselessly.

"Nasty fucker," Pomeroy said under his breath. "Least he seems to know what he's doing."

Berger grinned a friendly greeting as he passed the platoon sergeant.

"Glad somebody's having a good time," Pomeroy said.

Mulvaney looked away as he came even with Pomeroy. Danny had avoided him since the ARVN compound.

"I thought you were going to waste that gook," Pomeroy said.

"Should have," Danny said.

"Worked out okay. We don't want to tangle with so much as a crack Boy Scout troop with this bunch of FNGs all spread out along a trail. Best to stay cool 'til we get to the blocking position." Pomeroy began to say something else but, Danny walked on. Pomeroy mumbled, "Nice talkin' to ya," and moved ahead to regain his position in the file.

❦❦❦

Berger was imagining his next opportunity to use the deadly toy that the army had seen fit to bestow upon him. The corporal's deft handling of the weapon had impressed him. As Pomeroy stepped in front of him, he jerked the barrel up to snap closed as he had seen Mulvaney do. The recoil, as the grenade launcher discharged, surprised him.

Pomeroy felt the shock wave as the forty-millimeter projectile whizzed past his shoulder. In a split second, he knew what had happened. He shouted, "Hit the deck!"

The grenade exploded high up in a huge teak tree. Thousands of tiny bits of steel buzzed through the branches as the tightly coiled, notched spring surrounding the charge was released by the energy of the blast. The thick foliage in the canopy absorbed most of the deadly shards, saving the men below from injury.

Pomeroy rose to wheel on the hapless Berger, who stood dumbfounded. The sergeant checked his forward motion with considerable self-restraint. "What the fuck are you? A VC infiltrator?" he spat through clenched teeth. "Keep that fuckin' thing broken open until you're ready to use it, asshole. The safeties don't work most o' the time. Corporal Mulvaney," he snarled at Danny, as the agitated squad leader rushed to join them, "put a leash on this monkey, or I'll shove that thing up his ass."

Danny pounded on the mortified new man's helmet to ensure that the message penetrated. Pomeroy hurried to inform the lieutenant that they had better vacate the area quickly. Charley would know where to look for them now.

ᠸᢳᠸᢳ

Fuquette heard the faint crackle of AKs. The fight sounded far off, but the deadening effect of the forest made it difficult to gauge distance. The only thing he was sure of was that the firing had come from the other side of the river.

The sniper was annoyed with himself that he had slept so late—well past dawn. He checked his watch, but the crystal was so completely clouded it was impossible to read the face.

"AK's only," he whispered to the trees. "Let's hope Charley's having a mad minute." The lack of return fire from M-16s was ominous. Fuquette prayed that the VC had not sprung a perfect ambush in which the targets had been wiped out without fighting back.

The crash of grenade launcher concussions, moments later, was insufficient to determine the outcome.

"Charley's got Seventy-Nines, too," Fuquette said.

He decided he'd wait at the river for a time before heading upstream. It would not be beneficial to walk into a running battle.

His skin was raw wherever it rubbed against his sopping uniform. He was caked with mud and slime, and he was conscious of his discomfort for the first time. Fuquette's ample reserves were running low. Sleep had failed to refresh him. Caution was paramount now. He was too close to let himself be tripped up by a careless mistake.

CHAPTER 68

Ducking down to shield the handset from the sheets of rain pelting him, Charlie-Six strained to hear the reply from his Second Platoon leader. "Say again, over!" he yelled, to be heard above the background noise of falling water.

"I say again," Johnson's disembodied voice came back, "we have taken fire and evaded. The platoon is moving to the blue line in a north-westerly direction through—"

"Break! Break! Break!" Arnold bellowed, cutting off the transmission. "Do not indicate the size of the element on the net. Same-same location and direction. What the hell is wrong with you? Over."

Johnson reddened at the rebuke. He knelt in the mud, lowering his voice to hide his shame as he examined the puddle of water beneath him. His eyes darted up to see if anyone had overheard. The men were watching the jungle. Only Pomeroy saw the flustered look on his face. Did the captain really believe the enemy was listening? What if they were? There were hundreds of rivers. How could they know which one he was referring to? "Wait one for map reference," Johnson finally replied.

"Negative," Six fired back. "I know where you are. Proceed as ordered. And don't hesitate to report contact from now on. Six, out."

Johnson thrust the phone at his radioman and rose to his feet. "Continue mission, Sergeant," he snapped. "Get 'em moving."

⁊⊃℮⊃

Nearly two miles away, Beecher caught the handset Charlie-Six tossed to him.

Arnold fumed at the rotten breaks he was getting. The operation had barely begun, and the unit least likely to deal with it properly had been the only one to make contact. He regretted his weakness in letting that inept mamma's boy maneuver him into changing his plan. As he walked through the dripping foliage, the cool rain calmed him. No one had been hurt so far. It was done. Johnson would have to muddle through. Pomeroy would not let him get too far out of line. Maybe it was best. The experience was necessary, and a moving target was harder to hit. If they set up early, as originally planned, Charley might swoop down on them.

Captain Arnold wished for a little luck. He couldn't bear to lose another platoon.

One thing had been learned. There were active VC in the area. The little people who had shot at Johnson's platoon were not the crack troops they were hunting. They would have executed the ambush perfectly. Arnold knew the chances of surprising these fellows were slim and none. The most they could hope for was some signs pointing to their location. They would have to be cornered and pounded to death. First, they would have to be drawn out. He thought of Andy Syzmanski's crack about hanging their asses out and waiting for someone to shoot them off.

He sighed. "Helluva way to fight a war."

CHAPTER 69

Sergeant Vinh watched the pathetic creature in the tiger cage through narrowed eyes. He had little pity for the American. These rich meddlers from the far side of the world deserved whatever evil befell them. The American officer either didn't know what Captain Tran so passionately wished to learn, or he was too stupid to understand. A quick death was the most this dog could hope for. Why didn't he see that? Surely, he could not last much longer. Even the meager meals of rice and rancid fish that they fed him wouldn't stay down. But he had to admit this man had courage. As much as he hated the Americans, he had seen them do valiant deeds in the years he had fought them. He wondered how a nation as corrupt as Hanoi professed America to be could spawn such strong young men. Maybe, under different circumstances, their peoples could learn something from one another.

Vinh toyed with the idea of helping the prisoner along on his journey to his ancestors. Death was inevitable, and a soldier should not be tormented this way. He could smother the man, and it would appear he had simply succumbed to dehydration and exposure. Captain Tran, however, was irrational enough to blame his sergeant, even if the American died on his own. Better to wait and watch.

The men were becoming impatient. Vinh thought Lieutenant Sau should confront the captain, but he knew that would never happen. The younger officer was so much in awe of his superior that he was oblivious to the madness that gripped him.

Had they come all this way to torture one worthless American to death? How could they crush the morale of the enemy if they hid in the forest, tormenting one man whom the enemy didn't know was their prisoner?

Even the shock of the slaughtered unit they had attacked would not be capitalized upon if they did not follow up with further ambushes. This was to be a reign of terror, not one isolated incident. He looked with pity at the unconscious form curled in the bottom of the cage.

"What is so important about you?"

☙❧☙

Simms placed each step along the trail with deliberate care. Walking on such a well-used path was unwise, but the surrounding woods were so thick it would take the platoon days to travel a click. This was, beyond doubt, the most eerie place he had ever seen. Monster trees, with malformed trunks held prisoner by vines as thick as a man's wrist, groped for the sky. Moss drooped from gnarled branches and creepers. Spider webs, strong enough to snare small birds, stretched across likely openings. Every square yard of low-lying ground was immersed in fetid green water. Rats, bigger than the average alley cat back home, darted and squeaked in the underbrush. Simms dreaded the night.

As he rounded a bend, he noticed a lightening in the gloom ahead. He turned to signal a halt to the man behind him and then inched his way forward.

The trail opened up into a man-made clearing dotted with short tree stumps. A few elegant palms had been spared to conceal the leveled ground and the hootch at its center from the air. Ducking behind the nearest palm trunk, Simms pointed to the man at his back and then crooked the same finger for the man to approach. Bringing the finger to his lips, he signaled for quiet.

PFC Carmody, puffing with his load, waddled to within arm's reach of his squad leader, where he imitated his posture.

"Charley's little hideaway," Simms whispered.

"Is this what we're looking for?" the new man huffed, fear and excitement making him hoarse.

"I hope not," Simms breathed, feeling terribly alone. "Go back and tell Pomeroy what we've got. Move slow and quiet. Bring them up easy. I'll wait here."

Carmody nodded three times in quick succession and then

hustled back down the trail, his equipment rattling much too loudly to please Simms.

Pomeroy crept close a few minutes later with several men fanning out behind him.

"Looks deserted," Simms observed, "but the door to that hootch must be on the other side."

Pomeroy eyed the blank thatched wall. "It's too small for there to be many of them if they're in there. We could try to flank it, but it'd take all day in this shit, and I have my doubts about this bunch sneakin' up unnoticed."

Simms nodded fervent agreement. "Have to rush it," he said. "You stay here and cover my ass. I'll check it out."

Pomeroy motioned for a machine gun crew to cover the clearing. Simms swapped his grenade launcher for Pomeroy's M-16. If the hut were occupied, he would stand a better chance with an automatic rifle than with the one-shot M-79. The sergeant replaced the shotgun round in the chamber with high explosive. Simms had loaded buckshot for close quarters, as point man. If it hit the fan, Pomeroy would blow the hootch, and the gunner would open up simultaneously. Simms would have to do his best to get out of the line of fire.

When all seemed prepared, Simms nodded that he was ready and took off in a ground-eating lope across the clearing. He stopped ten feet from the corner of the shack, crouched, and began to circle toward the front, his weapon pointed at the building, his eyes flicking from it to the woods and back. Simms knew not to get in close and edge along the wall. That worked in the movies, but Charley expected it. If he heard you coming, he would look there first, and if Pomeroy dropped a round into the hut, the bamboo and palm construction was not going to stop the blast from coming through.

As soon as the doorway was in view, Simms dove on his belly and rolled to his left, his rifle muzzle trained on the opening when he stopped in a depression in the earth.

Nothing happened.

Simms counted to three, rose to his feet, and rushed the door. Four of his platoon mates followed his route as soon as he charged.

The hootch was empty.

While Lieutenant Johnson reported what they had found to

Charlie-Six by radio, Pomeroy and the squad leaders deployed the men in a loose perimeter.

Wyman stepped down into the shallow hole Simms had rolled into. Standing in its center, he observed, "This was dug."

Johnson asked the captain to wait while he examined something one of the men had found.

"You can see how straight the sides are, sir," the observant trooper explained. "The rain has eroded it some, but this is the beginning of something—a foxhole or a bunker—maybe a grave."

Danny joined the group as Simms said, "Not a grave. Gooks bury their dead in above-ground tombs. Water table's too high in the Delta for dirt naps."

Johnson looked puzzled but bobbed his head in agreement.

The pop of a sniper's rifle took them by surprise. A geyser of dirt spouted inches from the lieutenant's foot. Danny grabbed the officer's harness and yanked him backward. Johnson landed hard on his backside with a grunt. He began to protest such rough treatment when a second shot ricocheted off a stump near his knee. Scrambling backward on his hands and the seat of his pants, Johnson scurried up against the wall of the hootch. Two more shots rang out in quick succession. The slugs bored into the earth near the lip of the hole Wyman had now completely disappeared into.

"Wyman, you all right?" Danny yelled. "Are you hit?"

"Can't talk now, Corporal. This feller's tryin' to kill me," came from the hole.

"Stay down. Anybody see him?" Danny sang out.

The platoon searched the area, trying to see without being seen. Danny did some basic geometry in his head. Wyman was in front of him, and the hootch was at his back. To draw a bead, the sniper had to be—

"In the trees!" he shrieked, "the fucker's in the trees."

"I'm on him," Paco called.

"Get him!" Pomeroy barked.

Paco shoved his machine gunner aside and took over the gun. He let go a long burst into the top of a large palm.

"I think I got him," the Mexican hollered.

Silence fell.

"Check it out," Pomeroy ordered.

Warily, Paco and three men from his squad advanced across the clearing. They worked their way back up the trail to the suspect tree with their weapons trained on the canopy. The platoon waited, breathless, watching every leaf, ready for anything.

Paco trudged back, dejected, a scowl on his face.

"You missed," Simms accused.

"Paco don't miss." The Mexican's eyes flashed. "They musta dragged him off."

"You found a blood trail?" Pomeroy's doubt was evident by his tone.

Paco winked. "They musta dragged his blood off too."

Simms laughed. "Wetback greaser couldn't hit his ass with both hands."

"Fuck you, gringo."

"No time, my horny friend. We better beat feet. This place ain't fun no more."

Johnson didn't seem capable of leaving the safety of the hootch. He stepped to its corner and peeked around it then stepped back to stand with his spine to the wall. "Sergeant Pomeroy, I think we should go after that gook." His voice lacked conviction. He was sweating profusely.

"That's more'n likely just what he wants, sir. Best tell Six we got a probable on a lone sniper and *di di mau*."

"If you say so, Sergeant. Issue the necessary orders."

Pomeroy had the platoon withdraw by squads to the continuation of the trail. He relieved Simms's squad from point, substituted Lance and his people, waited for Johnson to summon the courage to take his place in the file, and then hung back until Danny brought up the rear. "Mulvaney," he warned Danny as they set off again, "you're gonna need eyes in back of your head. That's twice today Chuck stepped on his dick, and that just *don't* happen. Charles is playing games with us, and there's no way of knowin' what's up his sleeve. There's too many well-traveled trails in this AO—high-speed trails—and so far, no booby traps. That's weird. They either have so many men running around in here that they don't set traps to avoid wasting their own..."

"Or?"

"Or they're channeling us in a certain direction."

"I don't like the sound of either choice, but the second one *really* sucks."

"Roger that. Door number two looks to be the most likely to me. What's one lone sniper doing out here all by hisself with no spotter and no security? One thing Charley ain't is stupid. We're in some deep shit. You keep that head on a swivel."

Danny nodded affirmation.

"I'm counting on you, man." Pomeroy stared straight into Danny's eyes. "Be cool."

"Ice wouldn't melt in my hands," Danny whispered to the departing back of his platoon sergeant.

They followed the meandering trail until noon when they stopped for a break. Paco came back to tell Danny that his squad was switching places with the Second for the resumption of the march. Pomeroy liked to change the point and tail squads frequently to relieve the pressure and to keep both ends of the column fresh and alert.

Danny was walking in the middle of the file with Lieutenant Johnson when they came upon a ghostly swamp. All of the trees were devoid of vegetation. The branches, stripped of bark, resembled bleached bones. The rain tapered off and then stopped just before they entered the perished woods. The clouds parted. The sun boiled the moisture from sopping fatigues. Steam rose from their clothing as they dried out like ceramic figures in a kiln. The material became stiff from dried sweat. It chafed as it rubbed against flesh softened by moisture.

The only path through the defoliated area was a raised trail resembling a dike. With a sigh born of reluctance, Pomeroy ordered Lance to start across.

"Keep your intervals," he said. "Go quick but careful. This ain't a good place to be."

Danny was in the exact middle of the swamp when the enemy opened up.

Two AKs, one directly opposite Danny, the other, near the front of the column and at a forty-five-degree angle to him, triangulated their fire to converge on the middle. The platoon dropped flat and rolled into the muck behind the raised trail. Danny hesitated, eyeing the slime-covered water, so reluctant to resume being wet that, for an instant, speeding bullets were preferable. Pomeroy whirled, lost his footing, and fell over sideways. The new guys panicked. No one was shooting back. They were all trying to be invisible. Two slugs slammed into the dike beneath

Danny's feet. He felt the impact vibrate through the soles of his boots. He dropped to one knee. A burst zipped over his head like a flight of rocket propelled mosquitoes. One tracer round burned a hole in the air as it passed. Danny flashed back to his father.

They had been watching a war movie on TV together. Just he and his dad, staying up late, feet on the coffee table, munching popcorn and bonding. A sniper was zeroing in on the good guys with tracer rounds. Danny thought the special effects were cool and said so.

"The problem with tracers," his dad had said, "is that they work both ways. You see where your bullet went, but the other guy sees where it came from. No sniper worth his salt uses tracers."

The memory had flashed through his mind in an instant. Deliberately bringing his rifle to his shoulder, Danny sighted on the starting point of the incendiary round. He popped off two shots on semi-automatic. He was rewarded with a scream from the bush. He flipped to full automatic and unleashed two bursts of three at the same spot. Out of the corner of his eye, he saw the muzzle flash of the other sniper as the enemy soldier fired a long, wild burst to take the heat off of his comrade.

Danny pivoted to engage the new target and fired one shot at the sparkling hot gases.

The enemy fire ceased.

The platoon poked their heads up, a couple of men at a time. No one tried to kill them. They rose from the ooze as Lance bounded atop the trail and rushed to pound Danny on the back.

"Holy shee-it." Lance laughed. "Did you see that? Mulvaney, the one-man army. Audie fuckin' Murphy and Sergeant York all rolled into one. We was fucked until old Dan'l just iced them muthafuckas slick as you please."

"Nice shooting," Pomeroy admitted, climbing onto the dike and looking at Danny with awe. "Corporal," he said to Lance, "take your squad in there and make sure. And be careful."

Lance and his people split into fire teams and then slogged through the water into the brush at the edge of the swamp. They came back dragging two bodies and the enemy weapons. The dead men were dumped at Danny's feet. The first—the one with the tracers—had three bloody holes in his collarbones and throat. The second had one neat hole in his forehead and a red mass of pulp where the back of his skull should have been. Danny was saddened by the youthful appearance of both men. *Guys like me,* he thought.

"Guess these are yours." Lance proffered two Kalashnikov assault rifles.

"You keep 'em," Danny mumbled. "I don't want 'em." He walked slowly along the trail until he reached the end of the defoliated section. He sat with his back to a tree to watch the jungle ahead, heedless of the admiring stares of his platoon mates.

Pomeroy suggested they do likewise and get out of the open.

Johnson grudgingly complimented Danny on the bravery of his action as he called the captain to report the body count, all the while scraping mud and filth from his uniform. He had flopped flat on his face in the swamp when the first shot rang out and on the wrong side, the exposed side, of the dike.

Danny was the picture of alertness as his eyes roamed the jungle. No one watching could know that he saw nothing. His mind had turned inward. There was no gratification, no vindication. He had not evened the score. He had simply extended the game. Someone from the enemy's side would now feel compelled to avenge their own. Danny wondered who would have to die because of his killing. *War,* he thought, *is the theory of relativity taken to hideous extremes. Death is the only winner.*

Charlie-Six surprised them all when he ordered the bodies dusted off.

"G-Two wants a look at all enemy KIA," Johnson explained to Pomeroy's scowl.

"What the fuck for?"

"You have your orders, Sergeant. Prepare the bodies for extraction."

The only place suitable for an extraction by air was right where they were, so Johnson read the coordinates to the chopper pilots. He threw smoke into the swamp when he heard the inbound bird. The submerged grenade fizzled and went out. A second attempt resulted in the same failure. The pilot circled, demanding marking smoke before he would attempt to land.

"Sir," Pomeroy said, "you got to let the thing get started before you throw it in the water. Let me—"

Johnson pulled a third grenade to his chest and stepped back.

Pomeroy mumbled, "Be my guest."

The lieutenant stood in the center of the dike, yanked the pin, and held the grenade aloft. The veterans looked at one another, amused and dismayed. No one said a word.

Johnson's triumphant grin changed to a howl of pain when the burning canister blistered the skin of his bare hand. Attempting to fling the blazing cylinder from his grip, he was horrified to find it stuck to his skin. It shook loose when he snapped his arm like a whip.

When the helicopter touched down, Johnson was on his knees with his burned hand submerged in the filthy water. While the men loaded the bodies on the chopper, Doc bit his tongue to keep from laughing as he bandaged his moaning officer's hand.

"You're supposed to get it started, sir," Simms said, "not play Statue of Liberty with it."

Johnson ignored him. He refused medivac with the dead VC, in spite of pleas to the contrary from his *"concerned"* troops.

When the bodies were gone and the lieutenant ministered to, they set out again. Johnson checked his precious boxes to satisfy himself there were no bullet holes. He chastised the bearers for leaving them exposed when taking cover.

"If he's so worried about these damn things," E. Z. grumbled, as he and Berger hoisted one of the crates, "why don't he hump one hisself?"

They reached the river without further mishap. Berger beamed lie a kid dismissed unexpectedly from school when Johnson informed them they would carry their loads no farther. The lieutenant unsheathed a custom-made combat knife, which he used to pry the lid from one crate. The black-stenciled identification nomenclature had been obliterated by spray paint.

The platoon waited expectantly for the unveiling.

Johnson produced a green metal cylinder and then a heavy bundle of green rubber. His expression was one of irrepressible pride.

"Very nice," E.Z. sneered. "What the fuck is it?"

Johnson ignored him. He ordered the other parcel opened and the contents of both brought to the water's edge.

"Rubber boats," Pomeroy exclaimed, as the lieutenant assembled two-piece plastic paddles. "Sir, I'm not so sure about this," he cautioned, as the officer showed the men how to connect the compressed air bottles to the valves.

"Captain Arnold approved this operation," Johnson lied.

The staff sergeant thought that unlikely but could not challenge his platoon leader openly.

Johnson hovered like an over-protective parent as he supervised the inflation and launching of the craft. They were surprisingly large, given the relatively compact size of their containers.

"Each one can carry half the platoon, Sergeant," Johnson informed Pomeroy, showing off his expertise. "We'll glide effortlessly downstream. It'll take hours off of our timetable."

"We'll be sittin' ducks," Pomeroy warned.

"We'll gain the element of surprise," Johnson argued. "Charley will never expect an amphibious insertion."

"He'd never dream he could be so lucky," the worried sergeant proclaimed.

"*Daring*, Sergeant Pomeroy, that's what wins wars," Johnson preached, "*daring*."

"Whad'ya think, Sarge?" Danny asked, as Johnson arranged the squads in boatloads.

"I think John Wayne here has read too many comic books."

They pushed off minutes later to begin their excursion. Johnson had envisioned them slipping silently along, swiftly and surely, to spring upon the unsuspecting enemy at the culmination of their trip. What he got bore no resemblance to his dreams of glory.

The men straddled the pontoon-like gunwales of the inflatable boats while their packs occupied the rubber deck. Three men per side paddled. The rest rode with weapons at the ready. An M-60 machine gun was perched on the bow of the lead boat. Johnson in the first, and Pomeroy in the second, manned the plastic tillers, aft.

What Johnson had failed to consider was that six men who had never paddled a raft as a team would not be synchronized. Most of them had never rowed any kind of boat. Some had never been afloat. The non-swimmers were apprehensive about drowning, and the few swimmers were anxious about losing their gear, stowed in the bottom of the craft for ballast. All were aware that the rubber skin would do nothing to ward off bullets. The disorganized, uneven strokes of the oarsman, magnified by the differences in strength of the men, caused them to spin in the sluggish current. The width of the river, or more accurately the lack of it, sent them crashing into low-hanging branches and shrubbery.

Before long, anxiety was replaced by joviality. Mischievous young men soon found that they could batter their humorless leader against every obstacle.

Johnson quickly lost patience, cursing their ineptitude, but fought a steadfast verbal battle to maintain unison among his oarsman.

"Stroke! Stroke!" he called, like the coxswain of a racing shell.

Even the rain, which began to fall once again in sheets, failed to dampen the spirits of his crew. They merrily caromed off of every available overhanging tree.

"Sounds like Fearless Leader is conducting a circle jerk," Doc said, laughing in the second boat. The men pounded the rubber sides with glee.

"Knock it off," Pomeroy hissed. "Y'all be laughing outta new holes if Charley catches us out here."

That sobering thought renewed the crews' seriousness. The men concentrated on doing it right.

As the lead craft rounded a bend, the M-60 in the prow roared. Men clutched weapons tighter, straining to see through the gray curtain of water pouring down on them. Everyone thought they were dead as the helplessness of their situation dawned. If Charley was waiting, he had them cold.

Another long burst split the air. The boats drifted lazily on the current. Rowers dropped their paddles to retrieve weapons. Time stopped as the men waited to die.

"Cease fire, you bastards," came a voice from the bank ahead. "I'm on your side."

The men gaped at the source of the sound.

"I'm coming out, goddammit, and I'll drop anybody who twitches."

Danny's eyes grew wide as he recognized that voice. He stared with disbelief at Pomeroy.

"That's—"

"Davy Fuckit," Pomeroy finished Danny's thought. "I'll be a son of a bitch!"

CHAPTER 70

"Where the hell have you been?" Lieutenant Chicarelli demanded of the officer in charge of the .155 Howitzer battery.

"Listen, buddy," First Lieutenant Beaumont Stuart snarled as he sprang from his jeep. "My boys and I been jackassin' all over the goddamn Delta since we got deviated from our initial mission. We been from Vinh Long to the Wagon Wheel and back. We put more rounds through them tubes than you can count, even if'n your whole damn battalion took theah boots off, and we done it on less sleep and some of the lousiest chow you ever dreamed of in yaw wust nightmare. I am in no mood to take shit for somethin' I had no say to begin with." The tall, lanky Virginian glared defiance at Chicarelli.

"Well, excuse me, Lieutenant." Chicarelli grinned. "We been up to our asses in dancing girls here, and we were hoping you fellas would cut in and give the men a break."

Stuart pursed his lips and looked at his boots. He had a broad grin on his face when he looked back at Chicarelli. "And thank y'all fo' yaw kind understandin' too, Lieutenant Chicarelli."

"Chick," Chicarelli said, extending his hand.

"Beau," Stuart replied, pumping Chicarelli's right arm. "Where you want us?"

"Have to put you across the road. We just put out the No-Vacancy sign. We'll put a perimeter around you for security." Chicarelli walked toward the convoy that was dragging the heavy Howitzers. Stuart fell in step beside him. "We've been taking some mortars at night, now and again," Chicarelli said, "but no sniper fire for the past few days. You should be okay."

"If recent history is any indication, we won't be here long enough to worry about it." Stuart sighed. "We're supposed to put out some H and Is tonight to support whatever y'all got goin'." He shrugged. "Leastways that's the plan until some asshole orders us to move again."

H and I fire was Harassment and Interdiction. Shells were fired blindly at trail junctions, river crossings, and various suspected VC staging areas in hopes of catching the enemy at work. The big guns could land tons of explosives on targets well beyond the horizon.

"You boys seem to be in demand of late," Chick observed.

"You'd think these here were the only guns in the goddamn war."

"We'll send over some hot chow when you get set up," Chicarelli promised. "Real food."

"Like Momma used to make?"

"Only if your momma was an E-Seven."

"Momma was first class, but she weren't no sergeant."

"We'll do our best. Stop by the CP when you've had your fill," Chicarelli said, as he left him at the road. "I've got some Jim Beam. We can take a taste after we lay out your fire missions for tonight."

Lieutenant Stuart smiled. "I knew there was somethin' about this place I liked."

CHAPTER 71

He's alive?" Pomeroy gasped. "Tyler's alive?"
The survivors of the old Second Platoon crowded around
David Fuquette as the sniper sprawled against the base of
a tree beside a trail skirting the river.

Fuquette took another swig of water from Danny's canteen,
and said, "He was when I left a couple or three days ago. I better
give this back before I finish it." He extended the plastic flask
toward Mulvaney.

"Keep it, Davy. I've got three more. God, it's good to see
you."

"Likewise." Fuquette grinned through his exhaustion. His
complexion was sallow, his cheeks sunken, his eyes red-rimmed
and glassy.

Lieutenant Johnson elbowed his way in.

"I'll need a complete report, Sergeant."

Fuquette squinted up at him. "Yes, sir. But we best be gettin'
out of here. Charley's got patrols all over the place. I've been
ducking them ever since I left the camp. That racket your gunner
made is going to attract some attention."

Fuquette was obviously sick, but the determination in his eyes
was almost tangible.

The men milled about, still asking questions. They were not
going to make any progress until he gave them some answers. He
outlined the story of Tyler's capture and the flight to the enemy
camp while his friends stalled, making more of a chore of sad-
dling up than was necessary.

The recounting of Tyler's treatment by his captors made them
nauseous with anger. The new men listened, silent, awestruck by

this ghostly soldier in tattered rags. Even Doc, who had seen badly wounded men do extraordinary things, was amazed at the
stamina of David Fuquette. He treated his friend's abrasions
while Fuquette talked, and then, with suturing thread, sewed the
larger rents in Fuquette's uniform.

"If your personal tailor is finished with the alterations—"
Pomeroy grinned. "—we best get gone." He turned to Johnson.
"We'll have to ditch the boats, sir. Too dangerous to continue on
the river now. Let's call Six and sky up."

Johnson looked pained to have to part with his cherished flotilla, but even he could see the wisdom in Pomeroy's words.
"We'll sink the boats here, Sergeant, but I don't want to contact
the captain until I have a complete report."

He fiddled with his compass, which he held at a steep angle,
and made a show of studying his map. A Lensatic compass will
not give accurate readings unless level. Fuquette queried his
friends with a look. The rolled eyes and wagging chins he got in
reply confirmed his suspicions. Johnson was lost, in more ways
than one.

Pomeroy took control. "We'll follow the river downstream
until we can find a place to cross. It goes in the general direction
of our objective, anyway. Carmody, Phillips—poke some holes in
the boats. Put something heavy in them to be sure they sink."

"Right, Sergeant," Johnson agreed, giving up on finding his
location since Pomeroy obviously had. "Sergeant Fuquette, you'll
accompany me on the march to fill me in on the rest of the details.
Can you point out this enemy camp on the map?"

"Not exactly, sir." Fuquette frowned. "But I think I can maybe
find my way back there."

The veterans glanced at one another. Fuquette's navigational
abilities were legendary. He could probably state the coordinates
of the camp from his mental picture of the site. If he was reluctant
to show the way, he had a reason. Fuquette made eye contact with
Danny, Pomeroy, and Simms. Gentle nods confirmed agreement.
They were with him.

"With all due respect, sir," Fuquette went on, "talking while
walking is a bit reckless in these parts. Chuck zeroes in on chatty
troops. Why don't we relocate first, then I'll be happy to enlight-
en you?"

Johnson considered this, his hand gripping his chin. "Very

well, Sergeant Fuquette. Are you up to taking point? You seem to know the terrain."

Fuquette mimicked the lieutenant's thoughtful demeanor. "Roger that, sir. Good idea."

Pomeroy turned away to hide his smile.

Johnson showed Fuquette the spot on his map that Captain Arnold had assigned him to set up the blocking force.

"No problem, sir. I'll get you there. But what about Lieutenant Tyler?"

"I'm mulling that over, Sergeant. No need for you to concern yourself. I'll handle it."

Fuquette turned to Pomeroy who blew a puff of air through pursed lips.

They followed the river until it was nearly dark. Radio silence was maintained except for the occasional negative sit-rep. Johnson still did not report the return of the sniper or his news of Tyler.

They set up for the night on the far side of a banana grove. The VC had planted the trees after clearing and cultivating the area. Fresh fruit was plentiful. Many of the hands were ripe enough to eat. The men helped themselves as they passed through and were overjoyed to find wild grapefruit trees in the forest beyond as well.

"Amazing little motherfuckers, the VC," Simms commented as they feasted. "Set up this little truck farm way out here in the boonies. If Marvin the Arvin were as self-sufficient, we could've all stayed home."

Charlie-Six was angry when Johnson reported that they were stopping short of their objective. Johnson's excuse of unexpected delays due to the terrain met with snide remarks. Captain Arnold reminded Johnson of his insistence of the day before. "Falling short doesn't fit my idea of a 'more active role,' Two-Six."

"Why hasn't Peckerhead told Six about Davy?" Danny asked Pomeroy as they deployed the platoon in an ambush to cover the grove.

"Don't know. I suspect he's got ideas about keeping this to himself until he can find a way to cash in on it. In case you haven't noticed, this boy's got stars in his eyes. Let's talk to Davy."

The men watched, incredulous, as Johnson blew air into his rubber air mattress, arranged a mosquito net on poles around it, and spread his poncho liner like a quilt over his bed.

"Where did you find this guy?" Fuquette whispered, wagging his head as he watched.

Danny snickered. "He was hand-picked."

"So was this." Fuquette waggled a peeled banana, "but I ain't about to follow it. And what asshole dreamed up the rubber boats?"

"Two guesses," Pomeroy said, "and the first one don't count. Can we get Tyler out?"

"I'd say yes." Fuquette nodded. "But it's gotta be done quiet-like, and not with this bunch. That's why I haven't told this eight-ball where he is. If he calls it in, Division will charge in there like the thundering herd. They'll kill Tyler before anybody gets close."

"Desmond thinks Johnson is out for glory," Danny said in low tones.

"I agree." Fuquette nodded again. "Otherwise, why hasn't he told Arnold about me or Tyler?"

"So, what in the hell do we do?"

"Be patient," Fuquette advised. "Desmond, can you convince this asshole that West is South?"

"Humph. I can convince Lieutenant Peckerhead that trees grow down."

"Good. We can't do anything tonight. But tomorrow..." Fuquette whispered the outline of his plan.

❧❧❧

Captain Tran sat on a reed mat, honing the edges of his bayonet. The gentle rubbing of soapstone against steel had a soothing effect. When the blade was as sharp as a Samurai sword, he peered over the edge of his sleeping platform, erected eight meters above the suspended cage in which his prisoner languished. A freak sunbeam stabbed through the leafy canopy to illuminate a bare, bruised foot protruding between the bamboo bars. The toes hung within arm's reach of the jungle floor, a sight that would stir compassion in most men, but Tran was beyond compassion.

The stubborn American was wearing on his nerves. He had not imagined the man could hold out for so long. It would be necessary to force the information from him quickly now. Tran no longer found enjoyment in the man's suffering. His men were beginning to doubt his strength. The American officer was mocking him. He must break him soon. General Quoc would be flabbergasted when he, Captain Ngo Din Tran, rescued his sister from the hands of the enemy as well as completing his mission. He would show the insurgents the foolhardiness of their cause and, at once, show the high command his resourcefulness and daring. Mai would be returned to the home of her birth where she would be safe. Lieutenant Tyler of the United States Army would not stand in his way. Tomorrow he would talk.

Sergeant Vinh cleared his throat. Tran looked up to see his senior NCO poke his head into his leaf-shrouded perch.

"What is it, Sergeant?"

"Sir," Vinh said, climbing in, "a word, if I may."

Tran nodded.

Vinh settled himself in a squat, facing his commander. He toyed with a loose strand of jungle vine that lashed the bamboo floor together. "I would like permission to lead a patrol," he said.

"Is Lieutenant Sau ill?"

"No, sir, but he has been occupied with perimeter patrols and shallow reconnaissance." Vinh hesitated before saying, "I would like to go farther afield, possibly to Highway Four." Tran's frown of disapproval made him hasten to conclude, "We need information and food."

"Sergeant, if the information I believe the prisoner possesses is forthcoming, and I am determined it shall be, it will become necessary to move the entire unit, and quickly. That is why I have kept our men close at hand."

"What sort of information, sir?"

"Never mind that." Tran wasn't sure how his men would react if they knew of the extremely personal nature of his plans. They were becoming exceedingly suspicious. They were dedicated soldiers—professionals. And professional soldiers valued duty and mission above all else. Anything was possible this deep in the jungle, even mutiny. He had seen Vinh looking in an odd way at the prisoner—thoughtful, almost pitying. Perhaps a token gesture would relieve their apprehension. "Take four men." He reached for his map. "There is a tiny village here." He pointed to a spot where the highway ran through the U-Minh. "It is more of a marketplace for travelers on the road and close enough to the new

American base for the merchants to have dealings with the troops there. See what you can learn. Be back by tomorrow afternoon."

"Yes, sir. Thank you, sir."

CHAPTER 72

The Second Platoon was moving at first light. They were now heading in the direction of the prison camp, thanks to Pomeroy's clever subterfuge, so Fuquette didn't have to give Johnson too much information yet.

Last night's C-Ration meal and fresh fruit had played havoc with Fuquette's digestive system. Amoebic Dysentery was playing hell with his innards. The tiny beasts within him were gorging themselves. His guts were on fire but he would not let it show. There would be time enough when this was over to purge his body of the bugs that threatened to devour him from within. He would just have to hang on a little longer.

As he walked, he took stock of the new platoon. They were so cherry they belonged on an ice cream soda. His old pals were solid enough to pull this off, but he had to find a way to ditch the rest of these jokers, especially their idiot lieutenant, if this was going to work. He glanced back to watch Mulvaney redistributing an FNG's load. The new kid looked all in.

Danny seemed to have aged since last he had seen him. Not surprising. Killing and fear took a toll. Usually, the process went unnoticed as the metamorphosis occurred gradually in the company of other men in similar circumstances. Fuquette assumed it must be like watching your kids grow up. You saw them every day, and you didn't realize they were aging until one day you realized they were grown. Fuquette saw Danny as an older brother must see his sibling after a long separation.

Lance had bragged of his buddy's proficiency with a rifle to Fuquette during a break yesterday, recounting, and embellishing, Danny's actions in the defoliated forest. Danny had refused to talk about it.

In a private moment, Fuquette told Danny, "You saved your buddies. You did your job just like the gooks were doing theirs. Okay, so two young men died. Would you rather it had been some of yours? The price is high, my friend, and the bill ain't paid yet. Move on. This won't last forever. You'll need something left of you to take back home to that girl of yours. Don't let it eat you. Go from here."

Danny had said nothing, but Fuquette thought he had gotten his point across. He hoped so. Some men were too sensitive for this work. He knew because he had once been one of them.

e⁄ɔe⁄ɔ

The trail petered out. They were moving through heavy undergrowth when Page, a hard-headed Oklahoman who had insisted he could spell Fuquette on point, saw a blur of white move across his path. He brought his rifle up and froze, afraid his mind was playing tricks.

e⁄ɔe⁄ɔ

The VC trying to draw the American point man's fire stopped, cursing his foul luck. He would have to show himself more plainly to pull the American in. Stepping behind a tree, the guerrilla stood still for a moment, framing himself in the V of its split trunk.

e⁄ɔe⁄ɔ

Page reacted. He ripped off a long, wild burst with his M-16 and screamed, "I see one. I see a gook."

Several men behind Page opened fire, spraying the woods. The point man ducked as the rounds whined over his head.

"Knock that shit off," Pomeroy barked. "You'll be shootin' each other."

"I saw a gook, Sarge," Page yelled, lying flat.

"Point squad," Pomeroy rapped, "move on line. Check it out, careful like. Rest of you move up. Cover."

Page got to one knee. As soon as he saw the others start to move, he sprang ahead, determined to kill his first enemy soldier.

The new man was too inexperienced to know the cardinal rule—Never charge Charley. When the grenade sent him cartwheeling into the brush, Page felt the searing heat of the blast and white-hot steel fragments slamming into his flesh, but he did not hear the sound of the explosion.

Lance got to the wounded man first. The sight of his squad's first casualty sickened him. The kid's leg looked like hamburger. He shook his head to clear the vertigo overwhelming him. Dropping to his knees, he inhaled a lungful of lingering smoke and coughed. He dropped his rifle to press both hands to the wounds to stem the bleeding. His eyes bounced from tree to tree, fully expecting to see the screaming murderers of his nightmares coming back to finish him this time.

Frantic, awaiting the fatal onslaught he feared, Lance whispered the litany of first aid he was desperate to remember from training. "Stop the bleeding. Clear the airway. Uh—what the fuck is next? Treat for shock!" He tore his eyes from the jungle to look down at his hands. Crimson streams poured through his fingers. Tendrils of smoke rose from the wounds. "Oh, shit. *Medic!*"

Doc, skidding to a stop beside him, was the most welcome sight Lance could have wished for.

"Don't watch me, my friend," Doc said. "Watch the bush. Pick up your Matty Mattel pop-gun there and keep those murdering little motherfuckers offa me." Doc's hands shook. He inhaled sharply.

Lance's head whipped around to face away from the wounded man as his sticky fingers groped for his weapon on the spongy earth.

"Okay, Doc. Do your thing. I'm on it."

"Outstanding." Doc turned to Page. "You're okay. Just a little booby trap, nothing serious. Where you from?" Doc smiled while he worked.

Page began to feel the pain. He scrunched his head down until his chin was on his chest. He saw his own blood and tried to sit up to survey the damage.

Doc's mouth moving, just inches from his face, with no sound coming from it, frightened him. He stiffened, his hands went to his ears.

"You took a little shrapnel," Doc said, louder now, easing the man back down. "You're a little deaf from the concussion." He

pointed to his ears and shook his head. Page nodded, wide eyed.
"It's okay." Doc mouthed the words. "Happens all the time. It
will pass."

With facial expressions and hand signs, Doc convinced Page
he wasn't in bad shape. The panic subsided. He laid back and put
himself in the medic's care.

When the wounds were dressed and the man resting, Doc
turned to Pomeroy and Johnson. "He'll be all right if we can get
him out of here. He'll need blood and a surgeon aysap if he's going to keep that leg."

"Can't get a dustoff in here," Pomeroy said, "shit's too thick."
Checking his map, he announced, "Best bet's the road. It's about
a click and a half that way."

"We'll never be able to carry a wounded man that far in this,"
Johnson whined, indicating the dense foliage with a sweep of his
hand.

"What do you suggest, sir? Should we shoot him?" Pomeroy
snarled.

"No need," Fuquette interjected, cutting off Johnson's response. "It's easier goin' on the other side of the blue line. I've
been there."

"Then let's get across," Pomeroy ordered, turning his back on
the lieutenant.

They rigged a hasty litter with a poncho and bamboo. Lance
took point this time, determined not to lose another man. Fifteen
minutes later, he saw their way across the river.

"There's a fat log across a narrow part up ahead," he reported
back to the lieutenant. "Looks like a good place to cross."

"Let's have a look," Pomeroy said.

Johnson, trying to regain his authority, followed close behind.
His RTO fell in step with the officer.

Intercepting a narrow trail, Pomeroy looked down a ten-yard
stretch to the riverbank. A partially submerged fallen tree pointed
straight across.

"Looks adequate," Johnson announced.

"Yeah," Pomeroy muttered, "adequate. Charley might say
perfect. Shit. No choice. Okay, listen up. Point man goes across
to set up security on the other side. We follow one at a time.
Somebody's going to have to carry Page. No room for stretcher
bearers on that log."

"I'll take him," E.Z. volunteered, as Danny's squad joined them.

"You got it, soldier. You're second to last. Mulvaney, cover our asses. I want six dudes fanned out here to cover the far side. One Seventy-Nine. One Sixty. Four Sixteens. Grab some trees, people. Hunker down and wait your turn. Move it."

Lance trotted down the slope and crouched at the water's edge. Swallowing the lump in his throat, he edged out onto the log like a tightrope walker. When he was halfway across, Johnson followed, his radioman in tow.

"What the fuck is he doin'?" Fuquette whispered.

Pomeroy grimaced. "Tryin' to show us his balls."

"I don't want to see 'em, dammit."

Lance looked back, surprised to see the lieutenant standing exposed on the trail as if he was waiting for a bus. Johnson picked that moment to inform his CO of his progress. Snapping his fingers for the handset, he summoned his radio operator. The sandy-haired kid from Montana dutifully stepped into the open to hand his officer the phone.

℘ℴ℘

The VC trail watcher did not believe his luck. The American officer was almost standing on the land mine connected to the detonator in his hands, and his radio operator was on his heels. As the lieutenant reached for the handset, a black soldier broke from cover to run down the trail, shouting a warning. The Viet Cong guerrilla depressed the plunger as the man drew near.

℘ℴ℘

Johnson heard the pop as a small charge sent a Bouncing Betty mine into the air. He saw something black, moving fast, erupt from the earth between himself and the radioman. He had time to think, *What the—*

The bomb exploded in his face at the same time a huge, homemade Claymore mine, connected by a submerged wire to the other end of the log, detonated. Lance disappeared in a red fog that was quickly overtaken by the black cloud of the blast. Johnson's back was peppered with roofing nails, broken glass,

and scrap steel from the Claymore, while his front was obliterated
by the Bouncing Betty. The kid from Montana never knew what
hit him. His head was nearly severed from his body when the
mine exploded. Pomeroy caught a burning shard of hot steel in
his left eye as he ran to warn his careless officer.

The platoon lay stunned. No one moved for several seconds.
Every mouth hung open.

Doc broke the shocked silence, yelling, "Let's go. Everybody's a medic," as he bolted for the scene of the carnage.

Danny tried in vain to stem the pulsing blood that squirted
from the carotid artery of the kid from Montana.

"He's dead, Danny," Doc said, kneeling beside Johnson.
"Help Pomeroy."

"No, he's not. I got a heartbeat," Danny pleaded. Hot tears
burned his eyes.

"His head's half gone, Danny," Doc whispered. "Help the living."

Paco and Cooper were attending to Pomeroy, so Danny turned
to Johnson with Doc.

"It's a trap," Johnson gurgled through torn lips. "Get the platoon out of here."

"No shit, asshole," Danny mumbled, cradling Johnson's
bloody head.

The lieutenant's helmet lay beside him, split like a shattered
melon. Danny felt the death rattle vibrate the shattered officer's
body as he tried to raise him from the mud. Then Danny's gaze
fell on the middle of the log, the last place he had seen Lance.
The chips and slashes in the bark and a slick red stain told the
story.

"Spread out." Fuquette's hoarse cry sent the gathering men
scurrying to cover. "Recon by fire."

The dazed men looked at the sniper, the unspoken question on
all of their faces.

"The far bank, shitheads. Open up," Simms ordered, lobbing
an M-79 round at the woods across the river.

The platoon followed suit. Their fire tore up the opposite bank.
Inexperienced as they were, the new men emptied their magazines in long bursts and were fumbling to reload in the ensuing
silence when Fuquette hollered, "Cease fire! Cease fire! They're
gone." Rushing to Danny, who still had Johnson's head in his lap,

he saw the hopelessness on the young man's face. "Dead?"

Danny nodded. His eyes went to Johnson then to the kid from Montana and, finally, to the center of the log bridge where Lance had been. Kneeling in the dirt, Mulvaney visibly slumped.

"Grieve when there's time, man," Fuquette said. "These kids need us to get them out of this."

"What do we do?" Danny asked, as if in a dream.

"Get on the horn. Call Six and tell him our situation. Now, Danny!"

The radio lay beneath the dead kid's mangled body. Danny would have to get it off his back. He forced his mind to concentrate on the task and to ignore the sticky blood that soaked his fingers as he worked. Stifling a sob, he tried to read the nametag on the kid from Montana's shirt, which was black with blood. *I can't even remember his name.* Guilt tore at him as he realized the kid was carrying the radio that once had been his. As Danny twisted the shoulder strap to pry it over the dead man's shoulder, the kid's fatigue jacket popped open. The boy's intestines wormed out of his lacerated middle.

"Jesus, help me," Danny moaned. The rucksack, with the radio, fell away from the body as the quick release was accidentally sprung. "Charlie-Six, Charlie-Six, this is Two-Six-Oscar, over," Danny repeated again and again.

"Anything?" Fuquette asked.

"It's dead," Mulvaney whispered.

"Oh my God, not again," Paco groaned.

"Take it easy," Pomeroy cautioned. "Get 'em across. Try again later." With his one good eye, he sought to calm them with a confident stare. The veterans moved sharply to organize the platoon. Each of them hid the panic welling within by barking orders. The green platoon would come apart if they failed to see cool professionalism in their squad leaders.

It took nearly an hour, but they got them all across. The dead were difficult to handle on the precarious bridge. Danny now knew what the term "dead weight" meant. He couldn't manage the radio and the lieutenant too, so Soloway and Cooper half-dragged and half-carried the officer's corpse. The kid from Montana was slung across E.Z.'s broad back in a fireman's carry. He negotiated the slippery log as if he did it every day. Pomeroy helped Page.

"You help me see, and I'll help you walk," he told the wounded man.

They lay panting on the far side for several minutes before resuming the march. Danny carried the radio in front of him, fiddling with the dials and checking the connections. It didn't look damaged. The kid's body had taken the brunt of the blast. Why wouldn't it work? Maybe the internal parts had been broken.

Then he saw it. The handset connection was ajar where it hooked up to the set. He disconnected it to clean the contacts with the tail of his shirt. When he reassembled it, he heard the welcome hiss of static in the earpiece.

"I got him! I got him!"

"Let me talk to him." Pomeroy grabbed for the handset, leaning Page against a tree. A hurried conversation followed. The platoon circled into a defensive perimeter at the urging of the squad leaders.

"How many Claymores we got?" Pomeroy wanted to know.

A count was made.

"Everybody's got some C-Four, right?" He waited for the nods of agreement. "Six wants to know if we can blow an LZ like they do up north."

Fuquette looked around at the trees. They were mostly palm. "Tell him that's a rodge," he answered. "I've seen it done. We can do it but only big enough for one bird."

"That's all we'll need." Pomeroy began to give their position to Captain Arnold, signaling the men to get started.

The men set to work in earnest with Fuquette supervising placement of the charges. They pried open the plastic anti-personnel mines and wrapped the plastic explosive insides around the base of the stoutest trees.

"Leave the pellets in," Fuquette counseled. "Press the side with the buck shot against the bark. It should act like a shaped charge and cut 'em in two."

Blocks of C-4, the same high explosive found in the Claymores, were wadded around as many of the tallest trunks as possible. A length of Det-Cord found in Johnson's pack was wound tightly around several trees and used to connect the charges. Det-Cord was an explosive fuse used to do maximum damage to bridge supports or communication poles. It worked on palm trees as well.

"How big is the rotor dish on a Huey?" Danny called as he worked.

"It better not be bigger than the hole we can make with this shit," Simms grunted, packing white plastique onto a sturdy bole. "We got enough stuff to do this?"

"Rotor dish is forty-eight feet," Pomeroy yelled. "Add half of that for the tail boom, and I think we got it. Use grenades if you have to, but go easy on them. We may wish we had more later."

Pomeroy's admonition reminded them all that they weren't alone in these woods.

"Everybody out of the blast radius," Fuquette yelled when all looked in order.

"How far is that, Sergeant," Berger asked.

"You'll know if you ain't far enough," E.Z. chuckled.

"Funny," Paco smirked. "Figure 'bout a hundred yards. And find a big tree to get behind to be sure."

"Fifty from the nearest charge oughta do it." Fuquette mentally pictured the shock wave. "The big tree's a good idea though. Face away from the blast. Watch our backs. Charley ain't forgot about us. Wounded stay together and be ready to go when the bird gets here. Squad leaders, detail some men to carry the dead. We'll wait until the dustoff's inbound to blow it. No sense advertising our location before we have to. Danny, monitor the radio. Let me know when they're two minutes out. You guys with the detonators, wait for my signal. Everybody pushes the plunger on three. Got it?"

Scattered in a loose circle, the Second Platoon found cover and waited. A light rain began to fall. Danny prayed the splices in the wires would not be grounded by a puddle.

The medivac chopper called, "Five mikes out."

"Roger, Dustoff-One-Five," Danny replied. "Give me two mikes warning so we can blow the Lima Zulu."

When the call came, Danny sang out, "Now!"

Fuquette showed himself. All eyes were on him. He counted with a show of fingers, dropping to the ground with the third digit raised. There was total silence for a beat as the jungle seemed to hold its breath.

A deafening roar shattered the stillness, followed by the cracking and crashing of tortured wood. Acrid clouds of smoke obscured the scene.

"Pop smoke," the pilot called.

Danny could hear his grin. "Foxtrot Yankee," he shot back, choking on the gray cloud that burned his eyes.

"And the horse you rode in on," the chopper jock said, completing the insult.

Like a giant fan, the blades bit into the smoke, sucked it up, and spit it out. The pilot hovered until he saw the stumps and splintered trunks clearly. He dropped to within three feet of the earth, unable to set the vibrating bird on the blasted landscape.

"Get 'em on!" Fuquette ordered.

Men rushed to help load the casualties. The bodies were handed reverently to the waiting medics first. Then the wounded were guided forward.

Danny grabbed Laffin by the arm as he helped hoist Page aboard.

"If you want to go," he yelled in Doc's ear, "we'll understand."

Doc looked down at the ground, and then into Danny's eyes. The temptation to be out of this was enormous.

"You've done enough," Danny assured him. "It's okay."

"No, it isn't." Doc wagged his head. "Fuck it. The suspense would probably kill me anyway." He smiled, stepping back for Pomeroy to climb on.

The platoon sergeant balked. "I'm not goin'."

"You're half blinded," Danny pushed. "You're outta here."

"No time for bullshit heroics, Dez," Fuquette yelled over the roar of the clattering blades. "You'll be in the way here. We gotta move fast."

"You goin' after him?" Pomeroy refused to budge until he got an answer. The crew chief made a pleading gesture.

Fuquette grinned. "Soon as we get your ugly ass airborne."

"I ain't gone yet?" Pomeroy smiled his big, toothy smile, his face grotesque, half covered by the bloody field dressing taped over his ruined eye. He stood his ground, his loose clothing flapping in the wind, and looked them over as if memorizing their faces. Grabbing Danny's hand and then Fuquette's, he shook them fiercely. "Do it."

"Tell Six what we're up to when you get back," Fuquette hollered. "Tell him we're going, no matter what, so he best back us up." He motioned with his head. "Go!"

The medic in the helicopter looked relieved as he hauled Pomeroy inside and then jerked the sliding door shut.

They watched in silence as the ship wheeled about and shot skyward. "We better pull this off, or we're going to be in deep shit," Simms muttered, watching their last link to safety climb out of sight.

Danny and Fuquette turned toward him. They burst into laughter at the worried frown on his face.

"What are they gonna do?" Danny asked. "Send us to Vietnam?"

CHAPTER 73

A ndy Kowalski was quick to examine the new Alpha Company arrivals at Dagger with an eye for entrepreneurial opportunity. Before long he discovered that some of them had smuggled a few cases of beer in with them. There were no rules against a soldier drinking beer on his own time, but alcoholic refreshments had a low priority on the supply list. Space on convoys and aircraft had to be efficiently utilized. Material deemed mission-critical occupied most of it. Once the base was better established, S-4 would be more willing to ship creature comfort items to the defenders. In the meantime, ammo, food, and building materials would have priority.

The majority of the men, however, had a different view of what was necessary. While local brew was plentiful, American brands were more pleasing to American tastes, and what young soldiers want they find ways to have. Beer was easy to obtain in the larger bases and just as easy to transport in small quantities. With the growing number of thirsty troops at Dagger, private stashes of the liquid gold were jealously guarded.

The other problem the keepers of the brew faced was temperature. Americans like their beer cold, a preference difficult to satisfy in a climate where the thermometer seldom dips below the triple-digit range. The mess hall now had refrigeration as long as the generator ran, but no trooper in his right mind would leave his beer in such an accessible public place. Ice was the method the experienced soldier preferred to cool his beer. Ice was versatile, portable, and sadly improbable this far into the hinterland.

Enter Andy Kowalski.

"What are you guys? Teatotalers? Or are you assholes just cheap?" Kowalski needled the group of A-Company soldiers huddled in the cramped bunker. The Alpha troopers smelled a hustle, but Kowalski had access to something they wanted.

"Ten bucks a block is a little steep, don't you think?" The Alpha sergeant looked at the truck driver the way he would look at Lucifer himself.

"Did I say I wasn't going to make a profit? Nothing wrong with that, is there? I mean, that's the American way, right? We are capitalists, after all, aren't we?"

"Jesus, Kowalski, give us a break. You trying to prove Ho Chi Minh's bullshit all by yourself?"

"Hey, man," Kowalski said, "if you don't want *nuoc da*, you don't want it. Drink warm beer, for all I care. Just don't come begging tonight when me and my guys are sipping cool suds, you *bic*?"

"You sure you can get it?"

"Piece of cake." He grinned, looking the sergeant in the eye. "All it takes is a little money and a truck. Oh, and in case you forgot, I'm the guy with the truck."

"Okay. Deal." The sergeant looked to his friends for affirmation. They nodded begrudging agreement. "Five blocks, right?"

"You got it." Kowalski put his hand out. The NCO reached to shake it, but Kowalski pulled it back, saying, "Cash up front, please. Fifty bucks."

The sergeant shook his head. "We'll pay on delivery."

"No way, Jose. I got to pay papasan when I pick up the ice. What am I going to do if you dudes have an attack of the stingies while I'm gone?"

With a sigh, the sergeant relented. Collecting the money from his buddies, he warned Kowalski, "You cheat us, we're going to frag your greedy ass."

"Like I've got someplace to go, right?"

Kowalski stuffed the bills in his pocket, turned, and jogged through the rain to his own bunker.

"Wake up, Stevens." He shook the man in the top bunk nearest the door. "We're going for a ride."

"It's fucking raining, Andy." The man yawned. "Tell Alpha-Six we'll haul his garbage when it stops."

"This is a little unscheduled trip in the name of free enterprise." Kowalski leaned close to Stevens's ear. "There's five bucks in it for you."

"Like I said, let's go." Stevens flipped his legs over the edge of the bunk and dropped to the floor.

"Kowalski Trucking rides again." Kowalski laughed as they drove through the gate, slid onto the road, and headed south.

"You sure this is safe?" Stevens asked as they left Dagger behind.

Kowalski looked pained. "Would I lie to you?"

"I wish you hadn't said that."

❧❧❧

Sergeant Vinh and his team made good time through the forest. Moving a small unit such as theirs swiftly was easy, especially with the rain covering their advance. They had no trouble locating the tiny cluster of slapped-together shops at the edge of Highway Four, midway between Camau and the American fire support base.

With stealth born of years of experience in the jungle, the NVA sergeant and his men set up in the forest at a point where they could watch the comings and goings in the marketplace. Vinh's plan was to observe for a time and then move in to question the shopkeepers. He would, of course, impress upon them the need to forget they had ever been there.

Traffic was light due to the weather and the shopkeepers were all indoors sheltering from the rain. Smoke from three stovepipe chimneys suggested the business owners were preparing a meal. Vinh was ready to make his move when he heard a truck approaching from the north.

❧❧❧

Captain Tran ate cold rice. Lighting a fire in this accursed downpour was impossible. The rain had obstructed his interrogation. The fish trap was less effective when the skies dumped as much water on the captor as the prisoner sought to avoid. He had left Tyler tied to a tree near the tripod and had returned to his sleeping platform to wait out the monsoon. There was no sign of it letting up.

Let the pig wallow in the mud, he thought, *until it pleases me to return to him. Perhaps anxiety will loosen his tongue.*

Tran slid the finely-honed steel blade from its sheath. He wondered if he should begin with castration or end with it? Perhaps he should pluck the American's eyes out. Or would it be best to take fingers and toes, one by one?

The American would tell him what he wished to know, or he would die. Tran had no intention of relenting until his captive succumbed, one way or another.

ぐぺ

"If we keep pushing, we can make it in a few more hours," Fuquette said.

The platoon was taking a break. The rain fell so heavily it was difficult to see ten feet. They had to raise their voices to be heard above the din of cascading water.

"They're getting itchy." Simms indicated the men with his chin. "They've doped out what we're up to, and they know we're doing it on our own. They're grumbling about disobeying orders."

"They're scared," Doc put in.

"Who ain't?" Paco said.

"Maybe we should ask for volunteers," Danny suggested.

"Good idea," Fuquette said sourly. "Anybody don't want to volunteer for this here suicide mission can stay here for this *other* suicide mission."

"He's right, man," Paco agreed. "These assholes wouldn't stand a chance out here without us."

"Maybe we should call Six and let the battalion get Tyler out," Danny said. He waited for them to overrule him, hoping they would, yet wondering if they should.

"If you want to back out, do it," Fuquette said, teeth clenched, huddling against the rain. "I'm going."

"I'm going with you," Danny vowed. "I'm just not sure we have the right to drag them—" He tossed his head at the new men. "—into this."

"If it comes from you, they'll go along," Simms stated.

"Me?" Danny paused to look at each man in turn. "Why me?"

"You don't see it. We do." Simms cast his eyes to each of the others. They nodded agreement in unison. "Since you broke up that little ambush single-handed, they hang on your every word.

They think you're the coolest thing since peanut butter. They'll
follow you anywhere. You say the word, and it's law, Danny."

Danny didn't know what to say. He had sensed new respect
from the FNGs, but he could not put a label on it.

"Looks like you're the boss," Fuquette said. "Call it."

"Wait a goddamned minute, now." Danny rose from the jungle floor. "Davy should be in charge. He's got the rank, and he's
better at this than any one of us."

"We ditched the rule book back at the river," Fuquette said.
"This new platoon of yours is about as fucked up as can be. They
don't know shit, but they're all we've got. If you're the man
they'll follow, then you're elected, bro."

The upturned stares of his friends confirmed it. They had mu-
tually agreed. He was their leader. The crushing responsibility
weighed heavily.

"Saddle up," Danny sighed, "we're moving out."

He talked to each of the men as he worked his way up the line.
In hushed tones, Danny spelled out the job to be done and the
difficulties they could expect. He left plenty of room for argument, making it plain that no man should feel obligated. Tyler
was *their* lieutenant, the *old* Second Platoon's. They had to
try.But the new men could decide for themselves. They listened
but they left it up to Danny.

E.Z. alone voiced an opinion. "I'm goin' along for one reason," he said. "I want to see the white motherfucker that soul-
brothers are willing to die for. This dude best be super honky or
E.Z. goin' to have a serious case of the ass."

Danny couldn't help but laugh.

When he reached the point, Fuquette stepped ahead of him to
lead the file. He did not look back. Danny tried to emulate him
but couldn't resist a rearward glance.

The new guys really were following him. He swallowed hard
to ease the lump in his throat. Awash in uncertainty, he caught up
to Fuquette, and whispered, "You sure about this?"

Fuquette said nothing but slowed his pace and turned to Danny with raised eyebrows.

"I mean these guys are probably more scared of being left on
their own out here than anything."

"Probably," Fuquette said.

"They don't really know what they're getting into, do they?"

"Not even close."

"So, do you think this will work?"

"You're in charge, my friend. Make it work."

The rain allowed them to move rapidly without fear of detection. No one could hear them in this racket of falling water. Captain Arnold repeatedly called on the radio to order them to turn back. Danny ignored him but was pleased to know that Pomeroy had made it back and had reported their objective. Charlie-Six alluded to the ad-hoc operation in jargon designed to confuse the enemy.

"Two-Six-Oscar, this is Six. Understand your good intentions. We want to see the coach, too. Let the big leaguers go for the pennant. The farm team doesn't stand a chance against the eastern division champs. Think about it. Do you want this on your conscience?"

Danny monitored but made no reply. Fuquette saw the consternation on Mulvaney's face. He grabbed the handset and listened as the captain repeated his message.

"Charlie-Six," Fuquette whispered. "Do you know who this is?"

"Affirmative," Arnold came back. "Talk some sense into those people. You know what's ahead."

"Roger your last, Six. The ball is in play. Knock off the negative bullshit and get behind the home team. We're going for the series, with or without you. With you is better, but either way, we're at bat. Out."

Fuquette slipped the plastic bag over the handset and clipped it to Danny's shoulder strap. "Let him chew on that for a while," he said. With a grim smile, he added, "We can do this. Stay cool and keep your eyes on me. This is the same trail I came out on. It's clear all the way to the camp. We can be there by this afternoon if we hustle. We'll stop short of the place to make some last-minute plans. If the rain keeps up, it'll help. Pray that it does."

಄಄಄

Tyler lay on his side, his arms bound tightly behind his back at the shoulders and elbows. The ropes pulled until he thought his chest would burst at the breastbone. His hands were free but numb from blood starvation caused by constriction of the vessels.

They were useless. His ankles were also tied.

The drenching monsoon had begun to swell the stream. The fish trap overflowed and flooded the area around him. His neck ached from straining to keep his face out of the water, two to three inches deep where he lay. Rolling on his back to breathe made him quickly twist back to his side, nearly drowning from the pummeling shower. Wriggling like a fish, he slithered under a leafy branch to gain relief from the deluge. The thick foliage slowed the downpour enough to let him catch his breath. He blessed its green canopy, thanking it for deliverance.

His guards, sheltering beside the stout trunk of the same tree, laughed at his plight. Tyler rested his head on an exposed root, wondering if it might not be better to drown in the mud than to await the resumption of the captain's interrogation. He had decided to die without telling Tran about the nurse. She was all-important to the NVA officer and silence was Tyler's only means of exacting revenge. That Tran would kill him in the end, he was certain. No sense giving up all the marbles. When the rain let up, the vicious bastard would return. Tyler steeled himself to hold on. Blood ran in rivulets from the small slices Tran had made in his skin. He had shown Tyler where the next step, mutilation, would begin. His fingers were split at the first knuckle, his Achilles' tendons nicked. His cheeks were scratched below his eyes, and his nose marked at the bridge.

The guards had held his legs spread-eagled as Tran had tickled his scrotum with the point of the bayonet until Tyler bled from several small punctures. Gone was the fog of delirium. Hate had burned it off like morning mist. He was in no danger of bleeding to death from the tiny cuts, but they were burning warnings of how bad it would get before it ended.

℮ᴂᴄᴐ

Captain Arnold was livid. Beecher thought his CO would slug Smitty when the man asked what had been said on the radio.

"They're southwest of us. That's all we know," Arnold snarled, pulling his poncho over his head, holding it up like an awning, glaring at Smith until he got the message and held it in place. Arnold dug his map from a leg pocket, spread the acetate-encased paper on his knees and pointed.

"Dustoff was here," he growled. "If they ran into Fuquette somewhere back here, like Pomeroy says, they must be moving in this general direction. We'll cut to the south and try to intercept. Call the Third Platoon and shackle these coordinates," he snapped to Beecher. "I want them moving along this axis. Tell them to haul ass."

"Sir," Beecher said warily, "how do we intercept them if we don't have a fix on where they're going?"

"I just want to be in the vicinity when the shit hits the fan," the captain said. "Let's hope we can get to them before it's too late."

ↄↄↄ

Kowalski pulled to the side of the road and stopped. The windshield wipers bounded to and fro, slinging raindrops aside as they reversed direction.

"What are you doing?" Stevens asked. "There's nothing here."

"Change places with me," Kowalski said, opening the door and hopping out.

Stevens watched him run around the front of the vehicle and then yank the passenger door open.

"Come on, Freddy, slide over," Kowalski insisted, "I'm getting soaked."

Obediently, Fred Stevens scooted across the seat, lifting his legs over the gearshift as he went.

"You drive." Kowalski motioned with his chin at the road as he bounced into the passenger seat and slammed the door.

"What?" Stevens made an exasperated face. "What the hell for?"

Kowalski dug into his pocket and produced two silver eagles, which he began to pin to his collar points.

"Because officers don't drive trucks, especially bird colonels."

"Aw, Andy, I don't know about this."

"And neither will anyone else. Just you, me, and the little dink that runs the ice factory. Stop worrying. This is gonna be good. Let's go, Specialist." He pounded on the dashboard. "Move out."

ↄↄↄ

Sergeant Vinh heard the motor moments before he saw the

vehicle approaching. He signaled his men to stay low as he
watched the American truck roar by and then swing around to
head back the way it had come. It stopped in front of the icehouse.
Two soldiers emerged from the cab to walk briskly into the building.

Checking to be sure the road was clear, Vinh pointed to the
man nearest him, then back to himself, and finally, to the rusty
corrugated tin shanty across the way. The other man nodded understanding. Vinh motioned to the rest to stay put and to cover
them before he sprinted across the highway.

Using the truck for concealment, the two sappers edged their
way to the back of the vehicle where they began to duck-walk the
few feet to the ice factory. Vinh raised one finger to his partner
before moving in a crouch to a window. Removing his hat, he
slowly raised up to peer inside.

An elderly, obsequious Vietnamese bowed repeatedly to the
larger of the two Americans. Vinh's eyes widened when he saw
the symbols of rank on the man's collar.

This was too good to be true.

ℰↄℰↄ

Stevens sighed as Papasan scurried away. "I don't know about
this, Andy."

"Will you relax," Kowalski hissed. "Nobody's going to be the
wiser. We get the ice for two bucks a block and some rice whiskey thrown in for free. Papasan thinks he's making friends in
high places, and we make twenty bucks instead of ten."

"Twenty bucks?" Stevens whined, "And all I get is five? That
ain't fair, Andy. I should get half."

"Whose truck is it? And whose idea?"

"The truck is Uncle Sam's, Andy."

"Okay, seven-fifty." Kowalski looked put out. "Only because
we're friends, and I'm feeling generous today."

"Thanks, Andy."

"Shhh! Here he comes."

ℰↄℰↄ

Vinh ran back to his comrade. He whispered orders. The sapper spun in the mud and bolted across the thoroughfare. Sergeant

Vinh went to the driver's door of the truck, stepped up on the running board, and, reaching into the cab with his rifle, cocked the rearview mirror at an angle. He then dropped down to crawl under the truck.

Five minutes later, the double doors at the factory's front swung wide. A rusty length of steel-wheeled conveyor was hoisted onto sawhorses dropped in place by the Vietnamese workers. Five-foot long, hollow blocks of ice covered in brown rice for insulation were slid along the rusty rollers to be grabbed by the men with iron tongs as the steaming frozen rectangles threatened to topple from the end. The blocks were then lifted onto the bed of the truck, where they were slid along its length. Eight blocks were loaded, stacked, and covered with a green canvas tarp cut from the roof of a squad-sized tent.

Vinh lay prone, watching from his hiding place as the bare feet of the Vietnamese padded back into the icehouse. As the doors closed, he saw the soldier's boots walk by on opposite sides of the vehicle. He waited until the engine coughed to life before slithering to the rear of the undercarriage. He was on his feet, with both hands on the tailgate, his rifle slung across his back, when the deuce-and-a-half started to roll. In one fluid motion, he was up and over the tailgate and on his belly in the bed behind the ice.

๏๛๏

Kowalski was occupied with some mental arithmetic, figuring how to con the artillerymen into buying the surplus ice to add to his profit, when Stevens interrupted his calculations.

"Where do you want me to stop, Andy?"

"What for?"

"So you and me can switch places. And so you can take off them birds. You're making me nervous."

"I'm just beginning to enjoy being a full bird colonel and you want to demote me back to PFC. What are you? Jellicks in disguise?" Kowalski rummaged in the sandbag he held in his lap. Producing a Coke bottle, corked and filled with a clear liquid, he pulled the stopper with his teeth, spit the cork and gulped a mouthful of the contents. "Whooee, that's some potent shit." Eyes watering, he turned to grin at Stevens, who was adjusting the rear-view mirror. The way Freddy's mouth dropped open as he glanced in the mirror would have made Kowalski laugh if Stevens's head hadn't exploded all over the windscreen just then.

Kowalski screamed and swung the bottle at the muzzle of the AK protruding through the rear window. At the same time, he slapped at the door handle and bailed out of the out-of-control truck. Tumbling headlong into the ditch at the verge of the road, he saw a lithe figure leap from the side of the cargo bed as the truck skidded into the forest on the opposite side of the highway. Kowalski landed with a bone-jarring thud, flat on his back in the mud. He reached for his .45 but his hand slapped an empty holster.

"*Dai ta, Dung lai,*" he heard from behind and above him.

Looking up, he saw the image of an enemy soldier with a gun, feet wide apart, the weapon braced against his shoulder, the sights leveled between his eyes. Kowalski was puzzled. Who in hell was this guy talking to? There was no colonel around.

And then, Kowalski remembered the collar insignia. "Oh, shit."

eↄeↄ

Fuquette outlined the layout of the camp for the squad leaders. The rain plastered his hair to his head. Water dripped from his chin as he spoke. Doc watched him closely. The sniper was aware of the medic's eyes on him. Fuquette could not explain what drove him or where his reserves were coming from. He just knew he could keep going until the job was done. Killing that NVA son of a bitch was his most avid wish. Getting Tyler back was secondary. Watching a bullet splatter that gook prick's head was his goal. Fuquette couldn't remember ever wanting to kill anyone so badly.

Fuquette explained that he and Danny would reconnoiter the camp before they went into action. Fuquette wanted to be sure nothing had changed since he left.

"You ready?" he said to Danny.

"We are about to find out."

eↄeↄ

They crawled through the muck together. Danny froze as Fuquette's hand came up. He pointed. Danny saw the outline of a man walking slowly toward them. One of the roving sentries was making his rounds. His head was down, trying to shield his face from the punishing drops. An AK-47 hung by its sling from his shoulder with the muzzle pointed down. His drooping posture demonstrated his self-pity. The NVA soldier had been trained that Americans did not attack in such weather. His only worry was surviving the downpour.

Fuquette was signaling something. Danny lay still and tried to comprehend. A finger across the throat left no doubt as to Fuquette's instructions. Danny was horrified to realize that he wanted *him* to do it when Fuquette wriggled into the underbrush. Danny pulled his bayonet from its scabbard and nodded once.

As the enemy soldier slogged past his prone form, Danny mentally reviewed the lessons of basic training. The rear-strangle-hold-and-take-down had been a lesson he had never thought to use. This was Green Beret stuff, something from the movies. Regular GIs didn't do this shit.

The man was just past him when Danny sprang. He had the distinct impression of watching himself perform the moves like a spectator at a championship match. Flawlessly, his left arm encircled the man's throat. He yanked with all of his might. The smaller man's feet came off the ground. Danny felt him tense with surprise. The knife glanced off of the receiver of the assault rifle and went in above the kidney. The man stiffened, but Danny's hand crushed his throat to prevent his outcry. He dropped to the ground, his weight dragging the man with him. The sentry's neck was bent at an odd angle as they hit the mud. He shuddered and lay still.

Danny was pulling the blade from the man's back as Fuquette rushed up.

"Nice," Fuquette whispered. "Shove him in the swamp and let's go."

Danny did as he was told. As he turned to follow Fuquette, he was mildly in shock but struggling to calm the pounding in his ears as he left the man in the water. They were only a few yards away when they heard the sentry moan. They turned to see him fighting to get up.

With a look of disgust, Fuquette ran back, motioning Danny to follow. The sniper slid to a halt behind the stricken enemy soldier. Without hesitation, he clamped his hand over the man's mouth as he forced him onto his back. The stiletto in his boot seemed to appear out of nowhere. Fuquette plunged it into the man's chest. Blood gushed from the dying man's mouth to ooze between Fuquette's fingers. The NVA guard lay still.

"That got him," Fuquette whispered. He motioned Danny to go.

They were a few steps away when they heard the sapper groan once more. They looked back to see him sitting up.

"This boy's heart's literally not in the right place," Fuquette said with a short, sardonic laugh.

They fell on him together. Danny held his head under water while Fuquette sat on his back. The soldier's weak attempts to dislodge them ceased with a rush of bubbles. They sat on him for a minute more to be sure that he was finished. Convinced the sentry was finally dead, Fuquette nodded once, and they took off again.

Something made Danny look back. The bloody heap was stirring again. Fuquette whispered, "Shit," and ran back to pounce on him again. He grabbed the man's hair, exposing his throat. Danny slid to a halt beside him and slashed with his bayonet. Hot blood gushed along his forearm. There was a sound like a balloon deflating. The man's eyes rolled back in his head. They saw his body go slack.

"Fucker's got more lives than a cat," Fuquette whispered.

They sat with the corpse this time until there was no question. Both men half expected him to stir to life yet again. When, after several minutes had passed, he did not, Fuquette slid him under the muddy water. They finished the recon without further incident. Upon their return to the platoon, Simms saw the pallor in Danny's face.

"What happened?"

"Tyler's not in his cage," Fuquette replied, ignoring the fact that the question had obviously referred to Mulvaney's expression. "Relax. We found him. He's alive, but we gotta move fast."

CHAPTER 74

Kowalski thought of his uncle's prophetic prediction. "I'm telling you, Andy," the first sergeant had said, "you'll get it into something someday that you won't be able to talk your way out of and I won't be around to save your ass."

It had finally happened. The gun butt that slammed into his back emphasized it.

These were some of the gooks that had wasted the Second Platoon of Charlie Company. He was sure of it. And now they had him. They were driving him like a stray calf, urging him to be quick, anxious to get their prize back to their nest. The guy in charge was probably having a wet dream about the R & R in Cambodia his boss would give him when he brought *this* package in. They were going to be miffed, to say the least, when they realized their mistake. Kowalski was not looking forward to the discovery.

⌁⌁⌁

In the TOC bunker at Fire Base Dagger, stress made the very air taught.

"I know it's raining, dammit." Colonel Conte gripped the radio phone so tightly his knuckles were white. "I want a heavy fire team ready to go as soon as it breaks. Get me some fast-movers loaded to the gills with nape, rockets, bombs—the works. Call the General. See if he's serious about those B-Fifty-Twos. I want those bastards blown to hell as soon as they're found. Do you copy? Over."

The harried Specialist on the Brigade HQ end of this one-way conversation rogered the battalion commander's orders and added a heartfelt, "Wilco." Conte thrust the handset back at the operator and said to Chicarelli, "Looks like we got here just in time. We'll nail those bastards now."

Chick wasn't sure that right now really was the best time for the colonel to arrive at Fire Base Dagger with the rest of the battalion. The situation in the field was greatly unknown. He would have preferred to have some time to sort things out before calling in the heavy stuff. They were far too likely to drop something on their own people the way things were at the moment.

"Sir, Lieutenant Tyler is a prisoner of those people," Chicarelli reminded Conte. "Wouldn't it be best to hold our horses until we get some hard information?"

"From a mutinous platoon running around without leadership?" Conte sneered. "How the hell did Les let this happen?"

"Colonel, you can't blame Captain Arnold for this fiasco."

"It's his platoon that's out of control, Lieutenant. Who else should I blame?"

Chicarelli had no reply. He looked at the radio and then at the doorway leading from the TOC. A drenched soldier bustled in, saying, "It's like running through a car wash out there." Chick lit a cigarette and willed the rain to continue. They couldn't bomb if they couldn't fly.

"Get me that battery commander," Conte barked. "One-five-fives don't have to wait for the rain to stop."

e/ɔe/ɔ

Impatience interrupted Tran's prolonging of the prisoner's angst. He would finish this thing now. The guards jumped to their feet as their commander approached.

"Last chance, American," Tran said softly in Vietnamese, stroking the blade of the bayonet with his mangled hand.

Tyler didn't have to understand the words. The malevolence smoldering in the enemy officer's eyes made his meaning clear.

Tran produced the picture. He squatted in the mud, close to Tyler's upturned face. Shielding the photograph from the rain with his torso, he held it for Tyler to see through blinking eyes pummeled by the heavy drops.

"*Bacsi de?*" Tran said, almost kindly. All will be forgiven, his tone implied. Tell me where she is.

Tyler smiled, and said, just as softly, "Fuck you."

Tran shot upright, screaming orders to the guards. They dragged Tyler by his feet to the tripod over the fish trap. Grunting, they hoisted him up to hook his ankle bindings to the notched wooden hook fashioned for that purpose. Tran, cursing under his breath, paced back and forth like a caged hyena while his men struggled to raise Tyler. The bayonet swung like a pendulum at the end of his arm in time with his steps.

Crouched in the bushes less than fifty yards away, a few feet above the small clearing the NVA had set up as their torture ground, Danny and David Fuquette watched their lieutenant's agony.

"Now, Danny," Fuquette whispered.

Danny whispered into the radio phone, "Four-Six, Four-Six, this is Two-Six-Oscar. Fire mission, over."

"This is Big Six," Colonel Conte came back. "Who is this?"

Danny was startled. What the hell was the colonel doing there?

They had worked it all out, set it all up, and put their plan into motion. They would radio for artillery and tell Lieutenant Chicarelli that they were calling in the shells from a concealed observation point out of range of the bursts. Danny was supposed to say that Tyler was dead if Chicarelli balked. Captain Arnold would monitor, of course, but why should he interfere? They were giving them what they wanted—a fat target. The rest of the company would converge on the designated area once they reported it. That was good. They might need all the help they could get to get out of there.

Colonel Conte showing up had not been part of the plan.

Fuquette tried in vain to line up a shot at the NVA officer. The scope was worthless in this weather. He couldn't be sure of dropping the man without hitting Tyler. The artillery barrage might give him the distraction he needed to get closer. He looked at Danny, mouthed, "No shot," and stabbed a finger at the radio.

"This is Charlie-Two-Six-Oscar," Danny hissed into the phone. "I have a hot target. Enemy troops in heavy forest. These are November Victor Alpha, Big Six, the same fellas you've been looking for. Well, we got 'em, but we ain't got all day."

The colonel fumed at the insubordination but bit back his retort and handed the phone to Chicarelli. The lieutenant had heard the exchange on the speaker.

"This is Four-Six. Say target map reference, Two-Six-Oscar."
Danny sent the coordinates in the clear.

"Are your people well out of the target area?"

That question would normally have been unnecessary and
Danny chafed at the inference that he didn't know what he was
doing. But the question had been anticipated.

"Roger, Four-Six. We are well up-range. Give me a marking
round, over."

"Shackle your position, first. Over."

Chicarelli was taking no chances on wiping out a green platoon based on fire direction from a questionable forward observer.
Danny wagged his head but he was ready for this. He gave a ficti-
tious set of coordinates, using the company *shackle*, a prearranged code word of ten non-repeating letters to correspond with
the numbers zero to nine. The platoon was actually farther away
than the location he was giving and farther still from the fire mission coordinates. They had reasoned, when they made the plan,
that if Chick knew just how far from the target they actually were,
he might not trust their ability to call in the shells at all. And, if
he knew that Danny and Fuquette were closer and separated from
the platoon, he would almost definitely balk.

"What about Two-Six?" Chicarelli asked, the dread in his
voice painful to hear.

"KIA," Danny lied. "We found his body."

Chicarelli's sorrow hung poignantly in the dead air. The pro-
nouncement was the expected outcome, but the finality made it
no less crushing. Danny was about to ask if the lieutenant had
copied his last when a voice hardened by grief and anger came
back, "Roger, Two-Six-Oscar. Do you want one round smoke?
Over."

"Negative smoke. HE on the deck. One round. I will correct."

"I copy one round HE on the deck. Are you sure you don't
want smoke?"

Tyler was flopping on the end of his string like a hooked bass.
The gook officer was prodding him with a long knife.

"Hurry," Fuquette whispered.

"Affirmative, Four-Six. Delta Foxtrot confirms. We don't
want the little bastards to go to ground." Danny gambled that
Chicarelli would trust David Fuquette more than he would Daniel
Mulvaney.

At the TOC, Chicarelli relayed the instructions to Lieutenant Stuart via landline. The artillery officer said he was ready.

"One round HE in the tube," Chicarelli announced.

"Roger. Shot," Danny whispered.

"Shot out," Chick told him as he heard the big gun's thunderous report.

Several seconds later there was a sound like a passing freight train overhead and then a terrific blast in the forest five-hundred yards away. The enemy soldiers at the fish trap froze, staring wide-eyed in the direction of the missile's impact.

"Drop fifty and give me another," Danny ordered, his calm tones belying the pounding of his heart.

The next explosion was still out of sight but sounded much closer. Danny repeated the last transmission and got the same result. The NVA guards looked to their captain for orders. Fear filled their eyes. Tran seemed distraught as his own eyes flew from Tyler to the distant explosions and back.

"Drop seventy-five and fire for effect," Danny commanded.

He had planned on a hundred. Three-hundred yards out would be close enough to distract the gooks but still far enough away for comfort. The unexpectedly loud shell bursts made him hedge.

In moments, the air was filled with the continuous shrieking of plummeting shells, and then a cataclysm of blasts shook the forest. The catastrophic crescendo unnerved the enemy and friendly troops alike. Everything solid reverberated with the rumbling pressure wave emanating from the impact area.

Tran pointed to the center of the camp. He yelled something at his guards. They hurdled the stream and ran to join their comrades. As their feet hit the earth on the far side, the Second Platoon opened up from deep within the woods. Their fire was meant as further diversion. Danny was unwilling to endanger these novices in direct conflict with the hardcore sappers. Fuquette had agreed that shock and confusion would be as useful as concentrated fire, possibly more so. They hoped to rattle the enemy by denying him targets upon which to retaliate.

As a bonus, Simms was doing a professional job on the treetop emplacements with his M-79 Grenade Launcher. Fuquette's accurate depiction of the layout of the camp and its installations gave him a very good idea where to place his rounds.

"I don't have to see 'em to hit 'em," Bert had boasted, and apparently, he didn't. Men poured from the lofty perches like human rain to escape the whizzing steel shredding the branches. The grenade bursts doubled as Berger joined in, firing alongside Simms, mimicking his teacher like a gifted prodigy. The bespeckled FNG became so excited he began to laugh maniacally.

Simms knocked on Berger's helmet with his knuckles to get his attention. "Down, Igor," he said. "Let's stay with the program."

Tran was visibly torn between his duty to lead his men and the final confrontation with his prisoner. His head whipped left and right, from Tyler to his men and back again in rapid succession. Danny dumped the radio to crawl forward, paralleling Fuquette.

Tran made up his mind. He snatched his assault rifle from its resting place against a tree, sheathed the bayonet, and took aim at Tyler.

"Noooo!" Danny screamed. Tran hesitated, took two steps back, looking for the source of the sound.

Unable to shoot without hitting Tyler, Danny sprang to his feet and charged.

e/ɔe/ɔ

Mindful of the dangers of retracing one's steps, Sergeant Vinh had led his team and their captive in a circuitous route to re-enter the camp from another direction.

Without warning, one heavy-artillery round shattered the swamp directly in his path. The point man screamed and toppled over, his right arm gone at the shoulder. Yanking the prisoner's tether—a length of rope tying Kowalski's hands in front of him—the NVA Sergeant pulled Kowalski to the ground as the sapper team hit the dirt. Before Vinh could catch his breath, another shell screamed in. This one landed farther away. Vinh glowered at Kowalski, curled in a fetal position at his side.

Kowalski saw how the sergeant's mind was working by the look on his face, weighing his chances of evading the barrage with his prisoner in tow. Kowalski shrugged. "Depends how bad you want that R and R."

With a snarl, Vinh barked orders to his men. Kowalski was jerked to his feet and dragged like a pull-toy as the enemy soldiers charged toward the smoking jungle.

"That bad, huh?" Kowalski said, fighting to keep his balance as he ran.

෬౭෬

"Third Herd's converging on our poz," Beecher advised Captain Arnold. "We should link up any time now."

"Good," Arnold grunted. "Set up recognition signals. We don't want to ambush each other. Smith," he rapped, leaving Beecher to use his imagination in establishing the contact, "what's happening on battalion? Mulvaney still transmitting?"

Smitty had been listening to dead air for several moments when Chicarelli came on.

"Charlie Two-Six-Oscar, do you read? Say sit-rep. Over."

Mulvaney failed to answer. Chicarelli kept repeating his transmission over and over again. Smitty had an idea, a way to get even with Mulvaney once and for all. He answered the captain. "He's calling corrections but Dagger's not reading him, sir. Maybe his battery's weak. I can hear him but they can't."

"Relay, dammit."

"Roger that." Smitty turned slightly so that the captain wouldn't see him smile. "Dagger-Six, this is Charlie-Six-Oscar. I have commo with Two-Six-Oscar. Will relay his fire corrections. Over."

"Roger Six-Oscar, go."

"Target is moving. Right one-hundred. Fire for effect."

"That's a little close, Six-Oscar. Are you certain of Two-Six-Oscar's instructions?"

"Most affirmative. Shoot."

Smitty had gotten a good idea of the situation as he had monitored Mulvaney's calls. Captain Arnold had pointed out the Second Platoon's location on his map from Danny's reply to Chicarelli's insistent demand. He had heard nothing from his erstwhile friend Mulvaney in a good while. Danny might already be dead. Why else would he have broken off? But he had to make sure. If this failed and Mulvaney somehow survived, Smitty knew he would have some explaining to do. It would be his word against Danny's, but that had worked in his favor once before.

෬౭෬

Tran whirled and snapped off a burst at the new threat. A bullet pierced Danny's side and sent him spinning. His rifle flew into the brush. He fell, rolling down the gentle slope.

Fuquette was up and moving the instant Danny broke cover. He saw the NVA Captain react, but could not fire before the enemy soldier opened up because Danny ran into his line of fire. Dodging left, Fuquette fired as he dove. Tran was lifted off his feet from the force of the heavy slug that smashed his shoulder. Fuquette landed hard on his belly. The impact knocked the wind out of him. He tried to get his elbows set for a prone shot to finish the man. Tran let loose a long burst, one handed, from the ground where he lay. A bullet splintered the grip of the match grade rifle and shattered Fuquette's shooting hand.

҂ѻ҂

Kowalski felt the concussions rippling through the trees as his captors dodged through the brush, trying to run around the retreating curtain of explosions that preceded them.

Vinh cursed his commander for refusing to let him take one of their two radios. He had to know what was going on in the camp, but the only way he would find out was to run blindly into whatever awaited them.

҂ѻ҂

Danny saw the enemy officer knocked back by Fuquette's fire as he tumbled to a stop when the ground beneath him flattened out into a clearing. He spun in the dirt, feeling a sharp pain in his side. He clapped a hand over the spot, and it came away bloody. Craning his neck to check on Tyler, he saw the lieutenant go limp and his head plunge into the pool. His side on fire, he crawled through the mud, past the maddened Vietnamese jerking spasmodically on the trigger of his weapon. The rifle clicked again and again on an empty chamber. With superhuman will, Danny got to his feet. He wrapped both arms around the drowning man and heaved. Tyler's weight sent him toppling backward as the rope came free of its hook. He pushed the lieutenant's body off of himself and scrambled to his knees. His heart leaped as he saw

Tyler vomit water and choke on his first breath. Fuquette lay unconscious where he fell, bullet shock finishing his depleted reserves. Danny rolled Tyler on his back and began to saw at his bonds with his bayonet, vaguely aware that the artillery had shifted. It sounded like the shells were landing closer to his platoon.

He was only partially through the ropes when he looked up and saw the Vietnamese coming for him with that long knife. He fought the dizziness that made his brain reel as he staggered to his feet. Holding his bayonet in his fist like a street fighter, he braced for the onslaught.

With a cry of animal rage, Tran lunged. Tyler blinked through the fog that threatened to engulf his tortured brain and kicked at Tran's shins with his bound feet as he passed. The blow partially deflected Tran's thrust, but focused his full weight into the point of the blade as it pierced Danny's hip. The sharp point lodged in the ilium. Danny fell backward into the fish trap, wrenching the bayonet from Tran's hand.

Tran fell on Tyler, intent on strangling him with his one good hand. With strength born of desperation and hate, Tyler snapped his partially parted ropes. Blood rushed to starved veins. Nerves, still immobilized, snapped back to life like electric shocks. Tyler pummeled his attacker with fists and forearms aflame with awakening. Loss of sensation made his blows like clubs until one strike landed hard on Tran's broken shoulder. Screaming, the wounded Vietnamese rolled off of his intended victim. He staggered to his feet and stumbled into the stream.

Danny was upside down, wedged by the knife protruding from his hip in the watery hole. He didn't have the strength to pull himself out.

"Follow through," his father cheered in Danny's mind. "Finish what you start."

"I can't," he heard himself say. "I'm all done."

"You promised you'd come back," Amanda wept. He could see her standing behind his father.

"I know, but..." So strange, he thought, how he could never say no to her.

His fingers found the handle of the knife and yanked. It came out. His body convulsed with the pain, but he was rising, the air in his bursting lungs buoying him up. He stabbed with the bayonet into the sides of the pit and pulled. His feet felt the lip of the pool. Hands were clawing at them. He thought the NVA officer would finish him off. Instead, he was wrenched from the abyss and lay gasping in the mud as Tyler dragged him, feet first, from the fish trap.

Across the stream, Tran and his men had formed a tight perimeter and were firing wildly into the trees. As his vision cleared, Danny could see the enemy officer's back as he issued orders despite his wound, gesturing madly. The NVA were beginning to rally and concentrate their fire on the platoon's positions. Three men were setting up a mortar.

The artillery barrage was falling dangerously close to Danny's people. The radio was nowhere in sight.

Danny eyes searched madly for a weapon. The enemy's bayonet was the only thing he saw.

"Help me," he said to Tyler, getting to his knees. Together they pulled the bamboo tripod down. Danny set to work separating one pole from the others. Tyler watched, confused, but too exhausted to ask.

With one stalk freed, Danny hastily dug a pocket in the end of the green shoot with the point of the bayonet. He then reversed the blade and plunged the handle, up to the guard, into the pole. He quickly wrapped a length of thin vine around the top of the pole and tied it tight.

"Watch me skewer that son of a bitch," he told Tyler.

On his knees, Danny hefted the makeshift spear to find the balance. Tyler could see what Danny planned now but, gauging the distance through the tangle of vines and branches to the target, he croaked, "It'll never work."

Danny grinned evilly. "One gook kabob, coming up."

෧෨ങ

Beecher relayed Charlie-Six's orders to advance in parallel columns to the Third Platoon. They could hear the distant rumble of the exploding one-five-fives now, and all that remained was to keep moving until they made contact with the Second Platoon or with the enemy, depending upon the disposition of forces at the battle site.

Smith was still talking to Mulvaney and Chicarelli on the battalion freq, trying to control indirect fire while moving—a handful for the most seasoned radioman. Beecher decided to see if he could lend a hand.

"Three-Six, Three-Six, this is Charlie-Six-Oscar. Leaving the net for zero two. I'll be on Higher's push if you need me. Over."

"Roger, Six-Oscar. Advise when back up on this push," Third Platoon's RTO acknowledged.

"Roger, Three-Six-Oscar. Six-Oscar, gone."

At a dead run on the narrow jungle trail, Beecher hit the quick release and caught the strap as the rucksack dropped. Shrugging the other shoulder strap, he swung the radio to his chest and twisted the dial to get to battalion's frequency, never breaking stride as he moved along the trail. In seconds, he was listening to Smitty.

"Keep it coming!" he heard Smith yell. "Pour it on!"

There was silence for a moment and then, "Two-Six-Oscar says to expand burst radius. Enemy is scattering. Spread your fire in a widening circle."

Beecher stopped, his brow furrowed in puzzlement. Why hadn't he heard Mulvaney's voice?

"Two-Six-Oscar, say again your last," Beecher said into his handset. Looking at Smitty, he saw the excitement on his counterpart's face turn to astonishment as they locked eyes. Smitty's features registered shock, guilt, and then—terror. Instantly, Beecher knew what Smitty had done.

"Cease fire! Cease fire!" he screamed into the horn. "Cancel fire mission. Disregard last fire correction. Cease fucking fire!" With a howl like the wrath of the damned, Beecher dropped his radio and lunged for Smitty. "You murdering motherfucker!"

Captain Arnold turned in time to see Beecher's haymaker smash into Smitty's jaw.

ෙංෙ

Getting shakily to his feet, Danny filled his lungs, held it for a moment and, shifting all his weight to his good leg, leaned into the throw, snapping his arm like a whip.

The crude javelin wobbled as it flew before it leveled off and then dove on its target.

Tran half turned, sensing something.

The blade of his own bayonet pierced both lungs as it slammed into his ribcage through his side to slice through to the opposite chest cavity wall. Agony gripped him. His hands groped for the spear but they had no strength in them. He fell like a downed tree, his weight driving the point into the earth as he struck the ground. He lay dying, watching the rain wash his life force into the swamp, drowning in his own blood. As the jungle around him faded from his vision, he saw Mai, smiling, arms outstretched, welcoming him. He went to her eagerly.

಼ಌಌ಼

The thunderous detonations moved off once again. Vinh led his unit in a mad dash for the camp. A burst of automatic fire cut down another of his men, and he and his surviving team members dove for cover once more.

"Stop! Stop shooting," he screamed. "It is Sergeant Vinh. Hold your fire." He waited a beat and then tugged hard on his prisoner's cord. "We have a prisoner," he warned, lest his comrades resume firing at the sight of the American.

Lieutenant Sau was dead, hit by a shell from a grenade launcher and blown out of his bed. The surviving sappers were crouched under cover in a circular redoubt around their dead commander. The North Vietnamese firing slackened and quit. They awaited Vinh's orders. The Second Platoon ceased firing too. The jungle became still.

Vinh and his men ran into the small perimeter. He took in the scene at a glance, noticing the pounding of the shells had stopped as well. Americans scurried through the trees on the far side of the stream, taking advantage of the eerie silence, tightening their strangle-hold on his decimated force. It didn't take long to ascertain that their position was untenable. A frontal assault, which he saw as his only logical solution, was impossible because of the stream to their front. His men would be cut to ribbons, slowed by the restricting water as they struggled to advance. There was nothing to be gained by continuing this fight. The Americans would soon tire of wasting ammunition and call in an accurate artillery bombardment to finish the battle. He gave sharp commands and the Peoples' Provisional Captive Force sank lower, their weapons trained on the woods. Vinh could think of only one possibility.

Prodding his prisoner with the muzzle of his rifle, he forced

Kowalski to stand. Kowalski looked at his captor, stupefied. Vinh gestured insistently with his head toward the American positions.

"Hey, guys," Kowalski called, as he got to his feet. "Hold your fire. I'm an American."

"Andy?" Danny said. "Andy Kowalski?"

"Danny?"

"What the fuck?"

"I think this guy here wants me to talk to you." Kowalski felt the gun nudge his ribs. "Yep. He definitely wants me to talk to you."

Kowalski gave the NVA sergeant a plaintive look. Vinh motioned to his men and then to the far side of the stream. He made a flattening gesture with his hand and quick steps with his fingers.

"I think he wants you to stay put while he and his men get away." Kowalski had a strong urge to urinate.

"We won't shoot if they let you go."

"Sounds like a plan to me." Kowalski looked down at Vinh, raised his eyebrows, and motioned with his head toward the stream.

Vinh nodded.

As Kowalski began to walk, he saw the enemy troops slithering backward. He was still expecting a bullet in the back when he stepped into the warm, gentle current. In mid-stream, he took advantage of the camouflaging waters to relieve himself. On the far side, he dropped to the ground and then rolled under a bush.

The Second Platoon edged forward until they could see their comrades. Simms led them into a hasty perimeter defense, surrounding the tiny clearing.

"Save the cheers," he warned the elated young men, flushed with victory in their first engagement. "Mr. Charles don't quit so easy. Be ready for a counterattack. Kowalski? How the hell did you get here, man? And since when are you a fucking colonel?"

Kowalski peeked through the brush. "Are they gone?"

"Looks that way. What were you doing with the bad guys?"

Kowalski didn't answer. Instead, he stood on shaky limbs to peer across the sluggish body of water. When no one tried to kill him, he stood straighter and replied, "Would you believe I just went out for a little ice?"

Simms shook his head. "Truck drivers," he sighed. "Paco!"

"Yo, bro."

"Find the damn radio. Doc!"

"Way ahead of you, man." Laffin was making a beeline for his wounded friends.

ↄ⁄ↄↄ⁄ↄ

Danny leaned back on his heels. His vision blurred as he looked down at Tyler. The jungle started to spin when he turned his head to check on Fuquette. Raising his face to let the downpour wash away the dizziness, he wondered where his helmet had gone.

"Stay still, Danny," Doc said gently. "Let your friendly neighborhood doctor have a look at you."

Danny felt light as a sparrow. He looked for Paco but found he couldn't focus. Doc was ripping bandages from plastic bags. He looked upset.

Danny grinned stupidly. The rain was diluting the blood that flowed from his wounds. He looked up at the rain and said to Doc, "Damned Mexican left the water running." The jungle floor undulated beneath him like the deck of a storm-tossed ship. "Doc?"

"Yeah, Danny."

"We did it, didn't we?"

"Yeah, man. We did it."

"Anybody else hurt?"

"One of the new guys caught a splinter from a tree burst when the arty shifted. It's minor. He's okay. Why did you change the plan?"

"I didn't. The arty shifted?"

"Never mind. Rest. You've lost a lot of blood."

"Davy?"

"Took one in the hand. The guys are patching him up. He'll be fine."

Danny panned the clearing, groggy. "Tyler?"

The lieutenant gave Danny a thumbs-up from where he lay while Simms and Wyman ministered to him.

Danny watched the foliage on the far bank fade in and out and then begin to swirl before his eyes.

"Fuck you, Mister Charles." He raised his middle finger in a single digit salute and collapsed.

CHAPTER 75

1969, Delaware Water Gap, New York State:

Danny could not sleep. His eyes would not stay closed. All of his senses were in high gear. The darkened forest was a brooding malevolent entity surrounding him, waiting for him to drop his guard.

Relax, he told himself. *No way*, his little voice replied.

He was not alone in the tent, the other man's breathing sounded like an alarm.

Didn't he understand? They couldn't both sleep at once. Somebody had to stay alert. He wasn't ready for this. How had he let himself be talked into this stupid camping trip? *Why would anyone sleep in the woods when they didn't have to? This was supposed to be* fun?

His right hand slipped under the field jacket serving as a pillow and caressed the warm checkered grip of a 9-mm Browning Hi-Power automatic. The fingers of his left hand stretched out to brush the butt of the Japanese bayonet, hanging inverted in its leather sheath, suspended from his rucksack shoulder strap. Only slightly reassured by the close proximity of these familiar tools, Danny rolled onto his back feeling relieved on one level and disturbed on another. The security that the instruments of death provided troubled him more deeply than he could explain, even to himself.

Right from the very beginning, when they had arrived at the campsite after dark, he knew this was a mistake. As they picked their way along the trail leading to this place, he felt near panic, searching for booby traps that he knew could not be there. He knew he was being ridiculous when he slipped his pistol from its holster and placed his thumb on the safety, but there was a war going on his mind. Logic kept whispering in his ear that he was safely back in The World but something far more powerful than intellect, and certainly more primitive, refused to allow him to listen to the voice of reason. The self-preservation instincts that enabled mankind to bludgeon his way to the top of the food chain were now so much a part of his being they had taken control in spite of his will.

Now, in this claustrophobic canvas cocoon, his ears strained to hear any sound alien to the normal rhythm of the night. His pupils stretched wide to gather any light from the blackness. He lay in wait as if he were a kindergarten infant expecting the Bogeyman to come calling. But unlike the pre-school kid, he knew he would kill the son of a bitch if he came nosing around. The trick was to get the jump on him.

Danny sat up, wiped the sheen of sweat from his face with his hands and whispered, "*You,* Daniel Mulvaney, are fucking nuts."

The air in the tent was so dense he could feel its weight against his skin. He couldn't fill his lungs. It felt like something was sitting on his chest. He was getting less oxygen with every breath.

He had to get *out.*

Stop! Deep breath.

Okay now. Easy does it. Gather your shit and move out. Slowly. No panic. No sudden moves. Just. Get. Out.

He rolled over and knelt to grope in the dark for his jacket and pistol, and then began crawling backward on hands and knees. On an impulse, he went back for the bayonet.

Dragging his sleeping bag, he unzipped the screened flap, poked his head outside and began to gulp cool air. In a few moments he felt calmer, and he slipped out to stand erect under the blazing whirlwind of stars—tiny bright holes in the inky backdrop of space.

Danny stared, entranced by the dazzling display for several silent minutes. A meteorite streaked across the heavens, trailing white flame. The spell was broken. A shooting star was an omen of good fortune he had been told when he was a kid.

"Day late and a dollar short, God," he whispered to the heavens, "but I'll take it."

Bundling his gear in his arms, he made his way across a clearing, walking cat-like until he reached a makeshift square of pine logs arranged corral-fashion around a campfire pit that he and his boyhood friends had erected in days gone by. They had staked their symbolic claim to this, their secret place in the mountains, back when they were in high school. He thought of those times now as when he was young although he had not yet reached his majority in the eyes of the law.

He spread the sleeping bag beside the warm rocks encircling the still-glowing coals, put on his jacket, and sat cross legged—pow-wow style as he had called it as a boy—to face the heat of the smoldering charcoal.

The nights were cool in the mountains in early spring, the air clear and crisp. He remembered vanilla wafers, hot chocolate, and toasted marshmallows. He shivered.

Laying the pistol beside him, he tried to resist looking around. He couldn't. Methodically, he quartered the surrounding woods, searched each quadrant thoroughly until he assured himself all was well. Feeling foolish, he stirred the embers with a branch. The sleeping fire stirred, winking at him with red eyes.

He fanned the coals with a scrap of cardboard he found within reach and fed the fire dry twigs until orange tongues licked at the growing pile. The slumbering blaze awakened.

A rustle from the tent brought his attention to a shape moving toward him ghost-like in the gloom. *Probably woke him up*, Danny thought, embarrassed. Still, he was glad of the company and not at all surprised. They shared the wariness of sleep, he and his friend—that strange subconscious ability to watch and listen while the body rested. Either of them would be instantly alert at the mere hint of anything out of sync. He wondered if it would always be so. Somehow, he knew it would.

Gino nodded a greeting as he sat down beside Danny and tossed a small log on the fire. Sparks leaped into the air and they watched them whirl.

"You okay?" Gino asked. There was concern in his tone.

"Yeah," Danny breathed, "just couldn't sleep in there." He motioned with his head to indicate the tent.

Looking into each other's eyes, seeing the flames dance there, each glimpsed hell remembered.

"'Paranoia strikes deep,'" Gino said.

"'Into your heart, it will creep,'" Danny sang.

"'It starts when you're always afraid,'" they sang together.

Both men broke into quiet laughter. They sat for several minutes, gazing into the fire, grinning humorless grins, nodding wordless agreement, understanding, sharing a bond that only warriors know.

"Want to talk?" Gino asked.

"No. Think."

"Bad for you." Gino grimaced. "Fucks up your head. How about a beer?"

Danny laughed. "Why not?"

Gino stood up, bent over the top rail of the enclosure and fished around in the ice in a Styrofoam cooler. He tossed a can to Danny, stuck another under his arm and climbed up on the logs to sit with his feet hooked onto the lowest rail. Once settled, he leaned his forearms on his knees, popped the tab-top, pulled it loose, and reached into his shirt pocket. He extracted a long chain of tab-tops and bent the end of the new one to form another link. He then held his beer between his knees, pulled off his bush hat and stretched the chain around the crown.

"Almost," he said. "One more six-pack oughta do it." He then showed the shiny hat-band in-the-making to his friend.

"Cool," Danny said.

"Naturally," Gino nodded.

Taking a long pull from the frosty can, Gino held it up, aping a TV announcer.

"Doctor Gino's medicine. Makes the pain go away."

"Sure it does." Danny smiled his disbelief.

"Gonna stay out here all night?"

"Yeah. Can't get comfortable in there."

"Get a little spooked?"

Danny's head snapped up, denial forming on his lips, and then he shrugged his shoulders. No sense lying to Gino. He knew.

"Wanna be alone?"

"No," Danny whispered, "definitely not."

With that, Gino jumped lightly to the ground, set his beer down on a flat rock, saying, "Mind that for me," and went back to the tent. He emerged moments later to roll out his bedroll opposite Danny's. Bedding down, he spied a glint of blued steel amid the folds of Danny's sleeping bag.

"You don't need that out here you know," he said, pointing to the gun with his chin.

"You don't have one?"

"I don't need mine either," Gino said and winked.

They laughed until their sides hurt.

"As long as we're staying up," Gino said, "why don'tcha tell me the whole story?"

"You first." Danny poked a log further into the flames. "I still can't get used to seeing you alive."

"Thank you very much." Gino feigned pain in his heart with a hand clapped to his chest.

"You know what I mean. I thought you died in that snake-eater camp. Then, out of the blue, you show up at my uncle's door with a carload of camping gear to drag me off to the wilderness like nothing happened. Now, give."

"Okay." Gino raised his hands in surrender. "You want war stories? War stories it is." He took a pull on his beer, staring into the fire. "You know about the gooks over-running the camp."

Danny replied in the affirmative with a slow blink of his eyes and a nod.

"It happened so fast it was unreal. They hit us with a mortar barrage at about three a.m." Gino paused to look at Danny. "I don't mean the usual half-dozen rounds, man. I'm talking about an honest-to-God barrage. It rained fucking mortars. They were coming in so fast you couldn't tell where one explosion ended and the next one began. I didn't think Charley had that many tubes in all of Southeast Asia." His eyes dropped to the fire as he said, "Before the shit lifted, they followed up with a ground attack—hundreds of 'em. We mowed 'em down, but they just kept coming."

Danny pulled his sleeping bag in tighter, sipped his beer, and waited for Gino to continue.

Gino took a breath, held it for a moment, and then let it out in a rush. "I was having a beer with a buddy of mine in the team house when it started. I had just gotten off berm guard. We were standing down the next day so we were already in party mode. The CO was up, writing a letter to his old lady. When the first rounds hit, he says to me, 'Git your ass to the commo bunker.' We could tell from the onset that we were gonna need some help." Gino's eyes flashed as he relived that terrible night. "The

place was lit up like strobe lights flashing when I got outside.
Remember the Electric Circus in The Village? Like that, but
without the psychedelic shit. Things were going boom everywhere I looked. The guys on the wall were burnin' up ammo like
there was no tomorrow." He shrugged and then sighed. "There
wasn't. Maybe they knew.

"Anyway, I saw the first wave hit the wire. Jesus, I was scared.
I broke the land-speed record getting to that bunker. I dove in and
was just picking up the mic when the lights went out. I couldn't
move. Everything went black, like I was suspended in time. I
didn't know it then, but the bunker took a direct hit and caved in
on me. I was buried in sandbags and shit. My back must've taken
a helluva wallop from a roof beam. I was paralyzed. Couldn't
move a muscle. I remember thinking, *I'm dead.* Weird much, let
me tell you. I was expecting that bright white light you hear so
much about, but it was pitch dark.

"Then I felt the heat. The gooks were burning everything they
couldn't carry off. Some of the shit on top of me was on fire.
Then I thought, Uh oh, looks like old Gino gonna wind up someplace else he don't want to go. I mean, I fully expected to meet
little red guys with pitch-forks next.

"I musta passed out about then. Next thing I knew, some guys
were dragging me out in daylight, the day after the next. I was
buried alive for almost two fucking days. When our guys moved
back in and started sifting through the rubble, they found me."

"And you weren't hurt?"

"My sacroiliac ain't ever gonna be the same, but otherwise
I'm good as new." He spread his hands and looked down at himself, inviting inspection. "'Course, I'm permanently disabled, you
understand. Uncle Sam has to send me checks every month for
the rest of my life. But between you and me, old buddy, Gino is
fine. I can't do any heavy lifting, but I hadn't planned on a life of
hard labor to begin with."

He sat back, leaning against the logs, ankles crossed, seemingly pleased with himself.

"How come the part about you surviving didn't get in the papers?" Danny asked. "Anybody else make it?"

"Not sensational enough? Good news don't stir up the students? Who the hell knows?" Gino threw the empty can into the
fire. "In answer to your second question—no." The loss Gino felt

was evident by his expression—something Danny understood.

"I'm sorry, Gino."

"Me too. Okay. I showed you mine. You show me yours."

"Not so fast, wise guy. Why in the hell didn't you let me know you were all right?"

Gino inhaled deeply. "Probably because I wasn't." He sat staring into the flames for a minute. "I went to DaNang, and then to a hospital ship for a while, and then to Japan before I wound up in a VA hospital in Seattle. I needed some physical therapy for my back. At first, they had me in some kind of rig to keep me from moving. Then somebody decided I shouldn't be trussed up, I should be exercising. That seemed cool, but I soon found out it hurt like hell. They gave me stuff for the pain." Gino grinned. "Good stuff. I was so spaced half the time, I didn't know who I was, never mind where. When I finally got sent home, it seemed like such a bummer to be straight that I got into downers pretty heavy. It got so that I was blowing my monthly checks on pills as soon as I cashed them."

"Bad scene."

"You got that right. My old man had moved while I was gone. He forgot to leave a forwarding address so I slept in the subway for a couple or three weeks and then moved in with this broad I met. She was at least as strung out as I was. Funny thing is I never liked her. She was—I don't know. Useful? Whatever." He waved it away. "One day we were walking down Knickerbocker Avenue when we passed your mom on the street. I started to say hello and stopped. All at once I realized how ashamed I was—of who I was with, and of who *I* was.

"Believe me, Daniel. *You* would have called the cops if you had seen me then. I was that fucked up. Couple days later I moved out of the chick's place and I ain't popped so much as an aspirin since. Went to the VA Hospital until I got rid of the heebie-jeebies, and then moved to the Y until I got a job and a pad of my own. Now I'm thinking about school. You know, put the brain cells I got left to work."

"Good for you. Anything in particular in mind?"

"I'm thinking law school."

"No shit?"

"Know your enemy, that's my motto."

Danny's jaw dropped.

Gino winked. "Gotcha!"

"Smartass. Does my mother know you're alive? She'd want to know you're all right."

"I saw her last week. That's how I found out about you. End of story. You may proceed. Start from the beginning. Your moms wouldn't tell me shit. Just kept saying I should go see you."

Danny chuckled and then recounted the tale of Tyler's capture, starting with the massacre of his platoon and his guilt for not having been with them. His eyes got the same far off look that Gino's had, the thousand-meter stare. He went through the rescue operation and the events leading up to it.

Finally, he told of the fight at the fish trap, the end of Captain Tran, and the salvation of Andy Kowalski. "I crapped out after that," he said. "Doc patched all of us up as best he could. The gooks split. We just let them go. Not that we could have done much to stop them. Paco called in our real position, and the guys waited for Charlie-Six to catch up. The rest of the company hit a squad of VC on the way to us. They were pinned down for an hour. Arnold finally got some gunships to break them up when the rain let up. They couldn't get a dustoff in when they got to us. Shit was too thick. So, they carried us out. Must've been a bitch in the dark in that swamp. Took all night, but they got us to the road the next morning. A convoy was waiting for us." He laughed a short, sharp laugh. "Kowalski paid some dude to let him drive the truck that brought us back to Dagger. I have no idea why. I was in and out most of the time. They put us on a chopper and sent us to the Third Surge in Dong Tam. Tyler, Davy and I went to Japan a few days later. Davy lost his arm. He couldn't fight off the infection. They sent him home. He wrote to me a couple of times."

"Jesus," Gino whispered. "So, how come you're not on the cover of *Time Magazine*?"

"What the hell for?"

"Are you kidding? For the only successful rescue of a POW since this shitass war started."

"Tyler came to see me in the hospital in Japan once they let him out of bed. It was months later. He looked pretty good except for a few scars from that bayonet." Danny glanced at the knife on his pack.

"You mean that's the one you were talking about?"

"He gave it to me as a souvenir. I guess the gooks left it behind. I was pretty sick for a while. My wounds got infected. They even talked about amputating my leg. Then I got pneumonia, probably from the shit in the water. I damn near drowned in that fish trap." He laughed softly, remembering his surreal visitors and their encouragement. "Anyway, except for a few scars and a bad case of malaria, Tyler's all right. He said that there was a big hullabaloo over what to do with me. Some of the brass wanted to make us all heroes. The rest wanted us court martialed, especially me. They called me the 'ringleader.' Tyler put me and Davy in for the MOH."

Gino gaped. "The Medal of Honor?"

"Yep. I told him I wouldn't take it. 'No matter,' he says, 'they turned it down.' We did affect the rescue, but we broke every rule in the book doing it, and we disobeyed direct orders to boot. They said we got the kid from Montana killed. Funny, they never mentioned Johnson. The army decided it would set a bad example to make a fuss over us. Tyler squashed the court martial. He threatened to hold a press conference and tell the whole story." Danny wagged his head. "I doubt if that will do much for his career. In the end, they struck a bargain. I got the Silver Star, two more Purple Hearts, and busted to PFC. Davy got a Silver Star, a Heart, and a hundred-percent disability if he keeps his mouth shut."

"The rat fucks."

"Roger that. While I was recuperating, Tyler pulled some strings. He got me promoted back to corporal and then to buck sergeant before I came home. Now I'm officially on what they called 'convalescent leave with no definite term.' I suppose I could keep drawing my pay until I ETS. I haven't decided."

"What happened to the rest of your buddies?"

Danny drew a breath, pausing to recall. "Simms went home on his DEROS date. So did Paco. E.Z.'s a squad leader now. Pomeroy got out on a permanent disability. I hear he's fighting it. He wants back in. Doc extended his tour to get an early out. Berger shot himself in the foot. They say it was intentional." He laughed quietly. "No way. He was showing off for some new guys. Twirling a Forty-Five like Gene Autry, you know?"

Gino nodded, smiling.

"It went off. Paco was there. The round took off two toes. He wrote to me—Berger, I mean. Says he's going to write a book some day when it all blows over. I hope he does." Danny took a pull on his beer, thinking. "Arnold took a job at Battalion. Wyman tried out for Sniper School. I bet he made it. The kid was a natural." He sipped the beer again and laughed softly before he said, "Kowalski reenlisted. Go figure. I don't know what happened to the rest. The letters stopped coming after a while."

"What about Smitty?"

"Smitty disappeared somewhere between the NVA camp and Highway Four."

"Somebody mete out a little jungle justice?"

"That's what I thought, but Tyler says no. He talked to Beecher, who swears the bastard just wandered off in the dark. No one bothered to look for him. He was unarmed as he was technically under arrest. He's probably dead. Officially, he's MIA."

Gino could see Danny's mind wandering. "What about that gorgeous brunette from Manhattan? I thought you'd be marryin' that lady."

"We broke up," Danny mumbled, rising for another beer.

"That bitch dumped you?" Gino saw the sparks flash in Danny's eyes. "Time, good buddy." Gino made a T with his hands like a football referee. "Ex-chicks are fair game. It's in the rules."

Danny laughed at Gino's contrivance, and then said, sadly, "I broke up with her, Gino."

"Why?"

"I was a mess in the hospital, feverish most of the time. I did a lot of thinking, most of it incoherent, I suppose, but the one thing that I was sure of was that I had changed. She wouldn't even know me anymore. The guy that kissed her goodbye at the airport is dead. Vietnam killed him."

Gino started to say something, but Danny was still talking, almost whispering.

"I miss him," he choked. "I never knew how much I liked that guy until he was gone. Now I've got to learn to live with the guy who took his place. Amanda wouldn't know how. I'm not sure that I do. So, I wrote her a letter—a *Dear Jane* you might call it. When I got home, I moved in with Uncle Mike to sort things out. My own mother looks at me like I'm from another planet."

"Your mom is worried about you. Talk to her. She'll understand. Give her a chance. That might not be bad advice with regards to Amanda, either. The old Danny's not dead, my friend.

He's hurt bad, but he'll be back. Give him time. I know him well. Vietnam couldn't beat him. It ain't tough enough."

Danny lit a cigarette and wiped his eyes, pretending the smoke had stung them.

"At least now you know," Gino breathed.

"Know what?"

"That Daniel Francis Mulvaney can hack it. That's what you needed to find out, as I recall."

"Did I?"

Gino said, "Let's go into town."

"What the hell for?"

"Wine, women, and song. What else?" Gino rose to go.

"You're nuts."

"This is news?"

"It's after twelve, you idiot." Danny laughed. "This ain't The City. They roll up the sidewalks at dusk up here."

"What sidewalks?"

"Precisely. Forget it."

"I'm going."

"I'm not."

"Suit yourself. If I find two chicks, I'll screw yours first."

"Be my guest. Take some bread crumbs."

"To find my way back?"

"To feed the pigeons when you wake up on a park bench all alone."

He could hear Gino laughing all the way to the car.

Danny cracked open another beer. He watched the flames until his eyelids became heavy. Telling his story for the first time to someone he knew would understand had helped. The woods had almost lost their foreboding. He lifted his gaze to the river, partially visible through the trees as the moon rose. He watched the pale blue, dappled surface, rippling in the light breeze.

Once again, he thought of himself as someone else, someone he used to know a long, long time ago. Fatigue finally set in and Danny dozed. Smoke from the dying fire smarted his eyelids. He squeezed them tighter until he was asleep.

The dream came again. It was good to be with his friends.

He awoke to the sight of the Delaware River below him, dark now that the moon was down. Curling into a tight ball to ease the ache in his guts, quaking with sobs, Danny cried himself back to

sleep, where mercifully, the dream didn't come again—that night.
The sun on his cheek woke him the next morning. Gino had
not returned.

"It would be just like that clown to get lucky in that one-horse
town." Danny smiled as he started the fire to make coffee.

He was sitting on a massive granite rock, overlooking the river, sipping coffee, thinking that all places are beautiful at sunrise,
trying to ignore the tingling in his spine that warned him to watch
his back when he heard Fuquette in his mind, and he mouthed the
words. "Go from here."

The morning light bathed his gear in pink. The hilt of the bayonet drew his eye. He walked softly to the campfire, poured another cup of coffee, and sat staring at the weapon.

Go from here.

Danny set the cup down and withdrew the long blade from its
scabbard. It shone like a tracer in the dawn light.

Go from here.

Follow through.

Eyes focused on the shimmering steel, he stepped to the edge
of the bluff overlooking the river, laid the bayonet against a rock,
and stared at it.

*What is the spirit of the bayonet? To kill! To kill without mer-
cy!*

With a sudden stamp of his boot, he snapped the blade in two.
Without hesitation, he stooped to retrieve the broken halves of the
weapon, stood up, and threw them as far out into the river as he
could. He then nodded once, turned, ran back to his sleeping bag
and pulled the Browning from its folds. Breathless, he strode
back to the edge of the bluff, releasing the magazine, field strip-
ping the pistol as he went. Once more on the precipice, he scattered the parts and ammunition to as many points in the river as
he could. He was still standing there, puffing, slightly dizzy,
when he heard Gino's car on the road at the top of the hill.

CHAPTER 76

1988, Brooklyn, New York:

Danny's eyes were starting to adjust to the dim light in the tenement hallway when he heard the peephole cover snap shut and the security chain rattle. One second later the door flew open.

"Hi, Mom."

"Daniel! Oh, how nice of you to visit." His mother took his face in both of her hands and kissed him. Tears of joy welled up in her eyes as she stepped back to look at him, still holding fast to his cheeks. "You look great. How's the writing going? I'm so proud. My son, the author. Your father would be thrilled." She stood on tiptoes and peered over his shoulder. "Where are my grandchildren?"

"In school, where they belong. It's just me. I, uh—I wanted to talk to you."

"Well, don't stand in the hall. Come in, come in." She took his arm and walked him into the kitchen, took his jacket and sat him in his favorite seat at the kitchen table, the one facing the window.

Like a sudden storm, Joan Mulvaney dashed about the tiny kitchen, pulling cups and saucers from a cupboard, milk from the refrigerator, ground coffee from a canister on the counter beside the sink. Finally, she filled the coffeemaker her son had given her for Christmas with water from the tap.

Danny let his eyes roam the small apartment he'd grown up in, so familiar, so completely known. There wasn't a square inch of the place he wasn't intimately acquainted with, but something was missing. He knew in that moment what he realized he must have known subconsciously for some time. This wasn't his home anymore. He knew, too, that he wasn't sure when it had stopped being home. He just knew that it no longer was. It heightened his sense of loss.

"I'm the envy of the neighborhood since your book came out," Joan Mulvaney bubbled while her hands flew from one task to the next. "Did you know the library has a waiting list for their copy?"

"Copy? As in—one." He winced. "Sid will go bananas."

"What, dear?"

"Uh, my agent. He'll like that."

She smiled and prattled on about little things until the pot began to gurgle and the aroma of fresh coffee filled the room. As if that was an awaited signal, she dropped into the chair facing her son to say, "What's wrong?"

She had that look of total concentration he had only seen on her face when something serious, something that affected him, occurred.

He said, "This place needs a paint job. You pick the colors, and I'll come over and play Rembrandt for a couple of days." He looked into his empty cup and then out the window. "I should caulk these windows, too. The old place needs some work. How about a new rug for the living room?"

"Sold. Now, what's wrong? Is one of the kids sick? Are you getting a divorce?"

She wouldn't relax that penetrating gaze. *How old did a man have to be before his mother stopped reading him like a grade school primer?*

"No, the kids are fine, and I think my marriage will last a little longer, but, to be truthful, there has been some tension of late. How did you know I have a problem?"

"It's not my birthday, Mother's Day, Christmas, Saint Patrick's Day, Easter, or any day that might remind me of your father, but here you are."

"Have I been that bad?"

"Of course not." She took his hand and smiled. "You're exactly the son I prayed for. If I wanted you underfoot all the time, I'd never have let you start kindergarten." She got up to pour the coffee, saying, "And I wouldn't be the kind of mother you deserve if

I didn't know when my baby was in trouble." She slid the sugar bowl in front of him and sat down again. "Out with it."

He slipped a cigarette between his lips and stopped.

Joan Mulvaney raised an eyebrow. "That's not a good sign. I thought you quit."

"If it bothers you, I don't have to smoke."

She popped up again and rummaged in a cabinet until she found an ashtray.

"Puff away. We'll worry about your lungs later. Now, talk."

Danny plucked the letter from his shirt pocket and slid it across the table to his mother. The feeling of deja vu was overwhelming. Thirty-five years before, Danny had presented his draft notice in this same room, at this same table, in the same manner. Her hands trembled as she took it, so she pressed it flat on the tabletop and began to read.

Danny tasted his coffee and smoked his cigarette, watching her eyes scanning the page behind her glasses. Her hair was snow white, thinner than he remembered. He wondered why he hadn't noticed until now how the years had overtaken the woman he loved as no other.

"Who is he?" his mother asked.

"I don't know."

"Are you going?"

"I want to."

"Alone?"

"Yes."

"Why?"

"If I knew that, I probably wouldn't be sitting here."

"Have you talked to Gino?"

"Oh yeah." He rolled his eyes. "I called him. He thinks I'm nuts."

"Is that his considered legal opinion?"

"Hardly. He says I need a shrink, not a lawyer."

She smiled. "How is his practice going?"

"Rather well. He says his larcenous tendencies jell quite nicely with his chosen profession."

"He's a character—and a good friend."

"And I should listen to him?"

"I didn't say that."

"You were thinking it."

"Leave the mind reading to your mother. It's not your forte."

Danny shrugged. "I asked Gino along. He said, and I quote, 'Not without a B-Fifty-Two and tactical nukes.' *Sheesh.* Talk about bitter."

"He's entitled. You all are."

That shocked him. It made him angry. "I never expected that from you, Mom. What about all that stuff you filled my head with when I was a kid? Forgiveness? Compassion? Empathy? What was that? Motherly rhetoric?"

"Mind your tone, Daniel." The simple, sotto voice admonition brought him up short. She pressed on. "You have no idea of the motives behind this invitation, Daniel. You don't even know who this person is." She slapped the page for emphasis, but Danny saw it as if she had a subconscious need to punish the writer. "You almost died there. Why would you want to go back? It's a communist country now. Who knows what evil this man has in mind?"

"How do you know it's bad? Maybe it's something good."

"Oh, sure. You won the Vietnamese lottery, and they want you to collect your fortune."

"Sarcasm? From a Mulvaney? I don't believe my ears."

She bit her lip. "I can still spank you."

"Uh uh. I may be slowing down, but I can still outrun you."

The twinkle in his eye was mirrored in her own. She banished a tear with an arthritic knuckle. "The Kid? Slowing down? I should live so long." She produced a wadded-up Kleenex from nowhere. He wondered if he would ever learn the secret of how she hid them. "Peace?" she said, holding up two fingers in a V.

"Always." He reached across the table to cover her hands with his. "Look, Mom, I've been a mess since I wrote the book. It brought back all the bad stuff I've buried all these years."

He gave her hands a quick pat and stood to walk to the window. The view of the fenced-in back yard, with its carefully tended flower beds and vegetable garden, struck him as incongruous, surrounded as it was by ranks of tenements buildings huddled shoulder to shoulder—unbroken rows of perpendicular sameness—except for the back yards. He could look down the rows to see behind every house on the block, viewing the marks of individuality each of his neighbors had made. No two yards were alike: there were swing sets and shade trees, trimmed lawns and junk heaps, clotheslines and tool sheds, religious grottos and patio furniture.

Danny faced the back yards to avoid the pain in his mother's eyes as he continued with his confession. "I've felt like I was in mourning the last few months."

"For your friends who died?"

"Partly. And partly for me. You say I almost died over there? Well, sometimes I feel like I did. It's not just the letter. None of it has ever gone away. It's like it only slept. But it's awake now. It's out of the box, and I have to face it."

She started to say something, but he turned and cut her off.

"Don't ask me to explain it. I can't. I just know this is something I have to do."

She took a breath, sipped her coffee, and reached for his cigarette. He watched her take a drag, make a sour face and cough, "Filthy habit. Now I remember why I quit." She stubbed the butt out in the ashtray. Then she said, "My turn?"

He leaned against the windowsill, and said, "You have the floor."

"One of these days you'll have me lying on it."

His eyes widened in exasperation.

"Cheap shot. I'm sorry. I try very hard not to be the kind of mother who uses guilt as a weapon. It's unfair and it's weak." She waved it away. "I watched your father eat himself up inside until he found oblivion in a bottle." She sighed. "We women don't know what war is like except that it's horrible and that it does things to the men we love—things that we hate. I couldn't bear to watch you wither away as your father did. He was a wonderful man. I wish you'd known him before the liquor got him."

"I did. I don't remember much, but the memories I have are good ones."

"He loved you very much."

"I know."

"He'd say, 'Follow your heart,' and I'd agree with him."

"That's what you guys taught me. I've always tried to."

"Yes, you have. You're so much like him." Tears welled up in her eyes. "Now, leave an old lady to have a good cry." She gathered the crockery and went to the sink with it. "Don't leave without saying goodbye, and call me when you get there." Her brow wrinkled as she peered at him over the rims of her glasses. "They do have phones there now, don't they?"

"Yes, Mom, they do. Probably have fast food and flush toilets, too."

"I'll keep your wife sane while you're gone, and I'll keep the kids occupied while their daddy slays his dragon."

"Mom, I—"

"Git, before I change my mind. And remember, you owe me a paint job and a rug when you come back."

He hugged her as he passed, kissed her forehead, grabbed his coat from a hook by the door, and left without another word.

With hot tears burning her eyes, Joan Mulvaney washed the dishes and prayed, "Saint Jude? It's me again…"

ഏഌഏ

Gino was on the stoop, leaning on the handrail, when Danny stepped out the front door.

Danny said, "Deja vu is working overtime today. And you look ridiculous in that ponytail, Gino. Nice suit, though."

Gino swung his head, and the five-inch tail wagged with the motion.

"The chicks at the courthouse love it," he said. "You should try it. Makes the gray hairs sexy. But stay clear of Armani. You're too big for the Continental cut."

"I'll try to remember. What are you doing here?"

Gino looked at the sky, checked his watch, and said, "I heard that a Russian satellite is supposed to hit Brooklyn today. I'm selling T-shirts."

"Nice seeing you, Gino."

Danny started down the steps but Gino grabbed his arm.

"Your wife told me where you'd be. Let's talk about this."

"If she sent you to talk me out of it—"

"You know better than that."

"So?"

"Come on, I'll buy you a drink."

It was Danny's turn to look at his watch.

"Suggest coffee or bowling, and I'll deck you," Gino said.

Danny laughed. "Just one."

Gino led Danny to a midnight-blue, Mercedes 450SL with a

tan leather interior. Before stepping into the car, Danny asked, "It isn't hot, is it?"

"Please. You're talking to an officer of the court. It's even paid for. Get in."

As they left the curb, Gino said, "Did I tell you I defended Nicky Marino last month?"

"Let me guess—Grand theft auto."

"Seven counts. Nicky diversified too, you know. Had a chop-shop-slash-coke smuggling operation going."

"You get him off?"

"Nope. Three-time loser. Houdini couldn't have gotten him out of it this time. Twenty-five to life."

They were still laughing when they pulled up to a bar and grill on Wyckoff Avenue where they had both been served their first legal liquor two years *after* they had been served their first illegal liquor in the same bar. The place looked like dozens of rundown corner gin mills that dotted the neighborhood—monuments to working class despair. Two elderly, washed-up patrons sat at the bar, two stools apart, tended by a barman Danny thought interchangeable with his customers.

The bartender sized up the two middle-aged, middle-class newcomers, and said, "Afternoon gents. Phone's in the back next to the men's room."

Danny was vaguely annoyed that they should be dismissed as strangers but stayed silent while Gino ordered.

"I don't believe this place is still here," he said, as they slipped into a back booth with a pitcher of beer and two glasses. The smell of stale hops and tobacco smoke brought back memories, most of them fond ones.

"There's a lot about the old neighborhood you wouldn't believe," Gino said. He poured for them both.

"What's that supposed to mean?"

"Just that I've missed you. The old haunts aren't the same without my sidekick." Gino raised his glass, and said, "To absent friends."

Danny acknowledged the toast, clinking glasses with his old friend.

"Is this the preamble to the speech on why I shouldn't go?"

"We've been friends for too long for that to happen. I just want to know why. I swear," Gino raised his hand as if he was on

the witness stand, "no arguments from me. But I think you owe
me an explanation."

"Fair enough." Danny sipped his beer, gathering his thoughts.
Then he told Gino about the recurring dream that had haunted
him for years after he had returned from Vietnam.

"Not bad for a 'Nam dream," Gino said. "I used to have some
beauts. But that was a while ago. And you're having it again, after—what? Twenty years or so?"

"Yeah. It started again when the book took off. And then I got
the letter."

"From some gook you don't even know."

"They're not gooks. They're Vietnamese."

"Old habit. *Xin Loi.* Who do you think he is?"

"Wild-assed guess?"

Gino nodded.

"Someone who was involved in the U-Minh operation, maybe
one of theirs."

"What makes you think so?"

"The tone of the letter."

"I thought you said the wording was ambiguous?"

"It was, sort of, but I can't imagine what else it could be. He
talked about old friends reuniting. I wasn't there all that long. I
certainly didn't make any lifelong friendships with any goo—"

"Whoops. Politically correct's a bitch, isn't it?"

Danny reddened.

Gino poured himself more beer. He proffered the pitcher to
Danny, who gulped half of what was in his glass and slid it across
the plywood tabletop, glad for the distraction.

"Go on," Gino prodded, concentrating on pouring a perfect
head.

"I miss it," Danny said, shame flushing his face until he felt
like a thermometer about to explode.

"Vietnam?" Gino slid Danny's glass to him.

"The war," Danny whispered, "the guys."

When he thought of them, it was like the dream. They were
always smiling such bright, cheerful smiles—hopeful adoles-
cents—forever young. So many were gone. It was sad. But the
stories lived on. Wistfully, he remembered the bull sessions with
guys who had "seen the elephant." He'd been there and done that.
He had looked the pachyderm in the eye. So he told the stories.

Maybe that was why he had survived—to bear witness. And if one story had turned up on the bestseller list, so be it. The guys were rooting for him. He could feel it.

He looked at his beer. He'd done more drinking in the past year than he had in all the years since the war. Was be belatedly following in his father's footsteps? Maybe it was genetic, something embedded in his chromosomes, as inevitable as the seasons.

Danny thought he had made a kind of truce with his God and his conscience after many years of introspection and confusion. The writing had been the key to his tortured soul. There was peace in those pages of pain and suffering. Setting it down for all to examine had released him from responsibility somehow, for a time at least. You don't lose faith. You don't abandon those you love. You do what you have to do: you risk it all and leave no one behind. Isn't that what he had done then? When had he lost sight of the truth? Or did truth change, like people? And now, here he sat, being scrutinized like an alien life form by someone who should understand. Resentment bubbled up in him.

He stopped himself. What was he doing? Spinning like a top. Classic delayed stress.

Gino said, "Don't feel like The Lone Ranger."

"What's this? The return of Tonto?"

"Never left, old buddy." Gino patted his pockets. "You got a smoke?"

Danny tossed a pack on the table. They both lit up.

"This is what you miss," Gino breathed a cloud of smoke above their heads. It twisted and curled in the yellow light from the low-wattage swag lamp suspended there.

"Drinking and smoking in the middle of the afternoon?" Danny smirked.

"Maybe. But what I meant was being tight with people you love." Gino held up one forefinger. "Hey, don't let the ponytail give you the wrong idea." He stole a glance around the bar. "I ain't looking to pick out furniture or anything."

Danny chuckled, nodding. "No problem. I get the drift."

"Why did you write your book, Dan? After all these years, why now?"

Danny toyed with his glass for a moment, and said to it, "Berger. It was Berger." As if suddenly remembering Gino was there, he looked at him and went on. "I've been writing anonymous pieces for veterans' organizations for years. Nothing major. Keeping my hand in, if you will."

"I never knew that. Maybe I've read some of your stuff."

"*You* read veteran's magazines?"

"Old Gino's not just a fancy suit, Dan. I started doing pro bono work for Vietnam Veterans of America a few years back. You know, helping vets who get jammed up and can't afford a decent lawyer."

"I thought you'd written it off."

"As I thought you had. Humph. Who were we kidding? Wasn't Berger the screw-up?"

"Yeah." Danny shook his head. "Berger gathered information for years, trying to put his book together. He did extensive research on the whole mess. And I do mean *extensive*. He somehow got a hold of records from Hanoi. I had to fabricate some of the stuff, but most of it was gospel.

"He died three years ago. Cancer. Agent Orange. At least that's what his family thinks. He sent me his notes when he knew he wouldn't have time to finish it. I remember thinking that my first impression had been correct. Berger would not survive Vietnam." Danny took another pull on his beer. "I dabbled with it at first, not really believing I could do it. A book—*Jesus*. How could I write a book? And then it was almost as if he was guiding my hand. I couldn't help it. I had to write it."

Gino sighed, nursed his beer, and said nothing. The silence became uncomfortable for Danny.

"You must think I'm as nutty as a fruitcake."

"Always did." Gino winked. "What do you hope to accomplish by going back?"

"I don't know. Maybe nothing."

"Bullshit. You want to end the pain."

"I guess so."

"It won't work."

"How do you know?"

"I tried it through chemicals, remember?"

Danny shot him a scoffing look.

Gino spread his hands. "Same difference. You get to a point where you can't hack it, right? It hurts like crazy. You'll do anything to make it go away. You, you bastard, you absolutely amazed me. I didn't go through half the shit that you did and I completely fell apart when I came home. You just went on with your life."

Danny twisted his face into a grimace of disbelief.

"Really." Gino blew a cloud of smoke through his nose. "You got your shit together. Got a job, got married, had kids, bought a house. In-fucking-credible!"

"And you went to law school and became highly successful while I struggled for years to make ends meet selling shitty industrial supplies. Gimme a break."

"I had Uncle Sammy helping me out. I still get a tax-free check every month."

"You earned it."

"Like you didn't? Daniel, that check is my vote of thanks from the ungrateful bastards who sent us over there. I still don't know how the rest of my brothers survive without it."

"What choice do we have?"

"Precisely!"

"*You*—" Danny pointed a finger. "—are not making any sense."

"Let's get back to my original question. What do you think you can accomplish by going back?"

"Lots of guys have gone back. Maybe I can do something to make amends. We fucked those people. We owe them."

"We got caught in the middle of something that was none of our business. You worried about the Vietnamese people?"

"Aren't you?"

"Fuck, no. Those tough little bastards have survived more than the coming of America. We're gearing up to bail them out financially even as we speak. You watch. Before we die we'll be buying Vietnamese cars and wondering how the hell we can compete with them in the world market."

"I never knew you were so racist."

"Racist my ass. History, my man. If we don't learn the lesson, we do it again. And the lesson is right there in front of us. Nobody knows it better than we do. It's what's tearing you up. We lived as brothers in combat. Why the hell can't we all live that way all the time?" Danny's mouth fell open. "Simple, isn't it?" Gino continued. "Care for each other like we cared for each other in combat. That's what we learned. That's what we miss— brotherhood."

"It's too simplistic."

"The smartest things usually are." Gino shook his head. "Don't you get it? You don't want to go back to see how Vietnam is doing. You want to find the starry-eyed kid you think you left there. You're an incurable romantic."

"And you're melodramatic."

"Think about the dream. As fucked up as the war was, it gave us something we've never been able to replace."

"You're telling me that, after all this time, my stomach is in knots over losing touch with my friends?"

"Pay attention for once. There might be a quiz later."

Danny's eyes narrowed. His patience was stretched thin, but Gino wasn't letting up.

"*You* dove right into civilian life when you got back. Buried your hurt like a C-rat can and continued to march. *I* caved in. Rolled up in a ball and grieved until I couldn't stand myself. By the time we went camping, I was on the way back to the world of the living. You were so busy with shoring up the bunker you didn't take time to lick your wounds. Now, what's happened?"

Danny opened his mouth, but Gino answered for him. "You hit the jackpot. You're a success. New house. New cars. Kids are almost grown. No more work-a-day battle. You won. But, lo and behold, you notice little gaps in your armor and ghosts are peeking out of the cracks."

"But the letter—"

"Ah, yes. The infamous letter." Gino smiled and shook his head. "Feel flattered. You're in great company. Colin Powell got one. So did Stormin' Norman Schwarzkopf, John McCain, Dave Hackworth, Dennis Franz, Oliver Stone, Nelson DeMille, and about a hundred other Vietnam vets who have made it to the big time. Each got the same invite. You ain't exactly a household word, Daniel, but lots of people know who you are now. I did some checking when you called to tell me about it. You should get on the internet, Dan. It's gonna be big."

Danny looked perplexed. Before he could verbalize the question, Gino answered it.

"I may not have had the most illustrious military career, but I *was* in Special Forces, and that counts for a lot in certain circles. That pro bono work I mentioned has gotten me some contacts in places the average dude couldn't begin to crack. I know a guy in the Pentagon who can reach out and touch people with pipelines all the way to the Joint Chiefs and beyond."

Danny shot Gino a skeptical frown.

"I shit you not. Word is your gook's a player. Real estate. Hanoi's answer to Donald Trump. He's selling futures on beach front property for the Riviera of the Orient."

"You're bullshitting me."

"I've got the proof in my office."

"Why isn't it in the news? What you're describing would definitely get serious media attention."

"Oh, it will. The list of recipients guarantees it. You can bet the State Department, FBI, CIA, NSA, and every other agency in Washington's alphabet soup are checking this out six ways to Sunday. He probably didn't expect anybody to actually show up, but what better way to get a shit-pot full of free publicity in the target market? *You* were in business. Think! It's damned clever. They need investment capital, not care packages. Partners! That's what they're shopping for."

"You're telling me this guy is peddling land to guys with clout all the way to the White House. But they're communists, not capitalists."

"Come on. They're humans. Humans are opportunists. They'd be goddamn Democrats if Truman had had a little more vision. Communism's a great way to rally the troops." Gino did his commissar impression. "Let's all be equals, comrades. And let's kick the shit out of any capitalist pig who disagrees." He wagged his forefinger as he slid back into Ginoese. "But, when the smoke clears, maybe some comrades want to be a little more equal. Americans like to jump-start anything slow off the mark, and we are absolute suckers when it comes to rebuilding countries we fucked up. Hell, if the Arabs had any brains, they'd declare war tomorrow. But we get bored when the machine starts to hum. So we sell the whole kit and kaboodle to the poor schlepps that we felt sorry for to begin with. Or maybe we just hand them the reins and walk away. We're pigeons. Who knows that better than the goo—*xin loi*—Vietnamese?"

"I doubt that most of the people you mentioned would be willing to invest in something like that." Danny frowned.

"Probably not. But the word would go out via the media to lots of people who would. They learned how to make us jump through hoops during the war by using our own free press. The Vietnamese are going to be fine. We, on the other hand, are in deep shit." He settled back to stare at Danny, defying him to contest his logic.

"So, this," Danny spread his hands to indicate their conversation, "really *is* all about you showing me why I shouldn't go."

"Wrong. This is about you and me leveling with each other, nothing more. You want to go back to Nam? Go. I hope you find whatever it is you're looking for." He finished what was in his glass and set it down before saying, "If it means that much to you, you're going, no matter what. We both know you well enough to know it. But, if I had what you've got—and I don't mean the material shit—I'd think twice." He reached for the pitcher.

Danny sat watching while Gino topped off his glass.

"When you leaving?" Gino said, reaching for Danny's glass.

"Is that florist still there? The one on St. Nicholas and Greene."

Gino froze in mid-reach, "You got a sudden yen for posies?"

"I'm going to start over from where I got lost."

"How many beers have you had?"

"I'm incurably romantic, remember? It's part of my charm."

"Try a ponytail."

"Come on, let's get out of here. I've got things to do."

As they drove, Gino asked, "What ever happened to Amanda?"

"No idea. I never saw her again. When I met Karen, I—I suppose it was just as well. Amanda wasn't for me. We had nothing in common. I don't think she really loved me anyway. Karen's my kind of woman. My mother says she's the glue that holds me together."

"Don't you ever wonder?"

"About Amanda? Maybe once in a while. Why?"

"No reason, just reminiscing. She probably got old and ugly."

Gino waited outside the florist while Danny bought two-dozen roses. With twelve, long-stemmed beauties for each of the women he loved, he climbed back into the car, and said, "Home, James."

Gino eyed the flowers, and said, "Somebody wants to get laid."

"Shut up and drive."

As Gino pulled into traffic, a jet thundered overhead. Danny watched it lumber into the sky, and whispered, "Silver Dustoff, Freedom Bird—two good titles for a book."

Gino dropped Danny at his mother's apartment. He waited down the block until he saw Danny come out and get into his car. He followed him until Danny swung onto the eastbound ramp to the Long Island Expressway, and then he hung a U-turn to head back to Brooklyn. He punched buttons on his car phone as he wove in and out of traffic. He listened to the whirring ring until he heard a female voice say, "Amanda Russell's office."

"Miss Russell, please. Mister Sebastionelli calling."

She came on immediately, breathless. "Gino? How is he? Did you talk him out of it? If anything happens to him—"

"Oh, ye of little faith. Relax, gorgeous. Gino is on the case. Mission accomplished. Daniel Francis Mulvaney is going home—all the way home this time—and for keeps, I'd be willing to bet."

"Thank God."

"God's busy, beautiful, but I'm free for dinner. How about you?"

About the Author

James D. Robertson was a contributing editor for two non-fiction works, *Doc: Platoon Medic*, a Military Book Club selection by Daniel Evans Jr. (Pocket Books, 1992) and *Steel My Soldiers' Hearts*, a New York Times bestseller by the late Colonel David H. Hackworth (Ruggedland Books, 2002). Mr. Robertson served with the authors in Vietnam.

Robertson is a member of the Mystery Writers of America, International Thriller Writers and Long Island Writers' Guild. *For Good Reason* is his debut novel. *The Woodstock Murders*, a thriller, will be forthcoming from Black Opal Books in 2019. Robertson lives with his wife on Long Island where he is working on his third novel.

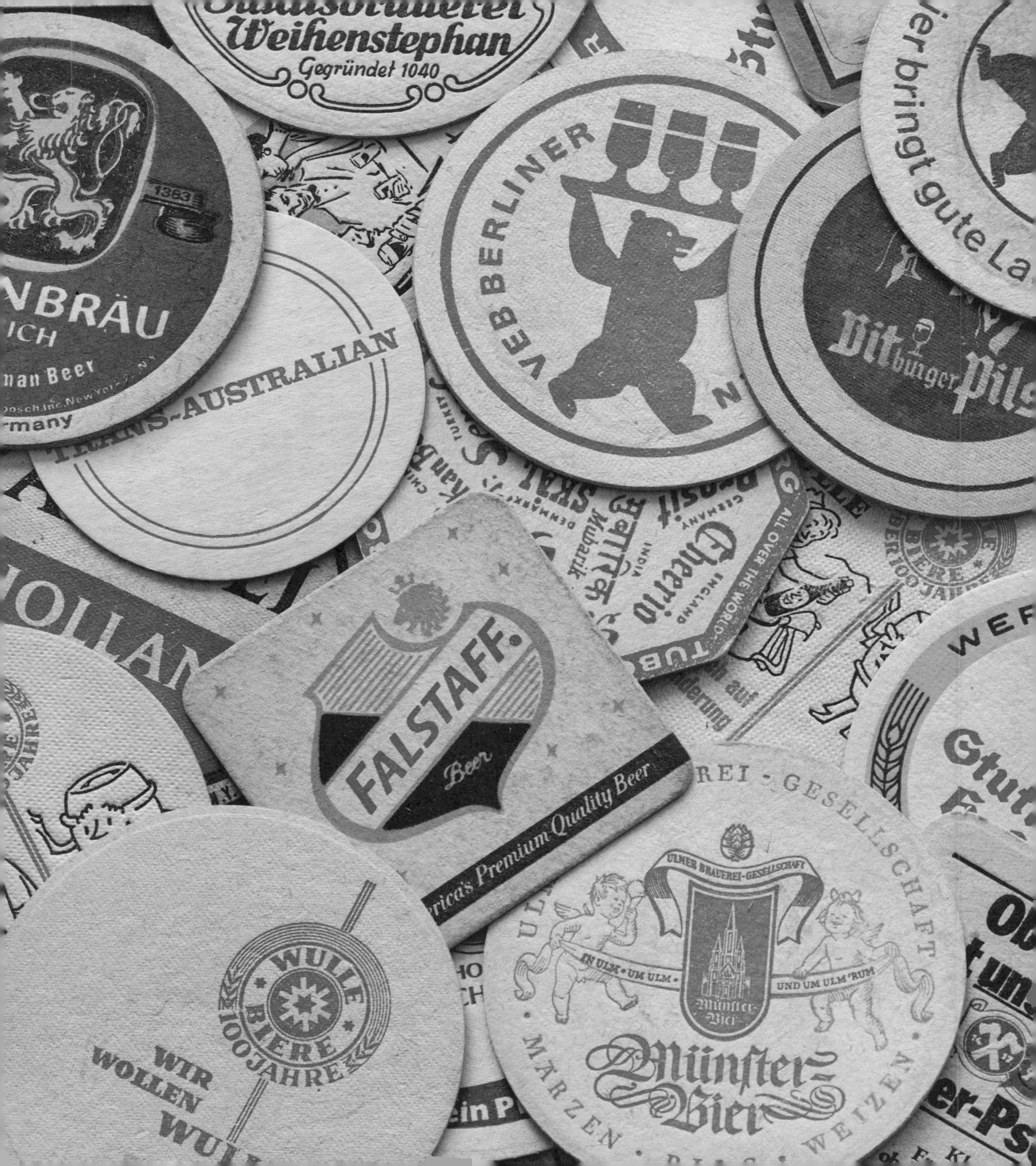

Weihenstephan
Gegründet 1040

VEB BERLINER

bringt gute La

Dit bunger Pils

NBRÄU
ICH
an Beer
Germany

TERNS-AUSTRALIAN

Cheerio

WER

HOLLAN

FALSTAFF·
Beer
America's Premium Quality Beer

Gtu

REI · GESELLSCHAFT

ULMER BRAUEREI-GESELLSCHAFT
IN ULM · UM ULM   UND UM ULM 'RUM
Münster
Bier

WULLE
BIERE
100 JAHRE
WIR
WOLLEN
WULL

Münster-
Bier
MÄRZEN   WEIZEN

BOOZE CRUISE

A TOUR OF
THE WORLD'S ESSENTIAL
MIXED DRINKS

ANDRÉ DARLINGTON

Running Press
PHILADELPHIA

Running Press
Hachette Book Group | 1290 Avenue of the Americas, New York, NY 10104
www.runningpress.com | @Running_Press

Printed in Singapore

First Edition: April 2021

Published by Running Press, an imprint of Perseus Books, LLC, a subsidiary of Hachette Book
Group, Inc. The Running Press name and logo is a trademark of the Hachette Book Group.

The Hachette Speakers Bureau provides a wide range of authors for speaking events.
To find out more, go to www.hachettespeakersbureau.com or call (866) 376-6591.

The publisher is not responsible for websites (or their content)
that are not owned by the publisher.

Print book cover and interior design by Josh McDonnell.

Library of Congress Control Number: 2020947159

ISBNs: 978-0-7624-9785-0 (hardcover), 978-0-7624-9786-7 (ebook)

COS

10 9 8 7 6 5 4 3 2 1

*To the many bartenders around the world
who have made me feel at home.*

Cramers Kunstanstalt KG, Dortmund

98087-C

MW 45
10 ¢

"ONE'S DESTINATION IS NEVER A PLACE, BUT RATHER A NEW WAY OF LOOKING AT THINGS."

—HENRY MILLER

CONTENTS

CHAPTER 4
THE AMERICAS

CHAPTER 5
OCEANIA

Author's Note

The research and travel for this book was completed in early 2020, as COVID-19 spread around the globe. Every attempt has been made to ensure information is accurate and as up-to-date as possible. However, since the time of the first printing there may be changes and closures due to the unprecedented headwinds caused by the pandemic. This book is a celebration of the Craft Cocktail Movement as it has impacted mixed drinks around the world, and of the dedicated people who have made it possible. The bar owners and bartenders highlighted are among the best in the world, and their perseverance in the face of adversity continues to inspire.

Pack Your Bags

"Bizarre travel plans are dancing lessons from God."

—Kurt Vonnegut

When drinks writer Charles H. Baker Jr. traveled around the world in pursuit of cocktails in the 1920s and '30s, he visited a number of remote locations connected by steamship. Some of his stops were hardly more than refueling stations, and the drinking landscape he discovered was one of lonely outposts—hotel bars and private clubs—where thirsty expats huddled around precious bottles of familiar spirits. In the record he made of his trips, *The Gentleman's Companion*, Baker recounts how he and his fellow travelers were often forced to make their own cocktails using whatever they had brought with them. Because for every well-stocked Raffles Bar in Singapore, there was a "bungalow out in Ballygunge" where the Martini-parched had to fend for themselves. The portrait of the world drawn by Baker, one in which mixed drinks were confined to exclusive oases sparsely dotted around the globe, is an accurate depiction for much of cocktail history.

How things have changed.

Now, long sea travel has been replaced by quick airport connections. When eager cocktail aficionados depart for top drinking destinations, they do not head to well-worn ports but to fast-growing major cities. Mixed drinks have firmly taken hold in the commercial centers of the world—at restaurants, nightclubs, rooftop bars, speakeasies, cafés, taverns, and the occasional grocery store. There are serious cocktail establishments in even medium- and smaller-sized cities all over the globe, with many towns boasting full-fledged cocktail scenes.

Today the planet is experiencing a mixed drinks renaissance, and it has all happened relatively recently. Since the new millennium, a cocktail revolution fomented in London and New York has spread to all continents except Antarctica. Not only are classic cocktails now available in large supply, but there are craft bar programs combining honed skills, quality ingredients, and new technology to help reshape mixed drinks as we know them. Add to this a gigantic distillery boom, and there has truly never been a better time to imbibe on Earth.

The book you hold in your hands is a snapshot of cocktailing around the world, of where to drink, what to order, and why. Plus, a little history and necessary how-tos for reproducing each location's signature drinks. The collection is a result of time I have spent as a roving drinks writer, culminating in a circumnavigation of the globe in order to conduct "liquid field research." Like Charles H. Baker Jr., I have traveled in pursuit of exciting potations. I am also interested in how local drinking cultures are making this current global "second cocktail wave" their own. That research is stirred into these pages.

From the world's established and emerging cocktail cities, I have been forced to choose the most distinctive, exemplary, and alluring—whether because of quality, size, value, or vibrancy. Section headnotes explain more about specific traits of major geographical areas. Forty-four cities are represented, a huge endeavor that nevertheless remains just a sampling of the contemporary tableau. Inevitably, there were deserving places I love that were left out.

I hope the selections here will give you a taste of the dizzying variety and creativity of today's cocktail world, and I am excited to share a number of recipes that otherwise would require a voyage around the globe to sample. Above all, I hope this book will inspire you whether you are a drinks maker, adventurer, armchair traveler—or a happy combination of all three.

Getting Around
(How to Use This Book)

Within the five geographic areas listed in this book, I have organized cities alphabetically. In the entry for each city there are two drinks. These are must-try cocktails while in the city or good representations of the drinks found there (the ones that are reproducible). Some cities have multiple signature drinks, and in these instances, I mention the other notables. In some cases, the first selection is historical and the second is a drink that shows what is currently happening in that location. I have included food recipes for a number of cities because nosh helps contextualize liquid culture. Occasionally, I have profiled bartenders around the globe who I think are doing fascinating work. There are also notes on local spirits, what to look for, and, also, what to beware of. When ingredients may not be widely available, I have suggested alternatives. General notes on what craft cocktails are and how to make them are in the Appendix (page 199).

TRAVEL ITEMS

- "Whiskey" is the correct spelling in Ireland and the United States. "Whisky" without the "e" is how it is spelled in Scotland and the rest of the world. Exceptions include US-made George Dickel, Maker's Mark, and Old Forester, which follow the Scottish spelling. I have spelled it "whiskey" to avoid confusion unless a specific product is mentioned.

- By "cocktail" glass, I mean a coupe or martini glass (i.e., the drink is served up and without ice). By "rocks" glass I mean a tumbler, and by "highball" glass I mean a tall cylinder. These are also sometimes called a "collins" glass, although the two are not the same. Collins glasses are taller and thinner.

- Liquor brands are included only when they are specified by the original creator of the recipe or provide a highly specific flavor such as is the case with cucumber in Hendrick's gin.

- Instructions for batching cocktails are on page 199.

- When I use "bar spoon" as a measurement, I mean a few dashes or approximately ¼ of a teaspoon. More cocktail equipment specs and recommendations are found on page 201.

CHAPTER 1

EUROPE

Mixed drinks as we know them today may be the result of American ingenuity, but the[y]
from Old World drinking culture. Europe is where the story of the cocktail begins. As Eu[ropeans]
explored the globe, they brought together rare and prized ingredients. In particular, the[y]
created a beverage called punch, from the Hindu word *paunch*, which was composed of [expen-]
sive ingredients from their East India trade: citrus, spices, and sugar. This punch was cons[umed by]
groups gathered around a big bowl, much like at a fraternity party.

Following the revolutions in America and France, drinking from such communal bowls [fell out]
of favor. Modern, egalitarian-minded citizens desired the luxury ingredients in punch, bu[t would]
not swallow the class-driven culture surrounding it. That, and the hurried new age did not ha[ve time]
to linger over a big vat of anything. Enter the idea of a bespoke drink served quickly. Essenti[ally, a]
cocktail is a single serving of punch made *à la minute* for a busy individual. This "cocktail" we[nt on to]
find great success in the United States until Prohibition sent it into exile abroad. There, it s[urvived]
at bars like the Savoy in London and at Harry's American Bar in Paris. It was in such establis[hments]
that mixed drink culture was preserved and extended.

Today, Europe is gripped by a new wave of cocktail fervor. The continent is a hotbed o[f inno-]
vation, and mixed drinks are becoming as much a part of a night out as traditional beer an[d wine.]
The culinary renaissance that has included a "molecular" revolution in Spain, a multicultur[al boom]
in England, and the rise of New Nordic Cuisine in Denmark, has spilled over into beverage[s. In all]
of Europe's major cities, you will find mixed drinks making inroads. Huge strides have bee[n made]
in a few short few years in cities as diverse as Athens and Stockholm, where cocktail cu[lture is]
relatively new but already extensive. In this chapter, you will encounter recipes based on [classic]
winter warmers as well as sunny refreshers that are recent creations.

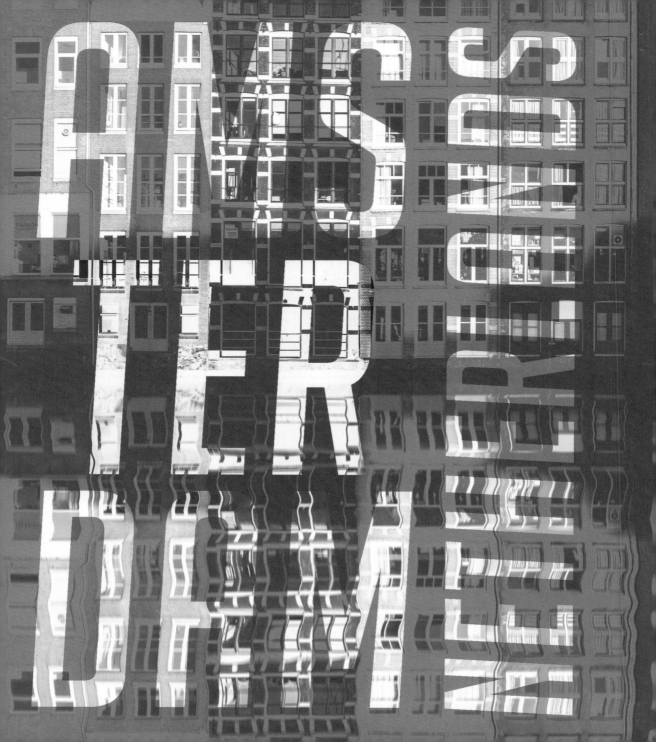

Charming canals and flat streets perfect for bicycling—what makes Amsterdam's pancake-like topography so easy for getting around also makes it a thrilling spot for imbibers. The Netherlands was once a maritime power, and the latticework of Amsterdam's waterways brought the world's spices and fruits back to the heart of its trading empire.

We have the Dutch to thank for curaçao, the orange liqueur hailing from the Caribbean. But more importantly, we have the Dutch to thank for gin. Gin, or *genever* in Holland, is the country's tipple of choice and widely available at tasting rooms around Amsterdam called *proeflokaalen*. It is consumed cold and neat, filled to the brim of a small fluted glass (lean over for the first sip to avoid spilling). Note that genever is different from the London Dry style you are likely familiar with and is more of a funky-flavored malt wine than a gin at all. Once you develop a taste for it, you'll be hooked—which is good, because when classic cocktail recipes call for "Holland Gin," genever is what they mean.

Amsterdam has been trying to chase away its reputation as a stoner and stag party destination for years. Not to say it still isn't one of the great party cities on Earth, but now alongside ladies-for-sale and college students frozen to the sidewalk after popping mind-altering truffles, there are a number of buzzy cocktail bars. A wide range of Prohibition-era speakeasies, molecular cocktail labs, and easygoing watering holes all serve exceptional takes on classics in addition to new inventions. Between all the drinks, don't forget to take in Amsterdam's sensational art.

THE KOPSTOOT

Wander into any Amsterdam bar and the way to get started is a kop-stoot, which translates as "headbutt." This is the Dutch version of the Boilermaker, a beer and a shot. Being Holland, the shot will be local genever. Genever comes from the Dutch word for "juniper." The spirit sailed to London with William of Orange when he ascended the throne of England in 1689, which is the abbreviated explanation of how this lowlands barley liquor made the jump from the land of windmills to the global cocktail stage.

Gin Cocktail

This is one of the original clear spirit cocktails, and it takes pride of place at the beginning of the first cocktail book ever printed, Jerry Thomas's *Bartenders Guide* (1862). The drink combines Holland's two most famous contributions to the cocktail world: genever and curaçao. Think of this as the ancestor to the Dry Martini. In the United States, there are a number of genever brands available. Chief among them is Bols, a company that makes both a line of flavored liqueurs and genevers. Gum syrup, sometimes spelled gomme syrup, is available at specialty cocktail stores and online.

2 ounces genever
1 bar spoon gum syrup
1 bar spoon orange curaçao
1 dash orange bitters

Stir ingredients with ice and strain into a cocktail glass.

Genever Old Fashioned

It would be a sad cocktail world indeed without Holland's fruit brandy contribution, curaçao. Without curaçao there would be no triple sec (the French version), meaning the combined loss of Sidecars, Margaritas, Cosmopolitans, Mai Tais, and more. The story of curaçao goes that when the Dutch took over the eponymous island in 1634, they found orchards full of bitter Valencia oranges. The oranges were unsuitable for eating, but good for making liqueur. This cocktail harkens back to a type of drink called a "smash," in which fruit is muddled in the glass in order to express flavorful oils from the rind. While it might look similar to a Gin Cocktail, it is worlds apart in depth of flavor.

1 sugar cube
2 dashes Angostura bitters
2 dashes orange curaçao
1 orange peel
2 ounces genever

Muddle sugar, bitters, curaçao, and the orange peel in the bottom of a rocks glass. Fill glass with ice and genever, and stir.

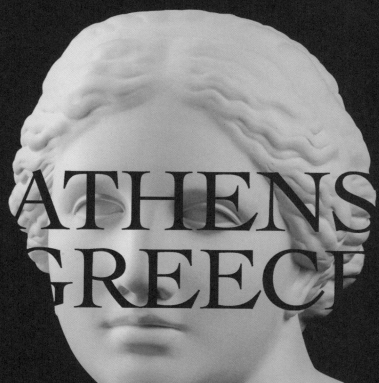

ATHENS GREECE

Nikos Kazantzakis writes in *Zorba the Greek* that all you need in life is a glass of wine, a handful of chestnuts, and something to roast them on. Agreed, except replace the wine with a proper cocktail. Kazantzakis's celebration of Grecian simplicity rings true even in the country's bustling and chaotic capital, Athens. All it takes to be happy in this ancient city is food you can eat with your hands and a stiff drink.

Greece's economic troubles are still a recent memory in this relatively small (as European capitals go) city, but in the wake of the upheaval there has been a flowering of creativity reminiscent of Berlin after reunification. Athens surges with creative energy. It is strange, then, that so many visitors perceive it as merely a jumping-off point to the Greek islands. This is a big mistake.

Athens is one of the most exciting places in which to have a mixed drink. Elegant rooftops, sexy cocktail dens, and modern taverns all seduce with their inventive menus and command of flavors. There is excitement here, and the Grecian love of nightlife makes the city a mecca for bar-hopping. For the adventurous, Athens offers up an experience that is arty and gritty, with a connection to elementary ingredients as primal as Zorba the Greek.

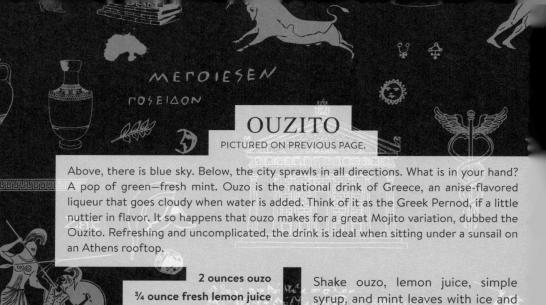

OUZITO

PICTURED ON PREVIOUS PAGE.

Above, there is blue sky. Below, the city sprawls in all directions. What is in your hand? A pop of green—fresh mint. Ouzo is the national drink of Greece, an anise-flavored liqueur that goes cloudy when water is added. Think of it as the Greek Pernod, if a little nuttier in flavor. It so happens that ouzo makes for a great Mojito variation, dubbed the Ouzito. Refreshing and uncomplicated, the drink is ideal when sitting under a sunsail on an Athens rooftop.

2 ounces ouzo
¾ ounce fresh lemon juice
½ ounce simple syrup
4 mint leaves, plus a sprig
2 ounces club soda

Shake ouzo, lemon juice, simple syrup, and mint leaves with ice and pour into a highball glass. Top with soda and garnish with a sprig of mint.

SKINOS HIGHBALL

Skinos is a liqueur made from the resin of the mastiha tree. Hailing from the island of Chios, the sap from this rare plant has been prized for centuries and commercially harvested at least since 600 B.C.E. Skinos has a musky pine flavor with just a touch of mintiness. It provides a unique base for cocktails and immediately conjures up a sense of place—you are, without a doubt, in Greece. A highball is a good way to experience this complex liqueur.

2 ounces Skinos Mastiha
4 ounces club soda
Cucumber slice, for garnish

Pour ingredients over ice and stir. Garnish with a cucumber slice.

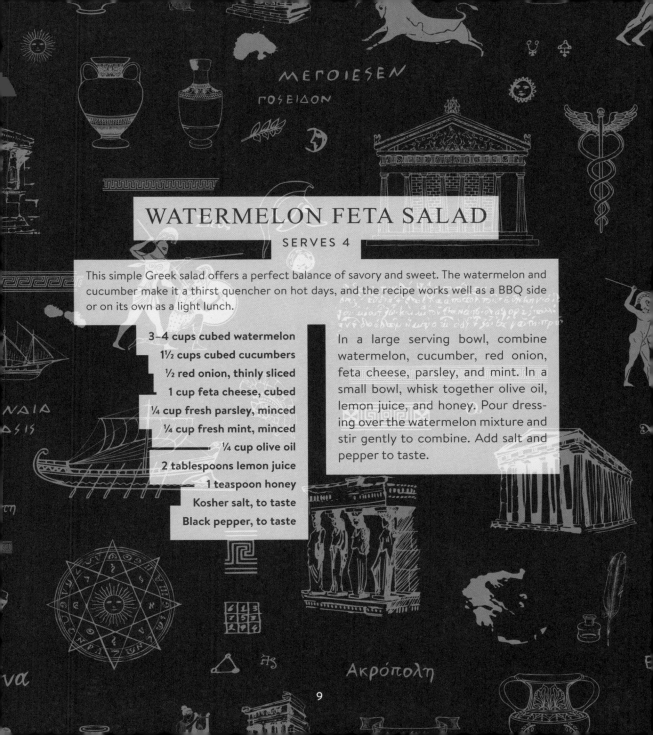

WATERMELON FETA SALAD

SERVES 4

This simple Greek salad offers a perfect balance of savory and sweet. The watermelon and cucumber make it a thirst quencher on hot days, and the recipe works well as a BBQ side or on its own as a light lunch.

3–4 cups cubed watermelon
1½ cups cubed cucumbers
½ red onion, thinly sliced
1 cup feta cheese, cubed
¼ cup fresh parsley, minced
¼ cup fresh mint, minced
¼ cup olive oil
2 tablespoons lemon juice
1 teaspoon honey
Kosher salt, to taste
Black pepper, to taste

In a large serving bowl, combine watermelon, cucumber, red onion, feta cheese, parsley, and mint. In a small bowl, whisk together olive oil, lemon juice, and honey. Pour dressing over the watermelon mixture and stir gently to combine. Add salt and pepper to taste.

BERLIN

GERMANY

Berlin defines cool. It is youthful, sexy, and layered in complex strata like a dark and tempting cake. It is a city of fantasies—a place where everyone is free to create their own path, however strange. To this end, Berlin parties hard and exists as a kind of anarchic judgment-free zone in which all are invited to exorcise anxieties and inhibitions. Young or old, Berliners are searching, evolving, and dancing into the future to a techno beat.

In a town where the main industry is clubbing, it might be unexpected to find a developed cocktail culture. But that would be to misunderstand Berlin; here everything is possible, even a well-made cocktail while wearing a latex bodysuit.

Although gentrifying fast, Berlin is still inexpensive compared to other European capitals. The city is a bargain in terms of service and quality. Note that mixed in with the bars and pubs (called *Kneipen*) there are unique businesses called *Spätis*—late-night grocery stores that function as staging areas for those inevitable big Berlin nights out. These humble spots occupy a gray zone somewhere between bodega and local tavern and are an experience unique to the city. Think of Spätis as the rest stops on the Autobahn of excess.

SPÄTI "GOLDEN RATIO" COCKTAIL

Spätis are holdovers from East German culture that are now an integral part of nightlife in unified Berlin. Meeting friends at these little stores is so popular that the activity has its own slang verb, "kornern"—as in, "to street corner." Inside a Späti you will find liquors and juices suited to making cocktails on the fly. While the available ingredients won't exactly make for high-end libations, they do provide great opportunities for practicing cocktail ratios. With a little math, it is possible to make a good drink. Below is the most helpful ratio for Spätis:

2 ounces base spirit (vodka and gin work well)
¾ ounce sweet
¾ ounce sour or bitter

Pour ingredients into a plastic cup filled with ice and stir.

KAISER SOUR

Kümmel is a clear caraway liqueur that boasts notes of cumin and fennel. It is difficult to overstate how enjoyable it is in cocktails. The taste is anise, but it is also wonderfully citrus-y and peppery. Kümmel is widely available in liquor stores and online.

2 ounces kümmel
1 ounce fresh lemon juice
½ ounce simple syrup
Lemon peel, for garnish

Shake ingredients with ice and strain into a cocktail glass. Garnish with a lemon peel.

OLIVER EBERT & CRISTINA NEVES

"The flavor of Berlin in a glass is kümmel, or caraway seed," says Oliver Ebert, owner of the bar Becketts Kopf with his partner Cristina Neves. Known for its gigantic stock of local spirits, the couple's bar in Berlin's Prenzlauer Berg neighborhood is a study in curation. Ebert and Neves have spent years collecting obscure bottles from Germany, Austria, and Switzerland—including a category called *Kornbranntwein*, a kind of German vodka. *Korn*, as it is referred to, is often consumed as a shot along with a beer. When drunk together this is called a "Herrengedeck," translated as "Gentleman's Menu." Also on offer are *Obstbrands*, or fruit brandies, from local distillers. The brandies come in many varieties, distilled from oranges, rhubarb, sunchokes, and more—and all find their way into the bar's creative cocktails. By sourcing ingredients from regional makers, Ebert and Neves have turned Becketts Kopf into an homage to distillation itself, and the bar's drinks exhibit a distinct sense of place.

BUDAPEST
HUNGARY

Straddling the wide Danube river, the capital of the Magyars is a romance of stunning architecture. There are art nouveau–style buildings, Hapsburg palaces, Ottoman monuments, and even a few Roman ruins thrown in for good measure. The city is a wild pastiche, and it helps to know that it was formed when three cities were merged into one: Buda on the western bank, Pest on the eastern side, and Óbuda to the north. More important for cocktailers, however, is the fact that Budapest is the nightlife hub of central Europe. What's more, here liquor reigns supreme. Spirits run in the city's blood—literally—so do not be surprised when you see locals downing shots in the morning before work.

The city's main party district is in the old Jewish Quarter, the hub for so-called "ruin bars," which are arty, makeshift establishments that feel a bit like flea markets. They offer an eclectic backdrop for getting soused. Budapest is a nocturnal wonderland, and one of the least expensive places in Europe to order a cocktail. Sophisticated options abound, and bars make use of local liquors such as fruit brandies called *pálinka*.

As an added bonus, thermal baths are a way of life in Budapest. Go early in the morning to avoid the crowds, and spend time relaxing and sweating out toxins following a night out. It is a shvitz (bath) and slivovitz life, and it is mighty fine. Note that on Saturdays some of the bathhouses throw raging pool parties called *sparties*, replete with DJs and club lighting. They get wilder than Vegas.

Pálinka & Ginger

Pálinka is Hungary's local brandy. It can be made with a wide variety of stone fruits. The most famous of these abroad is slivovitz, a plum brandy. There's good news for you, then, if you have been wondering what to do with that old bottle of sliv on your parents' shelf: mix it with ginger beer. In this version, apricot is the pálinka flavor of choice.

1½ ounces apricot brandy

3 ounces ginger beer

½ ounce fresh lime juice

2 dashes Angostura bitters, for garnish

Combine ingredients in a highball glass filled with ice and stir. Top with bitters.

Zwack Negroni

"You taste Zwack and you cannot really decide if you like it or not. But then you take the second sip and the third, and you end up loving it," says Zoltán Nagy of Budapest's well-known Boutiq'Bar. And it is true, Hungary's national liqueur, Unicum (made by the company Zwack) is something of an acquired taste. It is a bit like Jägermeister, but with an even more medicinal and bitter flavor. While a bit much to drink straight, it makes for a knockout Negroni variation.

1½ ounces gin

1 ounce Aperol

¾ ounce Zwack Unicum

Grapefruit peel, for garnish

Stir ingredients with ice and strain into a rocks glass filled with ice. Garnish with a grapefruit peel.

CHICKEN PAPRIKASH

SERVES 4–6

This famous Hungarian one-pot meal is aces for cocktailers. The dish can be completed entirely on the stovetop in under an hour (about the time it takes to consume a couple of mixed drinks), and delivers a full-flavored crowd pleaser. In this gadget-obsessed age, it is good to remember that special equipment is not required to make fast, delicious meals. Hugely popular in the 1970s and '80s, paprikash deserves a revival.

1 package egg noodles

2 tablespoons unsalted butter

6 chicken thighs

½ teaspoon kosher salt

½ teaspoon freshly ground black pepper

2 onions, diced

½ teaspoon caraway seeds

2 garlic cloves, minced

1 cup chicken stock

2 cups tomatoes, diced

2 tablespoons Hungarian paprika

½ cup sour cream

Cook noodles according to package instructions. Meanwhile, heat butter in a large saucepan over medium heat. Pat chicken pieces dry and season with salt and pepper. Working in batches, brown chicken pieces on both sides. Remove to a plate and set aside. Add onions and caraway seeds to the pan and sauté until the onions are tender, about 4 minutes. Add garlic and sauté 1 minute more. Add stock, and stir in tomatoes and paprika. Next, add chicken, skin side up. Bring to a boil, reduce heat, and simmer one hour with the lid ajar until chicken is cooked through and falling off the bone. Turn off heat, remove chicken from pan, and set aside. Stir sour cream into the sauce. To serve, place a piece of chicken on top of noodles and cover with the sauce.

The Danish capital is a global culinary and cultural trendsetter, so it is no surprise that the city's relatively recent adoption of mixed drinks is already showing huge promise. Following in the wake of New Nordic Cuisine (which made Copenhagen an international gastronomic superpower), cocktail bars have overcome Denmark's beer-centric roots to garner global acclaim.

Stylish and erudite, the Danes exude effortless cool. This natural élan comes across in their mixed drinks, which tend to be well-thought-out works of art. The stylish sippers fit right in with all the clean-lined Scandinavian furniture and lighting. Make no mistake, this is one elegant and design-y town in which to drink. But that is not to say Copenhagen's "Scandi cool" is superficial. In fact, this is one of the smartest and most environmentally conscious cities on Earth. Maybe the focus on sustainability contributes to why, according to a scientific study by the University of Lister, the Danes are among the happiest people on the planet. They are so happy, in fact, that there is a Danish term for a specific kind of happiness, *hygge*. Pronounced "HOO-ga," this untranslatable word means something like "the sense of coziness and conviviality that leads to a feeling of well-being." You find it in spades in Copenhagen's bars.

DILL AQUAVIT MARTINI

Aquavit has been produced in Scandinavia since the fifteenth century. It is a clear spirit made from either potatoes or grains that is then flavored with herbs. According to EU regulations, it must taste primarily of caraway and dill seed. While many versions are quite herbaceous, it can be of great benefit to add fresh dill in order to bring more flavor to cocktails.

2½ ounces dill-infused aquavit

½ ounce dry vermouth

1 dash orange bitters, for garnish

Stir aquavit and vermouth with ice and strain into a chilled cocktail glass. Garnish with a dash of orange bitters.

FOR THE DILL-INFUSED AQUAVIT
Wash and dry a few sprigs of dill. Place in a sealable container with aquavit and let sit in a refrigerator overnight. For a stronger herb flavor, steep longer. Once strained and stored in a sealed container, the infused aquavit will keep indefinitely.

CHERRY HEERING HOT TODDY

Nearly every Dane can agree on the flavor licorice, and it appears in many of Copenhagen's drinks. Cherry Heering is a liqueur made in Denmark and employed in a number of classic cocktails, most notably the Blood and Sand. It makes for an unforgettable toddy.

6 ounces licorice tea

1 ounce aquavit

1 ounce Cherry Heering

1 bar spoon fresh lemon juice

½ ounce honey, or to taste

Brew tea according to instructions and pour into a mug. Add aquavit, Heering, lemon juice, and honey. Stir and serve.

SMØRREBRØD

SERVES 4

Smørrebrød is a small, open-faced sandwich traditionally served on rye bread. Typical toppings are cold cuts or fish. You will also often see potato as a topping, and it makes an appealingly earthy accompaniment to aquavit. In this flavorful recipe, salmon roe, red onion, and cucumber add pops of color and flavor for a wowing presentation. This recipe makes an ideal centerpiece for a Scandinavian-inspired brunch.

4 Yukon Gold potatoes, peeled

2 tablespoons rice wine vinegar

⅛ teaspoon kosher salt

¼ teaspoon ground black pepper

1½ teaspoons grainy mustard

2 tablespoons chopped fresh chives

2 tablespoons olive oil

¼ cup crème fraîche

2 teaspoons horseradish

4 slices brown rye or pumpernickel bread

4 eggs, hard boiled and sliced

½ medium red onion, diced

2 tablespoons salmon roe

2 pickling or other small cucumbers, very thinly sliced

In a medium pot, cover potatoes with cold water and bring to a boil. Lower heat and simmer until potatoes are tender, about 15 minutes. Drain and set aside to cool. In a medium bowl, whisk together vinegar, salt, pepper, mustard, chives, and olive oil and set aside. When potatoes have cooled, cut into ¼-inch cubes and stir them gently into the dressing. In a small bowl, combine crème fraîche and horseradish. To assemble sandwiches, spread crème fraiche mixture onto the bread slices and top with potatoes. Place three egg slices on each bread. Top with small mounds of red onion, salmon roe, and cucumber.

DUBLIN

IRELAND

"Good puzzle would be to cross Dublin without passing a pub," reflects Leopold Bloom, James Joyce's protagonist in *Ulysses*. And it is true, the city is full of pubs awash in Guinness and whiskey—which is why it is fascinating that cocktail culture is making such serious inroads here. In the last few years, there has been a surge of interest in mixed drinks, and good examples are now available on chic terraces and at swanky rooftop bars. All this stands to reason as cosmopolitan Dublin comes of age on the global stage; young Irish have traveled abroad and returned home, bringing back visions of drinking scenes elsewhere.

What sets the Irish capital apart as it adopts global cocktail culture is Dubliners' unsurpassed wit, refreshing humility, and easygoing style. Drinking on the Emerald Isle is something special. For one, you will meet people at bars, whether you want to or not. For two, you will return with great stories. Dublin is a city of the tallest of tales and the most humorous anecdotes. The bartenders practically kill you with charm, and if you are looking for some of the best drinking companions in the world, no one beats the Irish.

POITÍN

You know the Green Isle makes whiskey, but be on the lookout for *Poitín*, or Irish moonshine. Made in monasteries and homes for hundreds of years—but suppressed by authorities until 1997—Poitín was finally granted Geographical Indicative Status by the European Union in 2008. Pronounced *potcheen*, it is a clear spirit with floral and grassy notes. Beware there are bad versions, which as the locals say, "taste like shite." Many new distilleries are getting into the game and making fantastic examples. Additionally, a few cocktail bars are using the native liquor in cocktails. Consider, however, that the Gaelic word for hangover is *poít*. You have been warned.

TRADITIONAL LIMERICK

Two foreigners joined with the crew
The captain roared out, "Who are you?"
The one from Bay Biscay
Said, "Letsav Awiski"
The other, "Don Cariff Fydoo."

23

Irish Coffee

The story goes that this drink was created in the 1940s by bartender Joe Sheridan for a group of seaplane passengers. The plane had just arrived at the port in Foynes, and when handed the drink, one of the shivering recipients asked, "Is this Colombian coffee?" Old Sheridan replied, "No, this is Irish coffee." The moniker stuck, and the drink has gone on to become a global sensation.

1½ ounces Irish whiskey
2 teaspoons sugar (preferably Demerara)
1 cup strong black coffee
¼ cup fresh cream, lightly whipped

Pour heated water into a glass or mug, swirl, and discard. Add Irish whiskey and sugar to the glass, stir, and add the coffee. Slowly pour cream over the back of a spoon on top of the drink.

Tipperary

This most famous of Irish cocktails first appeared in Hugo R. Ensslin's 1917 book *Recipes for Mixed Drinks*. It is likely named for the song, "It's a Long Way to Tipperary," which was sung by homesick Irish soldiers in the British army during World War I. The classic version includes ½ ounce of Chartreuse mixed into the drink. However, I follow the lead of legendary bartender and writer Gary Regan and recommend lightly rinsing the glass instead.

Green Chartreuse, to rinse the glass
2 ounces Irish whiskey
1 ounce sweet vermouth
Lemon twist, for garnish

Rinse a cocktail glass with Chartreuse. Stir whiskey and vermouth with ice and strain into the awaiting glass. Garnish with a lemon twist.

Traveler, Kyiv is epic. The city began as a Slavic settlement on the trade route between Scandinavia and Constantinople, thrived under the Vikings, was sacked by the Mongols, saw fighting during the Bolshevik Revolution, starved under Stalin, suffered through German occupation, survived Chernobyl (now a popular day trip), and remains engaged in a power struggle with Russia. What's not to understand? This town *needs* a drink.

Tossing off their Soviet past like another hassle in their difficult history, Kyivites are currently enjoying a renaissance. This includes mixed drinks, which are muscling their way into traditional drinking culture centered around vodka and beer. The city is cocktail-mad and teeming with excellent bartenders who know their technique.

Buildings that look like they are from a fairy-tale plus cool, hidden art galleries form an eclectic backdrop to the drinking experience in Kyiv. There are lush gardens, wide boulevards, and murals that are street-art masterpieces. The locals are gregarious and quirky and make for great carousing companions. All this, and the city remains shockingly inexpensive. Is Ukraine's capital cocktail heaven?

UKRAINE'S UNIQUE BEVERAGES

Ukraine boasts a number of fermented and distilled beverages that shape its drinking culture. These may appear in cocktails, and it is good to be on familiar terms with them: *horilka* is a grain distillate traditionally mixed with dried fruit and herbs. It might also contain nuts or milk. A moonshine version is called *samohon*, and a very popular style with spicy chile peppers is called *pertsivka*. A fruit liqueur called *Spotykach* is flavored with berries and spices. Liquor infusions, called *nalyvkas*, come in hundreds of flavors—a popular one being horseradish, called *hrinovukha*. *Medovukha* is a version of mead made with fermented honey and was once the region's most famous export. *Varenukha* is a traditional spice-infused vodka created by heating ingredients together in clay pots or in pumpkins over an open fire. *Ryazhenka* is Ukrainian fermented milk, similar to a runny yogurt.

BEETROOT SOUR

Kvass is a Slavic fermented beverage often made from rye bread, but it also can be made from beets, berries, and even tree sap (see sidebar on Ukraine's fermented beverages, page 27). The drink is slightly effervescent and tends to be a bit sour. Kvass of all kinds are widely available at health-food stores. Here, it is a fizzy addition to a wowing sour.

1½ ounces vodka

½ ounce fresh lemon juice

½ ounce simple syrup

1 egg white

2 ounces beet kvass

Shake vodka, lemon juice, simple syrup, and egg white vigorously without ice (known as a "dry shake"). Add ice, shake again, and strain into a cocktail glass. Pour kvass into the shaker and swirl to dislodge any remaining froth. Gently pour this mixture into the drink.

ROASTED CHESTNUT OLD FASHIONED

Kyiv is known as the Chestnut City because so many of the trees line its streets. By some estimates, there are over two million of them in Ukraine's capital. If you visit in spring, the trees' white-pink flowers are resplendent. As both a symbol and a readily available ingredient, the nuts frequently make their way into cocktails. Their sweet and earthy flavor, more similar to a sweet potato than a nut, make for one of the world's great Old Fashioneds.

¼ ounce chestnut simple syrup (recipe below)

2 dashes Angostura bitters

2 ounces rye whiskey

Orange peel, for garnish

In a rocks glass, combine simple syrup and bitters. Add ice and whiskey, and stir. Express oil from the orange peel over the drink by twisting it, and then place it in the glass.

FOR THE CHESTNUT SIMPLE SYRUP

Heat oven to 425°F. Using a knife, score 1 cup chestnuts (about eight) with an "x" on one side. This is important to do so the nuts do not explode. Roast for 15–20 minutes, or until skin is dark brown and peeling back at the score marks. Let cool for a few minutes, and remove outer shell and inner skin. It is easiest to do this while the nuts are still hot. Chop chestnuts roughly and add to a sealable container with 1 cup sugar and 1 cup water. Shake and rest mixture in a refrigerator overnight or up to 72 hours. Strain through a fine-mesh strainer and keep in a refrigerator for up to a week.

LONDON
ENGLAND

Ice crackin', garnish smackin' London. With a cocktail scene second to none, and being the city with the most bars on Earth, London is one of the world's top drink destinations. The Big Smoke positively wows with the variety of its establishments, as well as the level of service and ingenuity. There are Martinis served tableside from trolley carts, deluxe drinks presented inside smoky terrariums, and robust cocktails that will have you dancing the night away. From gilded gin palaces to rough-and-tumble whiskey bars, the full gamut is on offer here. A cocktailer's night can be spent in historic gin lanes or at new cocktail labs.

The reach of the city's empire brought the world's flavors to London's doorstep early, and as a consequence, a varied and multicultural drinking ethos runs deep. Add to that a craft cocktail revival that set the city apart early, and it is easy to see why London is such a global leader in mixed drinks. But what truly separates London from its peers is attitude. Here, a high level of sophistication is matched by an easygoing approach. In London, there is always a playful sense of adventure.

Pimm's Cup

This refreshing concoction was created by the owner of an oyster bar, and it is one of the best drink pairings with bivalves. The Pimm's Cup is the quintessential London cocktail, and it comes in a few variations; the most widely known employs ginger beer as a mixer. Because a single Pimm's is never enough, the drink is a great candidate for making by the pitcher for summer garden parties. To construct a larger version, convert ounces to cups in the recipe below.

4 mint leaves
Cucumber slices
½ ounce fresh lemon juice
2 ounces Pimm's No. 1
5 ounces ginger beer
Strawberry, for garnish

Muddle mint leaves and cucumber with lemon juice in a rocks glass. Add Pimm's, ice, and top with ginger beer. Stir and garnish with a strawberry.

Bramble

In the early days of the Craft Cocktail Movement, London cocktailer Dick Bradsell developed this drink as an English answer to the Singapore Sling. It is one of the great inventions of that era and is found on bar menus around the world.

2 ounces gin
¾ ounce fresh lemon juice
¼ ounce simple syrup
½ ounce crème de mûre
3 blackberries, for garnish
Lemon wheel, for garnish

Shake gin, lemon juice, and simple syrup with ice and strain into a rocks glass filled with ice. Pour crème de mûre over the top of the drink and garnish with blackberries and a lemon wheel.

THE GINAISSANCE

It is no secret that gin is experiencing a global boom. All over the world, the spirit is on the rise and getting a makeover with local herbs and spices. But it is perhaps in England where this explosion is most evident. The number of English distilleries has more than tripled in the last decade. In London, this means enthusiasts can visit distilleries, stop in gin museums, and even go to a gin school. Two brands to look for while in the Big Smoke are the legendary Beefeater Gin and the craft distiller Sipsmith. Sipsmith, opened in 2009, was the first new copper pot distillery in London in over two hundred years.

Maybe it is because Madrid lacks obvious tourist icons like the Eiffel Tower or the Colosseum that it fails to capture the global imagination the way other major European capitals do. This is curious, because Spain's biggest city is not only stuffed with some of the world's best art, but it has fully embraced the creativity of the country's gastronomic revolution. What's more, Madrileños boast one of the planet's most unique and enviable dining styles—let's call it "small bites carousing." After work, the city throngs to tapas bars and begins a frenzied adventure of drinks and snacks until the wee hours. Nights out in Madrid are something to experience—energetic and unfettered affairs that stretch on without end.

The ease with which Spaniards segue from work to play is likely the result of a long history of doing it. Spain is Europe's original world superpower, reaching its peak during the Age of Discovery in the seventeenth century. Hemingway was so impressed by Spain's cosmopolitanism that he called Madrid "the world's capital." Yet for all the variety and worldliness, one cocktail dominates at the expense of all others: the Gin & Tonic, or as it is known locally, *Gintonica*.

The Gintonica is religion in Spain the way Martinis were in 1950s America. At happy hour, expect to see the city's watering holes filled to the brim with patrons holding big, bulbous wine goblets overflowing with gin, tonic, and ice. Frequently, there will be dramatic seasonal garnishes. This is one of the world's great examples of a cocktail becoming a lifestyle. Mixing with this fanatic Gintonica culture, there are a number of craft cocktail bars. Expect well-made classic drinks with an occasional unique twist.

Gintonica

As much ritual as refreshment, the Gintonica is Spain's national cocktail. No matter where you go in the country, it will always be made by a bartender employing two small tongs to do the handiwork—and it will be impeccably constructed whether at a casual outdoor café or in a sophisticated bar. The Spanish are particular about gin, and prefer brands like Mahon, Larios, Gin Mare, and Tanqueray. They are also selective about tonic water and use either Fever Tree or Schweppes. Accept no substitutes.

2½ ounces gin

1 bottle (6.8 ounces)
Fever Tree tonic water

Lemon peel, for garnish

Fill a large wine glass to the top with ice. Pour in gin and tonic, and stir with a bar spoon. Twist a lemon peel to express the oil over the drink, rub the peel around the rim of the glass, and drop it into the drink.

Rebujito

The origin of this drink is murky, but it likely hails from the southern part of Spain, where English expats employed sherry in cocktails at home gatherings. It took hold in the 1980s and can be found throughout Andalucía as well as further north in Madrid. The name means, romantically, "a little tangle." Note there are variations that sport 7UP or ginger ale. Whatever the mixer, be sure to squeeze in some lemon juice to provide a lift of fresh citrus.

2 ounces fino or manzanilla sherry

4 ounces soda or tonic water

Lemon wedge

Sprig of mint, for garnish

Add sherry and tonic to a glass filled with ice. Squeeze a lemon wedge into the drink and garnish with a sprig of mint.

Pan Tomate

SERVES 4

Translated as "tomato bread," this classic bite is served in bars across Spain. Like all very simple recipes, the essence of the dish is in the details. It contains just five ingredients, but the quality and consistency of each is extremely important. Typically, the bread used is closer to ciabatta than baguette, but good French bread works as well. Also, if you can source good Spanish olive oil, you will be rewarded with its sweetness as compared to Italian or Californian. Serve pan tomate with cocktails and a bottle of ice-cold Manzanilla sherry such as La Gitana. To make a meal, throw in a large hunk of Manchego cheese.

4 cold roma tomatoes

1 loaf ciabatta, split in half horizontally lengthwise and cut crosswise into 3–4 inch slices

1 cup olive oil (preferably Spanish)

Flaky sea salt, such as Maldon or fleur de sel

Using a box grater, rub tomatoes over the grates using the palm of your hand. The flesh will grate off while most of the skin remains intact in your hand. Discard skin and refrigerate grated tomatoes. Adjust oven rack to top rack below broiler and preheat broiler to high. Place bread, cut side up, on a tray and broil until crisp and starting to brown, 2 to 3 minutes. Remove bread from the oven and spoon on tomatoes. Drizzle liberally with extra-virgin olive oil and season with flaky sea salt.

PARIS

FRANCE

Old men wheel down the street on bicycles, baguettes tucked under their arms. Women stroll past carrying baskets of flowers and chocolates. Paris is a movie set come to life, each passerby more charming than the next. If this sounds like a magical place to spend time quaffing cocktails, it is. With cafés dotting every corner, the City of Lights is one of the best spots in the world to just sit, drink, and people-watch.

Observing life from a bistro chair, it is easy to imagine the 1920s expats here, the "Lost Generation" as Gertrude Stein called them—Hemingway, Djuna Barnes, Fitzgerald, and Dos Passos, among others. They came because Paris was the cultural capital of the Western World and because they could drink. Prohibition had descended like a black curtain in January 1920, and droves of American creatives decamped to Europe. Paris was the top destination, a place where living was cheap and new ideas of sexual liberation created a heady mix when blended with absinthe.

The bar to go to in the '20s was Harry's New York Bar, so-named because its original owner moved an entire bar counter physically across the ocean. And it was at Harry's where so many Prohibition-era drinks received their due, particularly the French 75 and the Sidecar—both essential Jazz Age tipples.

However, it is a mistake to dwell only on Paris's storied cocktail history and not mention that the city boasts a dynamic, contemporary mixed drinks scene. While the New York Bar remains an unmissable destination, there are new essential stops such as Experimental Cocktail Club, the epicenter of the city's cocktail resurgence, and Le Syndicat, where bartenders use exclusively French spirits. With a new generation of cocktailers shaking things up, Paris's future looks as bright as its past.

FRENCH 75

Named for an artillery gun in World War I, this classic cocktail packs a wallop. It is also one of the world's great go-to drinks, owing to its near-universal appeal. Everyone enjoys gin, lemon, and bubbly together. If you find yourself in Paris, the cocktail is best consumed with Cognac swapped out for gin.

1½ ounces gin

¾ ounce fresh lemon juice

½ ounce simple syrup

2 ounces Champagne,
   or other sparkling wine

Lemon peel, for garnish

Shake gin, lemon juice, and simple syrup with ice. Strain over ice into a collins glass. Top with champagne and garnish with a lemon peel.

SIDECAR

This cocktail's origins are disputed, but what is sure is that it became famous at Harry's New York Bar in Paris. Bartender Harry MacElhone included the drink in his *Harry's ABC of Mixing Cocktails* in 1930, and it has been associated with the Lost Generation ever since. It is named for the sidecar of a motorcycle, an accessory that in the '30s was almost as popular as the drink.

Sugar, to rim the glass

2 ounces brandy

1 ounce Cointreau

¾ ounce fresh lemon juice

Orange peel, for garnish

Prepare a cocktail glass by wetting the rim and dipping it in sugar. Shake remaining ingredients with ice and strain into the prepared glass. Garnish with an orange peel.

Plateau de Fromages

Cheese and cocktails are a symbiotic match; alcohol cuts the fat and enhances the flavor notes in cheese, while a cheese board allows you to focus on making drinks instead of cooking. However, there are a few guidelines for constructing a successful cheese board: First, serve what is in season (ask your cheesemonger). Second, arrange a mix of colors and textures by selecting varying styles such as soft, washed rind, hard pressed, and blue. Third, always serve cheese at room temperature. Cheese must "relax" in order to yield up its full depth of flavor. Finally, to keep a board interesting, choose cheeses made from a variety of milks. Most cheese shops have signs indicating what animals were used for milk.

1 cow cheese
1 sheep cheese
1 goat cheese
1 blue cheese

Organize your plateau in progression of mildest to strongest-flavored cheese. Let cheeses relax on a board until they are at room temperature, about an hour. Serve with nuts, fruit jam, and warm baguette.

PRAGUE
CZECHOSLOVAKIA

The sunsets over Prague are stunners. They descend over the spired skyline, melting onto the city's fairy-tale buildings and cobblestone streets below. This is the ideal time to be nursing the evening's first cocktail at one of the city's rooftop bars. After the sun is down, then the partying begins.

Luckily, the capital of the Czech Republic is both sophisticated and rowdy. What's more, while it has a reputation as a serious beer town, cocktails flourish here. There is no shortage of dark, stylish bars in which to experience imaginative creations as well as classics. You will be intrigued, entertained, and likely even awed. Just keep in mind that Prague is no longer an undiscovered gem, and you will be picking your way past stag parties and mainstream dance halls to find civilized watering holes.

Happily, the effort is worth it. Prague is one of Europe's least expensive and most creative havens for well-made drinks. Friendly staff know their technique and like to put on a show. It is interesting to note that Prague has acted as an incubator for bartender talent worldwide. While out, you might spy the next big mixologist, following in the footsteps of a group dubbed the "Czech-Slovac Bar Mafia." Members have gone on to make their mark in London, Sydney, Singapore, and other major cocktail cities.

A word of warning about Prague's absinthe. Unscrupulous promoters have seized on tourist interest in absinthe that contains the active ingredient thujone. Thujone is illegal in the United States and elsewhere. Most absinthe in Prague is fake, green-colored vodka with added wormwood extract containing thujone. Look for reputable brands such as St. Antoine or La Grenouille. The staff at Hemingway Bar is particularly knowledgeable and can assist in further exploration.

BETON

This is a twist on the Gin & Tonic that employs local liqueur Becherovka instead of gin. Becherovka is a Czech favorite that is simultaneously bitter, herbaceous, and floral. It works beautifully combined with tonic and a squeeze of lemon and is magic when you need something to settle your stomach.

2 ounces Becherovka

4 ounces tonic water

Lemon wedge, for garnish

Pour Becherovka and tonic water into a highball glass filled with ice. Stir and garnish with a lemon wedge.

OAZA

A popular drink in Prague, the Oaza is something like a Daiquiri gone wild. It is compellingly complex, and the Becherovka's cinnamon notes combined with lime juice make for a truly engaging sipper.

2 ounces Becherovka

¾ ounce fresh lime juice

¼ ounce simple syrup

Lime wedge, for garnish

Shake ingredients with ice and strain into a rocks glass filled with ice. Garnish with a lime wedge.

PICKLED CAMEMBERT

SERVES 4

This classic Czech bar snack is a conversation starter. Either Camembert or Brie—with their soft, edible rinds—are fair game. An entire wheel of cheese gets pickled for a few days in oil, garlic, and spices to make a flavor-packed accompaniment to cocktails. Served with hearty dark bread or baguette, it can be a meal. Typically, pickled Camembert is rested at room temperature, but this is a safer version. Keep in mind that the resulting olive oil becomes a delicious dip or condiment for other dishes.

1 small white onion, sliced thin

1 cup olive oil

2 garlic cloves, sliced

2 teaspoons paprika

¼ cup roasted red bell pepper, diced

1 teaspoon juniper berries

1 teaspoon allspice berries

2 dried bay leaves

2 teaspoons dried thyme

2 teaspoons whole black peppercorns

1 Camembert wheel, 7–8 ounces, cut into eight wedges

In a small skillet, sweat onions on medium-low heat without letting them brown. Remove and let cool completely. Combine all ingredients except Camembert and stir gently until blended. Add onions and Camembert and store in a refrigerator in a sealed container for at least a week and up to a month. Be sure cheese is completely covered under oil, or it will spoil. To serve, place cheese wedges on a plate or in a shallow bowl and drizzle with the marinade.

ROME ITALY

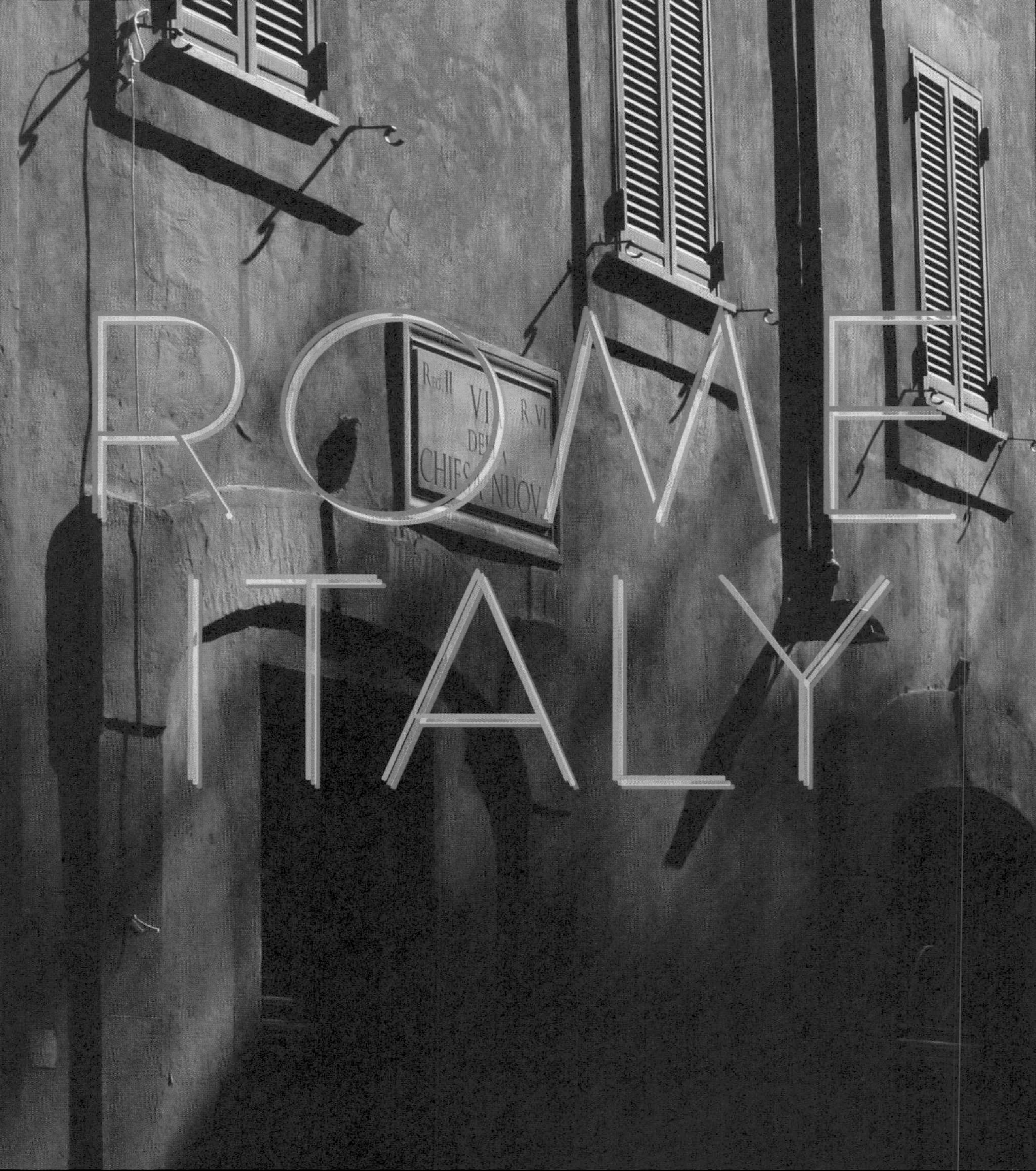

Rome has a particular quality of daylight—a majestic glow that casts onto its imperial buildings, ancient ruins, and broad piazzas. As the day wears on, this light signals the onset of evening, a time when the streets begin to cool and Rome's denizens find seats in the lengthening shadows. It is a glorious moment to be in the Eternal City, succumbing to the ancient ritual of aperitivo.

Aperitivo begins between 7 and 9 p.m. (go early if you want prime seats). As the sun finally fades, the city begins to drink in order to get digestion started for those big, multi-course Italian dinners. Typical aperitivo drinks include wines, beers, and amaro-based cocktails like spritzes. Beverages are traditionally accompanied by small snacks such as olives and nuts but can also be more complex plates like prosciutto-wrapped melon. As in Spain, snacks are often offered gratis with your order, and what you get depends on the type of drink you choose. Do not be surprised if you fill up while bar-hopping.

Carving out a place for themselves in Rome's aperitivo culture are a wide variety of relatively new cocktail establishments. These range from romantic little spots to swanky rooftops, from frantic singles bars to lab-like molecular establishments where glasses billow smoke. The bars are a stylish addition to the city and can often feel like impromptu cocktail parties casually spilling out into the street—because where Rome excels most is in its magnificent outdoor drinking atmosphere, and everyone wants to be outside. Where else is it possible to have a cocktail next to the Temple of Hadrian or within view of the Pantheon?

Aperol Spritz

Originating in Venice after the Napoleonic wars, this gentle sipper has since spread around the country to become "Italy's drink." It is the perfect combination of bitter to stimulate digestion and bubbly to lift the mood. This is the poster child for the aperitivo life.

2 ounces Aperol
3 ounces prosecco
Splash of club soda
Orange slice, for garnish

Pour ingredients into a wine glass filled with ice and stir. Garnish with a slice of orange.

PICTURED ON PREVIOUS PAGE.

Negroni

PICTURED ON PREVIOUS PAGE

The story goes that a certain Count Negroni was a fan of the Americano, but wanted something a bit more fortifying. Bartender Fosco Scarselli swapped the soda water out for gin, and the Negroni was born. Traditionally made with equal parts Campari, gin, and vermouth, today most craft cocktail bars "ladder" the ingredients to bring the gin forward and better balance the drink.

1½ ounces gin
1 ounce sweet vermouth
¾ ounce Campari
Orange wheel, for garnish

Stir ingredients with ice and strain into a rocks glass filled with ice. Garnish with an orange wheel.

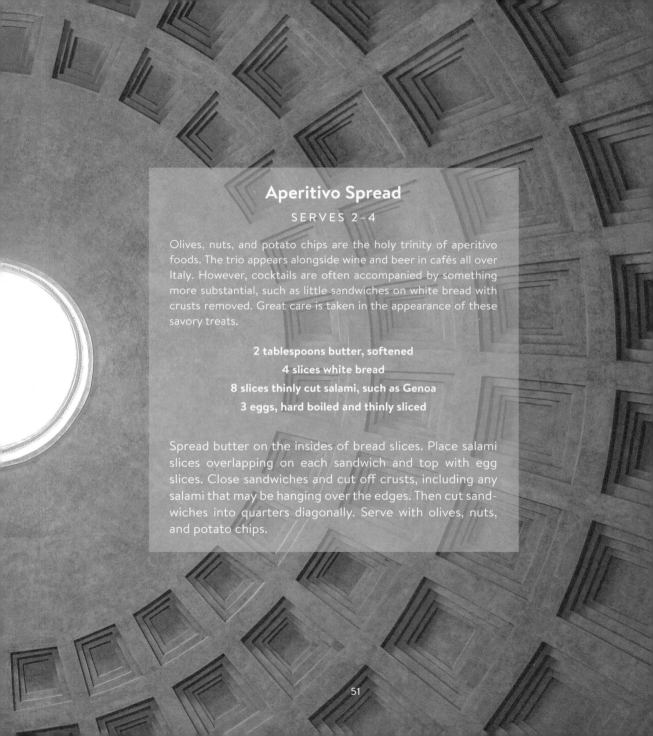

Aperitivo Spread

SERVES 2–4

Olives, nuts, and potato chips are the holy trinity of aperitivo foods. The trio appears alongside wine and beer in cafés all over Italy. However, cocktails are often accompanied by something more substantial, such as little sandwiches on white bread with crusts removed. Great care is taken in the appearance of these savory treats.

2 tablespoons butter, softened
4 slices white bread
8 slices thinly cut salami, such as Genoa
3 eggs, hard boiled and thinly sliced

Spread butter on the insides of bread slices. Place salami slices overlapping on each sandwich and top with egg slices. Close sandwiches and cut off crusts, including any salami that may be hanging over the edges. Then cut sandwiches into quarters diagonally. Serve with olives, nuts, and potato chips.

SAINT PETERSBURG

RUSSIA

Saint Petersburg was an imperial capital for two centuries, and it shows. There are ornate churches, grand palaces, and luxe ballet theaters making for a glamorous backdrop to the city's nightlife scene. Yet, despite all the outward glitz, the city's denizens remain down-to-earth and more easygoing than Muscovites. The vibe is less mega-club and more speakeasy, making the city ripe for serious craft cocktails.

Bars in Patis, as the city is called by locals, tend to have a theme. Popular varieties are English and jazz, plus a style best described as "Soviet nostalgia." Additionally, there are quaint spots that could be in New York's West Village, hidden tippling dens that feel like mod apartments, and arty bars that attract interesting crowds. With typical bar hours being 6 p.m. to 6 a.m., hopping between them can be an endless night's pastime. Get plenty of sleep before you arrive.

Vodka is the order of the day in Russia, but you would not necessarily know it from drinking in Saint Petersburg. There are whiskey bars and gin bars, and classic drinks are made correctly no matter the base spirit. Expect cocktails on par with the best in the world. When making a toast, it is proper to say *na zdrovye!* which means, "To your health!" To take a stab at being more profound, say, *za miravoy mir!*—"World peace!"

53

WHITE NIGHTS

Saint Petersburg is famous for its summer evenings that never end, when the sun barely dips below the horizon. These so-called "white nights," which peak in June, are a huge attraction and the centerpiece for the city's busiest season. "White Nights" is also the title of a short story by Dostoevsky, and this cocktail hails from the Orthodox Bar, a spot where drinks are inspired by Russian authors.

2 ounces vodka

1 ounce apple shrub (recipe below)

½ ounce pickle juice (from cornichons)

¼ ounce honey

½-inch slice of ginger

Shake ingredients with ice and strain into a chilled cocktail glass.

FOR THE APPLE SHRUB

Combine ¾ ounce apple juice with ¼ ounce apple cider vinegar.

VODKA-MORS

Russians love their tart berries. They feature in a drink called Mors, which is typically made from the juice of cranberries and lingonberries mixed together with sugar. Sometimes red currants or blueberries are added. Thus, ironically, if you want to feel like you are in the town Peter the Great built, all you have to do is pour yourself a Vodka-Cranberry. It is proof the United States and Russia are more alike than anyone cares to admit.

1½ ounces vodka

4 ounces cranberry juice

½ ounce fresh lime juice

Lime wheel, for garnish

Stir ingredients together in a highball glass filled with ice. Garnish with a lime wheel.

PICKLED HERRING

This recipe is inspired by a dish at Bar 8 on Bolshoi Prospekt. The bar is owned by chef (and force of nature) Katya Bokuchava, who also runs restaurant Mesto. Pickled herring frequently makes an appearance on Russian menus, and this is a particularly bright and herbaceous way to serve it. Sunflower oil lends a wonderful nutty flavor, but if you cannot find it, olive oil is a fine substitute.

1 cup pickled herring
1 tablespoon sunflower oil
4 scallions, chopped
½ cup dill fronds, loosely chopped

Blend ingredients in a food processor or blender until smooth. Serve with toasted bread and pretzels.

STOCKHOLM
SWEDEN

Set dramatically on fourteen islands, the boreal capital of Sweden is studded with pristine beaches and blessed with clear and clean water. The photogenic home of Vikings, ABBA, and Volvo is nothing short of an outdoorsy paradise. In the summer, it is a bathers' dream and, in the winter, the city is dotted with saunas. Both activities are often conducted nude. And why not? The Swedes love losing their clothes. Who are you to argue?

You might have heard it is expensive to drink here, a result of the state's strict control on the sale of alcohol—and cocktails do come dear. But look for happy hour deals, and you will find that drinks are not much more than in an American city. Note that if you want to imbibe at home, state stores called *systembolaget* keep strict hours and close at 6 p.m. most days. Also know that while the Swedes are lax about nudity, a drink outside will land you a fine.

It has to be mentioned that Stockholm lays claim to a special place in the drinker's pantheon because of actress Greta Garbo. Garbo grew up here, and famously spoke her first lines in a movie in 1930, helping to end the silent film era. And the first-ever words she uttered so memorably in her movie *Anna Christie*? "Gimme a whiskey, ginger ale on the side, and don't be stingy, baby." Let's concede that the Swedes know what they want and when they want it.

DOCTOR COCKTAIL

GLÖGG

The concoction of rum and spices called Swedish Punsch originated in the late eighteenth century with the Swedish East India Company. It remains a popular drink in Sweden. In the United States, Swedish Punsch is used primarily as an ingredient in Tiki drinks (made possible by a version imported by Haus Alpenz). The Doctor Cocktail hails from around 1916 and is one of the great fireside sippers.

1½ ounces Kronan Swedish Punsch

¾ ounce dark rum

¾ ounce fresh lime juice

3 dashes Angostura bitters

Lime wheel, for garnish

Shake ingredients with ice and strain into a rocks glass filled with ice. Garnish with a lime wheel.

This is the drink of reindeer races. A spiced holiday punch, Glögg is served warm in a communal bowl and dished out to individual cups along with a few raisins and almonds. Think of it as a juiced-up version of mulled wine. The recipe dates back to the 1500s, when it was thought to be a healing mixture for muscle injuries.

1 (750 ml) bottle red wine

3 cardamom pods, cracked

5 whole cloves

1 cinnamon stick

1 strip (3 inches) orange peel

1 piece of ginger, 2 inches long, peeled and sliced

12 ounces white sugar

12 ounces aquavit (or substitute vodka or cognac)

¼ cup raisins

½ cup sliced almonds

Orange slices, for garnish

Warm wine in a medium saucepan over medium-high heat. Place cardamom, cloves, cinnamon, orange peel, and ginger in a spice bag and add to the pot. Stir in sugar until it dissolves. Remove pan from heat and let cool, steeping spices for an hour. Add aquavit to the mixture and place over medium-high heat. Heat until just before the liquid boils. Add raisins and almonds. Transfer Glögg to a punchbowl, remove the spice bag, garnish with orange slices, and ladle into cups, being sure to scoop up a few raisins and almonds for each serving.

SWEDISH CARDAMOM COOKIES

MAKES ABOUT 20 COOKIES

Cardamom is Sweden's signature spice. These delicate, biscuit-like cookies make for wonderful holiday snacks and go well with cocktails. They are buttery, crunchy, and have just enough flavor to wow.

1 cup (2 sticks) unsalted butter, softened

½ cup sugar

1 egg

¼ teaspoon baking powder

2½ cups flour

2 teaspoons ground cardamom

¼ teaspoon salt

In a large bowl, beat butter and sugar until light and fluffy, 2–3 minutes. In a small bowl, beat egg and add baking powder. Stir until dissolved and add to the butter mixture. In a medium bowl, combine flour, cardamom, and salt. Slowly add to the butter mixture. Cover and chill for 2–3 hours.

Preheat oven to 350°F and line two baking sheets with parchment paper. Divide dough in half and lightly flour a work surface. Flatten dough with your hands, and use a rolling pin to roll dough out thin, about ⅛-inch thick. Cut cookies with a 3-inch biscuit cutter and transfer to baking sheets using a spatula. Reroll dough to collect scraps and repeat with second half of the dough. Bake cookies until edges are browning, about 8–10 minutes.

CHAPTER 2

AFRICA
and the
MIDDLE EAST

Africa is full of emerging cocktail hotspots. There are nascent scenes in Kenya, Ghana, Uganda, and also in the continent's largest city, Lagos, Nigeria. If this book gets an update in a few years, these areas will require their own entries. Today, two spots command the imbiber's attention: Tangier and Cape Town. Former expat haunt Tangier has seen development recently at its port and along its beaches. Likewise, Cape Town is in the middle of a cocktail boom and boasts an exciting distilling scene. Both tips of Africa offer compelling mixed drinks incorporating local traditions and ingredients.

The Middle East has long been dotted with serious drinkers' hangouts, being at the center of the trade route between Europe and Asia. However, in recent years, the once-major drink stops of Cairo and Istanbul have been experiencing challenges to tippling. Prohibition culture is on the rise in many Muslim cities, and imbibing is being pushed further into exclusive expat hotels and behind closed doors. Focus has shifted instead to the cities of Dubai, Beirut, and Tel Aviv. All three boast robust cocktail scenes. In each, Middle Eastern hospitality mixes with rich history for superb drinking experiences. Expect playfulness and luxury, as well as the thrilling flavors of the Spice Route in your glass.

BEIRUT

LEBANON

Seductive, orgiastic, chaotic. The brash and irrepressible city of Beirut perches on a promontory jutting into the Mediterranean like a beacon for the good life. The city is a trading port, a cultural crossroads, and a hard-partying town on the edge of the Muslim world. It is transitory, fickle, and unbearably beautiful. Just to the east lies the Bekaa Valley, the northern tip of the Rift Valley running up from Kenya. Humankind was born here, and sitting smack in the middle of the valley is the largest temple to the deity of drink, Bacchus, ever built. In this ancient place, alcohol is a god.

Beirut has a gravitational pull like a hypnotic dancer, and it confuses the senses. While it is almost a cliché to mention that the city is divided and war-torn, its buildings are indeed pock-marked with bullets. However, the city's citizens are strangely grudgeless and congenial. In fact, if all cities say something about the human condition, Beirut whispers, "Life is short. We may fight tomorrow, but we are together tonight." In the morning, what can you do but chase away the hangover with cardamom-laced coffee?

In hip neighborhoods like Hamra and Mar Mikhael, Lebanese hospitality, which is so rightfully famous, is on full display everywhere. There is always a promise of a good conversation over drinks. Bars are warm and welcoming, and it is easy to be pulled into someone's home for a round of arak, Lebanon's spirit of choice. To say "cheers" here is *késik* if addressing a woman, *késak* for a man, and *késkon* if toasting a group.

Arak Cooler

Arak, called the "milk of lions," cleanses the palate and sharpens the appetite. Its anisette flavor acts as a cool breeze on the many hot, dry days in Beirut. Note that the Lebanese are quality hounds. Arak here is typically made from local grapes, not from neutral grain spirits as you might find elsewhere.

1 cucumber slice plus 1 slice for garnish

4 mint leaves plus a mint sprig for garnish

1½ ounces arak

¾ ounce fresh lemon juice

Gently muddle a cucumber slice and mint leaves in a shaker. Add arak, lemon juice, and ice. Shake and strain into a rocks glass filled with ice and garnish with a cucumber slice and a sprig of mint.

FOR THE ZA'ATAR SIMPLE SYRUP

In a sealable container, add 2 tablespoons za'atar mix to 1 cup hot water and 1 cup sugar. Shake and rest mixture in a refrigerator for a few hours or overnight. Strain with a fine-mesh strainer and keep refrigerated for up to a week.

Za'atar Fix

A "Fix" is properly any drink with spirit, lemon juice, and another fruit served down on ice (the ice can be rocks, shaved, or crushed). The famous Lebanese spice mix, *Za'atar*, makes for an amazingly complex flavor alongside pomegranate.

2 ounces gin

1 ounce fresh lemon juice

¾ ounce pomegranate juice

½ ounce za'atar simple syrup (recipe below)

Lemon peel, for garnish

Shake ingredients with ice and strain into a rocks glass filled with ice.

MOUTABAL

SERVES 2–4

The most widely known eggplant dip in the West is baba ganoush, which traditionally includes pomegranate and walnuts and sometimes does not contain tahini. Its cousin, *moutabal*, is made with tahini and yogurt. If it sounds like you have been eating moutabal without knowing it, you are probably right; in the United States, baba ganoush has become shorthand for all Middle Eastern eggplant dips. Whatever it's called, this smoky spread is both an addictive snack and a great side dish. Note that eggplants can be roasted in the oven at 400°F for about 30 minutes, but cooking them on the stovetop produces more flavorful results.

2 eggplants
½ teaspoon table salt
2 garlic cloves, crushed
5 tablespoons tahini
¼ cup Greek yogurt
Juice of 1 lemon
¼ cup olive oil, for garnish

Place eggplants on the open flame of a stovetop. Keep rotating until their skins are charred and the flesh inside is soft and pulpy, about 20 minutes. Let cool for a few minutes, and peel off skins with your fingers while running under cold water. On a cutting board, add salt to the garlic cloves and mash with a fork until it becomes a paste. In a medium serving bowl, mash eggplant with a fork. Add tahini, yogurt, garlic-salt paste, and lemon juice. Stir with two forks to fully combine, and garnish with olive oil. Serve with pita or crackers.

IN THE EYE OF THE STORM

It is nighttime on November 30, 2019. In Beirut's old Muslim quarter, couples play backgammon in the cafés, smoke from their water pipes hanging in the air. Nervous shopkeepers stand at the entrances of well-lit stores. Despite signs advertising deep Christmas discounts, there are no customers. The scene feels expectant, as if I caught the street at the precise moment when a director yells, "Action!"

I had not intended to drink in Lebanon during historic times. The plane tickets for my circumnavigation of the globe (see page 189) had been purchased months in advance, and Beirut was my stop between Athens and Dubai. I'd heard the city's siren song and wanted to explore its vibrant cocktail scene. With concern, I watched Lebanon's October Revolution unfold on TV, and I hoped it would resolve by the time I arrived. It had not. Sectarian violence, everyone's worst fear, was breaking out. As my hotel concierge conveyed, this happened mostly on weekends. It was Saturday. Thousands of protesters gathered in Martyrs' Square a mile away, and Beirut was plunging, minute-by-minute, deeper into a political and financial crisis. Taxis idled. Restaurants sat empty. Soldiers clustered on the street corners guarding the ATMs.

In an expat bar down the street from my hotel, old regulars wore the glum faces of those who had seen these kinds of times before. Talk was hushed and the vibe funereal. But it is remarkable what a drink or two can do, because I found myself ordering a taxi, determined to complete a bar crawl. Soon my car inched through crowded Martyrs' Square, slipping into the buzzing neighborhood of Mar Mikhael. Here, bars were jammed with local revelers ignoring their precarious reality. For them, going out was an act of defiance. Jostling to get a drink, I heard the rattle of ice in shakers and, for an instant, I was transported to a time when the familiar sound was a rare beacon. It reminded me of the special place cocktails have carved out in our psyche; mixed drinks with their manufactured ice, distilled alcohol, and fresh garnish, are the beverages of civilization itself. The cocktail is a reprieve from our less-than-ideal reality, a temporary liquid reassurance that society's fabric remains untorn, conversations can be genial, and that—for the moment—there is nothing to do but order another round.

CAPE TOWN

SOUTH AFRICA

Situated next to the ocean and mountains, Cape Town possesses stunning natural beauty. This is the oldest city in South Africa, and an alluring melting pot of cultures. Increased tourism in recent years has meant a proliferation of bars and restaurants. Many of these are decorated in a dreamy Afro-chic style, lending a design-forward backdrop to a night out.

South Africa is experiencing a giant liquor boom, specifically a big surge in gin production. Industry estimates indicate the country is consuming twice as much of the spirit as it did just a few short years ago. Craft distillers are popping up around the country and infusing spirits with local plants like *fynbos* (flowering shrubs) and *buchu* (a medicinal herb). For those with an interest in distilling, it is worth traversing the Western Cape Brandy Route. Conveniently, it is possible to hire a car and use Cape Town as a base for exploration. To make the most of this local spirits bonanza, world-class cocktail bars such as Cause & Effect focus on the new artisan offerings.

When exploring Cape Town, be sure to seek out the local moonshine, called *mampoer*, made from peaches. Beware that at 80 percent alcohol it will level you, but it is a unique and exciting indigenous spirit. And want to truly drink like a local while in Mother City? Have a *Springbokkie*, a shot of Cape Velvet (a local brandy-based cream liqueur) mixed with peppermint schnapps. An acquired taste, but better than it sounds.

Capetonian

The Cape Town, or Capetonian, is a Manhattan variation that made its appearance in the *Savoy Cocktail Book* in 1930. Traditionally, it was made with Canadian whisky, but is best made today with local South African pot still brandy. The star of the show here is Caperitif, a rare vermouth that has been available again since 2014. The return of Caperitif makes another excellent Cape Town classic possible as well, The Biltong Dry: gin, Caperitif, sweet vermouth, and orange bitters.

1½ ounces brandy
1½ ounces Caperitif
3 dashes orange curaçao
1 dash Angostura bitters

Shake ingredients and strain into a cocktail glass.

Amarula-Rooibos "Latté"

This winning drink combines two of South Africa's most famous beverage exports, rooibos tea and the cream-based liqueur, Amarula. Rooibos is a plant that grows along South Africa's coast in a belt of vegetation along the Western and Eastern Cape provinces. Tea made from its leaves is floral, honeyed, and sometimes a bit smoky. It is enchanting when paired with the flavor of Amarula, made from the marula fruit, which is reminiscent of pear and passion fruit.

6 ounces rooibos tea
2 ounces Amarula
1 ounce brandy

Brew tea according to instructions and pour into a mug. Add Amarula and brandy. Stir and serve.

BUNNY CHOW

SERVES 4-6

So-named for Indian "bunia" vendors—not because the recipe includes rabbit—Bunny Chow is a classic South African street food. It is a blend of lamb or chicken, potatoes, chickpeas, and spices served in a hollowed-out section of white bread. This is a great snack for soaking up a few drinks, and one of the world's great takeaway foods. It is often accompanied by grated carrot and chopped cilantro.

2 tablespoons ghee or olive oil

1 medium yellow onion, diced

1½ tablespoons curry powder

½ teaspoon cinnamon

1½ teaspoons paprika

½ teaspoon ground cardamom

½ teaspoon cayenne pepper

4 curry leaves

5 garlic cloves, minced

1 tablespoon minced ginger

2 pounds boneless chicken thighs, cut into bite-sized pieces

2 medium tomatoes, diced

1 15-ounce can chickpeas, rinsed and drained

2 cups waxy potatoes (about 3), peeled and cut into cubes

1 cup chicken stock

Salt and black pepper, to taste

1 loaf white bread

½ cup chopped cilantro, for garnish

1 carrot, grated, for garnish

In a large saucepan, heat ghee over medium-high heat and add onions, curry powder, cinnamon, paprika, cardamom, cayenne pepper, and curry leaves. Stir until onions are translucent, about 2–3 minutes. Add garlic and ginger and cook until softened, about a minute. Add chicken and cook until pieces begin to brown on one side. Add tomatoes, and cook until they begin to reduce, about 3 minutes. Next, add chickpeas, potatoes, and chicken stock. Bring to a boil and simmer partially covered until sauce thickens, about 30 minutes. Add salt and pepper, to taste. Separate bread into stacks of three slices each. Using a cookie cutter or a knife, hollow out a hole in the center of the stacks. Serve chicken mixture in the hollowed-out bread slices, and garnish with cilantro and carrot.

DUBAI

UNITED ARAB EMIRATES

A few short decades ago, Dubai was a desert refueling stop for airplanes traveling from Europe to the Far East. It was a quiet town of pearl divers, merchants, and fishermen. Today, the city rises up from the sand as a futuristic vision of man-made islands and giant shopping malls sporting indoor snow-boarding mountains and wave pools. Dubai is a symbol of modern extravagance and synonymous with luxury. Everything that can be accomplished with technology and petroleum is, and travelers are swaddled in an air-conditioned fantasy.

In a fast-paced and overpopulated world, two things are in short supply: space and calm. It is these two things that Dubai addresses with great success. Whether in luxe hotel lobbies or on ocean-side verandas, there is an ever-present, lulling lounge vibe. This town is an amazing place to . . . chill, preferably with a cocktail in hand. To that end, Dubai offers some of the most posh and relaxing bars in the world. Expect soft couches to sink into and service that anticipates your every need.

DRINKING IN A MUSLIM COUNTRY

There is nothing to indicate from Dubai airport's duty-free shops, crammed to capacity with bottles of wine and whiskey, that the traveler has landed in a Muslim country. The United Arab Emirates is the most liberal of the Gulf States, and the country goes to great lengths to cater to international tastes. Hotel bars serve alcohol, and with the proper permit, it is possible for foreign nationals to purchase liquor at retail shops. However, even in this city eager to cultivate an image of openness, anecdotes abound of drunk expats getting deported. Punishment for public intoxication is swift for foreigners and severe for locals. It is best to consume in moderation. Do the locals drink? Technically, alcohol is only for guests of Dubai's hotels. In fact, if you are drinking in a hotel bar, you must be their guest unless you have a personal, government-issued liquor license. Yet there are a suspicious number of locals drinking from teacups when it is beastly hot. No one checks what the cups contain. For a fascinating book on the subject of alcohol and Islam, seek out Lawrence Osborne's *The Wet and the Dry: A Drinker's Journey*.

Hendrick's and Lemonade

SERVES 2

This gin-lemonade for two is quintessential Dubai, all repose and luxury, with an added dash of English pomp. It is inspired by a version served at a sleek bar called Play atop the H Hotel. You may enjoy it enough to make it your summer Sunday afternoon ritual.

2 sprigs fresh mint leaves

2 ounces simple syrup

5 ounces Hendrick's gin

2 ounces fresh lemon juice

2 cucumber wheels, for garnish

Muddle mint and simple syrup in a pitcher. Add ice, gin, lemon juice, and 1 cup water. Stir and strain into a teapot. Serve in teacups garnished with cucumber wheels.

Blueberry-Ginger Bourbon Sour

The famed Buddha Bar is a magnet for the glitterati when they visit Dubai. The swanky hot spot boasts an ever-changing menu of trendy cocktails, and the most famous of these is a version of a Whiskey Smash that became the darling of celebrities like Johnny Depp in the early 2000s. Domaine De Canton is a French ginger liqueur and is widely available in stores.

4 blueberries
1 ounce simple syrup
1 ounce fresh lemon juice
1½ ounces bourbon
½ ounce Domaine De Canton
3 blueberries, for garnish
2 candied ginger slices, for garnish

In a shaker, muddle blueberries with simple syrup and lemon juice. Add bourbon, Domaine De Canton, ice, and shake. Strain into a rocks glass filled with ice. Garnish with alternating blueberries and ginger on a cocktail stick.

For centuries, Tangier has exerted a powerful pull from across the Strait of Gibraltar. A gateway between Europe and Africa, the ancient city has had a myriad of influences, from the Phoenicians to the French. It has played host to sultans and slaves, pirates and spies. The "Door of Africa," as it has been called, has also been a refuge for creative expats like William S. Burroughs and Paul Bowles. There remains an edgy sense of mystery to the maze-like streets of the Kasbah, and it is easy to understand the fascination the place held for counter-culture icons like the Beats and the Rolling Stones. After years in decline, there has been a recent push to modernize Tangier, and this city of indulgence is full of renewed energy.

At one time, Tangier might have been the best place in the Western world to people-watch. Persons of interest from all over Europe, plus those arriving from the desert to the south, haunted the cafés, passed secret messages, and engaged in romantic trysts. Keeping a sharp eye out for interesting characters is still the right move, and a number of classic establishments still exist for this purpose; Cafe Baba, Cafe Tinga, and the Gran Cafe de Paris are all good spots to post up, order a drink, and wait for a fateful encounter.

Bars in Tangier are raffish and tend toward a movie set atmosphere. There is something James Bond about the waiters in their white coats and piano players tinkling the old ivories. Expect cocktails to veer classic with a few surprises. Often, the flavors of Morocco make their way into the glass: cinnamon, rose water, and preserved lemon.

Gin and Mint Tea

Mint tea, an ever-present beverage in Tangier, gets a lift here from a splash of gin. This is a refreshing sipper, made for hot afternoons.

4 ounces mint tea

4 mint leaves

¼ ounce simple syrup

1 ounce gin

Make tea according to package instructions and let cool. Gently muddle mint leaves and simple syrup in a glass. Add gin, tea, and ice, and stir.

New Morocco

Charles H. Baker Jr. includes an El Morocco cocktail in *The Gentleman's Companion* and goes out of his way to distinguish it from the New York nightclub of the same name. Yet, the recipe he provides could just as easily have been invented in America as North Africa; it is a miasma of his era, combining port and cognac with pineapple juice. This updated version is a better representation of the bold flavors of Tangier: cinnamon, rose, and clementine. Note that Combier makes a rose liqueur that is widely available in liquor stores and online.

2 ounces white rum

¼ ounce rose liqueur

½ ounce fresh lemon juice

½ ounce fresh clementine juice (orange is a fine substitute)

¼ ounce simple syrup

1 scant dash of cinnamon, for garnish

Mint sprig, for garnish

Shake ingredients with ice and strain into a cocktail glass. Garnish with a dash of cinnamon and a sprig of mint.

Fried Chickpeas

SERVES 2–4

All crunch and salt, fried chickpeas are a natural accompaniment to cocktails. They are healthier and lower in calories than many other bar nosh alternatives and can be made in a snap. Keep a few cans of chickpeas on hand for when you have unexpected guests.

2 15½-ounce cans chickpeas, drained and rinsed
8 tablespoons olive oil

FOR THE SPICE MIX
1 teaspoon ground cumin
1 teaspoon ground cayenne pepper
1 teaspoon paprika
½ teaspoon ground ginger
¼ teaspoon ground cinnamon
½ teaspoon kosher salt

Pat chickpeas dry. For best results, leave them uncovered in a refrigerator overnight. Combine spices in a medium-sized bowl and set aside. Heat oil in a large skillet over medium-high heat. Working in batches so as not to overcrowd the pan, add chickpeas and sauté, stirring frequently. Fry chickpeas until they are browned and crispy, 5–7 minutes. Using a slotted spoon, transfer chickpeas to paper towels to dry. When cooled, add them to the spice mixture and toss to coat evenly.

TEL AVIV

ISRAEL

Israel's coastal party center, Tel Aviv, boasts Bauhaus architecture, a thriving art scene, and a burgeoning cocktail culture. Dubbed the "Mediterranean Manhattan," it is a town of hip hotels and rockin' hummus joints. Plus, the city is positively abuzz with nightlife, from chill beachside bars to pumping rooftop parties.

As one might expect in a fun-loving seaside town, the beach spills into the city. Your Mojito may be served with a side of bikinis and flip-flops, and there will definitely be sand in your shoes. But this does not mean the city lacks an elegant side. In fact, Tel Aviv is one of the few major cities in the world where a day at the beach can be easily followed by a stylish, urban evening. Prepare to bring a few changes of clothes.

Cocktail bars range from funky bohemian to luxe hedonist. There are killer drinks, from speakeasy-era classics to modern, whimsical creations. Tel Aviv's hot and humid climate means that refreshment is key, and many cocktails are summer-y numbers that cool and rehydrate with the addition of citrus and soda.

LIMONANA

SERVES 2 | PICTURED ON NEXT PAGE

Limonana is the national drink of Israel, and is best consumed on hot days when lounging around is the only option. This spiked version makes for a thirst-quenching sipper and works best as a blended cocktail.

4 ounces vodka

1 cup fresh lemon juice

½ cup mint leaves, loosely packed

1½ cups cold water

4 tablespoons granulated sugar

2½ cups ice

2–4 fresh mint sprigs, for garnish

Combine ingredients in a blender. Pour into rocks glasses and garnish with sprigs of mint.

MYRTLE SOUR

This chic cocktail takes its inspiration from a gimlet variation served at Tel Aviv's Imperial Hotel Bar. Myrtle is an herb known for its calming effect, and it is also one of the four sacred plants of the Jewish holiday Sukkot. The leaves taste a bit astringent and orange-y—brilliant for mixed drinks. Myrtle leaves are available in herb stores and online.

2 ounces gin

½ ounce myrtle syrup (recipe below)

½ ounce fresh lime juice

1 ounce Sauvignon Blanc

Lime wedge, for garnish

Shake ingredients with ice and strain into a cocktail glass. Garnish with a lime wedge.

FOR THE MYRTLE SIMPLE SYRUP

In a sealable container, add 1 cup hot water to 4 tablespoons myrtle leaves. Steep 10 minutes. Add 1 cup sugar, shake until sugar is dissolved, and rest mixture in a refrigerator overnight. Strain and keep refrigerated for up to a week.

Lima Bean Hummus

SERVES 4–6

Restaurant Port Sa'id is a hipster hangout next to the Great Synagogue. Think diners with sleeve tattoos and a wall of vinyl albums. The place is high energy and there is usually a wait to get seated. One of Port Sa'id's popular dishes is a lima bean msabbaha (similar to hummus), which arrives garnished with tomato seeds, hot pepper, and red onion. In the restaurant's version, whole beans are cooked for hours and then mixed with more mashed beans. Below is an abbreviated snack version. I like to add pickles, but they are optional.

1 16-ounce package lima beans, thawed

½ cup olive oil, plus more as needed

2 garlic cloves

Zest of 1 medium lemon, plus 1 tablespoon lemon juice

1 teaspoon sea salt

½ teaspoon black pepper

¼ red onion, diced

1 small tomato, minced

1 jalapeño, minced

4 small gherkins, minced

In a medium saucepot, boil lima beans for 20 minutes to soften. Drain and let beans cool. In a large food processor or blender, mix olive oil, garlic, lemon zest, lemon juice, salt, and pepper. Add beans and blend until smooth. Add additional olive oil if the mixture is too thick. Top with red onion, tomato, jalapeño, and pickles. Serve with warm pita bread or challah.

CHAPTER 3 ASIA

Asia has become the center of attention for the world's cocktail cognoscenti. The region is experiencing a massive bar-building boom and has become a magnet for ambitious bartenders around the globe. Deluxe hotel bars have taken the lead, becoming the preferred stages for competition-worthy cocktails that boast jaw-dropping presentations. The biggest surprise in Asia's new drinking landscape is the ascendancy of Singapore, which is contesting long-established heavyweights like Tokyo and Hong Kong for dominance.

Bars in Asia often fall into two categories: rooftop and speakeasy. Because of a skyscraper boom, there are plenty of tall spots to sip while taking in an epic view (see page 99). Down below, hidden streets that once housed opium and gambling dens now boast alluring watering holes. Unlike in America, where speakeasies were something of a phase, Asian cities have adopted them as a part of the cocktail's DNA. This can be confusing to visitors, who assume it is a trend or that Asia is somehow "behind" the West. It is not; by some measures it has jumped ahead.

The big cities of Asia have young populations, and this energy translates into vibrant drinking cultures. Even though cocktail-making is very old in the East, things feel fresh and recent. Recipes often involve fruit, and local ingredients are finding their way into the glass. Expect everything from lemongrass to lychee, hand-carved ice to dry ice, ancient customs to contemporary twists.

BANGKOK
THAILAND

Bangkok is a city of calm canals and teeming markets, of quiet temples and raucous restaurants. It is modern, skyscraper-studded, and ultra-hip. With roughly half of the population under twenty, Thailand's capital is racing into the new millennium with fierce energy and eyes on the future. Yet the atmosphere remains filled with the past, including an ancient Buddhist belief that we live among the ghosts of our ancestors, called *phi*, who inform daily life. There is both clamor and serenity in this capital of a kingdom that was never colonized.

For the Westerner, Bangkok beckons with a siren song of some of the planet's best street food (plus over fifty thousand restaurants) and also unhinged nightlife. Thailand's dizzying capital is a mishmash of backpackers and addicts, paranoid ex-servicemen and ladyboys all out on the prowl for cheap drinks and a good time. But the dissonance between decadence and spirituality is exactly what makes Bangkok one of the most stimulating places to drink. Happily for the cocktailer, mixed in with the go-go bars and pubs are a profusion of world-class craft cocktail dens. These include some of the most exciting places in the world to drink, from breathtaking Lennon's to visionary Asia Today.

Going out for drinks in Bangkok has a conspiratorial aura of sipping somewhere magical. Magical and suffocatingly hot (it is the world's hottest city according to the World Meteorological Organization). Luckily, by settling into a chair on the street and ordering cooling drinks with a side of curried locusts, poetically called "sky prawns," you will grow accustomed to the city's temperature. Then, as the heavenly aroma of street vendor woks mixes with the smell of blooming flowers, you will dissolve into what the Thais call *annata*, or absence of the self. Now that is worth the price of a few drinks.

BANGKOK HIP FLASK

Although drinks are cheap and plentiful in Thailand's capital, many Thais (and expats) go out for a night on the town with their own hip flasks in tow. Often these are filled with whiskey, but sometimes a more refreshing mix is substituted. While makrut (kaffir) limes can be difficult to source in the United States, the leaves are always available at Asian markets. This recipe uses makrut leaves to make a flavorful simple syrup that is delicious in many other drinks. For instance, try it in a French 75 (page 39).

4½ ounces gin
1½ ounces fresh lime juice
1½ ounces makrut simple syrup (recipe below)

Shake ingredients with ice and strain into a hip flask.

FOR THE MAKRUT SIMPLE SYRUP
In a sealable container, combine twelve lime leaves with 1 cup hot water and 1 cup sugar. Shake and rest mixture in a refrigerator for a few hours or overnight. Strain and keep refrigerated for up to a week.

SABAI

This Thai welcome drink is a Southeast Asian version of a Rum Collins. It is best made with regional Mekhong "whiskey," which is actually more of a rum than whiskey at all. Thai basil contributes a glorious herbaceous note. A fantastic example is found at Tep Bar in Bangkok's Chinatown.

1½ ounces Mekhong or rum
1½ ounces fresh lemon juice
¾ ounce simple syrup
2–3 ounces club soda
Sprig of Thai basil, for garnish

Shake whiskey, lemon juice, and simple syrup with ice and strain into a highball glass filled with ice. Top with soda and garnish with a sprig of Thai basil.

BANGKOK'S COMMUNAL COCKTAILS

It is common in Bangkok for friends to drink cocktails together communally, sharing a bottle of liquor, mixers, and a bucket of ice. Bar staff will refresh the fixings throughout the evening. This is essentially a fun and convivial form of bottle service. If you are lucky enough to find yourself out with a group of Thais drinking, here are a few ways to say "Cheers!"

Chok dee—"Good luck!"   *Mote gaow*—"Bottoms up!"   *Chai yo*—"To success!"

Chone gaow—When proposing a toast, someone will say, "Chone!" This is a signal to clink glasses.

Vast, unruly, traffic-choked Delhi. Welcome to the dusty hub of the largest democracy on Earth. Car horns blast, motorcycles zoom by, and bicycle taxis lurch past offering rides for mere pennies. Everywhere, there are the eye-popping colors of India—saffron, crimson, and fuchsia. Now add in the smells assaulting your nostrils: smoke, gasoline, frying chickpea flour, animal dung, and flowers. Delhi is a city of cacophony and mayhem, of gloriously unfamiliar sights and sounds that defy the ability to process them.

Travelers often discover Delhi by passing through it as part of the "Golden Triangle" circuit formed by Delhi, Agra, and Jaipur. This is a region where the British colonial influence is still felt—in everything from food to government officiousness. And of course, in cocktails.

Drinks history looms large in Delhi. The cocktail was born from punch, which made its first appearance in India. It was also in India where the Gin & Tonic got its big start. The quinine in tonic was used to fortify soldiers against malaria, and the concoction spread around the globe to become one of the world's most popular mixed drinks.

India's capital offers a sprawling array of luxe bars in which to imbibe Gin & Tonics and other familiar classics. Additionally, because the city is supremely rich in seasonings, local ingredients frequently make appearances, evoking the flavors of India in the glass. On a night out, the drinker will be rewarded by bartenders digging into the country's unrivaled spice box: cumin, cardamom, coriander, turmeric, fenugreek, ajwain, tamarind, nutmeg, black pepper, cloves, fennel, poppy, and more.

MARIGOLD FIZZ

Marigold, or calendula, is ubiquitous in India. It plays an important part in religious festivals, its neon yellow buds symbolizing the sun. The flowers are frequently made into vibrant garlands, but the plant is also used medicinally to treat skin problems. Here, the petals are macerated in sugar for a simple syrup that is tangy and peppery.

2 ounces gin
¾ ounce fresh lemon juice
¾ ounce calendula simple syrup (recipe below)
2 ounces club soda
Lemon wheel, for garnish

Shake gin, lemon juice, and simple syrup with ice. Strain into a highball glass with ice and top with soda. Garnish with a lemon wheel.

FOR THE CALENDULA SIMPLE SYRUP
In a sealable container, steep ¼ cup dried calendula flowers in 1 cup hot water for 10 minutes. Strain mixture, return to container, and add 1 cup sugar. Shake until sugar is dissolved and keep refrigerated for up to a week.

ORIGINAL PUNCH

Communal punch was a favorite drink of the British stationed in India. The word punch comes from the Hindu *paunch*, meaning "five things"—in this case, alcohol, citrus, sugar, black tea, and water. The first known recipe for punch was recorded by a German traveler named Johan Albrecht de Mandelslo in 1638. This combination re-creates what the original punch in India might have tasted like.

Peel of 4 lemons
1 cup sugar
3 cups hot water (not quite boiling)
1 (750 ml) bottle white rum
1½ cups fresh lemon juice
4 cups tea
1 teaspoon rose water
6 lemon slices, for garnish
Rose petals, for garnish (optional)

In a large punch bowl, muddle lemon peels in sugar and let the mixture sit for a few hours or overnight. Remove lemon peels and stir in hot water until the sugar dissolves. Let mixture cool, and add rum, lemon juice, tea, and rose water. Cover and refrigerate for a few hours or overnight. Serve in a punch bowl with ice cubes or a block of ice and garnish with lemon slices and rose petals.

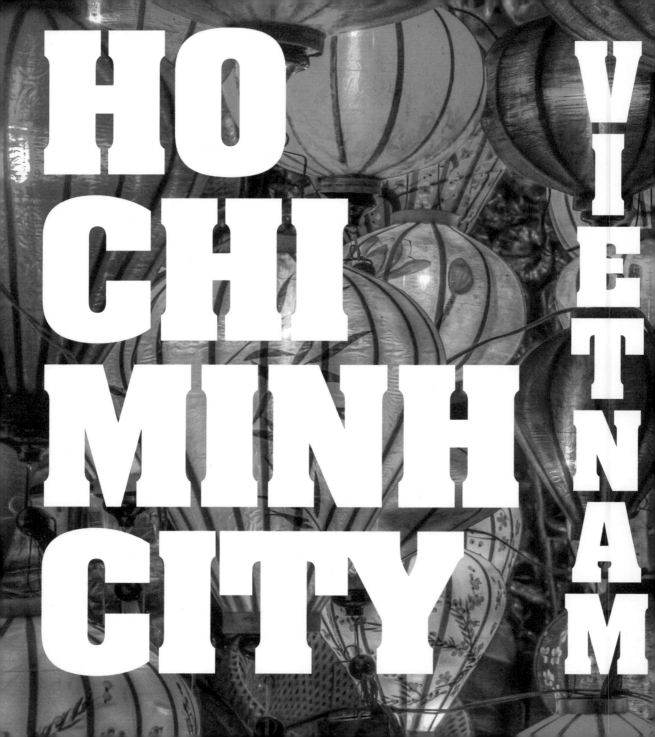

Scooters might outnumber people in Vietnam's largest metropolis. The city moves with the frantic pace of two-wheeled vehicles darting in all directions. While zipping around in traffic, you will notice how startlingly commercial Ho Chi Minh has become, a sign of the country's recent economic success. You'll tear past Starbucks and Louis Vuitton stores, new skyscrapers and air-conditioned designer malls. Yet despite the development, the city's urban landscape still oozes charm and elegance. There are spectacular French colonial-era buildings, quiet temples, and gorgeous tree-lined boulevards.

The boom that has brought luxury shops and swish hotels has also ushered in craft cocktails. There is no shortage of upscale nightlife haunts in which to find stellar mixed drinks. A great place to start your exploration is the glamorous Hotel Continental, where author Graham Greene wrote *The Quiet American*. It was here in 1955, in room 214, that the English novelist predicted the eventual outcome of the Vietnam War. Just know that while the war is still on Westerners' minds, it is a distant memory in this city more preoccupied with the newest craft beers than any old ghosts.

A welcome HCMC feature for the cocktailer is safe water, even outside higher-end establishments. If you have heard that consuming ice in Southeast Asia is verboten unless you want to get acquainted with your hotel toilet, relax. The cubes destined for drinks are made with filtered water, a legacy of the French. However, a word of warning regarding Vietnamese distilled rice wine, specifically *ruou thuoc*, which often contains exotic animals such as seahorses or snakes. These bottles are popular tourist items, but know that endangered species are being poached to make the wine, and that it is likely the mixture contains rubbing alcohol or formaldehyde. Do not buy and definitely do not consume.

LEMONGRASS-CARDAMOM COOLER

This cocktail employs the iconic Vietnamese flavors for a refreshing sipper that summons up all things Ho Chi Minh City. The lemongrass-cardamom simple syrup is a great addition to the cocktailer's arsenal, and can be used to add spice to a number of classic drinks. Try it in a Daiquiri (page 142).

- 2 ounces gin
- ¾ ounce fresh lime juice
- ¾ ounce lemongrass-cardamom simple syrup (recipe below)
- 2 ounces club soda
- Lime wheel, for garnish

Shake gin, lime juice, and simple syrup with ice. Strain into a highball glass with ice and top with soda. Garnish with a lime wheel.

FOR THE LEMONGRASS-CARDAMOM SIMPLE SYRUP
Cut two lemongrass stalks into 1-inch pieces. Using the flat side of a knife, crush stalks. Using the side of a knife again, crack ten cardamom pods. In a sealable container, add lemongrass and cardamom to 1 cup hot water and 1 cup sugar. Shake until sugar is dissolved and let the mixture rest in a refrigerator overnight. Strain and keep refrigerated for up to a week.

SPIKED VIETNAMESE ICED COFFEE

Coffee in Vietnam is a ritual. There is a special filter called a *phin*, which sits atop individual cups and drips coffee below. The result is a strong, bitter brew that is then mixed with the caramel-y flavor of condensed milk. The combination is ethereal, and adding a bit of whiskey makes it even better. To replicate a Vietnamese filter, brew a strong pot using a French press.

- 2 ounces whiskey
- 5 ounces strong coffee, cooled
- 1 ounce condensed milk

Combine ingredients in a highball glass with ice.

While this recipe may have a million ingredients, it is a breeze to make. Bun Cha—meatballs with noodles, fresh veggies, and sauce—is all assembly and no fuss. The result is a delightful, satisfying meal that is an antidote to strong drink. Bun Cha pairs well with sours, but also with more spirituous whisky or rum potations. Although originating in the north, and a specialty of Hanoi, this internationally recognized dish is also found in Ho Chi Minh City. Note that Bun Cha is what food writer Anthony Bourdain and US president Barack Obama ate when they met in Vietnam.

FOR THE NUOC CHAM (SAUCE)

3 tablespoons sugar

3 tablespoons fish sauce

2 tablespoons rice wine vinegar

2 tablespoons lime juice

1 bird's eye chile, seeded and finely chopped

3 garlic cloves, minced

FOR THE MEATBALLS

1 pound ground pork

2 teaspoons fish sauce

1 teaspoon sugar

⅓ cup finely chopped scallions

1 garlic clove, minced

2 lemongrass stalks, finely chopped

¼ teaspoon black pepper

2 tablespoons vegetable oil

FOR SERVING

1 3½-ounce package vermicelli noodles, cooked and drained

3 cups bean sprouts

1 head of lettuce such as green leaf or Boston, leaves separated

½ bunch cilantro, loosely chopped

½ cup mint leaves, cut into strips

1 lime, cut into wedges

In a small serving bowl, mix together sauce ingredients. Add ⅓ cup water, stir, and set aside. In a medium mixing bowl, combine all ingredients for the meatballs except oil. Form into six evenly-sized patties. Heat oil in a medium frying pan over medium-high heat and cook patties until brown on one side, about 3 minutes. Flip and cook on the other side until patties are cooked through. To assemble, divide noodles, bean sprouts, and lettuce leaves into bowls and top with meatballs, cilantro, and mint. Serve with accompanying sauce and lime wedges.

HONG
KONG

One of the few major commercial centers in the world that is also a tropical paradise, Hong Kong is a destination foodies, shopaholics, and outdoorsy-types can all agree on. Few other cities in the world can boast such a mix of restaurants, shops, and world-class museums all surrounded by a natural landscape. In this bustling city, the forest and ocean are always mere minutes away by advanced transportation system.

Hong Kong is a longstanding East-meets-West global crossroads. The smell of incense from old temples wafts up through new skyscrapers. The city is high-tech and fashion-forward, but also low key and spiritual. It is a town of ambitious bankers and kung fu masters, and the juxtaposition provides as much stimuli per square inch as anywhere on Earth.

Traditionally, Hong Kong bars have shown deep affinity for all things British. Even though the city is now part of China, there is a pervasive nostalgia for cricket, high tea, and Gin & Tonics. In addition, Japanese-style whiskey bars have long formed part of the backbone of the mixed drinks scene here. The result of these two influences has been a perception that Hong Kong is the fusty grande dame of the Asian bar world. However, exciting new bar openings demonstrate that the city's long cocktail history is less a hindrance and more of a head start. A new generation of bartenders is bringing up-to-date molecular gastronomy techniques as well as a hip sensibility to the glass.

THE HIGH BAR

Who doesn't enjoy a dramatic panorama while sipping a cocktail? Hong Kong lays claim to the world's highest bar, Ozone, on the 118th floor of the Ritz-Carlton. Following are other bars in Asia with breathtaking views:

Shanghai: **Cloud 9**, 87th floor, **Grand Hyatt**

Seoul: **Bar 81**, 81st floor, Lotte World Tower

Bangkok: **Vertigo**, 61st floor, Banyan Tree Bangkok

Singapore: **1-Altitude**, floors 61–63, The OUB Centre

Tokyo: **New York Bar**, 52nd floor, Park Hyatt

GUNNER

If Hong Kong has a signature cocktail it is the Gunner, a drink with origins in the British Navy. At one time, sailors were given Angostura bitters with their rations, and many popular drinks employing it were born on ships. This recipe is closely related to Australia's Campbell (see page 185), which has similar origins. The Captain's Bar at the Mandarin Oriental is the spot to drink a Gunner, although great versions can be found around the city. Here, rum is added to this otherwise nonalcoholic drink.

1½ ounces white rum

2 ounces ginger beer

2 ounces ginger ale

1 ounce fresh lime juice

2 dashes Angostura bitters

Lime wedge, for garnish

Sprig of mint, for garnish

Combine ingredients in a glass and stir. Add ice and garnish with a lime wedge and a sprig of mint.

SOHO SAUCE

SoHo, which in this instance stands for "South of Hollywood Road," is Hong Kong's sophisticated bar area. It abuts the party enclave of Lan Wai Fong, and the two form a symbiotic relationship between the elegant and the debauched. Inspiration for this drink comes from the sweet and sour flavors of this bar-studded area. Keep in mind that Hong Kong's craft cocktails are advanced and employ dry ice, sous-vide baths, centrifuges, rotary evaporators, and more. This is an homage to the kind of adventurous flavors found in SoHo cocktails. Shaoxing wine is widely available at Asian markets.

1½ ounces Earl Grey gin
(recipe below)

½ ounce Cointreau

1 ounce apple juice

½ ounce Shaoxing wine

1 egg white

Shake ingredients vigorously with ice and strain into a chilled cocktail glass.

FOR THE EARL GREY GIN

Steep two tea bags or 2 teaspoons loose tea in 6 ounces of gin for 30 minutes. Strain and store refrigerated in a sealed container for up to 2 weeks.

Made up of sixteen individual cities, the capital of the Philippines is more of a decentralized megalopolis than unified entity. Painfully difficult to get around with legendarily bad traffic, Manila nevertheless boasts vibrant pockets of some of the most exciting art and music scenes anywhere in the world—not to mention cocktails. In fact, this may be among the most underrated major cities in the world, a place where big things are happening under the radar and a little research rewards those who take a look.

It is important to know that cocktail culture is very old in the Philippines. When drinks writer Charles H. Baker Jr. dropped by the islands in the early 1930s, he noted that it was in Manila where he found Asia's "best and most consistent group of mixed drinks." Baker included a number of drinks by Filipino bartender Monk Antrim in his book, *The Gentleman's Companion*, and they are all worth exploring.

While it has been a protracted journey to take possession of the country's rich cocktail heritage, Manila bars are making up for lost time. Today, prestigious bar competitions are taking place in the country, and Filipino bartenders are becoming recognized globally for their exceptional skills and creativity.

Kalel Demetrio

Raised in the gritty streets of Manila, bartender and entrepreneur Kalel Demetrio worked his way up from being a sushi line cook to being one of his country's top drinks names. Inspired by the natural beauty and resources of the Philippines, Demetrio brought the jungle into the city at his bar Agimat in the Poblacion neighborhood. The restaurant, dubbed a "foraging bar and kitchen," features a giant vine-covered tree behind the counter.

"I've been on a lot of unbeaten paths just to search and discover ingredients," says Demetrio. "Some of it is undiscovered, and some is almost about to be extinct if we don't do something." Keen to discover native plants and incorporate them into drinks, Demetrio makes regular foraging trips out to some of the seven thousand islands that make up the Philippine archipelago. The results of his forays make it into cocktails, but also into Sirena gin, Demetrio's award-winning distillation project. "I meet a lot of people and those faces always give me a memorable experience," he says of his time searching for indigenous plants. "But the most unforgettable would be my days with the Albularyo, or shamans, who have taught me a lot of herbs that I never thought existed. Some are too bitter, some too sour, some too acrid, yet all work when concocted wisely."

GIN AND POMELO

This iconic cocktail was once served at the Museum Café in the San Lorenzo neighborhood. Pomelo looks and tastes like a giant grapefruit without the sourness or bitterness. It is a cash crop in the Philippines, and is joined in this drink by calamansi, a fruit that is something like a kumquat crossed with a lime. Gin is the base spirit. The Philippines is the world's biggest consumer of gin, leading the United States and Spain. Its popularity is a bit of a mystery, but the British brought it with them during their occupation of Manila in the 1700s, and it's conjectured that the spirit caught on with the city's Spanish settlers.

2 ounces gin
2 ounces pomelo juice
1 ounce calamansi or lime juice
¾ ounce honey
1 cucumber spear, for garnish

Shake ingredients with ice and strain into a rocks glass filled with ice. Garnish with a cucumber spear.

PINOY SOUR

Banana ketchup is a staple in the Philippines. The theory is that it appeared after Americans introduced tomato ketchup. Because there were no native tomatoes to re-create the condiment, bananas and food coloring were used instead. However, it is likely that a banana-based sauce was already indigenous to the islands. Whatever the origin, banana ketchup is rich and not too tangy, making it a wonderful addition in cocktails. It should be more widely used and can be found in Asian grocery stores or online.

2 ounces white rum
2 ounces mango juice
1 ounce banana ketchup
½ ounce fresh lime juice

Shake ingredients with ice and strain into a rocks glass with ice.

SEOUL

The capital of South Korea sits tucked dramatically between four guardian mountains. The largest peak, Bugaksan, acts as the city's backdrop, and at its foot sits the elegant *thirteenth*-century Gyeongbok Palace. The castle forms the ancient heart of this fast-paced and technologically advanced city. Seoul is a place of contrasts, where the modern and ancient coexist side by side, fashion-forward boutiques abut traditional stores, and Michelin-starred restaurants share street corners with noodle shops.

As one might expect of a wealthy city whose inhabitants love to go out, Seoul sports a serious drinking culture. There is a dizzying array of drinking options, ranging from street tents called *pojangmacha* serving soju (see page 107), to Western-style bars offering fine wine. With a top-notch transportation system, it is easy to hit a few places, and even a couple of neighborhoods, in a single night. As an additional bonus, it is legal to drink anywhere—a popular option being on plastic chairs inside convenience stores.

When in Seoul, be sure to sample *makgeolli*. This thick and opaque rice wine was once the tipple of the older generation, but has become a hit among the city's youth. For more upscale drinking options, Seoul's craft cocktail dens compare with the very best in the world and tend to pop up in secretive, speakeasy-style alleyways. Even the famed Charles H. bar in the Four Seasons Hotel is behind an unmarked door. At any of the city's craft cocktail bars, expect wowing, competition-style cocktails and impeccable service.

Soju Yogurt Cocktail

PICTURED ON PAGE 109

Soju cocktails made with drinkable yogurt and carbonated water are popular in Seoul. They come in a variety of flavors. A quick internet search will reveal just how many unique Korean yogurt drinks are available. Outside of the country, any off-the-shelf yogurt "smoothie" or "shake" will work. Try any flavor you prefer; a favorite in Seoul is peach.

3 ounces soju

3 ounces yogurt drink

3 ounces lemon-lime soda

Shake ingredients with ice and strain into a rocks glass.

Scotch-Plum Flip

Flips are an enduring class of cocktails, once concocted by sticking a hot poker into a drink and boiling the contents. That was three hundred years ago. Today, flips are typically served cold like a boozy milkshake. Korean plum extract (look for *maesil wonaek*) is a magnificent tool in the cocktailer's arsenal. It is sweet and sour without being either cloying or puckering. It is available in Asian grocery stores and online.

2½ ounces scotch (preferably Famous Grouse)

½ ounce plum extract

2 teaspoons heavy cream

1 egg yolk

Shake ingredients vigorously with ice and strain into a cocktail glass.

SOJU

Soju is Korea's version of rice wine, not to be confused with either Chinese *baiju* or Japanese *shochu*. Why the confusion of similar names? Because they are all derived from the same Chinese root word, *shaojin*, which means "burnt wine." Soju is made by fermenting rice with a wheat cake called *nuruk*, which acts as a starter. Soju is clear and tastes a little sweet from added sugar. In theory, soju is low proof, but be warned that it can be up to 50 percent alcohol. Although usually consumed neat, soju cocktails are popular around the globe. It might surprise you to learn that the spirit is one of the three most consumed alcoholic beverages on the planet along with Russian vodka and Brazilian cachaça.

SCALLION PANCAKES

SERVES 4

Snacks that accompany drinks, called *anju*, are a big part of Korean dining culture. They may take the form of nuts and fruits, or more complicated dishes like fried chicken. One of the most popular, and easiest to make, is a scallion pancake called *pajeon*. Crispy and a little greasy, they are an ideal accompaniment to cocktails.

FOR THE DIPPING SAUCE

4 tablespoons soy sauce

1½ teaspoons rice vinegar

1 teaspoon toasted sesame oil

1 teaspoon honey

½ teaspoon finely grated fresh ginger

½ teaspoon crushed red pepper flakes

FOR THE PANCAKES

2 cups flour

2 tablespoons cornstarch

2 eggs, beaten

1 teaspoon salt

1½ cups cold sparkling water

5 scallions, halved lengthwise and cut into 2-inch pieces

2 tablespoons vegetable oil

In a small bowl, combine dipping sauce ingredients and set aside. In a medium bowl, whisk together flour, cornstarch, eggs, salt, and sparkling water. Gently fold in scallions. Heat 1 tablespoon oil in a 10-inch skillet over medium heat. Pour half of the batter into the skillet, swirling the skillet so batter covers the edges. Cook until brown on the bottom, 3–4 minutes. Flip and cook until the other side is brown, 3–4 minutes more. Remove pancake to a cutting board. Repeat with remaining half of the batter. Cut each pancake into wedges and serve with the dipping sauce.

As China's most cosmopolitan city and a premier financial hub, Shanghai has played a huge role in the country's economic and cultural boom. The giant metropolis is China's showcase to the world, and it has been developed by the government to compete with the world's greatest cities. To this end, Shanghai boasts a number of record-breaking features. It sports the fastest train (267 mph) and the largest metro (400 miles), as well as a shocking number of skyscrapers—not to mention it has an exploding art and music scene as well as diverse food and drinking options. As a window into the mainland, Shanghai offers a glimpse of the Chinese "can do" spirit that is rocking the world.

Like other Asian cities, Shanghai's cocktail scene is a mix of luxury bars and cozy speakeasies. The latter often harken back to the city's Jazz Age heyday, and some even feature a sultry singer in the corner. At the glam Peace Hotel, the world's oldest jazz band (the drummer is in his nineties) plays while guests sip drinks that would not have been out of place a century ago. In the leafy French Concession neighborhood, hipsters sip cocktails at craft bars that use roto-evaporators, dry ice, and sous vide baths. At all types of establishments, you'll find complex and world-aware drinks. Excitingly, the city's cocktails are also enlivened with local ingredients: tea, lychee fruit, Sichuan peppercorns, goji berries, and osmanthus flowers all make their way into drinks.

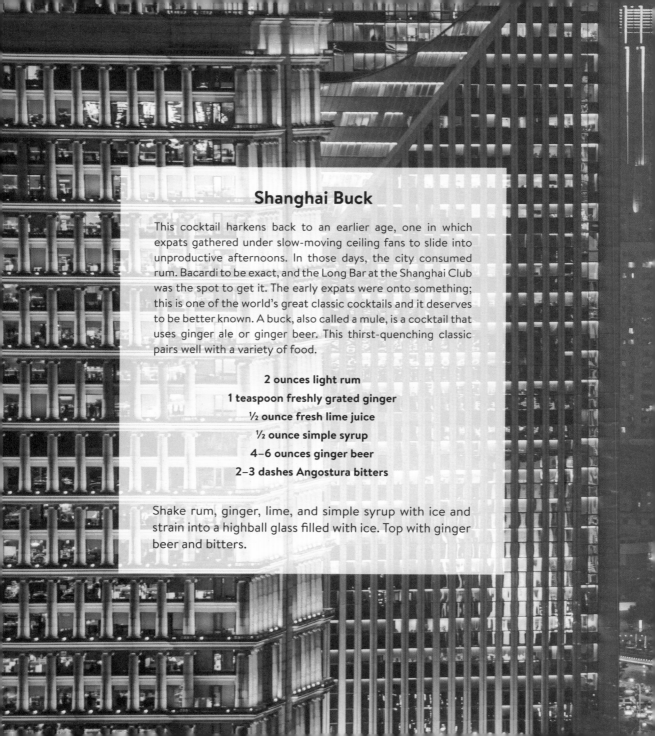

Shanghai Buck

This cocktail harkens back to an earlier age, one in which expats gathered under slow-moving ceiling fans to slide into unproductive afternoons. In those days, the city consumed rum. Bacardi to be exact, and the Long Bar at the Shanghai Club was the spot to get it. The early expats were onto something; this is one of the world's great classic cocktails and it deserves to be better known. A buck, also called a mule, is a cocktail that uses ginger ale or ginger beer. This thirst-quenching classic pairs well with a variety of food.

2 ounces light rum
1 teaspoon freshly grated ginger
½ ounce fresh lime juice
½ ounce simple syrup
4–6 ounces ginger beer
2–3 dashes Angostura bitters

Shake rum, ginger, lime, and simple syrup with ice and strain into a highball glass filled with ice. Top with ginger beer and bitters.

Osmanthus Martini

Osmanthus is common in Shanghai cocktails. The flower has a fruity aroma and flavor, reminiscent of apricot or peach, and can be found in tea shops and online. Here, the flower's delicate smell rises above the drink as you nose it. Taking a sip, it is a touch sweet. The result is a glorious Martini that is all subtlety and class.

2 ounces gin (preferably Plymouth)
1 ounce osmanthus-infused vermouth (recipe below)
Orange peel, for garnish

Stir ingredients with ice and strain into a cocktail glass. Garnish with an orange peel.

FOR THE OSMANTHUS-INFUSED VERMOUTH

Steep 2 tablespoons dried osmanthus flowers in 1 cup vermouth overnight. Strain and keep tightly sealed in a refrigerator for up to 2 weeks.

SINGAPORE

Nuclear. That is how best to describe the intensity of the cocktail scene in the city-state of Singapore. In fact, if you ask bartenders around the world where they would most like to drink, the majority will say this little island (just twenty-seven square miles) off the coast of Malaysia. All eyes have turned to the city's recent spree of high-profile bar openings.

The Lion City—*singa pura* means "Lion City" in Sanskrit—rises out of the jungle on the edge of the South China Sea like a futuristic movie set. Under British rule for a hundred years, it has gone on since independence in 1965 to become a kind of modern Asian Athens (minus the democracy). It is sophisticated, efficient, and self-assured. It is also famously one of the best places in the world to eat. Hundreds, if not thousands, of hawker stalls offer a dizzying array of cuisines perfect for soaking up booze.

While Singapore is the world's hottest city to go tippling, the traveling imbiber should be forewarned that it is expensive. Vices are allowed by the city's enlightened rulers, but are heavily taxed. The result of a 25 percent duty on alcohol is drinks that are pricier than New York or London. But then, it is possible to eat the best noodles of your life here for $2, so things tend to even out. An upside to a scene composed of luxury bars with dizzying prices is that drinks do not disappoint. From wild infusions to garnishes such as freeze-dried ants, every cocktail is an event designed to be a memorable showstopper. Singapore's bars wow. They also do an admirable job slaking an insatiable thirst driven by a combination of exploding wealth, Anglo drinking habits, and a young population. These days, the Lion City is roaring for a cocktail.

Singapore Sling

Based on an earlier recipe, the Straits Sling, this fantastic sipper was created in the early 1900s at the Raffles Hotel bar by bartender Ngiam Tong Boon. There are a multitude of conflicting versions. Below is the current Raffles Hotel bar recipe, but with my reduced amounts of pineapple and grenadine (it is too sweet otherwise). Note that while this may be Singapore's most famous cocktail, it is considered by locals to be a drink for tourists.

- 1½ ounces gin
- ½ ounce Cherry Heering
- ¼ ounce Cointreau
- ¼ ounce Bénédictine
- 2 ounces fresh pineapple juice
- ¼ ounce grenadine
- ½ ounce fresh lime juice
- 1 dash Angostura bitters
- 1 ounce club soda
- Orange slice, for garnish
- Cherry, for garnish

Shake all ingredients except soda with ice and strain into a highball glass filled with ice. Top with soda and garnish with an orange slice and a cherry.

Nasi Lemak Cocktail

Singaporeans love drinks that emulate the flavors of their famous food dishes. You can find cocktails that taste like Hainanese chicken rice, chili crab, and even the famed beef broth staple, *bak kut teh*. This particular winner employs all the flavors of the classic Malaysian specialty *nasi lemak*, a dish of coconut and pandan-flavored rice served with sides such as eggs, peanuts, cucumbers, anchovies, and hot chili paste. Pandan, also known as screw pine leaf, is ubiquitous in Southeast Asian cuisine. It has become a popular ingredient in cocktails around the world. Note that sambal oelek, or ground chili paste, is widely available in Asian grocery stores. Pandan leaves can be found in Asian grocery stores either frozen or canned.

- 2 ounces gin
- ½ ounce fresh lemon juice
- ½ ounce pandan simple syrup (recipe below)
- 1 ounce coconut water
- Sambal oelek, for garnish

Shake ingredients with ice and strain into a rocks glass filled with ice. Garnish with sambal smeared around the rim of the glass.

FOR THE PANDAN SIMPLE SYRUP
In a sealable container, add two chopped pandan leaves to 1 cup hot water and 1 cup sugar. Shake and rest mixture in a refrigerator overnight. Strain and keep refrigerated for up to a week.

Chicken Satay

Marinated and grilled meat served with dipping sauce may be the ultimate drinking snack. It is simple, delicious, and works as a casual finger food at cocktail parties. Satay likely originated on the island of Java and is descended from kebab. Muslim traders brought textiles to Indonesia to trade in exchange for spices, and a glorious food fusion occurred. Satay then spread throughout Southeast Asia and beyond. Note that this recipe must be started a day in advance—which is perfect because it is quick to finish, leaving time for making drinks. Galangal, sometimes called Thai ginger, is earthy and citrusy; it is widely available in grocery stores. Note that retoasting already dry roasted peanuts brings out their full flavor.

FOR THE CHICKEN

1 teaspoon ground coriander

1 teaspoon ground cumin

2 shallots

2 garlic cloves

1 lemongrass stalk (tender part only), roughly chopped

1 piece of galangal, 2 inches long, peeled and sliced

1 piece of ginger, 1 inch long, peeled and sliced

2 teaspoons salt

2 pounds boneless and skinless chicken thighs, cut into 1-inch-wide strips

2 tablespoons light brown sugar

2 teaspoons soy sauce

½ cup coconut or peanut oil (vegetable oil is a fine substitute)

In a food processor, combine coriander, cumin, shallots, garlic, lemongrass, galangal, ginger, and salt into a smooth paste. In a sealable container, combine chicken, spice mixture, sugar, and soy sauce. Stir and refrigerate overnight. If you are grilling with wooden skewers, soak 30–40 overnight in a pan filled with water to prevent them from catching fire.

To cook, reserve marinade for dipping sauce and place chicken pieces on skewers. Grill until browned, flipping frequently, about 15 minutes. If baking, cook skewered chicken pieces at 425°F for 15 to 20 minutes, flipping halfway through. Serve with dipping sauce.

FOR THE DIPPING SAUCE

1 cup dry-roasted peanuts, chopped

2 lemongrass stalks (tender part only), chopped

1 piece of galangal, 2 inches long, peeled and sliced

3 shallots, quartered

3 garlic cloves

2 tablespoons sambal oelek

2 tablespoons peanut or coconut oil

2 tablespoons soy sauce

2 tablespoons brown sugar

Toast peanuts in a skillet until brown, about 4 minutes. Set aside to cool. In a food processor, blend lemongrass, galangal, shallots, garlic, and sambal until it forms a paste. In a medium saucepan, heat oil and fry paste with leftover satay marinade until fragrant, about 5 minutes. Add peanuts, soy sauce, sugar, and 2 cups water, and bring to a boil. Simmer until the mixture thickens, about 10 minutes. Serve sauce at room temperature. Note: This sauce will keep for up to a week; reheat and allow to cool before serving.

TAIPEI
TAIWAN

The capital of the
Republic of China sits tucked at the
northern end of the verdant island of Taiwan, formerly called Ilha Formosa, or "the beautiful island." Taipei
is a hectic yet livable metropolis, brimming with lush parks and
inviting markets. Buildings from the island's Japanese era (1895–1945)
vie for attention with modern skyscrapers and make for an atmosphere
imbued with both history and futuristic élan. The city is a multicultural mishmash, rewarding the visitor with an ancient culture, but also with a delightful
quirkiness. This is underscored by a skyline dominated by the Taipei 101 tower,
which rises up like a wild bamboo stalk.

Taipei has been gripped by cocktail fever recently. New tippling dens range
from wondrously old-school spots stirring bespoke classics, to science-y bars
serving modern cocktails on draft. Mixed drinks here are a lesson in employing
local ingredients to make unique potations that strike a balance between
the known and the outré. In fact, going out in Taipei can be a bit like
entering Wonka's factory; there are a lot of wild things to explore.
Bars use modern techniques to incorporate herbs, fruits, and
teas from the city's surroundings. Expect to find mung
beans, fermented yams, sesame seeds, and
even cedar tree juice.

Dragon Well Daiquiri

Tea is an integral part of Taiwanese culture and in constant supply. Likewise, Daiquiris are a hugely popular drink in the tropical climate. Dragon Well tea, which is pan-roasted to give the leaves a nutty flavor, provides this cocktail with complex flavors. Note that the temperature of the water for steeping is important; if it's too hot, the syrup will become bitter.

2 ounces white rum

1 ounce fresh lime juice

½ ounce Dragon Well tea simple syrup (recipe below)

Shake ingredients with ice and strain into a cocktail glass.

FOR THE DRAGON WELL SIMPLE SYRUP

Steep 3 tablespoons Dragon Well tea in ½ cup of 180°F water for 5 minutes. Strain tea into a sealable container, add ½ cup sugar, and shake until sugar is dissolved. The syrup will keep in a refrigerator for a week.

Taiwan Tonic

Asian pear is a big crop in Taiwan. The plump, apple-like fruit is juicy and adds subtle flavor to cocktails. In addition, Asian pear juice has been shown in studies to be a cure for hangovers. Great news! This drink invokes Taipei in the glass with a combination of whiskey, pear, and oolong tea. Note that Asian pear juice can be found in grocery stores or online. It can also be made by juicing fresh pears. When using fresh, adjust the drink's sweetness with additional simple syrup if necessary.

2 ounces whiskey

2 ounces Asian pear juice

1 ounce oolong tea

¼ ounce simple syrup (optional)

2 ounces tonic water

Lemon peel, for garnish

Stir whiskey, pear juice, tea, and simple syrup (if using) in a highball glass filled with ice. Top with tonic water and garnish with a lemon peel.

Expansive, deep, and fast-moving—you had better know how to swim. Japan's capital is the largest city in the world by population, a megalopolis of such proportion that it feels boundless. Plus, sip on this: Tokyo has as many Michelin-starred restaurants as London, Paris, and New York combined. The city is a mind-bogglingly dense landscape of unending food and beverage options, including cocktails.

Tokyo has been the mixed drinks capital of Asia since the 1950s. In that time, the city's bartenders have exerted a big influence not only on its neighbors, but around the globe. Technique? Second to none. Attention to detail? Unrivaled. Dedication to craft? There have been famous career bartenders in Tokyo for decades. To add more complexity, Tokyo's bar scene boasts types of establishments that are not found in the West. For instance, a highlight of any trip to the city is its many record bars (see below). While these spots are not necessarily "craft" cocktail establishments, some offer similarly high-quality drinks. Because the Japanese are perfectionists, cocktails at humble bars are often on par with those at the best spots in other cities. Whether you order a complicated concoction or a simple highball, it will be extraordinarily well made.

The cocktail enthusiast should know a few additional things before jumping into Tokyo's mixed drinks scene: Whiskey Highballs are ubiquitous; advanced techniques like hand-carved ice were practiced long before any craft cocktail "revival" in the West; mixed drinks are part of broader Japanese food culture and they often refer to season and to place.

TOKYO'S RECORD BARS

Tokyo's record bars are descendants of the city's 1950s jazz cafés, called *kissa*. These were small, humble bars where enthusiasts gathered and listened to the latest LPs coming from America. Hi-fi equipment was too expensive to own at home, and the cafés filled a niche for obsessive music fans. At one time, there were over six hundred such establishments, clustered around train stations so commuters could stop on their way home from work. Some original vinyl bars still exist and have been joined by newer spots themed around specific genres; there are listening dens dedicated to soul, metal, drone, psychedelic rock, and more. The unique spaces provide a cozy and convivial atmosphere for music fans, and are also an essential part of the city's cocktail scene.

Whiskey Highball

Whiskey Highballs are religion in Tokyo. What sets them apart from just being whiskey and soda is the attention given to every aspect of the drink: glassware is chilled, ice is the correct size, bubbles are tight, and the whiskey is at perfect temperature. For best results, stir slowly so as not to lose the soda's bubbles. The ratio most common in Japan is 1:4 whiskey to water.

1 ounce whiskey | 4 ounces club soda
Lemon peel, for garnish

Stir whiskey and water in a chilled rocks glass filled with ice. Garnish with a lemon peel.

Yuzu Gimlet

Yuzu is a fruit that is tart and aromatic like a grapefruit, bright and refreshing like a lemon, and delicious like a mandarin orange. It is a frequent ingredient in Japanese cuisine, used to flavor vegetables, fish, hot pots, and custards. In this drink, the addition of yuzu's unique sour flavor makes for a nuanced and delicate Gimlet.

2 ounces gin | ¼ ounce yuzu juice
½ ounce fresh lime juice | ¾ ounce simple syrup
Zest of 1 lime

Shake ingredients with ice and double-strain into a chilled cocktail glass. Note: to double-strain, hold a fine strainer above the cocktail glass as you strain the shaker.

SWEET AND SPICY EDAMAME

SERVES 2-4

Edamame, or soybeans in their pod, are a lively, interactive bar snack. They are typically consumed with beer or sake, but are great with cocktails, too. In this version, they are given a sweet and spicy glaze for an extra punch of flavor.

2 cups frozen edamame in their shell
2 tablespoons soy sauce
1 tablespoon rice vinegar
1½ tablespoons brown sugar
½ teaspoon crushed red pepper flakes
1 teaspoon vegetable oil
1 garlic clove, finely minced
½ teaspoon fresh ginger, skin removed, finely minced

Cook edamame according to package directions. In a small bowl, mix together soy sauce, rice vinegar, brown sugar, and red pepper flakes with 2 tablespoons of water and set aside. Heat oil in a small saucepan over medium-low heat. Add garlic and ginger, cooking 1–2 minutes. Add soy sauce mixture and increase heat to medium. Stirring frequently, cook until sauce reduces to a glaze, about 5–7 minutes. Add edamame and toss to coat. Remove edamame to a serving bowl using tongs and pour any leftover glaze into a small dipping bowl.

CHAPTER 4

THE AMERICAS

When Europeans first came to the New World, they brought a limited supply of alcohol with them. The moment their boats hit the shores, a race was on to find ingredients that would ferment and make new drink. The settlers tried tree sap, vegetables, berries, and fruits like persimmons. Their need to forage and explore new ingredients played a big role in the creation of mixed drinks. Cocktails developed out of a spirit of innovation.

Over the years, three plants emerged as dominant sources for liquor in the New World: sugarcane, corn, and agave—rum, whiskey, and tequila (mezcal). Distillates from these three provide the base for the majority of cocktails in this chapter.

Today, the Americas are a cornucopia of ever-changing trends and drink styles. Each region has vibrant local traditions and can claim unique contributions to the world of imbibing: the Caribbean islands have been the source for the world's most famous hot-weather cocktails (Daiquiris and Mojitos); in South America, aficionados will find both laid-back aperitivo culture and terroir-driven drinks that speak of place, of the Amazon and the Andes; up north, the United States remains an epicenter for cocktailing and boasts thriving mixed drinks scenes in most cities. In all parts of the Americas, bartenders are creatively adapting to new technology and, thrillingly, returning to indigenous ingredients for inspiration.

The sprawling, high-altitude capital of Colombia is a dreamscape of Spanish colonial architecture set under dramatic Andean peaks. It is a city of big, inexpensive lunches and fascinating museums. In fact, Bogotá boasts over fifty excellent cultural institutions and museums worth a look. Between sights, markets brim with exotic produce, a constant reminder that the Amazon basin is not far away. Stir in the city's famously cool weather, and it's a paradise of manageable stops traversable by charming cobblestone streets.

Emerging from fifty years of unrest and civil war, Bogotá is on fire with energy and a renewed lust for life. Bars are open late and dancing is a must. Clubs play a compelling form of Afro-Colombian music fused with electronica—and do not be surprised to hear salsa and punk rock, back to back. The vibe is exuberant and experimental, a lively fusion of cultural influences.

Restaurants and bars celebrate Bogotá's diversity on their menus. Traditional spots serve beer and *aguardiente*, the local firewater made of raw sugarcane juice and aniseed. Newer cocktails bars are bringing mixed drinks culture to the capital. Most offer creations incorporating the many local juices, such as *tomate de árbol*, or tree tomato. Fancy a cocktail with coca leaf? That is available, too.

CANELAZO

This drink is designed for those cool nights high in the Andes. It is found throughout Colombia, Peru, Ecuador, and northern Argentina. While it is traditionally served around Christmas, Canelazo is appropriate anytime temperatures dip. Full of vitamin C, it also helps ward off colds.

SERVES 4

2 teaspoons brown sugar

1 ounce fresh lime juice

½ teaspoon cloves

2 cinnamon sticks

4 ounces fresh orange juice

4 ounces aguardiente or white rum

Orange slice, for garnish

In a medium saucepan, simmer 3 cups water with brown sugar, lime juice, cloves, and cinnamon sticks for 10 minutes. Remove from heat and add orange juice and rum. Strain and garnish with an orange slice.

EUCALYPTO SWIZZLE

Eucalyptus is an invasive species that grows on the hillsides around Bogotá. What better way to stop the spread of the plant than harvest it for drinks? Bartender Tom Hydzik does just that for his drinks at restaurant Mesa Franca. His take on a classic swizzle also employs *viche*, a sugarcane-based distillate primarily made by Afro-Colombian communities. The moonshine is consumed in *vicheras*, taverns that combine traditional music and drinking. In this recipe, viche can be approximated with cachaça or white rum.

2 ounces viche

¾ ounce fresh lime juice

½ ounce Fernet-Branca

1 ounce eucalyptus simple syrup
(recipe below)

4–5 dashes Angostura bitters

Eucalyptus leaf, for garnish

Shake ingredients with ice and strain into a glass with crushed ice. Garnish with bitters and a eucalyptus leaf. Serve with a straw.

FOR THE EUCALYPTUS SIMPLE SYRUP

In a sealable container, combine a sprig of eucalyptus (about six leaves) with 1 cup hot water and 1 cup sugar. Shake and rest mixture in a refrigerator for a few hours or overnight. Strain and keep refrigerated for up to a week.

PLANTAIN CHIPS

SERVES 2-6

Colombians love plantains. The bananas are consumed in every way imaginable: green, ripe, on pizza, in desserts, and even in coffee. Perhaps the best way to eat them is fried, as chips. They are an addictive bar snack.

3 green plantains, peeled
3 cups vegetable oil
Kosher salt, to taste

For best results, cut plantains in half crosswise and use a mandolin to make thin slices lengthwise. If you don't have a mandolin, cut bananas crosswise in diagonal ovals instead. A note that if plantains are very ripe, they can be cut with their peels on (remove peels after slicing). Heat oil in a sauté pan to between 375 and 400°F. Add plantains to the hot oil, being careful not to overcrowd. Fry in batches until chips are golden. Remove using a slotted spoon, and drain on paper towels. Sprinkle with salt and serve with salsa.

BUENOS AIRES

ARGENTINA

Buenos Aires is an elegant city, exuding a faded European glamour and decidedly Latin charm. Its inhabitants are elegant, too, and full of that signature Argentine passion. The vibrancy of the city's people makes it one of the most captivating places on Earth, filled with avant-garde art and *milongas* (dance salons), bookstores, and opera. Buenos Aires is also home to a food scene unrivaled anywhere in South America outside of Lima. There are steakhouses (*parrillas*) on nearly every block, as well as chic restaurants serving well-executed takes on Japanese and French cuisine. To wash down all the great food, there is local Malbec or Bonarda wine and also *mate*, an herbal tea made from dried yerba mate leaves. The stuff is religion in Argentina, and it is impossible to go anywhere without seeing people passing around the traditional drinking accoutrements of a gourd and metal straw.

Because such a large number of Argentines lay claim to Italian descent, the drinking routine in Buenos Aires is strikingly similar to Italy's aperitivo culture. Think relaxed early evening cocktails, heavy on the amaros. There are locally made liqueurs for this task, such as Amargo Obrero and Hesperidina, but the market is dominated by Italian brands Campari and Fernet-Branca. In fact, Fernet mixed with cola is something of the national drink, and Argentina boasts the only production facility for the minty digestif outside Milan.

Porteños, as the city's residents are called, are serious night owls. Bars get jumping around midnight, and clubs often get their push at 4 a.m. Craft cocktail bars are relative newcomers to the nighttime mix but already display a fierce sense of pride—evident in Argentinian interpretations of classic drinks.

TATO'S NEGRONI

At bar Florería Atlántico, owner Tato Giovannoni constructs an Argentinian take on the Negroni called the Balestrini. For his version, he employs his own Príncipe de los Apóstoles gin, Averna rather than vermouth, and locally produced Campari. He also adds a touch of seawater and then smokes the drink using eucalyptus branches. This is an homage to Tato's creation.

1½ ounces gin
(preferably Príncipe de los Apóstoles)
¾ ounce Campari
¾ ounce Averna
¼ ounce seawater (see note below)
Orange slice, for garnish
Sprig of eucalyptus, for garnish

Stir ingredients with ice and strain into a chilled rocks glass over ice. Garnish with orange slice and a sprig of eucalyptus.

Note: To re-create ocean water, add a shy 2 teaspoons salt to 1 cup water.

CLARITO

The Clarito was created in 1935 by the dashing Argentinian bartender Santiago Policastro. The drink was his take on a Dry Martini, minus the olives and with the addition of lemon and sugar. Wildly popular in the 1930s, the cocktail slipped into obscurity until bartender Federico Cuco revived it at Verne Cocktail Club in the mid-2000s. The Clarito is a prime example of a historic drink resurrected to newfound popularity. Thanks to Cuco's efforts, it is now found in bars throughout Buenos Aires. Note that the sugar is typically omitted and is optional.

1 teaspoon white sugar,
to rim the glass (optional)
2½ ounces gin
½ ounce dry vermouth
Strip of lemon peel
Lemon twist, for garnish

Coat rim of a chilled cocktail glass with sugar. In a mixing glass, stir gin and vermouth with ice. Express a lemon peel into the mixture and strain into the prepared glass. Garnish with a lemon twist.

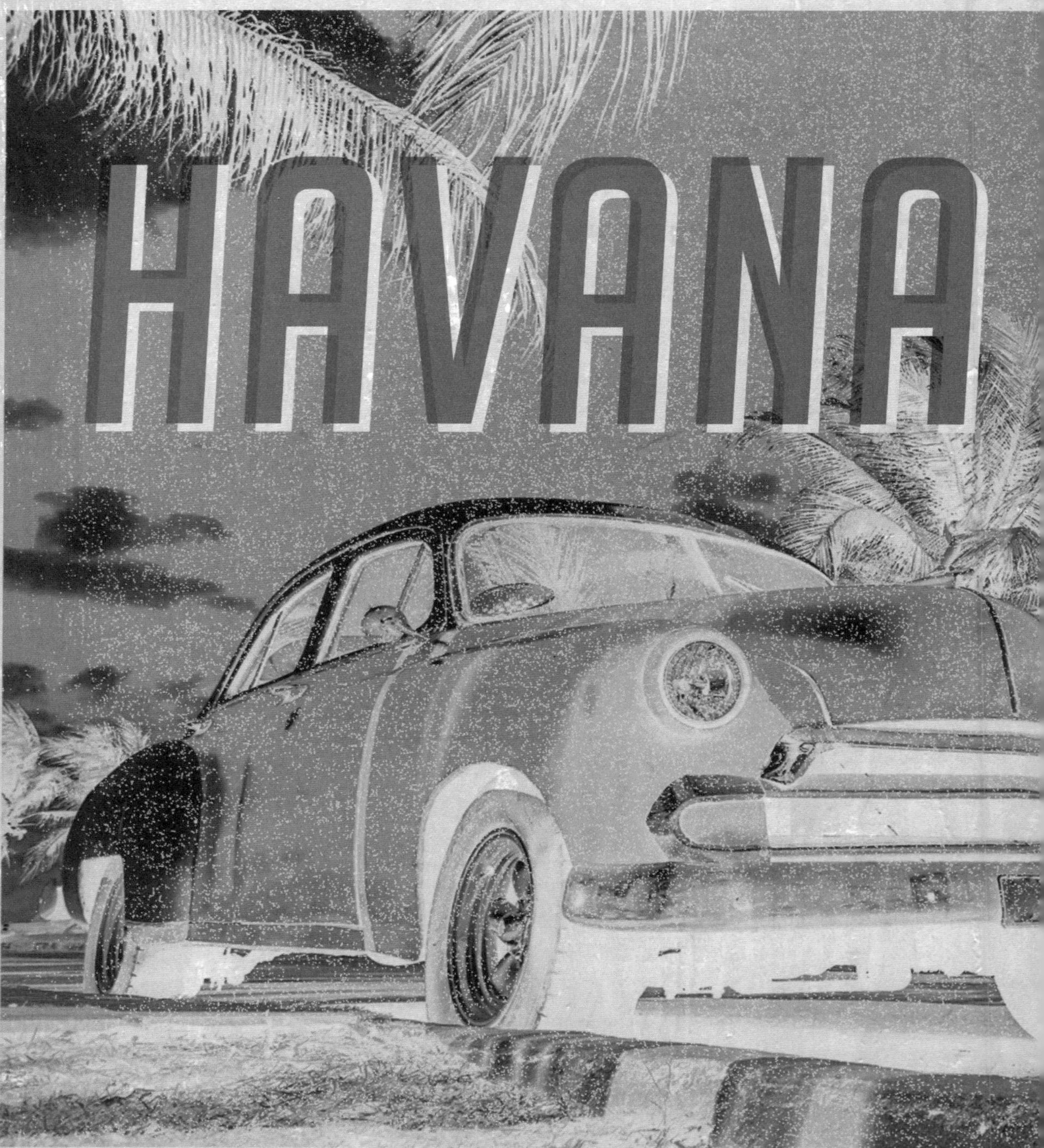
HAVANA

CUBA

Few cities strike a nerve in the cocktailer like Havana. Yes, Cuba's capital boasts famous music, dancing, food, and cars. But for aficionados of mixed drinks, this is all secondary to the city's role as an incubator for world-famous cocktails. Havana's bartenders have had an outsized global influence. Visit nearly any city on the planet and you will encounter Mojitos and Daiquiris. As if this weren't enough, Hemingway drank here, and any association with the Great Imbiber conjures memories of glamorous, early twentieth-century cocktailing. Indeed, the boozy writer still looms large over this biggest of Caribbean islands.

Only eighty-five miles off the shore of the United States, Havana is a long distance culturally. However, at one time, the city was the playground for hard-partying Americans. The nightlife was attractive enough that Hemingway bought a house here in 1940. Papa, as he was known, loved to frequent a couple haunts that are still operational today; the Floridita claimed his attention for its Daiquiris, and La Bodeguita del Medio was the spot where he spent afternoons downing Mojitos. The two bars are must-visits on any trip to the city.

In a way, Havana is a victim of its own success. Visitors expect to find a city that captures the mystique of Hemingway's era, a time when its famous cocktails were the toast of the world. The city caters to this expectation and can be museum-like in its reverence for another age. However, delving deeper, there are aspects to this island's drink culture that are less famous but just as noteworthy. Anyone interested in mixed drinks history should seek out cocktails created by the *mambises*, the island's separatist guerilla fighters. These soldiers had a hand in creating such classics as the Cuba-Libre, but also lesser known drinks like the Canchánchara (see page 143).

MOJITO

This hugely popular libation can be traced all the way back to a sixteenth-century drink named El Draque. Considered by some to be the first cocktail ever invented, El Draque is named for explorer Sir Francis Drake and is credited with saving the captain's scurvy-stricken sailors when they reached the Caribbean. The modern version, the Mojito, gained widespread popularity in the 1950s and today is one of the world's most popular cocktails.

4 mint leaves, plus a sprig for garnish
¾ ounce simple syrup
2 ounces light rum
¾ ounce fresh lime juice
2 ounces club soda

Gently muddle mint with simple syrup in a rocks glass. Add rum and lime juice and stir. Fill the glass with ice and top with soda. Garnish with a sprig of mint.

DAIQUIRI

The story goes that this classic was created in the late 1890s by a mining engineer named Jennings Cox in order to protect his workers from yellow fever. At the time, it was believed that lime and alcohol helped protect against the disease. Hemingway was drinking Daiquiris as early as the 1930s—he even created his own famous version—and the classic drink found widespread popularity later in the 1940s.

2 ounces light rum
1 ounce fresh lime juice
½ ounce simple syrup
Lime wheel, for garnish

Shake ingredients with ice and strain into a cocktail glass. Garnish with a lime wheel.

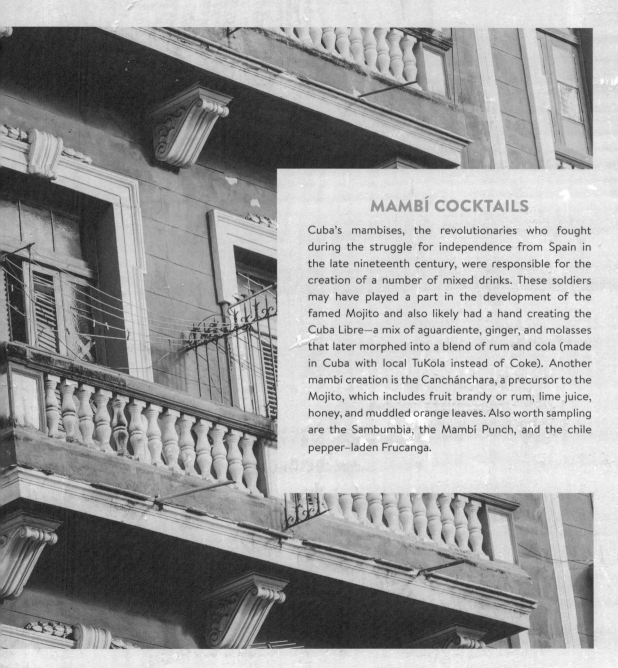

MAMBÍ COCKTAILS

Cuba's mambises, the revolutionaries who fought during the struggle for independence from Spain in the late nineteenth century, were responsible for the creation of a number of mixed drinks. These soldiers may have played a part in the development of the famed Mojito and also likely had a hand creating the Cuba Libre—a mix of aguardiente, ginger, and molasses that later morphed into a blend of rum and cola (made in Cuba with local TuKola instead of Coke). Another mambí creation is the Canchánchara, a precursor to the Mojito, which includes fruit brandy or rum, lime juice, honey, and muddled orange leaves. Also worth sampling are the Sambumbia, the Mambí Punch, and the chile pepper–laden Frucanga.

Originally a small encampment founded by the conquistador Pizarro on the edge of the Pacific Ocean, today Lima is a giant sprawl larger than New York City. Despite its massive size, Peru's capital is a town of contemplative flower gardens, graceful colonial buildings, and fascinating ancient ruins. The beach is never far away, and proximity to the seaside is a big contributor to the city's relatively subdued vibe. The nearby ocean is also home to one of the planet's premier fishing areas, and the wealth of resources attracts Japanese chefs. Their presence leaves no room for doubt: this is the best city in South America to eat.

The tipple of choice in Peru's capital is *pisco*, a clear grape brandy that can claim the distinction of being the first liquor distilled in the New World. The Spanish began cultivating grape vines in Peru as early as the 1540s, and Pisco appeared sometime in the 1700s.

A highlight of going out in Lima is a number of surviving "peña" bars, traditional spots where people gather to eat, drink, and dance to Peruvian folk music. The bars are a bit like tavern speakeasies, with festivities taking place behind closed doors. Check local listings to find them. Peñas are ideal spots to drink Peru's national cocktail, the Pisco Sour. The drink is everywhere, although the country's recent economic boom means chic cocktail bars have arrived, and with them, Martinis, Manhattans, and other classics.

PISCO SOUR

The origin of this cocktail is much disputed, but it was likely created by bartender Victor Morris at his Lima bar in the 1920s. It is a refreshing, frothy crowd-pleaser. Note that Peruvian and Chilean piscos are not necessarily interchangeable. Chilean piscos tend to be sweeter and slightly lower proof. You will need to adjust the amount of simple syrup and lemon juice accordingly.

2 ounces pisco

1 ounce fresh lime juice

½ ounce simple syrup

1 egg white

2 dashes Angostura bitters, for garnish

Shake ingredients vigorously and strain into a cocktail glass. Garnish with bitters.

SPIKED EMOLIENTE

SERVES 4-6

Emoliente is an herbal tea served by Lima's street vendors. There are many variations, but ingredients traditionally include toasted barley, flax seeds, dried grass, plantain leaf, and an herb called horsetail. The concoction is believed to have medicinal properties, and vendors will make bespoke versions depending on your ailments. Prepackaged versions of the tea are available in grocery stores and online.

1 package emoliente

16 ounces pisco

¼ cup honey

2 limes, cut into small wedges

Boil contents of emoliente package in 2 liters of water for 30 minutes. Strain, add pisco and honey, and stir well to combine. Ladle into individual glasses and squeeze a lime wedge into glasses.

CEVICHE

SERVES 2–4

Once you discover how easy it is to make ceviche, it will become part of your repertoire for wowing guests. Do not fear raw fish; it gets cooked by the acid of the lime juice. This basic recipe can be altered by adding other spices or more hot peppers. The serrano in the marinade adds subtle flavor, but adding minced jalapeños in addition also works if you like things *caliente*.

1 pound fresh, skinless snapper, bass, or other ocean fish fillets, cut into ½-inch dice

1 cup fresh lime juice

1 serrano pepper, stemmed, seeded, and finely chopped

½ red onion, thinly sliced

2 medium tomatoes, chopped

⅓ cup cilantro, chopped

2 tablespoons olive oil

Salt, to taste

1 avocado, diced

In a shallow bowl, combine fish, lime juice, and serrano pepper. Fish pieces should be completely submerged in liquid or they will not cook. Cover and refrigerate for four hours, or until fish no longer looks raw when a piece is broken open. In a medium-sized serving bowl, mix together onions, tomatoes, cilantro, and olive oil. Stir in fish and its liquid and season with salt. Let mixture rest, covered, in a refrigerator for at least 30 minutes. Add avocado just before serving.

MEXICO CITY MEXICO

Hear that? It is an organ grinder meandering down the street. In the distance, a marimba band is playing. Nearby, a market vendor calls out to advertise his wares while another one whistles. And what is that smell? The air is thick with the aroma of sizzling tortillas, roasting meat, and cooking chiles. CDMX (Ciudad de México), as the city is now named, is a feast for the senses, a colorful and tumultuous town of jostling humanity. It pulses with energy, both an inheritor of ancient Aztec culture and a young city with eyes on the future.

With an infectious zeal for living and a serious dedication to the good life, the people of Mexico's capital make going out for drinks a blast. Bar options range from humble beer and shot spots to elegant rooftops. Worth noting is that ordering a Margarita here will mark you as a tourist. Bars serve the drink because American customers expect it—but it is part of American culture, not Mexican. Instead, try drinks sporting local juices like passion fruit, guava, and hibiscus. At craft cocktail spots, bartenders are exploring their roots by incorporating unique regional ingredients like prickly pear and herbs such as *hoja santa*, translated as "sacred leaf." If you need a pick-me-up, try a *Carajillo*, Mexico City's ubiquitous cocktail blend of Licor 43 and espresso; it functions as the city's Vodka Red Bull.

PALOMA

This fruit-forward and crushable long drink is Mexico City's signature cocktail. A well-made Paloma sings with sourness, sweetness, and a touch of bitterness from grapefruit. And it is a taco's best friend. It is often made with grapefruit soda, but it's better with fresh juice. If you like bitter flavor, try an added splash of Aperol or Campari—an addition that helps stimulate the appetite.

Kosher salt, to rim the glass
(optional; sea salt also works)

2 ounces tequila

3 ounces fresh grapefruit juice

½ ounce fresh lime juice

2 teaspoons simple syrup

2 to 3 ounces club soda

Lime wheel, for garnish

Salt the rim of a chilled rocks glass and fill it with ice. Shake tequila, grapefruit juice, lime juice, and simple syrup with ice and strain into prepared glass. Top with soda and garnish with a lime wheel.

MARGARITA AL PASTOR

If you do drink a Margarita in Mexico City, let it be this one. Created by bartender José Luis León at Limantour, his version uses chile pepper, cilantro, and pineapple to mimic the classic flavors of tacos al pastor.

4 cilantro leaves

2 slices serrano pepper

2 basil leaves

1 pineapple wedge

2 ounces blanco tequila

¾ ounce Cointreau

1 ounce fresh lime juice

1 ounce fresh pineapple juice

Cilantro salt, for garnish
(recipe follows)

Muddle cilantro, serrano, basil, and pineapple in a shaker. Add remaining ingredients and ice. Shake and strain into a cocktail glass rimmed with cilantro salt.

FOR THE CILANTRO SALT
Combine 1 cup chopped cilantro leaves and 3 tablespoons kosher salt in a food processor. Pulse until mixed and store refrigerated in a sealed container.

THE RISE OF MEZCAL

Mezcal is a distillation made from various species of the agave plant. The spirit is produced by first harvesting the heart of the agave plants, called *piñas*, and roasting them in pits. These hearts are then crushed, water is added, and they are left to ferment. The resulting mash is distilled in clay or copper pots. Tequila is a specific type of mezcal that can be produced only using one species of agave, Weber Blue. Additionally, in tequila production, agave hearts are steamed rather than roasted. Note that contrary to popular belief, neither tequila nor mezcal should contain a worm in the bottle. This practice likely began as a marketing ploy in the 1940s, and today quality bottles do not contain a worm. Mezcal saw an enormous jump in sales in 2016 and is one of the fastest-growing spirit categories. Aficionados are attracted to the spirit's artisanal, non-industrial production methods as well as to its smoky and often herbaceous taste.

NEW ORLEANS USA

It's always a party in New Orleans. The city is happily stuck in a vacation state of mind, and street celebrations break out at the slightest provocation. Festivals and parades are a regular part of life here, and the sound of horns and drums continuously floats on the humid air. Arriving in Nola is like joining a rager that has been going for a couple hundred years.

One of the very few places in the United States with its own indigenous cuisine, the city's founding French, African, and Caribbean influences are very much alive in restaurants and bars. Food, and being passionate about food, is part of the city's identity. Drink is also part of it, and New Orleans can lay claim to being America's cocktail city (see page 159). In this hot and thirsty town, the glasses sweat Sazeracs.

The Big Easy is one of the only US cities where drinking in the street is legal, as long as cocktails are in a plastic cup; bars are happy to provide liquid refreshment to-go. Iconic stops are within quick walking distance of each other, and bar-hopping is an adventure because so many establishments are famous for a specific drink. In fact, no other American city has as many bars known for a signature libation: Old Absinthe House, Absinthe Frappé; Carousel Bar, Vieux Carré; Roosevelt Bar, Ramos Gin Fizz; Arnaud's, French 75; Erin Rose, Irish Coffee; Sazerac Bar, Sazerac; Bourbon House, Bourbon Milk Punch; Latitude 29, Zombie; Napoleon House, Pimm's Cup; Tujague's, Grasshopper; Antoine's, Café Brulot; Brennan's, Brandy Milk Punch. Just don't try to have them all in one go.

SAZERAC

Named after a cognac brand, Sazerac de Forge et Fils, this pre–Civil War drink is one of the most iconic New Orleans cocktails. The recipe is often credited to Antoine Peychaud, an apothecary who emigrated from the West Indies and made aromatic bitters that are still a key ingredient in cocktails today. The Sazerac is interesting for its peculiar manufacture involving the use of two glasses. It is as much ritual as drink.

1 bar spoon absinthe (to coat the glass)

1 Demerara sugar cube

2 dashes Peychaud's bitters

1 dash Angostura bitters

2 ounces rye whiskey

Lemon peel, for garnish

Swirl absinthe in a chilled rocks glass. In a separate rocks glass, muddle sugar and both bitters. Add rye and ice, stir, and strain into the awaiting rocks glass. Squeeze a lemon peel over the drink to express its oils and either drop in the drink or discard.

RAMOS GIN FIZZ

Henry Ramos invented this famous number at his bar, the Imperial Cabinet Saloon on Gravier Street in 1888. For a time, it was so popular he employed a fleet of "shaker boys" to meet demand. Think of this as a cocktail masquerading as a milkshake. Made well, it is one of the most enjoyable alcoholic drinks in the canon.

2 ounces gin

½ ounce simple syrup

½ ounce fresh lemon juice

½ ounce fresh lime juice

3 drops orange flower water

¾ ounce egg white

½ ounce cream

2 ounces club soda

Orange wheel, for garnish

Shake all ingredients except soda vigorously. Strain into a highball glass, top with soda, and garnish with an orange wheel.

Sit at any traditional cocktail bar in the United States and you will likely be served a bowl of mixed nut But does America have its own indigenous cocktail snacks beyond this simple offering? In fact, yes. During Prohibition, speakeasies introduced a number of finger foods. Canapés featured widely, as did cheese balls, radish roses, and deviled eggs. These drink-friendly bites were served at in-home cocktail parties for decades after. But there is an even older cocktail staple, originating from biscuits made by southern slaves. They became known as "benne" wafers—after the word for sesame seeds—and were sold by vendors on the streets of New Orleans and other southern cities. When a recipe for this uniquely American biscuit was finally published in 1950's *Charleston Receipts*, the *New York Times* reported they would "revolutionize cocktail parties."

½ teaspoon baking powder

½ cup butter

½ cup brown sugar

1 egg, lightly beaten

½ teaspoon salt

1½ cups flour

¾ cup sesame seeds, toasted

In a medium-sized mixing bowl, mix together baking powder, butter, sugar, egg, and salt. Add flour and combine until smooth. Stir in sesame seeds and chill dough for 30 minutes. Drop dough in teaspoon-size balls onto cookie sheets and flatten with a spatula or spoon. Bake at 325°F in a preheated oven for 15 minutes, or until edges are lightly browned.

THE CRADLE OF COCKTAILS

Situated at the mouth of the Mississippi River, New Orleans became a major economic hub in the nineteenth century. By 1840, it was the third-largest city in the United States. With the boom came cocktails. In fact, so many important mixed drinks recipes appeared around this time that books are devoted to tracing their history. The classic early study is Stanley Arthur's *Famous New Orleans Drinks and How to Mix 'em*. Arthur reveals how crucial the Big Easy was to the development and progress of mixed drinks in the United States. It is a role the city still plays to this day, as home to historic bars, the Tales of the Cocktail conference, and the Museum of the American Cocktail.

NY - NY - USA

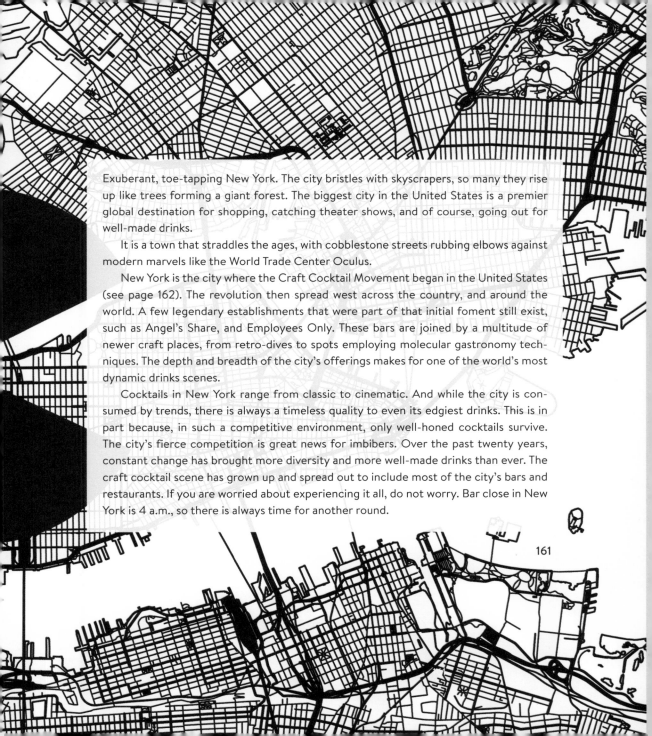

Exuberant, toe-tapping New York. The city bristles with skyscrapers, so many they rise up like trees forming a giant forest. The biggest city in the United States is a premier global destination for shopping, catching theater shows, and of course, going out for well-made drinks.

It is a town that straddles the ages, with cobblestone streets rubbing elbows against modern marvels like the World Trade Center Oculus.

New York is the city where the Craft Cocktail Movement began in the United States (see page 162). The revolution then spread west across the country, and around the world. A few legendary establishments that were part of that initial foment still exist, such as Angel's Share, and Employees Only. These bars are joined by a multitude of newer craft places, from retro-dives to spots employing molecular gastronomy techniques. The depth and breadth of the city's offerings makes for one of the world's most dynamic drinks scenes.

Cocktails in New York range from classic to cinematic. And while the city is consumed by trends, there is always a timeless quality to even its edgiest drinks. This is in part because, in such a competitive environment, only well-honed cocktails survive. The city's fierce competition is great news for imbibers. Over the past twenty years, constant change has brought more diversity and more well-made drinks than ever. The craft cocktail scene has grown up and spread out to include most of the city's bars and restaurants. If you are worried about experiencing it all, do not worry. Bar close in New York is 4 a.m., so there is always time for another round.

161

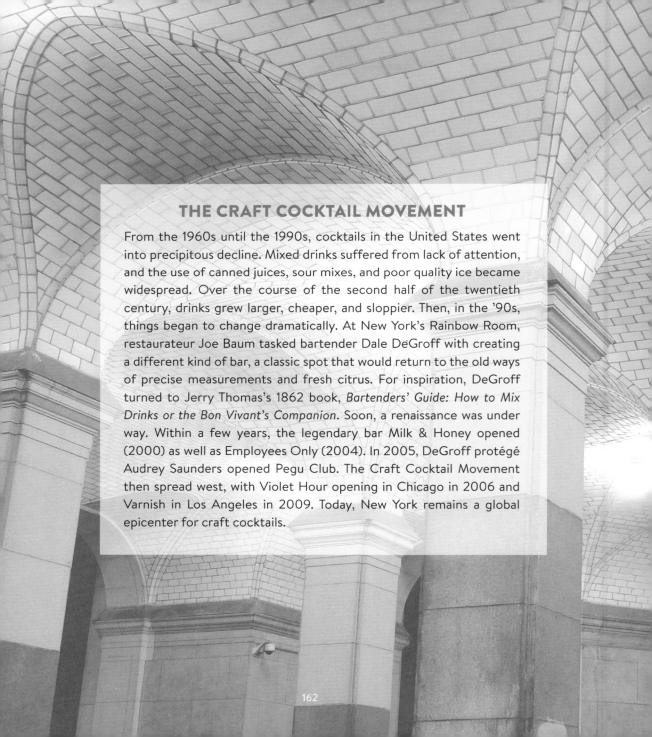

THE CRAFT COCKTAIL MOVEMENT

From the 1960s until the 1990s, cocktails in the United States went into precipitous decline. Mixed drinks suffered from lack of attention, and the use of canned juices, sour mixes, and poor quality ice became widespread. Over the course of the second half of the twentieth century, drinks grew larger, cheaper, and sloppier. Then, in the '90s, things began to change dramatically. At New York's Rainbow Room, restaurateur Joe Baum tasked bartender Dale DeGroff with creating a different kind of bar, a classic spot that would return to the old ways of precise measurements and fresh citrus. For inspiration, DeGroff turned to Jerry Thomas's 1862 book, *Bartenders' Guide: How to Mix Drinks or the Bon Vivant's Companion*. Soon, a renaissance was under way. Within a few years, the legendary bar Milk & Honey opened (2000) as well as Employees Only (2004). In 2005, DeGroff protégé Audrey Saunders opened Pegu Club. The Craft Cocktail Movement then spread west, with Violet Hour opening in Chicago in 2006 and Varnish in Los Angeles in 2009. Today, New York remains a global epicenter for craft cocktails.

Manhattan

The Manhattan is the most famous member of a group of drinks named after each of New York's five boroughs. The ultimate marriage of grain and grape, it is the poster child for the Craft Cocktail Movement. When the revival began, if a bar made Manhattans correctly it was a sign they were in the know. Did the bartender use rye whiskey? Yes. Fresh vermouth? Absolutely. Stir properly on quality ice? Naturally. Use Amarena cherries instead of artificially dyed? A must. Serve the drink in a correctly sized coupe glass? Of course. Today, we take these things for granted.

2 ounces rye whiskey

1 ounce sweet vermouth

2 dashes Angostura bitters

Amarena cherry, for garnish

Stir ingredients with ice and strain into a cocktail glass. Garnish with a cherry.

Penicillin

New York City is a fount of modern classic cocktails, from the Gin-Gin Mule to the Paper Plane, from the Red Hook to the Oaxaca Old Fashioned. However, by far the most famous drink from the early days of the craft revolution is the Penicillin, created by Sam Ross when he tended at Milk & Honey. The drink is all smoke and sweetness, hitting just the right balance of both. Today, it is known around the world.

2 ounces blended scotch

¾ ounce fresh lemon juice

¾ ounce honey-ginger syrup (recipe below)

¼ ounce Laphroaig 10-year

Candied ginger, for garnish

Shake scotch, lemon juice, and honey-ginger syrup with ice and strain into a rocks glass filled with ice. Top with Laphroaig and garnish with candied ginger.

FOR THE HONEY-GINGER SYRUP

In a saucepan, combine 1 cup honey and 1 cup water with a peeled and sliced 3-inch piece of ginger root. Bring to a near-boil, reduce heat, and simmer for 5 minutes. Remove from heat, strain, and refrigerate.

San José
Costa Rica

Although only roughly the size of Denmark, Costa Rica boasts 5 percent of the world's biodiversity, nearly two hundred times the amount of similarly sized landmasses. This is because the country acts as a land bridge between a temperate zone to the north and the tropics to the south. Every type of animal seems to find a home here, from jaguars to deer, sea turtles to raccoons. It is a wildlife enthusiast's paradise, not to mention a surfing mecca. All this explains why Costa Rica is the most visited country in Central America, with almost two million visitors a year.

Set smack in the middle of the country, San José is ringed by dramatic mountains and volcanoes. The bustling capital bristles with museums and theaters, lush parks and funky cafés. Manageably sized as far as Latin American capitals go, Costa Rica's capital is a compelling destination for gallery hopping, shopping, and dining out.

San José retains vestiges of a tapas culture, and a few bars serve small snacks called *bocas*. These are enjoyed in the late afternoon, similar to a happy hour, and are inexpensive if not totally free. Expect ceviche, tamales, fried plantains, and yuca as well as *chifrijo*—crispy pork belly with beans. The accompanying drink will be a local firewater called *guaro*, which is similar to unaged rum. Each village in Costa Rica produces its own version. The spirit forms the base of the local cocktail, the Guaro Sour, made like a Caipirinha (see page 178, substituting guaro for cachaça). Mixed drinks in San José frequently employ the country's diverse fruits and herbs, and are a great opportunity to try exotic juices—noni, guanábana, and cas—just to name a few. Plus, don't forget to have a *Chiliguaro*, the local shot, reminiscent of a Bloody Mary.

Pura Vida

Aged Rum Old Fashioned

"Pura vida" is a Costa Rican greeting meaning something akin to "the good life." Nearly every hotel bar in the country makes a drink by the name, with many using grenadine and blue curaçao to emulate the colors of the Costa Rican flag. Avoid these. Guava, a fruit common in the country, makes for a delicious version.

Ron Centenario is Costa Rica's most notable rum brand. The company makes young rums that are good in Daiquiris but is best known for solera-aged versions that can be up to thirty years old. These older bottlings are typically consumed neat, but are a revelation when used to make an Old Fashioned. Prepare to be amazed by the complexity of this cocktail.

2 ounces guaro or white rum
½ ounce triple sec
2 ounces guava juice
2 ounces club soda
Lime wheel, for garnish

1 orange peel
1 brown sugar cube
2 dashes Angostura bitters
2 ounces aged rum (Ron Centenario)

Combine ingredients in a glass filled with ice and stir. Garnish with a lime wheel.

Muddle orange peel, sugar, and Angostura bitters in a rocks glass. Add rum and ice and stir.

LIZ FURLONG

Self-described "jungle bartender" Liz Furlong has been shaking things up in San José since 2012. She has been a leading advocate for the use of native fruits, plants, and ferments in cocktails. "When I first got to Costa Rica, the only mixed drinks you could find in the country were Piña Coladas, Screwdrivers, and Rum and Cokes," says Furlong. "But that has changed, and the beverage scene has become more local-ingredient focused. I love that I can literally go pick ingredients from trees in the jungle, or pop into the market and still, after nearly a decade, find a fruit or herb that I have never heard of."

A sociology major in college, Furlong is interested in the role beverages play in communities and rituals. "From traditional Central American dishes to indigenous preparations of medicinal ingredients or ceremonial drinks, I incorporate that culture into my work with bars where appropriate. It's a personal passion of mine, and I work tropical ingredients into bitters, infusions, and sodas to try and keep menus hyper seasonal."

Furlong views bartending as more than just making drinks, and argues that cocktails containing foraged elements are a means for customers to learn about sustainability. "I use cocktails as a way to bridge the gap between tourists and Costa Ricans, and use drinks as a way of teaching visitors about local culture and ingredients which maybe they haven't been exposed to at home."

SAN JUAN

PUERTO RICO

Established in 1521, San Juan is the second-oldest European-founded city in the Americas. It is chock-full of stunning Spanish Colonial buildings, charming restaurants serving bold food, and bars. Unlike so many Caribbean island destinations—which require landing at an airport and then travelling further to a seaside destination—San Juan is an idyllic stop in its own right. Here, you can laze around all morning on the city's beaches and then walk into Old Town at night.

Puerto Rico's capital is full of lively establishments where all-ages crowds dance and carry on into the wee hours of the night. Sanjuaneros, as the locals are called, are a friendly lot, given to huge smiles and eager conversations. They are also über chic, regardless of age or station. Do not be surprised to find everyone dressed to the nines.

As if tropical beaches, great sightseeing, and sizzling dance halls were not enough, San Juan is experiencing a cocktail renaissance. The city boasts a cocktail week in addition to a bar listed by World's 50 Best Bars (La Factoria). As one might expect on an island that has distilled rum for 450 years, most drinks are based on the local spirit. The city is best known for classic Caribbean potations, but ambitious bartenders are also employing advanced techniques such as infusing bananas into rum using a centrifuge. Just be mindful of the power of the local shot, called a *Chichaíto*, which is white rum and anise liqueur.

PIÑA COLADA

The Piña Colada is many a cocktailer's guilty pleasure. And why not? A well-made version is pure pleasure, transporting the drinker to a relaxed paradise. The drink is commonly attributed to Ramón "Monchito" Marrero, who worked at the Caribe Hilton. This recipe replicates a 1950s version, and is shaken rather than blended.

2 ounces light rum
2 ounces pineapple juice
2 ounces Coco López coconut cream
1 dash Angostura bitters
Pineapple wedge, for garnish

Shake ingredients with ice and strain into a glass filled with ice. Garnish with a pineapple wedge.

COQUITO

SERVES 4–6

If you visit San Juan during the winter months, you will run into the Coquito, sometimes referred to as Puerto Rican eggnog. This decadent drink is great for sharing with friends during the holidays, and is always a crowd favorite.

Combine ingredients in a blender, place mixture in glass bottles in a refrigerator, and chill overnight. Garnish each glass with ground nutmeg and a cinnamon stick.

10 ounces white rum

1 14-ounce can sweetened condensed milk

1 12-ounce can evaporated milk

1 15-ounce can cream of coconut

¼ teaspoon ground cinnamon

¼ teaspoon ground cloves

1 teaspoon vanilla extract

Ground nutmeg and cinnamon sticks, for garnish

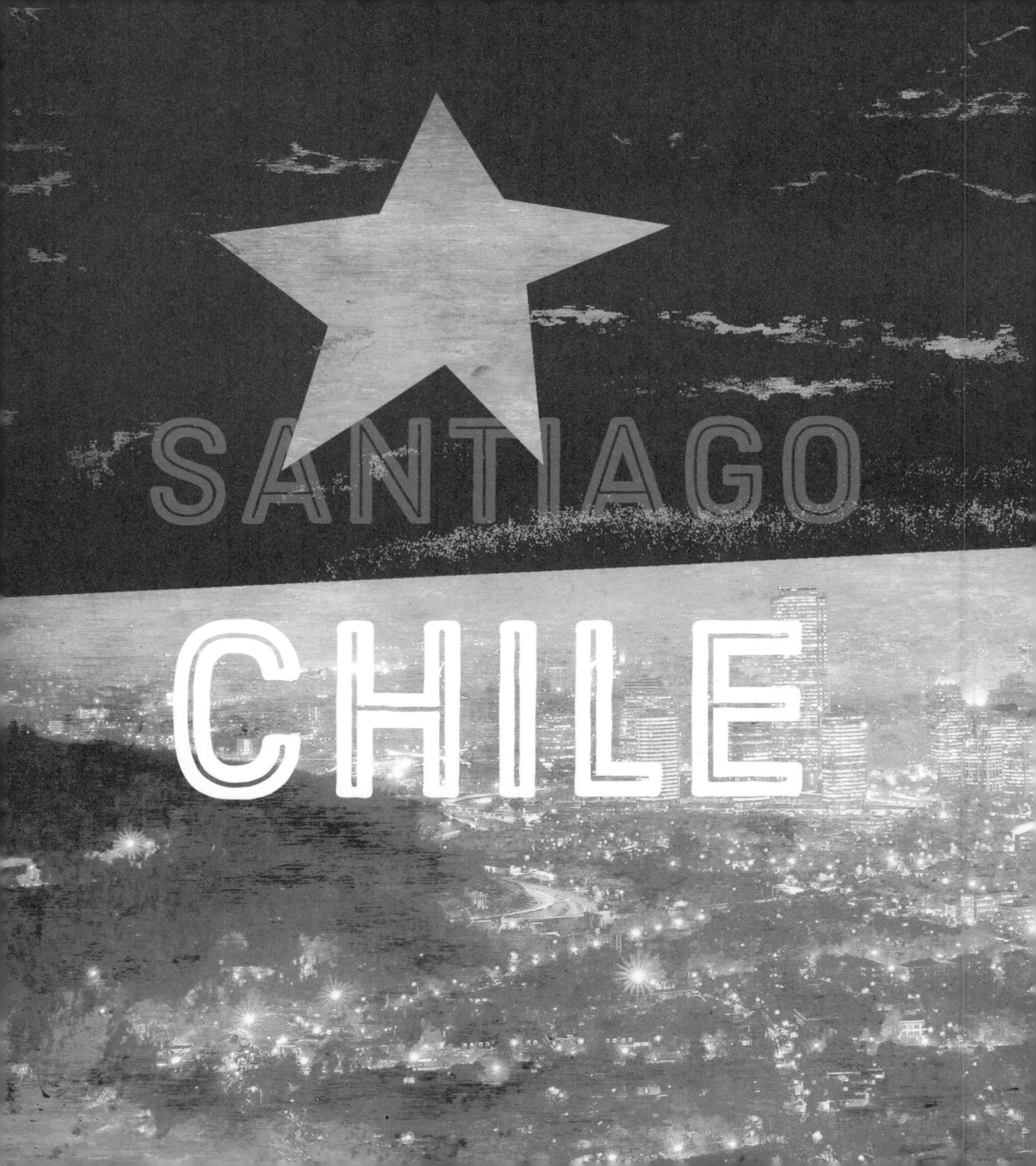
SANTIAGO
CHILE

"I stalk certain words . . . I catch them in mid-flight as they buzz past . . . I stir them, I shake them, I drink them, I gulp them down, I mash them, I garnish them."

—Pablo Neruda

Chile's capital is a laid-back town of unfussy, unhurried bars where dust collects on wine bottles and old men talk with animated gestures. It is a place to while away afternoons reading poems by the country's most famous writer, Pablo Neruda. Set against the dramatic backdrop of the Andes, the city also boasts a number of parks in the surrounding hills with magnificent views. This is a great town for hiking and reading, but also biking. In fact, Santiago is the most cyclist-friendly city in Latin America and offers a citywide rental system—it is a great feature when bar-hopping.

Santiago is full of *picadas*, old-school restaurants that serve budget-friendly, shareable snacks. These are hole-in-the-wall spots that offer traditional cuisine like squash stew and empanadas. They are also where to find drinks like Pisco Sours as well as *jote*, red wine blended with Coca-Cola. As a result of Santiago's recent economic boom, these humble establishments have been joined by modern restaurants and bars. The city is fast transforming from stopover into a major destination.

Like Peru, Chile is a pisco-loving country, and most drinks are based on the local grape brandy. With a strong pisco and wine culture, it has been a slow journey to embrace mixed drinks. But foreign liquors are appearing on menus, and bartenders are using them in creations that include native ingredients. Imbibers will find drinks employing Chile's excellent hard cider, as well as a medicinal herb called *rica rica*.

STRAWBERRY-MERQUEN PISCO PUNCH

The first Pisco Punch was created in San Francisco when the South American brandy hitched a ride up on ships carrying tallow and rawhide. There, a Mr. Duncan Nicol of the wonderfully named Bank Exchange & Billiard Saloon created this first recipe: pisco, pineapple, lime juice, sugar, gum arabic, and distilled water. The combination was famous enough for Mark Twain to write about it, but it sadly slipped into the fog of history with the passing of the Volstead Act in 1919. In this version, strawberries and a unique Chilean pepper, Merquen, feature alongside wine made from the country's Carménère grape. Merquen, a popular pepper for BBQ, is available in grocery stores and online.

2 ounces pisco

3 ounces Carménère wine

2 strawberries

1 dash Merquen pepper

½ ounce strawberry-Merquen simple syrup (recipe follows)

Strawberry, for garnish

Muddle ingredients and double-strain into a glass filled with ice. Garnish with a strawberry.

FOR THE STRAWBERRY-MERQUEN SIMPLE SYRUP
In a medium saucepan, combine 1 cup water, 1 teaspoon Merquen pepper, and 2 cups quartered strawberries. Bring to a boil and simmer until strawberries have lost most of their color, about 20 minutes. Turn off heat and add 1 cup sugar, stirring to dissolve. Strain into a sealable container and keep refrigerated for up to a week.

COMPLETO

SERVES 2

This is a Chilean version of a loaded hot dog and is sold by street vendors at bar time. There are many variations, and technically the recipe below is a "completo Italiano"—so-named because the red, white, and green ingredients represent Italy's flag. Use whatever kind of hot dogs you prefer, although the flavor of all-beef franks is hard to beat. Be sure to have napkins on hand!

2 hot dogs

1 large ripe avocado, halved and pitted

½ teaspoon fresh lime juice

¼ teaspoon kosher salt

2 hot dog buns

¼ cup sauerkraut

1 small tomato, diced

2 tablespoons mayonnaise

Grill hot dogs or boil them in water. Meanwhile, mash together avocado, lime, and salt. To serve, place cooked hot dogs in buns and top with sauerkraut, tomatoes, and avocado mixture. Finish with a thick strip of mayonnaise.

TERREMOTO (EARTHQUAKE)

This cocktail is typically reserved for Chilean Independence Day celebrations but deserves wider appreciation. The story goes that German journalists were served the drink and exclaimed, "This is an earthquake!" Certainly, too many can leave you shaking. Terremotos are traditionally made with pipeño wine, which is not readily available outside of Chile. Other sweet white wines such as moscatel or riesling work well.

5 ounces pipeño, or other sweet white wine

½ ounce Fernet-Branca

1 small scoop pineapple ice cream

Fill a glass with wine and add Fernet-Branca. Top with ice cream.

São Paulo

Paulo

BRAZIL

Long overshadowed by Rio, São Paulo is fast becoming recognized as Brazil's premier cultural center as well as its economic powerhouse. The city is bursting with creativity and youthful vitality. It is also chaotic, sprawling, and growing rapidly. This is not only South America's largest town, but the biggest city in all of the Americas. To visit is to step into a wonderful mess.

Paulistanos, as the city's denizens are called, enjoy their art. There are avant-garde theaters, cutting-edge galleries, notable museums, and serious music and dance scenes. Plus, the city boasts some of the world's best dining and nightlife. If living in this crowded, hard-working city is a grind, it is hard to tell when the sun goes down. As Brazilian singer Don L intoned, "In São Paulo, every day is a Monday—but every night is Friday."

Social life in São Paulo is centered around *botecos*, low-key spots that are a cross between a tavern and a café. Brazilians gather in these bars to watch futbol (soccer), dance samba, and hang out. On weekends, the botecos serve *feijoada* (see recipe). Some botecos have taken to serving cocktails, especially in more upscale neighborhoods. Expect Manhattans and Old Fashioneds along with the national drink, the Caipirinha. Mixed in with the botecos are a growing number of craft cocktail dens. São Paulo is on the move, as evidenced by the international bar and beverage trade show, Bar Convent, planting a foot in the city after launching in Berlin and New York.

Caipirinha

Cachaça, a distillate made from sugarcane juice, provides the base for the famed Caipirinha. The spirit is related to rum and dominates Brazil's bar shelves. A few São Paulo establishments specialize in it and boast hundreds of unique bottles. Just note that in Brazil some servers may assume you want vodka, so be sure to specify you want a Caipirinha made with cachaça.

2 teaspoons brown sugar
½ lime, cut into small wedges
2½ ounces cachaça

Muddle sugar and limes in a rocks glass. Add cachaça, stir, and fill the glass with ice.

Batida

Made with fruits like mango and guava, Batidas are something like a Brazilian version of a fruity milkshake. They can be shaken, but are most often made in a blender. The drink is a traditional accompaniment to feijoada (recipe follows).

2 ounces cachaça
2 ounces coconut milk (or cream)
1 ounce sweetened condensed milk
½ ounce fresh lime juice

Shake ingredients with ice and strain into a glass filled with crushed ice. Alternatively, blend ingredients with ice.

Feijoada

Classic feijoada has three ingredients that can be difficult to source: salt pork, trotters, and linguiça. Many traditionalists won't abide versions that additionally lack ears, tails, and other assorted piggy bits. Given the difficulty in sourcing these parts, US cooks often go in a different direction and make a deluxe version that substitutes chorizo or ribs. This is what I do, and while it may not be authentic, the result is delicious. In Brazil, feijoada is typically served on Wednesdays and Saturdays. It is traditionally accompanied by rice and collard greens.

½ pound smoked bacon, about ten slices

1½ pounds pork ribs, cut into individual ribs

1 pound sausage such as kielbasa, sliced

2 medium white onions, diced

½ teaspoon crushed red pepper flakes

4 garlic cloves, finely chopped

3 15-ounce cans black beans

1 tomato, diced

2 bay leaves

2½ cups beef stock

1 tablespoon white vinegar

Black pepper, to taste

Kosher salt, to taste

2 oranges, sliced, for serving

In a large stockpot or saucepan, cook bacon on medium-high heat until brown. Remove to a plate and drain pot of any excess oil, leaving about 2 tablespoons. Working in batches, brown ribs thoroughly on all sides and remove. Next, brown sausage and remove. Add onion, pepper flakes, garlic, and beans with their liquid. Cook until onions are translucent. Add tomato and bay leaves. Cut or break up bacon strips. Next, return the bacon, sausage, and pork ribs to the pan along with beef stock and vinegar. Bring to a boil and simmer, covered, for 2 hours or until beans are soft and ribs are tender. Adjust taste with salt and pepper. If there is too much liquid, cook with the lid off for the final hour. Remove bay leaves and serve with orange slices.

TORONTO

CANADA

The fourth-largest city in North America is also one of the planet's most multi-cultural urban areas. Immigrants from all over the world make their home here, with more than half of Toronto's residents born outside of Canada. A quick visit to the famous Kensington Market will underscore that over two hundred nationalities call Toronto home. The diversity makes for a thrilling food and drink scene.

As Canada's commercial and financial hub, Toronto boasts an easy metro system of subways and streetcars—although much of the cocktail action is conveniently located downtown. Note that like the United States, Canada suffered through Prohibition. Their failed experiment lasted only two years (from 1918 to 1920), but its effects are still being felt. In fact, the Temperance Movement ran so deep here that the last dry neighborhood voted to "go wet" (allow the sale of alcohol) as recently as 2000. Change is afoot, but the city still has restrictive liquor laws that include alcohol only being legally sold in state stores.

Toronto's cocktail bars tend toward classy and high-end, with the city's denizens enjoying a bevy of rooftop spots with exquisite views. The northern climate means dramatic seasonal mood shifts, and refreshing drinks on sun-drenched decks in summer transform into cozy fireside warmers during the winter. Cocktails range from classics to hyper-modern creations and, as one might expect, often feature maple syrup.

180

TORONTO COCKTAIL

This classic first appeared in Robert Vermeire's *Cocktails: How to Mix Them* as the Fernet Cocktail. It was popular in pre-Prohibition Ontario, and Canadian visitors likely told Vermeire about the drink while he was tending bar in London. It is considered the best of the classic Fernet-Branca cocktails and truly a concoction every drinker should know.

2 ounces Canadian whisky
¼ ounce Fernet-Branca
¼ ounce simple syrup
2 dashes Angostura bitters
Orange peel, for garnish

Stir ingredients with ice and strain into a cocktail glass. Garnish with an orange peel.

MAPLE MANHATTAN

Torontians love maple syrup in both food and drinks. This variation on the classic mix of whiskey and vermouth is a tasty sipper and especially good when the weather turns cool. It also pairs wonderfully with grilled meats and root vegetables.

2 ounces Canadian whisky
½ ounce sweet vermouth
½ ounce maple syrup
2 dashes Angostura bitters
Amarena cherry, for garnish

Stir ingredients with ice and strain into a chilled cocktail glass. Garnish with a cherry.

CHAPTER 5
OCEANIA

Oceania, an area that includes Melanesia, Micronesia, Polynesia, and Australasia, is a region with a big impact on the development of the modern cocktail. When the cocktail revolution was brewing in the United States and England, it was also taking root in the Land Down Under. Aussie acolytes of the late, great Dick Bradsell (see page 32) returned home and brought craft cocktailing back with them. These bartenders blended with a homegrown scene that already boasted influential bars such as Gin Palace and Der Raum (both now defunct). In fact, before becoming a legendary drinks maker in New York, Sam Ross (see page 163) owned a Melbourne bar called Ginger.

Today, craft cocktail bars are dotted all across Australia, with Melbourne and Sydney both featuring top spots that have won global acclaim. The country's drinks are creative and bold and feature bright flavors. Aussies are not afraid to make drinks a bit kooky—in the best possible way—and never shy away from making them boozy. With a long history of cocktailing and a pedigree second to none, the cocktail bars of Oz will ensure your evenings never run dry.

SYDNEY
AUSTRALIA

The opera house, buff bods on Bondi Beach, and cocktails. These are the takeaways from Sydney, Australia's posh-meets-casual big city, a town that is always game for a nightcap. Boasting one of the great harbors of the world, the city wraps itself around it like a koala hugging a tree—all charm and chill. And, of course, there is the food. If the city had to be summed up in a word, it would be *delicious*.

Sydney has gone from culinary snoozer to international destination since the start of the new millennium. The dining scene is sizzling, seemingly locked in competition with Melbourne to determine which city can create the most interesting dishes. The same energy that brought Australian food culture around the world—avocado toast and "flat white" coffee—is evident in its mixed drinks. Even Aussie wine has stepped out from its plonk-y past to find a foothold among the global cognoscenti.

The island continent's seafaring past has had a big influence on its cocktails, as has its membership in the British Commonwealth. Bartenders who worked in London have returned home to make Australia one of the top places in the world to drink. Expect interesting local ingredients in cocktails like finger lime, strawberry gum (a tree), and pepperberries.

CAMPBELL

Australia's national drink has its origins at sea. By the mid-nineteenth century, British ships carried Angostura bitters on board, and sailors mixed it with their gin rations. Drink recipes using Angostura spread around the colonies, and the Campbell took hold as an antidote to Australia's hot climate. This refreshing cocktail was once used as a cure-all, and is still prescribed for indigestion and car sickness.

½ ounce fresh lime juice

4 ounces lemon-lime soda

4 dashes Angostura bitters

Add lime juice to a glass filled with ice. Top with soda and add bitters.

SYDNEY SOUR

Using seasonal produce to make refreshing cocktails is the order of the day in sunny Australia. To that end, local mandarins show up on menus everywhere when they are ripe. Similar to an orange, but sweeter, and somehow orange-y-er, the mandarin makes for a tasty drink. Here, local shiraz (syrah) floats on top to make a colorful sipper with loads of flavor. This recipe is inspired by cocktails found at the Opera Bar and Bulletin Place.

1½ ounces gin

¾ ounce Cointreau

2 ounces fresh mandarin juice

½ ounce fresh lemon juice

2 ounces club soda

1 ounce shiraz wine, to float

Lemon twist, for garnish

Shake ingredients except soda and wine with ice. Strain into a highball glass filled with ice, add soda, and top with shiraz. Garnish with a lemon twist.

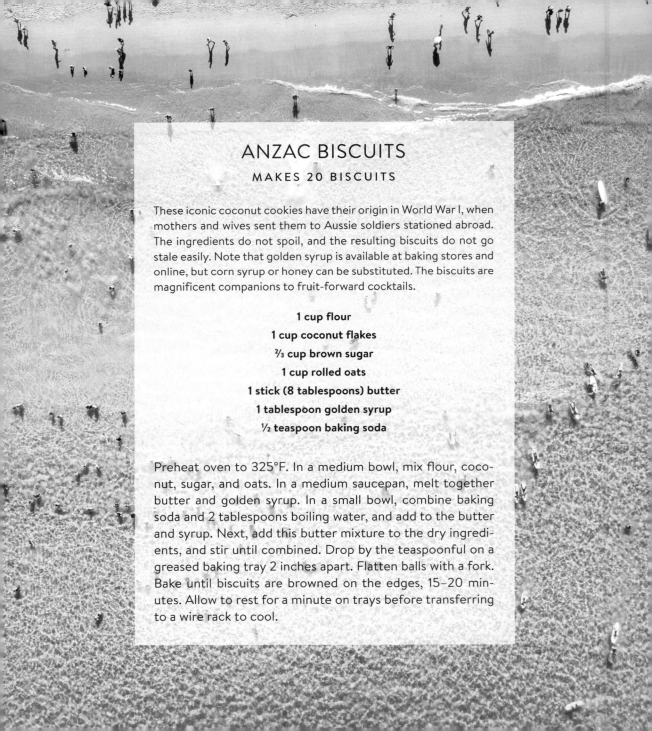

ANZAC BISCUITS

MAKES 20 BISCUITS

These iconic coconut cookies have their origin in World War I, when mothers and wives sent them to Aussie soldiers stationed abroad. The ingredients do not spoil, and the resulting biscuits do not go stale easily. Note that golden syrup is available at baking stores and online, but corn syrup or honey can be substituted. The biscuits are magnificent companions to fruit-forward cocktails.

1 cup flour
1 cup coconut flakes
⅔ cup brown sugar
1 cup rolled oats
1 stick (8 tablespoons) butter
1 tablespoon golden syrup
½ teaspoon baking soda

Preheat oven to 325°F. In a medium bowl, mix flour, coconut, sugar, and oats. In a medium saucepan, melt together butter and golden syrup. In a small bowl, combine baking soda and 2 tablespoons boiling water, and add to the butter and syrup. Next, add this butter mixture to the dry ingredients, and stir until combined. Drop by the teaspoonful on a greased baking tray 2 inches apart. Flatten balls with a fork. Bake until biscuits are browned on the edges, 15–20 minutes. Allow to rest for a minute on trays before transferring to a wire rack to cool.

The Cocktailer's Guide to Circumnavigating the Globe

In late 2019, I set out from New York to travel around the world with the express purpose of imbibing. It had been twenty years since the start of the Craft Cocktail Movement in the United States and I wanted to take a bird's-eye view of the world's fast-changing mixed drinks landscape. I hoped the journey would give me the kind of perspective Charles H. Baker Jr. achieved over the course of his three circumnavigations in the late 1920s and '30s. My route took me through eleven cities: Berlin -> Kyiv -> Athens -> Beirut -> Dubai -> Bangkok -> Singapore -> Hong Kong -> Shanghai -> Seoul -> Tokyo. In addition to a visit to some of the planet's best cocktail hotspots, the trip also became a catalogue of historic events affecting cities on my itinerary: I was in Kyiv shortly after ambassador Sondland called Trump on his personal cellphone (a call discussing withholding the funds to Ukraine that would get the forty-fifth president impeached); Beirut was a month into a revolution and financial crisis; following my stop in Dubai, the United States fired a missile killing Iranian General Soleimani in nearby Iraq; in Hong Kong, there were daily protests regarding Chinese extradition laws; holiday festivities in Seoul were overshadowed by Kim Jong-un's promised "Christmas surprise" (luckily none came); and finally, I entered and exited Shanghai right before the outbreak of the novel coronavirus. My journey gave me a snapshot of the global cocktail scene, but also of the world's precariousness. I was blessed with extraordinarily good luck, but my smooth trip was also the result of preparation. Below are a few tips for globe-trotting cocktailers that other travelers may also find useful.

WHERE TO STAY

Choose a hotel or apartment near the bars you want to visit. This seems obvious, but it is easy to get lured by deals, ratings, or inexpensive spots on travel websites. The easiest way to find the perfect place to stay is to research the bars you want to visit, pin their locations on a map, and search for hotels smack in the center of the pins. This way, you are ensured of being in the center of the action. A great benefit of this method is that cocktail bars tend to cluster together in fun neighborhoods, sometimes in neighborhoods that do not appear in guidebooks. When choosing a place to stay, be mindful that you also want a "home" bar that functions as your last stop at night. I prefer this to be in the hotel where I am staying, if at all possible. A great example is Michelberger in Berlin, one of the world's great hotel bars. Any sojourn is vastly improved when you can tread downstairs, have a drink, and chat with staff who are knowledgeable about a city's hotspots. A good bartender beats a hotel concierge any day.

FINDING BARS

When traveling, rank the bars you want to visit as you would other city sights. Make sure you have the bars grouped by neighborhood so you can easily hop between them. Note that finding the hottest bars can be difficult unless you know someone on the ground. Even online articles tend to be outdated—by the time an article's author visits the bars, and an editor finds space for the piece, things have changed. The best way to get intel on where to go is to ask staff at a good restaurant. Your waitress or waiter will know, since most are walking rolodexes of who is at what bar and when. As an added bonus, they will help cut through the hype and give you the straight scoop on bars that are actually good versus ones that are merely big names.

NO REALLY, WHERE IS THE BAR?

If the establishment you are visiting is a speak-easy, be sure to research how to find it and gain entrance. Look online to see if there is a password posted. Also, check if anyone has posted a picture of the unmarked entrance. Speakeasies can be surprisingly hard to find, even with instructions and a screenshot. Without this crucial information, you will be standing around in an alley watching and waiting for a door to open. Do not go across the world only to get lost or turned away.

CHOOSING DRINKS

Try not to order the same thing at every bar, even if you have a favorite drink or type of drinks. If you sip, say, Negronis across a city, it might make for an interesting magazine roundup, but it won't tell you much about a scene. When you receive a bar's menu, rank your choices. Start by ordering the lightest drink out of those choices. This way you have somewhere to go flavor-wise, and you don't fatigue your palate on the first drink. Cocktails, like wine, will typically be listed on a menu from lightest to heaviest. As an exercise, also identify the cocktail on the menu you are least likely to order; surprise yourself sometimes by getting it. This exercise almost never disappoints at good cocktail bars and will expand your range and understanding. Finally, take notes. Snap a picture of the menu when it arrives. Menus are rarely up-to-date online, so you will not be able to look it up later.

KEEPING YOUR WITS

When embarking on a bar safari, start at the establishment furthest from where you are staying. Then, throughout the evening, go closer to home with every move. Do not end up drunk on the opposite side of town from your hotel in a foreign city. Such adventures may be fun, but they do not make a successful habit. In fact, it's a great way to get mugged. Another rule is to reject offers for shots. If you do a shot, choose something low proof such as vermouth. Shots impinge on your ability to drink cocktails. However, do accept all offers by bartenders to sample liquors that you are not familiar with.

THE HANGOVER

It is impossible to tell how bad a hangover is until you start moving. Even if you have to return to bed, try to get out of it for a few minutes. Often, you don't need greasy, salty food. You just need salt. This is why Gatorade and Pedialyte work. By far the best way to combat a hangover is to prevent it by hydrating. Before going out, leave yourself a bottle of water on the bed as a reminder.

NITTY GRITTY (HARD-EARNED ADVICE)

Take out cash from the ATMs while you are still at the airport. These are almost always located just after Immigration and Customs (sometimes still inside the security zone). You never know when you will find the next one or when you will need cash—although it is usually the second you step out of the airport. In general, ATMs at airports give the same rate or better than you will find on the street. Even in advanced cities like Tokyo, cash is king.

Write down what $100 dollars equals in the local currency, not what $1 converts to. You will never take out $1 from an ATM, and after an overnight flight you will not be in a position to do math. Writing down the $100 equivalent in local currency can save you an expensive mistake (some airport ATMs will let you take out $1,000 or more).

Clearly print out the name and address of every hotel you are staying at. A cab driver who does not read the Latin alphabet will not be able to read an address displayed on your cellphone screen. Often, drivers are behind protective glass, and they will not be able to look at your phone screen. It is easier to pass forward a piece of paper with your hotel address on it in your language as well as the driver's. This way, the driver can keep the paper while entering it into their navigation system.

Find out in advance if the destination you are visiting observes tipping. What is the percentage? Should you leave a few coins, round up to the nearest bill, or leave 20 percent?

Note if the city/country has Uber or other car ride apps. If the country uses different travel apps, download them before you depart. Slow airport or hotel Wi-Fi is a painful option for downloading on the fly.

Google Maps does not work in some countries, and you may find yourself relying on Apple Maps. Beware that Apple Maps is accuracy-challenged. At best, it can be misleading, and at worst it will get you very lost. Know the current address of the establishment you are going to, because Apple Maps will often take you where it used to be instead (bars move frequently). It also helps to know any nearby landmarks to verify locations.

Worried about getting scammed? It is highly unlikely in a good bar or restaurant. At any reputable spot anywhere in the world, adding to a check would be easy to trace. Far more likely is that a clerk at a convenience store will double charge or overcharge your card after a transaction. I never think twice about using a card at a restaurant or bar, but use cash at convenience stores. Note that this advice is null and void if you are at any kind of establishment where hostesses are paid to talk to, or otherwise entertain, male customers. If you go to one of these, know that these spots are notorious for extracting big bucks from foreign targets. Your credit card company will not be terribly sympathetic and will assume that you did, in fact, order $3,000 in drinks and other activities.

BAR-OGRAPHY

Great bars are not made by fancy equipment or big liquor shelves, but by staff. When I am asked to share my favorite watering holes around the world, I invariably say that I seek out preferred bartenders, not specific bars. It's the people that matter. That said, this list is a starting point for finding some of the planet's best bars. These are exceptional establishments in the cities included in this book. Some are well known and appear on lists such as World's 50 Best Bars or have won Spirited Awards. Others are quirky, local favorites. Either way, they each play a vital role in the cocktail scene in their respective locations. I offer them as field notes; they are not ranked.

EUROPE

AMSTERDAM
Tales & Spirits
Hiding In Plain Sight
Vesper
Flying Dutchman
Bar Bukowski
Door 74
Super Lyan

ATHENS
Baba Au Rum
Bar Clumsies
BarroNegro
360 Cocktail Bar
The 7 Jokers Coffee &
    Cocktail Bar
The Gin Joint
Noel
Six d.o.g.s.

BERLIN
Buck & Breck
Becketts Kopf
Green Door Bar
Times Bar
Stagger Lee
TiER
Geist Im Glas
Michelberger Café &
    Wine Bar
Limonadier
Victoria Bar

BUDAPEST
Boutiq'Bar
Hotsy Totsy
Black Swan
Kollázs Brasserie & Bar
Warm Up Cocktail Bar
GoodSpirit Whisky &
    Cocktail Bar
Tuk Tuk Bar

COPENHAGEN
Duck & Cover
Curfew
Bootleggers
Baest
Kyros and Co.
Balderdash
Brønnum
Ruby
1105
The Barking Dog

DUBLIN
Vintage Cocktail Club
Peruke & Periwig
The Bar With No Name
The Liquor Rooms
The Lucky Duck
Drop Dead Twice
Farrier & Draper
9 Below

KYIV
Paravoz Speakeasy
Loggerhead
Pink Freud
Bar Ostannya Barykada
Alchemist
Barman Dictat

LONDON
Savoy American Bar
Connaught Bar
Tayēr + Elementary
Swift
Bar Termini
Hide Below
Hawksmoor
Milk & Honey
Kwãnt
Dukes Bar
Happiness Forgets
Oriole
Callooh Callay
Scout
Wun's
Nightjar
Three Sheets
Lyaness
Coupette
Satan's Whiskers

MADRID
Salmon Guru
Macera TallerBar
Bar Cock
Viva Madrid
Del Diego Cocktail Bar
Museo Chicote
1862 Dry Bar

PARIS
Experimental Cocktail
    Club
Little Red Door
Le Syndicat
Harry's New York Bar
Dirty Dick
Candelaria
Le Mary Celeste
Sherry Butt

PRAGUE
Anonymous Bar
Tretter's
Bitter Bar
Black Angel's
Bugsy's
Cash Only
Hemingway Bar
L'Fleur
Parlour

ROME
Jerry Thomas Project
Barnum Café
Salotto 42
Stravinskij Bar
Freni e Frizioni
Zuma
Co.So. Cocktail & Social

SAINT PETERSBURG
Orthodox
Apotheke
Kabinet
Tsvetochki
Tesla Bar
Big Liver Place
Imbibe Bar

STOCKHOLM
Erlands
Svartengrens
Tweed
Häktet
Riche
Tjoget
MELT
Lykke
Gemma
Pharmarium

AFRICA AND THE MIDDLE EAST

BEIRUT

Ferdinand
Electric Bing Sutt
Central Station
Ales & Tales
Vesper
Anise
Vyvyan's
Amelia
Godot
Internazionale
Rabbit Hole

CAPE TOWN

Cause & Effect
Harrington's Cocktail
    Lounge
Bascule Bar
The Art of Duplicity
Yours Truly
Chinchilla
Vicious Virgin
Asoka

DUBAI

Library Bar
Buddha Bar
Miss Lily's
Zuma
Vault
Play
Bahri Bar

TANGIER

El Morocco
TangerInn
La Luna
El Tangerino
Nord Pinus Tanger

TEL AVIV

Imperial Cocktail Bar
Double Standard
Jasper Johns
Spice Haus
Bushwick
223 Bar
Honolulu
The Library
Aria Downstairs
Bellboy

ASIA

BANGKOK

Tep Bar
Asia Today
Teens of Thailand
Lennon's
Rabbit Hole
#FindTheLockerRoom
Alonetogether
Havana Social
Bamboo Bar at the
    Mandarin Oriental
Sugar Ray
Vesper
Tropic City

DELHI

1911 Bar
Sidecar
The Library Bar
Farzi Cafe
PCO
Juniper
Blue Bar
Serai
Ek Bar

HO CHI MINH CITY

Snuffbox
Firkin
Saigon Saigon
Corked Tales
The Gin House
Qui Cuisine Mixology
Gallery Drinkery
Layla
Drinking & Healing
Monde Bar
The Alley Cocktail Bar &
    Kitchen

HONG KONG

The Old Man
The Wise King
Quinary
The Pontiac
Captain's Bar
Little L.A.B.
Tell Camellia
COA
J.Boroski
Stockton

MANILA

Agimat Foraging Bar
   and Kitchen
The Curator Coffee &
   Cocktail Bar
The Back Room
Proof Manila
OTO
Yes Please
Blind Pig

SEOUL

Charles H.
Southside Parlor
Le Chamber
Alice
Pussyfoot Saloon
D.Still
Get All Right
Bar Cham
HoneyHole
Bar Old Fashioned
Pocket Seoul

SHANGHAI

The Union Trading
   Company
The Long Bar at the
   Waldorf Astoria
Sober Company
Speak Low
Senator Saloon
Pocho Social Club
Botanist
The Odd Couple

SINGAPORE

28 Hong Kong Street
Manhattan
Gibson Bar
Live Twice
Tippling Club
Madame Fan
Junior
Shin Gi Tai
Jigger & Pony
Atlas
Native
Nutmeg & Clove
Operation Dagger
Skinny's Lounge
D.Bespoke
The Spiffy Dapper
The Other Room
Tess Bar & Kitchen
No Sleep Club
Back Stage Cocktail Bar

TAIPEI

Indulge Experimental
   Bistro
R&D Cocktail Lab
Ounce
AHA Saloon
RON Xinyi
Marquee
Alchemy Speakeasy Bar
Room by Le Kief
Fourplay
KOR
Draft Land
Bar Mood Taipei

TOKYO

Mixology Salon
Old Imperial Bar
Bar Orchard Ginza
MASQ
Bar High Five
The SG Club
Bar Kamiya
Ginza Tender
Bar Trench
Star Bar Ginza
Bar Benfiddich
Bar Gen Yamamoto
Rockfish
The Old Blind Cat
Ishino Hana Bar
Bar Sherlock

THE AMERICAS

BOGOTÁ
Ugly American
Pravda
Mesa Franca
Céntrico
Andrés D.C.
Apache

BUENOS AIRES
Florería Atlántico
Frank's
Verne Club
Rey de Copas
Boticario
Bar 878
The Harrison Speakeasy
Isabel
Pony Line
Presidente Bar
Gran Bar Danzon

HAVANA
El Floridita
Kilómetro Zero
O'Reilly 304
Madrigal Bar Cafe
Bodeguita Del Medio
El Chanchullero
La Guarida

LIMA
Carnaval
Ayahuasca
Barra 55
La Cachina Bar
Orient Express
Gran Hotel Bolívar
Café Victoria
Huaringas Bar

MEXICO CITY
Licorería Limantour
La Clandestina
Tokyo Music Bar
Bósforo
Hanky Panky
Xaman
Pulquería los
    Insurgentes
Cantina Tio Pepe

NEW ORLEANS
(see page 156 for
    additional listings)
Cane & Table
Cure
Bar Tonique
Barrel Proof
Empire Bar
Twelve Mile Limit

NEW YORK CITY
Employees Only
Dante
NoMad Bar
Clover Club
Death & Company
Angel's Share
Attaboy
Bemelmans Bar
Katana Kitten
Mace
Bar Goto
Dead Rabbit Grocery &
    Grog
Mother's Ruin
Amor y Amargo
Leyenda

SAN JOSÉ
Buchón
Mil948 Cocktail Room
Bebedero
El Cuartel de la Boca
    del Monte
The Publican
Azotea

SAN JUAN
Factoría
Jungle Bird
La Penúltima
El Batey
El Bar Bero
Bar La Unidad

SANTIAGO
Chipe Libre
Bar The Clinic
Ruca Bar
La Piojera
Sarita Colonia
Opera-Catedral

SÃO PAULO
Frank Bar
Riviera Bar
Guarita Bar
Sub Astor
Apothek Cocktails &
    Co.

TORONTO
Bar Raval
Cocktail Bar
BarChef
Mahjong Bar
Pretty Ugly
Shameful Tiki Room

OCEANIA

SYDNEY
Bulletin Place
Opera Bar
Eau De Vie

Maybe Sammy
The Swinging Cat
PS40
The Baxter Inn

Earl's Juke Joint
The Barber Shop

TECHNIQUES: MAKING CRAFT COCKTAILS

With a few basic bartending techniques, you can make cocktails at home that taste and look as good as drinks in craft cocktail bars. Here is what you need to know:

MEASURE

Always use a jigger to measure your liquids. Balance is the essence of every good cocktail, and by jiggering you will be able to construct exact drinks that are perfect every time.

USE FRESH ICE

Ice goes stale in a freezer, taking on the smell and taste of nearby items. Replace it regularly. If your home tap water contains a lot of minerals, consider making ice with filtered water.

USE FRESH FRUIT JUICE

As tempting as the bottled version can be, nothing replaces fresh-squeezed juice. Sealed tightly, it will last a couple days in a refrigerator. On average, lemons and limes will yield 1 ounce of juice per fruit.

GARNISH

Garnish is not just for looks. A lemon or lime peel twisted to express its oils adds aroma and flavor to a drink. It is best to think about garnish before making a cocktail. That way, it is ready to go when you need it.

WHEN TO SHAKE AND WHEN TO STIR

As a general rule, cocktails are stirred when they contain only spirits and liqueurs. They are shaken when they contain citrus, dairy, and/or eggs. When making cocktails that contain eggs, it is customary to "dry shake" first before adding ice. Some bartenders will add the spring from a strainer in order to help break up the egg quickly.

EGGS

Eggs add body to a drink and lend the signature froth to Whiskey Sours and Ramos Gin Fizzes. Eggs have grown in size since classic cocktail recipes were formulated, and it is common practice to measure out ¾ ounce of egg white for drinks.

SIMPLE SYRUP

Basic simple syrup is a mixture of equal parts granulated sugar and water. Often, recipes will call for heating the water—but beware that this can caramelize the sugar and change the resulting flavor; it is better to remove the water from the heat first, and then add sugar. "Rich" simple syrup is a ratio of 2 to 1, granulated sugar to water.

BATCHING COCKTAILS

To quickly batch a cocktail, convert ounces in the recipe to cups.

TOOLS: EQUIPMENT FOR MAKING CRAFT COCKTAILS

A Japanese jigger will get you the most accurate measurements, but an OXO jigger may be the most practical for home bartenders.

Originally composed of a metal tin and a glass pint cup, today the two parts of a Boston shaker are both metal. This prevents breakage if the glass slips from the bartender's hands. They are readily available online.

Mixing glasses and beakers have come way down in price in the past few years. Using one is recommended in order to correctly stir drinks.

If you want to properly stir cocktails, a bar spoon is required. Get one with enough heft at the end of the handle to crack ice.

It is worth having both styles of strainers on hand: Hawthorne and julep. In general, you will use a Hawthorne for shaken drinks and a julep strainer for stirred cocktails.

Invest in a decent juicer. Hand-juicers work for small amounts, but you will want one with a reservoir when making multiple drinks.

A must-have for garnishes, the y-peeler is the best tool for peeling citrus.

Get a muddler made of nonstained, nonreactive wood. Steer clear of any muddler that is painted, plastic, or metal.

There is no special glassware required to enjoy a good cocktail. However, you may like to invest in a set of coupe glasses. They are now widely available online, and the best size for these is between 4 and 6 ounces. Additionally, having good highball and rocks glasses on hand can significantly improve your presentation. Note that many box stores still sell oversized glassware, and these are to be avoided.

RESOURCES

A number of drink-related websites are helpful resources for the global cocktailer. Here is an abbreviated list of those I have found useful.

BartenderAtlas.com
Drinkmagazine.asia
Worlds50BestBars.com
ImbibeMagazine.com
Drinkspirits.com
ChilledMagazine.com
MinistryofRum.com
52Martinis.com
AustralianBartender.com.au
Alcademics.com
Indigenousbartender.com
ThirstyinLa.com
PunchDrink.com
TalesoftheCocktail.com
ParisByMouth.com
Thirstymag.com
DiffordsGuide.com
Drinkup.London
SmartShanghai.com
DrinkManila.com
TheSpiritsBusiness.com

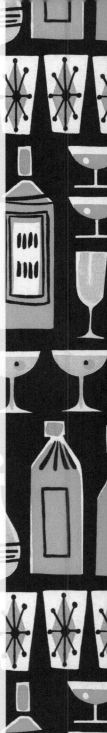

ACKNOWLEDGMENTS

This is my fourth cocktail book, and while the subject of all of them has been mixed drinks, writing every one has been akin to getting a master's degree in a second field of study; each has looked at drinking through a different thematic lens: *The New Cocktail Hour* is history, *Movie Night Menus* is Hollywood cinema, and *Booze & Vinyl* is popular music. The subject of this book is travel, and it is the project that has transformed me most. This book stirred, shook, rolled, squeezed, and peeled me, and—with the help of dozens of people around the globe—I have come out of the process a different and better person.

A heartfelt thank you is due to my editor Cindy Sipala and to my agent Clare Pelino for their unflagging support and guidance. Also, a giant thanks to my former publicist and now friend, Oleg Lyubner, who has worked as a trusted sounding board on this project. Plus, hats off to production editor Cisca Schreefel and champion copy editor Martha Whitt.

Amazingly, I was once again able to work with designer Josh McDonnell, photographer Jason Varney, and stylist Kristi Hunter. It has been a privilege to team up with these creative pros for a third adventure. I am grateful

for their amazing skill at bringing this book to life. For this round, we were joined by bar maestro Lee Noble on cocktail manufacture and chef Rob Marzinsky on food.

The research, writing, and travel for this project was a daunting undertaking and many people assisted in making it possible. To the friends and local guides who helped me navigate the cities on my circumnavigation of the globe, you made my journey magical, thank you: Gianna Leonards, Nicole Jilbert, Alina Virstiuk, Yulia Bevzenko, Marina Tsikou, Jean O'Halloran, and Vita Starkin. Additionally, a special thank you is owed to Tania Abiel Hessen for her incredible hospitality in Beirut.

To the bar owners and bartenders of Earth, your enthusiasm and hospitality knows no bounds. Thank you to those who made me drinks in person and also those who answered my questions by phone and email. This book has been profoundly improved by your wisdom. In particular: Anthony Zamora, Kurt Schlechter, Zoltán Nagy, Kamil Foltán, Demie Kim, June Baek, Oliver Ebert, Pietro Rizzo, Liz Furlong, Stelios Papadopoulos, Ronan Keilthy, Willy Park, Erin Rose, Aki Wang, Kalel Demetrio, Jay Kahn, Gagan Gurung, Sandeep Kumar, Joshin Atone, José Luis Léon, Shad Kvetko, Jeffrey Chang, Jerrold Khoo, Aki Eguchi, Gento Torigata, Sullivan Doh, Shelley Tai, Phúc Lê, Jad Ballout, Chabi Cadiz, Andy Ferreira, and Fatima Leon. Plus, an extra warm thanks to Indra Kantono, Gan Gouyi, Agung Prabowo, Keith Motsi, and Daniele Cervi for their extended time and company.

A giant thanks goes to Vivian Pei for her help and advice throughout Asia, and also to Moses Koh, who generously acted as my guide and drinking partner in Singapore. For additional help and guidance, a thanks is due to Jess Blaine Smith & Josh Lindley of bartenderatlas.com, Camper English of alcademics.com, Tatum Ancheta of DrinkManila.com, Ryan Opaz of Catavino.net, Cat Nelson of TimeOut Shanghai, Tara Fougner and the Thirsty Magazine Facebook group, Holly Graham in Hong Kong, as well as José Miguel Domínguez of foodtripchile.cl. Further, a shout out is owed Ed Rudisell for tips on Southeast Asia and beyond, Ryan Seal for his great suggestions wherever I am in the world, and also to Jessie Moore for her help and suggestions at key points in this project. Without our coffee breaks it is unclear if I would have finished a sane person. Plus, a debt of gratitude is owed Moore for her playful illustrations that adorn the social media posts for this project. Likewise, a huzzah is due to illustrator Bill Lutz for his tour poster.

A big, booze-soaked thanks goes to Kevin Lundell of Broad Street Beverage Co. for his help in recipe testing. This book is more accurate and tastier for it.

There is a select group of food and drink writers who have been the important influences on me over the years—Jonathan Gold, Gerald Asher, and Anthony Bourdain, to name a few. I count Lawrence Osborne among this circle, and it was an honor to share a number of cocktails with him for this project. I sincerely thank him for his time and sage advice.

Then, a colossal thanks is owed to my parents Sonja and Mahlon for their encouragement, as well as to my sister Tenaya Darlington, with whom I wrote three books that set the stage for this one. And lastly, but truly firstly, the biggest thank you and longest and loudest toast is reserved for my steadfast partner in life and travel, Janine Hawley, without whom this project would not have been possible.

INDEX

Note: Page references in *italics* indicate photographs.

PHOTO CREDITS

BARCELONA

SOUVENIR de la TOUR EIFFEL
PARIS

CITTÀ DEL VATICANO

EXP
BRUXELL

NAPOLI

ANACAPRI

AMSTERDAM

HOLLAND

VOLEN